Of
Amon

The Convergence
Book One

T.L. McVey

To my parents, for their undying support

The Convergence
Book One: The Fall of Amon
Book Two: The Blood of Amon
Book Three: The Apex of Amon
Book Four: The Heroes of Amon

T.L. McVey

Index

Donovini

Southern most country of Amon, home of House Pratt. Astrona, capital city of Donovini

- Nicolas Pratt - House lord of Donovini, eldest of three brothers to Landon Pratt
    - Maradyn Pratt - wife to Nicolas
        - Rayden Pratt - eldest son
        - Katlynn Pratt - daughter
        - Jerryn Pratt - youngest son
- Philip Pratt - First of Amon, House lord of Donovini, middle brother
    - Jessica Pratt - wife to Philip
        - Joanna Leir - eldest daughter
        - Winston Leir - husband to Joanna
        - Lillianna Pratt - youngest daughter
- Edmond Pratt - House lord of Donovini, youngest brother
    - Karen Pratt - wife to Edmond
        - Luther Pratt - only son born to Karen
    - Sara Wode - once lover to Edmond
        - Nathanial Wode - bastard son to Edmond

- Tristan Crane - Captain of the Astrona guard
- Iero - a Druid
- Yormi - Luther's personal assistant
- Belinda - handmaiden to Lillianna
- Hannah - a Druid healer
- Cullan Sambelight - House lord of old
    - Ferah Sambelight - youngest daughter of Cullan

Argonus

Eastern most country of Amon, home of House Rowe. Tessenul, capital city of Argonus

- Edfeld Rowe - *Deceased* - former House lord of Argonus
    - Christina Rowe - wife to Edfeld, House lady of Argonus
        - Allura Rowe - daughter
        - Gerald Rowe - son
    - Lurey Hillan - brother to Christina, Third of Amon
- Pendell Rowe - *Deceased* - brother to Edfeld
    - Brenda Rowe - *Deceased* - wife to Pendell

        - Jennifer Rowe - daughter

- Feko Hawbry - an odd fellow
- Alex - personal guard to Allura
- Frederick Pullman - former colonel in the Imperial Army, right hand to Gerald
- Clint - a tavern owner

Fallneese

Northwestern country of Amon, home to House Aylmer. Itopis, capital city of Fallneese

- Yelium Aylmer - *Deceased* - Former King of Amon
    - Dylinn Aylmer - wife to Yelium, Queen of Amon, House Lady of Fallneese
    - Yelium Aylmer II - son to Yelium
    - Maurdo Ulfini - cousin to Dylinn, captain of the Itopis Guard

- Lijid Nulittan - Fourth of Amon
- Gillar - head of the courts
- Talia - slave girl to Dylinn
- Niavona - a shadow

Ursan

Northwestern country of Amon, home of House Brocusk. Antuannee, capital city of Ursan

- Dehyllo Brocusk - House lord of Ursan
    - Eili - first wife to Dehyllo
        - Loh Brocusk - eldest son
    - Indulla - second wife to Dehyllo
        - Worveso Brocusk - son
    - Trayy - third wife to Dehyllo
        - Nahhn Brocusk - son
        - Qii Brocusk - son
- Ollifo Brocusk - cousin to Dehyllo

- Afeon - Second of Amon
- Phyin of the Night – Once lord of Ursan, legendary killer of Rocs
- Unther of the Dark – Once lord of Ursan

Genethur

Southwestern country of Amon, home of the king of Amon. Corovium, capital of Amon

Kwyantin

Secluded race of Amon. Rivermoore Down, hidden home of the Kwyantin

- Aldric - Historian of Amon
- Erian - apprentice to Aldric
- Ulladari - high councilor to the Kwyantin people
- Valencia - trader

Imperial Army

- John Shonnen - First General of the Imperial Army, Donovinian
- Isani Brocusk - Second General of the Imperial Army, Ursan
- Endry Dillerson - Third General of the Imperial Army, Argon
- Samuran Koit - Fourth General of the Imperial Army, Fallneesian
- Baldin Ascotte - colonel, Donovinian
- Tauven Ulfini - major, Fallneesian
- Pricilla Eynett - major, Argon
- Cy Kovar - captain, Argon
- Li Hollins - sergeant major, Ursan

The Guild

Organization in control of the merchants and fair trade. Prillian, home of the Guild lies at the northern border of Donovini

- Orpay - head of the Guilds, Argon
- Chal - a wealthy merchant, Argon
- Cylaa - high member of the Guild, Fallneesian
- Draven - right hand to Orpay, mixed race of Donovinian and Fallneesian
- Jadenine - a Guild member, Ursan
- Ebb - a Guild member, Ursan
- Drai - a Guild member, Fallneesian
- Keli - young tailor in Prillian, Argon

Moon Divide

- Deso - Fallneesian
- Nails - Ursan
- Scythe - Fallneesian
- Haze - Fallneesian
- Mortar - Donovinian
- Flint - Argon
- Aaron - Argon

Prologue

He watched as Jaa knelt silently, his pant legs rolled up as his knees buried in the sand. The Twin Moons rose high as they always had, casting down before them upon the Terrandonan Sea as waves steadily crashed against the white of the beach. The smell of salt water carried into the nostrils of Aldric, his lean arms crossed his chest as he took in the coastal breeze. He had followed Jaa here to the eastern shores of Amon, blindly and silently, as were the ways of the apprenticeship. It was not something he had selected, not something he chose to become, but the next Historian of Amon he would be nevertheless.

Jaa had held the position for the better part of nine hundred years. But no one, not even the Kwyantin people lived forever. The time had come to pass his duties to the next. All things considered, Aldric would have been just as satisfied serving his people another way.

We do only what we are meant to do. Nothing more.

The words of his master, not his own, though they echoed in his mind.

Aldric spent three silent years studying under the elder Kwyantin, his knowledge passing to him now, his duties explained in thorough detail. Endless hours Jaa pressed the importance of his role, of the recordings of Amon, of the passing of knowledge to future generations of people not only of Kwyantin decent, but of all the races of Amon. He spoke, but Aldric rarely listened. Certainly he absorbed the history but ignored much of the preaching.

This was a job, his life, one chosen by the elder council for him. He no more argued than he complained. Aldric accepted the role in the understanding that there were no options given, no decision to be made on his end. He would perform his duties. But he did not need to agree with them.

Soon Jaa would return to their village, return to their home within Ursan. He would begin to write down all of his knowledge, all of the information that he verbally exchanged with Aldric. Those volumes would be placed with the other writings of his predecessors, the previous Historians of Amon. His duties done, he would spend what remained of his days with the council. When he returned to the earth, he would be buried with the Historians of Amon's past. All the while, Aldric would be alone and be as Jaa once was.

The night enveloped them and he had not known how long it took before Jaa had finally spoken, his knees still pressed into the beach. "Do you know that for hundreds of years, you will remember every detail, every moment of every frail second of life?" the elder called back.

Yes, ironically since I do not forget things, I remember the dozens of times you drone on about that.

"Do you understand how tormenting it can be? Do you know how often I have prayed to the gods for ignorance?" Jaa stood and turned to face Aldric, the distance remained between them and the violence of the waves came dangerously close to the elder's back. "The priests believe that the separation of the Twin Moons mean that the gods have fallen, that they no longer listen to our prayers."

"The Twin Moons still rise high above us every night and every day," Aldric assured his seemingly depressed master. "And priests say many things from what I've heard. Not all of them coincide with one another. I somehow doubt they possess any great knowledge more so than anyone else."

The words did not seem to comfort Jaa. "I am beginning to lose my memory, Aldric. It has begun to slip away. And do you want to know the damnedest thing of it all? I prayed for this ignorance, for there are a great many things I wish I did not know, that I did not remember. But even as my memory fades, do you know what remains? Every horrid thing that our people have accomplished. Every error that the Kwyantin have committed in my life and lives past. They are with me, forefront of my memory . . . eternal."

Aldric took an unsteady step forward. These were not the words of his master. Jaa was a man of strength and honor, of undying dedication. These words . . . well they simply were not.

"The day has been long," the young Kwyantin offered up. "Come, let us move away from the sea. We can talk further elsewhere."

A hammering wave came down only several feet away from Jaa, spraying both men heavily with the water. *Why are the waves so immense on this day?*

"I believe we have been punished by the gods," continued Jaa. "They leave us with our fate, our decision. First they have empowered the other races, gifting them the abilities to manipulate the Realms. How can they utilize what we as a people discovered, unleashed even? Then our numbers dwindle . . ."

"Wait, what?" stammered Aldric. *Three years and he has never mentioned that!* "You say *we* discovered the Realms, as in our people?"

But the elder Kwyantin did not seem to hear his apprentice speak. ". . . giving us the inability to stop it. Then, when all seems forgotten, they will leave us, and doing such will uncover our secret, one that we attempted to bury so long ago. The Realms . . . we cannot stop the convergence. And when it happens, Amon shall fall. I cannot let that happen. I will not."

"I don't understand what you are saying, Jaa. Please, step away from the shore. The sea is more violent than I have ever seen it."

Another wave, another narrow miss against the elder. "Indeed it is. Our people will tell you to forget all that I shared with you this night. They will tell you my mind has been lost. Understand, Historian of Amon, you shall never forget this night even if you pray for ignorance. I know the empty results of those prayers. Promise me that one day when you train your own apprentice, when you pass your knowledge down to him as I have done for you, that you will tell him of this night. Tell him what I have shared with you. One day I believe that though we are to remain impartial to all that is around us, to never use our knowledge for gain, one day that may change. One day, we may need to atone. One day, the Historian may need to be more than just that. Let him know of my words, Aldric. Maybe then . . . you will understand what must be done."

A wave, larger than any of the previous, came down upon the elder Kwyantin and salt water splashed all about Aldric. The younger Kwyantin shielded his eyes against the power of the water, turning away from the ocean for but a second.

When his gaze returned, the beach lay empty, his master lost into the vastness of the sea.

**

A Short Reign

The death of a king is normally met by great sorrow. Thus, to claim oddity to the nonchalant attitude portrayed across the vast continent of Amon to the death of King Yelium Aylmer would be the gravest of understatements. Few questioned his death, as King Aylmer spent far too much time festering diseases in brothels, far too much time smoking of Chur'ash that both penetrated his organs as well as his mind. He was neither a foul king nor a cherished one, simply a man stricken with devastating vices.

As the Historian of Amon, I can harbor neither opinions nor favoritism amongst the House names of Amon, of the more difficult duties I once possessed. But if I mourned for any during that time, I mourned for his widowed wife, who did not birth his only child. A nameless prostitute did that favor, and the Chur'ash made him sterile, ensuring not to produce another.

For seven hundred years I watched the comings and goings of kings and queens within the capital city of Corovium. I did my duties as any other Historian had done prior to me, traveling across the continent to witness the crowning of his son. Irony would have it that upon what I had previously decided would be of my final trip to the great capital, I would be witness to a series of events that would signify the reshaping of Amon.

-- Aldric, Historian of Amon

I

"Earth and Flame," cursed Jerryn Pratt as he spat upon the soil before them, his steed reeling ever so slightly at his rider's recoil.

Rayden sat upright upon his own stallion, doing all that he could to maintain his temper at his younger brother. "What's there to complain about now?"

"He means something new," added their sister, Katlynn, who rode to his left. "Something we haven't already heard."

Jerryn rolled his eyes to his siblings. "I hate coming here. I'd much rather be home. I mean, how many Pratts must attend Corovium in order to make such an event official?"

Rayden contained his smile toward his younger brother. He was a good man, but his maturity simply lacked some to say the least. By most accounts, seventeen was far and away enough years to mature. But living within the House name, having an uncle as the First to the king . . . well an unfortunate amount of pampering took place. Rayden shunned such while Jerryn embraced it. Though the age differences between the siblings were minute, as Rayden now twenty-one years of age and Katlynn a year older than Jerryn at eighteen, the disparity in maturity could fill the gap between the capital and his home city of Astrona.

The elder brother turned behind him; seven of the Astrona guard trailed the Pratt children. Amongst them was their captain, Tristan Crane, darker than most Donovinians, short black hair and a well-trimmed mustache upon his young face. "Did you hear that, Tristan?" Rayden called back. "My brother feels that the crowning of a new king is trivial duty for Lord Nicolas Pratt's spoiled children. What say you?"

"I would say that Lord Nicolas Pratt would place the blunt side of a sword on the back side of Lord Jerryn Pratt's ass should he discover such whining," Tristan responded. "Utmost respect, of course, Lord Jerryn."

"To Shadow with all of you," Jerryn blasted toward them. "We are not some second family, cousin to a House name. We are Pratts. I just don't deem that we all need to be present for this. King Aylmer was a Chur'ash smoking fool. Let's hope his son is wiser. At best, you could have come here to represent the Pratt children alone, brother. Your name is the only one that matters."

"These are the duties of our House name. What kind of man our king was is of little difference in our honoring of his passing and paying homage to the new king. I'm glad you embrace all the perks of being the son of a House lord, and at the same time shun all of the responsibilities of that role." Rayden whipped the reins of his horse, pressing onward to the capital city before them. "Stiffen your resolve, brother, before I do so for you."

From what Rayden had learned during his younger tutoring, Genethur had once, long ago, been a desolate piece of land claimed by none of the races of Amon. But during the many talks of peace amongst the various races, a neutral site was needed, one for discussing the means to a peaceful resolve. Well over three millennia ago, were his readings accurate, but the dust and sand that were once Genethur now stood a vibrant array of open fields, long winded views of greens with cascading flowers that varied in purples and reds. An odd weather change occurred within this part of Amon, one that brought rain regularly from off the western coast. Some claimed that their now fallen gods, Turitea and Schill, had done such in their final act, to leave them a parting gift, to bless their newly created country in a plethora of rich soil that could plant a wide assortment of crops as well as fresh water lakes and rivers for regular civilization and cultivation.

Though his brother hated their rare ventures to Genethur and to the capital Corovium more specifically, Rayden embraced these trips. Their own homeland of Donovini felt bland in comparison. Recent droughts had dried up their lands. The once green landscape, even in the dead of spring, had browned and withered. Canals were dug, rerouting some of the precious water from the Huul River to their farmlands, though even that was not enough to maintain Donovini in its entirety. Thankfully the country of Argonus, their neighbors to the east, had partnered with them . . . for a fee of course . . . to aid in feeding their people. He had made the trip with his father personally, along with an ever-complaining younger brother, visiting with House Rowe to make the request for aid. That had only been a few months' past, and prior to that meeting, Rayden had very little dealings with the other Houses of Amon. But there were certain benefits to the meetings. Lady Allura of House Rowe, twenty-two and yet wed, blonde hair, green eyes, and there had been some talk between his father and Lady Christina Rowe . . .

"It *is* impressive, I'll give you that," mumbled Jerryn, interrupting his thoughts.

Rayden pulled the reins, bringing his steed to a halt. Spreading out beyond, engulfing the horizon, was their capital, home to the king of all four House lords. *Corovium.* By no means a fortress or castle as the eldest Pratt sibling had envisioned as a boy, the city was a trade metropolis with merchants from every corner of Amon selling anything and everything to travelers, petty politicians, aristocrats, and anyone with coin that lived within the capital. Genethur, while now a country on its own, had no original race of people. Here, all four races intertwined . . . five if the handful of tribal Kwyantin that still roamed Amon were counted. But the Kwyantin rarely traveled far from their hidden nest somewhere in Ursan. With the exception of the Historian of Amon.

The capital flowed as would a river; pushing forward, never backwards, progression never regression. He had only been to Corovium perhaps a dozen times, mostly to visit his Uncle Philip Pratt and his cousins. Each time the city grew, buildings rose as would crops in fields, or weeds as his uncle had been fond of saying. Industry, change, greed . . . all interchangeable, unbreakable things, Uncle Philip had claimed. *Maybe he is right, but little I can do to alter the world. Better you, Uncle. The First has a great sway over the government. So long as the new king keeps you as First, and pray to the fallen gods he will, as he will need you more than ever.*

"Come," Rayden pressed his siblings. "Father will be upset enough that we've taken as long as we have to arrive."

"Well . . . he's upset all the time anyways," commented Jerryn, a raised eyebrow to the obvious perhaps.

Katlynn chuckled a bit. "At you, dear brother. Save us your shit and we might keep Father from an early grave."

"We do what we can," answered the youngest.

Rayden pushed forward, listening to his brother and sister squabble back and forth behind him.

"Is it true, about the Chur'ash? That it killed him?" Katlynn inquired.

"He doesn't know any more than you," Rayden called back to them. "Don't let him deceive you."

"Bah, he only saves you from the truth. You *do* know why it's called Chur'ash right? Made mostly from Chur'rat dung."

Rayden did not need to turn to see Katlynn's flawless face cringe at the thought. "And someone would smoke that . . . *willingly*?" she queried, obviously appalled in learning the truth. "Earth and Flame."

--

Philip Pratt slumped into the chair within his office, papers littered amongst his desk, his work having been neglected for the full three weeks since King Aylmer's passing. Part had been his saddened state, having lost a man that he spent years attempting to repair, only to fail him, only to watch him deteriorate before his eyes. Another part had been in spite, leaving work piled for whoever the First would be upon the crowning of the new king. Philip enjoyed living in reality, and the bastard son of Yelium held no love for the First. The feeling, of course, was mutual. And as the king, the young Aylmer could shuffle the council and responsibilities of them any which way he chose, so long as his own House representative amongst the council was Fourth.

You will be lucky to be Third. Likely that shit will request a replacement from Nicolas come week's end.

Eighteen years since his appointment to the king's council, eighteen years spent as the First to the king, and he had worked hard to create Amon as a country of progress. Many ups, equally as many downs, but he felt accomplished at his body of work. Flame's embrace, his youngest daughter had been born within Genethur. Barely had she even known of her own home country of Donovini. Where was the time to usher her home frequently, to visit with her uncles Nicolas and Edmond, to spend time with those that he loved and missed? There was a country to be raised, groomed. *Indeed, where was the time?*

Guess you will have that time now, old man.

A solid knock on his office door startled the First as he watched it come ajar just enough for the familiar voice to call out, "Might I come in, First Pratt?"

"Of course."

The door came open fully, the shorter, stocky man entered with a sense of grace and style not fitting a man of his appearance. His beard grew wild and his red hair unevenly braided; the hair desperately needing to be chopped off. The man was from Ursan, the heavily forested northeastern lands of Amon, and his pale complexion had almost the look of an albino, though it was in fact a trait of his people.

"What do I owe the pleasure, Afeon?"

The Second closed the door firmly behind him, then strode across the small office to claim a seat across from the First.

"Your nephews have been spotted entering the outskirts. I've sent an escort to see them safely inside the royal demesne." His gaze turned to the disorderly desk. "I see you are as busy as ever, friend," noted the Ursan.

And you use the word friend too freely. "Thank you for word of my nephews, as well as their escort. And as for my lack of work lately . . . my mind has been on many things, Second."

"As have we all. I would make this visit brief, if it pleases you. As you have neglected some of your duties, they have in turn fallen to me to complete. And I understand that is my job, so I do not come to tell you the obvious."

"Get to it, Second," lazily remarked Philip, though not in harshness, only in hoping Afeon would skip the thoughts of dancing about formalities. There had not been much pride left to bruise.

Afeon nodded. "Something has fallen to me that I have no authority to fix, thus I must place this back to you." The responsibilities of the First was to govern all that belonged to the king, any and all duties to which he personally did not deem fit. Outside of that, the First directly oversaw the state affairs of each country, mostly when it dealt with military actions or internal conflicts. As for old King Yelium, he had not deemed himself fit for any of his tasks, so Philip had spent years running Amon fully in the capacity of the First. The duties of the Second were to oversee the economic state of Amon, namely in ensuring fair trade between the merchants and monitoring of the Guild. For what it was worth, Afeon performed his duties well.

The bearded man placed an envelope atop the stack on his desk. It donned a broken seal of the Imperial Army, addressed to the king. Philip made no attempt to reach for the letter; he had previously read it over a week ago.

"It's from General Shonnen," Afeon remarked after a silent moment between them.

"I know, Afeon. This was not meant to be passed to you. It was meant to be disposed," the elder Pratt claimed earnestly. "I apologize for this coming to you."

"*Disposed*? Philip, I realize that the death of King Aylmer was a great loss to . . ."

"This has nothing to do with Yelium. General Shonnen expresses concerns. He notes that the tides have been dropping by the eastern coast, that the Terrandonan Sea settles as the Twin Moons part. Earth and Flame, Afeon, I did not need to read that letter to know those facts. I can stare out my fucking window to see the Moons dip closer to the horizon every passing month. And General Shonnen has damn near a fourth of the Imperial Army at the coastline to tell me such? What exactly does he defend against? Whispers, dear Second. Nothing but whispers."

Afeon sat upright, his elbows upon the arms of the chair, his hands connecting between them. "How many wars has Amon seen in your tenure as First? None, same as me. Not even our Historian has seen a full-scale war in his life, and he is some eight hundred years old. Certainly we have had issues within our respective Houses. We've had skirmishes and fights and disagreements. We've seen our share of back alley dealings gone afoul. A jostling for position here that never seems to end. But this world has been free of a terrible war for hundreds of years."

"Your point?"

"Peace, for all its splendor, dulls the mind as easily as the thickest ale. When the gods fell, abandoning us, the Twin Moons parted, signifying both their departure as well as their separation from Amon. . ."

Shit, I forget sometimes how religious this man is.

". . . as Turitea and Schill left us broken, in a sense so numbing that we did not even feel it. There is nothing more naked than the loss of hope, First Pratt."

"And what does any of this have to do with General Shonnen's request for additional troops?"

"Across the Terrandonan Sea lies another continent," continued the red bearded Ursan. "Your belief in that land, or more importantly what lies upon that land, is mostly irrelevant. The departure of Turitea and Schill, the falling of the Twin Moons . . . it's all connected. The only thing keeping what lies on that continent from landing upon our shores is the ocean between us and the unsettled, unforgiving sea. That sea now calms, First. Every year the tide recedes. Every year the waves lessen. You have read the letter. His scouts have gone missing, his men have seen things . . . unnatural things against the moonlight. Whatever savageness lies beyond the Terrandonan Sea, we are unprepared."

But Philip only shook his head toward the Ursan. "Let me tell you reality, Second, since you live far away from such. King Aylmer did not believe much in the fallen gods, no more than he figured the parting of the Twin Moons to be anything but a natural phenomenon. I share his belief in that. But being that there are those such as yourself in higher concentration, we agreed to send out some men to Argonus to guard against fairytale monsters that live across the ocean. Few hundred not being enough to calm the religious fanatics, we sent out a thousand. When a few thousand would not satisfy the needs of those paranoid about an attack from whispers and legends, I sent out a fourth of the Imperial Army, led by the First General John Shonnen. All the while, the resources it costs to keep twenty thousand men fed and provisioned abroad is silently placing a strain on our economy."

"I know of money, First, as I have not neglected my duties," he hissed. "However, money will matter very little when we are invaded."

"Easy answer. But then what difference does sending more men do us if we are unprepared."

"True enough, First. We are dead peoples regardless. With our gods abandoning us, there is little hope against what awaits us." But he shrugged ever so slightly. "But we also do not know when such a thing will happen. Would you not agree that maintaining moral is an important thing for troops? Lost or not, they might like to have some reassurance from their king, from the First."

Philip Pratt's arms crossed about his chest. "The general is a reasonable man," mumbled the First, almost to himself. "I can't figure how he got . . ."

"Spooked?" finished Afeon. "Shadow knows, First, but something has your general concerned. I understand some hesitation in sending out more troops. These are strenuous times, with the crowning of a new king and all. We need the extra support here, as to reaffirm that House Aylmer still retains power."

Funny, as the only House that frightens me in taking advantage of the situation is yours, Afeon. House Brocusk is far too powerful to not eye the throne.

"But what harm," the Second continued, "in sending the Moon Divide?"

And Philip nearly choked on his own saliva. "You'd have me send criminals to the front?"

"No, I'd have you send killers to the front," he answered. "I can think of little that could rattle those soldiers. You would answer the general's call and respond by sending a crew brave enough to piss into the Flame Realm."

The Moon Divide was a group of elite killers, mostly criminals and cutthroats, thieves and assassins. Most of the men within the association had been given an option upon sentencing, either death by hanging, or death by enrollment into the Moon Divide. It was, after all, a lifetime sentence. The only way to depart from the Divide was to die in battle. Death by the rope or by the chain, as they were fond of saying. Never before had Philip integrated the king's Imperial Army with the king's lesser known assassins.

Wars? You think I have seen none? You sodden fool, I have seen plenty, only silent ones, those that did not call upon the army. Cults of rapists that needed purging, Shadowmancers united against the throne . . . oh I have seen wars, and I have seen blood. The Moon Divide has fulfilled the dirty work in the name of the king for years.

"Only about sixty or so left of them," noted Philip.

"And from my understanding, they are worth twenty times that."

You have no idea.

He did not like the suggestion, not even the slightest. But if it removed the Second from his sight, it was worth considering.

"Your point is made, Second. I will contact the Divide tonight. Do you have anything further for me?"

"No, First. I thank you for your audience." The Ursan stood, his eyes narrowing upon Philip in curious intent. "Tell me, First, you were closer to King Aylmer in life than our fallen gods in death. There is an . . . oddity I wish to question."

Philip knew the question before he asked it, but played the fool regardless. "And what is that, Second?"

"Young Yelium Aylmer II, his birth came as a rather . . . surprise to us all. When Queen Dylinn returned to Fallneese during her pregnancy, it left a great many to wonder the . . . legitimacy of the birth of this child." Though his pauses suggested his caution with words, Philip knew well that his words were well planned beforehand.

"You find it odd for her to return to her home country to birth her child rather than do so in a foreign land?"

"Did Lady Jessica not decide to remain within Corovium during the birth of your youngest?"

"Customs of Donovinians differ from Fallneesians, Afeon. Regardless, I regret Lillianna not being born in our country."

Afeon nodded to the statement. "As I recall, young Lillianna was due to be born in the midst of some disputes along the Fallneesian borders. There have never been questions regarding the diligence to your duty, First Pratt. But if, for arguments sake of course, say that our young, soon to be king was not born from Queen Dylinn, but from another . . ."

"Careful now, Second," cautioned Philip Pratt. "You are about to accuse a man crowned tomorrow of being a bastard son. Should he hear such, that borders treason." *Regardless of how true your accusation would be.*

"I cannot accuse with no evidence, First. I only make statement that if someone knew the facts and came forward with such a scandal, the lordship of Amon would fall upon the next in line to the late king. And since there is no other in line, it would fall back to the council to decide in honoring this boy as rightful heir or not."

"And would you honor a bastard child the throne of Amon?" pressed Philip, more prying into the deceptive mind of Afeon than playing along.

"Neither I nor Lurey would vote in favor of such. And being a fifty percent vote is all that is needed for the lordship to return to council, it would return to all of us to decide which House the strongest, which House the most . . . deserving of the throne."

You make a play for your own House, Afeon. But you do so with an empty hand.

"So you have talked this through with the Third, have you? Well I would suggest you find some evidence of such, and do so quickly. Young Yelium Aylmer is crowned tomorrow."

Afeon frowned deeply at the comment. "You understand that all that you have worked for will be lost shortly after the crowning, tomorrow. This work placed upon me, this desk of littered responsibility left unfinished tells me you understand such. If you comprehend the inevitability of your removal of First, and likely from the council altogether, why protect the young Yelium?"

"You assume far too much, Afeon."

"Do I?" Shrugging, the Ursan turned back toward the door. "Time runs short, Philip."

With that, the Second departed his office.

Philip sighed silently. *Perhaps not so empty a hand after all.*

--

"Rayden!" called a young girl's voice, and the elder Pratt brother spotted his young cousin Lillianna rushing through the courtyard to meet them.

He dismounted and embraced the girl. "It has been *way* too long. And you have grown quite a bit. Twelve are you now?"

She smiled, her young, slender face a shade darker than he and his siblings, no doubt thanks to the coastal sun. "Thirteen in only a few weeks, cousin." Katlynn now reached the girl, and his sister lifted Lillianna, groaning in the process, and kissed her upon her cheek. "A bit heavier I suppose."

"Flame's embrace," Katlynn cursed upon placing her down, smiling the entirety. "I suppose it's been a while since our last visit."

"I wish it were for a better reason," Jerryn added, hugging their cousin briefly.

"Jerryn," she acknowledged with a grin. "Come inside! Father is always busy, but I know he will want to see you all. He's been saddened by King Aylmer's death, but knowing that his nephews were arriving brightened him a bit."

"Is my father here?" Rayden inquired.

Lillianna nodded. "Arrived three days ago, I believe. I've seen him several times. Uncle Nicolas has spent most of his time with Uncle Edmond and some other House lords."

"Has he spent any time with Uncle Philip?" questioned Jerryn.

But the girl only shrugged. "If so, not much. Father's been very busy. All the king's duties have passed to him. He's had little time for much outside of his work."

Tristan Crane barked a few commands to the soldiers behind him, who in turn guided their own horses out of the courtyard. The captain moved toward the three horses of the Pratt children and grabbed the reins. Lillianna waved to him and he threw the blushing girl a devilish smile. "An honor as always to see you, Lady Lillianna Pratt. By your leave, I will take the horses to the lord's stables."

"I will join you," Katlynn offered willingly . . . perhaps too strongly so, Rayden noticed. "I will find you both inside shortly."

But her smile could not be refused in either case. "Fair enough. Lead the way, cousin."

While Tristan and Katlynn departed, Lillianna moved ahead, passing through the lush greens of the courtyard toward the capital building, which stood as the royal throne room, the council rooms, the homes of all of the royal family, along with the families of the council. The whole affair, crossing acres of land, was damn near as large as his home city of Astrona. Just beyond the monstrosity stood the Vurid Sea, the western coast of Amon. Difficult to see save for spotted glances through buildings and pathways, but the blues of the water could not be measured against any other color. The ultramarine brilliance called to him as would a siren to a sailor, his desire to submerge himself within the cool waters uncontainable.

"Gather up some aristocrat daughters later tonight, along with some wine, and we'll hit those waters," whispered his younger brother as they moved through the open gates.

"This is not a vacation, Jerryn," he advised.

To which his brother scoffed. "As if you weren't thinking the same thing."

Thinking and acting are two different things. Far too many responsibilities to run off and fuck with the local whores.

The pathway leading to the main entrance to the capital stood sparsely littered with a few familiar faces within the crowd, lesser cousins of Houses that he could not remember names to and did not care to try. A smile and a nod toward them carried the two Pratt brothers along. While the faces and the names fell from Rayden's knowledge, the likelihood of his name being unknown to them was close to nil. House Pratt had held lordship in Donovini for nine generations, since an elder kin had taken the lordship by force. Since then, they had not only governed Donovini, they had placed one of their own within the king's council.

Known and respected, but the Pratt's had yet to find the throne. The Fallneesian House, seventeen generations in lordship, had been voted into rule long ago, and with the crowning of the young Yelium Aylmer, it would make the eighth Aylmer to claim said position, and the eighteenth straight from Fallneese.

From the corner of his eye, Rayden spotted several members of House Rowe, and in the center of a group of chattering girls, Allura gazed in his direction, a smile flashed upon her flawless fair skin. Her blonde, almost golden hair fell carelessly down to her waist, an informal red dress pressed tightly about her, showcasing her curving woman's figure amidst a taller frame than most ladies from his own country.

Moving to them with intent was a middle aged, chubby Donovinian man. This particular man was insufferable, and though quite a talented Druid in his own right, not entirely stable either. No different than most who mingled in the Realms, searching within for power.

I sense a woman who may need rescuing.

"I'm going to say hi to Iero," Rayden stated to both his younger brother and cousin, of which Jerryn simply laughed aloud.

"You've got to be kidding me," the younger Pratt blasted back. "You see the group of young girls and leave me to . . ."

"Find Father and inform him that his children have arrived," finished Rayden.

"And so Katlynn gets to chat it up with our captain, you the same to some House ladies, and I get to find Father. Exactly where does any of that seem fair?"

"I don't believe fair ever goes into consideration when it comes to the youngest," Lillianna made note. "I should know."

"I bet," grumbled Jerryn. "Well I'd argue, but lose. So lead on Lilli. *Someone* should let Father know his children survived the harsh travel through the Donovinian heat and dryness, avoided death from the many bandits on the road, along with vicious animals looking hungry upon our passing as we . . ."

Rayden had barely paid his brother any mind during his continual complaining. Iero, the Druid, had now made it to the Argon women, and once engaged, it would be difficult to distract him away. If his eyes did not deceive him, a Chur'rat sat upon his shoulder, which would not bode well to a bunch of sophisticated noble women. The creature, slightly bigger than a house cat, both hung and draped over his shoulder, wrapped about as if it were a hairy, disgusting scarf. He quickly dusted off his tunic and did all that he could to look casual upon his step toward the group.

"It's a rat," Rayden heard one of the women comment as he came closer.

"A *Chur'rat* to be precise," answered Iero. "A slight difference. I find it ironic that you do not recognize the difference, as not but a dozen years ago, they were mostly found near the eastern coast."

"I was seven a dozen years ago," responded the same woman.

"Ah, the blessed ignorance of youth. Indeed, these Chur'rats dwelled upon the eastern coast of Argonus, and at times upward into Ursan. But for reasons unknown, these distant cousins to your standard sewer rats left the eastern coasts and were first spotted north in Fallneese, then many came here to Genethur. Some think the climate changes have created the move, while others are inclined to believe that their food situation has changed over . . ."

"Guess that explains the increase in Chur'ash here in Genethur," the lady commented.

"Quite possibly the very reason for the decline in your own home country. It is indeed a rare export, to transport excrement across countries in order to . . ."

"So, it's not a rat on your shoulder, it's a *Chur'rat,*" interrupted Allura, she now locking eyes with Rayden. "Outside of being bigger, hairier, and if possible, uglier, what's the difference? And why is it on your shoulder?"

"The why is because it's his familiar," Rayden quickly answered. "Druids have a tendency to caress the spirit of an animal to be their companions. They're almost like protectors to them. It's their connection to the Earth Realm that allows such. The better question, Lady Rowe, is *why* Iero chose a Chur'rat, of all creatures, as his familiar."

"Ah, do you lovely ladies know Lord Rayden Pratt? And to answer so many questions in quick succession, they are indeed a larger species, and what truly separates them is their choice in food. They are strictly carnivorous and hunt best in packs, known to take down much larger opposition."

"Humans," Rayden made mention through Iero's rants, to which raised many eyebrows amongst the women in attendance.

"Yes, at times," answered the middle aged Donovinian. "As to why it is on my shoulders, Lady Rowe, that is easily put. It's far more comfortable for him on my shoulder than walking, I'd presume. He hasn't ever told me why. Does get heavy at times. And Lord Pratt, to your question, the person does not choose the familiar, the familiar chooses the owner. Bird decided that I should be his master, and he my familiar."

"Bird?" Allura inquired.

"It is his name," Iero quickly answered.

"So your rat . . . *Chur'rat* . . .. is named Bird?" she pressed further

To this, Iero shrugged. "Indeed, quite odd, but that was the name he gave me. I only adhere to his wishes."

"At least that explains being on his shoulder," replied Rayden. "So Iero, I believe I saw the Historian inside the capital. Have you met him before?"

Iero's eyes lit up with excitement. "I have had the pleasure, by my count, fourteen times. This would be fifteenth should I find the great Aldric. I should make haste as to find him. Perhaps I should first look into the cafeteria, as a man of that stature would likely be hungry quite often."

The Druid continued his ramblings as he wandered away from the group, talking aloud to himself or perhaps his familiar, as he worked his way toward the entrance of the capital.

"Hopefully Aldric doesn't find out you sent him his way," Allura made comment, grabbing Rayden by his arm and walking away from the women in her group. "He may write horrible things about you that will echo into eternity."

"It was a wild guess that he would be here, so hopefully he will forgive me. And I rarely worry about eternity, Lady Rowe. I have far more concern about the present than to worry about what the Historian may write about me in the future."

Her smile widened, looking intently at him with her jade eyes. "So, you seem to be the master of knowledge about Chur'rats. Any truth in all that was said by the Druid?"

"All of it," replied Rayden. "Iero is a strange one, but honest."

"And what of you, Lord Pratt? What should a lady expect of someone such as yourself? We have met a handful of times, and each time I catch your eyes toward me."

"And certainly your brilliant eyes never find me," retorted the young Pratt facetiously.

"Who knows, Lord Pratt? Maybe I look beyond you, or perhaps behind you. Difficult to tell a woman's stare."

She had trouble masking her smile, as did Rayden. "Very well, perhaps I presume too much. And perhaps I ask too boldly that I would enjoy your company come dinner tonight."

Allura shrugged softly. "I might find room in my very busy schedule of gossiping for a handsome young lord from Donovini."

"I look forward to it," responded Rayden, his hand reaching over to hers, placing it gently to his lips. "For now, I must find Iero, and save Aldric from his grasps."

"I thought you weren't worried about eternity and all that."

"As I said, I am more worried about the present, milady. Have you *seen* the size of Aldric?"

--

". . . not opening them, but moving through the Realms. Who would break the only rule amongst us? How great is the quest for power to ignore the knowledge of our past? But the youth today have no care for history. Ah, Aldric, have you met Lord Rayden Pratt?"

"That I have," Aldric answered, watching the youthful, tan complexioned man approach. Taller than the average Donovinian, and carried himself well as he strode across the main hall of the capital. His brown hair a little wavy and cut short about his ears, his attire a basic tunic and loose fitting pants, comfortable traveling gear it seemed. In earnest, the Historian felt pleased at his arrival, if only to have the Druid breathe between statements.

"Pleasure again, Historian," Rayden bowed slightly, then gazed upward to Aldric's traveling companion. "Though I do not have the pleasure of knowing the one beside you."

The Historian's apprentice returned the formalities, bowing toward Lord Pratt. "I am Erian, Lord Rayden. I travel with Aldric as his apprentice, in a manner of speaking."

Rayden turned his eyes toward the Historian. "It is time, then?"

"As would it be for you," Iero continued to clamor, "should you walk for over seven hundred years. The Historian has been witness to the fine tuning of our great country of Amon, while finding his own race strangely vacant in the proceedings. It is a sad tale, one of the Kwyantin, his vast people slowly vanishing from . . ."

"Perhaps," Rayden interjected on the Druid's behalf, "a better topic might be at hand. I apologize for not knowing you were ready to pass your knowledge to the next. Erian, I am certain that Aldric will teach you all that is necessary of the Pratt House, and of Donovinians in general. Hopefully, he will not pass on his knowledge of my Druid friend, and you can erase his mention in the histories."

"Why astonishing you would slight me such, young Pratt," Iero began. "I have done much for not only this capital, or the late king, but for our country. Just the other day I spoke with a member from House Brocusk of the importance of a Druid and my privileged duties within Astrona. I find that . . ."

"You may want to depart while this continues," the young lord murmured to them.

"And so we shall. We shall speak soon, Lord Rayden Pratt." Aldric bowed, then moved along, the exceptionally powerful Druid still chastising the young Pratt even as the two Kwyantin men distanced themselves from the scene.

As Aldric moved to the rear of the main hall, heading toward the stairs that ascended to the living quarters of the capital, he could not help but watch the eyes of the people fixate upon them. There were many reasons why, and he knew each of them clearly. Firstly, they were Kwyantin, a people without a country, hidden away deep in the forests of Ursan. Not even the Ursan resident House Brocusk knew of their location. Lord Brocusk did not challenge their claim to any part of his land, however, as the Kwyantin had been in place long before the arrival of the Ursan people. That, and they posed no threat to the vastness of Ursan. Thus, for many of those within the capital, these men were the first and perhaps only Kwyantin they had ever seen and ever would. The second, perhaps more relevant than knowing *who* they were was observing their physical attributes. The Historian did not stand tall amongst his own people, but still towered at just over eight feet in height. His replacement, Erian, stood a solid foot above him, and at only seventy-three years of age, had room left to grow. And lastly, in understanding who he was, came an understanding in what he did.

Historian, keeper of knowledge of the people of Amon, teller of tales of the world as it shaped, how it formed. I am all of these things, but soon it will pass to Erian as Jaa once did for me. I only hope that this duty will not plague him as it has for me, as it plagued my master at his end. What is knowledge without purpose? To seek but not utilize that information, such a waste. Such a wasted life.

Some were like Rayden; simple, honest, proud people. The young Pratt's interest in Aldric seemed sincere, perhaps pity even. But many were like Iero, though only in purpose, as there was no one truly like the Druid. But to have their names retold in generations yet to come, to have their story echoed throughout time in Amon, that was the goal of many who approached the Historian. That was the power that he possessed. He could not extend to the Realms. He did not command armies. He did not lead people.

No, his gift was of pen and paper. Immortality was the power he provided, and many sought it with or without his consent.

"You will learn to ignore their stares," whispered the Historian to his young student. "Ensure you never embrace it."

"Why so?"

"Our role is not to influence Amon, only to record the workings of our country. To embrace the stares, you embrace every part of it, including the fame involved. You must understand, part of who we are place us immune, diplomatically immune that is. Should you accept fame within your mind, in your heart, you will defer from the path of the Kwyantin."

"Knowledge, not influence," echoed Erian. "That seems . . . difficult, Aldric."

"Understand that our knowledge ultimately will lead to influence, but not from our people. We harbor knowledge for future generations, not to shape current ones. Should we ever succumb to those feelings, that we should aid in the shaping of our world, we would lose all creditability as to what we are now, thus making our committed life to the gathering of history irrelevant."

"I hope I will honor you in all that I do," Erian mentioned, though with little enthusiasm.

The Historian chuckled. "Not I, dear student. Honor our people and our culture." *He looks at me the way I must have looked at Jaa. Half listening, half caring. How much truth should I even share with him? I speak to him as the council wishes me to speak. Should I tell him that I was once like him, reluctantly chosen for a job, to follow some old fool around until he relinquished his title? A title that I in fact never wanted and spent a lifetime doing regardless? No, best for him to formulate his own opinions.*

The stairs conquered through three stories before they reached their desired destination: the living quarters of the ruling House Aylmer. His path to Corovium had of course been two sided: the discovery of the fate of the old king and information on the man the new king would become. The information he had sought had taken him to those in witness to his death, as though illness had spread swiftly and taken him equally as quick, it had not been in much surprise. King Aylmer had fallen into a deadly trap of a horrifyingly powerful hallucinogen known as Chur'ash, an enormously addictive drug. For most cases, the only escape from Chur'ash was death. This had not proven any different with Yelium Aylmer.

Outside of witnessing the crowning of the new king, which had remained a priority to him, Aldric had come to meet and learn of the boy king. Yelium Aylmer II, sixteen and apparently an accomplished swordsman, would be the youngest king of Amon in centuries. There remained enough here to journal away, to make his final notes before stepping down to allow Erian to become the new Historian.

For what it was worth, Aldric had lived a full life, a committed life to his people. There had not been regrets, only tire in his aging mind. There of course was little to regret as his life was placed before him by the council. Aldric's only sin was distain, his overall lack of understanding of the position. He felt that would be a natural emotion for anyone that sacrificed an entire life, yet outside of writing things down, had little to show for that life.

But soon that would all come to an end. For the Kwyantin, the mind faltered before the body, and as the Historian, he could ill afford to risk that fate. He would likely live another hundred years, if he were lucky enough . . . or unlucky pending on certain circumstances. But soon his mind would wither, the memory gifted to his people would slowly expire. As the Historians before him, he would spend the remaining days of his sanity writing down all that he could recall, all that he had witnessed during his tenure.

Even that day on the eastern shore. Perhaps when the ink touches the paper for the first pen strike, that is where I shall start.

And then, one day, his mind would be lost to him. From Historian, keeper of knowledge, archivist of history, to one day waking and finding all of his memory gone, all lost, and purpose stripped, spending the rest of his days grasping for bits and pieces of a life he would no longer recall.

The thought was horrifying, to know that time ran short for him to catalog all the information stored within his mind before that inevitable day. But his people assured him of the serenity of that day, for it was not something to be feared. A life of purpose removed, to live whatever remained in ignorant bliss was the reward gifted by Schill, one of their now fallen gods.

What comfort can I have in the promises of a fallen god? Ignorance is bliss, as the old saying goes. Not for me. What am I, if I cannot remember all that I have done?

Then again, what exactly have I done? Ah, the curse of my existence.

Erian remained silent beside him, always observing, understanding his position in life. The young Kwyantin would make an excellent Historian. He knew the purpose of silent existence, something that took Aldric some time to both grasp and embrace. As they moved beyond the wide, extended hallway of the third floor, passing many dayrooms and living quarters, they reached the end, which opened in an explosion of color and extravagance. House banners of Aylmer hung from the ceiling before the widened, open entrance to the king's chambers, or at least the first room. Guards stood post before the entrance, still as statues. They gave no notice to the Kwyantin; they understood clearly that the Historian stood no threat.

"No, by the fallen gods, if you do not get this right, you will hang at my crowning tomorrow!"

The Historian found his first gaze and first impression of the young Aylmer to be of equal weight: underwhelming. The scrawny boy looked undersized, even with a year or two left to grow. If he was the swordsman others claimed, the weapon needed to be light based on his frame. As with all Fallneesian people, Yelium Aylmer II was dark complexioned, his eyes brown, attractive despite the frailty. His hair was shaven clean, but a thin mustache grew low, almost attached to his bottom lip rather than hover above it.

At the moment, the king was surrounded by servants and aristocrats, all silenced by his recent outrage. His eyes turned to face the Kwyantin, widening in excitement upon seeing them.

Abruptly he turned to those beside him. "Leave us, now," he commanded.

And the room scattered with the shuffling of feet, bodies departing into one of the rooms that looked to be the kitchen. Aldric and Erian both bowed deeply to the soon-to-be king.

"It is an honor, milord, to finally meet you," Aldric claimed. "I am . . ."

"Aldric, Historian!" exclaimed the young Aylmer. "Of course. Who does not know your name or your profession? And rumor has it that this is Erian, your successor. The honor is all mine, I assure you. I wondered how long it would take you to find me."

"I apologize for the delay. I had things to take care of before our formal visit."

"Tending to facts of my father's death." The boy shrugged. "I am well informed and have thick skin, Historian. You may speak frankly with me. I'm young, but there is little need to speak around the topic of his death. He was a father . . . many better, many certainly worse, but dead all the same. A lackluster king, though, and a lousy fucking Fallneesian."

His passing concern on his father, although not surprising based on his knowledge of Aylmer's lack of attention to both his parental and . . . marital affairs, it still remained baffling to hear the words outright.

"In either case, milord, we as a country are saddened by your father's loss. But indeed, the time was spent discovering the cause of death. Now that that is done, I can return focus to where it should be, on the new king of Amon."

The young Yelium smiled genuinely. "And I assure you that you will not be disappointed. Since birth I have been schooled on warfare, governing, political structures, as well as the means for monetary growth in a consumer based economy. Supply and demand, as it is."

"And are you proud of the empire you inherit, milord?"

"It is piss and shit from the fallen gods," replied Yelium. "We are bordering poverty, not that you would see such with all of the money being tossed around. Do you realize I have an army, about a *fourth* of my Imperial force guarding a sea? Fucking salt water being defended! Flame's embrace, are we guarding against ocean waves? Be just as effective to guard against whores to my bedroom. Both situations are inevitable. And strangely enough, in both situations . . . I get fucked. No, Historian, I am not proud of what my father has allowed to occur here in Amon, and I look to rectify that."

"So you would withdraw the army?"

"Withdraw? No, disband. I have already drafted the letter, it only waits my crowning. It will be my first great achievement as king. We have obviously survived without them for long enough to not need those men, and the money saved for the kingdom in just that will be astonishing."

And to leave tens of thousands of men without funds, jobs, but heavily armed and furious. Astonishing indeed.

"If it pleases you, milord," Aldric responded, "I would like to stay for the first month of your reign, silently observing you as a king, to write as my final entries into our history."

"I'd expect nothing less, Historian. I am certain you will write well of my accomplishments. I would like to read them once they are finalized, for approval of course."

Aldric felt the eyes of Erian turn to him, likely curious at his response. Indeed, as he was curious at his own response. "Milord," he began, "you understand that I write the histories of Amon within my village as my final duties to my people. I do not write them before I arrive."

"Yes, I am familiar with your customs," answered Yelium. "But you can write my excerpts while you are here. It would . . . please me greatly. I want to know what you think of me."

"It is not a matter of opinion, milord. I only write facts."

"Then I shall read the facts of my start."

Oblige the young fool. Not as if what I write here will enter the history, and not as if he would ever find my village to ensure the authenticity of my work.

"Agreed, milord."

"Excellent. Then if it is okay with you, may we continue these proceedings another time? I have much to attend to before my crowning tomorrow, and if my servants cannot tailor my attire properly, I will hang them in front of the entire ceremony tomorrow. Hopefully you all heard me! Hangings!"

"Of course, milord. Your mother, is she . . ."

"Other side of the hall, I'm afraid. She refuses to sleep in her old bed since my father passed. She is in one of the guest rooms now if you wish to record her sorrow into the histories."

Aldric bowed again to the young Aylmer. "An honor, milord. We shall be proud witnesses to your crowning tomorrow."

"As will all of Amon," he replied.

Something tells me your reign will not be short enough. Erian, may the fallen gods bless you with patience.

--

"Enter, Historians."

Queen Dylinn had not been surprised by the visit, but likely expectant of such. Her door had opened before they had made it half way down the final hallway, her words echoing through the passageway in anticipation of their approach.

The dark-skinned woman stood tall and slender, over six feet in height, only slightly above standard for Fallneesian women. Her hair braided in the back, her eyes almost golden in color, a middle-aged beauty unmatched by Aldric's vision, but saddened in an indescribable way. Not in the sorrow of one losing her husband, but of one losing purpose.

"I suppose you come to hear my account of things," she bluntly stated, moving toward a clear glass mug of water, pouring three cups while she spoke.

"If it does not trouble you," Aldric claimed.

"Much troubles me, Historian. My late husband is of the least." She crossed the room with elegance as she handed the two cups of water to her guests, keeping one for herself. "So have you met the young king?"

"We just left counsel with him, milady."

"He is a little shit, is he not?" Dylinn chuckled to herself. "His father's son, through and through. I weep for Amon, milord, and pray to the fallen gods for forgiveness against what will be unleashed unto our land."

"With proper guidance, milady, any man . . ."

"Guidance?" Again the queen laughed. "You presume I stay after the ceremonies tomorrow."

So he had. It took a moment for the Historian to respond to the latest revelation. "You leave Corovium?"

"What purpose is there in staying, Historian? I have already decided to ride back to Fallneese at week's end, to return to my family, leave this accursed capital that has stripped me of my pride and youth. Yelium will rule this kingdom as he sees fit, without council from the former queen."

"But your son takes the throne, milady," claimed Aldric, nearly crossing the borderline of impartial judgment, he realized.

Dylinn must have sensed much as well. "What you know is written in history, but not repeated to change our country," she stated as fact rather than question. But Aldric nodded all the same. "What if information that you knew could not only change our country, but completely shake the foundation? Would you still withhold those facts, remain sworn to your Kwyantin oath?"

"Any information I receive will be written within the histories for any to read, should they choose to seek the information out. But my information will not be made readily available for generations to come, my queen."

"Then have the histories read correctly to the knowledge of this House, Historian. When I left to Fallneese for the birth of my son, I did so in company with a servant woman, who in reality was a whore from some brothel here in Corovium. I was ushered with her far away from Genethur, somewhere private and hidden within Fallneese where I shared, in a manner of speaking, space with this whore for almost six months. I did so because she, not I, carried the child of my husband. Not once during our tenure together did I speak with this whore. Not once did I ask her for her name.

"Hidden away from the world, I sat and waited, visited from time to time by First Pratt to check in on the situation, the only man trusted with the truth. Not once did Yelium visit me. Not once did I receive word on his concern. Instead I watched the whore's child grow inside her, watched as my husband's indiscretion became truth upon every passing day. When the time came for the birth of the child, Philip Pratt was present, along with the whore's nurse and another nameless figure. First Pratt stood as an account to the legitimacy of the birth of *my* son, the nurse to deliver, and the nameless figure I found later to be one of the Moon Divide."

Dylinn placed down her water and turned away from the Aldric, her voice now lower and solemn. "Needless to say, the Moon Divide killed the nurse and the whore after the delivery of the child, and First Pratt escorted me and this child, Yelium Aylmer II, back to Corovium, the heir to the throne secure along with the secret of his birth."

The Historian could not mask his shock. "Milady . . ."

"The bastard, rightful name and all, does not have right to the throne without the council's approval. And being that he is not my son, even if he believes me his mother, I have no desire to remain here in counsel to that arrogant child."

"And Amon, my Queen?" Aldric inquired, knowing all too well her answer before she could reply.

"To Shadow with Amon," Dylinn hissed. "What has this country given me besides a husband whose seed impregnated a whore and in my absence during my fake pregnancy, he found Chur'ash and became sterile? And after raising a bastard child, I find myself beyond my prime, no children of my own, no husband to keep me warm at night. What is left for me to give to this world, Historian, besides spite?"

Aldric had no words for the queen. *Flame's embrace, Dylinn. Aylmer has no rights to the throne. And you hold this information from everyone, even to the boy that believes you his mother!*

"Not quite what you expected when you arrived in Corovium, is it Historian? Alas, at least your final venture to the capital will be a grand tale in your written account."

More than I wanted, milady. And a burden I wish you did not have to shoulder.

Earth and Flame, what will become of Amon?

--

If you want to ask me of the Moon Divide, I would advise that you just go ask them yourself. And good luck with that.

I am no fool. If the Divide wanted their names recorded in history, they would write the damn thing themselves.

-- John Shonnen, First General of the Imperial Army

II

Night had enveloped Corovium, the buzz of the capital building slowly dissipating as the evening progressed. The dinner feast in celebration of both the end of one rule and the beginning of a new one had just recently finalized. Most in attendance had begun to find their guest rooms, which had already been prepared for those Houses visiting from far throughout Amon.

Philip had not found himself at the feast. Instead, he sat alone with a glass of red wine . . . a merlot as it were . . . sitting outside his balcony, staring out at the Twin Moons.

The yellow is Schill, the red Turitea. How do I still remember these things? When is the last time I even stepped into a church?

First Pratt had little belief in the gods, fallen or otherwise. To believe in them meant believing in destiny and fate, of which he had little time for. Things happened. If they did not, then nothing would happen. That was as complex as Philip needed things to be. His life had been plagued of complexity, and the need to muddy it up with religion and faith felt trifling.

As First, Philip owned the entire east wing on the second floor of the capital. His daughter, Joanna, and her husband, Winston Leir, had been given half of the wing after their marriage a year prior. His youngest, Lillianna, had several rooms all for her own as well. His housing had been remodeled, a combination of seventeen different rooms, creating a large dining and living area, along with multiple dens and a bar, as well as a grand balcony that faced toward the ocean. This was his moment of faith, his religion. A glass of wine, the ocean air filling his lungs, the view of the Twin Moons, their light beaming across the ocean waters creating an interesting array of colors that cascaded along the coastline with the incoming waves. Here, his life, if even for an hour or two, became less complex. Here, Philip could pretend he was anything but the First.

From inside, he could hear the front door to his housing open and close.

Shit. Reality must return eventually, I suppose.

His wife, Jessica, strode across the room toward the balcony. The evening dress, strapless and elaborate, looked good on her, masking her weight. Her long black hair was braided and lifted, her tanned face still pretty though rounded. After the birth of Lillianna, Jessica struggled to return to the shape she had once been, the woman that Philip had loved. Philip hated the part of him that studied his wife with revulsion, hated that he was superficial enough to wish that his wife had looked the way she had when they married so long ago. It had not been fair, as she had birthed two beautiful daughters and was forced by the king to remain unemployed. Apparently the lady of the First should not find work as it would look bad if the council had their women out amongst commoners. No, the king had decided long ago that the council would be treated as royalty, as extensions of the nobility. That had not done much favor to the women of the capital as far as their physical shape was concerned.

Birth children and sit around all day. What did Yelium expect?

It was not fair of his judgment to Jessica; it was, however, unavoidable to deny it.

She walked outside, joining him on the balcony, saying nothing for a moment. Grabbing a glass, Jessica poured herself some wine, taking a sip, staring out into the ocean.

"You were missed tonight," she finally made mention.

"Was I?" he returned.

She turned to him, her eyes not indicating anger; more along the lines of frustration or disappointment. "You do know your entire family is here for the most part, right? Your brothers, their wives, their children. Have you even bothered to greet Rayden yet? You know how much he looks up to you."

Rayden was a good boy, one he wished he himself had. Philip envied Nicolas for his son. Proud, strong, handsome, and worthy of the Pratt name. Rayden would be admirable and ready to succeed the House lordship when the time came and Philip would be honored to claim him as the lord of Donovini. Jerryn was not all that could be desired, every bit as handsome, but childish and brash. Not to say that he did not love his own children, but his two daughters would not carry the Pratt name into the histories with them. That duty would fall to his Pratt nephews, including his brother Edmond's son, Luther, even though he was a shit, and an ugly one at that. Edmond would be lucky to find a woman to marry his son willingly, as horrid as it was to say about his nephew. Unfortunate for them all that Edmond's first born, Nathanial, had been born from a barmaid a few months before his marriage. Though he did not carry the Pratt name, Nathanial was worthy of such honor. Alas, that was not of his power to give.

"I have not spoken much to Nicolas or Edmond," he confessed, taking a long sip from his glass before continuing. "We are brothers . . . men. We do not need to find each other and gossip for long hours. When the time is right, we'll drink the night away and discuss all that we need to discuss of our lives. Then we'll likely all pack our things and make our way back to Donovini."

Jessica frowned at his last statement. "You say such as if it were a curse to return home."

"It is when you do so unwillingly."

"So you believe then the king will remove you."

He simply glared at her for few seconds. "The boy despises me, Jessica. He would be a fool to keep me as his First. And if he shuffles the Houses, he would just as well request a different council member altogether. Edmond has been itching for purpose anyways. Nicolas can have him take my place in whatever position the brat king gives our House, likely Third." Philip shrugged. "It would only make sense, if I were in his place."

"Philip," she said softly, her hand gently resting upon his shoulder. "You have a daughter that has grown without you, a life missed on the account of your duty to Amon. You have done all that you can. Should the king make a foolish decision after his crowning, then take it as an opportunity to not allow a second daughter to grow without you."

"I love my children," he mumbled, mostly to himself.

"And you love your country. I understand there is a balance. But you have been the First now for what? Seventeen, eighteen years? It was a marvelous run, Philip. You have done all that could be done. If Aldric is to write of you in his histories, he would write of a man that worked to make lives better."

And ultimately, nothing to show for that life. That boy will ruin all that I tried to create.

"I know you will miss this," she continued. "But I miss Donovini, my love. I miss our homeland. I miss seeing our family regularly, watching the children grow into their own adulthood. I miss the dry weather and the heat, believe it or not. *I miss Astrona.* And mostly, I miss my husband. Maybe I will yet have him back."

And I sense eagerness in your words. You look forward to the crowning of Yelium. You want me removed as First. Not to say I blame you. I have been a lousy husband and a rather disappointing father.

No different than my own.

"I have a meeting to attend," he claimed suddenly, her face unchanged at the announcement.

"And here we were talking of you leaving your duties."

"They are still mine, for as long as that may be."

"And what is important enough to have my husband sit here, mulling over something alone with a glass of wine, missing a dinner with his family? What takes my husband away this night?"

His eyes met hers. "I meet about the army in the east."

"At this hour?" Jessica's face shifted from perplexed to comprehension within seconds. "Let me guess, this has to do with the Moon Divide."

Woman is far too smart for her own good about these things.

"And best not to ask any further about the subject. You know I don't like you to even know of their existence much less our affiliation with them."

"Well I'd wager that you aren't setting this meeting up, so who is?" she pressed.

Philip knew better than to play cat and mouse with this woman when it came to his job. "Afeon thought it best to use the Divide to help aid the nerves of thousands of our men in the east. Shonnen seems a bit . . . shaken."

"And Afeon thinks a few dozen men will help? I'd wager eternity in Shadow that the Ursan are up to something. They have grown far too powerful. Probably feels more comfortable with the Divide as far away from Genethur as possible."

Ah, even you don't trust the Ursan. The prejudice against them is everywhere. Why do we fear them so? Numbers alone do not equal strength. And yet, Lord Dehyllo has built an army out of his people.

"True or not, the meeting has already been arranged. I meet my contact. Wheels are in motion."

Taking another sip, she nodded slowly. "Should I wait up?"

Lifting from his seat, his lips touched hers. "No."

Draining the rest of her wine, Jessica shrugged her indifference. "Enjoy your night then, First Pratt."

Though it was not said to be harsh, at least not by the tone, it was taken as such. But Philip shouldered the words, carried them, giving him weight to the burdens of his life.

I deserve much harsher words than that. If only she knew the remainder of my faults.

--

Sitting within one of the many day rooms on the first floor, Rayden sat comfortably upon the long sofa, his sister Katlynn beside him; he with a mug of ale, she with a glass of wine. Across from him beyond the coffee table on another sofa were his cousins Luther, son of Uncle Edmond, and Joanna, daughter of Uncle Philip. Joanna's husband, Winston, also sat with his wife. Missing amongst them were Lillianna, who had been ushered upstairs by his Aunt Jessica an hour prior, and his brother Jerryn, who had disappeared from their little family congregation immediately following the formal dinner, much to Rayden's chagrin. It had been a few years since they had all been able to sit as one, and he found himself angered that Jerryn likely found himself a foolish servant girl and made for the beach.

He resisted the urge to find him and drag him back inside at this late of an hour. It was not that Rayden did not understand the boy's youth, only his lack of understanding that he was a Pratt, that his uncle stood as the First in this very building. Perhaps there was a hint of jealousy in the free will of the boy, but the last thing they needed was some scandal, of him fucking the wrong woman that would bring unwanted attention to House Pratt. Hopefully his brother knew better than to embarrass their House. Their father was stern but understanding in many things, but respect was something that not even Rayden dared challenge the man in.

The passersby were few at this late hour, and only one attendant continually stood at watch for the Pratt children, refilling their drinks when needed. Winston smoked a small pipe, filling the room with an interesting aroma. He had claimed it to be a rare weed from Ursan. The legitimacy of that claim, Rayden did not know.

"Speaking of Ursan, did anyone get a count of how many people are within House Brocusk?" Joanna started, the eldest of them all at twenty-two.

"Forget people," Katlynn jumped in. "How many wives did each of the Brocusks have? Is there a limit?"

Luther chuckled to a bit, the attendant bringing him another mug of ale. "Why stop?" the eighteen-year-old added. "If you are allowed by your laws to have multiple wives, why not have dozens?"

"Have you *tried* marriage, my friend?" Winston Leir claimed jokingly, with Joanna punching him on his arm. "One is quite enough, my friend."

Joanna huffed loudly. "Seriously though, did anyone count? There had to have been a hundred present from House Brocusk. Just one House, not even his brothers or such."

"I believe Lord Dehyllo Brocusk has three wives and about thirteen sons, four daughters," Rayden stated, taking a swig of his dark ale. "And a few of those sons and daughters are married with kids of their own. So Shadow knows how many are under House Brocusk, being that we only saw Dehyllo's immediate family. He has eighteen siblings, as I understand."

"Earth and Flame," muttered Katlynn, her wine refilling.

"Well, save for your brother, it's nice to get us all together again," Luther shot toward Rayden.

"I agree, save for your brother as well, cousin," he quickly replied back.

"Why didn't Nathan show?" Katlynn inquired.

"Because this is a formal gathering for the king, you shit," lashed Luther. "You don't bring your bastard to these kinds of affairs."

Made of knives, this one.

"Nathanial is your brother all the same, Luke," Rayden cautioned. "Show him respect, being he cannot be here to defend himself."

"No but *you* can be, apparently," slyly he responded. "I meant no ill by the words, Rayden. I only speak truth. Ultimately my father did not invite him. It would not be proper. Like it or not, and I know that you don't, he's not a Pratt, and this invitation to the crowning of the new king was for House *Pratt*, not *Wode*."

"Is anyone at all concerned that no one seems to care that the king is dead?" Joanna mentioned, switching the conversation nonchalantly. "A boy younger than all of us is about to rule Amon, and we don't seem to be worried. By the fallen gods, we are arguing over Nathan of all things."

Finally a statement had been made to silence the room. Joanna, for all of her brilliant qualities, primarily her stunning looks, height, and poise, she at times lacked any inclination of understanding on what to and not to discuss. The woman spoke her mind, for better or worse.

"Well one of us seems to be worried," Luther mumbled.

"Maybe we should not talk about that inside the capital, Joanna," Rayden suggested. "Some things might be best discussed more privately, away from wandering ears."

"I only speak what the rest of you are likely thinking," she defended, but Winston placed his hand upon her arm, giving her a look to all but claim his thoughts on the matter.

"A discussion for enclosed walls, my love," her husband informed quietly.

"Another topic then," Luther stated and he took a healthy swig from his mug. "How did *your* dinner go, cousin?"

Katlynn nudged him gently, a smile upon her face. "Yes, brother. How was Lady Rowe this evening?"

Certainly he did what he could to retain his stern face, to not showcase for the others to see his excitement at his evening with Allura Rowe. Certainly, though, he had failed at such.

Luke laughed hardily. "Well, is someone smitten with that Rowe girl? Earth's warm bosom, Rayden, it is one thing to try and fuck this woman for a night, but another thing entirely to be infatuated with this girl. She isn't even Donovinian."

"I am ashamed to call you family right now," Katlynn stated, chuckling through it. "It shouldn't matter what country someone is born in. You are a horrible human being, Luther. Besides, my brother can be smitten all he wants with that light skinned girl, right brother?"

"Apparently you all already have your own opinions about my dinner, so there is nothing to share." It had, though, gone well in his mind. They had a separate table from their respective Houses, though there were the wandering eyes from both families at the two. He could not tell if his father completely approved of such a public meeting between them. Certainly Allura's mother, Christina, had been curious of the affair. They had known of the obvious attraction between the two and discussed privately of a possible union. Of course for them, it would be political with an enormous amount of meetings to uncover what the union would hold, which House they would represent, and a multitude of nonsense that Rayden would rather not become involved in. Not that he did not care for the status of his House, only his needs were of a more personal nature.

After spending only a few hours this evening with the girl, and he had trouble thinking or even focusing on anything other than her eyes, her smile. Allura was intelligent, his match in every way. It had been far more than just an oddity to find such a woman in Donovini, it had been impossible. Women of his country were shallow, hardened perhaps by their environment. Something about the women from Argonus, their prestige, the way they handled themselves, their wit and independence . . . it separated them from the rest of Amon. And no more illustrious of an example than Allura. To offend a woman in Argonus, and he might strike an intriguing debate that would match him. Do the same in Donovini, and he would likely get his jewels punched. Then again, an Ursan woman might as well chop them off and cook them. Tact did not always cross borders the same.

But if Luther had been right about anything, it had been on his comment of her country, her race. Certainly it was not unheard of, especially inside of the Guild, for people of different cultures to marry and have children. That concept, unfortunately, was still a bit taboo.

Rayden caught himself yawn for the first time and stared at a mostly empty mug that he had been nursing for long enough to know the hour was late. Besides, he had not truly noticed until he glared at his mug that he had little idea at how many he had this night. *Being that I can't remember, one too many, I think.*

"I think my night is ending." He raised his ale to his fellow Pratt House. "To a new king tomorrow."

"At this hour, I think today actually," Katlynn murmured.

"Even better," he remarked, downing the remaining contents of his mug.

--

The night fell further into darkness and Philip gazed back to ensure one of the capital guards remained close but hidden. Outside in the rear courtyard should not have been a harrowing experience, even at a late hour. No thief or assassin would dare make an attempt to breach the capital walls, at least not in a time which every House stood in attendance; the guard count higher than the guest count at such an event as the crowning of a king. But the First's nerves were on end, though not on the unknown assailant, but the known one. For indeed he invited a killer to meet him this night, and no matter how frequent his talks with the voice of the Divide, he hated every second spent close to him.

Not that Deso was a foul, ill-mannered man by any means. Part of the reason he was the liaison to begin with was his ability to articulate as a human rather than act like an animal like his companions. It was knowing what the man was capable of, what the man had accomplished in his life. More a healthy concern than fear, he convinced himself.

He turned again, the guard still remained close.

And when he turned back, Deso stood closer.

Philip nearly soiled himself in startle, and the Fallneesian killer seemed pleased at the effect.

"If I wanted you dead, First, I would have taken out the guard you have hidden in the shadows before moving to you."

"Comforting to know," Philip responded.

Deso was dark skinned, as most from Fallneese, with a shaved head and shaved eyebrows, but a cleanly shaped black beard that moved along his jaw line. Perhaps mid-thirties, if Philip were a guessing man, the voice of the Divide stood chiseled from stone, his tunic shirt tight enough to showcase his raised muscular chest, his thick arms and broadened shoulders. Philip would rather pick a fight with a Draywolf than this man.

He did not carry any weapons; at least none that could be seen.

At least he will have to strangle me if he wants me dead. Or rip off my arm and beat me to death with it. Another comforting thought.

"I thank you for coming at such a short notice," Philip began.

Deso snorted. "Aye, can we cut to the chase, First? You have taken me away from beers and whores, and I'm not so sure which upsets me more. Since it is up for debate, likely beers, because I need more to enjoy the whores." He paused for a moment. "Because they're ugly, First Pratt. Keep up."

Philip shook his head. "Do you know why I picked you, of all the Divide, to be the liaison to your crew?"

"Because I'm the only one that likes you," he replied.

"You don't like me, Deso."

To which Deso shrugged. "Aye. Well . . . by like, I mean least likely to kill you."

"Point taken." He knew the man well enough to know the difference between joking banter and a legitimate threat. This was neither. The killer made a truthful claim. If Philip's death had some sort of gain for Deso, the First would be face down in the grassy courtyard. "I selected you because you are the only one that understands the hierarchy of things."

"You mean I take orders, or understand the consequences otherwise." Deso's arms crossed his massive chest. "Not that the Divide misunderstands, First Pratt, only they don't fucking care. What happens if a dead man refuses an order? Does he become dead quicker? All the better, some might claim. For me, I'd rather stay alive as long as I can. Alive means more beers, more whores. See how it all comes full circle?"

"Well your understanding of the hierarchy, regardless of the reason, has you in the position you are in. Also, the rest of the Divide listen to you."

The Fallneesian chuckled at that statement. "If you say so, First Pratt."

"More so than anyone else."

And he nodded to that. "Agreed."

"Which is why I am electing that the Moon Divide be rounded up, with you in the lead, and head east."

"The Divide doesn't have a lead."

"They do now," First Pratt stated sternly.

Deso grunted. "How many do I . . . *lead*?"

"All of them."

"All of them?" Deso rubbed with his thumb against one of his shaven eyebrows, something he did when agitated. "I hope there is good reason to get all of the Divide together. And how far east?"

"All the way, to the coast."

Deso stood silent for a time, glancing over Philip's shoulder. "The Imperial Army stands along the eastern coast, First Pratt."

"And the Moon Divide joins them."

"Joins them to what end?"

"As soldiers. Welcome to the army, Lieutenant Deso."

The expression remained unfazed on the Fallneesian. "Captain Deso has a nice ring to it, I suppose."

"*Second Lieutenant Deso*," clearly stated Philip. "And the rest of the Divide are privates. I'd rank them kitchen attendants if I didn't fear what they'd serve the troops."

"The Divide will not listen to me or any authority within the Imperial Army and you know that. You have been a fairly straight forward man since I've known you, First Pratt," Deso made claim, one of the few statements where the Fallneesian made thorough attempt to sound sincere. "So hopefully you will be honest in your answer to my next question. Is this by the rope or by the chain?"

"By the chain . . . I hope."

Deso glanced again over his shoulder again. "Would either you or the Historian care to explain any of this to me?"

Philip turned about to hear the approaching footsteps long before he could actually see the large figures, two Kwyantin men, one instantly recognizable as Aldric. He adorned the familiar long robes of his people, with the hood draped over his elder brow.

"I apologize," started the Historian. "We were passing through, having recently finished meetings with several Houses this night. There was no intent to spy upon this meeting, but I am embarrassingly fascinated by the opportunity to meet with a member of the Moon Divide."

"This may not be the best of times, Historian," Philip noted, "though you of course are welcome to stay for this meeting."

Where is the harm in it? Besides, difficult to move an eight foot giant. Better they move on their own.

"You know it's not by design that you see me," Deso claimed to Aldric. "Dumb luck alone has us meeting."

"I find that dumb luck is how most of this world stumbles along."

"Aye, I'd drink to that. But if you ask questions of me, I would tell you to rightfully fuck off. I'd rather be kept out of your histories, if it makes any difference to you."

"*My* histories?' baffled the Historian, though not in a tone that would suggest objection; only genuine bewilderment. "My people write these histories for all of mankind."

"If you say so, Historian."

"Might I ask why you think such?" Aldric pried.

"No, now fuck off," he stated, turning fearlessly away from the giant Kwyantin and toward Philip. "Back to the topic at hand. What is the reason for the Divide on the coast?"

"Honestly?" started Philip. "Something is happening there, enough that the general has requested aid."

"What is it that they guard against?" Deso pressed. "I have heard they stand waiting for ghosts and hide from shadows. Now you want a volatile group of killers, thieves, and, let's be honest, assholes to travel across the entire damn country to do the same? If the Divide doesn't kill themselves on the journey, the Imperial Army certainly will, and not without a ton of causalities on their end. Answers, straight answers, or the next order you send will be to the rest of your army to hunt down the missing Divide. Or better yet, send the Guild after us, see what happens to them."

Now that was a threat.

"Not so much ghosts, Deso, as much as rumors, religious notions," was the First's answer.

"Not rumors entirely, First," Aldric commented. Both he and the Fallneesian turned to gaze upward at the Historian. "I have been able to validate some of what is speculated. If you like, I can tell you what I know. Or at the very least, what I have read."

Philip simply stared knowingly for a few seconds at the Kwyantin. "By all means, Historian. I'd love to know truth from stories."

"Truth I cannot validate, First Pratt, but I can say that I have found inaccuracies in the histories that I've read thus far. The continent deep across the Terrandonan Sea is called Espis, after an old word not easily translated from our language long ago. From what I have read, the sea was once as it was now. Calm, settled, not as it has been for many hundreds of years prior."

"Has the eastern sea been deadly your entire life, Historian?" Deso queried.

"It has, until now," Aldric added. "Thousands of years ago there stood another lost race of Amon, or so claim the histories, that lived here within Amon. They were different, savage as one of your own history books had proclaimed, at times more animal than man. Some books referred to these people as demons. Despite the differences, the people within Amon spent many years in peace and prospered off each other. I could never find the right text to discover what became of the flimsy alliance between Amon and this ancient race, but once things came apart, a war began."

"And your point to this entertaining history lesson is coming up sooner than later, yes?" further stabbed the Fallneesian.

If the Historian had been upset, it did not show in his face. "The war lasted lifetimes. Hundreds of thousands of lives spilled in this war. I do not know how the Realms played a part in this nor do I know how involved the gods were, but at some point, the Twin Moons began to rise from the horizon, slowly coming together as one in the sky. As they did, the Terrandonan Sea became unsettled, restless, devastating. The more the waves hammered away at the shores, the more the storms raged into the depths of the ocean, the less able those from Espis could cross."

"So sea rages, people of Amon win and exile the rest of the demons across the great sea, and all's well that ends well. That about right?" pestered Deso. "Believe it or not, Historian, that story is not so obscure amongst the common folk beneath you. I have heard similar tales sung by drunken bards in taverns that are dirtier than a few whores that I've fucked. Well . . . maybe not *that* dirty. Regardless, what makes your tale any more or less true than stories and songs? And moreover, what does any of that have to do with a piss scared general on the eastern coast, and my new rank of captain?"

"Lieutenant," mumbled the First.

"Whatever," Deso snapped in response.

Aldric waited a moment, his mind in apparent deep thought. "Your ministers, regardless of the religion, preach of the gods, tell you of the protection that Schill and Turitea give you. Religious or not, believe or not, the Twin Moons are separating again, and have slowly over a few hundred years fallen from the sky in opposing directions, heading closer to the horizon, threatening to leave us completely. Every year, the sea calms. The gods kept the eastern seas deadly in order to protect Amon from whatever lies on the other side."

"And the gods have abandoned us," said the Fallneesian killer.

"Leaving an opportunity for the end of days, as the ministers have warned us for years."

"Still, even if any of the books written by random people are true, what does that *really* have to do with anything?" Deso shrugged. "A war so far back that even you have to research it, against a race that existed before Amon had likely properly formed as a unified country. It's a war that we do not remember, save for songs and history books, books that seem more like fiction than fact. Demons across the sea, pray to the gods for wisdom so that we will survive when they return. Oh and give us gold coin so that we can continue to spread the gospel. How do we know anything lies across the sea at all? How do we even know if they ever existed? And even if some lost race of Amon lives on the other side, how do we even know they remember who we are to ever actually return?"

Aldric frowned some, a troubled look reflected on his brow. "My master tried to warn me once of the other side."

"Jaa the Knowledgeable was your master," added the First, feeling quite foolish afterward. He had leapt to the name as if he gained a prize for knowing that information. "His statue lies directly outside the throne room."

Aldric nodded. "Indeed. I wish I would have listened to him more often, more carefully before his . . . departure." The Historian straightened some. "There have been accounts of strange things that have washed ashore on our end. Unknown weapons, writings that could not be deciphered, things that would seem obvious that something once stood there. But whether or not something remains, not even I can say."

Deso turned to Philip. "Your general has shown fear. What has he seen?"

"I don't believe it is what he has seen," started the First, "more what he hasn't. Missing scouts, missing boats, strange things against the ocean horizon."

"So then they do in fact guard against ghosts. Only they may be more real than we make claim?"

The First shook his head. "Ghosts and whispers, nothing real. Their fear is of the unseen, which is normally far more frightening than reality."

In true form, Deso shrugged. "Why Espis?"

Aldric raised an eyebrow, taking a moment to realize that the Divide spoke to him. "How do you mean?"

"I mean the word Espis? What does it mean?"

"An old Kwyantin word, before we adapted to the common tongue. And I am certainly not a linguist. Knowing my old language was not really a priority, knowing that I would be spending the entirety of my life amongst the people of Amon. From what I can gather, it does not exactly translate, but it is somewhere in between the words gather and flee. Similar to withdraw, but in disarray."

"Would panic be the word you are looking for?" the Fallneesian offered up.

But the Historian shook his head. "No, more organized than that. It is more of a fear than a strategy, to leave because it is better than staying. Again, the word does not easily translate."

"Duly noted." The killer turned back to Philip. "So again, by the rope or by the chain, First Pratt?"

"Don't tell me that a member of the Moon Divide is spooked by some story by the Historian?" questioned Philip, almost immediately regretting it based on the returned look. *Flame's embrace, where does this false courage come from?*

"Tell me, First Pratt, how many do you have on the coast right now? A few thousand?"

"Give or take." *If twenty thousand is more than a few.*

"And something has your general concerned. Which means he is seeing something that may lay some truth to what the Historian has stated and what many of us have known from bedtime stories and late night drunken affairs. And now you, the most power man in Amon, are sending sixty-two men to calm a group of thousands. And you have also just made a captain out of a criminal."

"A lieutenant, but yes, to sum it all up."

"And how certain are you that there is nothing to fear on the eastern coast? If you are so certain of such things, why send us? I know the Divide exists for the dirty jobs, but this seems far too visible for us. Just send reinforcements."

"I am," answered the First. "They don't need more men, Deso. They need more balls."

"I am not so sure you want these kind of men delivering your vote of confidence. Very well. How long do we provide this . . . moral support?"

"For as long as General Shonnen deems necessary."

Deso shook his head. "I warn you, First Pratt, this will end poorly."

As is the story of my life.

"Noted, Lieutenant," replied Philip. "Any further questions before you gather your men?"

"None. It will take several weeks to gather them all, maybe even a month, but it will be done."

"A month?" the First stammered.

"We don't exactly bed together, First Pratt. I have to send out word, then they have to pack their shit and meet me. I'd wager not even you would want us all hanging out together at all times, especially this close to the capital."

True enough.

He turned and began to move back into the darkness.

"Have caution," the Historian called to Deso. "I do hope all that I have read, all that has previously come to pass shall not repeat itself."

"No worries," he responded without turning. "If we see these ghost people, I will tell everyone to *Espis*."

--

His escort seemed concerned and confused at his dismissal, but could not refuse the order from the First. Philip navigated slowly in the courtyard, the view behind the capital building astonishing as the grass and flowers bled seamlessly into the white sands of the beach beyond. Though appearances deceived the guard who likely still eyed him from afar, wondering perhaps where the First took his evening strolls and why so frequently, the reality was far more primitive.

Though this night his thoughts remained clouded. He was pleased at the swift departure of Deso and subsequent leave of Aldric and his apprentice, but the thought of war and the mysterious people of Espis spoken of by the Historian hung above him, tugged away at his courage. What truth stood in any of which was spoken? Certainly he knew *some* of that to which the Historian claimed. He was, after all, the First. Information was how he based his decisions, outside of his own instincts. But Philip never truly believed any of it.

The preachers and prophets had come to him, long after they had swayed the majority of the populace into believing that the end of days was upon them. At times it felt as if people had a morbid fascination with death, with the end of the known world. Yes, there stood some truth in these wars, but what difference did that really make to him? Send the troops eastward? If that appeased the people and removed the churches from his presence, so be it. That not being enough, then the army would have to do. Not once in his act did he think of what he was doing, only the result of that decision. And that result was simple: peace and quiet.

But now the reason stood forefront in his mind. What if these people still remained? What if they made their way across the ocean? How many would they or could they be? Would they come for peace or war? And how much, if any, did he *really* believe?

A low moan caught his ear, startling him, causing him to reach for a sword that was not there. He had not been foolish enough to arm himself while meeting a member of the Moon Divide. If he would draw his weapon to Deso or any of the Divide for that matter, he might as well stab himself with it, save them the annoyance of doing it themselves. But now, frightened of a sound, he wished otherwise.

At the same time, as the sound did not return, he wished for his dignity back.

Gather your wits. Deso spooked by a story? Laughable. There is irony somewhere in there.

Moving a bit more cautiously, again came the moan toward the beach, followed by a woman's giggle. Then his eyes finally caught a figure . . . two figures behind a series of palm trees that towered together at the edge of the sand. Philip smiled, remembering his own youth, and quickly decided to move along silently as to not disturb the lovers.

But when one of the voices, a young man, became distinct as he spoke softly to the woman, too distinct in fact, his decision to pass without pause had been erased. *Hopefully my ears deceive me.* Philip crept closer, hoping to identify one of the two lovers without being noticed, clarifying that the man was not who he had feared.

Neither of those two hopes came to fruition. Coming closer to the palm trees, he watched as a young girl rose up, riding the male beneath her as if he were a saddle, moaning and giggling, her youthful body flawless as her arms pressed above her head. Her hands moved through her blonde hair as she leaned back, her body coming into better view through the trees. Guilt pressed Philip as he moved forward, knowing full well that his intentions were to find out who the one underneath was. Innocent if a bit prying at best, but his eyes could not divert from the perfectly rounded breasts, the gyrating hips that forced down, pleasuring the mystery man beneath her. He could not see her face through the trees, as if that prevented the stiffening in his pants.

So distracted by the young woman's body, he paid little attention to his stealth. Something crushed underneath Philip's foot and the girl turned to the sound. She stood wholly unfamiliar behind the trees and the darkness.

She shrieked and dove for the blankets, while the young man rose, naked and ready to attack, until he realized who he stared at.

"Uncle Philip?"

And the First shook his head. "Jerryn, so help me, I am about to kill you." While his brother's youngest son stood in all his glory in the moonlight, Philip's attention turned to the girl beneath the blankets. "Whoever you are, I suggest you gather your clothes and get back to your House quarters before your family notices you are gone. And be lucky I do not escort you there myself."

Lucky for you. Unlucky for me, however.

The girl grabbed her clothes and with the blanket draped over her, she ran back toward the capital building, Philip forcing his eyes not to follow her as she left.

"Uncle, I can explain," started his nephew.

"Jerryn, what is there to explain?" Philip looked at two empty bottles of wine propped against one of the trees. "A little drink, a beautiful young girl you swooned to lay with you on the beach. Tell me Jerryn, what promises did you make to this girl? That her beauty alone would allow you to change your carefree lifestyle? Flame's embrace, Jerryn, you are the son of *the* House Lord! When will you act as such and not like some spoiled, lackadaisical little shit?"

The boy said nothing. He stood silent and still, his eyes unable to reach Philip's. "You piss on your father by your actions. The king is dead, we are hours away from crowning a new king, and you stand here naked for the world to see. Your father rules Donovini. How would it have looked if someone other than myself should have stumbled upon your stupidity? You piss on me as well. I am the First of Amon, Jerryn! Does that not mean anything to you, that your family has prestige in this land?" He turned back to watch as the girl finished clothing herself by the rear entrance of the capital, slipping through silently. The girl was Argon, which did not sit well with him. "Please tell me that she was not someone of importance in House Rowe? No, you know what, I'd rather not know. But I certainly hope that I do not have some father of importance yelling at me at how a member of my House cannot keep his pants on, if even for one fucking night!"

Jerryn only hissed under his breath. "You know nothing," he mumbled.

"Always the child, Jerryn." The boy was about plain useless, family or not. "Get back to your father's wing, and find a way to do so discreetly. *Discreetly*, understood? I might find this night forgotten in my talks to your father if you can manage that."

The boy nodded and scampered off toward the building.

"And get your fucking clothes on!"

--

"I said take your fucking clothes off, First Pratt."

He might have been a tad beyond his prime, but none would be able to tell based on his physique. Philip had not always been simply the First of Amon. Once, long ago, he had wielded a blade and defended Donovini as strongly and as proudly as his elder brother. With his shirt off, his muscles displayed, he gazed across at the Fallneesian woman, candles lit within her chambers that casted shadows of her nude body against the walls.

"I had thought to come here for a report, milady," he had replied in jest.

Queen Dylinn Aylmer, his younger by at least ten years, placed her hands upon her breasts, pressing them together, her eyes locked to his. "I'd have your report at some time after your clothes are back on, First Pratt. Not a moment sooner. But first, you must remove them. All of them."

She was, as she had always been, a demanding woman.

In fact, he was certain that she loved him. Never had Dylinn told him so, never had the two discussed their emotions despite their long term affair. But so long ago, he had been there for the birth of Yelium's son, the bastard about to take the throne. His friend, the king, had trusted him to be with his wife during the difficult time of coping with the distance from him, from Genethur, from home. He loved his king, but never had he betrayed a trust the way he had done then, the way he had done throughout the years.

A damaged woman, a broken woman who wanted nothing more than to be held, touched, loved. What he could not give to her emotionally, he had been able to do so physically. There had certainly been guilt, as despite everything, he still loved his wife, his family. But every man had a breaking point, a vice unable to overcome. Dylinn was a radiant, sexually demanding woman that might have been emotionally attached to him, but would never allow those feelings to interfere with his marriage, her duties, or their respective families. Ultimately, this led nowhere and would likely end soon enough. And he would leave her broken, perhaps more so than her late king. As for all his flaws, Yelium loved his wife. The man, however, had no capacity to display that love.

The problem with Philip was his weakness against the tests given before him. He watched Dylinn move slowly toward him, her hands moving down the sides of her hips as she walked. Every man had tests to overcome, and this woman was his. He could no more refuse her than he could cease breathing. Understanding and conquering faults were two separate issues altogether.

"You know I will not be here once Yelium's son takes the throne," he stated softly, watching as the queen removed his pants slowly, her hands gently rubbing against his stomach, her nails scratching just below his navel. She began to press her lips against his chest, biting hard against his nipple. Wincing in pain, he managed to state, "I will not be the First, and will likely not be in Corovium much longer."

"Nor will I be queen much longer, First Pratt," she stated, yet again refusing to call him by his first name. "Might we live out our last night, I as queen, you as the First?"

Her lips continued to move down his body. "Do you care to hear of Afeon's discussion with me earlier today?"

"Yes," was her response. "As I said, after your clothes are on. Not . . . a moment . . . sooner."

--

Rayden heard the door open and close to his living quarters and watched a shirtless Jerryn stumble in. The elder brother sat up from his bed, but quickly pressed his hands against his temple, his mind still swimming from the alcohol.

"Save any of your damned preaching," his younger brother bellowed as he fell face first into his bed, which lay opposite from his own.

After a moment of gathering his composure and reaching for a pitcher of water that he had wisely left beside his bed, Rayden stated, "Just tell me that no one saw you."

After a long, thought filled pause, he mumbled, "Uncle Philip."

And now I am truly a dead man.

"You have to be kidding me, Jerryn. If he tells father . . ."

"He won't," assured Jerryn.

"And you know this how?" After taking a large gulp from the pitcher and returning it, he continued. "If father comes at me for your stupidity one more time, Jerryn . . ."

An empty threat, he knew, but maturity would not reach the man.

"Whatever, Rayden. How often I forget how perfect you are, how you will one day succeed father and get everything you ever wanted. It must be so difficult in being the favored one."

"It's not about being favored," answered Rayden. "This is about you showing some respect. Acting as if you are a member of this House, not some skirt chasing fool."

"Not you, not Uncle Philip, not even father understands me, so quit pretending as if you know anything about what makes me who I am. Now if you don't mind, I am going to sleep. Maybe you should pay less attention to chastising me and more attention to the empty bed to your right."

As he turned, he saw nothingness atop the third bed in the room. Katlynn was nowhere to be seen.

His heart sank within his chest. "The gods truly have fallen," escaped his lips. "I am placed in Amon to babysit grown adults so it seems. Where in Shadow did she go?"

--

Once, as she understood it, reaching into the Realms, the worlds beyond their own, was considered magic. But since so few could manipulate the Realms, so few could find the mental capacity to *see* the doorways much less open them, it seemed an art rather than simple magic. Utilizing the powers held within the Realms was more like science than mysticism.

Even understanding such, some still knew it as magic. Perhaps most people appreciated the unexplainable rather than the obsessive need to categorize everything, discover the meaning behind it all as if they were all Historians of Amon. Katlynn accepted such thinking, as even being a Shadowmancer, she always felt the same.

Certainly since her youth, the Shadow Realm had been visible to her eyes, another plane of existence that led to somewhere that felt unfit for mankind. She had difficulty explaining her gift to others. Thankfully, her father had given her strict ordinance to never use her ability and certainly not let others know of this gift.

She could only describe seeing another Realm as in looking through a window. The focus of the eye was what was through the window, not the window itself. How many people thought of it as looking *at* a window? What was on the other side of that window was what mattered. Thus it became transparent in more than one way. Though just because a vast majority of people ignored the window and only saw through it, it did not change the fact that it was there.

The Realms crossed in such a way. To her, it was plain to see, plain to reach out and grasp it. Invisible to nearly all, many walked right by, around, yet completely ignorant to their existence. How it arrived, why it crossed their world, Katlynn neither knew nor speculated on such. It was there, she could see it, she could take hold of a power on the other side of it.

Katlynn used Shadow to envelope her, shroud her within the nothingness of the Realm beyond as she did now. Moving about in complete darkness, she passed guards that did not know of her presence. It was a trick she had learned at a very young age in Astrona, sneaking about the castle behind her parents and overbearing brother's back, allowing her a freedom that they could never offer.

The gods, Turitea and Schell, had gifted the Three Realms, so the religions stated. Some claimed them gifts for those powerful enough to see them. Other religions claimed them a curse, that they would destroy the known world. There were even some, a fewer lot, that claimed that the Realms were worlds altogether, and that they were in fact living within the Fourth Realm, that they all intersected each other. Those such as her could reach out and touch another world, borrowing power as if it were a part of her very being.

In any case, Katlynn spent very little of her time cataloging her belief. She had an ability and thus she utilized it . . . despite her father's constant bickering for her to hide such use. She could only see the Shadow Realm, not the others. There had never been someone who could see more than one Realm, none within the histories of Amon. Using the power, she grasped at shadows and wrapped herself in the emptiness, allowing her to appear as the night. Every time she opened the Realm, a rush passed through her very being, the hairs on her arms raised and goose bumps littered her body. Once hers, she possessed a variety of things to do with the darkness, such as her ability to maneuver undetected as she did now. Such a power, even simple, still required restraint. Katlynn had mastered her power well enough to know to use it in short, sparse intervals. Even in such times, there always remained the desire for more.

Katlynn had heard horrors of men that could not satisfy their cravings of the other side with restraint, that merely touching the other side was not enough, and found the payment of their treachery was far more than their curiosity and desire could sustain. Most stories were only that. But she believed in these stories, believed them as she had felt the fear, be it calming or not, in the reaching for the power. There remained the sense that even in her ability to take from the other side, the Realms were not meant to be disturbed, her stealing of power was dangerous and life threatening. Knowing something was wrong and acting accordingly was not of Katlynn Pratt's better qualities, but even here she dare not sway.

It had been passed to her the only rule, unwritten at that, amongst those with the ability to see the other Realms. Touch, borrow, but never cross over. Those that broke that rule were lost to the world. They were said to become something else entirely, something . . . not human. Likely just stories, she knew. Unwritten or otherwise, true or not, the desire remained, but Katlynn did not need the warnings to understand the dangers of the other side. She could feel it sure as a knife to the chest.

Passing several guards as she left straight through the main entrance of the capital, she worked her way silently through the wide open courtyard, moving with purpose to the chambers for the lesser members of the House staff. Besides the few guards who were posted at the entrance, the night had cleared the area of life, all save for a nasty, large Chur'rat that huddled down on all fours, apparently spotting something that it could eat somewhere near a corner of a building. Right as she approached about as close as she was going to get to the disgusting thing during her stroll, the creature stood up on its hind legs and spun about to face her, the eyes red and narrowed. There should have been no way for this thing to spot her, being shrouded in the shadows as she was, but there was little mistaking the creature's recognition of her passing. It did nothing save stare, cock its head a bit, then returned to whatever meal it had caught, as if her presence had never mattered.

The minor event had slipped beyond her having found her way to the officer's quarters, which were small, individual rooms for higher ranking members of either the Imperial Army or in this case, visiting House guard. Knowing exactly which one she wanted, she approached, opened the unlocked door, and entered, locking if firmly behind her.

"I wondered if you would show tonight," the familiar voice of Tristan Crane stated softly.

The darkness around her released, her form returning, she smiled to the captain. "I did promise you I would show. But I must admit, I might have had one too many glasses of wine tonight."

And the handsome guard rubbed down his thin mustache. "So, it may be fun for me tonight then?"

Lifting the straps from her nightgown, she allowed it to fall onto the floor, leaving herself fully exposed. "It may just be, Captain Crane."

--

Do you know why the Draywolf is of little concern to us here? The most ferocious killer in Amon, it can run faster than any land mammal, a mouth that can damn near swallow a man whole, a size that forces it to eat its weight four to five times a week, the Draywolf is a grand killer in its own world.

So why do we not fear such a killer? Unlike its wolf cousins, the Draywolf does not travel in packs. Instead they move alone, hunt alone, die alone. In Ursan, we know the strength that lies in numbers. I have many wives, who have given me many sons, many warriors. We move together, hunt together, die together.

We do not fear the Draywolf. It fears us.

-- Dehyllo Brocusk, House Lord of Ursan

III

Most cases, Nathanial Wode hunted without company. There was peace in the silencing of the world around him, the still of his mind, the edge of knowing a life would end; be it his or the thing he hunted, time would tell. Here, Nathan commanded his own life, crafted his own destiny. In Prillian, a trade city in the far northeastern corner of Donovini, he began to forge his own name in the histories of Amon. A grand hunter, they claimed. Unparalleled at the sword, they whispered.

Nathanial Wode, the hunter, the killer. In Prillian, far away from his home of Astrona, he was no longer a bastard within House Pratt. Here, he could be whatever he desired.

While he preferred his hunting solo, there were times when companions were needed. Several citizens from the outskirts of Prillian had been found partially devoured . . . or missing altogether. Some had claimed bears to be at the helm of such brutality, others certain a rogue Draywolf penetrated further south than normal this time of year. Either situation, Nathan felt better to keep a small hunting party with him, a few seasoned Guild members with keen senses and steady hands to help assess the situation. Bears . . . Nathan might have found a way to best them himself. A Draywolf on the other hand, that was not a beast to take on alone. Too much leg speed and maw strength to play nicely with.

Best be prepared for the worst. Rather be overly prepared than overly dead.

He moved carefully along the outskirts of the Lis'rial Wilderness, a dense but rather small forested area that shared the northeastern and southwestern border of Donovini and Ursan respectively. Here there had been rainfall; sparse, but better than a majority of his country. A drought had plagued the vastness of the area, dried up grass and crops causing towns such as Prillian to flourish as many of the merchants hailed from the bordering countries, bringing fresh goods to the market. Problem was that the merchants took advantage of the situation, raising the prices on even the simplest of goods, knowing full well that the residents would buy. Of course they would.

Supply and demand. Can't fault them for wanting to profit and work the system, but you'd assume them to have some form of mercy.

Checking the dirt before the forest, there had been distinct markings of something large that moved through recently. There as well had been a few spots of ripped clothing, perhaps a body being dragged into the forest beyond.

"Smells like a Draywolf," Ebb, a short, stocky Ursan, spoke behind him. "Just doesn't act like one."

"How so?" questioned the second man, Drai, a larger, Fallneesian fellow.

"What Draywolf have you ever heard of that stores food?" Ebb answered. "Definitely tracks here where one of our villagers was dragged."

"Storing for winter?" Drai inquired, sadly half serious.

"Summer's just started, you dumb shit," snapped Ebb.

"You're both fucking stupid," claimed the third and last member of his hunting party, an Ursan woman, Jadenine. "Female Draywolves care for their young until they are able to hunt for themselves, then abandon them."

Nathan turned to Jadenine, her eyes showing little interest in the hunt, if in anything at all. She was short, as were most Ursan, a few inches over five feet in height, but well defined and solid, easily far more useful in a fight than her two male counterparts. Slightly more tan than most of her race, but still very pale in comparison to Donovinians. She had long, curly red hair that she tied back and away from her face. There remained an attractiveness about the young woman, in a frightening, deadly sort of way.

"Real question remains on how many pups and how old," added Nathan, turning back to the forest. Even a young Draywolf could grow to be five or six feet in length before being left to fend for themselves. Sizeable enough to take a chunk out of any man, and the small pups would fight together, giving them a possibility of being even more deadly than their grown version.

If there was concern in his hunting party, Nathanial could not detect such. Ebb was a liar and a boaster, Drai a fool, but even they were hardened by experience and knowledge. Jadenine, perhaps a year or two older than he, had more experience than either man, as she had spent her entire life in the forests of Ursan, her tribe not within the protection of House Brocusk apparently.

Such a variety of races had been a rare thing outside of Genethur, outside of the capital of Amon more specifically. The races primarily kept to themselves, and even in the trade cities where mixture was bound to occur, the Donovinians stuck with the Donovinians, the Argons stuck with the Argons, and so forth. But the Guild did not care who they acquired and quickly pressed that race had little to do with skill. Talent was an individual trait, not a racial one. Nathan fully agreed.

Nathanial Wode adjusted the bow on his back, then repositioned the swords at his waist. "Do we continue on, or ask for more aid?"

Ebb shook his head vigorously. "And split the funds more than four ways? I'll take my chances against the bitch and her pups."

The other two maintained silence. Nathan pointed inward to the Lis'rial Wilderness and led them forward.

--

"Not sure I get you, Wode."

Nathan knelt against a large oak, turning to the whispering Jadenine. She leaned heavily on a neighboring tree, the sunlight barely creeping through the vast tops of the forest. The trail had gone cold an hour into their hunt. The signs of the Draywolf, or whatever it was they chased, had dissipated a mile back, and the four had been venturing further into the wilderness blindly. As the appointed leader by the Guild for this particular engagement, he had sent Ebb and Drai to circle their location in opposing directions in hopes to find some sign of their prey.

Leaving him alone with the normally subdued Ursan woman.

"What's there not to get?" was his questioning response.

She shrugged, hand upon the hilt of the short sword that rested at her hip. Jadenine appeared in no rush to answer, as it took several long moments to state anything at all.

"Ebb and Drai are both shits. I get why they do this. What else would there be for them? Join the army? Maybe, if they'd accept them. Go back and be criminals? Might pay better, but this will keep them in a bit less trouble. But you . . . you are not like us."

No, but I'm not like the rest of my family either.

"What of you?" he deferred.

"I am meant to be here."

Perhaps, perhaps not, but who was he to argue? He had heard that her tribe had been killed some time ago, she the only survivor. Rumors. None of his business, so far as Nathan was concerned. And if she had wanted him to know, she would have spoken such.

His eyes gazed upward to the woman, but her interest had already shifted. Jadenine was a difficult read. Funny, though, that she had spotted him. For several years he had been in Prillian now, returning home only on occasion to visit his birth mother and his cousins. He made attempts to visit his younger brother Luther and his father Edmond, though that tapered off some recently. No point in it. Not many warm receptions for the bastard of the family.

But here, no one knew who he was, that he was attached to a House name, *the* House name as a matter of fact. In Prillian, he was Nathanial, a Guild member, nothing more. Only Jadenine had seen through the ruse. But she knew nothing, of that much Nathan was certain. She might have guessed him a noble fugitive or a deserter to the army, someone with a bit more class and prestige than the standard issue Guild member. No matter what she thought, he did not see a point in sharing his identity. No point in that either, because what weight did that identity claim?

Only money if I needed it. Enough that the Guild could try and ransom me if they found out. But they don't know my father as I do. Try and ransom Edmond's bastard child and likely end up disappointed.

Pulling out a skin of lukewarm water, Nathan took a short swig, then replaced it. Spring was ending and the weather would eventually become unbearable, especially if the drought held through. Donovinian summers were already unnaturally hot, forcing him on more than one occasion to consider a migration north to Ursan or Fallneese during the hotter months. But not enough work for someone like him in those countries. His skin too dark for paying work in Ursan, too light for Fallneese. Oh there would be work, most certainly, but the kind that would be equal to cleaning piss from the streets with his bare hands. Not that Nathan was above such work, only he would rather be uncomfortably hot and paid well for quality work than underpaid, overworked, and treated like shit.

Footsteps approached without any attempt to conceal their presence, and Nathanial continued to kneel, relaxed.

Ebb emerged, his head motioning several times behind him. "Fresh tracks," he declared. "We missed a turn back along our old trail. Drai found it, already waiting."

--

Another half an hour and they reached the Fallneesian, his eyes intent upon their coming.

"Two sets of bad news," Drai began, whispering as Nathan came close. "About a hundred yards from here, I spotted the small clearing where our friends are hiding out. Jadenine was right, we got pups. Three of them, sleeping. Getting close to grown, so they are pretty damn big and nasty. Bad news."

"That *is* bad news," Nathanial confirmed. "Other bad news?"

"No sign of momma," he finished.

Ebb sighed heavily. "Even better."

"Earth and Flame," Jadenine hissed at Ebb. "Gather your balls. Did you think we came here to spear rabbits?"

"Yes, with your damned wit alone," he answered back.

"Enough," Nathan interrupted. "We will take the pups and hope we can kill them before the mother returns."

"What if she doesn't return?" questioned Drai.

To which Wode shrugged. "I'd gather there would be little need for her to collect food any longer. Problem solved. You three head around east, I will wrap around west. If they smell you when we get close, and they should, draw them your way and I will lay down some quick arrows to their asses. If we are lucky and they are still sleeping, cut their damn throats. Questions?" Silence returned. "Good luck."

They moved with a fluidity that would not lend one to believe they despised each other. Together and as one, the three disappeared from view. Nathan removed the bow from across his back and checked the bowstring, its strength still held as true as when he departed Prillian. Nervous as he had always been before battle, he fought back the urge to vomit. Enough times in this exact situation, he would have thought to be beyond such trepidation. But his mind and body did not agree with one another apparently.

He did not fear death, of that he was certain. He did not lack confidence in his ability, as he all but knew there were few he had met that could best him.

Stopping for a moment, he leaned over low and sprayed puke, quick and watery, onto the grass beneath him. Wiping his mouth, he moved forward with a double step, cursing his weakness. Perhaps, he had figured, that regardless of how good he had become at killing, his body did not agree with such even if his mind had grown numb to it.

The looming trees provided the cover he desired as he could spot the upcoming clearing a few yards away. He never kept a heavy supply of arrows, as they were meant only to gain counter against another archer or a quick attack upon an unsuspecting victim. His aim stood true, but his blades held truth. The Draywolves would not fall to a single arrow much less the eight that he carried. Slow and injure, perhaps, and that was all that he looked to accomplish with his attack. If the battle were to be won, such would be done by the sword.

Compact and gathered such as a storm, the oaks within the Lis'rial allowed him enough cover to huddle close to the clearing without entering into the open. It did not take long for him to find the three beasts. If they had been sleeping before, it had been spoiled by the possibility of a meal. The three Draywolves were up on all fours, each about six feet in length, about five feet from ground to jaw. The eyes of the beasts were along the side of their face, able to rotate about effortlessly as would a chameleon, nostrils somewhere atop their maw which extended out beyond their neck, thousands of teeth on display. They had the look of some kind of ungodly mixture of a crocodile from the deepest parts of the Ursan and the standard wild dogs that roamed the Donovinian plains. Deadly but frightened, these young Draywolves had likely never seen a human alive and moving, and though they could not yet spot their predators, instincts warned them of the danger.

They did not realize that their power could overcome four humans with ease, at least not yet. *Hopefully it stays that way.*

Coming as close as he felt necessary, Nathan knelt softly into the grass, his stomach tumbling again but he swallowed hard against it. Getting his arrow into the ready, he pulled lightly at the bowstring, steadying himself, breathing slowly, staring at the beasts that seemed to be all too aware of his presence in the forests before them.

Steady, calm.

Hairs on end, the beasts all spun eastward, their attention drawn to three Guild members that came out onto the clearing, weapons in hand. His breath held, Nathan aimed and released. Another shaft at the ready, and before his first arrow found a home, he released.

The first arrow found the side of one of the beasts. On his feet now, the second arrow buried again into the same beast; the first a surprise, the second a howling shriek in response. No hesitation as Wode came into the clearing, third arrow readied and released, fourth the same; his steps steady as he moved toward the Draywolves. Finally they had broken off, two wounded came toward the Guild members, the lone beast without an arrow protruding from its toughened skin barreled toward him.

Fifth released, puncturing the shoulder of the incoming Draywolf, sixth . . . the creature far too quick at closing the gap between them to attempt another arrow. Bow dropped, Wode unsheathed the sword at his side with his right, his left lifting a smaller, curved dagger with serrated edges. It attempted to rush him head on, mouth agape, but Nathan sidestepped the attack easily, his sword coming down, but only grazing the beast at best.

It turned and straightened some, circling slowly about him, understanding now that alone, a human was easy food. It judged correctly, but would not find its first human quite so willing to become a meal, nor so easily made such. The Draywolf snapped at him, Nathan's sword slapping hard against the teeth, each doing little to the other. Continuing to circle, it pounced, moving higher and swifter than expected, and Nathanial knew he was in trouble. Diving toward the creature, he spun and cut the beast's underbelly with the dagger, flesh opening, blood releasing. It did not save him from the claws that raked his right arm, his own blood emerging from three deep wounds. It did, however, save him from the jaws, which enclosed around the space where he once stood.

Rolling from underneath the creature, it yelped loudly from the wound it had received. Nathan wasted little time, ignoring his own cuts. With the creature stunned and bleeding profusely from his serrated dagger, he lunged forward and stabbed his long sword into the side of the beast, sliding part way in before hitting bone. The dagger then drove down on the Draywolf's back and he let his legs slip from behind him, placing his full weight upon the hilts of his weapons, the blades sliding down through flesh and muscle, as blood now came in droves.

Without enough wits to do much other than flail, the beast knocked him back several yards as it could do little else but bleed. Knowing full well this creature would be dead shortly, Nathanial turned his attention to the other two.

Ebb lay collapsed upon the earth, one of the creatures was down, the other backing down the injured Drai and Jadenine. Weapons sheathed, Wode reached down and reclaimed his bow, the sixth arrow still notched in place. Continuing toward the standing Draywolf, he aimed and released. Seventh at the ready as the sixth planted into the hindquarter, steady aim, released. Eighth at the ready, the seventh landing into its side, the beast turned from the other Guild members and gave way into a dead sprint toward Nathan.

Released.

A lucky shot, an impossible shot.

Bow tossed aside again, his weapons drawn, the eighth and final arrow caught a gust of wind and moved just enough to miss the massive jaw and found the left eye, puncturing through it, erupting in fluids.

The Draywolf reared its head, the approach slowed, the neck exposed as it flinched back from the blistering pain it must have felt. Nathan rose upward with his sword, cutting through the neck clean, the dagger slashing forth, cutting deeply down the neck, ripping away flesh, leaving a large slit that quickly filled with blood.

His sword retracted back and the beast fell, strength and life leaving the beast as it descended onto the earth below.

Weapons returned, Nathan began to cross the clearing, making his way back to the others. "Ebb?" he called out to the others in the distance.

"I think he's alright," answered back Drai, his voice carrying across the way. "I think he took a kick to his side, so maybe some broken . . ."

Jaws crunched Drai clean, his entire body filling a mouth that emerged from the wilderness beyond. Jadenine swung her blade to the new beast, but it did nothing. She leapt backwards, knelt low and ready, as the mother of the dead pups returned to the clearing. There was not even a scream from the now consumed Fallneesian, blood pouring from between the Draywolf's teeth, the maw so impressive it fit Drai between the jaws in a disgusting display. The mother was massive, at least twelve feet from ground up. Coming into full view of the clearing, her vision avoiding that of Jadenine, but stood focused on Nathan. He could not tell length at first as she continually poured from the trees, the body ceasing to end, and her pace was not rushed. She was a big one, even by Draywolf's standards.

She then came in full stride, and all Nathan could do was brace himself. No fear, no regrets, there was no time for that. Even his stomach calmed at the approaching jaws that opened wide, pieces of what remained of Drai dripping out as she looked to maim one more human.

So it ends.

And then, inexplicably, she stopped, just close enough for her breath to brush back his shoulder cut black hair, her drool dripping down before his face. Her head turned slowly, staring at something unknown, and for some reason, Wode turned to match her glare.

A tall, lanky Argon male stood solemnly with his arms crossed, his vision intense.

And in response, the Draywolf did nothing. Petrified in their equal stare, the stranger and the beast locked in silent content.

Nathan, knowing little else to do, brought his weapons up, finding the throat, the creature finding her end.

--

Steady, calm.

Ebb might have had several cracked ribs, maybe broken, but his hip was definitely shattered. One thing was certain: the Ursan was not walking out of the Lis'rial. The man could breathe, though, and that was better than could be said about Drai.

Wode had ignored the odd stranger, who in turn still stood patiently at the edge of the clearing, silent. He was trying yet fruitlessly to piece together what had happened in his mind. By all means, Nathan should have joined Drai on this day. They had not been prepared for the mother to return, not in the manner to which she had. Foolish, Nathan realized now, that they had not understood the relationship between mother and pup. Certainly, based on their loner mentality, her life would have easily been more important than her young, and should they be taken for bait in exchange for her attack, then it would be so. She had by no means simply stumbled back to the clearing when she did. The Draywolf mother had allowed her children to fight, perhaps in preparation for their adulthood, or perhaps self-preservation of her own. Regardless, the children had failed, and she should have torn him in half.

Instead, something happened, something unexplainable. And who was this man? None of it made sense.

His own wounds had been dressed by Jadenine, three cuts down the side of his arm. He would need stitches, that much he was aware, and that would need the attention of a medic back in Prillian. Ebb would need the same, if not a Druid healer, but their fees would be extraordinary. That decision ultimately would be made by the Ursan, but first they would need to make it back to Prillian, and that alone was a daunting task with a man that could not stand.

Thankfully Jadenine had several powders with her, one in particular to aid in sleeping. He had known her to use them to help with her sleep deprivation, and in this case, it came in handy in placing Ebb in a deep slumber. Easier to deal with his pain in his unconscious state, Nathan figured. She had not been happy to part with it, as expensive as it was to obtain, but Jadenine would have to deal with it.

It had not slipped by him that she had given several concerned looks his way, for multiple reasons. When she approached him, Nathan looking about for some sturdy branches, he could feel the conversation almost before it happened.

"You look to forge a makeshift sling to drag him?" she stated, more comment than inquiry.

"That I do," he responded regardless.

"I cannot drag him. His weight is too much for me."

"I realize that." Finding one sturdy branch, an arm's length, he moved about, looking for another.

She followed closely but not helping in any way. "You realize that you need stitches. You drag him, that strain will continually open your wounds, and you risk infection out here in the forest."

"Yes, I realize that too." A second branch located, slightly longer than the first, Nathan removed his shirt and began to tie it down to the branches.

"Do you realize as well that if in the same position, Ebb would have left you here?"

He nodded, then turned to the closest tree and began to use his dagger to bring down a few thin layers of bark. "To each his own, Jadenine. Perhaps he would sleep fine knowing he left me here to die. I, on the other hand, would not."

"And neither would I, now that you have given him my sleeping powder."

Having enough pieces, Nathan began to tie the bark together, then fasten it to his poor excuse for a sling.

"Are you going to speak to the stranger?" she pressed onward.

"Why don't you?" he snapped toward her. "You aren't doing much else, now are you?"

"I'm observing someone make a poor decision," she claimed. "And *he* is observing us, which makes me a bit on edge."

"You are free to make whatever decision you like, Jadenine. Leave. Stay. Help. Don't help. Talk to the stranger. Don't talk to the stranger."

"I am aware of my freedom to decide, Wode. Are you?" Her eyes gazed upward, the sun having already moved beyond their vision through the trees. "The day presses on. We should not want to be in Lis'rial at nightfall. Especially as broken as we are."

For what it was worth, Nathan finished his sling . . . or a reasonable facsimile. He marched by her and moved toward the stranger across the clearing. "Get him on the sling, if you want to at least pretend to help," he called back. He could feel her disheartening stare behind him as he moved further away.

The Argon man did not make any motion one way or the other to Nathan's approach. Middle aged, fair complexioned, he had unkempt, brown hair that reached beyond his ears and looked to have never seen a comb before. His beard equaled that in wildness, though not long, rather varied in length. Had his clothes not looked civilized, Nathan would have mistaken the stranger as a man on the run, or simply a man mothered by bears or the like.

"Hello stranger," he called out as he approached. "Is it you that I owe thanks for my surviving that encounter with the Draywolf?"

A single bushy eyebrow rose. "Me? I was as petrified as you were, friend."

"Are you a Druid?"

He chuckled at the response. "No, I cannot open any Realms, friend."

Am I imaging something? There has to be some reason for the beast to have simply stopped just short of killing me.

"I am Nathanial Wode. What is your name?"

"Pleasure, Nathanial. I am Feko Hawbry."

Wode opened his arms, motioning toward the dead carcasses of the Draywolves. "I, along with the Guild, have hunted the Draywolves deep into the Lis'rial. Might I ask your purpose here, Feko?"

"You can, but you may not like the answer."

What games are being played here?

"Humor me an answer."

The Argon shrugged his shoulders. "I come here to find you, as it were."

He did not appear armed, but Nathan had excelled and lived thus far in his line of work by taking caution. His hand reached and rested upon the hilt of his sword. "To what end, Feko Hawbry, do you seek me out?"

"I wish I could answer. I am only a vessel. But it looks like you could use a hand carrying that body. Are you on your way back to Prillian? I am assuming that is where you are headed, correct?" When Nathan nodded, the man continued. "Well I'd be more than happy to aid, if you'd like."

"What is your charge for this . . . aid?" Nathan suspiciously questioned.

"Only that you keep me in your service until the end of about three weeks."

What? "I am afraid I will pass, Feko."

"You do not look to be in the right condition to drag that man through the Lis'rial. Would you truly deny aid?"

"Pardon me," started Nathan, "but I do not know you, good sir. Your intentions may very well be sincere and I would gladly take them, but I will not keep you by any means when we return to Prillian. Understand that Amon is filled with those untrustworthy, those that would just as well take advantage of situations. I would gladly pay you the percentage of my fourth and lost member on this trek, if that would please you."

"No, the pay is not necessary. How about we revise the conditions? I aid you in this, and you help me find lodging for a time. You check in on me a few times during the next few weeks, and at the end of those . . . let's say three weeks . . . well perhaps we never see each other again. Agreed?"

The oddity of this conversation apparently knew no ends. "So find you housing for about three weeks, and then you leave. That's it?"

"Fair conditions I would gather, at least we think so."

"*We*?"

"Indeed. So is that agreed?"

The man was clearly odd, if not insane, and he certainly did not feel well about agreeing to anything with someone without mental stability. *Still . . .*

"I do need the aid, Feko Hawbry. I would hope that you are a man of your word and do not surprise me with further request. If that is all that you ask, then I gladly accept."

"Excellent. The day is late and we should press on immediately then."

His first steps were firm ones, direct as he stood up high and proper, statuesque in a way, as he simply walked by Nathan without hesitation, heading toward the sling.

"Might I ask you something?" Wode inquired as he caught up to the man. "What do you expect to happen at the end of this three week stay?"

Without turning to him, Feko replied, "I wish I could answer you. I am, after all, only a vessel."

--

Of all of his travels, of all of the companies kept by Nathanial during his years, nothing had been odder, nothing more uncomfortable than the walk out of the Lis'rial.

To his credit, the likely insane Argon had sizeable strength for his frame. Feko easily kept pace with Nathan and Jadenine as he swung the thin bark over a shoulder and heaved it along, Ebb's feet dragging just off the sling as they moved forward. Horrible to look at, certainly, but Nathan was rather proud that the whole thing held up to the strain.

His own cuts did not look good; the Draywolf clearly even in a grazing effort did far more damage than his adrenaline allowed him to feel. Now, hours after the fight, the pain was mind numbing. All of his attention remained focused on *not* focusing on the cuts, which in turn made him focus on it. Of course he did. Meanwhile, Jadenine seemed to toughen out the bumps and bruises she had received, but he could see she masked her discomfort.

Indeed, they were three broken Guild members, hired to hunt and kill, and could barely hold themselves up. If there was one thing that Nathan liked the least, it was to be in debt to anyone, especially someone he did not trust. Feko Hawbry was clearly a loon, without a slightest of doubt. At times, behind them, he mumbled to himself, answering his own questions, and even held private, hushed arguments. He seemed conscious enough about his insanity to keep it silenced as best as he could, but dementia could only be hidden for so long.

From the point where Feko began to carry Ebb until the night fell upon them at exiting the Lis'rial, not a word was spoken between them. Jadenine kept her thoughts to herself, which was nothing new, Nathan doing all that he could to ignore the throbbing in his arm, and Feko keeping his mumbling to a low minimum. None of them spoke to the other; a silent trek through the thick wilderness. But when they had finally broken the forest, the soft plains stretching before them, the light nighttime breeze that rushed through the open felt refreshing. Relieving in the knowing that Prillian, the Guild, and a medic were but an hour walk, an hour left until he might gain some comfort from the pain . . . and some much needed rest.

He would need to speak with Drai's family first. They deserved to know quickly of his fate.

Only fitting it should come from me, a brother in arms. I wonder if my family would even care if I suffered the same fate.

Not likely, he realized. His younger brother seemed to hate him. He could never understand Luther's distain toward him, as he did little besides make every attempt to show him love as would any sibling. But being a bastard had disadvantages, one being his inability to take his father's name. In Donovini, only a child through marriage could become a House lord, a House name. So Luther, being his only true son, would take the House name without question. But there remained such challenge in Luke. His direct lineage was never good enough for the boy. He had to do everything better than Nathan to prove his superiority, prove that he was worthy to succeed his father over Wode.

Problem was, sadly, there was nothing Luther could best Nathanial in. Nothing. Swordplay, strength, speed, agility, military strategy, hunting, skinning, fishing, horseback riding, survival instincts. The endless list grew on his brother's nerves, as it seemed, no matter how much Nathan allowed him to catch up, when he would gift him victory. Even when he made it appear as close as possible, if they ran and he gave up just a bit to let his younger brother win, Luther always knew he won by pity alone. It drove him bitter and angry.

As for Edmond, his father loved him as much as he should: just enough. Though he married his stepmother, Karen, after his own birth, Nathan always believed that a part of his father always loved his mother. But how could Edmond Pratt, a House name, brother to the lord of Donovini, proclaim love to the local tavern barmaid, Sara Wode? All Nathan knew was that his mother always loved Edmond, even after he abandoned her, discarded her as if she were some delusional whore.

But things were as they were meant to be, he realized. His brother's spite stood at the top of his lists for leaving Astrona. The further away, the better things were it seemed. If he did not have such a great friendship with his cousins Rayden and Katlynn, he would likely not return at all.

"You look like a man lost in thought," Feko noted, somehow coming parallel to him as he continued to pull the sling.

Looking back, Ebb now laid patiently, his eyes half open, drifting in and out of sleep.

"You still breathing back there?" Nathan called back.

Ebb did not answer; only lifting a single thumb upward to show he did fine, despite the pain.

That makes two of us.

"He is appreciative, I am sure, Nathanial Wode," the Argon offered.

Nathan shrugged. "Well he owes that to you more than any." Waiting a moment, Nathan thought to pry a bit into the psyche of Feko. There remained unanswered questions. "Tell me, Feko, what did you do before wandering the Lis'rial?"

"You mean my profession," he interpreted. "Actually I was an herbalist. Well, an apprentice."

"A bit old for an apprenticeship, don't you think?" Jadenine cut in from beside them both.

"Truth in words, my lady. But difficult to take over a trade until the master wishes to forfeit said claim. In this case, the master herbalist is only about twenty years older than I. And being an herbalist, not being much of a daunting or labor intensive kind of work, I do believe he will continue his work until he is senile or dead."

"So were you in the woods collecting herbs for your master?" wondered Nathan aloud.

"No, as I said, I came looking for you. And as I said, I am not sure why. I am only. . ."

"Yes, yes, a vessel. Well, all fine and well. But how did you know to find me where you did?"

Feko shrugged. "They spoke, I followed. Strange logic, but I did find you, did I not?"

"Wasting your time," murmured Jadenine.

Feko shrugged. "Look, I would be happy to answer your questions, but the further you pry, the more confused you will be. Perhaps we should wait out these next three weeks. If nothing extraordinary happens, then I was told wrong. If something does happen, then I will answer any questions you have. Seems fair enough."

"What do you expect to happen that will prove anything, Feko? A storm? A fire?"

"Well let's hope nothing that drastic, good sir," Feko Hawbry sincerely stated. "Let us hope that it is something far less . . . damaging."

"So you are looking for a sign?" laughed Jadenine. "Good luck with this one, Wode."

"Signs are everywhere, my lady. *Everywhere*. But to be honest, I'd rather not be needed."

Nathan shook his head, not able to piece together anything the man was saying. "Needed, Feko?"

"Yes. I fear for what is ahead of us. We are not prepared."

"Can you see the future?" pressed Nathan.

"Ha! What a gift that would be, would it not? But alas, no, nothing so grand. But those that have spoken with me have warned me of troubled times. Very troubling times ahead."

"And I suppose you will not elaborate?"

"Three weeks, Nathanial Wode. Three weeks."

Insane or not, Feko Hawbry spoke clearly and with conviction. At best, the Argon believed in his own words.

And even though Wode understood the man's insanity, it still gave him an uneasy feeling. The Draywolf found something in this man worthy enough to take her own life, for that was what she did on her last breath.

At the end of the day, he could not figure out between the Draywolf mother or herbalist from Argonus as to which of them confused him more.

Steady, calm. Not so certain I should be though.

--

What exactly are the Realms? I do not believe anyone will truly know. It is difficult enough to explain to the lament, to someone that cannot see the other side. They know that it is there, that it exists, but they can no more see it than they can see the wind.

Some claim them to be the makings of Schill and Turitea, other worlds that exist parallel to our own. Some believe the Realms were once part of our own, and were in fact sealed by the fallen gods in their final act for humanity, to save us against the powers that once claimed Amon. And those of us, the few and rare than can both see and manipulate the Realms, take from something that should not be, something that by the gods or otherwise, is locked away from us.

I do not fear the using of my Realm. I find that both Earth and Flame mostly require a need, a purpose to open. Healing, life, fire, warmth. These are things that have a design and are difficult to simply squander or experiment with.

What I fear is the Shadow Realm. There is never a need for that Realm, never a purpose, only desire.

-- Iero, a Donovinian Druid

IV

"Get up!" Nicolas Pratt boomed, his voice echoing into their chamber and Rayden nearly fell from his bed in response.

When did I even fall asleep?

He had consumed far too much alcohol, he only now realized, and his body ached, his stomach churned. Jerryn must have felt the same, but leapt to his feet at his father's entrance with ease. Their father was large for a Donovinian, with broad shoulders, a muscular upper body, but his beer belly left off some of the fierceness from his appearance. Still, much to be said for a man nearing his sixties and to hold himself the way he did. Nicolas Pratt stood tallest amongst his brothers, and not just in size, as there remained an intangible about his father, about the way he carried himself.

The man could not care less what others thought of him. And what they thought of him was a mix of fear and respect. But he pissed on fear and strangled respect from others. Rayden understood the impossibility of the shoes left to fill one day.

"So I hear my boys stayed up a little late with their cousins last night," their father spoke, stroking his long beard, grey mixed with black. "Had a few ales? Few glasses of wine, maybe?"

"No excuses, Father, I should . . ." Rayden foolishly began, knowingly full well that his father did not truly ask any questions of them.

"Of course there are no excuses, boy!" he exclaimed, veins popping out from his neck as the words released. "I am glad that my position allows my sons the opportunity to make fools of our country by getting themselves nice and drunk on the eve of the king's inauguration. Do you realize we are but two hours away from his crowning? We should be prepared to take our place with the First and our House name at the front of the ceremony. Instead, I come here to find both of you still in bed, the morning nearly beyond us."

His eyes had recognized that the room was well lit, thanks of course to the sun rising beyond the horizon. Indeed, it would not appear very prestigious if the Pratts showed late to an event of this magnitude, and Rayden knew such. It could not be helped, of course, as reversing last night was beyond their power.

"I would highly suggest," his father proclaimed, "that you find the quickest bath possible and gather your attire. And should that take longer than half an hour, you will need to find another House to take you in, because I will find other sons to take your places." Nicolas's eyes darted about the room. "Where is Katlynn?"

Rayden felt his chest sink inward just enough to sober him completely. Jerryn had arrived late, waking him, and he had seen her empty bed. He must have fallen instantly back asleep. If he were a dead man before, now . . .

His father was across the room in an instant, grasping hold of Rayden's sleep shirt and lifting him close against his face, enough to feel his father's breath upon his forehead.

"Where is my daughter?" The empty stare returned by Rayden answered his father's question. "You are to one day take this House, one day rule Donovini, and you cannot even task yourself to keeping sober and watching your younger sister?"

Nicolas released his grip upon his son and Rayden stumbled back upon his bed. "I will find her, Father," stammered the elder child.

"Do not bother," barked his father. "You cannot even take care of yourself, much less another. Bathe, dress, and be downstairs. *Now.*"

The door slammed behind the angered House lord, leaving the brothers speechless. *Humiliating.* An adult man now being chastised by his father. Rayden felt his pride bruised, but had little time to dwell on that now. Jerryn already stripped naked as he slipped into one of the three prepared baths in the room. At what hour they were prepared, he could not say. But they did not look warm . . . not in the slightest. And based on his brother's reaction, it could not be too pleasant; in fact, it was likely quite cold.

Rayden, disappointed in himself, assumed he deserved no less than a cold bath.

--

Aldric stood outside the throne room, his arms crossed at his chest, he remained as stoic as the lifelike statue before him. Jaa the Knowledgeable. For what it was worth, it looked just like the man, from the slightly hooked nose to the hanging ear lobes, every chisel to stone hailed true artwork to the sculptor. Staring into the blank stone eyes, a part of Aldric expected Jaa to come to life, to offer down wisdom yet untold.

Ironic how life worked, he realized. He spent only a few years in blatant ignorance of the teachings of the man, and after his death, spent the remainder of his lifetime wishing otherwise, grasping at strands of memory in hopes that somewhere within held the reason of his passing. Yet hundreds of years gone, and Aldric had no more figured out why Jaa had chosen to die before he finished the work of his people. The writings of his knowledge into the histories of his people left undone, leaving the council in eager anticipation for the day that Aldric would write both his life and the life of Jaa the Knowledgeable into the histories of Amon. Problem was Aldric could remember very little of what the man said. As a Kwyantin, he had the blessing and curse of his memory, his ability to take the slightest detail and engrave it eternally away in his mind. Of course he had to have *actually* been paying attention in order to remember. Certainly, there had been plenty to recall, but in most instances, he had found solace in his own thoughts rather than attentiveness to his master.

But he cared little for what the accounts would show when pen touched upon paper. Jaa had left him a riddle, both in the reasoning of his death as well as his claims of the Realms. Some seven hundred years later and he stood no closer to the solving those mysteries than the moment the sea swallowed Jaa from face of Amon.

What am I missing? There were no records of your claims, no accounts that we founded the Realms. Perhaps you were the crazy old man that no one else besides me knew. Maybe, but why can't I believe that? I wronged you in my lack of respect. I only wish I could find a way to make things right.

Erian hovered beside him, at first inattentive, then apparently must have noticed his focus on the statue. "Jaa . . . he is revered in Genethur," the young Kwyantin noted. "Why is that?"

Aldric turned slowly to the other. "They all believed themselves immortal, that worshiping the author of the histories would gain them eternal fame." He chucked a bit to himself. "How disappointed they would all be now to find that Jaa never completed his tasks."

"Shame that he died before he could finish his work." After a pause, the next question seemed all too predictable. "If I may ask, if I am permitted to do such, I would like to know how he died."

The details of his death belong to me alone. Best to keep lies to prevent the tainting of his good name in knowing he willingly gave his life at the end, rather than the accident that I claimed to have occurred. Jaa was a good man, if not a confused one.

"How he died, you ask?" repeated Aldric. He then shrugged. "At unrest, I suppose."

A side door along the hallway opened carefully, catching both men's attention. A single woman appeared, and the skinny, tall servant came out just enough to wave them in. "The king is ready for you sirs," she whispered softly.

The elder Kwyantin wasted no further words with his apprentice. Gazing once more into the stone monument of his former master, Aldric turned and moved through the door.

--

"Earth and Flame," hissed Philip upon entering the throne room, slowly moving to the front of the assembly. He had arrived a bit early, but the throne room filled quickly with the other Houses, along with the favored guests selected by House Aylmer. Large and elaborate, the throne room had been mostly an abandoned storage room while Yelium had lived. He was a great many things, but stationary long enough to sit upon a throne he was not. His son, however, did all that he could the moment his father hit earth to restore the throne room to what he envisioned it should be.

And his vision was decorations, crystals, banners, servants catering all types of food, bards strumming lutes, and all amounts of ridiculousness. Yelium Aylmer II would make a mockery of Amon in the process of undoing all that Philip had created.

Jessica walked beside him, her arm through his as they walked. Despite his late arrival home, she did not seem to be too frustrated with him, at least not outwardly. The crowning of a new king might have given her pause. But if Philip knew women, especially his wife, she would speak with him at great lengths on the subject at a time most inconvenient for him. Joanna and Winston stood several steps back, and Lilli walked beside her mother. With his family accounted for, he gazed about the room, spotting his brother, Edmond, near the front. Both his wife, Karen, and his son, Luther, stood upon seeing the First.

He approached his younger brother direct, their hands clasping hard upon greeting.

"So here hides my brother," called out Edmond, his smile genuine, if not in arrogance. "I know you are an important man in Corovium, but too important to see your brother?"

Philip faked a smile his way, then turned to his beautiful wife, some fifteen years his younger. "Karen," he stated, kissing her gently on her cheek.

"Ignore my husband," she claimed, blushing some toward Philip. "He is an ass and always will be, you know this."

"An ass to state the truth?" Edmond responded.

"A king has passed," defended Karen. "And in such, who do you believe the tasks have been passed to?"

"Bah," Edmond mumbled, throwing his arms upward. "You are a Pratt before the First. Never forget that, brother. *Family.*"

The First patted his brother on his shoulders, nodding to him, and smiling, as he moved on to shake the hand of Luther, and the pleasantries between their families began. He silently moved onward, taking his seat at the front row.

Family. You disloyal shit. What would you know of family?

He loved his brother, likely more so than his brother loved him. But Edmond fell from a different tree. Philip voluntarily admitted his flaws, if only to himself, and namely in his infidelity. Of course his infidelity could have shaken the entire nation had it surfaced that the First bedded Queen Aylmer readily and regularly, suffice it to say. And Nicolas was no more or less honorable in some of his indiscretions. Edmond, on the other hand, was a different breed. He convinced a barmaid in Astrona, Sara Wode, a wonderful woman by his own account, that he would change her life. Edmond gave the girl a romance filled existence, having her leave her work and life behind, moving into the Pratt estate. For a commoner, it was a dream. She was far too good for a man like his brother.

But the romance did end eventually . . . the precise moment she informed Edmond of her pregnancy. Their love could not have died swiftly enough for his younger brother, as he had her removed from the estate entirely. Had it not been for Nicolas who housed Sara back within Astrona and kept her financially cared for, Philip could only imagine where she would be. Dead, in all likelihood, and Edmond would have not paid notice one way or the other.

In the meantime, only two months after his failed relationship, he met and began fucking a then fourteen-year-old Karen, a daughter of a politician. Philip found the whole ordeal sickening, in more ways than one.

And the true loser in all this is Nathanial. Boy would have represented the Pratt name better than most. Better than me, certainly.

Edmond, still grumbling behind him, causing for Philip to turn and see what his grievance was. "What is it?"

"Where is Nicolas?" he barked, though to no one in particular. "The Rowes are almost all accounted for over there, and the Brocusks are rolling in like a damned monsoon." Philip gazed beyond his family to Lord Dehyllo Brocusk, a stern man if he had ever seen one, his three wives several steps behind him, the male children behind them, with their wives behind them, and so forth. The Ursan and his immediate family could have accounted for the entire assembly hall within the throne room if the king had allowed for such, which he of course would not. The king's House would take precedence, as it should have been. "Be a shame if we are the last family to show," Edmond finished, arms crossed.

As House Brocusk took their place behind House Pratt, Dehyllo did not falter in his steps toward the front of the throne room, heading toward Philip with a slow, purposefully step. The First stood, bowing his head well before Lord Brocusk had made his way to him.

Though not tall by any means, there remained an underlying sense of worth from the Ursan, his broadened shoulders seemingly as wide as a trunk, the beard groomed and braided, the scars mixed in with the wrinkles. Despite that, Philip would never claim the man old over experienced. He had a look that spoke for him, one that showcased his knowledge of killing. It was well known that the Ursan people were not completely civilized, at least not in the way of the other countries. They were far more tribal, even though they bowed to one lord, one House. But Dehyllo neither governed his country any more than he governed his own people. Ursan had a strong sense of fending for oneself, but stood together as one because of it. Should one fall, another should help them rise, only to allow them to fall again. How else would they learn to stand alone?

Philip did not understand, did not agree with how Dehyllo ruled his country, but he respected him. Anyone that could bring unity to that land earned the respect of all those around him.

And that was his look, that was what stood foremost on Dehyllo's brow as he came to a halt, staring upward some toward Philip, the skin of some beast draped about the plate armor upon his chest.

"First Philip Pratt," he stated after some time, completely ignoring Edmond, who had come to his feet a bit late.

"Lord Brocusk. It is an honor to have you in this assembly hall."

"Indeed, yet not honor enough to have a seat with us at the inaugural feast last night." He turned his head to Edmond. "You may sit, Edmond Pratt."

As his brother did as commanded, Brocusk moved over to take the hand of Jessica, kissing it with a smile. "If I might borrow your husband but for a minute, I promise I will return him."

To Jessica's credit, she said, "I know you will, milord. Please be gentle with him." She could have easily made any kind of snide remark of his continual departure from her side, but knew better. Jessica did well to keep their relationship woes behind closed doors.

Dehyllo moved slowly away from prying ears, toward the steps that led upward to the throne. "Perhaps your departure from last night's feast has something tied in to what Afeon speaks to me of. He says you grow weary, tired of the work placed upon you, angered that you will likely lose your position as First."

"The Second speaks quite freely, and with little tact," noted Philip.

"Indeed, and I assure you that I know there are two sides to every story, as you of all people should likely know."

It did not take much in the way of wisdom for Philip to deduce what Lord Brocusk implied. "If you are referring to what Afeon spoke of, I assure you . . ."

"Piss on your assurances," snapped Dehyllo. The Ursan moved beside the First, his voice calm yet firm. "Long before I conquered Ursan, my country bowed in the placement of this government. Agree or not, I find myself a slave to my predecessors. I accept it as what seems best for Ursan, for my people. For all of Nicolas' faults, he knew well to place someone of credibility on the king's council, his brother nonetheless. I may live far away from Genethur, First Pratt, but I too selected my representative on the council quite well. You may have a dislike of the Second, but the man has his sources, and his ear is uncanny. I am informed at who has really run this country of ours for many years. It would be a shame to lose such a man when the boy becomes king within the hour."

"A vacated throne would heavily favor someone with your position, Lord Brocusk," Philip sternly declared. "You may backhand compliment my work over the past two decades, but do me the favor of not hiding your true intent. You want the throne."

"You would rather have the boy on the throne? I would keep you as my First, aid me in running this country as you did with Yelium before. At this juncture, I could not care less if what Afeon believes is true or not. Bastard or not, all I need is an accusation. An accusation levees doubt, and doubt can pause this little crowning."

Philip shook his head. "Why are you so intent at this? Why does the throne mean so much to you that you would desire to destroy a family in order to claim it?"

Dehyllo's glare held true. "The end of days is upon us, First Pratt. While we bicker about a chair and who sits upon it, the gods have abandoned us and left us to our fate." His finger thrust toward the well decorated throne. "That wooden piece of shit means nothing to me. A symbol, nothing more. For as much as you have done for Amon, for as heavy as you have represented our country, you know nothing of Ursan. That throne is means to an end. What it gains me is an army to command and prepare for what is to come. Across the sea awaits death for us, First Pratt. Your commerce, your trade, nothing of that matters. Ursan is all that matters to me. And as best as I have done to prepare, my numbers, while great, are ultimately not enough."

The First took a careful step back and away from the Ursan lord. "Even if I had the evidence and information you sought, I would not trade a fool for a tyrant. At least the boy knows of government and economics. What do you know of such? You look to bring war to Amon."

Dehyllo chuckled, his shoulders shrugging slightly. "All I know is that when the Donovinians start to die in their sundried fields, there will be far less mouths to feed. At least my people shall be ready to face our ends, in one way or another. What does a man without faith say of that, First Pratt? How prepared will you be with your boy king on the throne as you piss away what remains of your life in Astrona?"

"I will say that during my tenure, there was no war between us, Lord Brocusk. Amon saw peace. I am content." Philip turned away from him, heading back to his place in the assembly. "Will you be able to say the same in the end?"

--

"What do you think?" bolstered young Yelium.

The outfit, without a better way to describe it in his mind, bordered lunacy. Aldric gazed carefully at the soon to be king, his armor looking to be so heavy that it would topple him to the ground upon his first upward steps to the throne. Paintings of his House symbol were forefront on the chest plate, while a cape that dragged several feet behind him, purple with the letterings of Aylmer down the side. A huge battleax by his waste, a shield beneath the cape against his back, a helm with three colorful feathers across the top, the boy had a stronger appearance of a jester heading into battle rather than a man about to be crowned king.

"It is . . . elaborate, my king," answered the Historian.

"Nothing less!" he exclaimed in return. He turned about to his many assistants, stumbling just a bit before regaining his composure. Erian turned to him, a look upon his brow to question the reality of this situation, and Aldric could do nothing but crack a smile at his apprentice.

Yelium snatched up an envelope that remained sealed upon his desk and handed it to one of the servants. "I wanted you to be witness to this," he called back to Aldric. "My first order as king, as I promised, is the disbanding of the costal army. The letter is addressed to First General John Shonnen himself. I basically tell him that his services are appreciated, but no longer required on the coast, and he is to inform his men that they are disbanded."

"Do you worry for their reaction?" Aldric questioned.

"Reaction? No, not at all. What would they do? Retaliate against the king? No, I have informed him that if they remain, they will be considered a rebellious force and treated as such. Regardless, that will make an immediate impact on our economy. The next bit of business will be to find this mysterious Moon Divide and deal with them."

"May be difficult," responded the Historian. "They have spent much time in secrecy."

"They are a relic from my father's time. I have no need for them. I know that First Pratt remains in contact with them, as well as the Second. I will beat it out of them before I have them both removed from my council."

Little surprise there. Remove your strongest opposition from the start.

Speaking to his servant, Yelium Aylmer II continued, "Carry this to the courier, inform them to ensure the finest hawk carrier delivers this to the frontline out in Argonus. It goes to General Shonnen, and no one else. And before you leave Genethur, take this second letter." Yelium opened a drawer and produced another sealed envelope. "Take this one to the treasury. This informs them that all funds are to be halted to any merchant, supplier, or even the Guild for any relation to the eastern army, effective immediately. Now be gone from my sight." With the servant scampering off, the young, scrawny boy smiled heavily. "Are you ready to witness greatness, Historian? Let us go make this official."

--

Philip turned, watching as his elder brother finally make his way through the doors into the throne room, Nicolas strolling tall and proud with his wife, Maradyn, by his side. Maradyn Pratt was an elegant woman, only a few years younger than Nicolas, but moved with the grace of a true lady of the court. Not all beauty could be beaten down by age, as was the case with her, as eyes were forced her direction when she moved through a room. A powerful woman indeed, but needed to be such to temper his brother, who was as much a brute as one could find in Donovini.

But to the First's surprise, the House lord and his wife moved through the throne room alone. Their children were strangely absent.

Grumbling as he came close, he barely gave notice to either of his brothers as Nicolas took his place beside Philip. The First stood and greeted Maradyn, her smile as genuine as they came.

"He's a bit upset," she whispered into his ear as she gently kissed his cheek.

"More than a bit," Nicolas growled as he sat, staring ahead rather than acknowledge any of them.

"He is discovering that his children are far more like him than he cares to admit," she noted.

Jessica stood and embraced Maradyn lightly. "Stubborn, head strong, too grown for their own good . . . does any of this sound familiar?"

Nicolas turned and took hold of Jessica's hand, kissing it quickly before returning to his cross armed stance. "At least *your* children are present, Jessica."

"Where are the kids?" Philip inquired.

"On their way," Maradyn offered.

"They'd better be," followed Nicolas. "Or the trip back to Astrona will be the longest of their lives."

Almost if on cue, the bards began to strum their lutes, others blew against their windpipes, and the side door opened to the sight of the new king of Amon.

Too late for the young Pratts.

--

Faces passed in a blur as Rayden rushed down the long hall toward the throne room. Only the House lord of their respective countries, their immediate families, major court officials, and the council could attend the crowning. All others were unable to attend but lined the corridor in order to be the first to greet and witness the new king. This of course dwarfed the much larger crowd that gathered in the courtyard outside the capital. Those that lined both sides of this hall were named men and women in some way or another. Some of those that caught his eye were easily recognizable as cousins and nephews and in-laws of House lords amongst Amon, some even related to him, but other faces were unfamiliar. Regardless, each of those eyes returned the puzzling look onto the two Pratt brothers. For even he did not know them, they of course knew who these two idiots were that ran down the hall.

But Rayden could hear the music inside the throne room long before they had even seen the double doors that would have granted them entrance up until now. The guards stepped in front and blocked the entrance to the throne room, their faces all but clear that no one would gain admittance now. The crowd outside was not where the Pratt brothers were meant to attend the crowning of the new king.

"Shit," muttered Jerryn as both of the brothers came to a halt well before they reached the end of the hallway. "Do you know how long of a trip it's going to be back to Astrona with our father if we are not in there?"

"Quite the long trip indeed," came a quickly familiar voice behind them. Rayden turned to see the portly Druid, Iero, and the Chur'rat clinging onto his shoulders. "Depending of course on your route of travel. Did you know that actually traveling north to reach the Sullein River and taking a boat ride east riding the current would be the quickest travel home to Donovini. Albeit not the most direct route, it is in fact the quickest manner of travel. I find that most people do not desire to . . ."

"Thank you Iero," interrupted Rayden. "That does not help us get into this ceremony, nor survive the onslaught of our father."

"Indeed," remarked the Druid. "There of course is the option of moving through his side passage. It would not mask you in unavoidably, but it would get you beyond the guards that stand at the door perhaps. I find that arriving late is better than of course not arriving at all. The complete removal of attendance is clearly more of an offense than . . ."

"Where is the side entrance?" Jerryn blurted out. "Can you guide us to it?"

"Well I am likely . . ."

"Yes or no!" Jerryn exclaimed.

The Druid, a bit taken back by the excitable Jerryn, nodded emphatically, the fat around his neck jiggling some as he did. "I will show you."

--

Loud knocking woke Katlynn in a startle, half her body hung off the bed while Tristan sprawled out, arms wide across the bed entire. Still nude, she reached down and grabbed her nightgown, slipping it on carefully, rubbing the sleep from her eyes. A stretch and a yawn later, Katlynn immediately began to think of breakfast.

What will I have Tristan fetch for me this morning? Eggs sound glorious right now. Or perhaps sausage and biscuits might do just fine. And what in Shadow is all of this noise?

A heavy clamoring echoed in her ears, as if hundreds of voices at once carried just outside the small chambers. As she took a step toward the closed and blinded window, the hard knock against the door made Katlynn nearly jump in startle. This time, the noise loud enough to wake the captain.

"Yes, yes, hold on," called out a waking Tristan, who covered the blankets around his exposed bottom. "What time is it?"

The noise, the knocking, and with her senses slowly returning from the sudden wake, Katlynn despaired at the knowing of that answer.

Late. It's very late. And I'm a dead woman.

Reaching out toward Shadow, she enveloped herself within the black, becoming nothing more than a dark corner of the room. Tristan Crane opened his door just a crack and a solider burst in, frantic and sweating.

"Sorry, captain," blurted a young soldier. "For interrupting, I mean. But Lord Nicolas Pratt sends me to you. Asked me to ask you, or asked me to tell you, I gather. In a manner of speaking, that is, and . . ."

"Out with it, soldier," demanded an agitated captain. "I was having a wonderful sleep."

"Yes, I know, part of the problem. Lord Nicolas wants you to locate his daughter, who has gone missing this morning. Also wanted me to let you know that . . . well he wants you to also inform him as to why you did not report this morning to him."

Tristan rubbed his eyes some, nodded to the soldier, and reopened the door. "Understood, soldier. Dismissed."

The nervous young man saluted, then stumbled about some before exiting from the chambers. "Earth and Flame," muttered Katlynn as she removed herself from the shadows. "It's the afternoon, isn't it?"

"Damn well close enough," answered Tristan. "Courtyard is already full of people. I need to get dressed and . . . and well I don't know. Probably be dismissed from my position after your father finds out that I was not in attendance for the inauguration. You can escape out of here unnoticed."

"And go where exactly?" she responded. "I cannot very well waltz into the throne room in my nightgown. And there's not enough time for me to maneuver through this crowd and back to my bedroom to get cleaned and dressed." Katlynn paused, staring blankly at the handsome captain, who seemed to return the same look. "What are we to do?"

His silence spoke volumes.

We are in the deepest of shit.

--

Rayden weaved aside the Druid as both he and Jerryn tore through the side room, the servants yelping at their surprise. More alarm might have been sounded if they did not recognize the sons of Nicolas Pratt. Instead they simply watched as the two foolish brothers moved through the king's personal dressing room and the hallway that followed.

Ahead they slowed as they could see the single door before them, the music halted as they could hear the start of the ceremony.

Jerryn threw his arm in front of him. "We can't go in now!" he hissed.

No, no we can't. We are two dead men once this is over with.

Iero finally caught up, his breath nearly removed from his larger frame. "The Pratt brothers are truly in magnificent shape," he managed to exhale.

Rayden did not respond. He listened intently to what sounded like Lijid, the Fourth, announcing the crowning of the king.

"It seems as we are still a bit late," Iero continued. "I would suggest that . . ."

The Druid suddenly stopped, his frame stood upright, and the Chur'rat upon his shoulder seemed to do the same. It would not have been as odd if it had been anyone other than Iero, a man that could barely find time to breathe much less pause in a statement.

"What is it?" Rayden inquired.

Iero took a step back, his eyes reflecting a horror of inevitability. "Shadow," he mumbled.

"What?" Jerryn pressed.

"Bird senses something. The Realms."

Rayden raised an eyebrow. He almost opened his mouth before he felt something brush beside him, as would the wind, save for the fact that they stood in a hallway void of windows. The feeling was altogether . . . unnatural.

"Both of you leave now," Iero commanded.

Jerryn stood his ground firmly, gazing intently at the Druid. "Flame's embrace, Iero, what's wrong with you?"

He only shook his head while he whispered something to his Chur'rat. In response, the creature leapt down and scampered off. "If you stay, I would suggest you find weapons. Now."

The change in both his demeanor and his talk were so drastic that Rayden froze in his place. Nothing about Druid gave any intent that he jested. His face clearly stated the extremity of the situation. His brother, however, read none of this.

"Are you a fucking fool, Druid?"

Iero only knelt to the ground below them. "Indeed, young Pratt. You at the very least may wish to take several steps back. Even Bird knows that to catch vermin, you must lay a trap."

--

If he does not shut up, I am going to leave. Damn Rayden's good sense of not showing to this.

Philip listened to the endless bolstering from the Fourth, Lijid Nulittan, on the greatness of the Aylmer rule. The elder Fallneesian, who some believed to be second cousin or some such from House Aylmer, was perhaps nearing his seventies now. Wrinkled badly and his receding hair line had ventured so deep that, for the life of him, Philip could not understand why the old man would not shave the entire thing off. He was old enough though for Philip to not know the validity to his lineage, though that mattered very little on being a part of the king's council. The king selected whomever he chose to represent his country, including this skeleton of a man.

As it were, his speech was meant as an introduction, but droned on and on for over fifteen minutes. Yelium this, Yelium that. The greatness of Fallneese here, the greatness of House Aylmer there.

To Shadow with Lijid. He knows damn well who runs this country.

Regardless of what he did or did not know, his loyalties remained strong with the new king. He spent much of his time convincing those in attendance that the boy not only *earned* a place on the throne, but in fact seemingly conquered it through diligence. The whole ordeal was nearly sickening, if not at the least boring.

All of his work, all that he had done to create the prosper that Amon had been witness to, threatened to fall so quickly, undone with but this crowning, that his life accomplishment would be piss on the Flame Realm. Bitter, rage . . . none of these words could equally describe his emotions as he watched the ridiculous outfit of this simpleton boy, who stood statuesque in front of the seated assembly, his grin unable to remove from his face. What Philip would not do to have five minutes alone with the boy; he would find a way to remove that fucking smile in a hurry.

Aldric stood on the stage with Yelium Aylmer II along with his apprentice who backed away in the shadows of the room. It was customary for the Historian to be present during these crowning, even if his people barely recognized the throne. They were a lost tribe, a lost race of Amon, but adhered deeply to the customs set by those that lived upon the land. As he understood it, the Kwyantin people had been in power long before the other four races of Amon. How the shift of power took place, likely only the Historian could say. And for all of the knowledge that Aldric possessed, his strange telling of the other continent of Espis had been the most he had ever shared in his tenure of knowing the man.

This had been Philip's third attendance of a new king. A boy when Yelium's father had taken the throne, a man as Yelium had taken his father's place, and the First, elder but still with life left to give as Yelium's son now stood ready to take his place in history. Likely, though, this boy would suck away the remainder of his life.

"We are blessed with the Historian of Amon," called out Lijid to the crowd, his longwinded speech finally coming to a closure, so it appeared. "Aldric, would you please be witness to the crowning of the new king of Amon?"

The large, elder Kwyantin took a step forward, his arm resting upon the shoulder of the boy king. "I, Aldric of the Kwyantin people, Historian of Amon, stand witness to the events that take place here in Genethur, within the capital of Corovium. As I once stood before your father and the many fathers before him in the Aylmer family, I acknowledge the legitimacy of this throne to you, Yelium Aylmer II, as the rightful heir to the king."

Horseshit.

Then it dawned on him, his eyes scanning the stage, then to the front row of House Aylmer, then his head turned to scan the hundred people in the audience quickly. Where was the queen? Where was Dylinn? Had spite truly kept her away from the crowning of the boy, son or not? Regardless of what the truth held, this boy thought Dylinn *was* his mother. Would she truly leave him to believe his own mother did not care about his crowning?

"First Pratt, it is to you now," Lijid stated, his arms extended to Philip.

Let's get this over with.

Philip stood, knowing full well that every eye in Amon gazed upon him, that somewhere in the crowd, Lord Brocusk and Afeon gazed heavily, wondering if he would shock the known world with his revelations. Only he and the queen could give witness to the truth. But that truth would remain buried. He would not disrupt this ceremony, regardless of what it meant for him. Yes, this boy would likely remove him from his council. But the consequences of him not taking the throne would likely place House Brocusk in his place. The strongest House, the most deserving House would take the throne in the case of vacancy, through war if the remaining Houses could not come into a unified agreement. Alliances would be quickly gained, but Brocusk almost literally bred an army. Somewhere between civilized and tribal laid a race of man that *yearned* for war, Philip believed. And they were tens of thousands deep, each with prolific skills in hunting and killing. A war with Ursan would plague Amon in blood.

As far as Philip was concerned, he would leave the country with an idiot boy. Better than Dehyllo, who would attempt to enslave the world.

The First moved up to Yelium, the slender boy still smiling, Philip still wanting to slap it off his face. The crown stood upon a small pedestal, a simple, gold thing that was far less elaborate than the feathered helm that Yelium carried by his side. The First took it into his hands.

"As First of the king's council, I have taken the duties of King Yelium Aylmer after his passing," started Philip, speaking loudly enough to be heard throughout the throne room. "I cannot speak more of House Aylmer that the Fourth has not already stated in thorough detail." A smattering of smirks and chuckles were swiftly suppressed in the audience, and he contained his own grin as the new king had not noticed his untimely humor. "Yelium was our king, he was my friend. As I here also acknowledge that bearing a son, that House Aylmer will remain upon the throne of Amon. This will be the eighteenth straight king from Fallneese, eight consecutive from House Aylmer.

"From this moment onward, I reclaim my duties as the First for as long they are given to me." *Not long, in all likelihood.* "And I forfeit my duties as ruler of Amon. As I place this crown upon the head of Yelium Aylmer II, son of Yelium Aylmer, he is no longer House Lord Aylmer." The boy bowed just enough for Philip to carefully place the crown upon his head. "He is now King Yelium Aylmer II, lord and ruler of Amon."

The ceremony completed, those in attendance stood and applauded. It was neither an uproar nor a pity clap, but somewhere in between, somewhere perhaps hopeful that this boy could make them proud. An applaud of question, of possibility, of hope. If only they knew.

If only they knew.

Yelium took several steps forward, his grin ear to ear now and he raised his hands into the air, as if he just triumphed over a grand foe, as if he won a jousting tournament of some kind. He won. And by all means, he had. He no more deserved to wear that crown than the First himself. But there he stood, a fool to it all, king of Amon, ruler of the world.

And then, in a splattering of blood, it ended.

It sprayed onto Philip's face, and the First stood in a moment of shock and startle that he had not realized that Yelium had been struck at all. As his mind cleared, he could see the blade punctured through the right side of the exposed ribcage of the new king, behind the blade was a darkness, only barely visible, a body of some kind without shape or a face. It had the look as if the shadows came to life and struck a lethal blow.

The crowd shrieked and panicked, and the guards rushed the stage. The next few moments felt like a blur to the First. He was shoved aside forcefully by the guards that stormed in and many in the audience began to dash toward the exit in fright and confusion. Complete chaos erupted. The formless figure removed the blade from the side of the new king and struck out at the first approaching guard, gutting him cleanly across his stomach, then disappeared only to resurface behind another guard, stabbing him straight through.

All the while Philip stood dumbfounded, mouth agape, staring like a fool at this shadow creature. It then disappeared, but not completely, not vanished. This figure wrapped itself back into darkness, into shadows, and became nearly impossible to see, like attempting to catch sight of a hummingbird's wings. They were certainly there, yet knowing such did not aid the eyes in seeing more than distortion.

More guards came about, but the figure moved, and Philip knew his death awaited him. He could hear Jessica call out for him, scream his name clearly above the rest of the chaos, but it was far too late. The sword came from outside the darkness, but rather than impale him, the figure only moved beyond him, brushing beside him, and through it he could see form to the nothingness.

The thing ignored him as it made its way to the side room, or so he believed, as after it moved beyond him, his eyes could no longer catch glimpse of it. Not it, as this was clearly a person. And the form was clearly not a man.

The assassin, that which spared his life, that which impaled the new king of Amon, was a woman.

--

"Here it comes," Iero muttered.

Rayden knew of the Realms; everyone did. His own sister tampered some in the Shadow Realm. But he rarely thought of it. The Pratts were a great many things, but religious was not one of them. Certainly he *believed* in the gods, fallen or otherwise. Existence formed somehow, and he could little think of a better explanation than Turitea and Schill, Twin Moons, gods of the night, or the many other names that people referred to them as. Some religions believed that they crafted different forms of existence, different Realms. Some could see these Realms. Some could touch the other side. But Rayden was not one of them.

Thus, he spent little time thinking of the art, those that could manipulate the other Realms. How often would fish wonder why they could not breathe on land? Did dogs spend their days wondering why they could not fly? No more, the young Pratt deduced, than he spent wondering about something that he could not even see much less comprehend.

But seeing the Realms and witnessing the effects of the Realms were two drastically different scopes. He no more knew of how the power worked, nor where it came from, but Rayden gazed in near horror at the incredible devastation they could cause.

The Druid went down to one knee and slammed his first to the floor. The tiles beneath them rumbled and the side walls shook. Roots and vines and rock from underneath them erupted upward, creating a wall through the explosion of stone. The act alone had been enough for shock, much less the destruction Iero caused.

"What are you doing? Why are you doing this?" repeatedly screamed Jerryn, both Pratt brothers stumbling through the devastation.

It was a sea of forested creation, a wall of roots that came from both outside the west wall and underneath the stone tiles. The roots moved as would snakes, slithering about each other, wrapping about themselves, forming together to prevent passage further between them and the side door to which they were previously headed. The path, for whatever reason, had become impenetrable.

Or so Rayden believed.

Almost as if to answer Jerryn's fearful questions, the wall Iero created went under attack instantly. A blade appeared in and out from behind the wall, slicing away at the roots, cutting through layers as would a hot knife through butter. In no way could a sword make such an easy display of these roots, but there was nothing natural about the blade. Rayden could not even see the wielder of the weapon. It was as if the sword was held by air alone.

"Run!" Iero screamed back to the brothers.

And yet Rayden hesitated, frozen. He had no idea what was going on or why. Much like his brother, the questions paralyzed him for the moment. But the sword was half way through the forested wall when Iero attempted to place down another layer. A second stream of roots tore through the western wall, creating several larger holes that led outside into the rear courtyard. Voices rose from behind the wall, the guards perhaps, but Rayden could not see beyond the roots.

Then arrows began to plunge into the wall, aiming for the sword, clanking harmlessly against the Druid's creation. The figure, the shadow . . . something that Rayden could not focus directly upon . . . well it must have noticed the predicament. Iero in front of the strange sword, guards now posted behind it. The sword ceased slicing away through the roots and disappeared from view. Certain now that a body could be seen somewhere in the darkness within the walls, Rayden watched as the form slid down one of the roots through an opening on the west wall. Now it was outside, away from them all.

Iero already began to withdraw his creation, the roots and vines plummeting back into the earth, leaving the gaping holes in both the floor and the wall. "Get after her!" the Druid screamed to the several dozen guards who in turn frantically rushed through the newly created holes in the wall. As the men followed after the figure, Iero stopped one of the men, grasping him firmly before he moved beyond them. "Where is the king?"

The solider shook his head. "I think the king is dead!" stammered the man, fear and panic in his voice.

Iero turned back to the Pratt brothers, his eyes stern and collected, unbelievable for the man that he knew the Druid to be. "Get the Pratt sons back to their room under lock and key. Do so now!"

"Iero . . ." started Rayden, but the portly man already moved toward the side door.

"Get to your room now!" screamed back Iero as he made his way to the throne room.

The king dead? A sword, darkness, the power of the Realms. What was going on? Nothing felt real. But the soldier mirrored that look in his own eyes. Three young fools gazing at one another.

Are we in danger? Why?

Hopefully not, Rayden realized, as the three of them simply stood about aloof. They would have been easy enough prey for the shadow assassin. Surprisingly it had been Jerryn to speak first amongst them.

"Lead us on," whispered the younger Pratt to the soldier.

--

Very rarely could Aldric claim to have seen something new. He had lived through generations of lives of men and nothing really surprised the Historian. Life moved on as it always had, one day following the next, each presenting similar challenges with similar results. A rock on the road would hit every wagon in its path until someone decided to move that rock. How much had life changed now that the road was clear of the rock? It of course was the same, minus the bump that was missed during the travel. And no matter how long that road would remain clear of rocks, eventually, inexplicably, a rock would find its way back on the road, awaiting to hit more wagons, and the chain would start again.

The other races of men had such short life spans and even shorter reigns of rule. If men made it into their seventies, it was both rare and considered a full life. House names could be interchanged several times a century, pending on their strength. Brocusk was an excellent example. He had conquered Ursan only thirty years back and had created an empire. The Pratts were some nine generations deep in Donovini. Their name seemed strong, but who was to say that another could not challenge their lordship, that an internal war would not change the face of their country. That was, of course, how the Pratts came into power to begin with.

The reign of a king varied. Young Yelium was the eighteenth king from Fallneese, but in real years, that was not eternally long. His father's reign was of the longer tenure's as king, standing at nearly twenty years. His grandfather's reign was only thirteen years. Their short life spans also carried with it the weight of age, that their minds and bodies left them long before they returned to the earth. Fit to be king was an old saying and in Genethur, the people truly meant it. Once that ceased to be truth, a reign would end.

Thus Aldric had seen kings remain in power for twenty years, he had seen some last as little as eight months.

Never, though, had he seen one such as this.

Philip Pratt knelt below, holding the boy in his arms, his hands placed over the gaping wound in the king's side. Blood emerged from the mouth of the young Aylmer as he attempted to speak, but only gurgled and choked through it. Nicolas stood beside the Historian, of the few that had the sense to gather his extended family together inside the room. There appeared no panic in the Donovinians, even in their youngest, Lillianna Pratt, who stood silently beside her mother Jessica awaiting further instructions. While the Pratts remained collective and calm, most of the remainder of the room had been chaotic, the screams echoed inside the chamber as some people still rushed to escape. House Rowe had disappeared along with what attended of House Aylmer. Even the Fourth, Lijid, had managed to hobble his way to the exit. Some of House Brocusk departed, though more orderly. Dehyllo himself still sat calmly, his elder sons of Loh and Worveso by his side, watching with an interested look upon their face as the life slowly faded from the king.

If Aldric knew anything about the man, he knew Dehyllo to be opportunistic. The Historian knew better than to jump to conclusions or gather his opinions, but it would not surprise him in the slightest if the killer had been from his House. Dehyllo, after all, had a throne to conquer.

Iero, likely the cause of the destruction in the previous room, emerged from the side room, frantically looking for a way through the guards. If the Pratts noticed the Druid, they did well to attempt otherwise.

"Is there anyone from House Aylmer present?" called out Philip, the king's blood all over him.

"Fucking lot of them took off," barked the youngest brother, Edmond.

Nicolas turned to one of the many soldiers that surrounded the Pratt family, protecting them as they knew little else what to do. "Give me your sword, boy," he demanded.

The soldier hesitated. "Lord Pratt, I . . ."

"The king is dead," he stated. "Give me the damn sword and let me end his suffering."

"Nicolas, this is not your place to . . ." started his wife, Maradyn.

But the elder Pratt spat upon the floor. "The boy was a shit and no one here liked him. His own family took off on him, left him here to bleed. That sword cut clean through organs, no doubts there. He will die, now or five minutes from now while he bleeds out. My place or not, I'm going to give the boy a clean death. Now give me the sword so that I can finish this, then the lot of you can quit protecting a corpse and find yourself out there trying to find the killer."

"They are not protecting the king," came a voice from behind them. Aldric turned to see the Druid had finally managed to make his way through the sea of guards. "They protect the First."

The First of Amon, when the throne is vacant, becomes the lord of the land. Temporary, but Philip Pratt is now the king until they figure out which House shall claim the throne.

Philip seemed to understand the gravity of the situation. Pulling apart the straps from Yelium's heavy waste of armor that did nothing to save him, the ornamental plate fell and clunked away. Afterwards, he waved to one of the soldiers. "Give me the damn sword. I will do it myself." Now there was no hesitation in the soldier this time. Sword removed from sheath, he handed over the weapon to Philip. The First wasted no time. "To the last Aylmer king, find peace." He stood over the body, whose eyes opened wide in frightful anticipation of the inevitable. Sword rose and fell, blade plunged into his heart, his death quickly followed.

Iero could not contain himself, unable to wait more than the mere seconds after the king's death to frantically tug at Lord Nicolas Pratt. "My lord . . ."

"Earth and Flame, Iero, now is not the time!"

"Make the time!" the Druid exploded. Aldric could barely believe his ears upon the forcefulness of his statement. He had never seen the man like this. Iero leaned in closely to Nicolas and spoke under hushed tone. "We need to get your daughter out of Corovium immediately."

"What? Why?" Nicolas inquired.

"You know why, my lord."

"If I knew why, would I really be . . ."

"The Shadow Realm was opened, Nicolas. I know how I appear to you, but I am no fool. Our assassin was a female Shadowmancer, which . . ."

Nicolas snatched the portly Druid by his tunic and brought him in close. "You dare accuse my daughter of assassinating the king?"

"No," answered Iero, "but can you say the same for your enemies?"

His eyes turned to the audience, and Aldric did not bother to follow. The Druid spoke of Dehyllo, and spoke wisely in his assessment.

"It does not matter truth from lies, you gained something in his death," continued the Druid. "The First is now lord of Amon until the council reaches a decision. Who knows how long that will be? There are those that know Katlynn is a Shadowmancer, and being that anyone with knowledge of the Realms witnessed the assassination, they will look at what is easiest and closest for an explanation. She will be detained. She will be interrogated. There will be a lengthy trial. And if the killer cannot be found, your daughter will hang to give the people the vengeance they desire. Then what do you believe will happen to the rest of your family after they determine her guilt?"

Nicolas released the Druid, his eyes all but displaying his deep thoughts against the matter. "You know I am right," Iero pressed further. "You are far too wise a man to not know the conclusion of this. Let me take her away from Corovium. *Now*. Before the Second has enough wit to take her into custody."

Silent for a moment, Nicolas calmed himself. "She is missing still."

"I know where she is," the Druid replied.

"Where will you take her?" Nicolas questioned, almost as a plea.

"Best you not know. Safe, I assure you."

Nicolas turned to the Historian, perhaps looking for guidance of some kind. *I can offer you none, yet if I could, I would tell you the Druid speaks the truth. Pray to the fallen gods that they find this killer, otherwise Katlynn Pratt will die, and the Pratts will fall.*

"What if the killer is found?"

"I will return her," Iero said confidently.

"How will you know if the killer is found?"

The Druid shrugged. "Likely when they stop hunting for us. Trust me, Lord Nicolas, I keep myself well informed. I hope they find this killer now and bring her back here, but we must act now before those against you would do the same. Her safety ties to the safety of the rest of your family and your name."

"But if she flees . . . it will look like guilt."

"Better to look like guilt and be missing than chained to a dungeon, waiting for the rope."

Slowly, hesitantly, Nicolas seemed to concede. "Go now before Maradyn finds out our conversation. Haste, Iero. If you let harm befall her . . ."

The sentence fell short, as the Druid already moved beyond the circle of guards, beyond the other members of the Pratt family that scattered about, heading toward the doors.

I thought that man was an idiot. Yet another thing new I have learned on this day.

--

First Pratt, temporary ruler of Amon, slayer of the king. Philip stood over the body, knew that his brother held an important conversation with the Druid, one that he should have wisely moved over and been part of. But none of that mattered. His eyes were locked onto Dehyllo Brocusk, and the Ursan's face stern and unwavering in return.

Did you send this assassin? Was this your plan all along? If I did not speak the truth of his birth, your Shadowmancer would strike from the darkness like a coward? What kind of way is this to die? No man, not even this shit, deserved such.

The blood-stained sword felt heavy in his hand, but he did not let go. Jessica, Lillianna, Joanna . . . they would all be staring at him now. How would they see him? Philip could not answer that. His mind was a utopia of thoughts and plots and possibilities. Nothing would be the same from this day forward.

And some part of him, the wiser half, knew that one day this may be his fate, lying in a pool of his own blood with a sword wielder above him.

Nothing will be the same.

--

If I am hungry, I find something to eat. I do not need to gather a council in order to discuss the hunger and decide on action plans and follow up appointments. I eat. No one stops me from it.

Ursan shunned away from lordship and kingship for many years, hundreds of years ago of course. I am not saying that I agree with that, no more than I am saying that I disagree with that. I only say that I understand.

-- *Afeon, Second of Amon*

V

When the knock came, Katlynn was uncertain of how frightened she should be. The crowd outside seemed frantic and confused. She had already missed the crowning of a new king and knew that her father would be furious at her for such. They had yet to even decide upon a course of action. Tristan had only barely gotten dressed. There stood a sense that once her father discovered that his captain bedded his daughter without consent, Tristan would be removed from his position and banished from Astrona altogether.

Tristan was her lover, not her soul mate, so she could not be so certain of how much she truly cared about the nature of his status. Though that was hardly fair. He was a good man. He was a better lover. He was a great captain. Katlynn could say in all honesty that she was not ready to see him relieved of any of those duties.

And for all of her careful planning and deception, of all her attempts to keep her secret relationship with the captain just that, Katlynn knew that they had now been undone. How could she explain that both the captain of the Astrona guard and the daughter of the House lord were missing, coincidentally at the same time?

Time to come clean, Katlynn. Best to just get the damn thing over with.

Her father's wrath would be . . . fierce.

"Just answer the door," she muttered toward Tristan, not bothering to gather herself into the shadows.

He did as she asked, opening the door, and allowing inside Iero, the Donovinian Druid, along with the disgusting creature that hung about his shoulders. In fact . . . the Chur'rat had a familiar look to him.

"Good Lady Katlynn, I greet you warmly but with haste. Are you all aware of the current events? Likely not, as you both are here together and strangely absent from the assembly hall. Not that I would jump to such conclusions as to why you both would be missing, nor would I assume that you being here in your nightgown would explain the departure from the meeting, only that . . ."

"Iero," butted in Katlynn. "Did my father send you?"

"In a manner of speaking, yes."

"How did you know where to find me?"

"Not I," confessed the Druid. "Bird keeps a watchful eye and informed me of such."

"Bird?"

"My Chur'rat, Lady Katlynn. A story for perhaps another day. I will say that haste is needed now, as we . . ."

"Look, Iero, I appreciate the visit, but I know that my father wishes to speak to me. I will do such on my own time. Ultimately this is my life, so I will live it as I see fit."

"My lady, I believe you misunderstand my visit. Apparently my assumptions are correct and you are not informed on the state of things. The panic and discussion you see outside is due to the crowning of the king and what has occurred. There is still confusion and misreports on such, so we have limited time to speak."

"Then Nicolas picked the wrong person if timeliness is at hand," Tristan offered up.

"The king was crowned and then immediately assassinated," Iero pushed on, the words almost falling deaf at first onto her ears.

"Say again," Katlynn stammered.

"The king was assassinated. By a woman. A Shadowmancer."

A moment passed, the words spoken, and it still took a bit longer to sink in. Iero was not here by way of her father on their absence, nor here to simply inform her of the tragedy.

"Are you . . . arresting me?" she questioned.

Iero shook his head. "I have no such authority. I am here to help you flee. Now. Before it is too late."

Katlynn could barely believe the words. "But I didn't kill the king."

"So you say."

"You know me well enough to know I wouldn't do such a thing. Why should I flee?"

"You are a woman and a Shadowmancer. You were not present during the crowning of the king. You will be the prime suspect of the crime."

"I can vouch for her," Tristan offered up. "She has been with me since last night."

"Indeed, and what weight will the testimony of her lover hold up in a trial? They would expect you to lie for her, thus not allowing you to vouch for yourself much less her."

Katlynn knew that her face turned red over the matter. "Do you think that I did this?"

"What I think is not truly important, Lady Katlynn. What I ask is that you wrap yourself inside the Shadow Realm and follow me out of Corovium."

"I will not!" she exclaimed. "You will take me to my father so that I can explain this situation! I . . . I . . . the king is dead?"

Iero nodded.

Earth and Flame.

She could feel her heart skip beats as she weighed in on the situation. *Assassinated. By a Shadowmancer nonetheless.*

"Happened quickly and painfully. The details I would be more than happy to share later. But if you stay, they will arrest you. Your gifts are not unknown to those in power. It is the business of some men to know the business of others. Strengths and weakness are always needed in evaluating friend and foe alike. If you remain much longer, the guards, the council, the courts . . . they will find you. You will be placed in confinement and, more importantly, the search for the killer will be called off until they determine your innocence or guilt. If you did not kill the king as you say, staying here would be a grave mistake."

"And running is better?" retorted Katlynn. "If I run, I admit guilt."

"You would not be running, as you were not even at the ceremony. You would be missing."

"And the difference?" Tristan cut in.

"The difference, my wise captain, is that missing allows her uncle to run the country and find the killer. If the killer is determined to be Katlynn, the Pratt name will go down in the worst of ways, I fear."

They would kill us all. Shit. This is unbelievable. Why is this happening? Why couldn't I have just woken up on time and been there?

"You must understand how these things work," the Druid continued. "They do not need evidence to prove her guilty. She needs evidence to prove her innocent. And sadly, Katlynn lacks that evidence. The best thing at this point is to disappear for a time until this can be figured out."

"And what if this can't be figured out?" she queried in desperation. "What if the real killer cannot be found?"

Iero raised an eyebrow as the Chur'rat repositioned on his shoulder. "Are you religious at all, Katlynn Pratt?"

"No. Well, I believe, but . . . well . . ."

"Then believe in luck, Lady Pratt."

Her arms crossed, her options danced in her mind. Stay, plead her case to council and hope that they would believe her. But why would they believe her? Her uncle would not allow her to be jailed, but without a king, many things would be set to vote. Katlynn felt ashamed to admit that she did not even know the names of every council member, much less trust in their decision making. Politics were not really her thing.

The only other choice would be to run as Iero suggested. How far could she get before they hunted her? The guards would not hunt beyond the walls and the army would not hunt far beyond Genethur. The Guild would be tapped and bounty hunters were positioned throughout Amon. No, running hardly seemed the right thing to do. That, and what did she know of the outside world? Katlynn had barely been out of Astrona in her life.

But if this is Father's will . . .

"You said my father sent you. This is his decision?"

The Druid nodded. "My lady, I would not be here if it were not under his consent."

"I'm not so sure then that I have a choice. I can't even speak with my brothers, to tell them . . ."

"Keep them close to heart but out of mind, Lady Pratt. Trust you will see them soon." Iero turned about to face Tristan. "So, good captain, can I presume you travel with us on our venture to . . ."

"You're fucking right I'm going," he interrupted.

"Where are we headed?" Katlynn questioned further.

To which Iero answered, "For now, out the door. We will find you clothes as we depart. Wrap yourself in shadows and head outside. And if anyone calls for you, young captain, do not stop. We make for the exit. Ha! I've always wanted to say that."

--

Blood still stained his hands and his clothes as Philip slumped heavily at the head seat. An hour after the assassination of Yelium Aylmer II, order did resume that left many prestigious men and women of House names embarrassed and a bit ashamed in their disarray. The army arrived and took the place of the capital guards, and in no slight hurry did the Second General Isani Brocusk assume temporary command. General Brocusk had been a son of a brother of Dehyllo, or some such mess that was the Ursan House name. Philip needed a fucking chart to track the Brocusk lineage.

Despite the confusing genealogy, Isani did well to calm and situate the masses, along with sending his best men out to hunt for the assassin. The council was quickly gathered and placed inside the war room upstairs in the capital building, outside the door and lined along the interior of the massive room stood the Imperial Army in all their glory, there to protect the council. More directly, of course, to protect him.

Lot of good they will do. Plenty of guards at the inauguration. Doesn't make the king any less dead.

For what it was worth, Philip's nerves had calmed. This was not the first nor the last time he had watched someone die before him. Flame's embrace, he had held more than one dying corpse in his arms in his lifetime. Irony, as in the aftermath Philip remembered holding the hand of the whore that gave birth to the young Yelium right as a member of the Divide killed her. It had not been a surprise, not like this one, as Philip of course knew her fate long before he arrived for the birth. Irony in how he was the last to touch their lives directly before he ended them.

The remainder of the House names were confined to their quarters under heavy guard. None of them had been pleased about it, at least none of the Pratts, but Philip did not yet stake his authority over the Second General. No need, as it was the wisest decision. At the moment, safety of everyone was needed, followed by the hopeful discovery of the assassin. Philip had spent very little time during this silent hour of sitting beside his fellow council members contemplating on who killed the king and why. Someone did it, and for a reason presumably. Knowing the killer and the motive did very little to bring back the king. In the end, the dead remained such. Damned shame of it of course was that the First could point a finger in any direction, even to his own, and find motive. He would have cursed the little shit to Shadow himself if given the opportunity. Not exactly the most likable of kids, that much was certain.

The war room was not immense, but sizable. The table stood at the center of the room, rectangular and lengthy at that. At the two points were chairs for the First on the side closest to the door, the king on opposite. Three chairs then positioned to the far of the room for the Second, Third, and Fourth. He only noticed it as even during the current state of affairs, all four council members sat in their exact positions, like school children in assigned seats.

Tools, the lot of us.

He gazed down again at the blood. He wanted a bath and a change of clothes.

"It was a clean death, First Pratt," stated Lurey Hillan, the Third of Amon. The Argon was a fatter version of his sister, Christina Rowe. Fair complexioned much as she, their blond hair equal in tone and length, the blue eyes a perfect match, their face similar in structure down to the nose that rose just slightly. Only real difference, of course, was that the moment Christina married Edfeld Rowe, the late House lord of Argonus, she had been required to maintain her body for his needs. Lurey, of course, no longer needed to worry about such. What need was appeal when he was the brother of the lady of the country? He could get whoever money could buy. And if rumor had it, he bought quite a bit . . . without much preference to either sex.

Philip gazed up from his slouch and barely gave the Third notice. "Funny, Third Hillan, as I did not see you there when he died."

After an awkward moment, the Third replied, "Well, from what I heard, the death was clean, First Pratt."

"No death is clean," mumbled Philip. "You die, then you piss and shit yourself. Nothing clean about that. Best you can hope for is to die surrounded by loved ones, maybe just your wife and kids and the such, letting the last thing you see or feel is the knowledge that someone cared for you, someone felt that the measure of your life was worth something. Worst you can hope for is to die slow, sit there helplessly bleeding while not a fucking soul cares whether you live or die, they just look to run and save their own asses. Worst you can hope for is to die in a room full of people that could not care less. Worst you can hope for is having the last thing you see being someone you hate giving you mercy, killing you because no one in your own House had the decency to stick around to give you that honor."

Philip shook his head. "No, Third, I wouldn't say that was a clean death. In fact, I would say that it was the *exact . . . fucking . . . opposite."*

Afeon seemed to find humor in the situation, as he only chuckled after the comment. "I think the Third only gave his condolence to your decision to give mercy."

"Save his fucking condolence," Philip cursed. "Last I checked, no one from his House was present and so I made a decision. I need neither approval nor pity to justify saving a man from further suffering. He was dead no matter what. And no one deserves a slow death. *No one."*

Best I can hope for is the same mercy in the same situation.

"So," Afeon pressed further, "should we start the discussion of which House is next to take the throne?"

Philip almost wanted to laugh at the audacity. "Earth and Flame, Second, do you want to let the corpse get a bit colder before we discuss his replacement?"

"Doesn't exactly make this any more or less difficult to discuss," was the Ursan's response. "Besides, we are not voting or deciding. We are just talking. Better than just sitting here in silence, waiting for the Second General to determine that it is safe to return to our rooms."

"Well since we already know where your vote will land, is it really necessary to speak on it?" Philip inquired trenchantly.

"Well the rules are plain," Afeon retorted immediately. "Not that we have had the opportunity to adhere to these rules during our tenure, but they are there for study nonetheless. The House that has forfeited the throne by any means cannot reclaim the throne unless voted unanimously by the remaining council. Other than that, the throne would be awarded to the most deserving House, which will relate to both military power and wealth. Let us be very clear here. We obviously have the military strength. Not to mention that Ursan is the wealthiest of countries, has been for some time."

Lurey raised an eyebrow to the statement. "Having the greatest number of trees, Draywolves, mosquitos, and diseases does not equal wealth, Second."

"True enough," admitted Afeon, "as we do not trade for gold and have the illustrious cities as do you, Third Hillan. But what we have are the herbs used for healing, skins worn for harsh winter months, vegetation to feed many mouths from across our great Amon, fresh water that can supply Amon should droughts continue, many ores from the vast underground caves throughout . . ."

"Want to wrap this up at some point?" Philip interrupted.

"What I am saying," continued the Second, "is that we supply many needs to Amon. Wealth is measured at times by need, Lurey Hillan, not always by cites and industry. Where do you believe a majority of the gold coins come from that you so happily enjoy? They are mined from my country, by my people. You measure it by the coin, we measure it by the need. And make no mistake, Third, we buy nothing from the rest of you, save for perhaps salt and spices from the Guild. And since you know for a fact that you cannot say the same, where do you think this money goes that we make from our three neighboring countries? Frugal, as you Argons may say."

"Asshole, as the Donovinians may say," mumbled Philip.

"Regardless," Lijid stated softly from the far of the room, "it must be voted upon."

"Thank you for your input, Fourth, and you are correct in such," sarcastically responded Afeon.

"What he is doing, Lijid, is pleading his case," Philip added. "But perhaps we should wait for the pleading until Yelium is properly buried with his father in the tombs with the remainder of the kings of Amon. And before we jump to any voting, we should make all attempts to uncover the identity of the assassin."

Afeon leaned into the table at the last statement, his interest suddenly spiked apparently. "So you believe that voting may be swayed based on the race of the assassin?"

"More the plot than origins," the First corrected.

"And what if the killer is your niece?" the Second pressed.

The remainder of the room stood still at his accusation. It did not bother Philip in the slightest, though. Katlynn would no more assassinate the king than she would bother with knowing the names of the king's council. Motive, she had none. But what his niece did match was the description.

Enough to bring her in. I have to, at least to question her. Nicolas will be furious, but I can't show bias. Not when the fate of this country is being held together by threads. I fear that one false step, and Dehyllo will take the throne by force.

Philip Pratt straightened in his chair as he responded. "If Katlynn killed the king, she would be hung, no different than the rest of us should we be found guilty of treason."

"Will you bring her in?" questioned Afeon.

"Yes, once we can get out of this damned room."

On cue, the door opened and Queen Dylinn Aylmer strode in. Her beauty could hardly be masked by the stress upon her face. Philip stood along with the remainder of the council, but she waved them down immediately.

"Sit, please," she stated insistently. "I come just for a moment to inform you that Isani is clearing off sections at a time. This will be the last to clear, and everyone save the First will be allowed back to their chambers unabated. The Second General wishes to speak with you before all is clear, First Pratt."

"Yes, Queen Aylmer, but . . ." he started but was swiftly cut short.

"I am not the queen, First Pratt. I am Lady Aylmer, head of my House in Fallneese."

"But my queen, clearly. . ." Lijid pleaded, but Dylinn would have nothing of it.

"Unless you are all blind, Yelium Aylmer II was crowed but an hour ago. That makes him the king. His death vacates the throne and my position as queen. I am nothing but the head of my House and ruler of my country, which is a hefty duty, but not to be placed amongst you four here. Once the word is cleared, I leave for Fallneese. I pray to the fallen gods that the decision amongst you all as to who takes throne will be a wise one. As for now, I wish you well."

When she turned to leave, Philip silently wondered if it would be the last time he would see her.

No, she will seek me out before she leaves. Won't she?

For the life of him, Philip could not decide if that mattered or not.

--

Rayden sat upon the couch in his parents' chambers, Jerryn beside him and the rest of the family scattered about their room. Katlynn remained missing and the Imperial Army had yet to allow any of them to search for her. They were confined and under protection until further notice from the Second General. It had been over an hour now. Plenty of time to think, plenty of time to be chastised repeatedly by his father.

Idiots and disgraces, along with a few disappointments were thrown into the jumbled cursing from one Nicolas Pratt. It would not have been quite as bad had it not been in front of his Uncle Edmond, Aunt Jessica, and the remainder of his extended family. Rayden truly did everything he could to be the son that this father wanted, to be the man ready to take the House lordship, to rule Donovini. Sadly, though, nothing short of perfection could ever please his father . . . which he repeatedly was informed that he was far, far from.

He rarely complained, though. Jerryn spent far more time bickering about the harshness of their father than Rayden did. His life was too prestigious to complain about his station or treatment in life. His brother would disagree, but the last thing Rayden wanted to be viewed as was a spoiled, rich kid. That, and if the unachievable expectations of a father were the largest of his concerns in life, so be it. The least he could do was attempt to live up to those expectations.

But he sat, humiliated as it were, chastised harshly in front of his family while his father let him have it. Thus was life. His focus did not waiver from the events that just transpired. Iero, the witnessing of the power of the Realms, the destruction it caused. None of it felt real. It was as if he heard the tale being sung by a bard at some local tavern in Astrona, disbelieving of the grandioso events. But it had been real, as real as his sight of the shadow figure as it cut through the wall of roots heaved upward from the Druid.

All of the chastising felt trivial. All of the yelling felt out of place. The king died. What would happen to the throne? What of the assassin? What of his sister? What of the power of the Realms?

Isn't that a bit more important than yelling at me for not being present to watch the king die? Isn't finding Katlynn far more important than any of this?

Instead the family moved about and mingled, discussing Yelium, both father and son, discussing the Realms, discussing Katlynn somewhat, discussing things of relevance. Nicolas took a breather from yelling and only paced the room, perhaps equally worried of his daughter if not showing such in his verbal lashings.

A firm knock on the door caught the attention of the Pratts as Uncle Edmond took a direct path toward it. Upon opening it, Christina Rowe stormed inside, her eyes finding Rayden first, then Nicolas second. She was perhaps in her late thirties if he were guessing, still a stunning woman in her own right. It was clear that Allura gathered her looks from this side of the family, from her blonde hair and blue eyes and near flawless skin.

"I am sorry for this interruption, Lord Pratt, but I must have a word with you. Your sector is not clear yet, but perhaps your family might move across the hall so that we can have a private word."

His father nodded his head. "Of course. If you will excuse us."

After a few seconds of hesitation, his mother took charge. "Come now, let's change rooms to give them some privacy," Maradyn spoke up. "The boys' room is just around the way."

As Rayden stood and made his way to the door with the remainder of his family, Christina put her hand out to him. "Not you, Rayden," she announced. "I wish for you to hear this discussion, along with my daughter."

If his face matched the skip of his heart as he watched Allura enter, he would have been more embarrassed than the chastising from his father. He had little idea what this meeting was about, little knowledge as to why the Rowes would need to discuss anything with the Pratts, much less a conversation needed to be attended by the children.

Unless marriage is to be discussed. Too wishful. Why would that be discussed at a time like this?

Allura stood radiant above all, though her face did not appear pleased to be in the presence of the Donovinians. He attempted to lock eyes with her as the room cleared, but she refused to meet his. Her stare stood to the ground, her demeanor slumped and sluggish.

As the room emptied, Christina pointed back to the couch, looking at her daughter. "Allura, sit. Rayden, do the same."

Little hesitation in either of them as they did as commanded.

"So what is this about, Christina?" his father questioned, his patience thin.

The House lady chuckled. "I like you Nicolas. Always have. If not, I would not have negotiated in the aid of your people during this drought. I respect you too much to not cut to the chase on this affair. You know damned well that the council is holed up, figuring out what to do with Amon."

"And that is their place to do such," his father responded.

"Maybe so, but perhaps it is our place to determine the outcome of such. Let us speak truthfully of things. The throne has been under claim of Fallneese long before our fathers, and their fathers, and so forth. This is the first time that it has come under grabs."

"You speak of it as if it were a prize, Lady Rowe," Nicolas stated with a half grin upon his face.

"Save your judgment for someone who might be offended," she hammered back. "Despite what you may or may not think of me, my desire has always been for the betterment of Amon. You know good and well the throne will fall to Ursan."

"It must be voted upon," replied Nicolas. "You know that Philip would not vote for them. You get Lurey to do the same and that saves that from worry."

"And what of Lijid? Any guarantees that he will not vote in their favor? Fear is an interesting beast, Nicolas. And a fifty percent vote is all that is needed for it to move to the courts. I believe we stand a better chance against Ursan if it the votes land there. We have stronger support in the judicial system than they do, thanks to their desire to only place one foot in the water as far as our government is concerned."

"So you look for a split vote," he deduced out loud. "Thus, you want the First and Third to place the same vote on the throne. But let me guess as to where the vote should be placed."

"Yet again, you judge me."

"Am I wrong?"

Christina shrugged. "In a manner of speaking, no. Look, I know you don't want an Ursan on the throne, but let us be truthful with each other. That possibility exists. I have little intentions of sitting idly by while Dehyllo takes the throne. An allegiance is needed to be made, and I do not seem to see why it cannot be made between us."

"To save the throne from Dehyllo?" questioned a skeptical sounding Nicolas. "For the betterment of Amon?"

"I know you think of me as some coldhearted bitch. I cannot blame you. I know that my boldness of coming here to request you to have Philip vote for House Rowe would be completely audacious, if not ludicrous. Thus, I have another solution for you."

"I would presume that is why you are here, so make your offer."

Christina gave a wicked smile. "Our eldest children marry. Unified, we would win the courts easily should it even come to that. Allura would take your name, Rayden would rule under my country."

There had been no pause as uncomfortable as this one in all of Rayden's existence. He did all that he could to contain the excitement of the offer, mixed in with the fear of his father's denial of the response. To Shadow with the politics, this was about Allura for him.

His eyes moved over to Allura's to see if her reaction was the same, to see if she had known this offer was to come. She still gave no glance toward him.

"So Rayden and Allura marry, Pratts in name, but rule under House Rowe. I got that about right?"

"And better yet, while young Rayden here learns to rule, Philip can and will remain as First to help him along the way. Only change would put Lurey as Fourth, Lijid as Third. Who cares what flag is flown by the king?"

"Besides you, you mean?"

"Your son is on the throne. You raised him with the intent to rule Donovini, only now he will rule Amon as a whole instead. What matters to me is that Dehyllo does not claim power. I would offer you my allegiance, but let us be honest, you are not to be trusted. That, and there is still the matter with your daughter. Best be under my name. We are clearly . . . untainted at the moment."

"What has Katlynn done?" stammered Rayden, completely out of turn and unwelcome, he realized.

"Become the prime suspect in the assassination of the king, young Pratt," was her response. "I do not believe those allegations, but that does not satisfy the Imperial Army, nor should it satisfy the council. We have no idea what that will do with your reputation amongst Amon, much less the courts should we need them. Rowe will be the House name to take the throne, but Pratt will be the name of the king. Your name, under Argonus. What say you, Nicolas?"

His father paced the room a bit, silent for a few seconds. What Rayden would not have given for silence before Christina arrived, and yet now he screamed inside for an answer. Again, with politics, Rayden did not truly care. He had not studied much in worldly affairs outside of Donovini. What were the chances that he would rule Amon? His destiny was to rule Donovini, one country, not all of them. But his thoughts were not on ruling, or governing, or even what happened to the last king.

Allura Rowe. No, Allura Pratt. Better yet.

"I need some time to think on this one, Christina. Definitely not a no, just need a little time."

"I understand, but time is not on our hand with Dehyllo and Afeon. They will look to quickly make their move to the throne. We must do the same, lest he take it from us."

"Agreed. I will get back with you after I discuss this with my wife. Is there anything else?"

"Yes," called out Allura. "Might I have a word with Rayden alone? I will be just a moment. I know this is a bit uncalled for, but. . ."

"Not at all," Nicolas cut in. "Christina, I can walk you out while our children speak some."

"Very well," Christina agreed. "Meet me back in my chambers when you are done, child."

"Yes, Mother," answered Allura.

Rayden watched as the two left, barely giving them a second glance as Allura waited until the door was closed and they were alone. He could not lie and not claim to have dreamt of this moment many times. The beautiful Argon woman, stunning in her walk as she stood from her seat and moved cautiously about the room, the many things he did to this woman in his mind were embarrassing to utter aloud. And now, here in the capital, the young Pratt finally had her alone.

"I do not love you," she finally claimed, her words stern and straightforward.

Whatever dream Rayden had been engulfed in, reality quickly retook form.

"I know that my mother wishes this marriage, and I understand why. But my being single has not been because of choice. I found another some time ago, one that I truly loved. But his name was not high enough in stature in order to be courted. So the remainder of my friends began to marry off while I grew older and awaited the opportunity."

Perhaps I do not know this girl as well as I think I do.

"Is marriage a means to an end for you?" Rayden inquired.

Allura shot back a look that could have killed a small child. "Easy for you to say, Rayden Pratt. What is in your future, marriage or not? To rule Donovini? What of my future? I am a woman of a House name. What skills do I possess that I might accomplish something in life? What, none you say? None because we are trained to look a certain way, act a certain way. We are bred to marry, spread our legs, produce children, grow old, and pray to the fallen gods not to be discarded for a younger woman when our men tire of us. When we become too marked from children, when we carry a few extra pounds from child birth, when the first spots of age hit us, what then, Rayden Pratt? Well guess what? I *am* a young woman still, but time is ever short. If now is not the time for my marriage, tell me, when is?"

"So, you want to be married . . . just not to me, is that where this is going?" inquired Rayden, both hurt and annoyed at this seeming attack. "Not that I need to defend all Donovinian males, but it is a bit harsh to assume we are all one way. Besides, I can attest that I do not love you either, not that you asked. But that does not change the facts that this union is what our parents need for the . . ."

"Come now, Rayden," Allura interrupted with a laugh. "I said I didn't love you, not that I didn't like you. Be honest with me, this has nothing to do with politics for you. I know we have only had a few meetings, but none of them have involved you speaking of Amon or your thoughts on ruling Donovini. The political world has little meaning to you. This marriage excites you because you get to marry me. It is not an arrogance thing, I promise you, only you have made every attempt to court me, save for reaching over and just grabbing my ass. It's flattering. You are a handsome man, and funny, and interesting. Every woman would die to be in this position I am in. Every woman would die to be in as many positions with you as possible."

"Every woman save you, I gather."

Allura sighed, a soft grin upon her face. "My heart is with someone else, despite the fact that I can never be with him. Trust me, Rayden, if your father agrees to terms, I will marry you. I will do so because it is asked of me. I will let you fuck me, as many times as you desire. I will have your children, I will stay looking as slim as you wish me to be, until the day you grow tired of me and cast me aside for another. I will do all of this because I *do* believe in the politics of this country, and I fear what will become of us under House Brocusk. I will do all of this because my mother asks this of me and I believe she knows the best interests of Argonus. I will do all of this because it is the right thing to do for Amon, my country, my family, my people. I will do all of this and anything you ask of me, everything . . . except love you."

Rayden did not exactly have much to say to her after that. His heart felt heavy and his throat tightened. Nothing worse in his mind than to believe that feelings were mutual, only to find out otherwise in vicious fashion.

The young lady Rowe moved across the room, rested her hand for a moment on his shoulder. Then she simply made her way to the door and departed, leaving Rayden alone with his thoughts.

Which, at the moment, was the last thing he wanted.

--

By the time Isani decided to show up, Philip had nearly lost what remained of his nerves. Almost two hours they had been held up without much word, save for Dylinn's information of course. But the Second General did finally show, midsized but a commanding sense of authority in the bearded man, Isani seemed proud to adorn the multiple scars upon his face. All good and well, Philip figured, as the man was as ugly as one could get. Scars could not possibly do him any further injustice.

The room cleared after his announcement that it had been safe to return to their quarters, but he requested they remain there for a bit while things sorted out. The courtyard and the surrounding area had been cleared of the onlookers, many citizens still trying to assess what happened. The entire situation was as close to shambles as could be.

The Second General waited patiently, then approached Philip, a single nod toward him. "First Pratt, as you can clearly figure out on your own, the situation is about shit down there. But it is maintained. I now relieve my control to you. Amon is yours, First. Orders?"

Just like that, he now officially stood in command. *A bit lackluster in the induction, but what else is new?*

"What have you found on our assassin?"

The Ursan general shrugged. "Not much, First Pratt. Obviously the side chamber to the throne room is a security issue, and I would have you not attend any business there until the repairs are completed. Or started, for that matter. But as brave as it was of Iero to attack and defend, especially with your nephews in the way, it created an easy access to the rear courtyard. From there, the guards stated they lost the . . . well whatever it was."

"Anything in the city?"

"Not that we have found, First Pratt. As much as I hate to say this, whatever did this managed to not only move into the capital without notice, but managed to sneak out all the same."

"Assuming she has left."

Isani nodded. "Yes, assuming *she* has left."

Philip began to move out to the hallway, with the general walking beside him. "Disturbing that this was done as clean and as easy."

"I recommend keeping us in the capital building for now. I know that having the Imperial Army may not be a complete sense of security, but still . . ."

"No, I agree, Second General. Rather you be here. If anything, gives people a peace of mind. In the meantime, I need your best men. We have someone missing, and we need her brought in."

"And who am I to tell them they are looking for?"

There really is no choice in this.

"My niece, Katlynn Pratt. She has been missing since before the inauguration."

"Interesting," Isani muttered. "That makes three people unaccounted for. I had not thought to check the House names for any missing personnel."

"Who else is missing?"

"Iero, for starters. I figured the Druid might have ducked away from us, knowing I might have had him rebuild the wall he destroyed. The other is your captain in Astrona, Crane I believe is his name. He is also unaccounted for as far as the guest list is concerned."

Tristan spent an interesting amount of time around the Pratts, namely Katlynn. And they were both strangely absent during the crowning. This clearly did not help her case of innocence. An accomplice perhaps, or the mastermind? This was how it would be viewed by the courts should they judge her. And Iero had spoken to Nicolas in the throne room when the king died. This was of course no coincidence. *Dear Katlynn, I hope you know what you are forcing me to do.*

"They will be traveling together, all three of them, likely making their way to Donovini. Have your riders press eastward to the border. They have a two-hour head start on us, but outside of Iero, they lack knowledge of the countryside."

"It will be done, First Pratt."

"And I cannot stress this enough to you, Second General, so I expect you to place the same amount of stress on your men. Katlynn Pratt is *not* considered the killer, but I need her brought in for questioning. She is *not* to be harmed. Is that clear?"

"If she is not the killer, why bother, First Pratt?"

"Because she is our only suspect, General Brocusk. Now go. And have one of your men bring me my brother, Nicolas, and have him meet me in the throne room immediately."

"But First Pratt," started the general, "I was clear that I think the idea of operating in the throne room is . . ."

"We will show no fear, Second General. We will not let this assassination break this country. Strength is needed, not caution. Bring me my brother."

"It will be done, First."

And if you are hiding Katlynn, damn you Nicolas. You better not get us all hung.

--

"So you leave Genethur, back to Fallneese?" Aldric questioned the former queen of Amon.

She did not stop barking orders at first to respond to him. Her servants were moving about her chambers, gathering her things, preparing for the trip. "Isani has cleared my departure," she called back eventually to Aldric. "There is nothing left for me here."

And perhaps she was right. The Historian watched, uncertain how to feel about any of the events.

I am not supposed to feel anything. That is the rule. But Jaa must have felt something. Guilt, perhaps? Remorse? How can emotion be removed from this? How can I not have an opinion?

"Strange," whispered Erian from behind him. "To think this was meant to be your last trip to Corovium."

"You say that as if anything has changed," he responded to his apprentice.

"Hasn't it?"

And in reality, Aldric did not know. Certainly he had lived long enough to see assassination attempts, even one that succeeded, but never something like this. And the race to capture the throne would likely be swift and brutal. Dehyllo would make his attempts, but neither the Pratts nor the Rowes would take such lightly. While the Houses would not fear much in the way of the fallout of this, Aldric did. He had seen small wars and skirmishes and battles in his tenure, but he had never seen a war of countries. That was what he feared the most currently.

It was not the only thing he feared. There stood a great chance that Katlynn would be caught and hung for her actions. The ramifications of that would pour downward to the remainder of the Pratts. They were a brash House, certainly, but noble and strong. Of all of the House names, the Pratts stood above them all. The throne would be best under their watch, regardless that by law Brocusk should claim it.

Opinions and thoughts, those of which he could not share nor have. He was to record the history, not become part of it. Thus his station in life. This was his crutch.

And as he watched Dylinn pack her belongings, he could not help but feel she fled in haste. There were still things to be done here in Corovium. Son or not, the country saw Yelium as that. She should remain to see him buried with the kings that ruled before him. She should mourn as she helped raise this boy, for better or worse, more latter than former. Dylinn moved without thought of how this may impact her House, her country.

But to express this to her would be to shame the Kwyantin, to dishonor his people. It was something he could not do.

The former queen stopped long enough to approach him, long enough to place a letter in his hand. "I know I ask you to do something that I should not, but can you deliver this to First Pratt? But not now."

"When you leave?" he inquired.

She smiled. "You know women quite well, Historian. Tell me, is there love amongst your people?"

It was an intriguing question. Very rarely had Aldric been in a position to answer questions about his own people. "We are certainly different from the remainder of your societies, Lady Aylmer, but there is love in my people. Love *for* our people in fact. We perform the duties assigned to us as proof of our loyalty. Kwyantin people have but one job, one station in life."

"And you perform this job out of the love and devotion to your people?" she pressed further.

"Yes, Lady Aylmer."

"And what of the women of your people?"

"They share the same passion, my lady," was the Historian's response.

But Dylinn shook her head. "What of love for each other, Historian?"

"Kwyantin are a whole, my lady. One society of voices. Each assigned a duty in life, and that duty is performed. Being the Historian is but one duty of our people, yet it encompasses my life entire." He shrugged his shoulders slightly. "Where is the time for such? We love each other as would we love our people, our way of life. To answer your question, not as the way you know such. Our procreation is decided, and the event is rather . . . let us just say planned."

"For the continuation of your people," she concluded.

To which the Historian nodded. "For the *love* of our people."

The former queen gazed at his hands, stared blatantly at the letter. "For some reason, Aldric, Historian of Amon, I feel sadness for you. Love of your people and your country is an emotion of pride. Love of another, just one person, is reckless, foolish, brash, and uncontrollable. All of that, and yet indescribably powerful."

He smiled. "I am not so certain it sounds altogether healthy, my lady."

"Love never is."

Not that I was without interest or desire. There was someone I was raised with, someone who caught my eye. Valencia . . . but that was not meant for me.

Aldric gazed to the letter as well. "Would you like me to say something to him, my lady?"

"Yes. Tell him . . ."

But her words hung, and Dylinn turned from the Historian. "Yes, Lady Aylmer?"

Dylinn shrugged. "I suppose nothing. What words can I give, Historian? I have no idea where I thought this would end."

"Where what would end?" he pried.

But she only shook her head to him. "Just the letter, Historian. And thank you."

Aldric held the letter as she turned back to her servants. He did all that he could to resist opening it right then.

--

Philip wasn't exactly certain how to feel. Dried, dark blood still stained the floor in the throne room to match his clothes and his hands. They of course had yet to remove the chairs, the tables, the appetizers, and the drinks. The throne room still had the same look as it had for the crowning as it did now that the First sat upon the throne. But he watched silently as the servants cleaned up the mess left behind. The fallen liquid and food swept and mopped, the chairs pushed and pulled back and away, clearing the throne room one section at a time. The First gazed at the staff as if he watched them clean and fold away the entire Fallneesian reign of the throne. Such prestige, such honor, despite it all. Yelium Aylmer II might have never been given the chance to prove him wrong, but his father had done well enough in giving Philip power. Leadership was not entirely about making the right decisions alone, the First knew. Sometimes leadership was placing faith in the right people. But even prior to Yelium, the Aylmer line did well to maintain and flourish in their position. From what he knew, there could be little complaint at their accomplishments. Good kings, all the way up to a poor decision by Yelium to bed that whore, to let her give birth to his child.

Ashamed to think it, but Philip always believed that the Divide should have been called in beforehand. Yelium should have had her killed long before the birth. It would have solved many problems, if not created new ones. Perhaps Dylinn would have been able to produce a child for him before the Chur'ash made him sterile. Perhaps a true heir to the throne would have emerged, preventing an assassination against the bastard boy. Perhaps, but foolish to think too deeply upon what ifs. It had happened exactly as it had and nothing would change it. Cruelty of fate, if such a thing existed.

The soldiers that guarded the steps to the throne straightened at the entrance of his brother, Nicolas, who casually made his way upward to the throne. This altercation would not be easy, he knew. The face of Nicolas showcased his annoyance at having to appear before his younger brother. But Philip did not turn his gaze away from him. A lifetime of being the superior brother had left Nicolas with a false sense of importance. Certainly the elder Pratt was important as a House lord, but he had never held much weight to Philip and his accomplishments. Irrelevant at the moment, as his brash decision may have cost them all their heads.

"If I walked all this damn way to just kneel before you, Philip, I will punch you straight through the fucking holes in the wall that Iero created," started Nicolas.

His tone had caused several of the Imperial Army to move from their standing positions to a direct path of the elder Pratt to impede his progress. But Philip only waved his hands. "You know damn well he is my brother. Stand aside."

"Wondrous," Nicolas exclaimed. "One minute into your rule and they are about to behead your brother. One minute into Aylmer's rule, and they let him get stabbed through."

"These are soldiers, not guards, Nicolas, so be fair," responded Philip.

Nicolas barely gave the soldiers notice as he moved straight through them, directly to the throne to which Philip sat. "What in Shadow are you doing?" was his first question to him.

"Taking my place as . . ."

"You are a substitute, you know that, right?" hammered his brother. "I don't care if it takes half a year or more, you will be replaced once the decision on which House will reign by a *king*."

"You are right," agreed the First. "A decision that I myself will vote upon. And in the meantime while we decide, I rule this country. The first priority that I have is finding the assassin. We have to find which House is responsible."

And Nicolas laughed at his comment. "That is why you summoned me, is it not? You want to know where Katlynn is. Well let me save you the breath, brother. I do not know where she is. You are much wiser than me, never disputed that, Phil. Iero did not tell me where he would take her, only that it would be best to keep that secret from me in case this very thing would occur."

"And you realize that she is the suspect . . ."

"She is your family, Phil, so watch yourself closely before you accuse her of . . ."

"I accuse nothing!" the First stammered. "But she must be brought in. You must understand that. Our name and credibility center on your daughter. Where was she during the ceremony? We need to gather the facts and we need her to come back in."

Nicolas shook his head firmly. "They will hang her and the rest of us if she does. At least this gives us all the opportunity to play ignorant."

"You do not understand. We need evidence away from us so that we can make some kind of allegiance, some kind of play toward the throne. If Brocusk and his House can be seen as a prime suspect to this killing, it will aid us in figuring something out, perhaps even forming some alliance with either Rowe or Aylmer, something to split the votes. If she comes in, we can find a way to prove her innocent."

"She will die, and you are smart enough to know this," he replied, though in earnest and pain rather than scolding. "You want to do us any favors as a family, as a name, I suggest you find the real killer. I would ask you to give her time before invoking . . ."

"I am sorry, Nick," claimed Philip. "The word is given."

His brother's eyebrows sunk inward sharply. "What word did you give?"

Philip's palms began to sweat. "That she be brought in. I sent out the army."

Nicolas reached toward him so quickly that the First had little time to react. His elder brother snatched his shirt with the left hand, his right slamming so hard into the side of his face that an eruption of white filled his sight, the sounds of the room muffled for a second or two. Somehow he had ended up on the floor and the coppery taste of blood filled his mouth.

His senses regained, the shock of the pain subsided, Philip spat blood down onto the floor, adding to the mess of the room. As he gazed up, Nicolas was held firmly by several soldiers, screaming from both his brother and the soldiers ensued.

"Silence!" Philip hollered over all of them.

"You damn fool!" hissed Nicolas. "That is your niece out there. Least you could do is give her a chance to . . ."

"You don't understand, Nicolas, and you never have. You understand how things are run back home but you damn sure don't understand things here. There are politics at play here. There are things that must be done a certain way. We must show good faith that we would seek prosecution of our own, even family, in order to progress the best interests of Amon."

Philip wiped his mouth clean and then waved off the soldiers. Reluctantly they released the angered brother.

"What has happened to you, Philip? What have you become?"

"This is not about me, Nicolas. I am trying to keep our name intact. I am trying to ensure that all we have done, all that Father did, does not die because of our stubbornness to adhere to the rules."

"You think I don't do my part?" continued a volatile Nicolas. "You think I would willingly shame the great Landon Pratt and his legacy? Perhaps you would like to know that Christina Rowe already made her play to our House, and I'm in the right mind to take her offer. She wishes to marry Rayden and Allura, our name, her House."

The First could barely believe what he had just absorbed. "She wants you to run Amon under her House?"

"But our name."

"Piss on that! Her House!" Philip laughed in anger, moving closer yet cautiously toward his elder. "She is using you, you understand. You take this offer, your line and our name is gone. We run this country under House Rowe, and the Pratts will become something of the past. You shit on Donovini if you take this offer."

"It is just for the rule, brother, to prevent Brocusk from taking it. Her name is in better shape than ours, should it go to the courts . . ."

"I know how the system works," interrupted the First. "And of course she's telling you that. She wants the throne. I don't fault her. We all do. But selling out our name to House Rowe is a mistake that I fear we will regret."

"No more than sending out the army after your niece, brother."

"Nick, you have to understand, there is danger in doing this. You place our entire fate in the hands of Rayden and House Rowe. You have no idea what risks you're taking in even thinking about this."

Nicolas chuckled. "Funny thing, is it not First Pratt? All of that power, all of your talk of saving our name, and yet you have no power over my House. And yes, this House and the decisions are mine to make, not yours. House lord *Nicolas . . . Fucking . . . Pratt.*"

As his brother looked to turn away, Philip reached out to him, his hand grasping Nicolas's shoulder. "Every moment she is out there, the longer we drag this out, she dives deeper into danger. The further away she is from us, the more difficult it will be to keep her protected."

And his elder shrugged away the touch. "If you still care for this family, call off your hunt and find the real assassin. If any member of the army harms her in any way, you will find that the next assassin will not be so mysterious or hidden."

No more words exchanged between the two as Philip allowed his brother to storm off, marching through the throne room doors. Anger swelled in the First, but there was little that could be done. After all, he was right. Their House was his to command, not Philip's. If he married his son to Christina Rowe's daughter, then he would do such with little say otherwise from him.

He did not want to send the army after Katlynn. He did not want to see their name shamed by treason. He did not want their rule in Donovini ended by the Rowes. And he certainly had not truly wanted to take the throne, least not in this fashion.

What power do I really have? Was this why you let me run this country, Yelium? Less than a few hours in and already I feel the crippling limitations of this power, old friend.

Gazing about, he suddenly had no desire to stay within these chambers.

"Fuck this throne room," cursed Philip Pratt to the soldiers about him. "Seal this off, not be opened again until the next king takes it. Escort me to my room."

--

The soldiers stood outside his room as he entered, Jessica moving to the First and embracing him.

"Phil," she whispered in his ear, her hand brushing the back of his head. "They would not tell me where you were."

"Safe," was his response to his wife.

Lilli was the next to him and he quickly embraced her. "I was *so* worried, Father, but I knew you would be just fine. I told Joanna and Mother that, but they worry too much."

"That we do," Joanna announced from the other side of the room, bringing over a bottle of wine, her husband holding the glasses. "I think we could all use a drink about now. Maybe you can talk about what we don't know. Katlynn has been missing, and there are all kinds of clamoring about her possible involvement. But we know that's not true."

His daughter was an amazing woman, but still never truly grasped his position nor his inability to discuss certain things. Or in this case, his lack of desire. "Jo, you know better than to ask me these things. Just know that whatever decisions I make, it will be the best for this family first, then Amon."

"And what of Nicolas's family?" murmured Jessica.

The woman, after all, was far too wise to be just a wife of the First. "I protect this family first, Jessica."

"But Uncle Nicolas and Aunt Maradyn will be okay, won't they?" Lillianna pressed. "You rule Amon now, so everything will come out fine in the end."

"I hope so," he stated truthfully.

I hope so.

--

The day pressed to night and Aldric watched from the balcony of his room as Dylinn Aylmer, former queen of Amon, rode off on carriage away from the capital building. Her departure swift as it was stunning. There remained so much for her to accomplish within Corovium at the moment. Her people were best represented by her presence here with the council, with the courts, with the many decisions that would certainly occur within the capital. Her voice would be well respected amongst the people, having been their queen for as long as she had.

Dylinn should have remained. And as much as Aldric wished to have told her such, he of course refrained. Instead he simply gazed at the scene, watching her disappear from view, entering the heart of the city on her way north, back to her country, back to Fallneese. Silently he stood, the letter she had given him still firmly within his hands.

"Should we deliver the message?" Erian quietly stated behind him.

"Yes," he answered. "We should."

But there he stood, motionless, eyes fixated into the distance. Another few minutes passed.

"Aldric," Erian called again.

The letter felt heavy in his hands. Nothing seemed as right to him as it once had. Nothing. For so long he had lived his life as his people had wished it, honored the Kwyantin as would any other. The Historian lived to serve the better of his people. And yet there remained an itch that he could not reach, a part of his memory that always came forefront.

Jaa's final moments.

All of his knowledge, centuries of information stored away, and yet it was meant for pen and paper, not to aid Amon. But what was the Kwyantin without Amon? What would happen to the country during these difficult times? They had lost two kings, father and son, within weeks of each other. And now their queen disappeared before them. But if the Kwyantin were nothing without Amon, what was Amon without people within? Would a decision to help Amon, therein, also help the Kwyantin?

Rationalizing. Why am I rationalizing? I should give this letter to the First, stay until a king is decided, then return home. It's time for Erian to take my place. It's time for me to record my part into the histories. I know this.

So why is this so impossible?

In Jaa's final moments, he had spoken of atonement, that a Historian may need to be more than just that.

The letter continued to weigh him down.

Erian seemed curious, if not impatient. "Aldric?"

The Historian of Amon, loyal amongst his people, dedicated to his profession, made his decision.

Aldric ripped open the envelope and unfolded the letter from within.

By the rope or by the chain, First Pratt? All of this, all that I have done is for the betterment of Amon. I pray to the fallen gods that you come through this still whole. I will not be able to live with myself if I know that my decisions have put you in harm's way. My heart is with you, even as I no longer can be. My savior, my friend, my lord, my love. -- Dylinn

"What are you doing?" Erian questioned behind him.

The letter folded, he moved to the closest burning candle and set the paper before it, engulfing it slowly in fire within his hands.

"Aldric?"

After all of this time, he had finally started to understand Jaa and his mindless rabble. He had even grasped his overwhelming guilt at the end to some degree. To shoulder such responsibility, to harvest the knowledge to which they possess, yet to horde that, to never use such, to allow mishap after mishap upon Amon without aiding . . . this was no life worth living. It was a life of regret, of ineptitude, of inadequacy.

A life that Aldric had lived far enough, in his mind.

Mostly ash, the Historian let the blackened letter fall into the wax to burn the remainder.

"What did it say?" his apprentice questioned.

"It said . . . it was incriminating, perhaps to a name that can ill afford more defamation."

Erian gave an inquisitive look. "But you have repeatedly claimed that . . ."

"Jaa the Knowledgeable once asked me to share with my future apprentice the final moments of his life," Aldric interrupted. "He believed in things that were not necessarily in the ways of the Kwyantin. It is time I share this information with you. From there, you must decide on your own where to go from here."

Erian returned his puzzled look. "I do not understand. Why would I decide anything? I observe, as you instructed."

"That I have," admitted Aldric. "But now I travel to Fallneese behind our former queen, to which you must decide to whether you follow me or not. There are truths I must uncover. I have many decisions of my own to make."

"I am bound to you, Historian."

Aldric only smiled. "You are bound to our people, not to me. More importantly, you are bound to Amon. Now let us walk and talk. As you hear the story of Jaa the Knowledgeable, you may decide your own path. The journey to Fallneese is long, and times such as these I wish we were not too large for the horses."

"Either that, or perhaps a Druid could train a Draywolf for us to ride upon."

Humor. So my apprentice does have character.

"An original thought, my apprentice. I think Jaa would have been proud."

--

Nothing Guaranteed

Jobs occur, you are assigned one, you perform it. There are no questions, there is no refusing. When the work is done, you are paid. It's just that easy. It's not really about right and wrong. At least not for me. It's just about work. I know I've done some good out there . . . just as much bad too. The fallen gods will sort out one from the other in the life after this one.

I'll say this. Last thing you want to do is mix swords with us. The Guild is unforgiving.

-- Draven, a Member of the Guild

VI

Nathanial Wode gazed down at his right arm, the wounds finally healed and the scaring had begun. Admittedly he had been fortunate to have received as few scars as he had in this line of work, but that did not aid him in grimacing at the sign of these new ones. Three wide black marks tore down from his shoulder to his elbow. Lucky to still have his arm at all, Nathan understood. But still it did little for the eyes.

He gathered his shirt and strapped on his leather armor. The morning was before him and one he intended to fill with more sparring. The Guild had yet to request his presence since his injured return from the Lis'rial, and he purposely and continually showed them that he had recovered. It took over a week before he could grip with his arm properly without opening his wounds again, another week before he could swing with it. But the last several days he had begun sparring with the other Guild members, allowing all to see that he still had no equal, even in a recovering state.

In Prillian, strength and wit were two parts of a whole. In Astrona, brute power ruled and conquered if needed. It was the Donovinian way. In Genethur, in the capital where his Uncle Philip stood as First, wisdom mattered most of all, as games were played daily. A knife in the back awaited a false step, an errant move. Here, the Guild ruled this city. Being at the near outskirts of Donovini gave the city the benefits of protection from the neighboring countries, namely Ursan, but far enough away to rule themselves. It was a civilized town in a way, sophisticated in the fact that it merged different cultures from the surrounding areas in a less than noble way of operating, yet those within also maintained certain codes and conducts.

Fear and respect, words that translated easily to any culture. The Guild governed Prillian. To cross the Guild was to cross Amon. There were no stretches of this land that their arms could not reach. Guild representatives could be found in nearly every major city within Amon, even within the courts in Corovium. After all, the Guild was a legal establishment on paper at least. What better place to establish their legal commerce than within the central government.

But Nathan had seen the reality of the Guild. For better or for worse, normally the former, the Guild stood as hired thugs that maintained order outside of the means of the Imperial Army or the government. They were the local force needed to sustain order far away from the watchful eyes of Genethur. When things needed to be done, the Guild was called upon. Certainly work for hire was hardly a noble profession, but sometimes, not always, the work was noble nonetheless. For Nathanial, the ends justified the means. Or so he told himself as often as possible.

He left his simple one room home and took a step into the uncomfortably hot and humid morning air. Even early, Prillian bustled with movement and excitement. Outside of being the headquarters to the Guild, the city also stood as an enormous center of commerce. So closely placed between three countries, merchants lined the streets from all across Amon, selling anything from exotic fruits to colorful beads to rare animal skins to hunting supplies and so forth. Much larger than the capital city of Astrona, Nathan had lived several years within the bustling city and had yet to truly explore it all.

His own home stood within a standard, working class area just above the slums. Elevation within Prillian counted as prestige, as the city was built around a slow developing hill in northern Donovini. At the foot of the hill, the entrance to the city, came the slums. The class of men rose as did the hill from that point, upward to the very top of the formation, ending with the Guild headquarters. An elaborate structure, beautiful really, and Nathan only found himself grumbling on his trips upward to the yards. Leaving the Guild, heading back downward, always felt better on the legs.

A few merchants called out to him, waving him toward their carts and wagons. Others called out to him by name, those locals that had heard of his deeds, that praised him for his body of work. In either case, Nathanial Wode smiled and waved. He had not come to Prillian for fame, necessarily, and did not thrive in it. But he found it difficult to not smile through it nonetheless.

For a bastard son of the Pratts, this was about a reckoning. This was about proving his worth to the family that shunned him. Not in spite, necessarily. Only to show worth of worthlessness, if not to them, to himself even. Because if they would not have him, then he would find his place elsewhere in the world.

"Heading up to the yards, Nathan?" called out a woman behind him, a voice to which he immediately recognized.

He stopped and turned, deciding it best to wait than be trailed. "Morning, Keli," Nathan called back.

An Argon girl, seventeen years old, was the daughter of one of the local merchants. A tailor by trade, her father ran a fairly impressive business within Prillian, if at best a permanent one. So many establishments came and left as quickly as the seasons, to find one that stuck around for a few years was as impressive as they came. He had known her since his young beginnings in the city, running errands for the Guild and, after finally earning enough coin, bought his first tailored outfit at her father's shop. She worked as a stocker on certain days, along with the remainder of her six siblings. After his first purchase, Keli always found a way to bump into Nathanial.

It had never been annoyingly bad, as the girl had her upsides. She was certainly pleasant to look at, with her dirty blonde hair and green eyes, rather short for an Argon, but her larger than average breast size all but made up for her lack of height. Though the girl was not much in the way of conversation, at least not on his end, she had not been entirely annoying until Nathanial made the unfortunate mistake of fucking her. After that, the girl found any number of reasons to simply be around him. Keli was smart enough to know better than to consider them a couple, but naive enough to believe that time would change that.

A woman, through and through.

The solution, of course, would be to stop bedding the girl and telling her to piss off. But he was human, after all.

"May I walk with you up to the Guild? Unless you mind a young girl's admiration for a recovering hero."

"Hero may be a bit much," noted Nathanial. "I work for the Guild and do as I'm told."

"And well enough, I might add." The light complexioned girl moved up beside him, then they walked together upward through the city streets casually. "I mean, I worried so much when you had to visit the Druids upon your return. But they say you bested *three* Draywolves. Flame's embrace, most men could barely handle one!"

"I was not alone in my confrontation, you realize."

Nathan did not think she had even bothered to listen. "I told my friends that *of course* you had done such, because there is no one in Prillian, likely Amon that could best Nathanial Wode in combat, not even a grown Draywolf! They of course are just jealous that I get to hang around someone as amazing as you all the time, and that I get to *personally* tailor your tattered equipment back to proper shape, if not make you new gear altogether. Of course Father normally does the mending, but they don't know that."

He faked a smile, not that she noticed, as she continued on about this and that. He had all but droned her babble out. Instead he focused on his day, his need to spar and prove himself. Without work, he did not get paid. Of course he had money stashed away for these kinds of circumstances. Never knew when injury would keep him away for a prolonged time. Three weeks was hardly an eternity, but long enough to get antsy by his standards. He stood ready to get into some kind of action. There rarely seemed a lack of work needing able bodies.

"What do you think about that?" Keli concluded some statement he had not even bothered to hear.

"Well . . . what do *you* think?" he slyly retorted.

"I think that the Pratt name is stained enough, so the First shouldn't be allowed to rule."

And for a stern moment, Wode did not know how to respond.

Keli chuckled at him, apparently noticing his lack of understanding. "Silly, don't you pay attention to *anything* outside of the Guild? I like to keep myself educated on the politics of Genethur. It's interesting to me at least. But they never seem to . . ."

"But why is the First ruling?" interrupted Nathanial.

And she returned a dumbfounded glare. "The king is dead, Nathan. Didn't you know that? Word hit the streets about a week and a half ago. People have it that the prime suspect is the Pratt daughter, Katlynn I think her name is. Apparently she killed the king so that the Pratts could gain power, but I don't understand why the Rowes wouldn't take over. I know that a Pratt is the First, but the situation being what it is, Argonus should claim temporary control. I know, I know, technically the Second should claim it, but Ursan is so . . . unstable, I suppose, that it should fall to the Third. I know you are Donovinian, but what do you think?"

At that moment, Nathan did not know what to think. Keli was a great many things and a gossiper was just one of them, but liar she was not. What she had claimed was obviously what she had heard. Now the question was whether or not what she heard was true.

"I think we should get up to the Guild," he responded without explanation to her.

He knew that if anyone had answers to the situation, it would be found there.

--

At the top of Prillian, the rather over-the-top building of the Guild stood alone amongst the sea of houses, an almost castle like structure that towered unnecessarily at the top of a hill. The yards came before the opening and many men gave pause at the sight of the approaching Nathanial Wode. Most of them he had beaten the shit out of recently and did not look willing to take up the challenge again. Even so, the yards stood as a testing ground for many of them, especially those that had yet been initiated into the Guild. Many young men and women from around Amon came here to attempt to prove themselves worth of admittance.

Nathanial remembered his time as a young whelp, looking for justification into his life. It had hardly been an easy entrance into the Guild. But that moment had been his and his alone.

Keli leaned over and kissed him gently upon his cheek, then leaned into his ears and whispered, "Perhaps I can come by tonight?"

Nathan only gave a single nod, and she grinned at the response. Not a moment later, she turned and made the envious trip downward, back to the trade district. Without hesitation, he moved forward, ignoring the both cowardly stares and equally challenging glares from both members and hopefuls alike as he pressed forward to the large doors of the Guild.

His head swam with questions and possibilities. His uncle, his family . . . were they ruling Amon? And what of Katlynn? He knew the girl too well to think her to play any part in the assassination of a king. None of this made sense. But if he were to sort it out, this would be the place. Nothing happened within Amon without notice from the Guild.

Doors opened, several Guild members on watch nodded at his entrance, gesturing him onward. The main hall stood elaborately before him, but that was not his calling. Immediately he took to one of the side doors, a long hallway filled with offices, each with a member of the Guild that involved some part of the whole. Nathanial did not pretend to care much for the politics of the organization any more or less than his care of the politics of Amon. If rumors of his own family had not been placed at the head of this affair, he would likely have cared very little for the death of a king, assassination or otherwise. As it were, he lost little sleep thinking much about how the other king had died.

Half way down the hall and Nathanial Wode found his destination. The door to this particular office stood open and he knocked slightly against the wooden railing to announce his presence.

"Nathanial, enter," the middle-aged woman stated.

Attractive if not a little overweight, Cylaa was a dark, Fallneesian woman, stern and to the point. Whether or not the woman liked him, Nathan could not say. But something about a woman that could take charge certainly earned his respect, for what it was worth. Within the room with her was Draven, a man made entirely of muscle and testosterone. Nathan did not know his entire story, but he knew that one of his parents was Donovinian, the other Fallneesian. While that made him as a bit of a rarity outside of Prillian, it was well accepted here that those things did happen on occasion. He was either a light skinned Fallneesian or an off complexioned Donovinian, pending on whose eyes did the looking.

In either case, Nathan was no fan. That was largely due to the fact that Draven was a bit of a mystery, used for secret operations that were trusted for his ears alone. That fact gave Draven a sense of superiority over everyone else in the Guild. And he hated to admit it, but the half breed was the right hand to the Guild head, Orpay, and easily one of the most important members within the organization. It was an envious position. Thus . . . he was no fan.

Also, he was fairly certain that Draven wanted to kill him.

"I didn't mean to interrupt," Wode began.

Cylaa finished scribbling whatever it was that she wrote upon her many stacks of paper upon her desk, then placed the long quill pen back into the ink bottle, her eyes rose to meet his.

"We are concluded here," she claimed. "I believe Draven was just leaving."

"And at the perfect time," was his immediate answer. He turned and barely missed brushing against Nathan. He was huge, an absolute monster of a man with an impressive battleax strapped to his back. "Maybe I will catch you in the yards before I deploy again. Hate it that I always miss your little shows."

"Something tells me you don't miss them as much as avoid them."

And Draven flashed a grin. "We will give the gods a good show one day. Of that . . . I am certain."

He carefully watched the half breed move off and down the hallway before taking a step inside the office.

Cylaa locked her hands together atop her desk. "You look well, Nathanial. I have seen you in the yards during a few of your spars lately. You quickly gain your form back."

The Guild had many members and many heads of their organization. Nathan was but a tool, closer to a hired mercenary than an actual voicing member of the Guild. Cylaa, however, stood as one of the heads. She commissioned all work out of Prillian, making her within this city of its most important citizens.

"Thank you, Lady Cylaa," replied Nathanial. "I am ready to . . ."

"Patience, my young sword. You should take this time to recover. Very little jobs requiring a sword arm the last week or so, nothing that others could not do in your stead."

"Like Draven?" he questioned.

"No, not like Draven. He is used for . . . let's just say jobs that are more suited for his abilities."

"Like smashing things with his face? I'm sure that anything entrusted to him, I can do as well."

"Draven is an equal to you in skill with the blade, make no mistake of that. But it's not uncommon to have two alpha males battling for supremacy. I can accept that. But don't let your distain for him remove his deserved respect. He is the right hand of Orpay for a reason, and that reason is simple. You can't fake experience or trust, Nathanial. And Draven has both."

Wode chuckled some to that comment. "I'd feel better if you gave him that same speech about respect."

"You work just as much as him, regardless of the importance of the job. And you are on the rise. There should be no envy between you two." The Fallneesian woman leaned back a bit in her chair. "If money is your concern, I can advance you whatever you need. I would prefer that you are one hundred percent before returning to work."

"No, Lady Cylaa, money is of no issue right now."

"Good, I am glad to hear you are able to manage your finances well enough. So then if not for money, you should not be rushed back into work. Let's put this Draven business behind us. Unless there is another reason that you visited me."

"I have heard rumors. About the king."

"Ah, I didn't think you one to concern yourself with politics, Nathanial," Cylaa claimed. "But you are from Astrona, yes? I can see why you might be interested, especially dealing with the claims against the Pratts. Many times, rumors are just that, tales told in inns by drunken men and gossiping women. I am afraid, though, that this time it's true. Our newly crowned king was assassinated at his inauguration, and the killer has yet to be found. While First Philip Pratt is currently watching the throne, the council will soon decide the fate of the next House to claim it. That selection will be of their decision alone, unless they cannot make a unified choice. In which case it would fall to the courts, and then we will be heavily involved from that point."

"What can you tell me of the killer?"

The woman shrugged. "A Shadowmancer, and a woman. Outside of those facts, nothing else is known. It's because of the limited information that we haven't been more heavily involved into the search. The Imperial Army has already lost the scent of the prime suspect, Katlynn Pratt, who is none other than the House lord's only daughter. The entire situation is a mess, to be honest."

Nathan hesitated, thinking of a way to pry further. The last thing he needed was suspicion on his inquiry of this. "You said *more* heavily involved. So something has fallen to us."

"Indeed," she replied cautiously. "First Pratt has given us the unruly task of finding the girl, alive of course. Cold trail right now, unfortunately, so I am not wasting more resources until I get a stronger lead as to her location or destination. For the time being, we have eyes in every city in Amon. If she is foolish enough to step foot in them, she will be caught. We have, however, had a small lead . . . one that I am obligated to follow up. An outpost inside Livensburg believes they spotted her but a few days back, traveling with two other Donovinians. The descriptions match what we know, of course, in that she travels with a Druid and a soldier. So I am sending someone out to investigate the area, spot any truth in this."

"No better hunter than me, Lady Cylaa," jumped Nathan, perhaps too eager in his statement. "I am hungry to get back into action, and this would not force the need of my sword arm being one hundred percent. Let me look into this for you."

She did not look convinced. "We are dealing with a Shadowmancer, a Druid, and a captain inside the Astrona guard. If this Katlynn Pratt is in fact guilty of the assassination of our king, she did so in front of hundreds of witnesses, able to sneak by guards undetected in doing so, and able to escape thanks in large part, from my understanding, to a Druid that nearly tore the capital building into rubble. She has also managed to elude the Imperial Army to boot. This may not be as safe as you seem to believe it to be. If this lead bears fruit, the Guild member assigned to this is to not engage, but follow and track only. I don't need a sword arm for this."

"Then you need an experienced hunter, which you know I am."

Cylaa's expression hardly changed. "Unfortunately I gave the job to another. If it means this much to you to get back into things, I can look into finding . . ."

"Who got this job? Draven?"

After a few seconds, she answered, "Jadenine."

Just great. Convincing her to do anything other than her job exactly as written . . . might as well piss into the Flame Realm instead. I'll get equal treatment regardless.

"Jadenine is an accomplished killer, for certain," he said. "But you need a hunter, and smarts at that. Let me take this job from her, and assign her something else."

"Why are you so persistent on this job, Nathan?"

To find Katlynn and ask her what is going on. Outside of that, I have no idea. Even if I find her, I can't turn her in. Betray the Guild? I will end up face down in a river.

"Because this has to do with my home, Cylaa. Certainly I am not educated well on the politics of our nation, but that does not mean I don't have pride. If Katlynn is guilty, I would like to bring her in, as she has placed a black stain upon our people. That, and who knows Donovini better than I? Certainly not Jadenine. Besides . . . I *am* getting a bit stir-crazy. I was hurt last time out, not killed."

"Thankfully not, and I can understand your sense of . . . shall we say impotence the last few weeks. But you do realize that there may be nothing in Livensburg to follow up upon. This may be a simple hike from one end of the county to the next."

"And I have something better to do in the meantime?" challenged Nathan. "Worse case, I get there, nothing to be found, I get back. Only this time I will be one hundred percent and ready for anything you have."

"I *have* quite a bit," announced Cylaa. She leaned back in her chair, arms crossed before her. "Very well, Nathan, I will fund you for this trip . . ."

"Thank you for . . ."

". . . as well," concluded Cylaa. "That is, if Jadenine accepts the company."

Whatever victory he thought he had won quickly dissipated into the nothingness.

--

As always, the travel back down to the working class was a joy, despite the sun rising to high noon by the time he descended. What seemed like a busy morning only turned into a monstrous early afternoon. A battle ensued, political in nature, one that could shape the fates of these crowded streets, these filled plazas. How many of these people knew of the king's death? How many of those even cared? Which House would ascend to the throne? It was such a pivotal event, and yet here, deep in the northern corner of Donovini, Nathanial Wode wondered how much of that *really* mattered. Would that truly change how these people lived their lives? Increased tax here, decreased tax there. Move the Imperial army to the eastern shores and funds increase to suppliers, from blacksmithing and tailoring to farmers and couriers, but to fund such an operation, some new tax would be levied to the populace. Such things took place from their last king and wheels still turned within Prillian regardless. Perhaps they knew well enough of the unstable nature of the throne, and perhaps they could not care less.

Even him, directly linked to the House lord, and his own concern was minimal. The thought at the foremost of his conscious was finding Katlynn. How did she get herself mixed into all of this? Worse yet, how was *he* going to get her out of all of this?

His cousins were good people, at least as far as Nathan was concerned. But Katlynn and Rayden were his closest kin. Many years in their youth did they spend together, and the two siblings never treated him as anything other than their family regardless of being the bastard that he was. Even with such a convoluted youth, those memories were of the few fond ones. She was like a sister and her involvement in this was insane. Perhaps more curious was the fact that his uncle had requested the Guild to find her. For show, or was he uncertain of her involvement in the assassination?

Plaguing his mind with questions did little to answer them. Sadly he knew next to nothing of the political world to assess any of it. For Nathan, he knew the sword and the hunt, and like it or not, this was his kind of game. If Katlynn was out there, he could and *would* find her. There stood little waiver in him that it would be done. The real question was if he could find her before she inadvertently walked right into the Guild's arms. Cylaa made no mistake in her assessment of the Guild's vision. Even in Corovium, they were always watching. If Katlynn were ignorant enough, and as much as he hated admitting that she was in this case, the Guild would find her easily. So the question of who would find her first was the only real relevant one at the moment. Well that, and what to do once he did find her.

For Katlynn, for his family, Nathanial Wode would betray the trust of the Guild. Certainly he would not be the first to betray the Guild, but since his induction, Nathan had not known any to have done such and remained amongst the living. No one left the Guild, no one betrayed the Guild. At least not without deathly consequences.

Thus came another interesting question as he maneuvered his way from one of the lesser bazaars to a housing area below his own, more affordable but less spacious than even his one room home. Stopping at his destination, he knocked once loudly upon the door and waited patiently.

Now, what exactly what am I going to do with . . .

The door opened inward and the flaming red hair of the short Ursan appeared before the woman herself.

"Jadenine," he stated.

And she spit onto the ground before him in response. "Earth and Flame," she hissed. "As if I do not hear enough about you in the yard, now you come to pester me at home."

Before he could retort, the woman walked back into her home, leaving the door open. Nathan took that as an invitation and took a step inside.

The room was much smaller than he thought, and if he had brought a friend, that would have been exactly three too many for this amount of space. As it were, he could barely close the door without bumping into her bed, which extended into her kitchen area.

Her travel pack was sitting upon the small counter before him, and Jadenine motioned to it. "As you can see, I *am* a bit busy packing supplies, so whatever you have come for, make it quick."

"Very well," started Nathanial. "You are heading out to Livensburg to investigate the possible sighting of our assassin, yes?"

Jadenine, who had just folded a small blanket to fit inside of her pack, stopped working for a moment and stood motionless before him. "I presume the Guild has told you of my assignment for a reason."

"That they have. Cylaa has had a change of heart and is now funding two for this operation."

Her open palm pressed intently against her forehead. "And I suppose if I were to guess who my travel companion would be . . ."

"You would guess correctly," finished Nathan. "So are we planning on leaving tomorrow morning?"

Jadenine did not respond immediately; rather she continued to rub her forehead, as if the pain of taking him along was too much to bear. He had known that she was no fan of his, but her reaction seemed a bit over the top.

"Jadenine?"

She returned silence, her eyes now locking with his. The Ursan moved over and stuffed the blanket into her pack.

"It would seem best if we moved at . . ."

"I don't like you, you know this right?" hammered Jadenine. So taken back by the announcement, he had no immediate reply. "As a matter of fact, I can barely stand looking at you."

"Well . . . I don't exactly like you either."

"No shit, Wode, and neither does anyone else. That puts you right along with the rest of Prillian and the entire fucking Guild. But you, *everyone* loves you. You are the golden boy here. Most believe you will be the youngest to ascend to a named position within the Guild. You are damned good with a blade, no faults there, and so far as Donovinians go, you look better than a Chur'rat, so that's a positive."

"Appreciate the extended compliments."

But she basically hissed at his statement. "Looks, skill, and a fake smile. Enough there to get you where you need to be in life. But me, I could do for much less of you, better none at all. Yet for reasons I will never understand, I have to pair with you more often than not."

"They put the best together," answered Nathanial. "Odds are better if . . ."

"Piss on odds, I'd do better with someone that I trusted."

And there it was, the root of her issues toward him.

"Yes, I don't trust you," Jadenine pressed on. "You may have the rest of Prillian and the whole fucking Guild convinced, but not me. You are a liar, somehow, someway, and I know one when I see one. You may be the finest swordsman I have seen in these parts, but that doesn't mean shit in a real fight, in a war."

"Amon hasn't seen war in lifetimes."

"Don't tell me what I have or have not seen, boy. Deep in the forest of Ursan, I have seen plenty of it. The only thing more important than the blade in your hand is the person watching your back, the one you trust to keep a sword from burying into your skull. A person that you can trust without seeing, that is worth more than anything. It keeps your focus before you rather than all around. A person you trust halves a battlefield."

She shook her head slowly. "Someone like you, someone you can't trust, they add to the battlefield. Not only do you have to watch in front of you, you damn sure have to watch that person too. Who knows if the battle presses too deeply if someone like you wouldn't just switch sides at the end, bury a blade in my back just to show good faith. Someone like you has to be watched more than the enemy. At least the enemy is predictable. They will come right at you. But you, who knows?"

"And have I really garnered the sword in the back metaphor?"

"Yes, because you are a liar. Who knows who you *really* are? I only know what you are not."

"And what am I not?"

Jadenine grinned. "One of us."

"And what are you?"

"A nobody." She shrugged, suddenly indifferent in her demeanor. "You know there is one similarity between us, and probably the one trait that you could do less of in your quest for success. We like to work alone."

"Look, the Guild was clear that . . ."

Her hand rose though, cutting him short. "If it escapes your mouth, I take it as gospel, Wode. They want two for this journey, so be it. Yes, the morning, before dawn, we ride. Be at the entrance or spend the better part of the morning catching up to me. Just because the Guild works us together, doesn't mean I have to like it, them, or you. It has been a peaceful three weeks without having to see your face."

Three weeks. Has it been that long? It has to be close to that. No, more than close. Tomorrow would be three weeks to the day.

Earth and Flame.

"I think we will need to make room for one more person you can't stand."

--

"Yes?" answered the voice of Feko Hawbry from the other side of the dingy, lower Prillian inn door.

"It's Nathanial, open up."

"Ah, yes, of course, of course." The door latch clicked and opened, and the scrawny Argon stood before him. "Pleasure, of course, Nathanial Wode. What can I aid you with on this day?"

"You can start by telling me how you knew all of this?"

One of Feko's eyebrows rose slowly. "Knew what exactly?"

"Three weeks, wait three weeks," hammered Nathan, his voice hushed but harsh. "You kept on about it, claim to be just an herbalist from Argonus, claim to be a vessel of some kind. No more games. Three weeks has gone by and certainly something *has* happened worthy enough to raise some questions. So time to come clean."

"You will not like my answer. Tell me, you have not visited me but once after my housing. What has happened?"

Nathan hesitated a moment, then motioned for him to move inside. The Argon complied and the two entered the inn bedroom, which consequently was larger than Jadenine's home.

The door closed, Nathanial began. "The king was recently assassinated. The boy king. Now the daughter of the Lord Nicolas Pratt is lead suspect to this crime. The job of finding this girl has fallen into the Guild's lap, which has now fallen to me. Jadenine and I leave tomorrow to find Katlynn Pratt, almost three weeks to the day of our meeting in the Lis'rial. A bit too coincidental to be just that."

"I see."

"You see what?"

Feko flailed his arms harmlessly. "Not you. Hold on a moment. Yes, well, I should accompany you tomorrow morning."

"Of course. And can I ask you *why* would I drag you with us?"

"Because they want me to. I can hardly say why, because they won't tell me. I'm not even sure that either of us are very important in this entire thing, only we are pawns in this whole mess. All I know is that I am meant to follow you."

"Who talks to you, Feko? Who's telling you all this shit?"

A long pause stood between the two men, an uncomfortable one, before the Argon finally answered. "I believe Turitea and Schill."

Morbid curiosity prevented him from bolting to the door. "The fallen gods? They speak to you?"

"And now you see my reluctance to tell you."

"That I do." Nathan turned to the door for a moment, then stopped himself.

You don't believe this. You aren't even religious. Even if *the fallen gods were real, why would they speak through this man? Walk away. You have enough problems on your hand. Come on Nathan, just leave this loon to his own accord.*

"I am a man of my word," offered up the Argon. "I told you if something happened at the end of the three weeks, I would answer your questions. I did not say you would like them. But all things being equal, I would rather not have them speaking to me. It does get . . . a bit crowded to say the least. Almost half of what they say is above a simple herbalist such as myself, and another half is spoken in a language I cannot understand. So only a little bit gets through every now and again, just enough to keep things vague but to the point."

Clearly the man was insane. And yet Nathan already knew that. He wasn't sure what he expected to find. Perhaps the strange confrontation in the Lis'rial was just that; strange, but nothing more. Fate, destiny . . . that was for the religious, for those that held firm to beliefs. Nathan did not disbelieve in the fallen gods, but he certainly did not put much weight behind them either. And yet some part of him desired explanations, the need for validation. The Draywolf mother should have killed him, but did not. The whole thing was . . . unnatural.

He supposed that he wanted there to be a reason for his fortune, for this bizarre man to be the cause of it. Nathan wanted the world to make sense. He asked for too much, he presumed.

"I will not be taking you with me, Feko. I fulfilled my part of the bargain and housed you for three weeks. I hope you find peace with yourself."

He reached for the doorknob and listened to the babbling of the Argon behind him.

"I know you want me to go," he whispered to himself. "What do you want me to do? He is leaving without me. What more do you want? Well, maybe you should give me something more . . ."

And Nathan did not wait for any more embarrassment. Door opening, he moved through, and right before the door shut closed, Feko Hawbry gave one final cry.

"Katlynn Pratt is your cousin!"

The door closed.

Shit.

The door opened.

--

Keli's breathy snores were soft against his ears, but annoying nevertheless. Her breasts pressed against his body, one arm draped across his chest while she slept peacefully. Nathan, on the other hand, lay silently awake, staring at his ceiling, wondering at what moment his life had fallen out of his control.

Shouldn't have taken that last job. I don't show up to fight the Draywolves, I don't meet Feko, maybe none of this happens. Then again, maybe I don't find out in time about Katlynn. Then again, maybe all three of them die to the Draywolves rather than just Drai. Of course, at least Jadenine would be out of my hair.

He almost chuckled at his thoughts and felt embarrassed by them at the same time. Jadenine hated him, but the feeling was far from mutual. He certainly was not fond of her, but he did respect her. The Ursan woman could hold her own in a fight, which was most of what he wanted in a traveling companion. Especially when they worked a job bound to be dangerous. And here he was, at odds with the one worth her weight, and even with the one that was as close to a babbling lunatic as one could be.

Feko had added nothing else to make claim to his accusations. For what it was worth, Nathanial still could not believe. But somehow this Argon knew who he was. Somehow knew exactly where to find him as well. Strange that he knew of his relation to the Pratts? Of course. But was it information that only the fallen gods could share with him? Of course not.

At this point, he wondered if Feko Hawbry was somehow involved in the assassination. That would explain better as to why they would approach him. If they knew his blood tie to Katlynn, they would also know that he would seek her out. Play tag along with Nathanial Wode and he would lead them right to her. Of course, who *they* were, he could not say. Someone that wanted the king dead and Katlynn framed, at minimum. But while logic would suggest that if that were in fact truth, distancing himself from Feko would be wiser, Nathanial figured it best to keep him close . . . at least until he could uncover his plot and hopefully uncover the truth behind the *real* killer.

And yet there remained an annoying thought that refused to escape, the possibility of this Argon being earnest. In which case he was simply foolishly lucky in his guesses and completely insane. Unless, of course, the fallen gods spoke with him in truth. And if so, what did that truly mean?

His hand moved down the back of the young Argon girl. She moaned a bit and reached her hand down to his stomach, then continued down and found his manhood. Keli lazily stroked him, still half in and out of sleep, and did nothing to arouse. Almost as soon as the mundane task had begun, it had all but ceased, her hand resting on his cock and her annoying, breathy little snores reappeared in his ears.

Nathan sighed. Little seemed to matter outside of the facts at this point, he realized. First things first, he had to find Katlynn. After which, he would need to figure out what to do with Jadenine, Feko, and the Guild. In all likelihood, his life would never be the same after this night.

Steady, calm.

And yet no manner of convincing could acquire him any sleep.

--

Hard to tell where the real power lies. The council is headed by the appointed members of House lords, so one could make argument there. The courts are headed by appointed members of assorted trades and businesses, but are mostly controlled by the Guild, so one could make claim with them as well. A king was in charge of them all, but a slave to them all.

Since you're asking me, in my opinion, the real power lies just outside the throne. But good luck convincing everyone else that. Because nothing is more important than the throne in Amon. Nothing.

-- *Lurey Hillan, Third of Amon*

VII

Allura Rowe watched as the same familiar faces piled into her mother's corridor for yet another morning of frivolous debate. The large table separated the two countries as cleanly as would a river, and the distance between their stances felt equally as wide. Nicolas hung his head high but had lost a step since these proceedings had begun. A proud man, no doubts there, but one without a single leg left to stand upon. His daughter, the only known suspect in the assassination, had remained at large; neither hide nor hair from her, the captain of the Astrona guard, or the bizarre Donovinian Druid that had all disappeared together. The strain of such showed upon his brow. And with the credibility of the Pratts now in question, his ability to successfully negotiate anything for his House name proved difficult to say the least.

Nicolas's wife, Maradyn, made another appearance, only making this the third time she had decided to attend. She was quiet but attentive, always listening, always reading between every fine line. Without knowing the inner workings of their marriage, Allura presumed that when alone, Maradyn had quite a bit to say, and likely more than just insightful.

Of course Rayden was present, hunched over and completely oblivious to any topic at hand. Not that she entirely blamed him for his attitude, but he had the demeanor as if someone had killed his puppy. *Very* prestigious for a grown man, especially a man who stood closer to the throne than any. Allura had not given him much in the way of reason to be excited about the prospect, of course. She could have been nicer.

I could have been many things, but straightforward is who I am. Blessing or curse, who can say? But better that than lie, I'd gather. At least he knows that my true intentions are for Amon and not for him, not for my mother.

First Pratt sat silently in the back during these negotiations. Still the strongest of the Pratts in her mind, but he looked every bit as crippled as he was. What say did he have in such affairs? In the real world, First Pratt commanded the entire country. In that same world, he had no power to enforce his elder brother to do anything, nor declare that his nephew could or could not marry. Here, he held no power. He sat and watched and listened as a part of his family, not as the First. Here, he was an uncle and a brother, and by the look of his face, an upset one at that.

Allura's mother held the lead on many of the topic points as only Christina Rowe knew how. Her mother was outspoken and demanding, and above all things, she knew what she wanted and how to get it. As much as she admired her mother's determination, at times Allura questioned her motives and intents. Was this surge a push for Argonus or Rowe? There was a difference, at least in her mind.

Her uncle, Lurey, had made all of the meetings as well, and much like his counterpart in Philip Pratt, maintained distance from it all. As the Third, he had plenty to handle outside of these events, and like the First, had little influence here. His appearance felt more obligatory than interest. Though she knew that Lurey truly did care for the future of Argonus, his ability to control his sister was null. In fact, Allura was convinced that no one could control Christina Rowe.

Today had the feeling of a breaking point between the two sides. Over three weeks had come and gone since the death and burial of Yelium Aylmer, and things had begun to settle within Corovium. Many of the lesser House lords departed home, as their need to be present at the moment bore no fruit. The council would decide the fate of the throne, and if not them, the courts. The time to decide was soon, and the First could not press away the constant assault by the Second Afeon and Dehyllo Brocusk forever. Ursan pushed for a swift vote as they had all but bullied the old man Lijid Nulittan, the Fourth, to accept their bid. At this point, even if Pratt and Rowe voted together for one or the other, the split vote would move to the courts. There, money would play a factor as the Guild held the real power.

And despite her reluctance to admit it, the barbaric tribes of Ursan had little use for money, but did well to horde it. As much as her peers thought of the Ursan people as ignorant, Allura knew better. They exported many items, such as furs, ivory, medical herbs, spices, as well as livestock. Even the largest supply of horse breeding was handled in Ursan. All of this, and they required nothing. Completely self-sufficient and yet they played the part of a country all the same, even if they did not consider themselves truly part of Amon. All export and no import meant that even though they did not live in elaborate cities or possess the fine clothing and jewelry that others so adored, they had more wealth than all three countries combined. And since the Guild was comprised of nothing more than thugs and mercenaries, the rich would win their vote.

If her mother could not work a deal with Nicolas Pratt, House Brocusk would take the throne. From there, Allura did not desire to think too deeply into what would become of Amon.

"So where did we leave off the other day?" Christina began, her eyes rummaging through the paperwork that scattered about the long table to which they had all seated.

"Time grows short," barked Nicolas, his eyes square upon her mother. "My brother Edmond and his family have departed back home two days ago, and I myself am starting to wonder what keeps me here. My tolerance is thinner than most today. Can we skip the recap and get directly to the point?"

But Christina did nothing to back away from the elder Pratt. "You think this is easy, Lord Pratt? You come in and grumble over points, we negotiate and we bend. I have my scribes redraft documents so that we can come closer to finalizing our deal, only to have you grumble some more. We are merging countries, Nicolas. This is not supposed to be easy or quick. I would hope that you wouldn't want it to be."

"And yet I am tired of talking about it. Get some of my grievances figured out before Dehyllo figures out how to rush this vote to the courts."

"I am not worried about the Ursan," assured her mother, "and neither should you. They have no grounds to rush a vote. We are neither at war nor in an economic recession of any kind. Since there is little need to panic, there is little need to convince anyone of a hasty vote. We have months before First Pratt can announce this country ready, despite the hounding of our Second and his whip master."

"And yet with their money and power, do you *really* believe we have that long?"

"If the First has a spine about him, we will," she lashed out. If the First was offended, he did well to mask it. "This may seem tedious, but deciding how we split profits and share wealth is important enough to tread carefully. This is a treaty, not a takeover."

"You're damn right."

Her mother seemed to roll her eyes just for a second before continuing. "But until you realize that every point must be fleshed out cleanly, these talks will carry out much further than needed."

"Patience is not my better virtue, Christina," Lord Pratt admitted.

"No, and yet you still carry wisdom in the decisions you make. Believe it or not, Nicholas, but I *do* respect you. Would never have offered my aid in this unfortunate drought otherwise."

"Yes, so our money has nothing to do with that aid, I presume," First Pratt offered up from the back of the room, mostly to himself as it appeared.

Surprisingly Maradyn turned about to face her brother-in-law. "Nothing is free, Philip, not even aid. It costs money to dig canals and transport fresh supplies across the country. You cannot expect them to pay for those expenses on their own."

"No, I expect it to be tax free," responded the First, his own eyes narrowed some, his vision against her mother.

"And if you are in such grievance with this," started Christina Rowe, "then pass your own law. You are king now. Require my aid to be tax free."

"You know damned well that law would never make it through the courts. I'd wager with as much Guild help as you have recruited for the transporting of these supplies that they would find a way to veto or alter that command. In charge or not, I'm still not the king, just a temporary fill in."

Nicolas chuckled. "Just now realizing that, are you brother?"

"I have always realized that, brother," the First snapped back. "Whether any of you realize this or not, I have done what I have done thus far to better aid Donovini through aiding Amon. Like each other or not, you know damn well that Dehyllo looked to the death of Yelium as a way in to the throne. I could have easily denied my responsibilities, given them to Afeon instead. Wouldn't have been too far out of my mind to do so, having watched what happened to the last person to be in charge of Amon."

"How daring of you to perform your duties to your country as defined by your position," Nicolas slyly retorted. The two brothers had been on edge since day one of these meetings, and nothing seemed to have changed over the weeks.

"You think this is easy?" continued the First.

"No, but so far in your regime you've buried our late boy king and hired the Guild to find your niece. Am I supposed to applaud your reign thus far?"

"Gentlemen," called Christina. "Your bickering hardly helps us out any. I know this is a family affair, but to offer a bit of insight from someone on the outside, there was little else the First could do in his place. We all know Katlynn is innocent of her crimes, or at least in this room. But that does not change the fact that she needs to come in to offer up her alibi."

Nicolas balled his fist and bit hard against his lip. "The courts would execute her if only to satisfy the facts that no other suspect has surfaced."

"Nothing that we could not fight as united Houses. Besides, if your brother did not send for her return, Afeon would have grounds to speak to the courts of his collusion to the crime, perhaps suppressing evidence or failing to follow leads that could lead to his removal. His removal puts Afeon in charge, and how quickly do you think at that point would we gather a vote for the throne? Not enough time for a marriage and unification of our countries, that's for certain."

A long pause hung in the room and eyes mostly centered on the table before them. Her mother had a way of bringing collective thoughts to align with her own. It was a gift; Allura was quite certain of that.

"Is there anything else before we start?" Christina Rowe waited a few seconds before continuing. "Very well. So where did we leave off the other day?"

--

After wasting away all morning, Rayden could not have been more pleased when his father agreed to have his scribes look over the copies of the paperwork over the weekend. Anything to get him out of this room, away from the political ridiculousness that this had shaped out to be.

Perhaps his noble sense was a bit old fashioned, or at least naïve at best, but Rayden had always thought that marriage was about love and passion. He wanted to run his House after his father's passing, but he had thought to choose his own wife, the one that would give him love and many children. Instead, his father and a woman from Argonus hammered out details of financial impacts and territory issues and profit sharing. All the while his bride-to-be stared intently and added points to the matter, obviously far more interested in working this out as some sort of deal rather than a partnership of commitment. The partnership was ink to paper, and the commitment was a unified country.

All he wanted was someone to understand and care for him. Instead, he was getting a stone-cold bitch.

He hated thinking the way he did, especially when not but a month ago he had thought a possibility that a marriage could occur, this very marriage, but under a vastly different set of circumstances. Rayden had also misjudged her affection for him. One of many events that seemingly spiraled out of control.

He missed Katlynn, gravely in truth. As much as he loved his sister, he had not truly understood how attached he was to her until her disappearance. It did not take a genius to understand that the disappearance of all three Donovinians meant that either they were connected into the crime or fleeing in understanding that their very presence screamed guilt. A female Shadowmancer had been the culprit in this crime, and the only known one in the area, albeit not publicly but known enough, was Katlynn. Certainly there were others, he presumed. To touch the Earth and Flame Realms seemed vastly more common than Shadow. Rayden took no pleasure in admitting that she seemed a likely suspect, and fleeing with the captain and the Druid did her little justice in proving otherwise.

And Rayden did not doubt his love for his brother, but it simply was not the same as his love for his sister. Jerryn played a constant game of one-upmanship with his siblings, even when the others had little idea the game was being played. His superiority complex prevented a relationship of substance. Always Jerryn looked to be better in everything. A thirst that could not be quenched, an itch that always remained just out of reach.

As those within the room stood and began to depart, Allura Rowe took a quick step around the larger table to stand in his way.

"Rayden," she whispered a bit, her face still cold and harsh. "I was hoping you could find time so that we can begin to arrange our wedding."

To which he chuckled a bit. "Let's let my father press the quill to the parchment, then we can discuss things."

"I understand," she continued, "but it's quite obvious that this will happen. I see no harm in discussing and planning our . . ."

"In my experience," interrupted Rayden, "nothing is obvious, nothing is guaranteed. *Nothing*."

He moved around the girl, ignoring the scowl on her face as he moved out into the hallway, out to find his way for some fresh air.

--

A knock on his door startled Philip, and he wondered silently if he had dozed a bit at his desk. His work area had surprisingly not cleaned itself since his appointment as temporary king of Amon. Apparently no title held within the country could make paperwork disappear, at least not without complete neglect of duty. Then again, perhaps the real king had such a position and a council member to ensure of that.

Remembering what had brought him about from his either sleep or daydreams, he gazed up to his door. "Enter," he called out. It would have been someone important to make it through his many guards to even bother knocking, which likely meant it was but one man.

"Pleasure again, First," announced Afeon as he opened the door, a smile both wide and false.

"As always, Second."

Afeon closed the door and moved across the room. After losing the argument of Philip's relocation, Second General Isani Brocusk had demanded then that guards be posted inside his room in case of another assassination attempt. The general had lost that battle as well. He didn't need the Imperial Army inside, disturbing the only good sleep he had received since Dylinn had left back for Fallneese. Certainly that would leave him open for an attack, but very few were allowed free reign to come and go as they pleased nowadays in the capital. The Second stood as one of the few, and should he make an attempt at his life, Philip was convinced that the Ursan would find that he was quite unlike the elder Aylmer that once stood at the throne. He was far from drugged and incapacitated, far from sodden and helpless.

"What can I do for you today, Afeon?"

The usual smugness of the Ursan did not show on this day. He had the look of all business, which Philip did not take as a good sign. Moving across the room casually, the Second seated himself across from the First.

"I see your brother Edmond and his family have departed back to Astrona."

Philip nodded. "That they have. Someone still needs to run Donovini during these times."

"Quite true," Afeon continued. "Strange that it would not be Nicolas. Is there some reason he remains in Corovium?"

"Look, if you have come again about the vote . . ." started Philip.

"I have heard of your meetings with House Rowe."

Of course you have, you inquisitive bastard.

"Then you have heard incorrectly," noted the First. "I have not had any meetings with House Rowe. But what my family does is not of my choosing. That you may wish to bring up with my brother."

A half grin appeared on the side of Afeon's face. "I like you, Philip. I really do. I was a bit envious of Yelium's trust and affection for you, but that spite was not against the recipient of that, but the proprietor. And before his death, I thought you did your job fair and just. I have no reason to lie to you, as you have always known the truth of things. Dehyllo always sought to find a way to replace you with me. He understood the power that the First held and knew that in order to make changes, the correct changes, somehow he would have to find a way to convince Yelium to change the House order. But his love for you prevented that from taking place."

"I presume this little talk has some sort of point," mumbled Philip.

"You are an idiot, Philip Pratt," Afeon announced. "Your fear of my House has caused you to align yourself with someone untrustworthy. Are we so feared in Amon that you would run to an enemy in hopes to prevent our rise?"

"So you admit to wishing to ascend to the throne?"

"Don't we all?" Afeon retorted. "What country would we be if we did not *believe* that we could do a better job upon the throne than others? Certainly Dehyllo wishes the throne. That does not mean he would find himself comprising himself in order to gain that power."

"Such as murdering the king?" he accused.

The Second leaned steadily back into his chair. "Funny, Philip, as your niece is still the only one tied to that crime. And seeing how you still maintain power within Amon, you are the only one to gain from it as well."

Philip held no proof, heard no whispers, yet knew that Ursan, namely Dehyllo, stood behind the murder of the king. Despite his own gain, it was temporary at best. With a vote impending, Ursan stood primed to take that power, positioned to claim the throne for themselves. They had the most to gain in the death of the king, despite the initial appearances.

"If you have come to speak of the meeting or learn something from me, you will leave disappointed. I attend as a family member, not a voice. Whatever is decided, if you should choose to sway anything, you are speaking to the wrong man. Find my brother and tell him of your concerns."

"You do understand what will happen, do you not?" pressed the Ursan. "Without being present, let me guess at their proposition. They think your name has been tainted and you will be required to claim the throne under House Rowe. I bet she lets you keep the Pratt name though. How will that feel, I wonder, for you to see Pratt make claim for the throne under another House?"

"Again, Second, get to some point if you intend to make one."

"She will betray you." Afeon stood slowly from his seat, his hands pressed firmly down unto his disorganized desk. "You fear us so much, and yet you do not understand. Our quest for power is due to our understanding of the real issues in Amon. Fallneese, Donovini, Argonus, Genethur . . . all of you look but do not see. This trivial dispute amongst us is minuscule in the eyes of the fallen gods. So much more is at stake than your throne, your power."

"And yet you seek that power all the same," replied the First.

"Only to ensure that the preservation of Amon remains, First Pratt. Not your economy, not your names, but life as a whole. Tell me, First Pratt, do you truly believe that Christina Rowe has intentions of involving your people in her quest of the throne?"

At this point, there stood little reason to play quaint with Afeon. He had known of their meetings somehow, and Philip did not desire spending much time contemplating how. Far too many bodies within to not expect one to speak, not to mention the guards that had watched them gather. From knowing the frequent talks, those wise enough could easily deduce the meaning behind them.

"Allura makes claim, not Christina."

"And is her child not just a puppet for the mother?"

Philip shook his head. "Rayden would not allow Christina to control the throne while he sat upon it."

"Ha!" bellowed the Ursan as he stood upright, arms crossing before him. "Your nephew is a good man, of that there is little doubt. But politically savvy enough to know when he is being manipulated by a woman who is the master of deception? No, First Pratt, your family signs over your entire country, your very name over to Argonus, and for nothing more than to prevent our inevitable ascension."

"You are dangerous people," stated Philip silently. "Despite the fancy attire and the knack for politics, your people are hunters and killers, not kings and nobles. I don't trust what you will do on the throne, Second. No one does."

"So you support this marriage, this unity of countries?"

"I do."

Disappointment reflected in Afeon's face. "I fear that you will not live long enough to truly regret your decision, First Pratt."

"A threat, Second?"

"A warning," answered the Ursan. He moved toward the door, stopping halfway to call back to him. "Once the ink dries, call for a vote, First Pratt. If this union is to happen between you and House Rowe, Ursan shall place their full support behind it."

"You vote for us to take the throne?"

"For House Rowe, yes."

The First could hardly believe him. "And you would do this without gain?"

"That is the difference between us, First. You require one thing for another. In Ursan, we recognize strength. Your union would be strong, unfortunately stronger than us. Should it happen, we would place our vote for your unification. But I warn you, First Pratt, things will end badly. One day you will look back to this moment and wish that your alignment had been toward Ursan, toward me, toward Dehyllo Brocusk."

Not a fucking chance, you crazy shit.

"Can I have your written word on that?" questioned Philip.

"You do not need such," the Second responded. "My people still believe in honor. No other country can say the same."

Before he could think of a reply, a solid knock hammered upon the door as it opened slightly, the head of the Third Lurey Hillan peeking through.

"I am sorry to interrupt," he started, "but you both may wish to come with me to the courthouse."

Afeon turned to the First with a bewildered look upon his face. Philip could only gather that his own reflected the same.

"And why would we wish to attend that?" the Second claimed, as if attending local affairs and issues not involving the council were far below his thoughts much less his presence. Which in reality, Philip concurred.

"The Guild has just filed a grievance against us. They are about to hear their case."

"Us?" stammered Philip. "The council?"

The thought alone was preposterous. The Guild barely walked along the line of legality, much less to file any type of grievance against the king's own council in the courts. That, and being that the Guild practically owned the courts, any grievance should be dismissed based on conflict of interests.

"What the hell for?" pressed the First.

But the Third waved his arm to the door. "Well I don't know, First Pratt, that's why I figured that you may wish to come with me to the fucking courthouse."

--

The three council members moved through the streets of Corovium with many a heavy stare from the standard pedestrians. Seeing the councilors together in stride might not have garnered such attention; however the accompaniment of a few dozen from the Imperial Army might have caused a bit of the stir. The soldiers called out ahead of them, attempting to clear a path through the early day crowds. Corovium was of substantial size, and Philip regretted spending very little time within the actual city he called home. His duties kept him buried within the capital. At least he convinced himself of that.

With so much going on in his mind, Philip found very little time to focus on the things that mattered. Foremost, there had been no word from his niece. The army had long since given up the chase for her and the Guild had yielded no results as of yet. Far too soon, he knew, but that did not ease his trepidation over the events. His brother had yet to forgive him or even spend much time speaking to him since their discussion in the throne room several weeks back. Nicolas was proud, but brash. No amount of talk could ever get through to him and Philip would know. After all, he had known his brother since the moment he entered into this world, and if Nicolas was going to change, he would have likely done such before now.

The interesting proposition from Afeon had yet to truly sink in. This stink with the Guild had muddied up his thoughts. Certainly he would relay the information to Nicolas and in all likelihood he would consider it a victory. The First presumed he should as well. But he did not trust Afeon and certainly did not trust Dehyllo. Why should they vote for this unified House? Why not take their chances in the courts? Perseverance and treachery would be at grand display should the courts become involved, to which both Christina Rowe and Dehyllo Brocusk would feel quite at home with. Bribery, threats, and back alley deals would spread from slums to the capital building, from pavement back to dirt. And who could say which House would come out atop in the end? Certainly not the First. Had his House not been involved, he would even find intrigue to the affair.

The problem, at least for him, was his distrust of Dehyllo barely outweighed his distrust for Christina. How long before she made the attempts to erase the Pratt name from Donovini? The fighter, the warrior in Nicolas blinded him to the true intent of that woman. And yet she still stood the lesser of two evils.

It had not taken the three councilors long to reach the stairs to the courthouse. The courts stood only three stories tall, but had three sublevels as well. Some of the higher ranking officials lived within the lower levels of the courthouse, as did the councilors and their families within the capital. The other levels were separated into different factions of law, everywhere from fair labor proceedings to local crime hearings. Different days presented different trials and efforts, but only once a month did the courts open for public hearing of grievances. The complaints could be as small as a domestic dispute that needed clarifying, to a request from a small village for financial aid or support. Some waited months to be seen, but others such as Orpay, head of the Guild, could be seen at any point in time. He ran the Guild, who financially supported many areas within the courts as well as lined several pockets that sat in judgment. There was no waiting for a man of his stature.

The soldiers parted the way as they reached the start of the stairs that led upward to the courtroom. The building stood above a small incline, and the stairs started early and ascended slowly for no apparent reason other than dramatic effect by the architect. Philip cursed that fucking architect.

Orpay sat patiently in front of the courthouse, as fat as he was ugly, and the elder Argon was plenty of both. He steadily chewed on some root, moving it about around his mouth as if it were some trick to be marveled at. By the time Philip reached the top of the stairs to which led to the wide double doors of the courthouse, he could smell the musk from the heavy Argon from several feet away, discouraging him to move much closer to the bench where Orpay was seated.

"Wondering when you boys were going to show up here," wheezed Orpay, the words marred with exhaustion.

The First smiled to the Argon. "I heard that the Guild was filing a grievance against us. I came quickly, but in honesty, if I had known that the great Orpay would have made this trip himself, I'd have not bothered to show up at all. I wouldn't have guessed you to make it up all those stairs and live to speak the tale."

Orpay did not seem to find much humor in his statement. "A fat joke. Humorous, First Pratt. I'll ensure to remember that the next time one of my men asks me on the condition of your niece's return once captured. I keep saying alive and untainted, but damned if I can remember that each and every time."

And now that the pleasantries are out of the way.

The man was from Argonus, but hardly a true Argon. The Guild controlled the trade, commerce, and just about anything to do with finances in Amon. Like them or not, the First was forced to have dealings with them. They secured trade routes, created new ones for suppliers, ensured laws were enforced, ensured that fair trade occurred within every civilized city in Amon. Certainly they were also mercenaries and hired thugs, but there stood larger use from their existence. Without them, crime would increase, monopolies would be difficult to control, there would be little to no fair trade in the larger cities, especially those far and away from Genethur. No, Philip had no love for the Guild, but understood they were a necessary evil.

If anything, he only wished that the head of their Guild had been someone other than the pompous Orpay. Perhaps someone less compulsive, more open minded, or even someone that did not struggle mightily to conquer stairs. At this point, Philip was convinced he would simply take someone that smelled less repulsive.

"No witty retort, First Pratt?" started Orpay. "Very well. The grievance has already been delivered and those in the hearing will reconvene with you all by week's end to discuss and decide the outcome. I stay here awaiting you, as I know how quickly news can travel in Genethur."

"News travels as fast here as anywhere, Orpay," noted Afeon, who moved up beside the First.

The Guild leader looked steadily at the three men. "So where is the Fourth?" he inquired.

Lurey chuckled. "Likely pissing himself or wondering where the rest of his damn House went. What difference does it make? Now will you tell us what this is about?"

Slowly Orpay stood from his seat, in no hurry as it appeared, the smug look upon his face not finding an end. "You boys will be able to hear in detail if you wish once the judges meet with you, pending on if the courts allow my little grievance through. In which case you will have to find a way to pay me an enormous amount of funds, along with those merchants out of work now."

"Speak straight, Orpay," demanded Philip, his patience with the elder limited.

"Very well. The king, in his only order at the throne before his assassination, disbanded the army on the eastern shore. In doing so, all of the funds that were once routed to the merchants that supplied the army, as well as the transportation costs that the Guild received, have ceased."

"You've got to be kidding me," murmured Lurey, almost laughing in disbelief.

No need to confirm this. That idiot boy thought he was a genius, and being king meant he was above his council or the courts. If I knew you would have done this, I'd have asked the assassin to kill you long before you became king.

But then again, why did the assassin wait for that moment in the first place?

Afeon shook his head. "You must understand, Orpay, that order is void, as it was made obviously before he was king."

"And how does that matter?" Orpay questioned. "The letters were sealed with the Aylmer stamp. Funds did stop. The notice of their removal has reached the eastern shore. Word quickly reached me that the merchants and craftsman did not receive that courtesy letter and are still owed funds for services rendered to the former army during this unpaid time. That, and since they were contracted to work, are owed money for the breach of that contract. I am here as their . . . representative."

"As the Second claimed," Lurey interjected, "the boy must have given that order before he was crowned, being he didn't last all of two seconds as the actual king."

Orpay gave a long, exaggerated shrug of his shoulders. "Truth being told, do you really think that when General Shonnen received that letter, he had any idea whether or not the boy had written that before his crowning? Is the treasury going to question the legitimacy of a sealed letter with the Aylmer stamp? What is done is done, Third Hillan. Be thankful it was not more severe. Or worse yet, he had actually *remained* in power to continue his idiocy."

"The eastern army should have never been disbanded," added the First. "We will simply start the funding again."

"Ha! We shall see how easy you have at that task, First Pratt. You may be in charge here at Amon, but a king you are not. Do you think it as easy as snapping a finger?"

The First frowned heavily at the Guild head. "Why not come to us with this? We had no idea that Yelium disbanded those men. We are talking about thousands of men who served Amon to the order of their king at the time, some who have been out there for as many as two years, away from their families, away from all that they know. We thank them by simply disbanding them, leaving them without a job, money, or life?"

"Not us," Afeon corrected. "Our dead king gave that order. And rather than come to us so that we could set this right, you go to the courts to . . . well to what exactly? Extract money from the council?"

Orpay's face displayed his indifference. "Set what is right, councilors. Your lack of knowledge of this situation does not change the fact that you have an army on the eastern shores of Amon that are now out of work. Their plight is not mine, however. The merchants that spent years supplying them, feeding them, clothing them . . . they are now also out of work and are owed money due to the contracts that the former king had in place, and they look to the Guild for help. You do not have the power to tap the treasury for funds of this nature. Not without going through the courts. And even then, how long will it take for them to reestablish this army and redraft contracts with merchants? And what are these former soldiers supposed to do in the meantime? Wait? We will be damned lucky if this doesn't start a revolution from those men."

"Earth and Flame, Orpay, you should be helping us fix this," hissed the First. "You could push the courts, get them to reestablish the funds and get word out to these men that they were disbanded in error. You have the disposable money to help us out, knowing full well that we have access to repay you plus more for your service. Why not help us? Why go through this grievance?"

And the Guild head only raised his index finger to his forehead in a half attempt to salute. "We all have our agendas, councilors. The Guild is of no exception to that. I will be seeing you soon."

Orpay moved beyond the councilors and began his long flight down the stairs. The First turned to Lurey, and the Third could only stare with an angered fury in his eyes toward the Guild head. Philip had no words and little thoughts on the matter. So much was happening at such a rapid speed that he had trouble catching his breath much less sort it all out.

The situation did have one positive, so far as the First could tell. Afeon stood silent, his glare intent, his mind obviously flooded with thought. In all his years, it was the quietest he had ever known the Second.

A silver lining, I suppose.

--

"Do you love her?" Lillianna questioned softly, her deep brown eyes intent upon him.

Rayden shook his head. "This isn't about love, Lilli. This is about a unifying of two countries to the betterment of Amon."

Sitting casually in the dayroom of their western wing, the day pressed forward sluggishly, as did most days since the beginning of these negotiations. He could remember loving to travel, making his way across Amon, across the vast greens of Genethur and into the bustling and thriving crowds of Corovium. Now . . . he felt trapped, alone, and more than anything, just wanted to ride home to Astrona.

Wonder when I will ever see home again.

It had been Jerryn who had done the complaining at their arrival, and now he seemed the content one. They did not speak much as of late, but his brother did not seem bothered. Still he spend several nights a week out far too late, creeping into their chambers in the morning hours in hopes that Rayden would not notice. To both of their misfortunes, Rayden was a light sleeper. Every creek on the floor board, every late night stumble to dress, the elder brother heard it all. He was not exactly sure how much he cared. If his brother snuck out to fuck some different whore nightly, why should that bother him? It should not, and yet it did get under his skin some. Perhaps because he was simply bitter that his own love affair had not turned out so fruitful.

The fact remained that with Katlynn gone, the two brothers did little besides annoy each other. She had been their median on many sibling rivalries, always the one to bring them together on the worst of spats. Without her, the brothers simply sat in the same room and mostly ignored each other, save a few parting phrases here and there. Ultimately, Rayden knew that Jerryn missed Katlynn as much as he, only he had no capacity to express those emotions. All the same, the elder Pratt supposed.

"I wouldn't marry anyone I didn't love," Lilli said after some time.

"I envy that you'll likely have that option," replied Rayden. "And don't compromise that for anyone."

"Well, why would you compromise?" she queried.

Rayden shrugged. "We do what we must for Amon, I gather."

"You don't believe that," mumbled Jerryn, his eyes staring out the window of the large dayroom.

"Maybe not," admitted the elder. "But I have little choice. Father makes the decisions for our House . . . not me, not any of us."

"My father says that everyone has a choice," claimed the young girl. "I think he says some kind of quote, like by the rope or by the chain . . . or something like that. I don't really know if I get what that means, though."

"Actually, I think that means the opposite of choice," corrected Rayden. "You are a bit young to understand where that came from, but that actually means to be cornered by two options that lead to the same end."

"One quicker than the next," Jerryn added, making a quick visual display of being hung by the rope.

"Oh," Lilli sighed. "Well, I still think that everyone has a choice. I mean, Joanna married Winston, and that wasn't my father's first choice."

"Your sister fell in love and would not be swayed. Very few fairy tale endings, Lilli, but be hopeful knowing that one such ending is within your very family."

"I know, Rayden. I guess I just thought you deserved something better."

You and me both.

--

Inside Nicolas's chambers in the western wing, dinner had been served and both their families sat in the dining area, tenseness within the air that would not dissipate with the richest of red wines. Certainly there was talk, casual conversation around the room, but there remained an odd sense of separation between them all. Katlynn missing, Edmond and his family traveling back to Astrona and the Pratt estate, Jerryn and Rayden in a silent struggle of some kind, and the obvious dispute amongst himself and Nicolas clear enough to see in darkness.

All in all, a typical Pratt dinner as of late.

And as much as it pained him to admit it, Edmond would not have allowed all of the bickering. He seemed to embrace the role of instigator and enjoyed his lack of popularity. Somehow, at least as Philip imagined it, he would have diverted all of the extra animosity toward himself so that the rest of the family could coexist normally. As much as he disliked his younger brother in many ways, the man had his uses.

Nicolas, regardless of Philip's urgency, would not see him until after the main course had been completed. Roasted lamb with string beans and carrots, with a potato soup to start. An exquisite meal by all standards, but he had rushed it in hopes to speak with his brother over the day's events. But the House lord would have nothing of it. Patience in his eating, the man enjoyed every bite on his plate, as if knowing such would further infuriate the First. Every moment it looked to be his last bite, as if he could eat no more, his fork went back in for another helping of something, another round of wine.

"Nicolas," called out Philip and the table seemed to silence at the same moment.

"It can wait, brother," replied the House lord.

"It can," admitted the First, "but I'd rather it not. It's important."

After a long, awkward moment, Nicolas refilled his wine glass, then made a head motion for his balcony view. Philip grabbed his own glass and both brothers stood and moved through the door to stand out in the early evening air.

Opposite view here from Philip's chambers, the balcony gave way to the many lights of the city. It was easy to forget, at least for the First, that people lived below them, that there was more to life than this political shit that he sat in. Despite the kings and councilors and judges and politicians and Guild members, there were merchants and smiths and tailors and farmers, as well as schools and churches, children and the elderly. Lives came and went, regardless of the king that sat upon the throne, regardless of which House took power.

All that we do, all that I have done for Amon, and yet . . . I wonder how important all of this is in the end.

Alone outside, Philip wasted little time.

"Afeon knows of the talks between you and Christina."

Nicolas chuckled once. "Shadow take that bastard, but I expected nothing less. He's the smart one in that mess of a country."

"All fine and well, but I'd gather you wouldn't expect his take on the situation. He wants you to finalize the deal and wants me to call for the vote. He claims that he will support this union and that House Rowe will take the throne."

The elder brother took a sip from his wine glass, then his elbows leaned heavily against the rails. "Baiting us somehow."

"Normally I'd agree . . . but I sensed honesty in his tone."

"Can't trust those Ursan bastards, Phil. What they say and what they mean are likely oil and water. You should know that well enough."

"I do," replied the First. "But something was different about this talk. He sounded defeated, lost perhaps. I think Dehyllo knows that if you unify, there will be little chance for them in the courts. Two Houses, two countries coming together is strong enough in the voting to outweigh them. Money can't buy everything."

"It can buy a damn lot," was Nicolas's response. "I have trouble believing they are going to simply roll over and die after all of this. They are too poised, too close to taking what they have wanted for lifetimes. But I suppose this all changes very little. We are close to solidifying this merger to force the courts to pull favor our way. If Ursan chooses to vote for us rather than allow it to fall to the courts, then so be it."

"So then should I call for the vote?"

"Do you press me to sign this agreement?" Nicolas did not turn to him in his question. His eyes focused out into the city, wine glass still firmly in hand. "You have been the one against this union. Even Edmond believed it to be the right call, for Donovini, for the Pratts."

"I still don't think it's the right call," admitted the First. "But damned if you will listen. And since you won't, you might as well sign it and force the Ursan to make his call one way or the other."

"I suppose I can be difficult," Nicolas confessed.

"A bit."

The elder sighed heavily. "Do you know how difficult it was to be the eldest son of the great Landon Pratt? The greatest swordsman in all of Amon, they used to say. Nothing I could ever do would ever live up to his giant fucking shadow. But I did not take this House from Father with the thought of just signing it away, pissing on his legacy. Our elder Pratts fought to the death to claim our country, and a part of me feels that I betray them."

In a way, brother, you are.

"But ultimately, I suppose, is Amon more important than Donovini? You would gather that answer to be yes, and yet . . ."

His voice trailed off, and Philip understood his confliction. Amon was everything, that which he spent nearly two decades maintaining and striving for betterment. But where there should have been no separation in home and country, it was difficult at times to not draw the line between them.

"Donovini is our home," offered Philip. "It's everything to us. I *am* angered, and I don't agree, but I do believe as you do. Dehyllo takes that throne, he will disband the courts, pit the countries against each other, and topple the economy in his quest to have us all revert back to his primitive ways. And he will come for us first, fast and hard, to take out his only threat in the country. I don't agree because I would rather die fighting against him than unify with another enemy to hold him at bay. We stop nothing, we only postpone the inevitable. If we are to fight, we might as well start that now."

"You say that until we start dying, brother."

Philip took a strong swig from his glass. "A defeatist attitude, Nicolas. You can't blame the killing on the killed. And there is always the notion that what if Ursan doesn't do what we believe? What if our fears are without merit and they run Amon as would any leader beforehand? Will we have signed this treaty, given up our country for nothing?"

"We do not give up our country. We share it."

"And that differs?"

"No."

Philip shrugged gently. "You have made it abundantly clear that the decision is not mine to make. I just find it ironic that you are making the political decision in this matter, and I am taking the complete opposite."

"You choose to fight. Perhaps had you asked me of this when I was younger, when my children were younger, perhaps I would have answered differently. If you lost Joanna or Lillianna, I wonder if you would feel the same as you do now."

"Nicolas, I am certain that Katlynn will . . ."

His hand firmly rose to silence the First. "She has grown, and the decisions she makes are her own, as for all of my children. The decisions I make are for Donovini, and for the safety of our people, our families. Had you asked me many years ago, when the Twin Moons were not as pressed to the horizon, perhaps, Phil. But now . . . I only want is best for the children I have left."

Another sip, another pause later, and Nicolas finally turned to him. "Clear the room and call for House Rowe. Tell her I will sign the papers. Flame's embrace, Philip, I hope I am making the right call for our family."

Philip gave no response. What more was there to say?

--

Allura sat cautiously at the beach, buried and hidden behind a group of palm trees that rose behind the capital building. Clouds moved before the Twin Moons, keeping all surrounding her shrouded in the darkness. The soft waves rolling ashore were the only sound save for her breath . . . and perhaps the heavy heartbeat that pulsed in her mind. Curling some sand in between her toes, she exhaled deeply, calming herself, assuring herself that no one had seen her, that no one knew she was here.

This was the only place she could relax. The only place she could be herself. Certainly this changed nothing of her stance on Amon or her placement in life, Allura reassured herself. The final signing took place and she would marry Rayden no matter what. But here, on the beaches of the capital, she could pretend that her life had choices, that it could end up as did the stories in fairy tales.

Just dreams, Allura. Nothing more.

But what harm were dreams?

And a figure that appeared beside her nearly caused her heart to collapse altogether. She gasped, heard the laugh, and then spotted the wide grin from the gorgeous Jerryn Pratt.

"Did I scare you?" he pestered, knowing damn well the answer.

"You almost fucking killed me, you ass," she hissed back.

And before she could give him a solid punch to the arm, he leapt to her and pinned her down, his body atop hers, his breath against her cheek.

They had been here before, long before the capital, long before the crowning of the king. They had first met in Argonus, his father looking for aid in their drought. He had taken her during that trip, and any such time they could find the opportunity. They wrote in secret across the countries, knowing full well the dangers of discovery. But she could not resist him. His short black hair, deep brown eyes, perfectly tan skin, his deep voice . . .

So strong, so firm in her beliefs and understandings of her country and her House, and yet this man, this Pratt . . . he was all she ever wanted.

"We must talk," she whispered, the words that escaped barely her own.

"Then talk," he said back, his mouth against her neck, his hands removing the straps of her dress.

Allura let him continue, her breasts exposed, his lips moving downward to her chest. "Your father is signing the papers."

"Let him sign them," continued the young Pratt.

His mouth moved over her left nipple, his hand moving downward to her naval and continuing southward, and she bit hard against her bottom lip.

"I will have to marry your brother," she reluctantly claimed.

"I know."

"I don't want to."

"I know."

His hands moved between her legs with intent, his mouth still working back and forth between her breasts. Wiggling an arm free, she quickly worked her hand into his pants, grabbing hold of him tightly as he quickly hardened upon her touch.

There was no need for words after that.

--

Of all the nights of all the many that he ignored his instincts, perhaps this was the worst of nights to finally succumb to curiosity.

Rayden was not sure why he decided to follow Jerryn, why he had finally decided to uncover the mystery of his brother's frequent disappearances. And as he had seen the two, both his brother and his bride to be, naked and rolling about the sand like a pair of fish out of water, he had found himself in a full flux of emotions, with only one taking precedence over the others.

Betrayal.

--

People have many different opinions of us, many different views. I am cognizant to what is out there, if for anything else, assessment.

Eventually, everyone needs our help. And when that time comes, how receptive might I be in supplying aid to someone who distrusts the Guild, someone who has openly spoken against us? Not as receptive, you might realize, as one who accepted our role in Amon.

We are here to shape Amon, create a better land for us all. We do so not as a race or a country, but as a unified people. What better way to represent Amon than by those standards? Why would anyone speak against us, outside of fear?

And they should fear us. We do not bend for any who stand against our ways. Any who oppose us, they will know our resolve.

-- Orpay, Guild Headmaster

VIII

In hindsight, Livensburg had been a horrible idea. Certainly they had been spotted by the Guild back in that small town, which Katlynn had been painfully reminded a dozen times over by Iero. Before they ventured into that village, Tristan had assured them both that despite the previous warnings of the Druid, the Guild would not have been involved yet in the hunt for the young Pratt.

Since then, they both followed Iero's lead.

Thankfully, Livensburg was a small, nothing of a town on the outskirts of Donovini. The Guild's outpost had all of two, perhaps three associates representing them there. Spotting the trio of fugitives was one thing. Following and apprehending them was another ordeal altogether. If those Guild members had known what they were looking for, they had equally known the threat. A Shadowmancer, a Druid, and a captain of the Astrona guard were nothing to gawk at. Though Katlynn never used her abilities for harm, she could easily understand the fear of it, understood the potential of it. The Shadow Realm was, for obvious reasons, a feared thing. Anyone that doubted the power could try and ask the king. Except he was apparently already in the dirt.

But if their ignorance in Livensburg had done anything, it had alerted them to the gravity of their situation. Katlynn, all the way leading to that point, had secretly questioned the truth in anything that the Druid had claimed. Their escape had been unabated. And despite the commotion and the talks of the assassination amongst the common folk during their flight from the capital, there had been no link to the death of the king and her. She whispered to Tristan her doubts, who felt the same in return. They began to wonder if the Druid had led them astray for reasons they had yet to surmise. So much so even, that despite his warnings, they strolled into the first town available to them inside of their home country of Donovini for resupply. Foolish, as if they were not fugitives on the run, as if message could not have found the Guild sooner by horseback or a carrier bird. Their disbelief had given them a false confidence, and after catching wind of the wanted posters and the immediate attention drawn from the Guild, reality shaped quickly for Katlynn. All that she attempted to dismiss had been in fact truth by the Druid. Her innocence in the aforementioned crime did not matter.

The path set before them had one road and no forks. Only one country had minimal Guild presence, only one place that they could hide for an extended amount of time while they waited for this whole mess to subside. Ursan.

And it had been a grueling travel. The limited supplies that had been gathered in the capital had been reduced to dried meat and water, and they used those shortly into their flight. Some days they found game, a rabbit or other small rodent, normally whatever the damn Chur'rat didn't get to before them. They ate and kept extras for a day after, anything longer spoiled so there stood little need to ration it. Other days they ate berries or nuts or other random edible leaves. Other days they ate nothing. Thankfully Iero had known his way through Genethur well enough to keep them on track for the routes with fresh water and away from any roads to keep themselves hidden. A pond here, a small lake there, each time they stored up water for the trek ahead. And despite the Druid's chubby exterior, the man could move at an exhausting pace.

All in all, now reaching near a month since she had been on the run, a month since she had seen her family, taken a proper bath, eaten a proper meal, slept on a bed, and most of all, not cried at some point in her sleep over the entire ordeal . . . well it began to numb. Katlynn missed her brothers, her father, her mother. She missed the life she once lived, certainly. But it began to dull the senses the longer she spent away from it all. She cried less. The hunger did not bother her as it once did. The acceptance that she did nothing wrong, yet had little choice to flee sunk well into her conscious, taking it as fact rather than question. Katlynn had far from hardened since her departure from the world she had known; at best, she had learned to cope.

The night had been heavy and hot in central Donovini, and both Iero and she waited patiently in the outskirts of the town of Uvull. Larger than Livensburg, but still a rather small mining city, Uvull had been a heavily traveled, but sparsely lived area. Several deep underground caverns kept the miners at work at all hours of the day, bringing up precious gems and gold regularly enough to garner the attention of the Guild. For a rather small population, Uvull had a large faction of Guild members here, which of course was the last thing they needed.

Unfortunately, the first thing they needed in the drought filled lands of Donovini was water. That was something they could not afford to pass on.

Tristan had braved the city knowing that he, more so than either her or the Druid, could pass amongst the commoners. At this point, Katlynn felt that she had looked so horrible and likely smelled worse that the only thing that she could be mistaken for would be a homeless hag. But Iero assured her that the Guild would be looking for someone of that exact description.

She had argued enough with the Druid during the first half of their travel that at some point, she had accepted what he said, if for anything else to keep him quiet. Which of course was damn near impossible.

But strangely, as the two sat silently for a change, staring through the darkness of the sparse wilderness near the outside of town, Iero had kept silent for longer than several minutes, which was a welcome change. For reasons unbeknownst to her, she broke that silence.

"What do you believe?" she inquired, her eyes still cutting through the darkness, looking for movement of any kind.

The Druid sat cross legged, his Chur'rat draped over his shoulders sound asleep, the heavy breathing of the repulsive thing irritated Katlynn to no ends.

"Believe what, Lady Pratt?"

"In what we do, what we are?"

"You mean the Realms?"

Katlynn nodded, even though she doubted he had seen her do such.

Iero chuckled a bit. "I do not know if it matters so much of what you do or do not believe, so much as you believe in something. Truth in the matter, many religions dance around similar topics, while keeping many of the core beliefs out there intact. I find it humorous that many churches do not support the next, despite subtle differences between their reasoning behind existence. Personally, I think . . ."

"Iero," cut in Katlynn abruptly. "What do *you* believe?"

The long pause told the young Pratt that Iero thought long and hard about his choice of words.

"I believe in Turitea and Schill, Lady Pratt, for whatever that is worth. I believe they crafted four different Realms of existence, four different planes that at one time, shared each other in balance. With Shadow, Earth, and Flame laced over our plane of existence, men could but reach out and take that which they needed to build their world. But men were wicked and found power in the shared existence of the Realms, destruction over creation. The gods became furious over our misuse of their gifts and separated the Realms, removed the power from our very hands. The problem was that even as gods, they were not powerful enough to destroy the Realms entirely. So instead they hid them in plain sight, so much so that men could no longer use what they could no longer see."

"Save for a few of us," she noted.

"Indeed. Very few, and very rare. Some believe the reason that each individual can see but one Realm, never more than just one Realm, is because the sheer capacity to see one is strenuous enough. Others believe that since no two brains or eyes are alike, none of us can see anything quite the same as the next. What I see and what you see differ greatly. I find that Bird here on my shoulder is a beautiful creature, while you find him a vile repulsive rat. There is an old saying about the eye of the beholder, but it is true in many more ways than one."

"So by that rational, I can see the Shadow Realm and you can see the Earth Realm only because we see the world differently?"

"As good of an explanation as any, Lady Pratt."

She repositioned a bit, her knees now pressed into her chest. "What does the Earth Realm look like?"

"I do not know, milady. I would gather you already know that. It is there, certainly, but difficult to focus upon. Like a mirage that remains just beyond sight."

"Sometimes I wonder . . .," her words hung for a moment, deciding whether to voice her thoughts aloud. "There is so much power that comes from whatever the Realms are and yet . . . sometimes I wonder what it even looks like within. I mean, we open the Realms and borrow from them, but what is it that we borrow from?"

The Druid's eyebrows rose. "Careful, Lady Pratt. That is a dangerous line of thinking."

"Dangerous in wanting to know more of our power?"

"Danger of breaking the only rule of our kind."

"Never cross over," she whispered the one and only rule ever passed to her in the use of her Realms. A Druid healer had spoken to her of this rule when she was maybe ten, which was around the age when she first started to understand that she was different from other people. "Who made that rule?"

"Someone wiser than either of us, I would gather." Iero closed his eyes and seemed to return to his steady breathing. "It is there for a reason."

"Have you ever thought of crossing over?"

"No." His response was stern, certain.

"And have you known of anyone to cross over?" Katlynn pressed.

"No. And if I did, I would give you the same answer. Anyone that crosses over is no longer one of us."

"Us?"

"Human."

Her mouth opened then clamped shut. Prying further would do little, she realized. Just because he had seen many more years than she and had the gift of experience in his use of his power did not necessarily translate into more answers or more insight into the origins of the Realms. Any more questions and he might fully break from his meditation and began his longwinded explanations of anything and everything that would pop into his mind.

So instead she turned her attention to Tristan, hoping he would not take much longer in gathering their supplies.

The only rule . . .

Katlynn hated rules.

--

The dreaded sun came down heavy on this afternoon and Nathanial wiped the beads of sweat from his forehead. He walked casually about the small forested area just outside of Uvull, both Jadenine and Feko Hawbry remained on horseback as they stared impatiently at him.

"What do you hope to see here?" pestered Jadenine.

"Something," he mumbled in response, gazing about the patches. Someone had been here, that he could easily see, but they did a well enough job covering up their tracks. At least two had spent some time here and were on foot. Outside of that, Nathan could tell little more. Not only had he not found any signs as the direction they departed, he had no real idea if this had indeed been his quarry.

"Maybe we should continue onward to Livensburg?" offered up Feko. "Not to pry into what you do, but did I misunderstand where this assassin had been spotted?"

"You did not misunderstand," noted Nathan. "I only know that they would not be there anymore. If their destination is where I believe, this would be a great stop for water and supplies in their trip."

Jadenine laughed at his statement. "And now that you have spent all morning in the town and half the fucking afternoon out here. Exactly when do you intend to give this up?"

She had been right, of course. Nathanial had thought himself so damn smart that he was above reproach in his ability to hunt. Beasts were one thing: predictable, habitual. People were something completely different. Even still, this *felt* right. Katlynn was too smart. She would not have made an attempt to return to Astrona; the Guild stood waiting for her there. He knew that this was where she would have stopped on her way, but wasting away in the heat did little to bolster his confidence.

He had almost apologized to the Ursan woman before accidently kicking a large brown pellet that sat behind a few small bushes. In doing such, he almost laughed at himself.

I've been tracking the wrong thing.

"We've got our scent, quite literally," Nathan called out.

Jadenine gazed at him as if he had lost all sense. "You found shit, quite literally."

"Not just any shit, my negative companion. Chur'rat shit."

She shrugged. "So sell it to some Chur'ash fiend and be done with it."

"I think you fail to realize the point. Chur'rats are not indigenous in Donovini. However Iero, the Druid that moves with our Katlynn Pratt, has a Chur'rat familiar."

"Ha, so we are on the trail then I see!" excitingly claimed Feko.

Jadenine did not seem as thrilled, but turned her mare about with authority. "Northeast I am gathering?"

Nathan nodded. "They are heading to Ursan."

--

The night drew far and deep before Iero had decided they traveled enough for this day. Katlynn remembered how difficult the task had been to start, to march continuously, to rest only to gain water and nothing more. To move until her legs burned, her thighs chaffed, her feet blistered and bloodied. No, the trek had been anything but pleasant, but she recalled some old Ursan saying about perseverance through tribulation. Truth in words.

As a House lady, she trained with the sword as much as she practiced manners during her childhood, and she was a far cry from out of shape before the trip began. But no amount of casual conditioning could prepare her for this kind of torture.

But she was a Pratt. She cried alone in her sleep, even away from Tristan. Part from the pain of her legs and feet, part from the feeling that she had done nothing to deserve such treatment, part in her thinking that she may never see her family again. Tears dried. Bodies toughened. She was a Pratt after all, and that was something that she repeated in her mind as often as possible.

They had moved through what at one time in her childhood been a vast forest in central Donovini. The Roseglenn Wilderness had been transformed by the long, painful drought into a barren area of downed or simply hallowed out dead trees. What grass stood from the dirt below was brown and hardened, bushes now just a mere growth of sticks. A graveyard of nature and a far cry from the luscious greens of Genethur they passed on their way here. It was at the Roseglenn that Iero had stopped and waved his arms, calling for them to rest for the night.

She placed her pack down and sat beside it, her shoes slipping off, the pressure against her feet relieved for the moment. During their swift flight from Corovium, Tristan had grabbed and purchased her a loose-fitting tunic and slacks, but the shoes had been a size too small. It had not been his fault, though he apologized to no ends over the mistake. How often had Tristan purchased women's shoes in his lifetime? They were not unbearable, but certainly did little to relieve from the blisters. Her feet were wrapped tightly with bandages, these now stained red from blood and puss. Certainly her body strengthened, but the constant pace and little pause had not given her body time to heal properly.

As she reached over and began to undo the bandages, Tristan dropped down and began to aid her in the task. She flinched away.

"I'm fine," she whispered, not harshly. But she could see in his face that damage had been done regardless.

"Very well."

The captain stood and moved across from her and began to unpack some of his food rations, part of his most recent and last purchase. What money Iero and Tristan had upon them during their flight had now been spent, though the Druid assured them that money would do them little good in Ursan.

She watched him for few moments longer, then started again at her bandages. Her feet were horrendous and the last thing she wanted was her lover staring at them. The captain meant no harm and would not have cared in their appearance, but *she* did. He would not understand. So she did not bother to explain.

Katlynn cared for Tristan Crane, but just like a man, he did not seem to know when to leave things well enough alone. She was an emotional wreck and he wanted her to talk it through, ask her if she was okay at every step of every moment, constantly apologizing as if he had anything at all to do with any of this. Flame's embrace, he was insufferable. He was, after all, only a man, and despite his many great attributes, primarily below his waist, he suffered the same fundamental flaw as any other man she had known: he had little idea *how* to help, and thought the answer was to ask her over and over what she wanted him to do.

Shutting the fuck up was a good start.

Problem was that this was something that could not be fixed. That fact alone bewildered Tristan into his childlike pestering. He *wanted* to help, *wanted* to fix this. But what could he do? Could he bring back the dead? Could he find the real killer? Could he send message to her family? Earth and Flame, he could not even buy her proper fucking shoes.

What she needed was time to sort it out. He wanted to hold her, kiss her, fuck her in all likelihood. She was a disgusting wreck that likely smelled worse than the shit pellets that the Chur'rat left everywhere. Again, where he might not have cared about how she smelled or appeared, she certainly did. And though she missed sex just as much as he did, she did not feel like having sex on the dry ground, give the Druid a nice show of things, smelling the way they smelled, all while dealing with the fact that they were all fugitives. Of course she was an innocent fugitive, but Katlynn knew better than to hope that she would make it out of any of this alive if caught. If the Guild found her and delivered her back to the capital, she would die, if for anything else, to please the crowds. Whether or not their king was a good man or bad, he had been murdered. Punishment would be swift and unjust.

No, what time or place had there been to talk about her feelings? They ran, poor and underfed with tattered clothes and bloody feet to show for. All she wanted was for none of this, not a single second of it, to be real. But every morning she woke up disappointed while she put on her tight, blister inducing shoes.

Katlynn wanted to explain to him, tell him that all this would pass. Somehow she would end up back in Astrona, back to the life she once lived. Perhaps she could attempt to convince her father to allow her an actual relationship with the captain. Perhaps she could get to know the man in more than one way, regardless how good that one way was. She wanted to tell him that soon this would all be over and that, at the very least, they could go back to how it used to be.

But since she did not believe any of that, she instead reached into her pack, found a new bandage, and began to rewrap her feet . . . alone.

--

Jadenine had not questioned his knowledge of Iero's familiar. Nathanial had of course known for the simple fact that he met the man. The nature of his Chur'rat friend was not completely public knowledge. Of course unless someone asked the man, in which case he would drone on about the differences between a Chur'rat and a standard rat for hours. Perhaps she had not taken it as anything more than face value since Nathan had been annoyingly good at nearly all that he did. He knew this and could do little about it. He was no more a braggart than he did boast. But that alone might have made him that much more insufferable.

I could let people win and best me. Would that make people like Jadenine and Draven pull back on their venom? Not likely. Just like my damn brother. Somehow, inevitably, they know I back off. Nothing worse than being allowed to win I suppose.

Instead she had remained on her horse, back to her silent self, staring out into the night, the Roseglenn Wilderness still a little ways yet. It seemed that since he had known the woman, she had two modes: hate and silence. Ironically, Nathan hated silence. It made their frequent pairings that much more enjoyable.

"Shhh, let him work," mumbled Feko to himself. Nathan gazed up at the Argon involuntarily, and he smiled in response. "Sorry, Nathanial. I did not mean to interrupt. Continue on."

Their time together had done little to determine sanity or otherwise, but Nathanial easily leaned upon the latter. Feko Hawbry seemed in constant battle with his mind, speaking to himself under his breath frequently, and spent more time actually trying to hush whatever voices he thought he heard. In this case, Jadenine had been correct. The man was insane, though that fact changed very little. Somehow Feko had found him in the Lis'rial Wilderness combating the Draywolves. Somehow he had known of his relations to the Pratts. Somehow he had known that his cousin would be framed for an assassination and hunted. At the very least, he had agreed to keep his knowledge of Wode's lineage to himself for the time being, and thus far had been true to his word.

No, he was certain now that he wanted the Argon close. If he was involved somehow in framing Katlynn or had any knowledge to the assassination whatsoever, they would need him alive. That was if given the chance. If Feko had been wise enough to seek him out and use him to find Katlynn, he was not the blubbering lunatic that he had outwardly betrayed.

One way or another, the man deceived the eye. The luckiest madman ever or a clever charlatan. Dangerous and unpredictable described him. Turning back for a moment to Jadenine, he began to wonder which of the two he was more concerned with. Almost a week out of Prillian and he had not even conceived a plan beyond finding Katlynn.

Well, that is the most important part of the plan at least.

How would either react when he captured the girl and did not intend to return her to the Guild? Would Jadenine part her separate way or make an attempt to kill him? Would Feko play his hand and reveal his employer and intent? Nathan had no lack of confidence in his ability with the sword, but even he was lucky at times.

And inevitability, eventually, luck ran out. Never at the best times, either.

He spat to the earth, frustrated that his mind continued to wander rather than find a new trail to follow. The Chur'rat dung had led him to a fresh set of footprints, the dried grass doing little favor to those attempting to hide passage. The indentations had shown three different sets of prints, three travelers, three fugitives. They had gained quite a bit of ground and by the set of the last prints, Nathanial gathered them not even an hour behind. But now he had lost their trail, momentarily he realized, but frustrated nonetheless. Dismounting he moved about, gazing for some sign to show him the way.

Problem was the clouds moving steadily across, covering the Twin moons, blocking the light they produced. He knew they were within reach, but without the proper light to be able to find their trail, he settled into the realization that they would likely need to camp for the night and catch them in the morning.

Feko must have seen that contemplation upon his brow. "Perhaps," started the Argon, "we should think to rest our horses for the night, Nathanial Wade. It has been quite a day, and it seems you have gained quite a bit of ground on our alleged assassin."

"I rarely agree with him," Jadenine commented, still gazing out at neither of them. "In fact, I've never agreed with him. But my ass is rightfully sore enough for one day."

Nathan almost agreed until he caught sight, faintly, of a set of prints. Then a second, and a third. And then a fourth? He looked carefully, a fifth set, and a sixth. These had been recent. Seventh. Very recent, under thirty minutes if he were a guessing man. And he was at that.

"They are being followed . . ." mumbled Nathan.

"What was that?" Jadenine called out.

He quickly rushed back to his steed and mounted. "They are being trailed by another group, larger group, maybe seven or more."

The Ursan woman finally met his gaze, her look equally intense. "Guild members from Uvull?"

"Possible. I'd like to make sure they don't damage our prize. She's wanted alive."

"She's a Shadowmancer. You damn well better have a plan that doesn't involve us dying if we rush in."

Against Katlynn, no problems. Against whoever this new player was in their game, he could not say.

--

She had barely slept, despite her exhaustion. Partially due to her aching feet, but mostly due to her conscious weighing heavy against her.

Katlynn rolled to her side and gazed over at a snoring Tristan. Handsome and caring, if not forcefully so, he was a good man. By all rights he could have stayed back in Corovium, in which case he would have likely been back in his own bed by now, back home in Astrona. Which was a sight better than a wanted fugitive, she gathered. There had not been a true decision to flee with her as much as it had been an actuality, a reality. While Katlynn struggled with the facts laid out to her by Iero back in the capital, the captain had swiftly known his move. He would join her, and that was that.

How could their lives *ever* be the same? They fled with the elder Druid toward Ursan in hopes to escape the army, the Guild, and anyone else looking to capitalize off her capture. It would not take long for all of Amon to be out hunting her. How could she prove her innocence? Her word against whose exactly? A dead king? Perhaps the real killer would step forward and take blame? She made little claim to know the judicial system as well as she knew fashion, but naïve she was not. Standing in the courts, she would state her night, her relationship with the captain, her oversleeping and missing the crowning of Yelium Aylmer II, and finding out from the Druid the outcome. Her testimony would certainly be heard and dismissed. Evidence was clear. A Shadowmancer had killed the king. She was a Shadowmancer and questionably missing from the ceremony. All three of them would hang and if lucky, the courts would only remove the Pratts from their House status and give it to another family name in their place. If unlucky, her entire family would hang with her, the captain, and the Druid.

Knowing this, why would anyone, lover or otherwise, choose to come with her? They had never claimed love for one another. Their relationship had been mostly physical and he had played his part damn well. But as close as they were, she could not say that she really *knew* the man. She would have just assumed him to have excused himself during the conversation back in Corovium rather than offer up to join her. And since his accompaniment, he had done nothing but try to aid her. And up to this point, she had all but spit in his face for his attempts.

Of course she had. She felt alone, betrayed, confused, and most of all, scared out of her mind. She was a Pratt, so she hid it well. Her bane of him was the defense against her emotions, against her anguish.

Should I apologize?

The archer rarely apologized to the tree for using it for target practice. How else to strengthen skills, hone ability? And the tree, for all of its great purpose, could do little but be patient in hopes that the archer eventually stopped impaling it with arrows, or at least moved on to another tree.

And since Katlynn did not have another tree, Tristan could only hope she would toughen up quickly before whatever they had between them became unsalvageable.

She did not apologize. Instead she rolled to her opposing side, her back to him now, and only then did she spot the shadow outline of several figures just beyond through the dead trees.

For a moment her heart froze, paralyzed with uncertainty. As the figures began to move, it had been clear that these were men and not tricks of her imagination. One broke off east, the other west, perhaps looking to surround them. Who were they? That answer seemed obvious. The Guild.

Part of her wanted to scream in fear of the realization of this attack, that they were seconds away from capture at the very least. The other part though, the primal part, took over as she reached into Shadow. The feeling, regardless of the number of times she reached to the other side, scattered her arms with goosebumps. The sense of power in the Realm, the part where her hand borrowed but a small portion of Shadow, always left her unsatisfied, always left her feeling the need for more. Despite the feeling of euphoria, Katlynn pulled her arm back, cloaking herself in the darkness, then rolled back and onto her feet, uncertain of what her next move would be. Only now did she think of having Tristan purchase a weapon with their limited funds. It seemed as if water and food were of higher priorities, until this moment of course.

In hindsight, Uvull had been a horrible idea.

Losing sight of the two men that moved to either side of the small camp, her eyes focused in on the larger group to the south, maybe five it appeared, one stepping forward before the rest. He did not mask his approach; there stood little need now. With his men in position, they had the upper hand. Katlynn, for all her wit, had no idea what to do. Taking another step back, she stepped on the damn Chur'rat, who in turn hissed, lifted up from its slumber, and Katlynn stumbled backward, falling directly into the legs of the sleeping captain.

Tristan woke with a start, in which doing so also woke the Druid, mumbling to himself as he came to. Katlynn kept herself in Shadow as she came back to her feet, still lost in her own mind whether to flee while the opportunity still presented itself.

"Katlynn," muttered a half-asleep Tristan.

Where he was still sorting things out, the Druid had already pieced together the puzzle.

"Run," Iero muttered, stepping forward diligently, brushing past her as he moved ahead of them all.

The figure from beyond came into view, a short Donovinian man armed to the teeth in knives. It was as clear as the night sky that there would be no escape for the three fugitives. Tristan now stood, apparently also having collected himself, moving next to Iero.

"If you are still here," he stated softly, "please go."

She wanted to desperately. Her feet, however, would not move.

He didn't leave me when he had the chance.

"I won't leave you to die," was her answer.

"You staying will not change that, milady," Iero retorted.

"Make to Ursan," Tristan urged. "Find a way to survive."

I can't do it alone.

For all her thoughts at being a Pratt, how long would she live without the two of them? Hell, the Chur'rat contributed more than she. All she had done since their departure was endure. And treat the captain like shit. And badly blister her feet.

The Donovinian man clapped his hands loudly and obnoxiously, a smile upon his smug, elder face. "You have done well to last as long as you have on the run, but as you can guess, that time has ended. I know the girl is still here and we know what you are capable of. Remove yourself from your Realm and no one is going to die."

"Are you from the Guild?" called out Iero. "As if you are so, you should know that several important laws are in place to uphold the outline of your contract, some of which are punishable by death if broken. Should we be part of that contract, then we ask to be taken to the contract holder so that we may find out . . ."

"That's enough stalling," the man stated firmly. "I cannot see you, but I can see your friends just fine, Shadowmancer. I have two archers placed to either side, both with arrows pointed directly on the talkative one. So if I were you, Druid, I wouldn't make any sudden movements." He flashed a devilish smile to Iero, then turned back to her while gazing blindly about the area. "After his death, we kill the captain here. Without them, not so certain how long a House bitch is going to last out here alone. Not long, I'd gather. And since we won't give up pursuit, you aren't going to get very far anyways. And if you did manage to evade us for a bit, you will be hungry and thirsty and begging for us to capture you."

He paced about, his eyes still gleaming in the satisfaction of winning. "I get more money with three of you alive. I'd much rather take you all in and let the Guild sort it out. But I get no pay without you, Shadowmancer, so I will take what I can get. If you force my hand, I will kill these two and be done with it. But if you come out, I will spare them *and* you. What the Guild does with you, I cannot say, nor do I care. All I promise is the three of you will remain alive up to and leading to me dumping you off in Prillian. You have one chance, this chance, to make your decision."

Almost as if reading her thoughts, Tristan muttered, "No . . ."

But her decision had been made. She was not sure if it was bravery or cowardice, but at least it had been decisive.

Shadow removed, Katlynn Pratt stood behind her companions in defeat.

"Wise, Lady Pratt. Very wise."

The men from behind the Guild leader came forward, three of them with ropes in hand and approaching with purpose.

"Iero . . ." Tristan began, but trailed off, perhaps uncertain in his own words.

If Iero had planned anything extraordinary in an escape attempt, he hid such thoughts well.

"Nothing rash or stupid, Druid," warned the Guild leader. "Just let the boys tie you up, then we make our way to Prillian. No one needs to be hurt."

Faint at first, then loud and predominant, the sound of hooves slapping against the dead earth echoed into the empty space of the Roseglenn Wilderness. The men who approached paused to the sounds of someone imminently close and the Guild leader quickly withdrew two knives in response. Bowstrings somewhere in the distance could be heard pulling back, and the other Guild members unsheathed their weapons as well.

"Hold! Hold!" called out a voice from just outside of view.

Three riders fast approached, one kept intentionally distance while the other two made their way into view. The first was an Ursan woman, fiery red hair, her pale skin even detectible in the darkness of the night. The other was a Donovinian, handsome and tall . . . and remarkably familiar. Unbelievably at that.

Nathan . . .

--

"You have done well, gentleman," Nathan called out, the mercenaries before him both nervous and edgy. "But this is a Guild matter. We have chased our quarry for a solid week, and now we look to take them back to Prillian."

If the mercenary leader had been impressed with his bravado, then Nathan would have been pleased with his odds. It turned out he was not.

"Who the fuck are you?"

"Have you heard the name Nathanial Wode?" A sea of dumbfounded faces returned after his statement. "Then you are no more Guild members than these three fugitives. We appreciate your work and you will be paid your due for a finder's fee. But again, this is now a Guild matter."

"And how might we receive our finder's fee if you are dismissing us? Suppose we should just trust that you will make it back to Uvull and find us?"

"I would gladly take your names and send a representative . . ."

"With all due respect, Nathanial Wode, you can kiss my Donovinian ass. These three come with us. Now since we are obviously heading in the same direction, we don't mind the company, unarmed of course. And if you are Guild members as you claim, you would be able to perhaps pay us a little extra for the escort service. No offense, but how are the three of you planning to subdue a Shadowmancer and a Druid?"

"Mercenary, I will show you exactly how I can subdue someone should you give me an order again."

Nathan was uncertain if his blatant, over the top aggression would scare any of these men into backing down, but he had no idea as to how this could end without bloodshed. If he surrendered to their demands, his weapons would be gone. Unarmed, he would have no opportunity to free Katlynn during their trip to Prillian. And in all reality, he would likely be bound right along with them. Thus, if he could not talk his way through this . . .

"We are not disarming," Jadenine snapped toward the mercenary. "You had best come up with a better comprise that doesn't involve me handing over my sword."

"Guild or no Guild, we are not having you armed and traveling with us," said the mercenary. "We don't know you, and we aren't leaving these three until we have coin in hand."

One of the other mercenaries took a step forward, his confidence shaken. "Look, Erik, maybe we should rethink this. Money isn't worth the Guild coming down on us."

"Shut up, you fucking coward," the mercenary leader bellowed back, immediately returning his stare to Nathan. "Some of us have hungry families waiting for our return, and we damn sure won't be heading home empty handed. I'm only going to say this once. Remove your weapons or we drop you dead here in the wilderness."

"Erik, I'm not . . ." another began, but the leader had little patience for the shaken resolve.

"We are *not* giving these fugitives up! Drop your weapons and dismount, now!"

Nathan turned to Jadenine. He wondered what she thought, wondered if she had understood his stubbornness to not work with this small mercenary group. It was sad, indeed. These men were no warriors, no trained soldiers or Guild members. They were likely miners or farmers, out of work in all likelihood, starving and attempting to find ways to feed their families. The drought had placed many in this same kind of situation, forced to look for other ways to provide necessities. They were not killers, but desperate times created desperate men. And there was no mistaking the glint in their eyes. These men were in dire straits.

Jadenine returned a look, one that Nathan could only translate as pity. He knew the look well, as he presumed it mirrored on his brow.

These were not bad men. They were hungry and broke men, but not bad. It was a shame that they would all have to die.

Steady, calm.

His stomach churned, and he did all that he could to avoid it. His bow was in his hand before the mercenary leader yelped in startle, and Nathan slid intentionally off his steed just as the twang of an arrow could be heard from the western archer, then a second from the east, both planting into his horse. The poor beast neighed heavily, raising and thrashing as Nathanial rolled away from the animal. An arrow notched firmly, he rose to a knee and aimed in the direction of the western archer and released. Another shaft at the ready, he turned to the eastern archer, who in turn did the same, his arrow readying. Not quick enough.

Released.

He flung the bow to the ground and unsheathed his blades, his steps moved maliciously toward the leader. An eruption shook him from his balance, likely from the Druid's abilities, and Nathanial struggled to gain his feet. The mercenary struggled equally, and his first knife throw missed terribly. As they both gained footing, the second knife came directly to him. Both weapons crossed, Nathan managed to deflect the throw. The foolish mercenary leader made an attempt for another knife, and while he found the time to wield it, he could not find time to use it. Nathan was upon him, his smaller, serrated dagger slicing the wielding arm, ripping apart flesh and spraying blood. His right hand followed through with his long sword, puncturing the mercenary's gut straight through, the moan evident that the man went into shock from the pain.

Nathan pulled back the weapon and spun about to the rest of the field before him. One engaged Jadenine, one stood impaled by branches and roots, and two rushed toward him blindly. The first man swung wildly with his blade and Nathan deflected the blow with his sword. The second man followed with his own sword swing, this one Wode caught with his dagger, both strength and a notch in the serrated blade holding the attack firm. Nathanial came quick with his sword arm and, while the opposing man was caught motionless for the moment, removed his hand clean from the rest of his body. He screamed, the sword and hand dropped to the ground, and both Wode's weapons rose in time to block another wild swing from the first mercenary. After the defense, he lifted upward with the dagger, again the notch keeping the attacking blade firm, then slashed with his right, the sword opening the guts of the mercenary. Before he could fathom the pain, Nathan tucked in his right elbow then extended hard into the chest of the man, sliding between ribs and penetrating organs, blood oozing out instantly.

His weapons removed from the mercenary, he kicked over the dying, bleeding wreck and moved over to the handless man, who cried in agony on his knees. Nathan jammed his sword through the man's neck, his screams gurgled and then faded entirely.

As he turned to Jadenine, she stood over the body of the last man, her sword red with his blood, the man bleeding and mostly dead.

The scene calmed and a heavy silence hung over the Roseglenn Wilderness.

Nathan then keeled over and vomited.

--

It ended as quickly as it had started, and the defenseless Tristan and Katlynn could do little but observe. Iero had reached into his Realm, into Earth, and killed a man. It had been a side of the power she possessed herself that she had not known, had not utilized. Never had she thought of the ability as an offensive weapon, as a means to kill. But her uselessness had all but showcased her need to learn that side of her gift.

Her cousin had been magnificent in his ruthlessness. It was a sickening display, one that she could not decipher whether to applaud or join him in the vomiting. In all her eighteen years, she had never seen a man killed. The whole thing was . . . surreal.

Katlynn was uncertain of what to do, so completely removed from the reality of the situation. She stood frozen, gazing steadily as Nathanial Wode wiped his mouth against his sleeve, then proceeded to use one of the dying men's shirts to clean the blood from his weapons. Sheathing them, he moved toward her, unable to suppress his own discomfort with what unfolded on this night.

As he came to her and extended his arms, she felt guilt as she embraced him. These men died, likely for nothing more heinous then looking to bring justice to Amon, and Katlynn could do little to feel pity. Disgust, certainly. But she could only feel relief. It angered her, but she could not fight the emotion. For at least one more minute of one more day, she had been alive and free.

"Nathan, I . . ."

"Later," replied her cousin. "We have plenty to discuss, but we need to gather what supplies we can from our friends and make some distance between us." He smiled. It warmed her.

"Maybe one of them has small feet," was her reply.

--

Jadenine finished the killings to the half dead men. It was mercy, but Nathan did not even have the stomach for that. He would much rather have been good at knitting. Instead, he could fight and by result, end lives. It was what he did well, but it did not mean he enjoyed it.

The Ursan did her task and asked no questions at first. Her eyes reflected her understanding, her concern perhaps. He had spent no time explaining his related ties with the fugitive, but he did not need to. They embraced, signifying one way or the next they had known one another, and she had meant enough for him to risk life to save her. Jadenine might not have been educated by normal standards, but she was no fool. If she had thought anything at this point, it was escape. He would say fear, but Nathan doubted that woman feared anything.

"Shame about your steed, Nathanial Wode," stated Feko, who had rode his own horse up to him.

Indeed it had been, as he gazed at the poor animal, part of the mercy killings that Jadenine had performed. Sadly enough, Nathan did not have the stomach to even end his own beast.

"I'd like to claim it better him than me, but that isn't really what I think."

"No, I'd suspect you the kind to loathe your ability to swordfight. But you do it to protect. Nothing dishonorable in that."

"Your gods give you any insight as to our next move?"

The Argon shrugged. "They seem to think that Ursan is where we need to be for now. We are supposed to find something there. Information it seems, but we can't do it alone. I am supposed to find someone else to help us find that information. I have no idea what they refer to. It's more encrypted than I can begin to explain."

Nathan watched as Tristan and Iero moved about and collected weapons and food supplies from the dead. His cousin removed the mercenaries' shoes and tried on multiple pairs, while Jadenine finished killing the last of the dying and made a direct path toward him once done.

"You might want to give me some space, Feko."

"I would wager that to be a wise estimation, Nathanial Wode."

As Feko Hawbry turned his horse and galloped away, the Ursan woman made haste toward him, though her demeanor appeared unaggressive.

"Let me explain," started Nathan as Jadenine approached.

"Not sure I get you, Wode." Her arms crossed, but her face was calm. "Do you kill me now?"

"I'd rather not," was his answer.

"You cut me loose, what assurance do you have that I don't relay all this information to the Guild?"

"I'd presume you would. And me killing you would not change their opinion on what happened out here. It would only delay it."

She hesitated, searching for words it seemed. "Tell me everything."

"What?"

Jadenine did not budge. Not that he thought she was capable of such. "I think I deserve to know. You dragged me out here blind, damn near got me killed, and now place me in a situation where I am likely a dead woman no matter what happens."

"The Guild would . . ."

"You know the Guild as well as I do. I return to them empty handed and retell this story, they would think either I am incompetent or a coward. In either case, they will likely kill me. Or worse, remove me from the Guild and make me unemployable in Prillian. What the fuck would I do then? Return to Ursan? I have no family there."

"You have no idea if the Guild would banish you."

"And neither do you." She bit down hard on the side of her cheek, her face all but displaying the mix of emotions. "I never much cared for the Guild, to be honest. But they took me in. They took me in when I was just some nothing teenage girl trying to survive. The Guild is shit, Wode, but at least they kept me from whoring myself in Prillian to live."

"What happened to you in Ursan?" he pressed.

"Fuck you, Wode. This isn't about me. Tell me everything. Who are you? You owe me that much."

"And what happens when I tell you everything? You feel better about yourself?"

"No, but I decide my next move, whether I risk death from the Guild or death from you. You brought me here blind. Could have told me something, warned me, clued me in. I know we hate each other, but we have been on enough missions from the Guild to have a bit more respect for one another. So instead of being honest, we get here and pick a fight with a bunch of miners. That easily could have been worse and you know it. So yes, you owe me an explanation. Remember that whole thing about trust? A blade in my back? Well talking about what the fuck is going on right now is the least you can do."

At this point, he could see little harm in being honest. In the end, the truth always surfaced.

"Not so certain the truth changes anything. You should take your leave while I still allow it."

Her eyebrow rose. "You ever heard of the Moon Divide? Met one of them once, or at least so he said. I was pretty young, but he had this saying, one that stuck with me. By the rope or the chain. Do you know what that means? They are dead men anyways, but at least they have the choice on how they go." Jadenine shrugged. "If you are going to kill me, fine. If you are going to cut me loose, fine. If you are going to let me decide on my own, that's fine too. But you owe me the explanation. Who are you really?"

"Somehow, you always could see through me." A pause and a hesitant moment later, he began with, "I am the bastard son of Lord Edmond Pratt."

--

It's not the rise that defines a country or the people within. It's the fall.

Dylinn Aylmer, House Lady of Fallneese

IX

The further north the Historian traveled during his month long trek, the more pleasant the trip had become. The summer months ahead would bring heat as it would with any of the countries of Amon, but the further north, the better. Nothing worse than a Donovinian summer. And by consequence, nothing worse than a Fallneesian winter.

But this was no vacation. In fact, Aldric could barely piece together his reasoning for this trip. Katlynn Pratt was a wanted fugitive, likely being hunted by the Guild at this point. Within Itopis, within the capital of Fallneese, the Historian had his suspicions that the true killer lay in waiting.

And why exactly had this mattered to him? Seven hundred years and he had never intervened in the daily affairs of Amon. There had been deception. There had been murder. And each time the knowledge came to Aldric by one means or another, it had been recorded away in his memory but never once used otherwise. So why now? Why did this disturb him to the point of traveling to central Fallneese? And for what? A suspicion?

To his credit, Erian had not questioned much. Aldric spoke the details of Jaa's death, and in doing so doubling those in the know of such. He silently listened, asked limited questions, and remained in thought. There had been many opportunities for his apprentice to leave his side, to return to their home and leave the Historian to his fate. And in all reality, Aldric would not have blamed him in such. But the young Kwyantin remained, understanding at the very least their purpose in Itopis.

Did Dylinn have Yelium killed? And if she did, why?

And exactly what am I going to do with this information?

Questions, no answers. A long month of walking and his mind remained riddled with the same inquiries, the same blockade of rational thought. His people had been mindful of the world, of Amon, but lived in solitude from it. What the Historian did now was against every spoken word, every written page of Kwyantin history and law. Aldric wanted this information for his own gain, his first error. And when the truth was found, he was not altogether certain what to do with that information, his second error.

I will do what is right.

But for his people or for Amon? As those two needs were not directly correlated.

Itopis stood in the open plains several miles away from the distant yet towering peaks of Zliin Mountains. A grand city and one of the many marvels of Amon, it stood as home to House names only, along with the families of any of those within the courts in Genethur. There was no class separation here. The workers came and went daily, commuting from the village just east of here, Molovand. The guards, cooks, maids, servants, and any other worker within Itopis lived in this eastern village, including many of the merchants as well. The capital remained a place for the upper echelon of peoples and there was no amount of modesty upon the building of such a city.

Stone and marble interchanged to form the streets, giving a unique look and feel, and the homes and buildings had been crafted against white stone, giving an almost porcelain glare against the sun. Fountains stood at every other corner, each more elaborate than the next as if they competed against one another in elegance. It was as if the gods themselves had come down and blessed the city with wealth and beauty.

Aldric had never been envious or intimidated by Itopis; rather mindful of the difference, coming from his own simple village. Many of these Fallneesians had known no other life but this wealth. It at times could prove difficult to overlook their arrogance. But the Historian did not find fault in such, lest none that he could not explain. To live a pampered life would certainly dull the mind as sure as strong wine.

His arms crossed, he gazed at Itopis from the entrance.

"Have the terms of our diplomatic immunity ever come into question before?" questioned his apprentice.

All Historians, all Kwyantin had been deemed diplomatically immune to any laws or customs in Amon. It was part of the arrangement that they had with the other races. It was what enabled them to move anywhere, see anyone. Who would say otherwise?

"To imprison us would be to start a war, Erian," he answered.

"A war? All of our people combined couldn't conquer a small village, much less the capital of Fallneese. Who would come for us if something were to happen? Better yet, who would even know of our disappearance?"

More questions, no answers.

"I suppose," Aldric started, "that we will not know those answers until they occur. I would not think differently of you should you decide to . . ."

"I only ask," interrupted Erian, quick to dissolve any doubt in his voice. "It was only a question."

The Historian nodded slowly. *They are good questions, nevertheless.* "Very well. Let us move to the capital building."

--

The guards at the front entrance to the Aylmer estate gazed heavily, cautiously at the two giant men. It may have been the first time they witnessed a Kwyantin, so caution was certainly understandable. But for the extended delay in their admittance, that bordered on the line of offensive.

"I appreciate your patience in this," noted one of the guards.

"Patience?" Aldric chuckled. "Live as long as I have and you will understand patience. Lives come and go as would days and nights. This is not an issue of patience, good sir. I am curious why you must suddenly seek permission to allow admittance of the Historian of Amon?"

The guard shrugged. "Historian or not, I was given specific instructions to not allow entrance to anyone. You *are* someone, are you not? So I cannot allow you entrance. I have, however, asked for permission, as you so clearly witnessed. The fact that it has taken so long tells me that Lady Aylmer is still deciding."

"You are certain that the courier understood the message?"

"The Historian is here to see you," repeated the guard, spitting to the earth after saying such. "Difficult to fuck that up, pardon me for saying."

What gives you pause, Dylinn?

Aldric paced back and away from the guards, back to where his apprentice stood patiently. He locked his hands on opposing arms, of the few bits of flesh exposed from his hooded robe.

"Do you think she knows why we are here?" Erian inquired.

Aldric shook his head. "I doubt such. I am not so certain myself."

His apprentice seemed to smile some. "You believe Dylinn to be guilty of assassinating her son. Or the person everyone believed to be her son that is."

"And yet . . . it is against everything our people have preached to us, against the meaning of the Historian."

"I have been meaning to ask you that."

A single eyebrow rose. "Ask what?"

"What is the meaning of the Historian? You have spoken before of love. You said that what we do is for the love of our people."

Aldric nodded in agreement. "It is. Our love is why we do this."

"Take our entire lives and devote it to the comings and goings of the people that live on our world?"

He knew this man, Aldric realized. It was the same man that once stood before Jaa the Knowledgeable and ignored his preaching. And yet he could not say that he was any wiser then than now.

"We share this world with the other races. Our job, before this moment, was to record the histories into our own account. In doing so we hope to educate Kwyantin of the future, not the present."

"So we are together, yet separate from the other races of Amon?" his young apprentice questioned further.

"I would say we consider ourselves part of the whole," was his answer.

"Then could you not say that what you do now is for the same love? What good will it do to watch idly as Amon falls into ruin? How will we have honored our people when war spills onto our village and we did nothing to prevent it due to our overwhelming sense of duty? There is no love in that decision, Aldric. None, at least, that I can gather."

It was the same man. A younger version of himself. It was likely the most Erian had ever uttered in a continual sitting. And it held a due amount of weight.

"If we are not banished from our people, Erian, you will make a much finer Historian than this land deserves."

"Historian!" called out the guard by the gates. Aldric spun about swiftly to face him. "Dylinn will see you now."

--

Seven hundred years was a long life by most accounts. Certainly it was nothing to the average Kwyantin, but the average Kwyantin knew nothing of the world outside their village. They could live a millennium and still find themselves surprised at the most mundane thing. But to walk amongst the other four races, to see them, hear them, live with them, walk with them, watch them build and destroy, love and hate, live and die . . . there could be little to surprise the Historian.

Yet to walk into the main chambers of the Aylmer estate, to find Dylinn wearing little more than an open-ended robe, exposed to the dozens of men and women that lay scattered onto her floor, many naked or close to being such, some even sexually engaged with at least one other partner . . . Aldric could say with all honesty, he was quite perplexed.

There was an odd sense of freedom within the chambers, with everyone socializing, drinking heavy amounts of wine and ale, laughing and gossiping, some even ignoring the people having sex only a few feet from their very presence, others watching intently while they touched themselves. It was a strange party of sorts, one that made Aldric instantly uncomfortable upon his entrance. Yet the people did not seem to notice nor care about the two Kwyantin men that entered into their foray. Dylinn sat mostly naked onto a large throne, her eyes intent on the Historian. A woman sat by her side, naked and silent, a nervous servant girl in all likelihood. As the two of them made their way around the exterior of the room carefully, avoiding the partygoers and sexual encounters alike, Dylinn pointed to an eastern door. She grabbed her servant girl by the hair, kissed her passionately while grabbing the girl's small breasts, then shoved her forward into the rest of party where some people instantly began to grope her. The House lady strode across, tying her robes together, casually covering herself as she moved across, heading toward the same eastern door she had pointed out.

Aldric arrived first, his apprentice closely behind, opening the door and entering a side room, a den as it appeared. An elaborate bar along with many chairs and couches adorned the room as well as several card tables and dart boards. The door closed solid behind her and soon only the three of them stood alone in this new room, the sounds of the party now only a soft muffle through the walls.

"Do you play cards, Historian?" she questioned, not waiting for an answer as she strode across to the bar, pouring herself a glass of wine. "Have you heard of the game called chained? It is a complicated game played by the Moon Divide. First Pratt told me that should I meet them, to never enter into this game regardless of how tempting and easy they made the game appear. Even knowing that I would never play, he still felt the need to explain the rules. Waste of breath. I am damn sure convinced that no one save the Divide could understand or win such a game. I'm not even sure *they* understand the game. What I do know is that there's a tremendous amount of coin to be won should anyone actually figure out the rules and win the damn thing. Would you like a drink?"

Aldric smiled, but waved his hand against the drink. Dylinn shrugged and took a long sip from her glass. "I have only met one Divide, Lady Aylmer," he stated calmly. "His name was Deso. It was the eve before the crowning."

"Ah, yes. Afeon removing the world's greatest killers from his sight. Convinced the First it was a good idea. It will be an interesting thing indeed when the Divide arrives at the shore of a disbanded army. My husband's son was something else, was he not?"

Another strong sip later, and she reached over and topped off her glass again. "So I presume," she continued, "that you know that First Pratt and I were fucking. And I might guess that what you witnessed here must take you by surprise."

"There seems to be a sexual freedom in the next room for certain," Aldric noted. "A bit of a shock, yes Lady Aylmer."

"My secret meetings with First Pratt was all that I ever got for many years, Historian. Kwyantin are different people. You speak greatly of love and other emotions, but for us, for mortality below you, we are primal in a way. First Pratt was an amazing lover. But our visits were not as frequent as I wanted. Problem with affairs is that in order to maintain secrecy, you also have to keep the visits casual and infrequent. Meanwhile, my late husband couldn't even get his cock up to do much of anything. Chur'ash was far more important than making love to his wife."

"Lady Aylmer, I am sorry to hear . . ."

"Yes, I am going a bit over the top since my return to Itopis, I agree. But I have gone through sixteen, seventeen years of sexual frustration. I am a free woman now, Historian. I can do whatever I please, whoever I please."

"I do not argue with you, Lady Aylmer. Only that it is quite a surprise."

"Life is full of surprises," was her answer. "Speaking of which, Historian, why are you here? I mean no offense, as you may come and go as you please. But why here? Why Itopis at a time like this? Shouldn't you be in Corovium, to stay with the council as they battle at who should claim the throne?"

"Perhaps," admitted Aldric. "But I do not feel as if I am done asking questions of you. Many new ones have surfaced."

"Have they now?" she responded, a half smile creeping across her face. Her lips moved slowly across the tip of the wine glass. "And you've crossed half of Fallneese just to ask these questions. Well then . . . ask what you must."

"Tell me of your affair. How long was it going on?"

"From the beginning," Dylinn admitted. "I knew how close the First and Yelium were. When I was holed up and alone for those months with the whore, he came to spend a few days in the beginning, then spend the final month entire. Between those visits, I knew how I could pay Yelium back for impregnating this whore. I would seduce his only friend, his trusted council. It was a simple thing. It was just sex after all, and I know that I look good. I do not find it arrogant to admit to your own looks. Many still find me attractive even now, Historian. Imagine me sixteen years ago."

Another sip of her wine and a pause later as she leaned against the bar, her robe barely concealing her breasts, her aptly defined legs crossed as the only thing preventing sight from anything below the naval. Dylinn was a stunning Fallneesian woman, even though Aldric stood mostly numb to her beauty. He was Kwyantin, different from the other races of Amon, but a mortal man as the same.

"Needless to say seducing him was easy. Letting him go, ultimately that was what I found impossible. Perhaps it was his power. Maybe it was just the attention. Maybe just the feel of a real man inside me. I don't know."

"So you fell in love with him?" questioned Aldric.

"Not right away, but certainly there was . . . *is* something about First Pratt that is difficult to explain. He always held himself tall and strong above any other I knew in Genethur. Something about Donovinian men, Historian. Confidence without arrogance. Two things difficult to separate. Some cannot do such."

"I presume you refer to Ursan men."

"Ghost faced pigs, if you ask me," blurted Dylinn, taking a longer sip from her glass. "Sorry for that. I suppose that was a bit racially insensitive."

"I would gather you can say whatever you like in your own home, Lady Aylmer."

"I suppose so." Another soft sip of her wine later and she continued. "My plan to ruin my husband, and perhaps the First in the process, obviously never happened. Our single sexual encounter quickly found a sequel. Twice turned into many times, and when we returned to the capital, I found myself secretly wishing that he would show nightly." Lady Aylmer laughed softly and pathetically, if only to her own thoughts, topping her wine again. "A sixteen year affair. Can you imagine, Historian? I suppose that does not sound like such a long time when you have lived as long as you. For the rest of us, it can feel like a lifetime."

"What did you expect would happen? From the affair, I mean."

"I expected nothing," she claimed firmly. "First Pratt was devoted to Jessica. She mothered his kids. An asshole enough to cheat on her, but not an asshole enough to leave her. I knew that well into our meetings in the capital that he would stay by her side and one day return to Astrona with her. I held no notions that it would be different. Perhaps . . . well the woman in me likely only dreamed."

"Of what?" continued Aldric.

"A life with him. One away from the politics, away from the capital, away from everything." Her glass lowered to the bar counter, her head turned away from them for the moment. "Then one day you wake up, a middle-aged woman without children, without purpose. All that was once good in you stripped away, until you have nothing left but hate."

Again she snickered a bit sadly. "Do you know how old I was when my family sold me to Yelium?"

"Thirteen," answered Aldric.

Dylinn turned, the half-smile that had once adorned her face all but vanished now. "I forget who you are sometimes, I suppose. Of course you know. You know everything about me, at least what was made public. Yes, thirteen, eldest daughter of a wealthy merchant, sold to make more money for the rest of my family and to raise the status of his House name. I never forgave my father. I was still a child, *his* child. Yelium used to rape the shit out of me. My father must have known what would happen. I was a thirteen-year-old girl, Historian! Thirteen! Tell me what child deserves that?"

"You were innocent," the Historian offered up, but felt foolish in doing so.

"This is Fallneese. What my father did was within his right. And what Yelium did was within his as well. He was almost thirty years old at the time, marrying a child, approaching his time to take the throne."

Her hands shook some as she reached again for the wine and took a wide mouthed gulp. Quiet took the room for a few moments while her mind must have wandered to places that Aldric dared not travel. Dylinn had a difficult, if not all too familiar life in Amon. Not all races had been such toward children, namely in Argonus, but even in Donovini similar things could be found. Edmond Pratt himself married a girl far too young at the time, but such was life. Right or wrong, fair or otherwise, these things occurred, only far too frequently in Fallneese.

Lady Aylmer turned again to the Historian, the smile on her face returning. "Why are you here, Historian? I doubt you made this trip to uncover the mystery of my affair or the difficulty of my upbringing. You came here for a reason. Might I ask you a question? What happened to the letter I gave you? Did you deliver it as I asked?"

A lie, he knew, would have been better.

"I did not."

"If you didn't deliver it . . . did you by chance read it?"

For the first time in many years, he felt apprehension. He should not have felt worry or concern. There were laws in place for Kwyantin. But he was far removed from his role and he was no longer convinced on what Dylinn was capable of.

"I read your letter," he reluctantly admitted.

Dylinn reached behind her and grabbed her half full glass and emptied the contents. "So you did not, of course, travel all this way on foot to apologize to me. That would have been more acceptable. Instead you travel all this way to accuse me of killing the king."

"I would not accuse you," swiftly corrected the Historian. "I would but ask you of it."

"And are you so certain that this inquisition is but a search for knowledge, not personal gain?" she asked sharply. "Your impartial judgment seems less so than it has in the past. It is a bold move for you to travel here to Itopis, enter my home, accuse me of treason. Bold, Historian. Perhaps too much so."

A side door opened, one that he had not spotted before, and from within several guards entered, armor clad and swords at their hips. This had been most unexpected and his heart raced in fear. He had mistakenly misunderstood her own anguish, her own desperation.

She moved closer as her half a dozen guards enclosed around Aldric and Erian. Dylinn took her precious time, closing the gap between them. "So concerned you are with the nature of my involvement in the death of the young Yelium. What would you do with such knowledge?"

He shook his head. "I had yet to decide. Ultimately, whatever would be best for Amon."

"I know little of your people, but I do know of the nature of the Historian. You are to be impartial to the world around, record but never influence. Am I right?"

"You are."

"And what happens when you are no longer such? What happens when you look to influence this world with the knowledge locked away inside your mind?"

"I would return to my people and admit my failure, to which I would be replaced immediately."

She now stood before him, her head tilted upward to stare into his eyes. "You have no idea how deep my treachery goes," Dylinn Aylmer whispered. "And it is far from over. In fact, I believe it has just begun."

I pity you, Dylinn. I always have. But I once thought you helpless. I was wrong.

"Did you kill the king?" the Historian questioned directly.

Dylinn's eyes did not waiver. "Which one?"

I am a fool. How gravely I have misjudged you.

Taking a step back, she looked to her guards. "Take the Historian and his apprentice below."

"Lady Aylmer," pleaded the Historian. "You realize that the law states . . ."

"You broke your own laws when you came here, Historian. And now where do we stand? I let you leave and accuse *me* of assassination? What would you have me do?"

What did I hope to accomplish here? All these years I honor my people, did my duty as instructed, and then the moment I falter . . .

Dylinn's eyes, in retrospect, refused to yield. "*Take . . . them . . . below.*"

--

And by below, she meant below. While there was in fact a dungeon on the underground floor of her estate, they moved past that, further downward, into the darkness of a catacomb. All of the standard stereotypes found their place here as one guard led the way with a lit torch, the others pressed the two Kwyantin down the passageway from behind. Cobwebs lined the corridor, a distant scurrying of rodents dashing between holes in the walls could be heard, and the pungent smell of mold filled the air. It was stuffy, narrow, and most of all, frightening.

It was a new emotion for Aldric. Fear. He had understood it, of course, but never found the situation to truly feel it. Exhilarating, save for the fact that he likely marched to his death. And yet for the first time since watching Jaa wash away into the Terrandonan Sea, the Historian felt alive. In the end, what was life without emotion?

Honor, respect, love of his culture and his people. How much he had missed. *Time lost. My whole life a waste. Why did I listen to the elders? Why did I so readily accept the role of Historian without challenging it? Why didn't I listen to the pleas of Jaa?*

At the end of the long, stone hallway they reached a heavy wooden door, to which the lead guard opened with a key. The door looked quite thick and creaked heavily as it swung open, the stale air from within somehow overpowered the mold and fungus smell from the hallway. The guard entered and began to circle the new room, lighting torches around the perimeter. As torch fire began to illuminate the room, Aldric realized that his was no cell, no torture chamber of any kind.

He stood inside a vast library.

Columns of bookcases lined parallel to one another, each with multiple shelves filled complete with book upon book. Tables and chairs littered the area as well as several small sleeping cots, along with a few desks that looked quite worn. This room had the feel of stern use, as if many spent lifetimes here in the pursuit of some unknown knowledge.

After the guard had lit most of the room, the other guards nervously standing by the only entry or exit from this extensive new room, he moved over and placed several empty torches on a table with a container likely filled with pitch and flint.

"I wouldn't get crazy with that," the guard announced, motioning to the dozens of shelves of books. "They are quite old, and you wouldn't want to catch your own ass on fire."

"How long are we to spend down here?" Aldric inquired.

"Until Lady Aylmer tells you otherwise."

A fair enough answer, and he was not so certain what other answer he expected.

The guard strode back to the large wooden door and quickly shut it, the loud click all but signifying that the two Kwyantin were now imprisoned. The real question, of course, was why here?

"I suppose we could try to burn the door down," noted Erian.

"Did you see how thick that door was?" Aldric replied. "We would likely die from the smoke inhalation before we would burn that thing down."

"Just trying to think of ways . . ."

The apprentice's words trailed off all the same as himself, moving over to one of the book shelves and examining one of the hundreds of books on display.

"I am sorry," admitted Aldric. "For everything."

"The decision to lock us in this room was not yours," called back the apprentice. "There is little need for apology."

"Regardless, I do not believe I thought my course of action to conclusion."

"Well, have you ever?" queried Erian. "By that I mean, when have you ever made a decision in your pursuit of recording all of current history? You simply move as you feel fit, follow where the largest events occur. Where is there a need to think through an action?"

"When I leave the well-traveled path, my apprentice," answered Aldric. "I should have understood that I bordered against all of the teachings of my past, all to which we hold true to our people. What did I think would happen?" He shrugged. "I wonder if Jaa knew something like this could happen."

"If he did, perhaps he knew we would end up here."

"For what purpose, I wonder."

"Perhaps," announced Erian, "to find out more about his claims of the Realms. These are not your standard books, or so it would seem."

The Historian moved over to where his apprentice stood and examined one of the shelves. Certainly by title, there appeared to be volume after volume of research books, each mentioning something with the Realms. He pulled one out at random and thumbed through the pages. These were journal entries into the studies of the Realms, as well as . . . experiments.

"What is this place?" Aldric mumbled.

Erian shrugged beside him. "Maybe we should just start reading some?"

The Historian found some measure of a smile. "I suppose we have time."

--

A fumbling of keys, a click, and a loud creaking door later and Dylinn Aylmer stood at the doorway, several guards behind her. It had been more than a few hours since both the Kwyantin had been imprisoned in the library, and the House lady now stood fully dressed before them, her demeanor solemn.

"When I first arrived here as a girl, Yelium had these catacombs sealed," she began, as if nothing stood out of the ordinary, as if she did not have two Kwyantin illegally imprisoned in her underground library. "He told me what his father had told him, that whatever occurred within these catacombs had happened long before his becoming of House lord."

Both Aldric and Erian had been seated at one of the many tables and before the interruption from the House lady, scanning through books as they awaited their fate. He had not read much yet, but plenty had been revealed in his readings thus far. Treachery occurred within this estate.

Several steps forward and as her guards started to follow, she raised a hand. "Stay there. I will be just a few minutes with the Historian."

"But Lady Aylmer . . ." started one of the guards, but could not complete.

"The Kwyantin are many things. I do not believe assault on a defenseless woman would be one of their traits. I will be fine."

And how defenseless are you really, I wonder.

Reluctantly the guards remained by the entrance while Dylinn continued toward them. "I spent far too much time avoiding my husband during my early years to give much thought to this dungeon. Avoiding rape was a more pressing issue. Some nights you win. Other nights . . . well not as lucky. Though many would argue that a husband cannot rape his wife, as keeping her husband sexually pleased is a duty and privilege. But that is neither here nor there, I suppose. In my early twenties, right as we were about to make the transition to Genethur for the crowning of my husband, something reminded me of this place.

"I had men excavate these catacombs, but they remained off limits to anyone once the paths were cleared. It was no easy task, from my understanding, and this was done without my husband's knowledge. Of course much more than just excavation was done without my husband's knowledge, as you now understand better than most. Thus the men chosen for the task were trustworthy and few in number, and patience became a virtue. During one of my trips back home years later, this very room had been uncovered. I was the first person to enter and found what you now examine."

"Your House has broken the only rule," blatantly stated Aldric.

"Yelium's House, not mine," she swiftly corrected. "And what do you know of the only rule?"

"Never cross over," he replied.

"And who made this rule?"

"Likely someone that understood the dangers the Realms possess."

"Or someone that wanted to horde the power for their own." Dylinn now stood before them, her arms crossed at her chest. "Whoever made the rule must have either crossed over themselves or known the dangers first hand. Touch, borrow, but never cross over. The only rule."

"And this House ignored the rule."

"You know nothing of the Realms, Historian," she breathed more than spoke. "The power they demand." Her pause gave light to the weakness behind her resolve. Her strength and determination, even when acted upon, could not hide the frailty behind her mask. "I have lived such a life that the end may not justify the means."

The opportunity for truth seemed to be at hand.

"Are you responsible for the death of your husband's son, House lord of Fallneese, king of Amon?"

A long moment later, and a single nod was her response.

"And what of your husband?"

"Many long months of poison that ate away at his insides," she whispered. "Everyone knew of his addiction to Chur'ash. Why would anyone think his death was caused by anything other than that?"

A perfect crime, if such a thing exists.

"It does not end there, Historian," Dylinn readily claimed. "Many years before, I sent the Moon Divide out to kill my father . . . before my very eyes, so that I may lay witness to it."

Aldric could hardly believe that this was the same woman who appeared beaten and distraught within Genethur. The same woman, certainly, with the same weaknesses, but a rage unbeknownst to those in her path.

"For what was this all for?" he managed to question through the shock of her admittance. "Revenge? Is it something so trivial as that? Katlynn Pratt is on the run now because of your decision."

"Regrettable."

"We are speaking of the niece of First Pratt, one you hold so dear."

"Regrettable," she repeated with more authority. "But unavoidable. Someone must be blamed. She was the obvious choice."

"And what of your House? By having the king killed, you forfeited the throne."

"It is due time for a change."

"But Fallneese . . ."

"All that I do, I do for Fallneese." Dylinn turned away, her back facing the Historian. "It's not the rise that defines a country or the people within. It's the fall. And Amon shall fall, Historian. I shall watch it crumble beneath me. And with it, Fallneese shall rise." A short pause, then she made her way to the door. "Keep reading, Historian. Find more that you can uncover about this House, about the Realms and those that can cross over. Your fate may depend on your use."

A loud creaking door, a fumbling of keys, and a click later, and Aldric and Erian were alone in the sparsely lit library once more.

--

Dreams are for fools. I could spend much of my time crying over my upbringing, of my arranged marriage, of how different life could be. What exactly is the point of that?

No one respects frailty.

-- Christina Rowe, House Lady of Argonus

X

"The courts have ruled against you and your council, First Pratt."

The voice within Philip's chambers belonged to Gillar, a short, Fallneesian fuck, pompous and boisterous beyond his measure. Both heavyset and balding, the middle-aged man stood as head of the courts in Genethur. Which made him about as worthless as First Pratt had felt in more recent times. In fact, every successive week increased the crippling, crushing feeling of his inadequacies.

"So are we even allowed to speak our case, Gillar?" Philip inquired.

"Honestly, First Pratt, what is there to speak?"

Afeon, who sat across from his desk, did not even bother to turn and face the Fallneesian. "Perhaps that our late king had yet been crowned before his order."

"That did little to stop the treasury from ceasing funds to the Guild," Gillar noted. "Nor did it keep word from reaching your troops on the eastern shore. Speaking of which, have you heard from General Shonnen yet? Has there been a reply?"

"Not a one," answered Philip. *The most frightening response . . . silence.* "Still, you should have given us an opportunity to speak to the courts before making your decision."

Gillar huffed. "Had we thought that any input would sway a vote, we would have. You owe the Guild money, councilors. It can be no simpler decision. Based on Orpay's figures, you owe them one million, one hundred and seventy-three thousand gold coins for services unpaid to be distributed equally amongst the merchants."

"And how much of that is promised back to you, Gillar?" Afeon blatantly accused.

But the court head simply widened his smile. "The Second is far too untrusting of the courts. We are no more bendable in our resolve than you are, I would gather."

To this, the Ursan turned his head about toward Gillar. "I am quite bendable when the occasion presents itself."

"Let us hope for otherwise then."

"Where would you like me to extract this money?" Pratt stammered between the squabbling men. "We are not exactly in the position to simply grab the money from the treasury and hand it to Orpay."

"Take it from your own personal account for all I give a shit," responded the Fallneesian. "I deliver the ruling, not the action. You are the First and ruler for the time being. I'd gather you can find a way to come up with the funds. While you cannot take the money yourself, as there is no king, you can simply put in a request to the courts. I am certain that we may look at pushing that through."

"You make decisions without thought of repercussion," muttered the Second.

Ignoring Afeon, Philip shook his head toward the short, stubby man. "Little good arguing would do me, I suppose. If the courts have decided, we will find the money. In the meantime, tell Orpay to hold his fucking breath for it. I have a pile of paperwork on this side of my desk comprising of work that I will get to before I die. His request goes on the bottom of that pile."

"Another reason I am here," Gillar announced. "The paperwork has arrived at our doorstep, to legalize the union of House Rowe and Pratt. I presume you have looked over this paperwork, yes?"

"I have not."

That did not seem to be the answer he was looking for, as he raised an eyebrow to the admittance. "Well . . . it is perhaps in your best interest to look it over. I do not believe that any decision will be made until early next week. But to be honest, I see little reason for the rejection of the request. There is, however, time to remove the paperwork from our desks, I am sure."

"And why would I do such?"

"Well . . . I only find it odd that you would relinquish your hold to your own country. Certainly we have not had the greatest of relationships in the past . . ."

Wanting to stab you in the face with my quill is not great?

". . . I still find that the Pratts have done an exceptional job in Donovini. It is not the easiest of countries to run, we all know. The frequent droughts, the starving families . . ."

"The point, Gillar."

"The *point,* First Pratt, is that many respect your brother's rule. Many respect yours as well. The same cannot be made for Christina."

"And where would your vote lie, I wonder?" Afeon commented casually. "Should the vote end in the courts, that is. Would you vote for House Pratt? Or would the vote be swayed by coin?"

Gillar did not flinch from the inquiry. "It is an honest question, Second. The problem lies in the fact that everyone has their own agenda. The Pratts would be the honest choice, the Brocusks the rightful one . . . and yet here we stand, before two councilors representing each House. Yet we are bound to kneel before Rowe."

"You did not answer his question," pestered Philip.

And the court head shrugged. "It is not always coin that can influence a vote. Most of the time it's politics alone. We would not vote for your House, First Pratt, while your niece is at large."

"In which case your sentiments for my family are appreciated, but about as useless as a torch in Shadow."

"A torch in Shadow. Quite clever First. But I would gather that it could prove useful to a man that knows how to wield it." Gillar waved a single hand to them. "First. Second."

As he departed, the door closing behind him, Afeon returned his gaze to Philip. "At times I wonder what life would be like without the courts. Just a single ruler over all of Amon."

"You gave your word, Afeon," the First almost growled.

"And I am a man of that word," he affirmed. "I only speak aloud what is on my mind. And now it shifts to the paperwork I better start drafting to request that gold from the treasury."

"You do that," said Philip, standing from his table, "and I will take a stroll to the courts."

"For what purpose?" the Second queried.

"It's time to end this madness. We need to reinstate our men on the coast. We need to mend our relationship with the Guild. Mainly, we need to get this capital back in order."

"You were always good at that, First Pratt," claimed Afeon with a smile. "Cleaning up messes."

"Not of my favorite duties."

"No, I'd gather not. Tell me, First Pratt, now that it makes little difference. Was the boy the son of Dylinn or not?"

"He is buried with his father and his ancestors as a once king of Amon. What he was changes very little as to what he is now."

"Dead?"

"And cold."

The Second stood along with him, straightening his tunic. "I hope that your nephew is ready for the toll of power. It can erode more steadily than the river on the earthen soil."

"He is stronger than me," the First admitted. "I have faith in him."

"Well . . . at least you have faith in something," mumbled the Second.

--

In the end, it was quite humorous. He could not figure out why it was so funny, but he laughed nonetheless. It stood the only way to get Rayden through the day to day. His sister still missing, his brother fucking his fiancé, his father signing away his country . . . there was little to smile about. And yet he stood outside the balcony, the morning well underway, and had a smirk upon his face.

Rayden had asked for very little in life and taken even less. He trained with the sword, he wooed a lady or two in his time, but never did he ask for his name to hold the proper weight it deserved. Never had he taken what was born to him for granted. He had mistakenly presumed that all men were like him, that all men had a sense of honor and respect. And where others had proven his thoughts inaccurate, at least his family could not be corrupted. The Pratts were honorable. The Pratts stood taller than any other House name in Donovini, in all of Amon.

Except for his Uncle Edmond, who abandoned a woman who birthed his bastard child. And his Uncle Philip, who conspired with the Moon Divide. And his father, who now only stood the approval of the courts to signing away his country to Argonus. Luther was an ass, Nathanial a glorified killer, and Katlynn wanted for murder. And of course his brother a backstabber, likely in more ways than one.

And so he smiled. *So highly thought of, without merit.*

He heard his brother stir about within their chambers inside. After some mumbling about too much wine while relieving himself, Jerryn stumbled about to the balcony. "Why are you still here?" he began, wiping the sleep from his eyes. "Shouldn't you be in another meeting about your marriage?"

"No meeting today," Rayden answered. "We await the approval of the courts."

"I suppose you should be excited." The younger stared blankly at him. "You seem anything but."

"Difficult to be excited about marrying someone who does not love you."

"She may yet grow to love you," Jerryn encouraged, but his words carried no weight. "I would kill to be in your position."

I bet you would, you dishonest bastard.

"Have you spoken to her recently?" he continued.

Rayden shook his head. "About a week ago, when she asked to meet and start planning the wedding."

His brother did not seem comfortable with the thought. There had been plenty of time for confession since the start of these talks, from either of them. Instead Rayden avoided them both at any given moment. Rage turned into sorrow, sorrow back into anger, and now he simply felt empty and lost. And betrayal. Plenty of that.

"Well that's a good thing I suppose," responded the younger.

"Without heart, I see no need to plan a marriage. We should simply sign documents. What need is there to plan anything. I told her . . . the last thing I said to her was that nothing is guaranteed. I believe that, Jerryn. I truly do."

"Well . . . I suppose at this point there is little changing . . ."

"How long have you been fucking Allura Rowe?"

And there it was. The moment the words left his mouth, rage returned. And only shock and disbelief stood in reflection upon his brother's face.

"What are you talking about? I mean . . . Rayden . . . where did that come from? I have done nothing of the sort!"

"And so here, with only the two of us alone, you would still lie to me in my face. I will ask you once more, and I certainly hope this time you will answer honestly. *How long . . . have you . . . been fucking her?"*

Confusion in Jerryn's face now switched to fear. He had never seen Rayden like this. Rightfully so, as neither had Rayden.

"Many months ago, when the drought started and we requested aid from Argonus. We met there. That was our first time."

"But far from the last time."

"Yes," Jerryn admitted, his tone low and ashamed. "It started harmless, I swear. Just another girl I could pull, just a harmless House girl from Argonus. But . . ."

"It turned into more than that."

"It did. We returned from that trip, and she wrote. Often. I wrote back. We found any excuse to meet. She went as far as to ask her mother about me even."

"Christina knows?" stammered Rayden.

"Yes. She denied our . . . union. My name is right, but my status in this House was not."

"But mine was. So of course that was the past. Now that you know that I am about to marry her, that the courts are looking to approve our union, certainly now you have stopped fucking her. Right?"

There was little need for his brother to answer.

Rayden reached over and grasped his brother's neck. *"Right?"*

"No!" he choked in response. His hands wrapped around Rayden's wrists, attempting to pull them off, but lacked the strength. Rayden, meanwhile, tightened his grip. "I . . . care . . . for her."

He released him with a shove back into the rails of the balcony. "You once cared for your family and your country as well, two things that you have known far longer than this bitch. You piss on those that have loved you back in earnest. You piss on me, brother. Earth and Flame . . . Earth and Flame . . ."

"Rayden . . ."

But he already moved, making his way back into the bedroom. He did not want to be here any longer. The politics, the betrayal, everything that took place here in Corovium, in this cursed place.

"Rayden. I'm sorry. I don't know what to do. I didn't know how to even tell you."

The words were spoken, but Rayden barely heard them. All he could think about was leaving. No, running.

"Please, Rayden. Forgive me. It will stop. It will all stop now."

And so his door opened, his brother called after him, and he moved. One foot in front of the next, without destination, without thought.

Where to?

Away.

--

Patience was a virtue, or so Allura had heard before, and she had considered herself to have had an enormous amount of it. But the cup had filled with Rayden's childish behavior over her confession of emotion. No, she would not love him. That was held for his brother, to which she knew would be best to keep from him. But she *would* marry him, and she *would* bare his children. Was that not good enough?

He had skipped the last two meetings of their families, and while Nicolas made all the excuses he could for his son's absence, she knew better. The pouting, the frustration . . . what did he expect? Was she to swoon over him the moment the talk of marriage began? Her being unwed was of her mother's doing. Certainly it was not from lack of offers. Allura did not think she could stop the Twin Moons from parting with her beauty alone, but well above average she did give herself. Offers came, offers went. Some interesting, others quite thankfully removed from the table. Single and available Allura remained until the right situation, the correct pieces stood before her mother.

And in a bizarre, puzzling perfect storm, that happened with the death of a king.

And Shadow take her, she was not about to let Rayden ruin her chance to take the throne as queen of Amon because of his infant notion that marriage was about love. It might have been in the world outside of this capital, outside of their respective Houses, but not within the world they lived. Marriage stood about positioning and not in the fun way. It was about power. They should be thankful that each was at least pleasant to look at. Rayden may not have been Jerryn, but still an attractive man nonetheless. In fact, the Pratts were well bred, for whatever that was worth. All were attractive, if not a bit rugged, save for maybe Luther.

She stormed through the capital, heading directly toward the Pratt's quarters in the castle. It was time to discuss their marriage, time to discuss their lives. Strange, though, as all she could think about during her walk was Jerryn.

If the gods were real, why would they put me in this situation to begin with? My love is so close . . .

An impossible situation. She loved everything about Jerryn. His touch was soothing, his words powerful. She let him believe what he wanted when they first met in Argonus. Just another girl in all likelihood. But Jerryn was gorgeous, to the point that even knowing his words were just words, that all he wanted was to fuck her, she allowed it. In fact, she pursued it. To this day, Allura could not figure out why she allowed herself to be used. Maybe she had enough confidence in herself to know that Jerryn would not be able to walk away satisfied with just once. He would have to see her again.

When she wrote him, she did so with a trusted courier and left the letters unaddressed for obvious reasons. There stood little reason for their families to know of their connection. There was no knowing if he would even write her back, if she was simply another notch against his belt. But somehow she knew otherwise. He wrote her. Of course he did, with a letter far lengthier than even hers.

They met once in what was meant to be a diplomatic meeting between Jerryn and an assistant of Christina in Obline, a small city on the eastern border of Donovini. A small matter, one that did not require either Nicolas or Rayden to attend. Of course, she was not required to attend either, but convinced her mother that her presence was necessary. Allura had never had as much sex in as many different ways as she had that week.

He was damn good and he knew it. But she must have had something to offer all the same, as he could not stop wishing their next meeting. And that became their relationship. Waiting. One meeting to the next, one letter to the next. Always waiting.

She strode up a flight of stairs with haste as she moved with purpose. Fully expecting to catch him off guard by her appearance, she stood rather disappointed in her near shock at seeing Rayden round a corner and made his way toward her.

"Rayden . . . I . . ."

She could not even get her sentence in before he stormed passed her, moving back toward the stairs.

"Rayden!" she called out forcefully.

To his credit, her tone got the point across. He stopped, but did not turn to face her at first.

"I spoke with Jerryn," he spoke through his teeth.

And what more was there to say?

She could claim a million different foolish things. Easily she could deny it all or simply stand defensive. Allura instead remained silent. Not the greatest defense or explanation, but she had no idea what to say.

Rayden turned slowly to face her, his face no longer the sad defeatist. Now only anger stood in its place. "When exactly do you think is a good time to stop fucking my brother, Allura? Perhaps our wedding day? Or maybe the days following?"

"I told you my heart belongs to another."

"But not my *fucking* brother!" screamed Rayden, loud enough that certainly anyone within Amon could have heard him. "I think you left that little detail out!"

"Calm yourself, Rayden. I did not tell you because this would be your reaction. I met him before our talks of marriage you understand."

"And our marriage talks did not stop your meetings with him, now did it?" Again, she said nothing. "Did it?"

"No!" she hammered back. "But it should have. It's my fault, one that shall never occur again."

His eyes narrowed toward her. "You would end this foolishness? You would walk to Jerryn and tell him that it ends now?"

She hesitated. "Yes," she said, but uncertain if she believed.

Rayden shrugged. "I never wanted to be king. I never wanted any of this. In fact, you know what? I am not sure I ever knew what I wanted for myself. Sure, I knew I would take over my House at some point. But it was not something I looked forward to. It wasn't until I saw you for the first time that I finally found something that I wanted."

"Something you are getting," she assured.

"Earth and Flame, Allura. Like this is the way I wanted things. Our marriage a *union?* I don't want a union. I want a wife."

"You would have a wife."

"I'd have a fucking partner," laughed the Pratt, an awkward one at that.

"You laugh at us? You laugh at our marriage?" She felt her face heat up at his discovery of humor in any of this.

"No, I laugh at the thought you think this would work," he responded.

"Work? Are you that much an idiot? We have an opportunity to control Amon. You and me, together! We can change and make a difference and . . ."

"Now who's the idiot?" Rayden turned back and made his way to the stairs. "You want to see how things work? Look to my uncle, look at the frustration on his brow. See how much change he has made in his tenure. You live in a dream, Allura Rowe, the same dream where I marry for love and devils live across the Terrandonan Sea. Dreams. And maybe I'm ready to wake up."

And before she could stop him, Rayden took the stairs down, leaving Allura alone in the hallway, wondering exactly what in Shadow he meant by that.

--

Philip swore that if he found the descendant of the architect of the fucking stairs to the courthouse, he would have them killed for pure spite. Though in great shape, he was no young man, and every successive step felt longer apart and crushing against his legs. Yes, a painful death stood waiting for any relative of this architect.

Two of his escorts that jogged up ahead opened the doors to the courthouse before he arrived, and he could hear the uproar long before he ever moved through the entrance. Men stood and yelled across to other men in the large, theater like building. The courts consisted of men equal in number across all four countries of Amon, twenty-five each, totaling almost one hundred fools. Even those from Donovini were foolish and greedy, much like the rest. Corruption knew no race, no gender. In his experience, every man had a breaking point, and for most, the jingle of coin from the Guild was enough to turn and sway any man in any direction necessary.

At the moment, all stood present, save for Gillar, and all stood barking out, arguing, so much so that the reasoning could not be heard through the rumbling. But through the mess of egos and testosterone, the First caught sight of the man likely responsible for the uproar in the court. And in return, Lord Brocusk smiled.

"It will be done!" the House lord bellowed over the others, and the room calmed in response. Turning to one side, with those of his own country in the foremost, he continued. "We have no place here, in this capital, in the courts, anywhere within Genethur. We have tried this system for many years, long before Brocusk ruled Ursan. But I fear it is time that we embrace the old ways, those that have kept us alive for so long."

"But who will be the voice of our country?" one Ursan man challenged.

"Afeon remains on the king's council," Dehyllo answered. "He will act on our behalf for all our country. We do not need many voices to represent us. We never have. We need but one, and he will supply it."

"And what of our affairs here?" another inquired. "What of the choices we make for . . ."

"*Their* affairs are of *their* concern. How many issues have you ever settled for Ursan while you have sat upon these seats and grown fat and weak? This is not our way. It will never be. You will all regain your resolve when you return home."

"And why would they return home?" First Pratt interrupted, making his way through the now silent crowd. "Each man here represents a voice of Amon, even those from Ursan."

"They represent your gold coins and where they land," Brocusk made claim.

"Are you not part of Amon?"

Dehyllo huffed loudly. "We are, First Pratt. I fear we are the last race of men to be such."

Philip waited until he made his way directly to the House lord before speaking under his breath, "Earth and Flame, Dehyllo, what are you doing?"

"I am pulling my people from your courts. They have signed their consent to the union of House Rowe and Pratt. You shall have your wedding and crown your new king. There is little need for my people to remain."

"Don't you feel as if there are more important things to take place than something petty such as this? We have an army that needs to be reinstated along the coast, something that I would have thought you would aid me in."

"Why? Do you suddenly believe in the unknown, that to which you cannot see?" Dehyllo chuckled some. "Or is it your fear of their retaliation for your decision to leave them hungry and untended?"

"Damn it, Dehyllo, you know that was not me," whispered the First into his ear.

"It was under your watch, one way or another. You are a man without faith, without belief in what will be upon us. Your need to aid your army is out of fear in their numbers rather than fear of what they stand to protect."

"You have men in their numbers as well."

"Men who ceased to be Ursan when they joined the Imperial Army. They are part of that family now, not mine. You look to reinstate them, speak to what remains of your courts once I am finished extracting my men. Speak to that useless fat Orpay if you desire to reestablish a supply route. But you will do all of this without my aid."

Philip shook his head in disbelief. "All of this because you did not win the throne? Your plan to take it has backfired, so you run like a whipped dog?"

"There was never a plan to take the throne, Philip. We *earned* the throne. Your brother and that Argon bitch have schemed against us, formed a foolish union to do nothing more than keep us from taking what is ours by right. As you have no faith in the gods, I have no faith in this court or those that run it."

"Careful," cautioned the First. "You border treason with those comments."

"I did not say we would no longer adhere to your government. We simply abstain from its presence." Turning back to his people, he spoke aloud yet again. "Take only what you need back in Ursan. Leave your useless luxurious possessions here, as they will do you nothing but slow your trip. They are worth nothing back home. Have your families ready to leave by nightfall and meet at the eastern entrance. Those that do not join us will never be welcome in Ursan again so long as I breathe."

He flashed a smile to Philip. "My House is no longer one of your fears, First."

"You are making a mistake in taking your men from these courts. Good men, with your country in their hearts."

"And gold in their pockets, wine in their bellies, whores on their cocks. They have forgotten the strength of our people. Living within these walls has dulled their minds. I shall sharpen it once again for them, and they will remember who they are. A war is coming, First Pratt, and not from us. We now head home to prepare for the coming storm."

"You are a fool."

Dehyllo stroked his lengthy beard, his arms seemed to tense. *Where does my recklessness stem from?* For a brief moment, he could have sworn that the House lord was seconds away from smashing in his skull. Instead he laughed, a sympathetic one, and shook his head in dismay.

"You have been given many chances to align yourself with Ursan, with House Brocusk."

"I know, Dehyllo. Your Second has all but told me that he feels I will regret my decision. I think otherwise."

"Indeed. I hope that your last thought before life leaves your body is how things could have been different if you would have learned to fear the right thing and trust the right men."

The First stood motionless as the many Ursan men in attendance began to gather their things and follow their House lord out the door, leaving many others agape in attendance. Philip could not determine whether or not Dehyllo had threatened him in his final statement. One way or the next, he did not believe for a moment that Lord Brocusk had given in to his desire for the throne. In fact, he was damn near certain that the games had only just begun.

--

"What do you mean?" harshly questioned Allura's mother. "If he would not speak of marriage, you force the talk from him. We must arrange this so that all can see the union. Simply signing names to paperwork is not sufficient enough. The public needs to know of this union, and that together, both Rowe and Pratt shall rule Amon."

"I know," she answered, "but it was not as easy as that. He knows."

Christina stopped for a moment within her chambers, staring blankly at Allura with her piercing eyes. "Knows what, child?"

"Of his brother."

After a brief pause, her shoulders shrugged. "So be it. It should change little. You will marry him and unify our Houses regardless."

"I never said I wouldn't," Allura quickly defended. "But convincing him may be a different discussion altogether."

Her mother chuckled some, rolling her eyes. "Hopeless romantics . . . I believe it resides solely in youth at times. I wish your father would have been such."

Her mother rarely spoke of him, at least not as much as Allura would have liked. "Did you love Father?"

"I loved Edfeld in my own way, child. Duty can lead to love, whether you believe so or not is for you to decide. I certainly did not love him when he chose me to represent his House as his wife. I did for him what I ask of you. I spread my legs and gave him two children."

"It *is* romantic when you say it in such a way . . ."

"Your brother Gerald will take over this House in due time, when I am damn well ready to release it from my grip. I endured much to be in the position I am in. But we all make sacrifices. Certainly I did not have the personal life that I wanted, but I am in charge of our country, as you will soon be in charge of all of Amon."

Allura knew of her mother's resolve. She was far tougher than Allura would ever be, and had eyes that drove fear into the soul. Christina wanted her children to be the same, a decisive killer not afraid to backstab and betray in order to gain a step in life. Yet Allura always found herself disappointing her mother.

So rather than confess that she too did not want this marriage, that she in fact loved Jerryn Pratt, she chose against it. Silence seemed the better play at the moment.

"Find him again and tell him this," Christina demanded. "If he will not begin arrangements on the wedding, we will ask Nicolas to replace him with Jerryn on the throne."

Her heart jumped a beat at the thought. "But . . . you said . . ."

"I know what I said!" snapped her mother. "You do not think I was foolish enough to place a name on the signed agreement. It simply names that you shall marry a son of Nicolas Pratt. If something tragic happened to Rayden or he refuses to marry, then it would fall to Jerryn to complete the union."

Something tragic . . .

"He will come to his senses once you tell him this. Knowing your relationship with Jerryn will force him to marry you quickly in spite. Now go from my sight and find this foolish Pratt boy and get him to commit to a timeframe. No more than a few weeks away."

She stood and made her way to the door, attempting unsuccessfully to remove ill notions from her thoughts.

Maybe I can yet make you proud, Mother, and still make me happy in the process.

--

The afternoon was upon him and the rain began. *Of course.* Rayden had no real idea where he was within Corovium, only that one foot went before the next, the afternoon was upon him, and he had no more desire to continue in the rain than he had to stay within the capital.

I should get used to it, if I am to marry. This would be home . . . forever.

The luscious greens of the valleys, the blue of the ocean, the clean air, the rain. And yet he missed the heat, the dryness, and the tumbleweeds. He missed the lizards than ran upon the earth, the blaring sun on his back, and the familiarity of his own people. As cloudy and rainy as it was, he would end up as pale as the damn Ursan if he stayed here.

There of course was another way. He could say no.

And have Father disown me and strip me of his last name.

But what was a last name? Nathan did well enough without the Pratt name, or at least he said as much. Certainly there might have been some bitterness to the bastard son, and Rayden could hardly place fault to that. But if Nathanial could make a place in this world without the name of Pratt, Rayden could do the same.

Couldn't I?

Some noises and standard drunken clamor came from a tavern to his right, and he quickly decided to duck inside to avoid the darkening clouds. A larger establishment and a rough one by the looks, Rayden wondered if he had made a good choice. Hard men stood about and ate and drank away the afternoon, some with interesting tattoos upon their skin, others with missing teeth and scars; the standard assortment of men that fought for a living. The capital, while housing the government, was still a city all the same. And a city still needed dirty work done at times, and none better to handle that work than the Guild.

A Guild hangout was not the safest of locations, but safe enough should he keep his nose to face. He maneuvered over to the back of the room and found an empty table and took a seat, careful to keep his eyes down and away from those that did the opposite.

"What can I get you?" a tough voice rang from an overweight, middle aged waitress.

"What do you got to eat?"

"Meat," she sneered. "But most people around here only eat beer and wine."

"Well then serve me whatever you got that's thoroughly dead," replied Rayden. "And the stiffest ale you got."

--

The entire walk back to the capital building, Philip had thought of kicking through the door to the Second's office.

Bad enough he had to spend a few hours getting through paperwork in order to just submit a request to reinstate the army, along with paperwork to be sent to Orpay as well. In all likelihood, the Guild would reject any subsequent request until they were back paid from their last bit of work, which would take another written request from the Second to just secure funds. In other words, hours of work, and nothing solved. And nothing would be solved for weeks, perhaps even months. Sad enough that he could not anticipate what General Shonnen was thinking or doing. His written apology and assurance that it would be rectified had gone unanswered by the First General. Probably too busy quelling a rebellion.

Bad enough it had been a waste of time, worse yet that most of the uproar had been over Brocusk's brash actions at the courts. He might as well just killed his men there in front of the rest. Yet another reason that any vote would be stalled, as the decision to replace twenty-five votes would need to be placed to . . . a vote? Voting on how to vote felt so strangely redundant that it almost made the First laugh. But he could not help but think that the move by Dehyllo had been for that very intent. All the requests in the world would do nothing until the courts could decide how to further proceed, and that would now take priority over anything. Good thing war was not upon the capital. The First could just envision himself requesting the invading force for more time while they figured out how to properly decide on *how* to decide.

Bad enough he wasted time, worse that Brocusk all but crippled the courts temporarily, and then there was the rain. It was a long walk back to the capital in the weather, and the horizon looked darker than pitch. A fierce storm formed over the ocean, which was nothing new for Corovium, but no less fun to deal with. And while he walked in the rain, he wondered how much of this was known to Afeon. He hated the Second and certainly the feeling was likely mutual despite what was said aloud. But soaked in the rain, a day wasted in the courts, and the Second could have saved him the humiliation.

Thus his thoughts remained focused as he backtracked all the way up to the Second's office. He would kick in his door to show his true ferocity.

But the door was open. Of course it was.

"Raining pretty good out there, eh First?"

And Afeon got in the first stab at him. The day got better by the moment.

"I finished your request for the funds. It just needs your approval, then I can submit it to the courts."

Philip made his way across the room. "A lot of damn good that will do. How much of this did you know before I made my way to the courthouse today?"

"All of it, of course," admitted the Second, a sly grin on his smug face. "I know you are angered, and obviously soaked. But to my defense, you never asked me what Lord Brocusk's plans were. And even if you had, I do not necessarily feel so inclined to speak on it. Not as if you offered up the information on the union between your brother and Christina Rowe."

"Then at least tell me this, Second. Does Dehyllo do this because he has lost faith in our government, or does he do this because he looks to send it into disarray?"

"Why can't it be both?"

"It does not have to be this way. We could help each other."

"The time for help is over. Remember our conversation before the crowning of our late king? Time is short, First Pratt. Shorter than you can perceive."

"Why is it I often feel that you or your people are constantly threatening me, Second?"

"You were given a chance to align with Dehyllo, and you did not. Should you seek guidance at how to move forward from here, speak to your new queen, Christina Rowe."

"She will not be the queen," corrected Philip.

"Don't be naïve."

You have me there.

"And I am not the one who aligned with her."

"No," noted Afeon, "but you did deny both me and Brocusk before the crowning. You could have shared what we speculated, of the bastard child of Yelium."

"What if it wasn't true to begin with?"

"Now you think I am naïve."

"It is never as simple as either of you make it out to be."

Sure, I could have admitted that the son was a bastard and handed over the throne to Ursan. Would have had to admit my part in the whole thing too. I gather withholding that information would be considered treason against Amon. The courts would not have likely shown mercy.

"Life is never simple," said Afeon. He stood from his seat and made his way over to the First, handing him the paperwork for the courts. "Neither are the choices we make in it. Now if you excuse me, I think I shall retire for the day. Close the door for me on your way out."

Watching the Second brush by him, Philip decided the day could get no worse.

--

Allura moved inside a small, broken down tavern on the east side of the capital. She had been bundled up against the downpour, and the day was moving beyond her, not that anyone could tell through the darkness of the storm. She had yet to find Rayden, though she knew he would be holed up in a bar of some kind, likely similar to this one, drinking himself stupid. She took a seat, deciding to wait out the weather a bit before continuing on her search.

"Two nines tops the jacks."

"My ass. This is the third engagement. Nines top the queens."

"I'll top the fucking queens, alright."

The four men at the center of the room had the look of killers, and she bundled up tighter in her robes. They were loud, obnoxious, and likely drunk. She drank occasionally, a glass of wine when she felt the need. But blistering drunkenness never seemed wise. In fact, it seemed to get most men in far greater trouble than it ever garnered success.

Rayden. He was but a child in the form of a man. A million different ways he could have handled this situation, a chance of a lifetime, but she should have guessed he would handle it this way. Perhaps the best thing was to convince him to deny the marriage. Perhaps the best thing for him was to simply . . . disappear.

It had not escaped her hearing at the verbiage used by her mother in the explanation of the possibilities. Something could happen to anyone at any time. Any doubters could ask the king, if he were alive. So what if something was to happen to Rayden? Everyone would get what they wanted in the end. Her mother would have the union of their Houses, Amon would have a new king and queen, and she would rule alongside a husband that she loved. Rayden would be the only loser in the matter, and that could not be helped. There had to be a loser in any game. No better choice in her mind than Rayden.

"Look, it's very clear here. This is the third round, but the fourth engagement. So eights top jacks."

"My piss is more clear than these fucking rules."

"Your piss is probably a stark yellow, you Donovinian fuck."

"Aye, truth there. Well fuck these rules anyway."

She could barely think through all the clamor behind her. All that she knew was that she needed to think of a way to remove Rayden from the situation. She needed . . .

"I would find another establishment," came a stern voice beside her, one that had her nearly jump from her seat.

In some circumstances, voices never match appearances, at least in her experience. This was not one of those circumstances. The dark complexioned Fallneesian looked as menacing as his deep voice, chest raised and arms thick, his eyebrows were shaven along with his head. Allura could only guess that the man worked for the Guild, or at the very least, hurt people for a living. And in all likelihood, enjoyed every moment of the hurting.

"I only escape the rain," she stated in her best attempt to match his authoritative tone, but sadly came out half shriek, all pathetic.

"Brave the rain," the Fallneesian stated. "Better than here."

There was something familiar about the man, though she could not gather how so. "I am a customer as anyone else here. I thank you for your concern, but I . . ."

"You are Allura Rowe, daughter of the House Lady of Argonus, Christina Rowe," the man claimed, and she scavenged her memory as to how he knew such, how he looked so damn familiar. "I may be here in an unsavory bar in the corner of Corovium, but that does not mean my finger is far from the pulse, milady. This is no place for you."

"I do not frequent Corovium often enough for you to know me."

"I know much I shouldn't," he continued. "Now leave before the men behind me realize who you are and get unfortunate ideas in their heads."

It then came to her. One night many weeks ago before the crowning of Yelium Aylmer, she had seen him about the rear courtyard. She had met with Jerryn that night on the beach, and this gentleman met with someone as well. Connections inside the castle for a man of this kind likely meant he handled situations best kept secret.

"Are you with the Guild?" The Fallneesian did not answer her question. "You have helped before at the capital, with some work that remains quiet, yes?" Again, silence from the big man. She was feeling more and more foolish by the passing second. "I am searching for a man here in Corovium, likely in a bar tonight."

"You will find plenty of men in bars tonight. But perhaps someone of your prestige should look elsewhere for cock."

She would have slapped him if she thought she would have lived afterwards. "I mean one man in particular. I need him found. Perhaps I can . . . hire you."

"Do I look like a man for hire?"

"Yes."

The big man chuckled. "Aye, suppose I do. Another time, perhaps. Me and these men behind me are meeting others tonight as we embark out on a job. Never wise to take on two jobs at once. We have but a few hours left in Corovium and I do not think we look to squander the opportunity to get shitty drunk just for a few coin."

"It is important. My . . . fiancé, of sorts, is somewhere getting himself right and drunk. I think I need to see him . . . well I suppose that . . ."

"Get to it."

There is no other way to ask. Just tell him what you want. Maybe, just maybe, he will agree.

"I want him . . . taken care of."

The Fallneesian rose what would have been an eyebrow to the statement, if he had one. "Do you make common practice in entering shady taverns and asking the patrons to kill your lover?"

"I didn't say kill, necessarily. Have you killed men before?"

His bulky arms crossed at his chest. "I give you credit, Allura Rowe, you are an interestingly bold individual. Certainly I have done things in my line of work. Goes with the territory. Tell me this. Have you ever backstabbed anyone in order to move yourself into a better position?"

"Whatever it takes," she answered.

"Good, because that is how I suggest you kill your fiancé. Blade to the back works just as effectively as a blade to the front, my dad used to say. Now get yourself out of here and do not speak any further of these things. You are lucky I'm in a good mood today."

"You have done these kinds of things before, yes?"

"You are bold indeed. Let me guess, your ladyship. Your mother has you marrying someone you do not wish to spend your life with, so now you look to have him killed just to get yourself off the hook."

"Like I said, not necessarily killed. I just need him . . . gone."

"Aye, but no better gone than in the dirt. My dad used to tell me that too."

"So what do you want in return?"

"You don't understand," he swiftly responded. "This is not a negotiation. There is nothing you can offer that I want."

"But . . . I thought that you worked for money. The Guild normally works for . . ."

"I never said . . ." The Fallneesian rubbed his thumb against his barren eyebrow. "Look, we are not killers for hire, or kidnappers, or anything else you need us to be. I also do not have magical powers to link me to your fiancé, so I don't know where he is."

"But you could maneuver yourself around this town easier than me."

"Aye, but why would I?"

"If not coin, what is it that you want?" He gave an empty stare toward her. She suddenly felt uncomfortable. "I am not sure that . . . I mean, I wouldn't . . ."

"Oh calm down," laughed the Fallneesian. "You are far too skinny and pink to tussle my trousers."

She sighed. "So if not sex or money, what is it that you need?"

"Nothing."

"Every man needs something. If Rayden disappears, I have an opportunity to become queen. I could grant you anything."

"Rayden Pratt?"

This man seemed far too informed for a standard Guild member. She took a grave risk in speaking with him, perhaps a graver risk in trusting him with any information. "Yes. I suppose you know of him as well."

"I may. How long does he need to be missing?"

"Long enough for me to marry another and take the throne. Anywhere from four weeks to forever."

"I would presume you are leaning on forever."

"Perhaps," she earnestly answered.

"Very well. Assuming I can find him out here, you have yourself a missing fiancé."

"Really? Well, what should the payment be?"

"Your memory," was his strange response.

"Say again?"

"Men of my kind do not barter in sex and money."

"And what kind of men are you?"

"Dead ones." The Fallneesian leaned in closely to her now, his voice nothing above a whisper. "Remember my face, Lady Rowe. You say every man needs something, every man has a price. Aye, we do. But we barter in power and favor. I need a favor. Or more like someone close to me needs a favor. But we will hold off on my needs until the job is complete. The next time you see me, you may not like my coming. But you will answer my call, to whatever ends."

Suddenly this deal sounded far worse than she could have anticipated. Coin was an easy thing to give away. Sex might not have been as easy, but normally ended just as quick as it begun for these kinds of men. At least the going price was up front and clearly stated. Agreeing favor for favor, without knowing the one in return, was normally quite foolish.

The chance to back out was now or never.

"We have a deal then," Allura responded.

The Fallneesian nodded. She felt a strange emptiness at the pit of her stomach. Striking a deal to have a man killed did not feel as rewarding or thrilling as she might have visualized. In fact, she felt like she wanted to vomit instead.

"Now leave," barked the big man. "You don't want any more witnesses to your stroll away from the capital."

She stood, nodded back to the large man, and left the tavern. Every step away she felt worse for it, sickened to the point of tears forming in her eyes. Regret? Fear? What would happen if these men simply walked to the capital and gave her up for the murderous whore that she was. She would deny it, but the damage would be done. Worse yet, what would Jerryn do if he found out what she had done? Would he be overjoyed or hate her forever? Allura knew she should turn about, tell the Fallneesian to disregard their conversation. It was a fool's wish to begin with. Maybe he would not even find Rayden?

Needless to say, it was a long walk back to the capital.

--

By the fallen gods, Rayden had to piss. But that would involve standing and he did not feel that would be in his best interest at the moment. In fact, not even thinking felt in his best interest at the moment.

On the bright side, it looked like the rain had ceased, giving way to the darkness of the night. How long had he been drinking in this tavern? Damned if he could remember. All he knew is that the ale was a thick brew and it did far more damage than he had intended.

Damn it all, he truly had to piss.

As the crowd cleared some, he noticed with a few new faces in the mix. Almost looked like they were clearing out the patrons. But he could not focus much. Hard to tell these kinds of things when steadying upon a barstool was a harrowing task in its own right.

A few walked up to him, his eyes though focused on the half empty mug in front of him.

"This the one?"

"Aye. That's him."

"Sure you want to do this here? Still got a few people watching."

"We want to be seen, just not caught."

"Whatever, *Lieutenant.*"

"Looks pretty shit faced to me. Maybe we just ask him to come along?"

Are they talking about me?

"Nails, you want to do the honors?"

"Why is it always me that has to do this shit?"

"Just shut the fuck up and do it."

Suddenly a sharp pain hit Rayden in the back of his head, hard enough to see an explosion before his eyes, and then he began to tear up as the world started to spin.

The last thing he could remember is no longer having the urge to piss.

--

"Philip," Jessica called out with urgency and the First startled awake.

"What?" he mumbled in response, his mind slowly regaining its sharpness from whatever dream had taken him. He was still within his room, the morning upon them, nothing immediately out of the ordinary.

Then the door rattled again, someone banging hard against it, calling out his name.

"Better be fucking important," the First cursed under his breath, knowing full well that he would rather it not be.

Do I ask too much for someone to simply knock on the door and ask how I am doing?

It was always bad news when the door knocked in the morning. Good news never traveled before breakfast. Good news could always wait. Only bad news had this sense of urgency.

Reaching his door, the handle opened almost simultaneous to his unlocking, his brother franticly bursting through. "They took him last night!" Nicolas bellowed, his voice filled with rage. Behind him cried Maradyn and an expressionless Jerryn.

"Wait, what? Took who?"

"Rayden! Damn you, Phil, why didn't you tell me?"

"What?" he stammered while waving the two other Pratts inside his chambers. The guards just outside moved into place, blocking any entrance. Shutting the door clean, he turned back to his family and found the quick embrace of a sobbing Maradyn.

"First Katlynn, now Rayden," she managed to state through the tears. Jessica gasped heavily, and Philip's thoughts went from bewilderment at first followed immediately by panic.

Door opened again, he called out. "Someone get my children and bring them here now!"

"Right away, First Pratt," announced one of the soldiers, darting off.

This time when he turned back, he suffered an embrace of a different kind. Nicolas grabbed his robes and yanked him close. "Why didn't you tell me about Brocusk?"

"Tell you what? What is going on? Tell me!"

"Someone has taken Rayden," painfully stated Maradyn from behind his enraged brother. "He was alone in town, and we have already found a few witnesses that saw him carried away from a tavern by several men. No one recognized these men, likely outsiders they said."

"By some strange coincidence," hissed his elder brother, "Dehyllo whisks away in the middle of the night, and my son goes missing as well. I find that far too convenient. Why didn't you tell me about Brocusk? Why didn't you tell me he planned to take his people and leave?"

"I didn't think it relevant . . ."

"He may have killed the king and framed my daughter, and you didn't think it wise to tell me of his moves?"

"Well why the hell was Rayden alone in the city to begin with?"

Nicolas released his grip on him, Philip thankful in the process. "Fair question. What do you know of this?" he inquired in the direction of his son.

Jerryn sat onto one of the sofas in the living room, his eyes never gazing up at them. "I don't know," he murmured. "He didn't seem pleased with the marriage. He got upset."

"Upset at what?" pressed Nicolas.

"I . . . I don't know."

"Then tell me word for damn word what you two spoke of yesterday!"

The First raised his hand slowly to his brother. "Easy, Nick. The boy has a sister and brother now missing."

"No thanks to you in any of this, so shut your fucking mouth, Phil."

"If he was kidnapped," started Jessica, "then we can expect a ransom. Or something. If they wanted him dead they would have done so last night and left him for us to find. Right?"

"If Ursan took him, there will be no ransom," his brother claimed. "They will keep him until the wedding is canceled, and Dehyllo may have claim to the throne yet again."

"Well he doesn't have much of a head start," stated Philip. "I will send out the troops to bring him back in."

"He won't be foolish enough to have Rayden with him," Nicolas gathered.

"No, perhaps not. But that won't stop us from finding out what he knows."

"He is a House lord," Maradyn cautioned, wisely so. What the First now spoke of could have easily been construed as heresy. All they had to go on was pure speculation alone. If Brocusk was *not* behind any of this . . .

"He is also a citizen of Amon," the First declared boldly. "If he is innocent, he will have nothing to hide. In the meantime, get a letter written and sent by bird carrier to Edmond. Have him keep our family carefully guarded and on the lookout for a ransom note in Astrona, just in case we are mistaken at the culprit and motive."

"I want Jerryn with constant guard until the wedding," Nicolas stated, and a swift hush took the room.

"We will find Rayden, Nicolas," noted the First, "but perhaps it is time to send Jerryn back to Astrona. It's no longer safe for him here. I will have armed escort ready at moment's notice."

"No, Phil. I will go and speak with Christina now. This wedding takes place as soon as it can, with Jerryn taking his brother's place."

If anyone had expected Nicolas to state that, they did a poor job of containing their shock. Even Jerryn sat with his mouth gaping like a thirty dog.

"Someone plots against us," continued Nicolas. "Two of my children are now missing because of this. I will not run, nor will my last remaining child. He takes the throne and ends this madness. He will be king of Amon and punish those responsible for this. We will see Rayden and Katlynn back to this family or there will be blood as payment."

His eyes raged like fire from a man at his very end, a cornered animal ready to strike with the last of his strength. Danger and peril stood within those eyes, and Philip should know. He had seen it before many times. Both men now walked a path that there could be little turning from.

As the soldier returned in a rush, both Lillianna and Joanna came to him flustered with Winston closely behind.

"Dad, what's wrong?" Lilli questioned, fear in her voice.

But Philip kept his gaze to the soldier. "Get to both General Brocusk's and Afeon's chambers with a few men and throw them under lock and key."

The soldier looked immediately confused. "Am I placing the Second of Amon and the Second General under arrest?"

"Phil," he heard Jessica breathe softly in warning.

There was no going back at this point.

"Yes."

--

A steady rocking, back and forth, back and forth, churned his already weak stomach. His head throbbed. His mouth tasted like a mixture of stomach acid, woodchips, and blood. Rayden felt something wrapped around his head, maybe a bandage, as he laid on something rather uncomfortable, and his eyes might as well have been sealed shut as heavy as they were.

All in all, Rayden felt like shit. To top it off, he was fairly certain he was about to vomit.

"Looks like you're finally awake," stated a deep voice somewhere to his right.

His reactions far too slow to be alarmed by the presence, he simply took his precious time and peeled opened his eyelids. A large, muscular Fallneesian sat upon some boxes before him. He looked to be below decks of a boat perhaps, which would explain the rocking. As he reached his hands about, he realized they were tied behind his back.

Then reality finally kicked in. He was a prisoner.

He had many questions.

"I think I'm about to puke."

That was not one of them, but they were the first words he managed to form regardless.

"Well now," the larger man started, "go right ahead. In case you haven't smelled yourself yet, you've already done that a few times. And since you've been bound and laying on them boxes right there since we casted off, you can gather where all that vomit has ended up so far. Yes, all over yourself."

Rayden felt humiliated along with frightened now. Fear did much to gather his senses, though did little to battle the pain at his temple.

"So questions, right? I'm sure you have many. Let's get some of the formalities out of the way. My name is Deso. What is your name?"

"Rayden . . ."

"Wrong! Rayden Pratt is dead, haven't you heard? Killed him myself and tossed him into the ocean. He's fish food now. The horrid smelling man lying before me is named Breeches."

"Breeches?"

"Primarily because you desperately need a new pair. Pissed yourself after Nails gave you a bit of a knock on the head. And he's rightfully sorry about that, I might add. He's not one for restraint. Well having carried you, piss pants and all, you also vomited on yourself once during the trip, which also ended up on your shirt and trousers. A man's shirt is easy to remove to help out. But sorry to say that we ain't removing a man's breeches. So they started calling you that, because they have to call you something, and thankfully they have no idea who you are. So Breeches is your name from hence forth."

The more Deso spoke, the harder his head thumped. "I have money to pay. I am a Pratt."

"No you are not, as I just stated," Deso growled. "We are men without last names here. And men without last names at times get hired to kill men *with* last names."

"Someone hired you to kill me? Who?"

"Does it matter? You are dead, and dead men ask very few questions. I suppose the better question, Breeches, is who wouldn't have wanted that man dead? Rayden Pratt, a man in possible line to ascend to the throne. Hell, the last king died a pretty gruesome death as I've heard. Apparently someone does not want the throne occupied."

"So . . . why am I *not* dead?"

"And there is the money question, Breeches. I am no stranger to your family, primarily First Pratt. I have no time for stories, but let us just say that there was a time when I faced a similar situation, death ready to take me for my crimes. Your uncle gave me a choice, a choice of servitude, but one of life. I breathe, and I figure that I might owe a man for that, one way or another. He may never know it, but this keeps us even in my mind. He saved my life, and I saved his nephew's, life is square now."

Somehow he doubted that this Fallneesian saved him for the simple honor of it all. "Where are we?"

"Currently? The Vurid Sea, but we are just about ready to turn into the Sullein River and ride it as far as we can."

"And will you let me go at some point?"

"Let you go?" Deso laughed loudly at the comment. "We certainly do not understand one another. The men here have no idea who you are. Once they know, you will be a tool for ransom, and nothing more. My dad once told me that the best hostage is a dead hostage. Words to live by. They grovel and cry less, along with eat less food and drink less water. And since at the moment they don't know you, they all think you are some swindler that owes me money and is about to work it off. Rayden Pratt is dead and gone . . . forever."

Rayden could hardly believe his ears . Was this a dream he could not wake from?

"Oh, cheer up, Breeches. Could be worse. I could just *really* kill you and be done with the trouble. Seems like you should be a little more . . . appreciative of it. But I suppose that will come in time. Well, let me go up and get you some food and water. That being alive is a pesky thing, needing to eat and drink and all. Well if anything, it might help with that headache you likely have."

A few steps away, and Deso turned with a wide smile upon his face.

"Welcome to the Moon Divide."

Oh shit.

**

As the Ursan Say

The forests of Ursan harden an individual. I lost a son to them when he was very young. But that is not a rarity. We test our strength against it and come away stronger, or do not come away at all.

Many outside of our ways do not understand us. They think us savages for our way of life. Let them cower against us. Let them fear our resolve. They only fear what they cannot comprehend. We could cut down the trees, build towering cities and castles. We could burn the land and place farms and cattle. We could hunt and kill off the life that threatens us daily within the wilderness, and life would be easier.

And we would be weaker for it.

-- Dehyllo Brocusk, House Lord of Ursan

XI

The night stood clear as Turitea and Schill both radiated brilliantly against the darkened sky. Admittedly, Nathan spent very little time gazing into the stars. He kept himself grounded, his eyes focused on what was in front of him versus forces outside of his control. That, and Donovinians were not known for the undying faith in the fallen gods. The Twin Moons were perhaps other worlds or just giant rocks hanging in the night sky. Or maybe they were the gods. Who knew for certain?

Religion took shape when logic held no reason, or so he had always believed. If it could not be explained, the gods were involved. The Twin Moons, gods. Realms, gods. He could remember a hail storm when he was a child that some thought to be a message from the fallen gods due to the severity of it. But in reality, it was just hail, a natural weather phenomenon. It was not that he did not believe at all, just he spent no time pondering on such.

His mother once told him that she felt it best to keep an open mind. Sometimes it was okay to not have an answer, to simply not know. Better to discover something new than be proven inherently wrong. Nathanial could honestly say that he had never known men to die solely because they kept an open mind on various possibilities. He had, however, known men to die because their refusal of accepting and learning something new.

Katlynn lay flat against the grass alongside him. The Twin Moons at the very least gave them some vision into the open plains before the Lis'rial Wilderness. She was brave and lucky thus far to have endured. But that was only due to her own lack of understanding on how frighteningly powerful she truly was. Nathan had minimal contact with those that could see or open Realms, though what he had witnessed in his lifetime had been eye opening. From Druids able to heal deadly wounds to Pyromancers that could turn themselves completely ablaze. Katlynn may not have killed the king, but he could certainly understand why they feared such.

Somewhere hidden well behind them were Iero and Feko. Both were useless scouts and thus he left them to speak with each other. He smiled, wondering exactly how fun of a conversation those two would be sharing. While his cousin was no better a scout than either of those men, Nathan refused to have her from his sight. He went through enough to find her, and there stood little reason to test his luck any further.

"Here they come," she whispered.

To the east he could barely see the hunched over figures running through the tall blades of grass. Both easily recognizable. Tristan arrived first with Jadenine close behind.

"She was right," stated the captain through short breaths.

"Of course I was," hissed Jadenine.

"A couple of scout patrols, but they are spread thin. They didn't expect us to come this way."

"Nor would I have chosen this path," the Ursan added.

"Good thing you are not in charge," snapped Nathanial. They were far too close to Prillian than he desired, and he did not look forward to another trip into the Lis'rial. But both were the most direct routes, and the most direct routes were rarely the expected ones.

"I don't see much of a problem getting passed them," Tristan finished.

Nathan motioned to the south. "Gather our eccentric friends. We make a run for it now."

The captain nodded and moved along, leaving Jadenine gazing at him with her typical discontent. "Hope you are ready for this, Wode. Or should I say Pratt?"

"Wode," he firmly corrected.

She shrugged her indifference. "That scar on your arm is just a small taste of the dangers in the wilderness. Night is a dangerous time to enter. Killers are on the prowl."

Nathan reached over instinctively to the recently closed wounds on his arms, the claws from the Draywolf still fresh on both flesh and mind. "Survival creates strength, isn't that an Ursan saying?"

But Jadenine spit to the earth in response. "Trust your sword arm more than your brother is another one."

"All fine and well, but . . ."

"If you carry a shield, do not let it defend against your swing. One of my favorites."

"Alright," Nathan conceded through her intentional annoyance. "I am a man of my word, Jadenine. You might hate me, but you know me well enough to trust I keep to my promises. Get us through the Lis'rial, you are free to go."

She nodded in response, but did not look convinced at such. He couldn't blame her. The wise move would be to cut her throat and let her bleed in the wilderness. It would prevent her from informing the Guild to their movements and it would likely keep a predator or two off their tracks for the night. But what was wise, what was easy, and what was right rarely, if ever, aligned.

Before the group behind them could even get close enough to speak in hushed tone, Nathan could easily smell the foulness from the Chur'rat seep into his nose. Yet another reason to keep the Druid further back.

"That fucking rat is going to give us away," cursed Jadenine.

And for once, he agreed with her. Turning back to them, he pointed to it. "I think it best to part ways with your rat."

"His name is Bird," defended Iero.

"Call him shit," barked the Ursan woman, "because that's what he smells like."

"We cannot be separated."

Jadenine extended her hand to Nathan. "Give me a blade. I will separate the two."

"Enough." He gazed heavily at the Druid. "That thing gives us away, I kill it where it stands. And at the first spot of water, after we fill our canteens, it takes a bath."

"Well you must understand that the traditional Chur'rat bathes himself when the time is right, but with the constant travel and weather, he has not been able to properly hunt or mark his grounds in order . . ."

"Bath, Druid. I don't care if you dunk that rat yourself. He smells a spot worse than us, and that's saying something. Understand?"

Iero nodded. "I believe I do."

"Good." He turned to Jadenine. "Let's go."

--

Her cousin might have possessed great luck, but that did not pass true to the children of Nicolas Pratt, or so Katlynn believed. Though they did well to make an attempt to pass between two patrols, they mistimed their movement greatly. Rather than avoid them, they unwittingly stumbled directly onto a group.

But as if to counteract their misfortune, there only stood three Guild members between them and the wilderness. Nathan did not seem eager to enter these forests, and upon seeing the darkness embedded within, she gathered that she agreed with him in that aspect.

Her feet still hurt, still bled. But they had healed some. Finding shoes that fit well enough from the dead mercenaries helped. Riding Feko's steed all the way until they abandoned them today helped more. Jadenine and Feko's horses were abandoned because they were running low on supplies for themselves much less the horses. She was still in no shape to run, and that did little to help their cause. Katlynn felt more like a square wheel by every passing day and wondered when exactly she would be able to start helping.

She might sneak into Shadow and cut the throats of these men in quick succession. But of course she was none to certain she had the stomach for that. She was not Nathan. In fact, she might have been the very opposite. He was a stone, or at least he appeared as such. He killed without mercy or thought. She, on the other hand, did not feel confident in holding a sword no matter how often she had trained with such in Astrona. Thrusting toward a target dummy did not truly prepare for stabbing a man for real.

If she needed to make any type of decision at the moment, it was lost to the rest. Nathan already pointed toward Tristan silently and she would have thought that these men had known each other for years based on their movements. The captain moved with a steady pace around, silent while the three Guild members talked casually amongst themselves, doing little to take their patrol seriously. And why would they? What chance would there be at the fugitives to cross their line of sight?

When she turned to her left, Nathanial was already far off and in position, his bow out, and an arrow notched into the bowstring. Her eyes turned back to the three men, and then caught the blur of a dagger to her right and the hiss of an arrow to her left. The arrow landed first with deadly precision through the gullet of one of the men. The dagger landed before the two could react, penetrating the arm of another, causing him to scream for but a half a second before an arrow embedded into his esophagus. The third man did not know immediately what to do. He went for his sword and held it up, but Nathanial had already drawn his blades and moved toward the Guild member.

But to his credit, he did what any man would have likely done in that spot. Dropping his sword, he took to flight, and ran as quickly as his legs could maneuver.

"Iero!" called back Nathanial, but the Druid was already moving, his hands pressed against the earth.

A wave of roots lifted up and grasped hold of the running man, wrapping around him as would a mighty snake to a rodent, squeezing so tightly that no screams could emit from his throat. The vines wrapped tighter and tighter, and Katlynn turned away in time to only hear the popping and crushing sounds, leaving whatever bloody mess that ensued only to her imagination rather than her eyes to witness.

Nathanial reached his arm to his mouth, coughing some, perhaps holding back the strange sickness he had when they fought. After a moment, he reached down and pushed one of the arrows all the way through the neck, placing it back into his quiver. When he repeated the action with the second, the arrow snapped inside the man's throat, and her cousin flung the half piece he held into the dirt.

"Fuck!" he cursed.

Iero stepped forward some, his Chur'rat climbing back onto his shoulder. "A clean victory is a victory nonetheless, young Wode. I find that breathing after such an ordeal is still event enough to feel pleased."

"Your words do not put more arrows in my quiver, Druid."

"The wilderness is before us," Jadenine announced. "And we should not stop once we move through until we reach Ursan."

"Should we drag the bodies out of sight?" Tristan questioned.

Nathan only gazed to the west. "Certainly, if you possess a mop and a bucket for our friend over there. If the other patrols spot this, and they will, they will not travel deep into the Lis'rial without the approval of Cylaa. We make it to Ursan, we will be safe from the Guild for the moment."

She silently wondered how safe they would be from the wilderness itself once they entered. There stood little time to ponder upon it. They again were on the move.

--

Nothing quite like darkness to hinder the ability to understand distance traveled. At least during the day, Nathanial could turn his head and see how far his ass had moved from the last time he turned his head. In the shroud of the night, he felt pleased enough to not run face first into a looming oak. The forest wrapped itself tightly around the fugitives like a warm blanket in a Fallneesian winter. And the density of the trees all but negated the brightness of the Twin Moons, leaving the group completely and solely dependent on Jadenine.

Assuredly not his most favorable position, but there stood very few other options. At the moment, she was unarmed, but that did not necessarily make her any less lethal. Tristan stood close to her as they all remained huddled to one another. He would have rather been the one watching the Ursan, but his focus remained on protecting his cousin while keeping a constant eye on Feko.

It was a problem he created by first speaking with Cylaa to begin with. Thinking back, he should have never gone to her, instead left Prillian in search for his cousin alone. He would have left both Jadenine and Feko Hawbry back in the trade city and made the rescue alone. Instead, he followed the protocol of the Guild to join with Jadenine and allowed his own intrigue to conquer his better judgment in bringing Feko. Now he could only hope that Jadenine would leave peacefully once she guided them into her home country, even though in doing so would leave them utterly lost. As for Feko . . . he found no immediate solution. Alive long enough to figure out his true intentions, short enough to not wake up with a cut throat.

While the rest of the group endured the long hike, even the overweight Druid, Katlynn struggled and more frequently fell a step behind. Her body likely tired and ached, and he knew that her feet had cracked and split and swelled. He had seen them the first night after the skirmish with the mercenaries. It was nothing that would heal overnight, especially if she kept on them. But at the moment, they did not have many options. Space was needed between them and Prillian, and then . . . well he had yet to figure the next part out. Hide? Run more?

Ursan might have had the least amount of Guild populace, but the Guild still found themselves stationed throughout the country. In the end, they could not run forever. Nathanial, of all people, knew this well. The only way to end this would be if the Guild were called off, and only the courts or the council could do such. Where was the strength and wisdom of their government when they needed it?

"You okay?" whispered Nathan to his cousin, extended an arm out to her while she struggled up a short but sharp incline.

She accepted the help, grasping his hand and lifting up. "I will be alright."

"Perhaps," started Feko just a few short strides away, "we might all benefit from a break."

Hearing this, Jadenine stopped and gazed heavily at his cousin. "Ursan is only a few miles away. We should be there within the hour."

"A few minutes," Nathan suggested, catching the rolling eyes of the Guild member. "For those less seasoned in travel than others."

Feko knelt over and stretched his legs while Tristan walked back to Katlynn, bringing out a flask of water to share with her. Iero nearly plummeted to the earth with the Chur'rat taking the opportunity to remove itself from his shoulder and move about the area.

"You could make your life easier and drop a few pounds off your travels if you allow me to cook that furry opossum on your shoulder," offered up Nathan as he passed beside him, moving toward their guide.

"Oh, I gather I need the exercise," justified the Druid. "We all do not swing as many swords as you do, Nathanial Wode."

"No, I'd gather not."

Jadenine hovered low to the earth, her elbows resting upon her knees as she did not bother to even look upward to him.

"I can't tell my head from my ass out here," Nathan noted.

"And that's different from any other day . . . how?"

"I mean . . ."

"I know what you meant," she snapped. "I keep my word, Wode. I will get you safely into Ursan. It will be a few hours outside of Prillian, giving you a little bit of time to rest for a few hours before you decide your next move."

Nathan nodded in understanding. "So I have always wondered something. Donovinians from Donovini. Fallneesians from Fallneese. Argons from Argonus. Why Ursan from Ursan?"

Jadenine finally met his stare. After a moment, she pointed beside her to a grand oak tree. "Do you know what that is?"

"Um, I believe it is the Lis'rial Oakwood, a hybrid if I read correctly. I believe it is a mix from the cross pollinating done between the western Argonus Redwoods in the Quoin Woods and the standard oaks here."

She blinked at him in dumbfounded silence for a second.

"It's a fucking tree," she stated in brutal fashion.

"Earth and Flame, I thought you meant what kind of tree."

"Are you a Guild member or a botanist? Perhaps you and Feko have something in common after all, besides deceptiveness."

"Fine, it's a fucking tree. What about it?"

"Now what's this?" she pointed back to another tree close beside her as well. "And before you answer, it's a rhetorical question. It's also a tree. That's a tree. Over there is a tree. They're all trees."

Apparently that was the end of her answer, as she returned her glare somewhere other than him. He waited a moment still before pestering further. "And what is that supposed to mean?"

Jadenine sighed. "You give the trees names. I do not believe they consider themselves different from the tree beside them. Neither do we consider ourselves different from the earth which we stand upon. So why should our name differ? Ursan is the land, it is the people, it is the air we breathe." She stood, brushing back her red hair, showcasing her full scowl toward him. "We are Ursan."

He did not know if he entirely grasped her concept, but he did not argue against it. Personally, Nathanial could use for less of nature and more of civilization, but perhaps that was the Donovinian in him.

"It's been a few minutes," Jadenine noted. "We should move along."

To that he wholeheartedly agreed.

--

In perhaps the longest hour march of her life, Katlynn could not have been more pleased to hear that they had arrived in Ursan. Which she found ironic, since she had never once held the desire to visit. The more frightening piece, the piece she kept buried in the deepest corners of her conscious, was not knowing exactly how long this unplanned vacation would be.

"We will rest a few hours," Nathan called out to the others.

She sat down quickly, removing the newer shoes that did a spot better than the ones before. Just then her cousin startled her, dropping to her legs within seconds, fresh bandages in hand.

"I can handle it," she whispered, quite differently than when Tristan had attempted the same thing many moons before.

"I am aware that you can," was his reply. "I of course didn't ask you." Nathan unwrapped the bandages, careful to hide his disgust at her damaged feet, but it was a difficult thing to mask. They were likely permanently scarred at this point, and little could be done to change it. Bloody, cracked, worn, and then bloody again, a repetitive cycle for well over a month without foreseeable end. Now calluses formed over split and withering ends in her feet, and that was but a few days ago. She did not have the heart to look at it any further.

"They aren't as bad as you make them out," he offered up, though she knew better than to believe him. "Why can't Iero take a look at this?"

As if on cue, the talkative Druid came close, the Chur'rat off again, likely hunting better food than they would have. "The Earth Realm is not the same for everyone, Nathanial Wode. For me, I can reach in and borrow an ability that allows me to speak with the nature around us. There are those that can hone in on a body, aid in the natural healing ability. Alas, I am not so fortunate."

"Is it different for everyone?" her cousin pried.

"No one sees the world the same way, young Wode," was the Druid's answer. "Thus, no one that sees the Realms gather the same ability."

"If no one sees the same thing, how do you know there are only Three Realms?"

"How do we know anything?" The Druid sported half a smile. "Faith."

Nathan huffed loudly and intentionally to Iero, and in response the Druid only shrugged, then stood and moved away. Apparently the Druid did not understand the Pratt's limited reliance on faith.

Nearly done wrapping her first foot, he carefully placed it down and worked on the next.

"I did not kill the king."

He met her gaze. "I know that you didn't."

"It's important to me that you believe me."

"I do." His words were stern and earnest.

"If you do . . . then I am sorry. Please believe me that I am. I truly did not want any of this to happen."

"Why would you?" he answered, only to raise of his eyebrow to her response. "It was a set of very unfortunate circumstances that . . ."

"Could have been avoided if I would have just woken up on time. Something so damn simple . . ." she said, letting her words hang for a moment. "Will you be able to return to the Guild after this?"

It took him longer than she would have liked to answer. That alone was an answer before he said it. "No."

He probably hated her. And how could she blame him? "How could I ever replace the life you gave up just to help me?"

"I did this on my own choosing. Family is more important than anything, Katlynn. And don't you dare blame yourself for this. The only person to blame is the one that killed the king."

"Still . . . Tristan, Iero . . . they can never go back home."

"You will all go back home once this mess is cleared up."

"And you? Will you go back home?"

Finishing with the new bandage, he lightly slapped her legs. "All done. Get some rest. It will only be a few hours, so get what you can."

He stood and moved over, Tristan waiting until he was well enough away before moving in beside her. The captain must have seen the look on her face and decided against saying anything foolish, anything needy.

Tears dried. Bodies toughened. Strange, as even though she discovered the truth in those thoughts, she as well uncovered that new wounds could open just as easy, and new reasons to cry could be found.

--

Tristan came awake after about an hour of rest, then moved beside Nathan, sitting down while rummaging through his pack. After procuring a small flask, the captain reached over and handed it to him.

"Last bit of wine left that I snagged from Uvull," he claimed. Nathan gladly accepted, taking a swig, the sour taste leaving him puckering his lips somewhat. Handing it back, Tristan finished the contents, tossing the flask aside. "You should get some rest."

"I will be fine," Nathanial assured.

"When is the last time you slept?"

He shrugged, gazing about at the sleeping group. He would take no pleasure in waking them soon. "We will need to be up shortly."

Tristan nodded in understanding. "So what are we looking at here?"

"What do you mean?"

The captain motioned with his head to Feko. "The one that mumbles to himself," he whispered. "And the woman."

"Keep your eyes on Feko," responded Nathan in a hushed tone. "I do not know his intent yet."

"Then why did you bring him along to begin with?"

"Long story, Captain, perhaps for another day. As for the woman, we are about to cut her loose."

"Are you certain? She could still be dangerous to us. What if she leads the Guild directly to us?"

"We left a trail of bodies back at the entrance of the Lis'rial. We don't need her to bring the Guild to us. We are doing a fine job of that on our own. Besides, she is partially to thank for helping free you from the mercenaries to begin with."

"Maybe," Tristan admitted. "I don't know about your company, Nathan. I am fairly certain that she wants you dead."

"You will get no arguments from me there." Nathanial stretched his legs out, getting the blood circulating in them once again. "We do not know each other well, Captain, but you sacrificed quite a bit saving my cousin. For whatever it's worth . . . thank you."

"No need for thanks. You should probably stop calling me Captain, though. I am not a captain of anything as of this moment."

"Some might argue with that. You are a ranking officer of the Astrona guard. You are defending a House lady. I would say you are doing your job quite well."

"We would not be in this situation if not for our . . ."

His words trailed, and he looked rather embarrassed at his admission. "You can go ahead and say it, Captain. I did not need to ask to realize that there would be more than just a simple reason to flee Corovium with an accused killer."

"I care for her," he stated. "Likely far more than she does for me."

"Love is a funny thing, Captain. What you want and what you need are likely not what you get."

"Suggestions?"

"Take what she gives you," he said, "and hope that you turn into what she needs. She wears her emotions on her sleeves, Captain. But she has short sleeves. Very, very short sleeves."

"Well so far I think that all I have managed to do is pester her. She is to the point with me, rarely speaks, and I am beginning to wonder what in Shadow I am even doing anymore."

"She is piecing this reality together, as are we all. Katlynn has never been separated from her family before. To go from that to becoming a fugitive all within the manner of seconds can be traumatizing. Give her time, and be patient. She will come to you when she is in need. For now, the only thing we *actually* need is to figure out our next move."

Tristan nodded. "Damn, I suppose I sound like a selfish ass. I know there are more important things to concern ourselves with. I did not mean to sound like my feelings were more crucial than . . ."

"And quit apologizing," Nathan interrupted. "Stand by your convictions. I am fairly certain that I have never apologized for anything, even when I am wrong."

As if the very presence of evil had been felt before them, both men gazed upward to see Jadenine standing before them. "I suppose we have just come to the root of my hatred for you, Wode."

"And here I was beginning to think it was jealousy alone." Turning to Tristan, he motioned him to the others. "Wake them. We should be on our way."

The captain stood and moved to the others, leaving the two alone.

"So what of me now, Wode? Shall you keep your word?"

Reaching for her sword that Tristan left with his belongings, he stood and moved before her. Extending the weapon, Jadenine hesitated before taking hold of her sword. And if Nathan were to rank awkward moments in his life, he just found his new number one. They stood and only stared at each other, stoic like figures in statuette form, gazing longer than he likely had ever looked upon her for the culmination of their acquaintance.

Then she nodded to him, and he did the same in return. It was the most honest moment between the two that he could recall. Nathan would have liked to believe that she thanked him for keeping his word. It could have gone a great many ways, but this was the right one, the honest one. He would have liked to believe that.

But in reality she likely told him to fuck off one last time, all with a silent nod.

Either way, the moment gone, Jadenine turned and disappeared into the wilderness beyond.

--

"Haroulvene is a small village," continued Iero, his mouth moving but words rarely absorbing Katlynn's conscious. "Just inside the border, it still garners the occasional hunter from time to time. It should not cause distraction for one or two of us to enter for supplies. But caution should still be taken as it is far too close to Prillian to not assume the Guild presence amongst them."

"Thankfully I brought some gold," Nathan, who walked in front of the rest, spoke back to them.

"I would say yes to that," Iero agreed. "Fortune best shines on those prepared to face all kinds of adversity. I would even stretch to say . . ."

"Shut it," Nathan snapped. "Whoever goes in, and I would likely say you, Tristan, we will need to focus on the supplies we need to survive. I need more arrows, we need water, flint, and whatever dried rations we can get a hold of in case hunting becomes sparse."

So is this what my life has come to?

It hardly felt fair. But then again, when had life ever shown itself to be *fair*. Her tears would no longer be for herself, but for those that traveled with her, sacrificing their own lives and well beings and ultimately for what? For one foolish House lady? Katlynn had never paid much attention to her responsibilities. Never had she asked Uncle Philip of his duties and the pressures of it. Not once did she speak to her father of his life as a House lord. Never, because she did not care. What usefulness came from such a line of questioning? Would she ever rule her House? Would she ever take the throne? Best case scenario for her, she might be held to marry someone within the high courts or some such, bringing more prestige to the Pratt name. Worst case, she would be accused of murdering the king in cold blood and forced to become a fugitive on the run. Seeing things in that new light, she could not understand her bleak outtake.

All the political ignorance, all the lack of concern in her family's affairs seemed ironic now. It was not her, but *someone* killed the king, in which now framed a House name, hers in particular. All the while she was nearly too dumb to even bother to run. This life left for her felt unjust and yet somehow deserved. She would sleep outside, reek of filth, and eat squirrel and rabbit for the remainder of her days.

What a life indeed. What girl could ask for anything more?

Katlynn pushed away a tear that formed and inhaled heavily. She could not change it. At least she was not alone.

"You should not have sadness," came the voice of the strange Argon, Feko. "You will be fine in the end. You will accomplish great things, I'm sure."

Tristan had cautiously moved between the two, even though Feko made no attempts to close the gap between them. Neither Nathan nor the captain had explained this man's presence. An oddity, as he spent many hours speaking to himself. It did not take a genius to understand that her cousin had very little trust in the Argon, and that transferred quickly to Tristan.

"I suppose you just know this," she replied.

"Well, in a way. Difficult to explain."

Pausing for a moment, she wondered exactly what he meant. "No more difficult to understand on this end either."

"You have purpose, Katlynn Pratt," he responded. "Not unlike myself, though in a grander scale. After all, you are you, and I am but a vessel."

"I don't know about the grander scale, stranger. At this point, I would be thankful for a bath and a hot meal."

--

The second day was brutally long and the pace slowed. Katlynn's feet did not get any better; in fact, he began to wonder if they were infected. Nathan would have much preferred reaching Haroulvene by now, but instead they would spend another night in the wilderness without proper supplies and with water becoming scarce. Though he did not confess to his group, he began to second guess his direction. He had been to this small village before, but only once, and there was no road to guide him. The Ursan and their damned culture of living amongst nature had many visual pleasures, all of which he would piss upon for a decent map and a proper bed.

"At this point, I would take a bath before anything," mumbled his cousin, who sat with her legs outward, alleviating pressure from her blistered and cracked feet. "We all reek."

"All the better," started the Druid, and Nathan half cringed as Iero found yet another reason to open his mouth. "In the wilderness, best not to smell wonderful or clean. A better idea would be to blend in, become one with the trees and the animals around you. And to be honest, Lady Pratt, the animals within the Lis'rial are known for many things, but fresh smelling would not rank as one of those."

"True," she agreed, "but I don't take pleasure in smelling like that Chur'rat of yours. Speaking of which, where did he run to now?"

"Eating, I am sure," Nathan added. "And a damn sight better than the lot of us."

"Oh, they are excellent hunters, Nathanial Wode. Alone they do quite fine at catching smaller creatures. They are even excellent climbers and can catch the occasional raven or sparrow. But as a group, they are quite deadly. Larger packs can take down a greater foe easily, just as easily as . . ."

"Enough," he interrupted. "Between Feko's mumbling and your inability to keep quiet, you might as well draw a lot of Draywolves directly at us, or worse."

"Draywolves don't hunt in packs," Iero corrected.

"You know what I mean," he snapped back to the Druid.

Feko looked visually disturbed. "What is worse than Draywolves?"

"These are ancient forests," answered Nathan. "Too close to Donovini for anything crazy. But who knows what lies in the depths of this. I have heard crazy stories, men that claim they still see Rocs fly and hunt in the north."

And his first miracle on the trip: silence. His eyes moved to his companions, from Feko to his cousin, Tristan to Iero, and not one of them had anything to say at the moment. Nathan exhaled. A moment of peace . . . strangely interrupted by the thumping against the earth . . . rhythmic thumping . . . horses . . .

Shit.

Tristan must have felt the vibrations as well, as he stood with sword drawn. Both blades were quickly in Nathan's hands, and he spun about to his cousin.

"Get within the Shadows," he demanded with such authority that Katlynn did not take a moment to question. For one instant, she was sitting, the look of fear in her eyes. The next, she was gone, lost within the darkness around her. "Iero," he stated, "I hope you are ready."

"I am always ready to . . ."

"And Feko," Nathan continued, not letting the Druid ramble on. The Argon stared blankly, fearful even. "Just hide and stay quiet."

"I will stand with you, if it is all the same," he replied.

"Should we be running?" Tristan questioned in a flustered voice.

"No point," Nathan whispered in response.

They will find us. There is no place they can't find us. I should know.

The Guild had found them quicker than anticipated. How foolish he had been to believe that there was any sanctuary from them, even in Ursan. They could move without laws to prohibit them, as they were an extension of laws. And yet they stood with the honor of mercenary and thieves, each looking to deceive the next. As easily as Nathan had found Katlynn Pratt, others found him all the same.

They fast approached, the sounds bouncing from the trees. They did not hide their presence. Seven, maybe eight. He had four arrows left. Luck would allow two kills with those, leaving maybe five or six. But these were not desperate men from Uvull. These were trained killers.

The shorter, serrated blade sheathed, his long sword planted firmly into the earth before him, the bow came from his back, his quiver dropped beside him. He lightly drove three of the arrows into the ground, iron tip first, and notched the fourth in place. On his knees, he waited patiently for the inevitable.

"I might add," started Iero, "that I have yet recovered from my last touch of Earth. My strength will not be what it normally is."

"We take what you can give."

"And it may also draw unwanted attention from the Draywolves, amongst other creatures. The perversion of nature does not go unnoticed by its inhabitants."

"I'm more worried about what's coming at us right now. Worry about the Draywolves later if we survive this. Now ready yourself."

The loud thumping finally slowed as they came to a steady trot just outside of his vision. Of course they must have known Nathan would be ready for them. Their numbers certainly could overwhelm him, but that was the difference between the Imperial Army and the Guild. The army fought as one, without care of glory or sacrifice. In the Guild, numbers or not, fear or not, no one wanted to be the first to die.

"I am Muul, of the Guild," a male voice called out from the shadows. "I come out alone. The boys won't be surrounding you or anything. They are going to wait patiently behind me. I ask that you not throw a dagger at me while I come out and make some sense of the situation."

"As an equal member of the Guild, you have my word on that." *Especially since I don't have any throwing daggers.*

On horseback, the Donovinian strode out into view, a fairly large man with heavily tanned skin, tattoos running down his exposed neck. An ugly bastard, that much for certain, but had likely seen twice the battles that Nathan had.

Muul reached back and elbowed a concealed rider hard, and the figure fell from his horse and hit the ground with a thud. It did not take more than a second to process who the bound prisoner had been.

"Found Jadenine here trying to make her way back into Donovini," Muul noted. "Of course she said that you had forced her along or some such horseshit, then let her go. I would have half believed it . . . if I was a dumb shit."

Nathan ignored best he could the pangs in his stomach. "She speaks the truth."

To which the Guild member laughed. "You likely do not know me, Nathanial Wode, but I know of you. A fucking killer you are. Only an ignorant ass would let someone go that could reveal his location and intent. And you are not. Now before you get any crazy ideas, I got eight more men behind me. No one wants a scene. I already sent one man back once we captured this bitch to inform the Guild that you and Jadenine have gone rouge. Captured Lady Pratt yourselves for some reason unknown, likely working for House Brocusk now. Either way, this forest is about to be flooded by week's end with Guild in search of you. What chance could you last?"

"No better than my chances now, I would gather," Nathan replied.

"Damn right," chuckled Muul. "So I am a loyal member of our Guild, Nathanial Wode. Don't so much care why you are doing what you are doing, not so much going to ask you one fucking question about it either. Just need you to put down your bow, tell the captain there to drop his sword, tell the Druid to keep his hands from the earth, and surface the girl you are protecting. Do all those, everyone lives. Don't, and only Lady Pratt lives."

"You assume she is here."

"I know damn well she is here. Especially since she is right there."

As Muul pointed, Nathan turned to see his cousin in plain sight, a short dagger in her hand. "I will be damned if I let you die for me, Nathan."

The Guild member laughed aloud. "Come, do not be a fool. You know this ends here."

He swallowed back hard, his stomach rolling about within him.

Steady, calm.

"She is innocent of any crime," he pleaded.

Muul shrugged. "Maybe so. Since when has the Guild been the judge? We are the fist."

"I cannot allow her to travel back to Genethur. They will kill her to please the masses."

"And that will not be of our doing."

"But we will have allowed it!" cried out Nathanial.

But the Guild member appeared unmoved. "We will have done our job, as requested by Cylaa and those above her. Flame's embrace, this order was sent out from the First of Amon. Since we have no king, there is no higher man amongst us living. Lady Pratt, Captain Tristan Crane, and Iero come with me for transport to Genethur to await trial for high treason. You and Jadenine will travel to Prillian to answer for conspiring against the Guild. And you . . ." his eyes wandered to Feko, arms crossing before his chest ". . . are free to go. I have no idea who you are."

"No once drastically important," answered Feko. "But I fear this ends in blood nonetheless."

"The fallen gods speak through him," Nathan announced, his arm slowly pulling back on the bowstring. "And they apparently know our course of action."

Muul's eyes widened. Clearly he had not thought Nathan this foolish. He must not have really known Nathan at all then.

"Did you not agree that your chances are folly?" stammered the Guild member.

"I did," answered Nathan. "But then again, what chance did you give yourself?"

"Uh . . ."

Released.

A clean shot that exploded in blood, his exposed neck the home of the arrow. Reaching quickly he grabbed another arrow and notched it into place. The roar of the Guild members now in full charge came up and his urge to vomit could have never been stronger. He would not make it out of this one alive.

Inevitability, eventually, luck ran out. Never at the best times, either. And this might have been the worst.

Horses came into view and he released.

A lucky shot, an impossible shot.

As he readied his third arrow, the second buried into the side of the lead horse. The beast neighed heavily and rose up on its hind legs, the rider tumbling back and into a horse behind him. The injured animal then fell over itself, taking an adjacent rider with it. Bodies flung everywhere, and horses flailed about, kicking wildly in their attempts to rise back to their feet. It had become a few seconds of pure chaos. And Nathan could not have asked for a better stroke of luck.

A steady aim and the third arrow released, it found a home in a helpless man pinned down by his steed. Fourth arrow notched and sent away, a man that once still remained on a horse now took one in the shoulder, enough that between that and the shock from his animal, the horse just threw him clean off. Nathan dropped his bow, unsheathed his smaller blade, and grasped hold of his long sword that had stood before him in the earth.

--

She refused to be useless any longer.

Iero had already placed his hands upon the ground before him, but she could tell from his face that he grew weary, that his touching of the Realm had taken a great toll and did not have sufficient time to recover. Katlynn, however, had plenty of strength within her. That was never in question. It was her resolve.

Nathan moved forward now to the mess of downed and confused Guild members with Tristan right behind him. She reached out, the Shadow Realm opening upon her touch, calling forth to her, willing it to be such. There stood a temptation that Katlynn always shoved aside, always refused to admit to others much less herself. But it was there, and the time for confrontation on the matter was not now. Need or not, desire or otherwise, she took from the Shadow Realm a portion of their world, the ability to shroud herself within the darkness of her world. And like wrapping herself with a scarf, the blackness of the night came around her, and she disappeared into it.

And then she rushed forward. Nathan already engaged with one Guild member, slicing open his stomach before moving to the next. Tristan parried back and forth with another man, and Iero had left up a few walls of vines and roots, more in an annoyance and deterrence than an offense. It did the task well, though, as it forced men to move about or around the barriers.

Katlynn moved up to her first victim, his eyes focused and intent on Nathan, and her dagger found the side of his neck, once, twice, three times. Warm liquid poured between her fingers as his hands reached up in attempt to stop each successive thrust with no avail. She had never killed a man before. It was not as difficult a task as she would have thought.

Quickly she moved to the next, and he too could not have been wiser to the assault. Her blade coming up behind and slicing deep into his neck, blood rushing out with a sickening, gurgling sound to follow. No time to think. Again Katlynn pressed on, except now she had been spotted. One turned in her direction, glancing about, watching his neighbor die horrifically to a shadow. She hesitated, wondering what direction she should move, all the while as the Guild member wondered where the mystery attack would come from. He could see the darkness but could not focus upon it, she knew.

Tristan once told her that in the heat of the battle, never worry about a blade from behind. No sense in that, he said, as the focus should be on the one swinging. The irony did not leave her in that the captain buried an unsuspecting blade deep into the shoulder of the Guild member, a cut so deep that it nearly took off an arm. The pain must have been so blinding that his mouth stood open, but nothing came from it. A second swing took half of his head off, and Tristan looked about for another, though Nathan was making easy work from the madness.

--

It was a quicker affair than he had anticipated. One Guild member stood left, an arrow in his shoulder, and he stumbled with a blade in hand over to Jadenine.

"I'm walking out of here," he made claim, lifting the bound and helpless Ursan to her feet.

"You've picked the wrong hostage," mumbled Jadenine, a smirk on her face. "You all had Nathan right. He is a killer. And he certainly doesn't care about me."

Nathanial took a few steps forward, his weapons still dripping from the blood of his foes. He would have been a much more menacing figure if he did not swallow back the starts of his stomach. He pictured himself looking like a spastic monkey or something similar.

"We made a mistake," the wounded man stated. "*I* made a mistake. I should have never come after you."

"Damn right," Nathan managed to say with some form of authority.

"Just stay back. I will hurt her if . . ."

The words were lost to a blade into the eye, a shadowy figure wielding the weapon. The Guild member struggled, but his cousin rose and dropped the dagger deeper, blood working freely down his face, his own weapon lost as he reached up in reflex only. In reality, the blade had penetrated deep enough the first time, but sometimes it took a few seconds for the body and brain to match. Reflexes had a strange way of making a man do bizarre things in death. Nathan should know. He had seen his fair share.

Katlynn came back into view, her powers faded or stopped or however it worked, and she took a few steps forward before kneeling over and coughing, some puke releasing from her.

"A family trait," humored Jadenine.

Nathan had a witty comeback, but it was lost to his own attempts to keep his stomach calm. Instead he walked over with his weapon and cut free the rope that had bound her.

Rubbing her wrists together, she looked again to Katlynn. "I only jest. First time you killed anyone?"

She nodded, still keeled over, still coughing some.

"No shame, Katlynn. It was the same for us all," noted Nathan. "Just some of us never seem to get used to it."

Surprisingly enough, Jadenine nodded to him, as if to say she understood. Somehow he doubted as such. "Killing is easy, Katlynn Pratt," the Ursan stated softly. "Living with the facts is much, much harder. But I . . . thank you, regardless."

"The Twin Moons give way for such a show of affection," Feko stated with all smiles.

"Fuck you, you crazy . . ."

"Alright," Nathan swiftly intervened. "Everyone is on edge, especially . . ."

His statement could not be completed, as Jadenine planted her fist deep into his gut. He vomited in response.

"Damn you Wode," she hissed. "What is left for me?"

"You are alive," Feko added in caution. "It is something."

"For how long? Two day ride and the entire Guild will know we are traitors. They will also know exactly where Katlynn Pratt is. How long until this place is swarming with more of these men? Only this time they arrive by the dozens."

Wiping his mouth, Nathan turned back to her. "I never wanted this for you, trust me."

She took a few steps over to his cousin. "Are you okay?" she stated, though still in a stern and direct voice. "We will need to move soon, get as much distance from us and the border as possible. No time better than immediately."

Katlynn nodded slowly and rose back to face them all. "I . . . don't want to be useless."

"You did well, but we need to push onward," Jadenine added.

Tristan moved over to Katlynn. "Come," he started, "let us see if any of the horses did not wander far. Hopefully we can get you off your feet."

His cousin nodded and trailed off with the captain while Jadenine brushed past Nathanial, giving him a cold, dead eye. "Damn you, Wode. You should have warned me back in Prillian."

Yes, but should haves and could haves were about as useful as giving caution to a harlot. Waste of time.

"For what it is worth," he called back to her, "and likely very little, I would not have let you die just now. I would have saved you."

"I know," Jadenine answered back. "And you're a fool because of that."

Damn, she is right. About it all.

Her death would have been one less questionable person to deal with. He had not asked her what she would do from here, but that answer seemed obvious now. She would trade in whatever stood of her life and follow him into solitude. The more the merrier.

Nothing quite like spending eternity with someone that wished him death. At the very least, it made things interesting.

Nathan was beginning to appreciate the little things in life.

--

I hear people speak of blind faith as if that's any different from faith itself. Any faith is blind faith. You follow your heart, because you believe, because you trust. All of those are abstract. Faith cannot be seen. That is why it is blind. But I am no more foolish for believing.

The only people with blind faith are those without it.

-- Feko Hawbry, an Argon Herbalist

XII

Allura was sleeping, yet cognizant of her surroundings. Jerryn slept beside her, silent, still. The room was filled yet empty and wholly unfamiliar to her.

Where am I?

Through a window a shadow appeared, moving up and into her room. The shadow was a figure, knelt over with blades in both hands. Allura made every attempt to stand from her bed, but was paralyzed. Frozen. She could feel the sweat from her head as she could only watch as the faceless figure approached, one ghostly step after the next.

"Jerryn!" she called out to her husband, but there was no answer. He was no longer there.

"I told you I required your memory," the figure stated. "I have come to reclaim that payment."

"What do you want from me?"

The blades lifted above her. "Your blood," he answered.

"No!"

Allura arose from her bed, sweat everywhere, and no figure to be seen. The room now seemed familiar, her chambers within the capital, her bed void of Jerryn. A dream. Nothing but a dream.

She must have screamed the words as the door forcefully came open and first through was her personal guard. Attractive, clean shaven, the man had closely shaven blond hair and the traditional armor of the House guard of Argonus, the colors black and green. His arm rested on his sword as he examined the room quickly. He must have surmised the situation as he eased back within a few awkward seconds and turned to close her bedroom doors again.

That quickly changed as scampering footsteps could be heard and the guard gave way to her mother. She stormed though, her nightgown only half thrown on in her rush. "Is she alright?" she questioned her personal guard, who nodded in response. "Are you fine, girl?" she then directed toward her.

Allura realized that she must have screamed loudly enough for her mother to have heard. "I am fine," she responded. "I am fine. Fine. Just a nightmare."

Her mother nodded, then adjusted her robes. "Two nights in a row. I can remember my fair share of nightmares before my wedding. Are you okay with this, child? I would assume you would be."

"I am. Of course I am."

"As I thought." Christina moved across the room and sat down at the end of her bed. She motioned for the guard to leave and he did as commanded, disappearing back into the previous room. "Nicolas has agreed that speed is best at the moment. Normally we would take months to plan this wedding, but with the conspiracies against his name and the unknown of Ursan, we need a power onto the throne as soon as possible."

"I understand the situation," Allura responded, wiping the sleep from her eyes. "What of the courts approval?"

"With Brocusk gone, the courts are crippled. They will decide nothing soon. At the moment, we do not need them. The council will approve House Rowe as succession after the marriage and we will crown you queen with or without the courts."

"And without Afeon?"

"So you have heard already?" her mother inquired with a grin. "News travels swiftly amongst these halls. You must admit, strange set of circumstances a few nights ago. Brocusk takes his court officials and leaves on the same night that Rayden is abducted, possibly killed. Very strange, as it is also on the same day that I misspoke, telling you of my stipulation in the agreement with the Pratts."

"I believe that's why they call it irony," she retorted, doing what she could to mask her fear.

"Indeed. Now you have had nightmares just suddenly, where you wake up in a panic. Is this all from the wedding or the pressures of such? Or perhaps something else?"

"It's nothing, I am sure."

"Is there anything you wish to tell me? Anything at all?"

Hesitating, Allura answered, "No."

"Can Rayden's disappearance be linked back to this House?"

"Earth and Flame, Mother. I had nothing to do with it."

Except everything to do with it. And I feel ill. And the nightmare felt more like a damned premonition then a dream. Why did I put myself above Amon? Love? Oh you stupid, stupid girl.

There were certain things she could tell in a look. She knew Jerryn was an amazing lover by the way he gazed at her the first time. Allura knew that the man in the tavern that she convinced to take Rayden was a killer by the gleam in his dark eyes. And she knew without pause that her mother did not believe her, not for the slightest of seconds.

"Very well, child." If she was disappointed, Allura could not tell. Christina strode across the room, stopping only for a moment to conclude, "You will meet with the tailor to ensure the wedding dress fits you properly. I have arranged for Jerryn to be with you all day today to help arrange things. We may rush this wedding, but . . . I still wish you to have one."

It may have been the only moment her mother had appeared human to Allura. And before she had the opportunity to get used to such feelings, her mother shut the door as she left.

--

"You know Lilli turned thirteen a week ago," Jessica stated softly, standing in their kitchen with a glass of wine. It was a bit early for wine, but he did not mind it much at the moment. Times were tense, and all things considered, Philip would have liked one himself. But he did not need his mind clouded. He had uncomfortable meetings about to take place, along with an impending wedding that would feel more like a military battleground than a moment of unity. Hard times were plentiful, and he had his share of nightcaps in order to get through those. No, he did not mind that his wife had a drink to calm her nerves.

Though he did mind that she insisted on making him feel like shit regularly.

"I did not forget," Philip responded. "You know I love my girls. I will see her today and speak with her after I finish with . . ."

"Work. I know."

"Do you?" Philip stood from the small dinette table in their kitchen and walked out to their living room. "I know that I missed out on her birthday, amongst many other things as of late. But we have a nephew and a niece missing, a wedding to arrange, a throne to claim, the courts to repair, and oh yeah, I have the Second of Amon locked away in the dungeons below. I am sorry, but it appears as if my hands are a bit tied in this political insanity along with attempting to get through this without any more of our family lost and running. I think that the least you could do is the simple task of keeping our immediate family together while I try to keep our country together."

"Of course. Because saying happy birthday to your youngest is far removed from your duties."

"I will apologize to her," he assured. "Do you intentionally pick the worst times ever to pester me?"

"I want to leave."

It took a moment to absorb the contents of her words.

Jessica took another deep sip from her glass. "I am taking Lilli back to Astrona, and I am going to ask that Joanna and her husband to follow suit."

A loud knocking interrupted the two, though Philip dared not let his gaze leave his wife's. "Enter!" he called out, and the door came open just enough for a soldier to step into view.

"First Pratt, you have visitors. Shall I allow them entrance?"

"Yes," he responded, and the soldier ducked back through the door. "We can talk later about this."

"There is little to discuss," Jessica replied as she grasped the bottle of wine and shuffled off to the bedroom, closing the door behind her. The time to ponder this new chain of events was certainly not now. The door swung open and Lurey Hillan came into view along with several guards, followed by Second General Isani Brocusk. He was not bound, as per the request of Philip, and strode in with his head held high. There did not seem to be any immediate animosity felt within the room at his presence, outside of the uncomfortable look on Lurey's face.

"Welcome, General," Philip stated. "Hopefully your stay downstairs was not altogether unpleasant."

"It was not," he answered. "I thank you for that. You could have made life more difficult if you chose it so."

"So you are not upset with me? Two days down in the dungeons is not always perceived as a vacation."

"True enough, but I am a military man, First Pratt. I understand that sometimes you must react with first instincts. Might I speak freely?"

Philip nodded toward the general. "By all means, General Brocusk."

"I will not denounce my people, nor claim war against Ursan," the general immediately laid out. "I will, however, denounce Lord Brocusk as my House lord, if that suits you well enough. I had no communication with him on his moves and no understanding of any plots he might have played here."

"But he is family to you, is he not?"

"Distant cousin at best," scoffed Isani. "When I gave my oath to King Yelium Aylmer, I did such with great honor. I devoted myself to no longer just protect Ursan, but Amon. If Dehyllo has kidnapped your nephew, he will have crossed a point that there can be no return from, and there is little need for him to lead my people any further."

"So far he has eluded your men," offered the First.

"He is a crafty bastard, that much is for certain. I doubt my men will catch him easily, if at all. He knows his way well enough into Ursan that it will be difficult. You could tap the Guilds again . . ."

"Who have not proven that they can even find my niece. Besides . . . this is not so clear. We cannot let the mass populace know that we are hunting Dehyllo. Bad enough that the word is spreading that he has withdrawn from the courts. They believe he denounces the throne and prepares for war."

Isani shrugged. "You do realize, whether he kidnapped Rayden or not, there may be truth to their panic."

"I do. So better to not involve the Guild until we find out his intent."

"Very well. So what of me?"

"What of you?" Philip questioned back to him. "I have just detained you long enough to make a decision on what to do. That decision completely depends on your outtake on the situation, which seems to be honest. If Brocusk marches his army across Amon, you know that many of your people will march with him."

"I do. And I will not be the one to kill them. Dehyllo will be responsible for such."

"These are difficult times, Second General Brocusk. Your name will draw much ire if your cousin does what we fear."

To which the general chuckled. "As if my name hasn't drawn ire before any of this."

"Point taken, General. Your temporary inspection of our dungeons has ended."

"They were in prime condition, First Pratt."

"And now you have a new job to immediately plan for. The wedding will be taking place in a few days between Allura Rowe and Jerryn Pratt."

Isani raised an eyebrow. "So it takes place regardless, then?"

"The fortune of having multiple offspring," humored Philip. "Following this wedding will be a crowning of a new king. I need these to go a fair sight better than our last crowning."

"I would imagine you would. I will meet with my men immediately and make the arrangements. If it's not too far above my station to ask, what is to happen to Second Afeon?"

"Life is never simple," the First spoke softly, the irony lost on himself. "Neither are the choices we make in it."

--

Jerryn stood about in presence and body alone, but not in spirit. They sat through meeting after meeting, between the florist and the tailors, to the bakers and the decorators, all the while the guards hovered about them by the dozens, as if it were their fucking war room. And each time Allura turned to her soon to be husband, he only sat about, lifeless, thoughtless.

"The day has been long," she said to him in hushed tone. "Perhaps we can go for a walk?"

"Fresh air doesn't much change the situation," mumbled Jerryn.

"No, no I suppose not." Allura leaned heavily back in her chair. They had a moment's rest between appointments, and it did not seem as if Jerryn sought to join her in taking advantage of the lapse. "I understand that you've gone through much, but I would have thought this would make you happy?"

Jerryn turned to her, his eyes reflecting his confusion. "Do not mistake my desire to marry you with the loss of my family. My sister has yet to be found, my brother kidnapped, and they could both be dead for all I know. How happy do you want me to be? How excited and enthralled should I pretend to be while sitting here planning our future? I was a shit of a brother, I admit that. But I loved them."

She refused to lose him to despair. Not now. She would be queen in no more than two weeks. In order for that to happen, she would need a husband.

"And what of me?" she queried. "Do you not love me?"

There was hesitation in his response. "Yes."

"Then embrace what is left, rather than cascade me against the cliffs."

"Earth and Flame, Allura, I do not toss you aside. I mourn."

"Then let me help you mourn," she offered. "I know that this isn't how we wanted this, but we *did* want this. Now that it's ours, should we spend our time weeping against our losses?"

"What do you know of loss?"

And her hand whipped about before she had thought better and struck him clean across the face. It was a clean hit, an unsuspecting one as well. For a briefest of seconds, she thought to apologize.

"My father died, you Donovinian shit. Or did you forget?"

She decided the opposite.

Allura stood from her chair and moved across the room, tears forming in her eyes. She could not figure why she was about to cry. This had been her fault, in part. Rayden's disappearance had been what she wanted. Jerryn had been the man to take the throne, with her by his side. Everything was going as planned.

So why, she wondered, did she feel like the worst human to ever walk Amon? Why did she feel so wrong in condemning Rayden Pratt? He was a good man.

"Wait!" roared Jerryn as she was but steps away from the door.

When she turned back to him, his face had the mark of her hand across it. It was . . . significant.

He stood, kicked his chair back to the ground, and turned to the guards that stood about. "Leave us," he ordered.

No one moved.

"Apparently you fail to realize that I am about to be your king," he continued. "I will have you all hung off the side of this building the moment I am crowned if you do not leave this fucking room. Now!"

Still, there stood a pause amongst them, but now they seemed to waiver, each looking to the next.

One brave enough decided to step forward. "We were given strict orders by General Brocusk to remain at your side lest punishment of death."

Jerryn reached out and took hold of the soldier by his armor. "When the dust settles, who do you think will be in charge of Second General Brocusk? Guard the door and leave me to my fiancé."

Something in the way that he said such had her wishing she could leave with them. There stood no more hesitation in the men this time. They marched out like good little soldiers, leaving only her personal guard who remained. His orders could only come through her. Though she wished him to remain, she waved him off with the others. Something in his eyes told her that he as well did not wish her to be alone. But he complied nonetheless, closing the door behind him, leaving Allura standing by the door, nervous and uncertain.

Jerryn moved around the table and began approaching her, slowly. "You expect me to be king? Of all of Amon? And you dare strike me in front of those that are meant to die for me?"

Allura could tell much on first looks. She knew Jerryn would be an amazing lover. But this look was new. Her assessment of this look did not bode well for her, of that she also knew.

"You are to be my king," she barely whimpered. "I should not have struck you."

"No," he agreed. "You *really* fucking shouldn't have."

He reached out and grabbed her arm, then flung her against the table. Her stomach hit against the edge of it hard, and she exhaled every bit of the air in her lungs. While she gasped for air, Jerryn grabbed her hair and wrenched her face back, his hot breath heavy against her cheeks.

"Is this what you wanted?" he hissed at her through his teeth.

By the fallen gods, no it was not.

"Should you ever strike me again, I would suggest you just kill me. Might be easier for you in the end."

He shoved her face back into the desk and let go while she slid down to the floor, her arms pressed against her stomach. The pain was steady and sharp, coming in and out in flashes. It had dawned on her that she perhaps did not know Jerryn as well as she initially thought she did. Certainly they had exchanged many letters, but what did that tell her about his character?

"You know what?" he stated. "Let's go for that walk. It's a beautiful fucking day today, right? You want to get off the floor there, my love?"

--

The air hung stale and heavy inside the dungeons of the capital. For the first year or so as the First, Philip wondered why they even *had* a dungeon within the capital building. It would seem that any dark or demented deed that needed doing should be done far and away from where they lived. There was an old saying about shitting where one ate, but it was lost to him at the moment. But as he aged, he discovered that having this kind of thing close was better on the legs, which was better on his overall wellbeing. He did not need to travel across the city just to interrogate or torture someone. Dig low enough, deep enough, and even a preacher would not notice or question. There was another old saying about out of sight, out mind. It was a damned sad truth.

The First of Amon moved with steady purpose through empty cells and darkened rooms. He had a great many things inside his head as to what he would say to Afeon the moment he spoke to him. But in all likelihood, it would matter little. Something about the Second always felt like he had the one up on him. Even now, locked away inside of a cell, Afeon would likely twist that situation as if he knew it would happen and hoped for such.

To Shadow with him, not this time.

At the last cell available, the guard that had stood quickly bowed respectfully toward the First and then swiftly shuffled along. Philip came to the cell and pulled up a stool that stood against the dungeon wall. When he gazed inside the prison, Afeon looked no worse for the matter.

"Ah, First Pratt!" he bellowed, a smile across his face. "A pleasure for you to visit me down inside my new quarters. A tad stuffier than my old place, certainly, but the hospitality is about equal."

"Are you done? Because apparently you do not realize the spot that you are currently in."

"I am no fool, First Pratt, and neither is Dehyllo." He pulled up his own chair inside the cell and sat down across from Philip. "I have been given instruction, as he assumed you would pull such a move after he removed his people from the courts."

"So he predicted your imprisonment, and left you to it?"

"Would you have us cower away from the inevitable? No, someone had to stay behind, First. We still hold on to hope that you can be swayed to understand the importance of what we do. One of the reasons I was selected to be Dehyllo's voice on the council was because I knew how to speak and play the games of this government. Many of Lord Brocusk's family are similar to him. They would have just bashed skulls when arguments did not go their way."

"I appreciate the chivalry," said Philip. "So why don't we discuss the location of Rayden Pratt? Did Lord Brocusk do you the favor of sharing that piece of information?"

"He did not. But I can tell you with some assurance that you are asking the wrong man, and the wrong House."

"And yet Brocusk departs in the middle of the night, same night that people witnessed Rayden being dragged away by strange men that no one could recognize."

"It's a strange coincidence, that is certain. You should be all too familiar, being Katlynn goes missing at the same time a Shadowmancer kills the king. But Katlynn did not kill the king and Dehyllo did not kidnap Rayden. Besides . . . kidnapping isn't our style."

"But killing is?"

"Ha!" Afeon slapped his hands together loudly, a smile appearing across his face. "Of that I would agree. I find it amusing, First Pratt. You think we were responsible for the death of King Aylmer, but we were not. You now think we have kidnapped your nephew, but we did not do that either. The only thing you have pinned correctly on House Brocusk is their desire to claim this throne. To which should be his by right, minus this wedding that your House plans."

"Fear of a tyrant."

"Fear of the unknown," Afeon responded. "In the end, all kings are tyrants. How they are perceived depends greatly on the character of their surroundings."

"We waste time here. Tell me what I want to know, and we can quit pretending as if either of us is interested in holding this conversation."

"I have nothing to tell you."

"What did Dehyllo instruct of you to do in staying behind?" pressed Philip. "Is there more to deal with here in the capital? Are you to disrupt the wedding or the crowning?"

"No on all accounts. Dehyllo has left me behind to be his voice. He did not kidnap Rayden. Why do you fear us so? Why do you presume us to be the suspect to every crime in Amon? Is it your fear of our faith, our understanding of Turitea and Schill, of the Twin Moons, of the dangers that lie beyond the sea?"

"I fear the number to which you populate," answered the First. "And the war upon your minds."

"We do have war on our minds, but not against you or your throne." Afeon sat back, the smirk still plastered onto his face. "Do you not believe that House Rowe would have more to gain from Rayden's disappearance?"

"No." The thought, in honesty, had never even dawned to him. "What sense would that even make? They looked to wed . . ."

"I heard whispers that they were not happy," interrupted the Second. "I heard that Rayden simply sat through the meetings like a corpse. Perhaps Allura was none too fond of your nephew."

"They were new," defended Philip. "That does not necessarily mean . . ."

"Do you know the convenience of having an Ursan as the general? When his people see things, they tell him. When they tell him, they tell me."

"For once, Afeon, speak straight if you have something to say."

"The guards caught many nights where Jerryn Pratt slipped out in the night, out by the beach."

Philip shrugged. "Jerryn has his flaws, one of those being his inability to keep his cock in his pants."

"Agreed," Afeon replied. "Interestingly enough, Allura Rowe was caught on the same nights as well, sneaking from her chambers into the night. To the very same beach as the young Jerryn Pratt."

That night . . . at the beach.

His memory took him to his meeting with Deso, to finding his nephew naked with the Argon girl.

You stupid son of a bitch, Phil. How did you not recognize her? They have been at this even before the assassination.

The Second smiled. "I see you are starting to understand."

More than understand, he realized. Now he struggled to comprehend the scope of the deception. Did Christina know? Was it her that planned for this? Did Rayden know, explaining his attitude and his late-night stroll into the tavern the other night?

Did House Rowe assassinate the king?

"So, what of me, First Pratt? You can't just let me go, no more than you can call off the Guild against your niece."

"No," he mumbled. "No I can't."

"In the end, someone must be responsible."

"Always."

"So how long do you perceive me staying locked away for a crime that my people did not commit?"

"Until the new king decides your fate," Philip answered. "This would be no different than if Katlynn is captured. The only person that can pardon you would be the courts, which are in shambles thanks to your House lord."

"The council could override the court decisions."

"One fourth of the council sits behind these bars."

"Who would support this pardon, I might add."

Philip shook his head. "Even if I thought in error, I cannot vote in right conscious to pardon you. Not that I believe I could get Lurey to join me in such."

"Ah Philip, do you understand the flaws in your system now?" Afeon laughed aloud at his last comment. "It took the death of one man to set this world aflame. One man! And to make matters better, Yelium Aylmer was a tool. He dies, and Amon falls apart. How can one man hold that much power to cripple this country?"

"I am not here to discuss politics with you, Afeon."

"No, I would gather you are here to believe me innocent and yet powerless to do anything about it." The Second shook his head. "This is also no real surprise, First Pratt. You are amazing at gathering the truth . . . and doing nothing with it."

Philip did not know what to say to the Second. Here they sat again, across from each other, and yet the First feeling the lesser of the two. Even bars could not keep the air of audacity from Afeon. No prison could lock away that ego.

"I . . . must go," Philip claimed. "When the crowning takes place, which should be no longer than a week, I will discuss the situation with Jerryn."

"Do not waste too much breath," he responded. "I know how this ends, First Pratt. By the rope, as your Moon Divide would say. By the rope. And if I were you, I would take caution that you do not end the same way. How long before Christina looks to eliminate the remainder of her threats. And to think you feared us? Ha! One day your people will beg for our assistance."

"I hope that day never comes," Philip claimed.

"It will," Afeon murmured. "Soon."

--

They ended up back in Jerryn's chambers, the guards posted outside. Meetings were concluded for the day, and Allura had little desire to find her mother and speak to her on how things went. She was not even certain how to feel at the moment. Jerryn had been himself in front of the public eye, in front of anyone that could see them. But there remained a darkness that she had not witnessed before. Her stomach began to bruise from the impact to the table. That hardly was the worst of her pains. The shock of his change in attitude still struck her worse than his strength.

"What a day," casually stated her fiancé, to which she only stared silently back. "Come now, you must have something to say?"

She shrugged. "My stomach hurts."

"Does it now?" He walked over to the small bar in their chambers and poured two glasses of wine. As Jerryn handed her one, she nervously claimed it, her shaky hands taking a good sip. "Look, Allura, you know my feelings about this. I will marry you because it is what my father and your mother wish of us. I will be your husband with all loyalty. I love you. *You.* But I could give a shit about Amon."

His words were like daggers to her. She recalled a similar claim by his brother, though not nearly as harsh.

"I have never really cared about what Uncle Philip did," he continued. "And since I was never going to be the actual House lord, I didn't pay any attention to Father. What use did I have of politics? I would be destined to be part of the council or the courts or just get drunk and fuck whores all day. But Rayden . . . not him. Rayden this and Rayden that. Rayden was the man to be the next amazing thing in Donovini. Do you know what I do well? Fuck. And drink. And I do both often enough that I better be damn good at them."

"We would be in this together," she managed to say.

Jerryn took a heavy gulp from his glass. "It isn't about that. My brother trained his whole life to be ready to run his country. But he was also a hopeless romantic. He wanted this, and not just you. He wanted all of the insanity that came with being a king. Kings and queens and heirs. I just want you, Allura. Of that I want to be very clear of. I do not, however, want to be king. I never have. I wanted us together long before this craziness happened, long before the king was killed. But I want *us*, not everything else. You were going to marry my brother. I was fine with it, to be honest with you. My brother, the king. So be it. I envied his bed partner but not his status. All I wanted was you. And I know that you want me. But I cannot be, and will never be the man you want. The throne is a thing to cripple a man. I do not want it. I am sorry for what happened to Rayden, I truly am. But he was the man meant for this, and truly the man meant for you. In the end . . . I am not much of anything. In the end . . ."

The words trailed off, and he was already pouring himself another glass of wine. She removed the straps to her dress and let it fall to the ground. When Jerryn turned to her, his eyes examined her exposed body.

"I will run this country then," she claimed. "You will sit on the throne and drink and fuck me endlessly. I will have your children until you have an heir, and we will have someone raise them for us. When you tire of me, you can fuck someone else. You will be fat and drunk and blissfully happy."

You and your brother are both idiots. The world in the palm of your hands, and you would let it slip away. And for what? Fear? Fuck you both then. Cowards. I will rule Amon.

He moved to her, his hands reaching out and grasping her breasts, his fingers pinching her nipples, and she groaned softly for him.

"I suppose Yelium was a useless shit," he stated. "My uncle ran this country."

"So why feel pressured about this? Why worry? Let your uncle continue his job, with me looking after the important affairs. I want you, Jerryn. I love you. But I also love my country. All you have to do is sit there on occasion and look the part."

Jerryn moved his free hand down and slipped them between her legs, his fingers entering her. Again she moaned to his touch.

"I must admit," he said with quiet intent, "perhaps I have thought of this whole thing incorrectly."

"That you have." She took a sip from her wine, then used her free hand to reach into his trousers and find his already hardened cock.

We both have.

--

Pratt slumped into the chair within his office, papers littered amongst his desk, and he could not help but think that he had been here before. There was just a familiar feel to it all. Come to think of it, with Yelium being the Chur'ash fiend that he truly was, it was more a wonder how Philip managed to get anything done during the entire tenure of his position. The country now felt more in peril than it ever had before, and Philip stood powerless to stop it.

And for reasons he could not explain, he found himself thinking of Dylinn.

Life was simpler in her arms. Had the two of them ever been caught, had even the hint of their union made its way to Yelium, it would have ended his life, destroyed his immediate family, and defaced his House name. But what was a man to do? She was the most beautiful woman he ever had the pleasure of bedding, and yet it was more than just that.

He might have loved her. It was a silly thought. *What was it? A sixteen-year affair, or some such? And now I think I might have loved her?* Humorous, perhaps, and yet there stood a chance of it. Worst yet, he had let her leave the capital without a single word, letter, or otherwise from him. What was he supposed to say? What was he meant to do? They both knew how it would end. Shitty. No manner of dreams could change that regardless of what they both wanted.

Now there stood this new revelation before him. It would have been much simpler had he executed the Second before allowing him to speak. Not but an hour ago, the Ursan had murdered the king and kidnapped the next in line. But now . . . now he was not so sure. How much did Jerryn know of this? Worse yet, how could Philip approach anyone on this subject? Should he upset Christina on the accusation, she could all but cancel the wedding and forfeit the union. Amon needed someone on the throne and swiftly. As much as he despised the admittance of such, Afeon stood correct in his assessment. Amon was caught in a spiral and the only direction it traveled was down.

A solid knock on his office door startled the First as he watched it come ajar just enough for the familiar voice to call out, "Might I come in, First Pratt?"

Damn this really does feel familiar.

"Enter, Lurey."

Lurey Hillan entered the room, a letter in his hand. The Imperial seal stood upon it.

"I am sorry," he began, "but a letter arrived via bird carrier for you. It was delivered to me in your absence. I have not opened it, though."

The Third placed the letter down upon the pile on his desk, then sat down across from him. Philip stared at the letter and did nothing.

"Would you like me to leave?" Lurey inquired.

"No," mumbled Philip. "Just thinking how that letter won't be good news. Thinking I would rather burn it and pretend someone shot the damn bird down for lunch."

"Stranger things have happened."

"Truth there." The First leaned back into his seat. "I have not seen the Fourth today. Is he okay?"

"So far as I know. Lijid has been busy, as have we all. These are difficult times, First. Makes you wonder."

"Wonder what?"

Lurey shrugged. "How we kept this world together while Yelium was here."

It was Afeon's point, through and through. How could one man cripple Amon? Certainly Dehyllo had done such with his removal of his people, but none of that would have been possible with a king in place. Oddly enough, those in high enough station knew how pathetic he truly was. But perhaps it was not about his true power in the system, but his leverage against the people. Amon might not have loved Yelium, but they certainly respected him. He was their king. And despite the fact that the council truly ran the country with Philip at the head of such, they could not do the task without someone, *anyone*, upon the throne. The people needed to believe that one man made their lives better. Not a group of men sitting about, mulling over this and that, tax this and subsidize that. One man. Just one.

The people in Amon held true power. But they did not want it. In the end, they only wanted to hold someone accountable.

He reached across and grabbed the letter, opening it and unfolding.

First Pratt,

I understand that we have been disbanded by the king, and while I appreciate your letter to assure us that the reinstatement of my men will take place, patience only goes so far. Money grows short, supplies even shorter, and keeping twenty thousand men in check can be more daunting than it sounds.

In the meantime, I have heard nothing of a new king yet much less a vote on the new House. Does this take place soon? I fear, though, that it will not be soon enough. Action must take place. The situation here grows tenser each passing day.

We have known each other for many years, First Pratt. I feel it best to be honest with you. If I do not hear back from you soon, I will be forced to find supplies for my men. Without money left, the only thing I have left to barter with is fear. If you cannot find a way to repair the situation with the Guild, then we will have little options left but to find our own way.

The situation is grave, Phil. Please understand that in the end, my men come before politics. I pray to the fallen gods that you can repair the damage done by the death of both Aylmers.

Time is utterly short. -- John Shonnen

"What news is it?" Lurey questioned.

Philip barely glanced away from the letter. "The only kind of news as of late. Bad news." He shook his head. "Now give me my pen. I must return the favor."

--

In the end, there is never enough time.

-- Jaa the Knowledgeable, Historian of Amon

XIII

At some point they moved beyond the Lis'rial and into the Forest of Entelar, not that Katlynn could tell the difference. As far as she could see, they stood amongst a bunch of trees. Only real difference was that within the Entelar, it had become increasingly difficult to move with her horse. The trees were wound together tightly, and what little light they had enjoyed in the Lis'rial had all but been a distant memory. According to Jadenine, the Forest of Entelar stood denser than any other within Ursan. She believed it, as if it had been any darker, she would have thought it to be night.

Her horse had done her well and her cuts had at the very least callused completely. Likely damaged beyond repair, but she now settled for comfort. When the Entelar had become too dense for horseback, she had finally felt the pain subside and the bleeding had ceased. Good timing. Her horse had done his job, and his hard work was repaid by his slaughter. Sadly food could not be wasted, not even a loyal servant such as the steed.

It had been two days since the attack, two days since she had killed men. Nathanial, Feko, and Jadenine had left the three of them alone while they scouted ahead to some village. Their food supply still held true but their water supply needed replenishment. The Ursan woman had claimed that she knew of a lake not too far off from their location if her village did not seem safe, though she seemed confident otherwise.

In the meantime, they were to wait. Nathan did not seem keen to leaving her behind, but he as well did not want to risk her to the Guild should they occupy this village. The separation would only be a few hours apparently, which might have helped his decision in leaving. That, and he took both of his questionable party with him. It also might have helped that Katlynn had just proved her worth, for better or for worse.

Mostly for worse, in her mind.

"It gets better, over time," Tristan sat beside her, whispering to her, careful not to wake the napping Druid. *By the fallen gods, please don't.*

"So says my cousin . . . and that Ursan woman," she replied. "It seems you all have experience with this kind of thing."

"That is one way to put it," he stated. "I always looked at it as being part of the unfortunate. I certainly have never wanted to kill anyone. Got sick myself a little the first time. Just something about the finality of it all. Ending someone else . . . it's difficult to get used to."

"But you have."

Tristan nodded. "I have."

Katlynn still felt sick. They did not sleep much during their trek, but what dreams she had were of the deaths. And when she did not dream of that, she dreamt of the power within her grasp. How easy it had all been was remarkable. Her father had demanded that she not use her gift. Perhaps this was the reason. Perhaps . . . he knew how deadly she could become, *would* become.

"I don't know if I could ever get used to it," she admitted. "And I am afraid if I do."

He said nothing at first. Tristan only sat patiently beside her, their backs against trees as the day moved onward. She turned to him, his eyes remaining fixed on the ground before him.

"You should probably get some rest," he recommended. "Catch even an hour of sleep if you can, like the Druid there. I will stand watch."

"Doesn't much seem fair," she replied. "I can stand watch too."

"I did not question your ability to do such. I only thought you might want some rest while there's time."

"I'd rather not dream, to be honest."

He sighed heavily. "I believe that is called an uncontrollable. Sleeping, however, you can control. Dreams or not, you need sleep."

Katlynn had not forgotten how good of a man the captain truly was. "I have been a shit to you, haven't I?"

It took a long moment for him to respond. "You have lost everything you love. I only wish I could be more for you."

"You are," she murmured back to him. "You gave up everything to help me. Who else would have done such?"

"Everyone." He smiled, though he still did not lock eyes with her. "Iero, Nathanial . . . they have volunteered their lives to defend you. Do you think that Rayden or Jerryn would have not done the same given the opportunity? You are adored, Katlynn. I am but one of many."

"You are one in hundreds of thousands." Katlynn smiled, then reached over and lightly kissed him, her lips pressed against his for several seconds, her hands reaching back and stroking his hair. "Can you . . . hold me, maybe, just for a little bit? Until I fall asleep at least."

His smile was the response. Katlynn curled up and pressed her head into his chest, his arms wrapping around her and squeezing her gently.

Please don't let me dream.

She could have easily asked for the winds to never howl, the sun to never rise, and time to never move.

--

Haroulvene was a small village in the middle of the Entelar Forest, no seeable beginning nor ending; it just appeared and vanished at a whim's notice. The Ursan stood with nature, lived amongst it, thus they did not knock down the trees to build their houses, rather they utilized branches and stones and anything else they could gather to build their shelters. Not to say they were primitive in any way, as the structures built could easily sustain the tests of nature. Some lived on the ground, others above the earth in the trees. And if Jadenine had not been in the lead, Nathanial would have undoubtedly stumbled into this village with the grace of a drunken teenager.

They decided to wait until dark, which was but an hour away, before Jadenine would enter and gather the water they needed.

"This will be one of the last villages to barter with coin," she stated, as the three travelers sat close together, hidden in the outskirts of town. "They still have use for it in Haroulvene. Not amongst themselves, but they are close enough to the border to still be able to trade with Donovini."

"An interesting life," stated Feko, who caught a glare from Jadenine. "At least we think so."

"It is a life like any other, Argon," she replied, though not in her typical shortness. "I do not claim it to be any better or worse than any other life. To live a life without coins, to earn and make everything you own . . . it hardens a person more, that much I can attest to. But better?" Jadenine shrugged her shoulders. "My father always told me that life moves onward, with or without you."

"You've never mentioned your family before," Nathan pointed out.

"You never asked," was her reply.

"I guess I was under the impression that you would never tell me anything."

She chuckled at the comment. "And like you are the shining star of honesty and openness?"

To which even Feko seemed to smile. "Curious indeed, Nathanial, how exactly did you hide your name from the Guild for so long?"

"It was hidden from most, save for you of course," Nathan stated.

"What do you mean?" Jadenine questioned.

Feko answered, "I told him within Prillian that I knew of his family ties. I only knew because the fallen gods told me such. It was because of that that Nathanial Wode decided to bring me along."

"Great. Anything else I should know before we continue any further, Wode?"

"That barely seemed worth the retell," was his response.

"Horseshit, Wode. You lied to me from the start. You didn't tell me why Feko joined us, you didn't tell me who you really were, and you didn't tell me this rescue attempt would all but ruin my fucking life."

"No," started Nathan. "But I suppose you might see where I would be timid about telling you all that information. I might not have made it very far out of Prillian if I had."

Jadenine laughed some, light and under her breath. "So tell me, Wode, how was it growing up for a privileged bastard?"

"The same as anyone else, I suppose. Inadequate. How often does birth become the very start of a life of disappointment in your father's eyes?" The rhetorical question was met by blank stares. "My father loves me as much as he could and should. I spent time when I was younger with him and my brother. But I never felt wanted. I was there because my father knew I was blood. My uncle helped out my mother, ensured she was housed properly within Astrona and that we were taken care of."

"To not let the little secret out about the bastard, perhaps?" Jadenine suggested smugly.

"More than likely, yes," was his honest reply. "My father accepted what Uncle Nicolas had done for my mother, but he did not aid in any way of his own. You ask me how I kept such a secret. I kept no secret. I am not a Pratt. I am a Wode. And that name holds no power or weight."

"Be easier if you were a Pratt, wouldn't you say?" Jadenine inquired.

"You say this while we escort an innocent Pratt girl into Ursan who is being hunted by the Guild, and meanwhile my Uncle Philip Pratt has all of Amon breathing down his throat for justice. Oh, and Uncle Nicolas Pratt has a missing daughter, and my father Edmond Pratt is hiding a bastard son."

"Point taken. What about you, Argon? You are a middle-aged herbalist from Argonus, I am certain your story must be fascinating."

"Not as much as you might think," answered Feko, to which even Nathan laughed as silently as possible.

"Well when did you start to hear your voices?" she pried further.

"Not too long ago. I was once just a simple herbalist. An apprentice, but I was happy with what I did. I was taking some time away from work, dipping the old feet in the ocean water, when one night the voices began."

"And exactly how do you know that these voices were in fact the fallen gods?" continued Jadenine.

"I just knew. There are always voices, constantly speaking. Sometimes it's so incoherent that it is more like a low hum. Sometimes . . . well it is difficult to concentrate. It is like they became trapped in my head, and are only aware of that annoyance on the rare occasion that they chose to speak to me."

"So they don't speak to you often?"

"Practically never," admitted Feko.

Jadenine returned a puzzled look. "So when you are mumbling to yourself around us . . ."

"Normally I am asking them to make better sense, if not just to shut up for a minute's peace," he interrupted with a smile. "I am here because they ask me to be here. All things considered, I would much rather be at the beach, my toes in the water and the sand. But I would like to believe that this happened for a reason."

Like the Draywolf mother in the Lis'rial. There must be a reason . . . unless there wasn't.

"Never dawned on you that you just might be completely fucking insane?" she queried bluntly.

To which Feko nodded. "Certainly, for a bit. Then I began to figure that if I were crazy and I made up these voices . . . seems like they would talk to me more, and maybe speak some sort of recognizable language more than half the time."

Nathan turned to the village, then back to Jadenine. It seemed like as good a time as any to enter the town, unless discussing Feko's insanity took precedence all of the sudden. He worried for leaving Katlynn . . .

"Relax, Wode," said Jadenine as she slowly stood. "No chance this time the Guild has reached us yet. And no great hunters of man in the Entelar. Too compact for any large creatures to effectively hunt. Some larger hawks then you are used to seeing, but none that attack us alive. Mostly squirrels, rabbits, and some standard sized foxes and wolves. Now give me whatever coin you have. We need to spend it now before it becomes useless." He did as commanded, tossing over a small coin purse. "Good, now give me your bow and quiver. I should look to resupply your arrows along with water and some dried meats and fruit."

He had no arrows left, but he felt strange in giving it to her. She now had his bow and the last of his money. What kept her from leaving them to figure things out on their own?

"Just give me the fucking bow," she hissed, obviously perturbed at his hesitation. "After all this shit, do you really think I would betray you? Where the hell am I supposed to go? Like it or not . . . well obviously not . . . we are stuck together, Wode. Not that I loved my life with the Guild, because I didn't, but at least it was a respectable line of work. A sight better than a fugitive, wouldn't you say?"

The bow did not leave his back, nor did his vision remove from the greens of her eyes.

"We enter open plains north of here," she continued. "That is Draywolf territory. Will *not* be a pretty trek, that's for sure. And at the moment, there is no other direction for us other than north. You got me in this mess, Wode . . . and you damned better believe that you are going to find me a way out. Now give me the bow. I need to look like I have a reason to buy arrows, and you need them."

"I hate you, Jadenine." Nathan removed the bow and quiver from his back and tossed them to her. "But I trust you."

She smiled some at the comment. "Damn funny thing about trust, isn't it? You don't even need to like someone to trust them. You just got to believe that in the end, they see something the same as you. And right now, we both have to trust each other, because we both want to live through this." Jadenine picked up the weapon and placed her arm through, the bow lying clean across her back. "Won't take much time, so long as they don't kill me. And then it still likely won't take much time in that."

--

Katlynn only thought she hated the Entelar. But once outside the forest's grasp, the vastness of Ursan could truly be felt and the nakedness of being without the cover of the trees. Lying out on the grassy plains she saw the horror of a Draywolf, a massive creature with chameleon like eyes on the sides of its face, a body larger than three bears combined. Until this moment, Katlynn had only heard or read stories of such a creature, of men brave enough to hunt and kill one. As she understood it, several tribes within Ursan held killing the beast as a rite of passage for the young men. Be it sport or tradition, they were mad for such. All she wanted to do was creep back into the Entelar and wait for the creature to leave.

Jadenine, however, stood nonchalant before them without her sword drawn. Instead she tied back her auburn hair and then readjusted her pack.

"Come, let us go." She took a step forward, then without looking she called back. "Do not fear the beast. They are far smarter than they may appear. Lonely creatures. Spend most of their adult life hunting and fending for themselves."

"Bet you can relate," her cousin jabbed at Jadenine.

To which she only chuckled. "Regardless, the fact that he has not even given us much of a look means that he's not foolish enough to attack. He has tangled with humans before, and likely picked his battles wisely. Low numbers, women and children, the elderly. Easy prey. But a group of four grown men and two people that can use the Realms . . . he would have to be hungry to try."

"How would you know for certain that he's hungry, Jadenine?" questioned Feko.

"The charging right at us the moment he smelled us might be a clue," was her answer.

They moved with Jadenine at point, cautious steps out into the grassy fields that stretched beyond the eyes. The Draywolf eyed them with suspicion, but did not bother to budge. His head resting upon his front legs, he watched, his attention focused primarily on Katlynn, or so she felt. But as Jadenine assured, the Draywolf never approached and the small group moved beyond the creature, continuing to move until he was nothing more than a blur in the distance.

"Our people believe that many animals in Amon have a keen sense of the Realms," Jadenine stated to no one in particular it seemed. "Animals always seem to sense things before us. Something about their instincts. They must have some understanding of the power. Maybe just a healthy respect."

She watched Philip turn his head to Feko, who did nothing besides continue to follow. He had such a visual distrust of the man. She still had little idea as to who he really was and what he was still doing with them.

When Katlynn gazed back to the front, she spotted Jadenine staring back to her. "He was watching you, you know. If you didn't spot that."

"I did," she responded.

Jadenine turned again to the front. "Dangerous art that is. I can see why they think you killed the king."

"I didn't kill him."

"I would gather that convincing me does you very little. You assume I care one way or the other. Doesn't change our current situation."

Iero coughed purposefully loud to garner the attention. "I would gather it is important for you to validate that this venture, at the very least, was worth something, wouldn't you say?"

"No, you fucking rat wrangler," she spat in response. "Thanks to Wode, I am stuck. If she killed the king or not does not change any of our fates." She flailed her arms to them. "We are all dead. Just a matter of how long we got left. All of you must know that by now."

"If that is the case," Iero continued, "then why bother even moving forward?"

"Mostly because I am stubborn and refuse to accept reality. I will live as long as possible, as long as I have the wits to stay focused and the luck to remain unnoticed. Until hopefully I can die with some form of honor."

Katlynn had little to say or dispute to her comments, and neither did anyone else for that matter. Save for Iero, of course.

"If I have you pegged wrong, and I do not believe that I do, then you may still be interested to know that I *saw* our assassin. It was not Katlynn Pratt. This assassin's power was . . . unparalleled, unnatural."

A second later after processing his statement, the words actually sunk in. "Wait. You *saw* the assassin? You never told me that. You saw her, and you wouldn't vouch for me in Corovium?"

Iero rose his hands and Bird leapt from his shoulders and scurried on ahead. "I knew that you did not do such, and so did your father when I suggested to him that you flee. You must understand the politics involved in this. The king was killed in cold blood . . ."

"You suggested to my father?" Katlynn reached him and grabbed the chubby man by his shirt. "You said my father asked this of me! You fucking liar! You said this was his bidding!"

"You remember what you choose to remember," Iero quickly stated, sweat forming at the top of his forehead. "You asked if your father sent me and I said in a manner of speaking, which was in truth. I told you that I would not have been there asking you to flee without his consent. And that was also in truth. But I was not forthright about everything. If I had told you that I convinced him that this was in your best interest, you would have never come along."

"And I might not be here in Ursan, away from my homeland, with bloody feet and a price on my head!"

Her cousin quickly moved between them. "Calm down, Katlynn," he said with a surprisingly relaxed voice. "Iero is right on this one. And that's painful to admit. He was wrong certainly in the way he told you, but correct in you being here. Uncle Phil is the one that sent the order for your capture. If our own family tapped the Guild for you . . . imagine what would have happened if you stayed, if you would have walked back in the capital."

"Iero could have told them what he saw!" Katlynn continued, tears forming again at her eyes. "He is a respected Druid, they would have listened! They would have listened! I am innocent!"

"Lady Pratt, you do not understand," Iero insisted, his voice low and saddened. "If I would have told any of them the truth in what I saw, they likely would have just killed you and been done with it."

"Tell me then, what *is* the truth?" she queried, harshness still in her tone.

"That they will never find this assassin. Never."

His words were so final that Katlynn released the grip on his shirt.

Iero straightened. "I am sorry, Lady Pratt. They won't find her unless she wants to be found. We missed our only opportunity in the capital. *I* missed the opportunity in the capital. I tried, I really did, but she was far more powerful than me. And that is because she is not human."

"Say that again?" Jadenine questioned, finally showing some genuine interest in their conversation.

"She is something else. She was not cloaked in Shadow in the same manner as you. She was . . . she crossed over."

Then it is true. Power, unbelievable power, is there on the other side. All that one must do is break the only rule. But how easy is it to come back from the other side?

"Horseshit," hissed Jadenine. "I've heard of people crossing over. No one comes back. Once you cross over, that's it. People coming back . . . that's just stories to scare children."

"To warn them," Feko corrected. "They tell me that many that break the only rule never come back. Many . . . but not all."

"And those that do," Iero continued, "do not come back as they once were. Our assassin was not a human. She was something else, something changed. Do you understand now? They will never find our real killer, because they do not even believe that such a thing exists. And if I would have told them the truth, and let us say that they actually believed me, more the reason to kill you publicly so that everyone would sleep better at night. The mass population isn't interested in details as much as they are interested in results. Politics aren't always about doing what is morally correct, Lady Pratt. Half of the time it isn't even sensible. But most of the time, it is what must be done."

"People need blood?" she whispered in horror.

"They need retribution." Iero took steps to her, his hand reaching up and resting upon her shoulders. "This was not what any of us wanted, Lady Pratt. But we must make do with what we got. Either that or turn yourself in to the Guild. It would be a meaningless death."

She wiped away the tears that formed out of anger as she slowly calmed herself. "What's the point of this kind of life?"

Jadenine moved close, her green eyes locked tightly with her own. "Get over it, Pratt. If death comes, move quicker, or so say the Ursan."

With that, the Ursan woman swung about and continued north, not looking back to see if anyone followed. One by one though, they all shuffled along. And why would they not? Death was coming for them all. It would have to catch up. After all, she was a Pratt.

--

"Not sure I get you, Wode."

A rogue tree out in the open plains proved to be a blessing that likely only he and the Ursan would appreciate, though she did not know such just yet. His small, serrated blade removed, he cut into the base of the tree and into one of the roots.

"What's there not to get?"

He was first up for watch on this night and Jadenine was the last awake save himself. His blade made easy work of the root, cutting deep into it and produced a few strands from the inside.

"Outside of what seems to be your strange knowledge of trees . . ."

"Jest if you will," Nathan stated, tossing her one of the root strands, the other he placed in his mouth, chewing on it as if it were a piece of liquorish.

She looked at it for a moment. "You are something else. Is this . . ."

"Ashroot. No business whatsoever being here either. Ash Pines grow out on the east coast, so who knows how this one got here. Just blind, dumb luck of pollination I suppose. Anyways, as I am sure you know, Ashroot will get us right and tipsy. It will also help you get some sleep. I know you have problems with sleeping."

Jadenine wasted little time chewing on the root. He detected the slightest of smiles. "You know I still hate you."

"I know."

"But I will say this. I hope your luck doesn't run out."

"It always does. And never at the best time."

"Is that a Donovinian saying?" she questioned.

"It's a Wode saying."

Jadenine shrugged. "We got a saying in Ursan about luck. Only dead men wager on luck."

"An interesting saying."

"That's not why I don't get you, Wode. Why the Guild at all? I presume you could have lived the glorious life of a bastard in Astrona. Plenty of money, no real responsibilities. And since you were an outcast, you had the ability to marry whoever you wanted. And yet you came to the Guild. Why?"

"How would you feel if you were less than worthless?" Nathan continued chewing down on the Ashroot, walking over to Jadenine, his vision upon those sleeping just a few yards away. "I had a chance to be something within the Guild. I would never be anything as a bastard Pratt. Not good enough lineage to rise within the ranks of the Imperial Army. An unwed barmaid mother is about as close to a whore as you can get by public perception. So what was left? The common job? Blacksmithing, butcher, baker? Yes, I could have gone into any trade I wanted, and would have felt empty. I wanted to do something to prove my worth, to prove that I was better than what my father thought of me."

"You sought glory."

But Nathan shook his head. "I seek purpose."

She steadily chewed on the Ashroot, her rear end planting down beside the tree. "My last name is Zo." She did not turn to him while she spoke; her focus remained on pulling out the grass before her for no apparent reason other than the sake of doing such. "It means nothing to you, but that name is still spoken of like the whispers against the wind. Many people came to follow my father. Some to challenge his strength and find themselves disappointed. Others to find leadership other than Brocusk. My father began to build a strong force in the east. Too strong."

"A threat to Dehyllo?"

"In Ursan, you either serve Lord Brocusk or you die. And by serving you must take a knee and proclaim him your lord. It is not an easy thing for an Ursan to do such. I would gather as a proud man, you might be able to relate. But as our tribe began to rise on the eastern border, against the Terrandonan Sea, Dehyllo began to take notice to my father. I was very young, you understand, but I remember him visiting us. He warned of the war that would ravage Amon and decimate our people, that we could not stand divided if we even thought to breathe the word hope. He preached of a terror that awaited us across the vast sea. Together, as one country, that was the only way to fight back the inevitability.

"But Dehyllo did not want a union. His terms were simple. Bow before him and proclaim his last name as law. My father . . . he would not kneel. As proud as a Zo . . . a popular saying once as I understood it." Jadenine exhaled a pathetic laugh. "That saying has a different meaning nowadays."

She drew silent, steadily playing with the grass before her, still chewing upon the Ashroot in her mouth. After a moment, Nathan dangerously inquired, "What happened?"

It still took a few more moments for Jadenine to continue, her face reflecting her discomfort.

"In Ursan, we famously battle one on one in disputes if both parties agree. A championed duel as it is known. My father was not a fool. He knew that in open war, Dehyllo would win. His numbers were too great to combat. So my father called for the challenge, and to his credit, Dehyllo accepted. Well, more weakness than credit I suppose. He was and is notoriously known for his inability to turn down a challenge. My father picked his champion, Dehyllo picked his. The conditions were simple. If Dehyllo won, my father would kneel before him and swear himself to Brocusk. If my father won, Dehyllo would leave the eastern shores to the Zos and never return. My elder brother Vilihame was the Zo champion. Greatest fighter I have ever seen in combat, perhaps save you. There was no way he would lose. But that was assuming a fair fight. My father should have known better. Dehyllo's champion was a damned Pyromancer."

Jadenine crunched her knees into her chest and wrapped her arms around them. "His champion opened the Flame Realm and engulfed my brother into nothingness. I watched, numb, not certain I understood what I saw. It was over before it ever started. A cowardly move by Dehyllo, but a wise one. Not playing fair and with honor was nowhere within the terms. And unless the rules are set and agreed upon on both sides before the start of the duel, living is winning, and dying is losing. My father's champion . . . my brother . . . had lost the duel, and by law my father was meant to kneel."

Her emerald eyes stared blankly onto his. "He would not kneel, Wode. Even after he lost, he still would not yield an inch to Brocusk. You either serve or you die. And since he would not serve, I presume you can figure out what happened."

"And your family?"

"Dead. All of them. Dehyllo rolled in with his force and fought a war that they still speak of today. Bloody, long, and down to the very last drop of blood. My people killed his by more than five to one. Unfortunately he outnumbered us twenty to one. A useless damn rebellion. And Brocusk is not known for taking pity. You have one chance to kneel, one chance and one chance only. Should you choose to pass on it . . ."

She trailed off for a moment, laughing to herself to hide her pain. "He killed everyone. Everyone I ever knew. My entire tribe was annihilated, save me."

"How did you live?"

Jadenine shrugged. "I was ten. I can still see Dehyllo's face staring at me. After killing all the people that served him, he then round up all my father's wives and children and made him watch as he killed them all in front of him, all save me. Maybe I was too young, but who knows? When they were all dead and my father was a broken nothing before him, Dehyllo killed my father. And there I stood, the last Zo and last member of my tribe. I knew death would come, but it didn't. He spared me. Fucking bastard spared me. I had a dagger in my right hand, held my father's lifeless hand in my left, blood was everywhere. I see him when I sleep. I see him looking at me. I see the bodies of my mother and brothers and sisters."

Nathan did not know what to say. What was there to say? "I know why you can't sleep now."

"No you don't," she snapped. "The blood, the death . . . I'm an *Ursan*. I can live through that. I can't sleep because I see myself, I see the dagger in my hand, and I see Dehyllo. I froze. I did nothing. That is what haunts me. I had him within range to kill and I let it slip away."

"Earth and Flame, Jadenine, you were ten."

"Blade slides through flesh all the same." She stood and tossed a rock out into the endless fields before them. "He didn't smile, or laugh, or gloat when he saw me. Dehyllo looked as if he gave me pity. Fuck his pity. In the end, I stood and did nothing, and he turned and walked away, leaving me in a sea of death. I watched him leave with his army. No one won on that day. My people gone forever, Brocusk minus a great army that should have fought at his side rather than die in a senseless rebellion. My father doomed us by his decision, his pride. But Dehyllo still called for the blood. But what choice did he have? My father went against the championed duel. He left Brocusk little choice."

"That doesn't excuse slaughter."

"No," she agreed. "But it does explain it. You cannot forgo the agreed terms of a championed duel. Unless you also forgo all your pride."

Jadenine was difficult to read, which of course was nothing new. Nathan knew she pained from the ordeal, knew that she scarred deeply and permanently from this, and yet he still had difficultly seeing it reflected in her eyes. She truly was an Ursan, through and through. Tough, hardened, and a realist. The past could not be changed.

"How does a ten-year-old girl survive on her own?"

"Anyway she can, Wode. Do you understand my respect of the Guild, now? I have no love for the things we do. Half are worthy, half are greedy. We are but the weapon that the hand wields. But that hand took a hungry girl in, one that had lost all hope. And more importantly, one that had lost all pride. There isn't much that a ten-year-old girl can do for money. Not much."

Nathan took a few careful steps toward her. "Why tell me all this? After all we have been through over the years, and after all this mess I have put you through, why now? You once told me that I would put a knife in your back in battle."

And then the strangest thing occurred. She honestly laughed. "Do you want to know the damnedest truth, Wode? You kept things from me, as have I from you. But your lies I understand. Why tell me your lineage when it could put you in desperate position, one that might have you bound and gagged and awaiting a ransom for life? Why tell me that you intended to rescue your cousin rather than turn her in, when I would have simply marched to Cylaa and ended that madness? Why tell me of Feko's discovery of your ties to the Pratts, when I would have likely just killed him in assumption of *his* ties into this whole assassination? And speaking of which, I hope that . . ."

"I don't trust him any more than you do, Jadenine."

"Good. Smart to keep him close. Might be able to guide us to the real killer. You think, Wode. I react. It is . . . a good quality in you. Of the few. But in battle, I know that you handle yourself better than any other I have ever seen. And like I said before, you don't have to like someone to trust them. And I do trust you Wode."

"So now I won't put a blade in your back?"

Her face remained stern. "Strange, Wode, for me to admit but these are desperate times. How I got here, I blame you and I will forever blame you. But I take life by the minute, and right now, survival is at the foremost of my thoughts. Has been since I was ten. So I evaluate my surroundings. Feko is a liar and untrustworthy, along with being worthless in battle. Katlynn is coming onto her own, but lacks confidence. The captain owns his sword well enough, but walks about like a lost child half the time. Iero is powerful, but a fool. At the end of the day, it is my blade and yours. If I must trust someone . . . I trust you, Wode. Or at the least, I trust your blade."

"It is difficult to tell if that is a compliment or . . ."

"Only a Donovinian would analysis things in the form of praise or not. It is fact, Wode. Take it as it is."

"Well you have kept your name a secret for a long time. I suppose I can take that as a step in the right direction for our new-found respect for one another."

"You told me your name, and now I have told you mine. Nothing simpler. You, a bastard son of a Pratt. Me, an orphaned daughter of a name that no longer exists. We are two broken people, you and I."

"But dangerous, I would gather."

She nodded. "Broken people often are."

"An Ursan saying?"

Jadenine Zo flashed a grin. "No, but it should be."

--

War is far simpler than politics. Two opposing forces that cannot find middle ground, thus they lay down their lives to fight for their beliefs. The one left standing wins the debate.

In the courts, nothing is quite as simple. Arguments must be supported by peers, or bought as the case may be. It must be presented, agreed upon, voted upon. Then it must be presented to the council, to the king, then ratified, then returned to the courts for full amendment. By the end of the day, the initial document looks nothing like the final one. At best, you can only hope that what you wanted is even included.

War. A far simpler thing.

-- Gillar, Head of the Courts

XIV

Darkness. It became a part of everything around Aldric. The underground library had become his home. Hours could not be counted nor determined, and the same could be said of the days or weeks. Even so, time made little difference to the Kwyantin. A day, a year . . . it bled together like paint on a canvas. However even the Kwyantin could find their resolve tested by isolation in this way.

The candles burned low as did the test to his patience. Book after book droned onward of the experiments within the Realms, but nothing came of such reading. Madness seemed to follow those that touched the other side, either that or death. The Historian had always thought that the one rule had been in place for a reason, and he was discovering the truth in such. Each volume of the experiments spoke in length of the day in, day out trials into opening the other side, to viewing into the Realms beyond. In the end, it mattered little. Some moved to the other side and never returned. Some returned but lost something of themselves in the process. Some completely went mad. Certainly there seemed to be great power on the other side, but he had yet to read anything to claim that their research had yielded results. What they seemed to be searching for was the ability to not only cross into the Realms and back, but the ability to find a way to cross into multiple Realms at once. But through his readings, it appeared as if they had yet to uncover someone with that ability. It seemed they were convinced that the more research they conducted, the closer they got to figuring out how to harness the power of every Realm.

There stood the other possibility of course. Perhaps there simply was no such person and no such gift. It was often said that a person could only fathom one Realm, that the mind could not comprehend the sight of any other. Anything more would destroy the body and the mind, or so said the many preachers. It added to the danger and peculiarity of the Realms.

One thing was clear: House Aylmer broke the only rule. Touch, borrow, but never cross over. The real question was why they had done such to begin with. Their House sat upon the throne. They *had* the power. What more could there be? A king and queen upon the throne, yet it did not seem to satisfy. They wanted more or perhaps they wanted to ensure they kept it. Either way, death took place here. And for what?

"How much longer will she leave us here, do you think?" Erian questioned, his patience thinner than even his.

"As long as she deems fit, I would gather," answered Aldric.

"What does she want of us? If she means to kill us, why not just end it now? Why have us go through volume after volume of these books, only to find little other than journal notes of experiments that did not go as planned? And why not have her own people go through these volumes?"

"Maybe she seeks answers," the Historian replied. "Answers that she might not trust with even her own people. But it would seem that if she meant to kill us, that would have already taken place. Take some comfort in that."

"I do not fear death. I only fear the uselessness."

"Get used to that feeling."

Erian turned to him, his book closing as the dust kicked about. "You have been the Historian for seven centuries. You have honored our people, our way of life. You would likely be on your way back to our people as we speak, preparing to write the long journals of your life into the volumes of our histories that would join the many Historians before you. And yet something changed. You uncovered the true culprit in the assassination. Why become involved now?"

Aldric knew that his apprentice would eventually ask that question. He had no better answer now then he did the moment he opened Dylinn's letter in the capital.

"I search for reason," Aldric admitted. "I feel as if Jaa knew far more than he was able to share. Perhaps we are in the wrong library searching for answers."

"You feel as if the Realms are a key to something."

He nodded. "I do. Most that believe the gods have fallen do as well. The Realms, our world, the wars of our past . . . this convergence. It is all connected to Turitea and Schill. But perhaps back in our village we would find better answers if we dug deep into our own histories. Perhaps that was how Jaa had learned whatever it was that caused him to give up his life. To feel that kind of guilt."

"Then why come here at all?"

"I am unsure. I had to know the truth. I felt that this was important somehow for Amon." The Historian shook his head. "I wish I could better explain. But this all feels like pieces that I am attempting to make whole. These experiments all but show that I am right, at least in the knowledge that others seek to possess the power of the other side. Or just an understanding of what lies beyond."

"So what *is* on the other side?"

"Questions without answers. But I do feel they start here. The assassin employed to kill our late king could open the Shadow Realm, but was no Shadowmancer. Or at least none that I have witnessed in all my journeys as Historian. She was not merely cloaked in Shadow, but a very part of it."

"If not a Shadowmancer, then what else could this assassin be?"

"I am unsure. I hoped to find answers. Instead we find imprisonment."

"We did find some answers," Erian noted. "They broke the only rule. That might explain our assassin. Maybe they succeeded to some extent and creating a powerful Shadowmancer. Maybe they created something that Dylinn used in this killing. Maybe it's here somewhere in this estate."

The lock worked and clicked, and the door creaked open. One of the guards appeared and waved them to him.

"Come," he announced. "Lady Aylmer is prepared to see you now."

--

They stood alone within the House lord's hall, a long, narrow room lined on the east and west with pillars that ran parallel to the throne. Tapestries with the crests of the many great names that ruled this hall hung down before the pillars, the coloring changed with each successive family. The ruling House Aylmer's tapestry hung behind the throne, a bright purple with the letters moving downward to form the name. An elaborate room, but not overdone. Aldric knew many great men that once sat upon that chair, many men of honor that once ruled Fallneese and ultimately moved on to rule Amon.

Those men were long dead, never to return. All that remained now tainted their honor. This House and all those beneath it would forever be known for their abominations. That was, of course, if either he or his apprentice could escape this madness.

"First we wait in the dungeon," started Erian, "now we wait in her throne room. Perhaps we should head back downstairs and wait for her to be ready for us?"

It was then that Aldric caught the slightest of movements in the corner of the room, behind the throne, huddled in the dark. "Hello?" called out the Historian, but nothingness returned.

His eyes narrowed as he attempted to focus upon the movement, catching some form . . . a figure perhaps. Aldric thought to call out again, but since that failed the first time, he changed his thoughts to moving forward. One slow step after another.

Not but four steps in toward the dark corner and the figure seemed to jump about nervously.

"Please, I won't harm you," assured the Historian, his open palms extended outward.

"As if you could," a raspy, female voice stated affirmatively. "Stay there."

"Alright, alright." Aldric crossed his extended arms about his chest. "I am Aldric, Historian of Amon. Who might you be?"

The figure seemed to chuckle some. "You write of history, tall one?"

"I do. It is how I serve my people."

After a moment, she questioned, "Who do you write this for?"

"All of Amon."

Again, the figure in the darkness laughed softly. "Amon does not need your history, tall one. She has little use for such."

"Maybe not the land," agreed the Historian, "but the people upon it."

"What use do they have of your history? Do they read it and study it?"

Reluctantly, Aldric shook his head. "They do not."

"Then what good are you?"

The figure shuffled about, both nervous and seemingly dangerous, like a cornered animal. There was something not right about this girl or woman. Certainly there were shadows in the grand hall, but not enough to shroud the figure in this manner. She appeared as would a blurred motion, something distinct and yet abstract.

"Whether they read it or not is of little consequence," he offered as a retort. "It is available nevertheless."

She huffed loudly. "Enough history written in the earth if people knew how to read."

"How do you mean?"

"I don't," she replied.

The darkness shrouding her is not natural. She is a Shadowmancer. She must be. And if that is true, then there stands a chance that she is Dylinn's assassin.

He no longer felt as comfortable and safe as he had before.

"Perhaps my writings and knowledge may save lives one day," he offered.

"Lives are of little importance."

Aldric felt a single eyebrow rise involuntarily. "What is the land without lives?"

"Land." The figure shuffled about some, still seemingly uncomfortable with either his presence or his questioning.

But Aldric, being who we was, refused to let up.

"What is your name?" She did not answer. "Do you live here, in Itopis I mean? Or perhaps outside in Molovand?" Again, silence. "Have you been to Corovium lately?"

"Do you always talk so much?" was her answer.

"No, I am a much better listener. Part of being the Historian. Tell me, child, have you touched the Shadow Realm?"

Though there was no immediate answer, he paused regardless. The figure moved awkwardly about, looking as if she were deciding upon flight or fight, of which Aldric was uncertain which he rather preferred. But she was unsteady, uncertain, uneasy even.

"What do you know of Shadow?" she whispered.

"I know that . . ."

"Nothing!" snapped the figure. "Do not speak of what you cannot begin to comprehend."

"Then you speak."

She stared at him, and though he could not see her eyes, he felt them. A part of him that was beginning to understand the concept of fear had the desire to take a step away from the Shadowmancer. But he could not change who he was. A Historian gathered facts and watched and inquired. So instead he took a step closer.

The figure looked poised to jump toward him.

The throne room doors opened and the former queen moved with steady purpose, guards at her side that remained stride for stride with their House lord.

"I told you not to speak with our guests," called out Dylinn to the figure, though with hesitant conviction in her voice. In response, the shadowy figure shuffled back into the corner, then became hazy for Aldric to even see. "I need to have a few words with the Historian. Leave us be for now and I will speak with you later."

And when the Historian turned back to the corner, his eyes could no longer see the figure. She might have been there, but now there was no telling. Only the dark corner of a throne room stood before him, apparently empty and void of life.

When Dylinn stood before him, the guards remained several steps behind. "It is good to see you still in health and in good spirits, Historian."

"Who was that?" directly questioned Aldric.

To which one side of her mouth displayed a grin. "Right to questions, I see. Tell me, what has your reading uncovered, Historian?"

"Not much, other than the knowledge that those that once called themselves House lords of this estate have experimented into moving into Realms. I believe they were attempting to find some sort of way to control the Realms, to move between them maybe. They were trying to create something unearthly." He pointed back to the where the girl once stood. "I think you keep from me something more valuable than books. What was she?"

"What do *you* think she was?"

Aldric straightened, gazing downward to Lady Aylmer. "Clearly she was a Shadowmancer. Or at least she was once. Is she something more?"

To which she frowned heavily. "All that damn reading you have been doing, and you cannot answer that question yourself?"

There was sincerity to her face that could not be masked, could not be faked.

"You don't know either, do you?"

You think because of who I am, because the vast knowledge that I hold in my memories that I have an answer for you. Where your own people could not decipher truth from fiction, you believe that I have those answers for you. Dylinn . . . I am right to pity you. You have no idea what dangers you toy with.

Dylinn turned from him and began to pace. "You have come to us at an interesting time, Historian. Wheels are moving."

"What wheels?"

"Those of war." Her arms crossed, her smile widened. "As I told you, Amon will fall. I will stand tall before it. You will be by my side as it happens, Historian. You will catalog every event, every victory."

"What do you speak of, Lady Aylmer?"

"Perhaps," she started as she turned to face him, "it is best you see."

--

They left the Aylmer estate and continued on a lazy, sluggish pace through the mix of stone and marble that lined the streets of Itopis. They made their way into town, her guards still about though at a relaxed distance. They knew well enough that despite their size, the Kwyantin men lacked any real threat, though that did not keep them from a relatively cautious proximity.

"So you ask many questions in your line of work?" asked Lady Aylmer.

Aldric turned to her, but her eyes remained focused ahead of her. "Yes, my lady," he responded. "It is the nature of my work. Though to be honest, most are quite liberal at the information they present without any line of questioning."

"How many have ever asked you questions?"

"I am not sure I follow your meaning."

"I mean of your life, your upbringing, your people." Dylinn shrugged gently. "The Kwyantin have history. Who has asked you these questions?"

"Save for your inquiries . . . very few, in honesty."

"Do you not find that odd?" further she pried.

"Most find themselves fascinated by the thought of immortality through my writing and are not focused on my personal history, Lady Aylmer."

"That is not what I meant. I mean, you are here as the Historian of Amon to record into the history all that has transpired during your tenure. Do you not find it odd that you spend no time cataloging your own people? Who is cataloging their time in this world?"

Historian, keeper of knowledge of the people of Amon, teller of tales of the world as it shaped, how it formed. I am all of these things . . . and yet I have no idea what my people are doing or how they live during the gaps.

"Since I left as an apprentice with Jaa the Knowledgeable, I have been back four times to see my people. Once to inform of the death of Jaa, twice to check in with the elder and read into the histories left before me, and the last to acquire an apprentice, as it was time."

Maybe this is the missing piece . . .

"I want to know of the Kwyantin," Dylinn said earnestly. "Tell me of your people, of what you know."

And now I question what I know.

"Time is a difficult thing to fathom," he began. "You begin to discuss who was here upon Amon first, and you start to discuss things that only religion can answer. When our history begins, we were the dominate race apparently. Enough documentation from your people and my own exists to validate that. Vast in numbers, rulers within Amon. I have found a difficult time uncovering the missing years in where we move from superiority to our current role. Several conflicting accounts, neither making much sense. The only unified consensus was that for reasons unknown, our numbers dwindled. War? Plague? It's an unknown."

"So your removal from power was due to the lack of numbers alone?"

"Difficult to rule the world without numbers," the Historian claimed. "And I do not know that for a fact. The only thing for certain is that we were once great in number, then dwindled to our current fold."

"So . . . why exactly do your people control your population? Because that is what you do, is it not?"

"Not necessarily. We are all given a task in this world. To give life is an honor, but not all-encompassing."

"Tell me more, Historian. I want to know about your people. I have always been intrigued."

She stated all of this as if they were friends, as if he were not a captive within her grasp, as if she did not possess a Shadowmancer within her command, as if his life did not hang within the balance of her mood.

"We live within the depths of Ursan, alone and hidden away. We have remained away from the views of current humanity and society in order to protect ourselves and our culture. You have asked me before of love, but that does not come into play the same way for us. It truly is an honor for those selected to give birth, but it is a task given in our life much the same as mine. Our numbers are kept low intentionally by the elder council. And before you ask, it is not my place to know why that is. It simply always has been. We have limited supplies and we are not to expand. That is the decision of our council, which was the decision of the council before them, and so forth."

"So what age are these women given the task of giving birth?"

"The council assigns all tasks at the same time, this being no different. Our council of elders evaluate every young Kwyantin and decide what would be best for their particular talents."

"And you had a good ear?"

He shrugged slightly. "I asked many questions. It is the reason many people of your species live and die without seeing a Kwyantin. And those few that have, they have seen me. Most of our chosen tasks in life involve remaining within our isolated village. Some are chosen to work on our homes, the repairs and upkeep. Others to farm. Others to hunt. Others to cook. Most of those entail remaining close to home. Certainly the need to barter and trade does come up every so often, and we have someone selected for that task as well. Some are meant to act as liaisons, so we do have a few of my people that will travel throughout Amon from time to time. But we are intentionally kept from the world because that is the will of our council. Even as the council ages, they select those that are meant to replace them, and the selectees spend decades, sometimes centuries in an apprentice role. We each are given a task, and we are set to perform it."

Dylinn continued to move through the city nonchalantly. "It does beg to question why you bothered to stray from your path."

"That it does."

Itopis truly was a marvel. Every street was made to display the wealth, the power that the former House king held. The few streets made of marble had a look of almost glass, the sun beaming off the dark surface and reflecting dully into the buildings. Every time he had entered Itopis, it never ceased to amaze. Some beauty not even time could erode.

"So your mother and father . . ." began House lady.

"Yes, they were around," answered Aldric. "But we are raised as a village, as a community. It is not the same sense as a mother and father as you know in your . . ."

He paused, wondering how she would take the statement he was about to make based on her upbringing.

"Continue, Historian," she demanded. "I did not have the typical childhood. Most people have a distinct mother and father. My situation was fucked up. Let's call it an anomaly. So continue. Your village raises the young. Do you simply bounce around from home to home?"

"The children all stay together in one home, similar age groups. While we live much longer lives, it also takes longer for us to mature. We are children for many years, into our thirties and forties before we are fully grown. Well . . . more like teenagers I suppose by then. At that age we are working, but our jobs are not selected for us. So the first years are schooling. In our twenties, we begin to work within the village in whatever needs the most help. Odds and ends, the kinds of tasks mostly needed for upkeep. Mostly hard labor that is not selected as an actual job. By the time we move into our fifties to seventies, our tasks have been selected for us and we begin the apprenticeship, much as Erian here."

She looked to his apprentice, then back to him. "So when do you stop growing?"

"In height? About a hundred, give or take."

"Any warriors amongst you?"

The Historian shook his head. "Too few of us to bother with that. We are herders and farmers mostly. Despite our size, we are quite passive."

"Certainly not a poor quality, Historian. I, however, am unable to relate."

She grew silent and the small group continued their march through Itopis. The streets were strangely sparse, and it dawned on him that the area had a strange feel to it. Far too many citizens at midday to be so lightly populated on the streets. Vendors were packing up, a few people rushed from one house to the next. There seemed no panic in their faces as much as purpose and intent. Something was afoot, something that did not seem altogether right.

One thing was certain; his mind had difficultly focusing. It had dawned on him now the reality of Dylinn's words, truth or otherwise. His entire life now came into scrutiny, at least in his own thoughts. The Historian spent a lifetime writing of the deeds of mortal men, but never of the Kwyantin. And the reason he knew little of the reasoning behind their fall from power in Amon was largely due to the fact that little was written of it. The Historians wrote of others. But who wrote of them? What was their history? Did they have none to speak of? Or was there something to hide?

Everyone has something to hide, or so I am finding.

No bigger secret then perhaps the thunderous roars just beyond the streets, passed the open gates, just outside the city walls. It did not take a grand genius for him to figure what the sounds were of: men, and many of them. He could spot several from the opening before him, but that was not the direction they traveled.

"Come, Historian," Dylinn urged. "We move to the wall."

He followed as she went to a set of stairs that led upward to the ramparts. His mind might have wandered for the previous moment, but now it sharpened to a point, and that point was the now.

I record history. It is all that I know, all that I have ever done. Nothing that I have recorded before this moment may be more important than this.

Dylinn made the wall first and a roar of men erupted from below. Aldric was second on the wall and he gazed downward to see thousands upon thousands of men, some armed in full battlement, others with nothing but regular garb and plenty of spirit. Together in unison they roared, united upon seeing their leader standing before them and she smiled as would any snake before their prey. For that was what she was . . . whether they realized it or not.

"I have more men that come as word spreads across the countryside," she spoke out of the side of her mouth to the Aldric. "Do you know what you witness on this day, Historian?"

He slowly nodded. "The wheels of war."

The fields before Itopis lined of fools, each voicing their love toward Lady Aylmer. The sea of faces varied in experience and stature, from young to old, weak to strong. No different from most armies, save for this one compromised of citizens mixed with the Itopis guard. It may have not mustered the same authority as the Imperial Army, but it could likely kill just the same. But as most mobs in history, they had little idea of the truth. But he could not be certain that the truth mattered any longer. They did not care for truth. A mob only called for blood.

And she would give it to them.

"My people!" she bellowed out to the thousands below and they quickly hushed in response, their eyes gazing upward to the wall. "There has been a tragedy and a crime in Corovium, one that goes unpunished. When my husband died, he left his son as rightful heir and ruler of Amon. And as you all know, there, within the capital of our land, he was murdered in cold blood before all to witness."

The crowd hissed their resentment of such a heinous act. "And as they send the Guild out to find the only suspect, Katlynn Pratt, House lady in Donovini," she paused, allowing another jeering to take place, "they spend their time jostling for position in claiming *our* throne. Do they give it back to Fallneese? No! They took it from us. And the Fourth, Lijid, tells me that none other than Jerryn Pratt, brother to the assassin, now stands as the one to take the throne!"

The roar of disapproval stood near deafening. She raised her hands, calming the crown once again. "Ursan has abandoned the courts and left the capital altogether. They lost faith in our system. Without the courts and without a king, Genethur stands crippled, along with all of Amon. If Brocusk looks to begin his own campaign, why should we stand about and do nothing, waiting for the very House that assassinated my son to decide the fate of Fallneese, the fate of Amon? Brocusk will assemble their troops. The Pratts and Rowes will have control of the Imperial Army, but they are weakened. So what are we to do? Should we wait and do nothing?"

The mob howled, the words no and never heard above all.

"Then should we fight?"

Yes came in a saddening abundance.

"Should we take back the throne?"

Again they agreed in booming fashion.

"Then those prepared to train and assemble remain here. We will begin to supply you and arm you, feed you and school you. Those that must make arrangements with your family and your loved ones, return home, but swear your loyalty now to me that you shall return. And while you are gone, spread our word. Fallneese shall bring terror to Amon. We shall see blood for the death of our king. Bring more. We need every able body if we are to march upon Corovium. We will need swords! Shields! Armor! We need revolve! We need retribution!"

The sound of thousands of men slapping swords against shields and fists against armor echoed throughout the plains.

"We will spread death like the plague! And when we reclaim our throne, we shall no longer serve Amon. Amon shall tremble before Fallneese!"

The crowd of men loved her, because she was Dylinn Aylmer, House lady of Fallneese, mother to the fallen king. Of course she was also the murderer of the boy and his father. And what could he do to convince them of that fact? Scream at the top of his lungs that she was a murderer? A sword would be through his neck before the words were ever released. And even if they released, no one would believe him regardless.

No, if one man could stop the wheels of war, he was not that man. At the moment, Aldric was just a spectator. Just an observer.

Just the Historian.

--

They sat at the dining table within Dylinn's chambers, the guards standing around the perimeter of the room while Aldric and Erian sat patiently to the left of Lady Aylmer, her servant girl beside her, naked with a chain around her neck that tied to the chair in which Dylinn sat. The girl looked frightened to breathe and Aldric gazed at her, his heart hurting. How could someone that lived such a painful life as Dylinn do to others the same way? The answer was unfortunately simple. At the end of the day, this life was all that she knew, all that she understood. Pain begets pain. An endless cycle.

"I am expecting a visitor," she stated, breaking the silence. "You should eat. I am sure the food before you is better than what you ate in the catacombs below."

"Tell me," began the Historian, ignoring her comment even if his stomach could not, "all that you have done, all those you have killed, you did such just to start a war?"

"Yes." Her answer felt absolute.

"You had Amon. Your husband could have lived longer with you in charge. His son thought you his mother. I'm sure you could have controlled him in time. If power is what you sought, you had it. Why have you done this?"

"Because we need a change," Dylinn answered. "This is not just about the throne. This is about the whole damned thing. Look what has happened since you left, Aldric. You have no idea because you were locked away. Dehyllo did pull his people from the courts and left Afeon there alone. Who, by the way, has been imprisoned because they believe that the Ursan conspire against the Pratts. And who knows, maybe they do. I kill one boy . . . one stupid, arrogant boy, and the world goes to ruin. Our system is broken. What we need is one voice, one person in charge. No more Houses, no more countries. Amon stands unified by one leader."

"One dictator," he added.

"All in the same, Historian. I did what I must to start anew."

"With you in the forefront."

"As I should be. Have I not suffered enough?" Dylinn grabbed a glass of wine before her and took a heavy swig. "It is my time. But also the time for my country. Besides, these changes could not have been in place with my husband or his bastard. They were both hardheaded and impossible, you should know that as well as anyone."

"And what of this shadow that you keep. What of her? Is it her time as well as yours?"

Dylinn placed her glass down, her stare intense onto the Historian. "The one you speak of is a weapon, nothing more." She then removed the chain around the girl by her chair and with a wave of her hand, the girl strode naked across the room and into the next, shutting the door behind her.

"Is that shadow girl . . . is she your assassin?"

"Yes."

"She seems unstable. Does she belong to you like this servant girl you just released?"

"No, the servant girl is for pleasure. The other is . . . something else entirely."

Aldric finally reached over and grabbed some fruit from the dining table. "Does she follow you?"

"Of course she does. And why wouldn't she? I uncovered her."

"Uncovered?" he repeated, uncertain if he heard the words correctly.

"Yes. I told you once before that the catacombs underneath this estate were sealed. When we broke through, we found the library. But that was not all that we found."

"The girl? Trapped underground?" The words were clear as spoken, but he found difficultly grasping them. *Impossible. How could she have lived?* "How long could she have been down there? You said it had been sealed before you left for the capital. That would have been years of isolation. What food or water sustained her during that time? How much air could have been trapped within?"

"Questions that I would have assumed you could answer for me during your time in that library, Historian."

"Experiments," he answered. "What more was I meant to find there? This House made attempts to create a weapon. Perhaps they succeeded, but I had not found that volume during my readings. You know more than I do about this."

"Then we together know nothing," she concluded.

"Let me speak to her," pleaded the Historian. "Let me find out what she knows."

The main doors came open slowly and several figures hovered just beyond. One of her personal guards took a single step forward.

"My Lady Aylmer," he announced, "the Guild is here at your request. Shall I allow them entrance?"

"That you may." Dylinn then turned to Aldric, the fierceness in her eyes returned. "Say nothing of what you know and I shall allow you to speak to the girl."

He nodded his agreement, uncertain though if it was wise to make deals with the Fallneesian woman.

The guard moved aside and only one Guild member moved into the dining hall, waving his chubby arms back to the guard, silently signifying his desire to close the doors. The guard obliged.

Orpay looked to have gained some weight since last the Historian saw him, and that was saying something. He moved with purpose across the room and sat down, barely making eye contact with anyone at the table before grabbing a plate, tossing food onto it.

"Lady Aylmer, an honor per usual to be in your presence," he wheezed while sitting down, the chair groaning some upon his weight. "And interesting to see you here, Historian. This must be a substantial meeting I have been summoned to for you to be here. Perhaps it has something to do with the six thousand men at the gate."

"It may," Aylmer claimed, sipping her wine, her smile widening.

"Well I must be honest, my time is short. Pressing issues send me back to Prillian, as it appears as if all of Amon moves at once." He spoke between chewing, food running down the side of his mouth without little care for manners or simple tact. "It seems we have found Katlynn Pratt, or at least we know where she is. There is also an issue along the coast. I fear the recently disbanded army of General Shonnen is getting stretched a bit thin as far as their patience is concerned. I am not completely convinced of what they are capable of. Nothing good, I'm sure."

"You are a leader," Dylinn stated sternly as she would to a child. "These are things that leaders must do. The decisions we make here may shape us for the remainder of our lives."

"Perhaps you are right. Regardless of our conversation, however, I leave for the south the moment we are done talking. Far too much to accomplish. I would not have bothered with this trip had it not been for anyone but you, Lady Aylmer. Ravens would have been sufficient rather than a face to face meeting . . . with anyone else."

"I don't completely trust Ravens. Some might fly the wrong path. Some might deliver a message to the wrong person. I've heard rumors that some are trained to fly off course on purpose. Face to face is so much more personal for these kinds of talks. But I am flattered at your words. So for your sake, I shall make this brief. I know that you play aloof better than most, but we should not play games now. You have many eyes everywhere as do I. You are well aware of the situation within the capital. Afeon did not leave with Dehyllo when the House lord took his council members and left the capital."

"No, no he did not," concurred the Guild Headmaster. "He sits behind bars beneath the capital."

"And so Lord Brocusk makes his moves. He has put quite a bind on the capital when he removed his men. Top that with Rayden's capture pegged on Dehyllo, the Pratts may make swift work at moving against him once they take the throne. It is due time he is removed from power. Now they have cause, control of an army, and the public support to do such."

"All of that you say is true. The wedding takes place shortly. They will have issues getting unified approval for the crown though, with one of their councilors jailed and all. The courts won't be much of any help either."

"I believe that Christina will find a workaround," commented Lady Aylmer. "The courts signed consent to the union of Donovini and Argonus before Brocusk removed his people from the council. A simple vote amongst the councilors is all that stands in her way. We will have a new king by month's end, if not sooner. And then comes the question of how quickly will they act against Dehyllo."

Orpay stopped eating long enough to smile toward her. "And that is what you wait for, is it not? A war against Ursan gives you an opportunity."

"It would certainly be opportunistic for someone who wanted to invade the capital, being that the Imperial Army would be thousands of miles away, engaged against Brocusk."

"Hypothetically speaking then, someone in your situation would need more men," bluntly stated the Guild head.

"Hypothetically speaking, we have more coming in."

"Highly unlikely you would have enough. Six, seven thousand men *might* gain you the city, but it would not hold it long enough to matter. How quickly would the Imperial Army disengage from Ursan to flee back to the capital should they find it under siege? You would need to take the throne quick enough to gain control of the Imperial Army, and do such decisively. The bridge you are crossing is as narrow as the ravine is deep. The likelihood that you make it across is slim to none."

Dylinn placed her glass out over the arm of her chair and one of her servants came over promptly and filled it with more wine. "All true, Orpay. So here you sit."

"Here I sit," he repeated.

"And knowing that you likely have eyes within my very House, you knew why I summoned you here."

"There is a possibility in that."

"So no games. You know what I am about to ask."

To which Orpay laughed. "And yet I will allow you to ask it all the same, Lady Aylmer."

A heavy sip from her glass later and began her request. "I do not need an army, Orpay. That I have. Numbers may not be on my side, but I have enough men to start a siege. I could use some more for the illusion. But make little mistake, it is an illusion. What I truly need are men to infiltrate. Trained killers, the kind that you likely keep hidden away."

"Sounds like something that the mysterious men of the Divide would normally handle, Lady Aylmer. Mysterious isn't really the Guild's style."

"The Moon Divide has been sent away. And regardless of that, they are under control of the First of Amon. Like you said, the throne needs to be taken quickly and decisively. I would need the Pratt boy and the Rowe girl killed or submitted during this siege or it would all be for not. Their deaths would allow me take it by force."

"Maybe. But who would honor your newfound title?"

"You would," she claimed. "The courts are under your control, Orpay. Like it or not, you are one of the most powerful men in Amon. If the courts were to support my name, so would Amon. And then I would have control of the Imperial Army. Then I would not need to stop their approach toward the capital, but could continue their press into Ursan to finish off Dehyllo for good."

The Guild head sat silent for a moment, deep thoughts showcasing upon his brow. "And what is it that you offer me, Lady Aylmer? I give you men, I give you support, I give you the throne. What exactly do I get?"

"What is it that you need?"

And now you are where you don't want to be, Dylinn Aylmer. In negotiations with a man that needs nothing.

Knowing such, Orpay's grin widened. "To be honest, I rarely play favorites amongst the Houses. It is not . . . financially wise to say the least. Nor will I find myself in a situation that if you fail in what you attempt, that would put me in a failing situation as well. You are on your own in this affair, Lady Aylmer. Treason normally ends with a rope around the neck, and I am not too fond of such thinking. But I might have men for hire, as that is the line of business I am in. What you do with these men is of your own accord. Of that the only cost is coin and your agreement that our conversation here never occurred. But of course the cost of my support should you win your little battle . . . assuming you win your battle . . . well that may come at a different cost."

"And that is?"

"First of Amon."

"What of him?"

Orpay shook his head, and pointed to himself.

Head of the Guild and First . . . from one of the most powerful men to the *most powerful man. Greed is boundless . . .*

"First Orpay," mumbled Dylinn, her own eyes in reflection of her contemplation. "It is a steep thing you ask of me. Technically you are not attached to a House. The council is meant to be appointed by each House as a representative of such. You represent the Guild, which is a conflict of interest to be honest."

"You would be the queen. If Christina can find a workaround to crown her puppet, I believe you can find one to make me First. The choice is yours. If not, then you march your people to their doom. Even if you succeed, you will be ripped from the throne and beheaded for treason. The courts will not recognize your name in succession. I will not bend on my demands."

"No, I would not gather a man like you to bend on his desires."

"You do not ascend to certain positions by giving ground, Lady Aylmer. A lesson that you should take with you in the future. Now, if there is nothing more, I presume that you will not have issue with me taking some supplies for the long ride back to Prillian?"

"Of course not," answered Lady Aylmer.

"Excellent. Well I will begin gathering some men for you. Say two thousand for your cause? I could have them to you by perhaps two months' timeframe. Add that with the rest of your men and you may be prepared to have them all killed by the end of summer. The cost of the deaths of my men to your country will be severe, financially that is. Of course you will likely be dead as well, so it will make little difference to you."

"You will have what you want," she made claim, though with no excitement in her voice. "I shall make you First of Amon if I succeed. And you give me court approval. It is yours."

"Excellent. I am glad this trip was not a waste of time for either of us." He groaned some as he stood from his seat, bowing his head to Lady Aylmer. "I will send message back to you when I reach Prillian and we can further discuss the details of our silent arrangement. Until then, I thank you for your hospitality in our brief visit today. Good health, Lady Aylmer."

"As to you, Orpay. Also . . . I want good fighting men from you. I don't want hacks."

The Guild head grinned heavily. "No worries, Lady Aylmer. I plan on sending some good men. I will also send the best warrior the land has ever seen to you. Of that I can assure you."

No more words exchanged between the two. The large Argon man walked to the doors which were opened for him and left without as much as a look back. There stood little need for him to bother with such. This round clearly went in his favor. He gave very little, received quite a bit. No better negotiations than that.

As the room grew silent again, Aldric turned to Dylinn, who took another drink from her half full glass.

"I will let you speak to the girl soon. Best to keep contact with her limited, even for me."

"Is that why you choose not to use her to infiltrate Corovium in your plans?"

"No," she replied. "I do such because I will be out in the front of this army. They will know that Fallneese approaches. I cannot kill the king the same way as I have their predecessor. That would implement me in an assassination."

"Is that not what you would be doing this time around?"

"This is an uprising, Historian. This is war. There are no rules in war. Only winning and losing."

"And what of your agreement with Orpay? You know that he would become more powerful than even a queen if he became First."

"I do," said Dylinn with a smile emerging on the side of her face. "Funny thing about making arrangements, Historian. You have to live long enough to follow through with them. Now *that* is a lesson that he might wish to take with him in the future."

Orpay may have been powerful, but Aldric began to see that there were none more dangerous than Lady Aylmer.

--

The fallen gods show little favor in the games played by men. Pain spreads equally amongst men of any race, of any loyalty, of any walk in life.

I have held enough dead men to know that while it may numb, it never fades. You still feel the sting of it, still wish that none of it was real.

But it's real. All of it. Every damn second. I would ask the gods to save us, but they won't listen. Little favor in the games we play.

-- John Shonnen, First General of the Imperial Army

XV

The River Vlate cut across Ursan, an extension of a much larger lake to the east. The name of the lake was lost to Katlynn, but she did know that it branched many of the rivers throughout Ursan. The river was more a gentle stream than a true monster such as Sullein or the Huul, at least in her mind. Despite that trivial fact, the calm waters held a large breeding ground for several types of fish and provided both food and fresh water to the village that shared in name: Vlate Crossing, though most of the Ursan locally simply referred to their village as Vlate. Far north from Haroulvene, this village seemed quite popular, as even though the River Vlate remained timid and mostly shallow in some areas down the hundreds of miles that it stretched, it was wide and very deep in other areas. It also housed several large predators, which were of no danger here in the populace, but alone along the river bank could prove deadly to a traveler foolish enough to make an attempt to cross. A natural bridge of rocks and stone aided in the crossing here at a point of high elevation and shallow depths, making this the perfect spot for crossing to and from the only large city in Ursan, Antuannee, home of Lord Brocusk. Thus the name . . . Vlate Crossing.

Though in honesty, the story seemed more interesting when told to her by the locals versus the retelling in her thoughts.

It was here that supplies grew short and the need to work came upon them. Vlate was one of only a few villages that allowed outsiders to contribute within their community according to Jadenine. The Ursan woman felt that they needed to press further north, closer to the capital where the Guild would not tread, but that trip would not be made without proper supplies. New clothes were needed to replace tattered and blood soiled ones, shoes needed to be replaced for all, though none more relevant than Katlynn's, as well as dried meats and fruits, proper sleeping gear, and medical herbs and supplies. The trip would be long and difficult still as they would need to move from village to village in order to find one that accepted their aid. No telling how long they would spend away from civilization. No telling if they would be accepted at all.

Not that they had money, but even if they had, it did them little good here. There were no coins exchanged here, only bartering and working. And since they had nothing to barter with, they worked. They were given a small cabin that had two rooms and one latrine, as well as a small bathing area. This was not free of course, as they had to work just to stay there. So outside of the occasional pause to eat and sleep, the six travelers worked continuously at whatever job the village had to offer. The village chief was in charge of distributing the work and there never seemed an end to it. But if they did not work, they did not eat, forfeited the roof over their head, and removed their ability to gather supplies. So they worked, all of them, and they worked hard and often.

And when Katlynn had her first bath, it almost felt as if the journey had been worth it. Clothes were the first thing they decided to acquire, and the moment she received her fitted tunic and proper shoes, a long, warm bath ensued before placing on her new clothes. She felt clean for the first time in . . . well time no longer mattered. Days went by and so did life. How many weeks and months had it been since she fled the capital? It was all hazy and blended together and of little importance now. Strange, as during that first bath, a small part of her actually relaxed . . . a small part felt comfort. This was obviously not the life she had envisioned for herself, nor the situation or place she desired to be. However it had also not been the killing grounds that she had pictured in her mind. She had thought of Ursan as a place where people killed one another for an inch of land and men raped multiple women and made them their slaves. But not so. Vlate's community was tightly wound, all working together for each other, all strong and with purpose.

A part of her began to find purpose as well, something she had difficulty explaining. Not the life she sought, but the life she got. Her tears dried. Her body toughened. She might have been a Pratt, but she was becoming something else, something new, something stronger.

Things between the captain and her had grown . . . better. In truth, the days went so quickly that they had not spent an enormous amount of time together, which helped. The men did a majority of the stronger, physical labor, so Tristan spent much of his time out of the village either hunting or gathering. And work was done all day and all night, pending on the task, so they did not always cross paths. But when they did, he cared for her while not speaking at times: rubbing her back, massaging her shoulders. Katlynn even allowed him to rub her feet, which although no longer pained her as much, still looked disgusting. Not once did he ask her if the work she did was too much, if he could help in some way, if there was something he could do to make things better. He simply shut up. And she could not have liked him more for it.

Every now and again they would discuss their day of work, what they had to do, how it went. Every now and again they fucked. Clean again, she became open to the idea of him inside her. It had been a long time for either of them, longer than she had ever gone without sex since she became sexually active in the first place. It was good to have regularity back in her life, even something as trifling as sex. They were cautious not to disturb others and mostly wandered off into the wilderness to do it. There were only two beds in the cabin they lived in, of which they rotated nightly on who slept upon it. A bit disgusting, she presumed, to have others lay in a bed that had been soiled with sweat and sex. Well in her mind at least.

Most of her days were spent washing, both dishes and clothes, pending on the hour and the day. Katlynn also prepped food on other days, though she was not entrusted to cook. Meals were also consumed as a community, as they had one large dining hall where they ate together as a village. It was such an interesting sight to see an entire community come together as one, to see the fruits of their labor as the hunted and gathered food by the men was prepped and prepared by the women and consumed by all. Each felt pride at what they did, each felt a part of the whole.

This did not seem like the Ursan that she and others had feared.

It had been about two weeks since their arrival in Vlate and Katlynn had spent the last three days in the kitchen. The locals were starting to get used to her presence. *Well, at least they don't stare as much.* The dishes cleaned from the large dinner, she was dismissed for the day. The hour grew late, the sun dipping behind the trees as she made her way to the small cabin. She had little idea who would be there, though she spotted Bird moving up from the forest beyond, walking beside her strangely as would a dog heeling by her legs.

"What do you want, you smelly little shit?" she mumbled to the furry beast.

"He likes you," announced a voice just off to her right, startling her to near death. When she turned, she spotted the unkempt Argon, Feko. "I think he is walking you home to ensure your safety. It would be quite adorable if it were anything but a Chur'rat, would it not, Katlynn Pratt?"

She held her ground, keeping the distance between them. He seemed earnest if not crazy to her, but Nathanial was very specific with her when it came to the Argon. He did not want her around him alone. But even without his warning, she did not trust him. And for the life of her, she could not gather why they would want to keep him around at all. It seemed better to just cut him loose if there was a lack of trust.

"Well it is good to be admired, I suppose," she offered up, remaining cautious.

"I agree. So I must ask something of you that you may not like, but understand that I have no choice but to ask you."

"There is always choice," Katlynn swiftly noted, hoping to prevent anything regrettable. She was not afraid. Her power was no longer the gift that she once thought it to be, but she understood well enough what it could do now to give her the confidence that she was certainly not defenseless.

But the Argon shook his head. "There is not always choice for some of us. I have been asked to take a long walk, one for several hours, and it was strongly recommended that you come with me."

"Who recommended this?"

Feko glanced away for a moment, muttered something indecisively under his breath, then turned back to meet her eyes. "I am sure that Nathanial Wode has spoken to you, yes? Of the voices?"

"Somewhat, Feko. Somewhat."

"Then you should understand the importance of this."

He took a step forward and consequently she took one back, her arms raised defensively, and Feko did the same.

"Stand your ground, Feko."

"Whoa, calm down, Lady Pratt. Calm yourself. I mean you absolutely no harm. I am trying to help you."

"I have had enough of people trying to help me, Feko. Right now, I just want to go home."

"Agreed, but this is not a good time. You should come with me. We will return, I promise."

"Enough, Feko. I will not walk with you, not alone."

"Then with company?"

What games are being played here?

"If it is that important to you, then yes. But not without Tristan or Nathanial."

"Then let us be swift then. I assure you that I will keep my distance as we walk to the cabin."

Feko took the lead, walking ahead of them as he made his way toward the cabin. The Chur'rat stood on his hind legs, staring with his head cocked sideways at the Argon as he passed, a look of perplexity on his little face.

"Believe me," she whispered to Bird, "I understand what you mean."

--

A lucky shot, an impossible shot.

"Ha!" called out Jadenine.

Her makeshift spear punctured three fish straight through. It was easily one of the best throws Nathan had ever seen.

Their pants were both rolled up and feet submerged in the water up to her knees, his shins. They did not eat today with the community. Work had them out fixing a few holes in the natural bridge which involved moving some heavy rocks, which involved *finding* heavy rocks to move in the first place. Needless to say, the task was tedious and it kept them out of the village for a majority of the day. As the task completed, they were beyond time for dinner. They could not tread too deeply into the Vlate, as even in these calmer parts, the depths further in could not be easily measured. They treaded just along the shoreline, which for Nathan was far enough. Stories of creatures in the waters played more than a few tricks on his mind. A brush of even a larger than average fish against his leg caused him to jump for no reason. Also they did not even have a fishing pole to catch anything, so it felt like a waste of time.

Thus Jadenine's insistence that she could catch enough fish for them without proper equipment.

"Damn lucky is all," Nathan commented lazily.

"Look who speaks of luck?"

Lifting the spear up, the three fish punctured in different areas of their body trashed mightily and fruitlessly about. Nathanial began to track back out of the river to the shore.

"Well I will grab my blade while you see if you can spear us a fire."

Jadenine laughed. "For as good of a hunter as you are, Wode, you are a horrible outdoorsman."

"Who said hunting and being an outdoorsman had anything to do with one another?"

The Ursan shook her head. "I suppose there is no written rule on such, but you would assume that someone as gifted as you in the hunt could better take care of himself out here."

"I am a bit accustomed to buying things still, I'm afraid." Making it to the shore, he shook off the water from his legs before unsheathing his serrated blade. "Do you miss this at all?"

"Miss what?" she inquired, lightly tossing the spear out toward Nathan while she worked her way into the forest, rifling the ground.

"Your tribe, your people, this life."

Several piles of fallen branches in her hand, she walked back over to him. "Earth and Flame, Wode, I was fucking ten. It was a long time ago. I'm not a Kwyantin, so memories come and go. Things I forget . . . well I am ashamed to admit."

"Such as?"

"Such as I am ashamed to admit. What part of that is difficult for you to grasp?"

"I just figured you have told me plenty so far, why not just tell me?"

One fish at a time and his blade came down, the head removed from the body, the flopping steadying shortly after. As she started on the fire, he began to work on skinning back scales with the smoother side of his shorter blade.

"I remember Brocusk's face as if it were yesterday," she admitted as if it were a crime of some sort.

"Well of course you do. He . . ."

"I can't say the same for my father." She looked away, forgetting the fire for a moment, her eyes out to the clear waters of the River Vlate. "Can't see him anymore. When I dream, he is just a faceless void."

"That is nothing to be ashamed of."

"Easy enough to say, Pratt."

"*Wode,*" he distinctly clarified.

She smiled at his annoyance, working again on the bundle of sticks. "That bugs you quite a bit, doesn't it?"

"You know that it does. I would gather that's why you jab that at me every few days with that."

"Never gets old."

"For you perhaps."

A spark hit and the small fire began, Jadenine leaning over to blow against the flames. Her shirt fit loosely and dipped low enough for the top of her breasts to be on display. He made an attempt not to look . . . but he was a man after all.

"Anything you like, Wode?"

He laughed and looked away. What more could he do? "I suppose I couldn't have made that more obvious."

"No, you could not."

"Sorry. Just kind of instinctual."

Jadenine rose and Nathan tossed her the fish, to which she caught and placed aside while she still prodded the fire, the flames slowly working.

"How old was that little whore of yours back in Prillian anyways?"

"Her name is Keli."

"Whatever. You know who I mean. The tailor's daughter. How old? Twelve?" she inquired.

"Fuck you," was his immediate response, to which she of course laughed.

"I really *can* get under your skin as of late, can I not, Wode?"

"Can we talk about something else besides *her* please?"

"Or my tits?"

"Yes. Something else."

She shrugged, spearing the skinned fish again and placing them over the fire.

"What I wouldn't give for a drink . . ." Nathanial muttered out loud.

With her free hand, Jadenine Zo reached into her pack and tossed over a black object his way, to which he caught and examined.

"What is this?" he queried.

"Not as good as Ashroot or ale," she began, "but a little something to get us by. It is a dried, poisonous mushroom. Not potent though, so don't give me that look. Break off a piece and throw the rest back to me."

"How potent is not potent when it comes to poison?"

Breaking in half, he threw the equal piece back to her. "Not enough to do much, but enough to do something. Just chew on the damn thing while the fish cook."

And he did. Squishy, tasteless, yet strangely disgusting . . . but he chewed all the same. And it did not take long for his mouth to feel a bit tingly, almost a numbing feeling. He could see Jadenine chewing her piece as well silently, her red hair tied back behind her, her face smooth and without blemishes despite her difficult upbringing.

"I suppose I only asked you if you missed this because this was not really what I thought tribe life would be like here in Ursan."

She continually turned the fish, the smell filling his nostrils pleasantly as they continued to cook. "As I said before, it is life like any other. I think so many times we analyze why our culture is better than your culture. Typical male sense of sizing things up. My cock is bigger than your cock."

"I wouldn't doubt it."

"Fuck you, Wode, you know what I mean. People spend too much time trying to figure out which way of life is better than the next. There is no answer to that question. Take Donovini for example. Strength is power there. I can respect that. The name is not as important as the strength. Once in power, the best way to stay such is to surround yourself with a strong family and strong allies. Anyone can move up in life, if you are strong enough to survive it. You will not rise far if you are not good with a blade. But in Fallneese, you had better be born with a prestigious name. If you are born a son or daughter of a servant, you will be a servant, along with your children and their children and their children after. The servants are paid and treated well mostly, and at least you know your station in life. Understanding what is expected of you is important to most. In Argonus, it is all about wealth. You can ascend if you have the looks and the influence, but you need thick skin to survive on top. It is a far more political world there, one of backstabbing and plotting. But if you dream of being on top of the world and are careful not to piss on the wrong people, you are likely to get where you want.

"Ursan, everyone has a place. Much like Fallneese, there is comfort in knowing your station. All is well and done until Brocusk lifts the banner."

She extended the now cooked fish and Nathan impaled two of them with his blade. "What happens when the banner is raised? What do you mean?"

They both took a bite into their meal, which was very good, at least for the fact that they had no spices or otherwise to cook with.

"If Lord Brocusk lifts his banner," Jadenine continued on a full mouth, speaking through bites of her fish, "that means he calls upon all those who swore loyalty to him. Which, as you can gather, is all of Ursan. Men, women, children. Should Dehyllo claim such, all would fight for him when he decides it. So this life that both you and your cousin seem smitten over, in a snap of a finger, it could all go away. All to follow one man and his ambitions."

Finishing her meal, she tossed the stick into the fire. "Like I said, a life like any other. None are better than the rest. They are just different. And since when has being different been a bad thing?"

"You and I see things differently than most of the world," he added. "The Guild works with anyone and everyone. For all of their faults, and they have many, that is one of their brighter sides. What difference does your race amount to when the goal is wealth and power?"

"None, but it does for most outside the Guild. So much fear and misrepresentation against Ursan and yet . . . justified in a way."

"If anything," concluded Wode, "I am beginning to understand better."

They sat, silent, staring off in different directions. Their meal finished, they should have been ready to head back into Vlate. But for the moment, Nathan felt good. Certainly his lightly filled stomach played a part, as well as that mushroom that had his body feeling loose and good but not out of his control. He just sat there, comfortable, content.

"Do you want to fuck?" Jadenine questioned.

She was certainly the most straightforward woman he had ever known. So taken back by her question, his immediate response was to stare back like an idiot. He must have stared blankly better than most.

"Well never fucking mind then," she hissed back and spat onto the earth.

"Hold on . . . I mean . . . I didn't say no or anything . . ."

"No," she stated, all the hatred back in her tone. "You didn't say any damn thing."

"Well sorry. I'm just a bit taken back is all. I mean, you pretty much hate me and all."

"What, you have to like someone to fuck them? Did you like that little whore back in Prillian?"

"*Keli*, and no, not really."

Silence.

Well . . . this is more than a bit awkward.

He coughed a little, feeling more foolish at each passing second. "I suppose if you . . . I don't know . . . decided to come over here and all. Closer that is."

And he was teenager back in Astrona again, with all of the worst things to say. *Well no repairing that line.* He just watched Jadenine, her green eyes focused for a second more on the fire before lifting her shirt up and off, her perfectly rounded breasts exposed in the firelight. She stood and walked over to him and wasted little time in plopping down into his lap. Her legs wrapped around him, both still sitting up and staring at one another for a second, eyes freely exploring each other before they began to kiss. His hands swiftly found her breasts as he squeezed hard upon them, his fingers moving to her nipples.

She bit down deep into his lip, and he was not so certain that she did not want to eat the fucking thing. His hands removed from her breasts, they worked down across her back and to her ass, hands sliding between her trousers and her skin, grabbing so firm upon her cheeks that she released the stranglehold on his lips and worked her mouth down to his neck. Her hands clawed at him for a moment longer before she shoved off some and wrenched his shirt off. Now her hands explored his chest, their mouths locked again as they kissed wildly, both sloppy and all over the place.

He hardened steadily and uncontrollably with her still sitting atop him, and Jadenine must have felt it beneath her. She began to move up and down his crotch, clothes over clothes, as her hands clawed heavy down his back. He flinched some as her fingernails drove into his flesh, and she smiled at his discomfort. *Damn bitch, even now.*

She stood abruptly and her pants were removed as she stood completely in the nude. His eyes moved up and down her near flawless, toned body for but one long moment. Then he fumbled to remove his own pants, struggling at first, then just falling onto his back and sliding them off. She did not let him up from that position. Jadenine was back on top of him, her hands reaching for his cock and guiding him inside. She was already wet as her fingers dug into his chest and she slowly at first began to sway back and forth. Nathan moved his hands to her hips, then up to her breasts and played with her nipples, enjoying the feeling of her riding his cock. She began to pick up the pace and he found himself enjoying the moment too well, and he moved his hands back down to her hips to slow her motion, to make it steady, to find rhythm.

Jadenine allowed him to control the movement and the pace for a few minutes, then she reached down and snatched his hands and returned them to her breasts. In control once again, she moved back and forth with a passion, moaning now, her eyes closed and thoroughly enjoying the moment. So was he. Damn it all if he was not. *Don't think. Don't you fucking think on this. Just enjoy it.*

She dropped closer to his chest and pressed the issue now, faster, faster, with more intent, her moans increasing. Nathan did what he could to control it, but it felt good, too good.

He moaned himself as he finished inside her, her eyes pausing for just a moment as she realized he climaxed.

"You're done?"

He felt embarrassed. "It's been a while. Shit . . . not like you haven't been with me every step of the fucking way to know that."

"You don't take care of yourself every now and again?" she inquired, though strangely not judgmental, only inquisitive.

"Well, that's not really the same. Doesn't exactly help endurance. Just kind of helps get me by."

Silence.

Still inside her, still hard, they waited for but another moment.

"You can . . . keep going if you want," he suggested, being the gentleman that he was. "I am ready."

Jadenine seemed to think it over for a few seconds, then pressed her face down to his chest as she began again.

--

"Do you want to run this by me again?" asked Tristan.

Katlynn could do little save shrug her shoulders. "He wants us to go for a walk."

"I am standing right here, Tristan Crane," Feko clarified, his hand half raised as if this cabin were a classroom.

He looked nervous. First sign of guilt was to look the part, or so the captain had told her once. And Feko looked, felt, and all but seemed a man with ulterior motives. He kept his distance from her during their walk back to their tiny cabin, but once inside, his comfort level decreased. He began to sweat some, mumble under his breath more than usual, and pace about the small area. Iero sat patiently, his eyes never leaving the Argon, while Tristan ensured he stood between the two.

No one trusted Feko Hawbry. No one wanted him there. At any point he could leave and be a free man without anyone hunting for him, and no one would think twice to ask him why.

Now it seemed as if he was beginning to come to terms with that.

"Feko," Tristan started, his tone firm and defined. "Perhaps you should take that walk. And perhaps you should think long and hard on if you need to return."

And there it was.

If the Argon waited for someone to jump in to defend him, to rescue him from the captain's comments, he was in the wrong cabin. Likely, he was in the wrong country.

"It is important," stammered Feko a bit. "I wish you could understand. I don't ask for much. Just to take a walk. If I knew why, I would tell you. But I think we all just need to go for a bit."

"We?" questioned Tristan. "A few minutes ago, you attempted to take Katlynn alone on a walk."

"I did. That remains to be true. But she will not walk without you at her side. So I am forced to add you in, even though you are not in their plans."

"What plans?"

"I don't truly know, Tristan Crane. I am but a vessel. But I know that you are not mentioned. Neither am I, I assure you. My path has led me to her. I am meant to protect her. And right now, I . . . I think we should walk."

"You are a fucking lunatic, Feko," Tristan blurted out.

"Calm yourself, Tristan," Iero cautioned.

"I will not. Nathan should have been wiser at choosing his traveling companions, and at least been more up front with us about you. I don't trust you. I am not sure what you're capable of. Why don't you take that walk, and if you come back, make sure Nathan is here to defend your presence."

There was a moment, a brief one, when Feko's eyes met hers, where Katlynn watched as he gave such a look that she questioned everything. Maybe he was insane, but that did not necessarily make him dangerous or insincere. It just made him crazy. The look he returned was of helplessness. Katlynn could not change the pity in her heart, the regret in her mind.

"Just go, Feko," she whispered.

Her chest ached at the comment. She could only imagine what the Argon must have felt.

"I tried," he said, saddened. "I will come for you. I . . . will not have a choice."

He wasted no more words. Feko grabbed his traveling pack and stormed out the cabin door in a panic. He began to run, circling about then heading west, away from the cabins and into the wilderness. Katlynn watched the bizarre scene until he was out of sight completely.

"That was . . . interesting," the captain declared.

"You could have been nicer," she chastised.

But Tristan only huffed some toward her. "Come now, like you weren't thinking any of that too. Of course you were."

"Doesn't excuse it. He has been with us for some time now and has yet to show us that kind of disrespect. Crazy or not, he has always treated us well."

"Did it ever dawn on either of you," Iero butted in, "that he may be telling the truth?"

Tristan crossed his arms before his chest defiantly. "Do you believe him, Druid?"

"I can reach into the Earth Realm and draw upon the power of nature to create walls with vines and weapons of roots. I even have a Chur'rat as my familiar that calls himself Bird. Let's just say that I have seen stranger things in this world. I like to think that I keep myself open to possibilities."

"Then you are as crazy as him," slammed the captain.

Katlynn moved to the cabin door, staring out to see if Feko had flubbed his departure when she felt the vibrations beneath her feet. Thumps, many of them. Soft at first and steadily rising.

"Can you feel that?" she called back, and the Druid and the captain turned to her.

Iero stood, his eyes now focused. "Close the door."

"But . . ." she started.

"Close the door!" he screamed.

Reaching for the handle, she did as commanded.

--

If he had to rank his most awkward moments again, he found his brand new number one. They walked back, not very far apart and not very close either. About the appropriate length for two people that were not very fond of each other, so Nathanial presumed. He glanced over at Jadenine, who in turn kept her glare straight forward. His eyes wandered for a second to her body before catching himself and turning his sight straight in front of him.

Sex had a way of mudding things up. A part of him wanted to ask her if this would be a regular thing, while another part wanted to ask her to maybe forget this ever happened. It was not because of her looks, because Jadenine Zo, while trained with the blade, tough as steel, and kept a permanent fortress up to defend against emotion . . . was also stunningly attractive and a damn good fuck at that. But the reality was that they really *did* hate each other. They fought all the time, they never saw eye to eye on just about anything, and he was fairly certain that she would still feed him to a Draywolf if it meant saving her own ass.

So exactly what's the problem?

The problem was that they just had sex, and it was damn good for them both. Difficult to find a pure sexual relation that was not complicated with too much thinking. Save for maybe a whore, but even then . . .

Wake up, Nathan. You just had sex. Not the first time. Let's certainly hope it's not the last time. Just sex. Nothing more. No need to really think about it. If she wants to do it again, great. If not, no big deal.

He had to admit, it would be nice to have some regularity returned to his life, even it was something as meaningless as sex.

Keli was perfect for him, he hated to admit. She did not hover too long after sex and she spoke enough about nothing that he found he could simply zone her out. Beautiful, young, and most of all, forgettable. Now the sex was mundane, but he finished every time regardless. Which was always satisfying in its own right, even if the journey there was less than such. Nathan was hardly looking to marry or commit, so someone such as that was perfect for him. He *knew* nothing would ever come of it, and that satisfied him. Face value was important in life, after all.

Nothing worse than amazing sex. Made men do foolish things, stupid things.

"Stop staring at me."

Damn it all, he *was* staring at her.

"Sorry, just . . . nothing. Sorry."

"Don't make this weird, Wode."

"Of course not. I mean . . . no, that's not at all . . ."

"Just sex, Wode. We are human, after all, right?" He nodded to her. "Good. And if your brain is wondering if that was a onetime thing, maybe your attitude will determine that."

"Maybe I was just thinking that I would hate you less if you walked around with your clothes off all day."

There you go. Get your composure back.

She chuckled at the comment. "Certainly would make meeting new people easier, at least for them."

"Help people forget about your *oh so* charming personality, I would gather."

"I aim to please."

He smiled. "That you do."

Sex, such a funny thing.

They continued onward, walking silently back toward the northern entrance to Vlate Crossing, passing a few locals with a concerned look on their faces. It was then when he first felt the vibrations against his feet. Horses, lots of horses, dozens of them. Jadenine must have recognized it as well. Their step increased but they did not run, did not want to alert any of the villagers to their panic. The Guild? Could they have made it this far this fast? It did not seem possible; in fact, he knew that it could not be. There was no way they would have pursued this far north yet, if they had even bothered to cross into Ursan at all. They would need Orpay to give direct approval, and even he would likely reach out to Brocusk for permission to move through his lands. All of that would take time, time that had yet to transpire.

So then if these horses were not the Guild, they were something else.

But what?

Some of the villagers began to huddle about; no fear in them, only curiosity. As they made their way toward the cabin, Nathanial caught sight of the village elder working though the forming crowds with haste, heading toward the southern entrance close to their cabin. They followed from a distance until their cabin was in sight, and so were their visitors.

Nathan grabbed Jadenine's arm and they both ducked behind one of the nearby cabins, outside of earshot but within sight of them. He gazed at the men on horseback . . . all Ursan, over fifty of them. Not a single familiar face amongst them. He sighed of relief. Maybe another group simply passing through.

"Not the Guild," he murmured.

Jadenine's hand reached the hilt of her sheathed sword. "No. It's Dehyllo."

Earth and Flame.

"Stand your ground," he hissed toward her. "He has fifty men about. You wouldn't get more than one step to him."

"Maybe one step is all that I need."

"And how would you make it out of there even if you could reach him?"

"I don't really care," she answered in earnest. "I will join my family in death."

"And kill the rest of us as well? The village elder would quickly tell him of the others that traveled with you."

"No worries," she offered up. "He's doing that already."

Sure enough, the elder was pointing toward the cabin that had been offered to them all, speaking in length. Dehyllo stroked his beard for a bit, listening for a few long seconds. He then waved back to his guard and his men dismounted, hands on weapons.

"He explains to him that his only available cabin is recently occupied," explained Jadenine. "Dehyllo asks of the guest, and he tells him four Donovinians work within his village along with an Argon and a lone Ursan. Four Donovinians sounds suspicious. Unauthorized Guild presence, or maybe something more? Maybe he is thinking he should open that cabin door and find out who is inside."

She of course could not hear or know what words exchanged, but the body language all but told Nathanial the same.

Jadenine wrenched free of his grip and took her step out into the open.

Nathan inhaled deeply.

Steady, calm.

He moved out into the open with her, eyes of the fifty something warriors all slowly and gradually turning to them. Nathan felt Jadenine about to rise up, about to unsheathe her sword and charge the murderer of her family, of her people. He appreciated the bravado, even understood her pain and rage. But he had lives to consider. Namely his cousin's.

"We are from the Guild!" he announced loudly, and Jadenine whipped her head in shock and confusion.

I have to try something.

"Stand your ground, Guild member!" Dehyllo Brocusk called back. "What business do you have this far north?"

"We are on official business, but did not mean to travel this far north. Shamefully we got ourselves a bit lost and found ourselves short of supplies. We did not inform these people of our affiliations to the Guild. Thought it best to leave that part out."

"And under whose orders are you to be out in my land to begin with?"

Oh we can play the name game, Lord Brocusk. I will pass this test.

"Cylaa, of the named members in Prillian. As I understand, Orpay himself gives her the order. We are in search of two rogue members of our faction that we believe have fled into your country. We do not stir any issues or cause any concerns. We only search for our own."

"And yet you stop for several days now?"

"We cannot hunt without proper supplies."

Brocusk nodded some. "I appreciate the honesty, as that can be a difficult thing to do. But you must realize who I am and what I am capable of. Perhaps that is why you are so upfront with me."

"Best to be honest and be done with it, so I've been told."

"Funny, we have a few sayings here in Ursan. One of my personal favorites, an honest stranger is a fool or a fable. So which are you, Guild member? You do not seem the fool, so perhaps you are a fable. Perhaps you lie to cover for your other companions in the cabin."

"Anything I say to follow that up," stated Nathan, the sweat now forming upon his skin, "you would simply brand me a liar regardless."

"The elder tells me there are four Donovinians in his village, on my lands. Surface your other three companions. Let me see them and judge myself to which you are."

He returned silence to the House lord. Instead his hands moved to his blades, his fingers tapping the hilts nervously.

"I am certain the cabin is locked," Brocusk continued. "Tell them to open the door before I lose patience and kill you, then burn the damn thing down."

"It was a fair attempt, Wode," Jadenine stated beside him. "Damn shame I have to die next to you."

The door erupted in an explosion of roots and vines, and the sound of drawn swords echoed against his ear. Jadenine rushed forward, sword in hand, and Nathan was not far behind. Tristan came out first, using the wall of vines as a shield between them and Brocusk's men, with Katlynn just a step behind him. But these were no miners from Uvull. They were no second-rate Guild members from Prillian. These warriors were part of Lord Brocusk's personal guard. If the explosion of vines was meant to startle and scare them, it did not accomplish the goal. Several of them already formed position around Dehyllo, and the others made a direct line toward Tristan, swords out and ready to strike.

Katlynn's face expressed fear. His did not. He knew this day would come. Death was an inevitability.

"Hold! Hold!" bellowed Dehyllo.

Several feet away, Jadenine and Nathan stood their ground, Katlynn and Tristan off to their right, pausing in their step as well. At least seventeen warriors stood only a few feet away, blood thirst in their mind, but held firm while awaiting the instructions from their lord.

Lord Brocusk gave a healthy and misplaced smile toward the group. "Welcome to Ursan, Katlynn Pratt." He then moved away from his guards, taking a few closer steps to their group while his guards remained readied just in case they were needed. "And Iero, come out and join us. And remove your wall of vines from sight. You know it will do you little good here. Far too many of us."

"You speak truth, Lord Brocusk," he heard Iero call out as the vines and roots receded back underground. "You cannot fault me for trying."

"Not at all. Is Bird still with you?"

As Iero moved beyond the now gaping hole in the side of the cabin, the Chur'rat leapt from the earth to the Druid's shoulder.

Brocusk clapped his hand. "I would have thought he'd have found better company by now."

"He has little sense of taste, that is for certain," Iero agreed.

"So," continued Dehyllo, his vision returning to his cousin. "Fortune continues to smile upon me. I have been apparently labeled an outcast as I removed my lazy, fat, pathetic court appointed officials from the council and made my way back home. First Pratt has taken this as an act against the throne."

"And where are your court officials now?" Iero inquired.

"They walk back. One of my men accompanies them. Some will die on their trek back, as they have forgotten how to be an Ursan. Those that remember will live and will be stronger because of it. So I travel with my men, back home, back to where I belong. And look what I find. Face to face with another outcast of the throne, the murderer of the last king."

"I did nothing of the sort," spat Katlynn.

"So you say, but your brother Rayden looks to take the throne. He apparently weds Allura Rowe in an alliance against us. So the last king is killed, and that leaves an opportunity for your family name to sit upon the throne of Amon. There is already evidence and now there is motive."

"I couldn't care less for your opinion. I did not kill the king. I am guilty of nothing save fleeing from an unjust hanging, which you know damn well would have happened."

"Of course I do," he admitted. "Do you see what's wrong with our land, Katlynn Pratt? The system is broken. And it falls to me to fix, I suppose." Brocusk slapped his hands together again. "So, the daughter of my enemy falls directly in my lap. I cannot pass on such a thing, you hopefully understand. It is nothing against you, but your father and your uncles are of men without standards or spines, and I look to break them all. You are valuable. The rest, however, are expendable. Take her and kill the rest."

"I am Jadenine Zo! I challenge you, Dehyllo Brocusk!"

And Brocusk's eyes widened as he took several steps forward, gaining a better look while wisely still keeping a good distance.

"The little girl I let live that day . . . oh, child, how sad this day must be for you. All of these years . . . and now we stand face to face and only death awaits you."

"Fuck you, Brocusk. I challenge you to a championed duel."

"A championed duel? Well, in order for such a thing, you must have something I want that I cannot obtain by force. What can you possibly offer me that I would willingly accept your challenge?"

She hesitated. She had nothing. "My blood!" she called out.

"I will have that regardless. If there is nothing else . . ."

"Another Pratt," Nathan announced.

That caught his attention.

"Another Pratt," Brocusk repeated, his eyes displaying hunger. "I do not recognize you boy, and I know all the Pratts. I know them all because I hate them all. Warriors playing in politics. Bah! They lost their sword arm. Nothing sadder than a warrior that forgets how to swing. But . . . there is something in your face, boy. Something familiar. So tell me, who are you?"

"I suppose you will have to accept the duel in order to find out," Nathan claimed.

"Again, you do not understand how the duel works. I can simply have my men capture you. Whatever I can acquire by force is of no use in a duel."

Nathan's blade reached his own neck. "I can take my life and you have nothing. I give you leverage. That is what you cannot take by force."

Lord Brocusk laughed out loud. "Perfect, perfect! This is how the game is played. But why, if I might ask, would you risk your life for *her* duel? Her family lost their honor. I accepted a duel with her father. I could not gain his people without the duel. I did it to prevent bloodshed. When I won, her father went against our ways, denied the conditions of our duel. She holds no honor."

"Then why did you let me live if I held no honor?" Jadenine screamed her question.

Dehyllo only stared intently at her in response.

"*Why*?" she hollered, spit forming as the words removed from her lips.

The crowds had formed. Every villager within Vlate Crossing had formed a wall north of them. All eyes gazed to the girl that screamed at the lord, and all awaited their lord's response.

"I accept your duel."

"Then draw your sword!"

"Calm yourself," he announced. "Firstly, I just accepted your duel. Now we must render terms and conditions. I have accepted that upon my victory, I acquire both Pratts and they surrender themselves willingly. What do you gain should you succeed?"

"Freedom, for all of us, without recourse."

"Very well. Those are acceptable terms. Now for the conditions . . ."

"The dead loses," Jadenine barked out, to which several in attendance sparked a grin at her boldness.

"That they do, Zo. As you know, we normally would choose our champion. I know how desperately you wish this to be between me and you, but that is not how a duel works. The champions cannot be us."

"Then I choose . . ."

"Hold your tongue, Zo!" bellowed Brocusk. "My conditions are simple. We choose each other's champions. It must be someone within our respective parties. Do you accept my conditions?"

Jadenine held firm, sword still in hand, her mind still pondering.

"Accept," pleaded Nathan. *There's no other way we make it out of this alive.*

"Silence!" she spat back. "I accept!"

"Then choose my champion," demanded Dehyllo. "And I certainly hope you have learned more honor than your father should you lose."

Jadenine sheathed her weapon. She spent little time as she gazed at the men that traveled with Dehyllo. Behind him stood a tall lanky kid, paler than most, thinner than all of them.

"Him," stated Jadenine, her arm thrust outward to the boy.

Dehyllo turned back, gazed at the one she pointed to, then turned back to her. "That is my escort, more like a squire."

"You did not name exceptions in your conditions!"

Lord Brocusk only shrugged, walking over closer, staring at those amongst them. "Well, who shall I pick as your champion? Obviously I can't pick you, Zo." His eyes met Nathan's. "And you are my prize, so not you." Over to Iero. "Not a chance, Druid. We did not set any conditions against Realms, and I am no fool to not think you cannot defeat even my best man one against one. I am aware of the power of the Realms."

"As you should be, being lord of Ursan. I heard rumors of a Pyromancer at your disposal during some past championed duels," Iero proclaimed.

To which Dehyllo only smiled. "Katlynn Pratt, you are also my prize, so it cannot be you." Then he turned, fixed upon the last of them. "Captain Tristan Crane. You have the dubious honor of being the least valuable here amongst those present. I choose you as the Zo champion. You shall face my squire, Ollifo, one of my many nephews. This battle is to the death."

The tall boy, who could not have been more than sixteen if Nathan were guessing, stood forward and drew the sword by his side. The men of Ursan backed away and space was given. Tristan understood what was at stake. His eyes did not waver, nor did he show any fear. Should he win, they would be free to go. Otherwise both Katlynn and Nathan would be the only two to walk away from this, and not the way they would have liked.

And where is Feko?

Tristan removed his sword and took a step forward inside the circle. Those from the village pressed closer and against Wode, their desire to likely both see the battle and also ensure the rules were kept. Honor stood above all in Ursan. It was worth more than life. The captain began to move along the perimeter, only staring at his opposition, his sword dragging down into the grass and dirt. The boy looked scared and kept himself at the center of the circle, allowing Tristan to move around him, sizing him up.

Do it, Tristan. Fucking kill him.

"Begin!" called out Dehyllo.

Tristan charged, his sword up and down, finding nothing but air as the squire stepped aside, his sword pressed against his chest. Again the captain came at him, this time a clean thrust that met a downward parry from Ollifo, and he sidestepped away. The boy was quick for his frame, and though he looked to struggle with the sword weight, he did not have any issues with fighting.

Everyone in Ursan fought, regardless of status, regardless of physical prowess.

Tristan came again, his sword swing ensuring accuracy as he made an attempt toward the legs. The squire defended the blow, then countered with a strike that the captain barely raised and defended from. Now the two men gazed at each other, perhaps a hair more of respect from the captain than before. Tristan swung, and Ollifo defended. Followed by a swing and a parry. Again the captain swung, left and right, high and low, and the squire defended.

The captain then spun about and connected a grazing cut against the boy's arm, a surface wound at best, but Nathan could see the confidence now return to Tristan. Short lived, though. The squire gave Tristan a straight kick to the gut, giving them separation and the captain had to duck and roll away from a heavy swing to save his life. The Ursan in the circle roared in approval while the captain held his stomach tightly for a few precious seconds, gathering his breath as he moved further away. The squire did not pursue. Instead he lifted his arms into the sky and gave a battle cry, which further enticed the onlookers.

Gaining his breath while losing his composure, the captain rushed forward, his sword flailing outward recklessly and the squire gracefully spun aside. His blade then came down hard into Tristan's back. The sword sliced clean through and blood filled the wound quickly. The captain yelped in pain, Katlynn screamed in terror, and Ollifo wasted no time.

The captain stumbled and dropped to his knees, his sword slipping from his hand. Ollifo then lifted his own sword and swung clean across the captain's neck, Tristan's head rolling off his shoulders. The body dropped and twitched about some after. Reflexes had a strange way of making a man do bizarre things in death. Nathan should know. He had seen his fair share. Someone once told him it would get easier to deal with death in time, but that was a damn lie. It never got easy. Nothing worse in fact. Especially someone he respected . . . trusted.

The crowd that had formed to watch the fight roared in approval. Katlynn fell to her knees, tears forming in her eyes uncontrollably. Jadenine beside him drew her weapon only to drop it, a strange content within her face.

All was lost. All for nothing.

"Ollifo is the winner!" Dehyllo announced. "Well done, nephew, well done. Now gather a paper and a quill. And get a bird carrier."

The boy sheathed his weapon and ran back to his supplies. Dehyllo stood forward and pointed to the Druid.

"I feel generous today. Bind the Druid's hands behind him. Place my mystery Pratt and the Zo under lock and key. I am not done with either of them yet. Katlynn Pratt stays with me at all times. Now carefully drop your weapon, Pratt."

He untied his belt and let it drop to the ground, sword and short blade included. Soldiers were atop them all quickly afterwards, pressed him hard into the grass, bodies holding him down should he decide to play the hero . . . which he did not. Nathan was a realist. There was no winning here, no escaping.

"Write three notes and send them to all three Pratts," he heard Dehyllo speak out to his squire. "I do not even know who I desire to read this more. Nicolas, Philip, Edmond. It is an equal hatred. Tell them all that we have two Pratts in our possession now. Tell them that we will hear their negotiations for their lives should they concede the throne to us. And if not . . . then we invite them north to try and take them from us."

Nathan felt himself being helped up, arms now bound behind his back. Jadenine was beside him and he could no longer see his cousin as he was forcefully guided away. He certainly was lucky.

But inevitability, eventually, luck ran out. Never at the best times.

--

A Wedding, a Crowning, and an Old Flame

It can be a difficult life here in Genethur, despite the wealth and the power. It is not wholly unfamiliar to me. My father was a wealthy merchant growing up, and when Philip was younger, he knew what he wanted and got it. I was a prize to him, and I could not have been happier. The Pratts taught me what life was about, real life. They had riches and power, and yet they worked and fought for everything they had. I learned how to live in Astrona, truly live.

And when we moved here, when we came to Corovium, things changed. Nothing uglier, nothing dirtier than politics. Nothing can beat a man down like the games involved. The wealth and power simply make you a target here.

Appearances aside . . . Genethur, Corovium in particular . . . you better have thick skin. This city will devour you.

Jessica Pratt, House Lady of Donovini

XVI

Allura could tell much from a look. The seamstress that had finished the last second alterations to her wedding dress prayed to the fallen gods that as she fit this dress upon the future queen of Amon, that it would be found satisfactory. Her personal guard barely seemed to notice she existed, which of course was a ruse. He watched her every move with great intent. The way Jerryn stared at her from across the room was of disinterest, and it was quite clear that he would have rather placed knives into his eyes than stand about, watching his fiancé play dress up. Maradyn Pratt clearly did not like the dress by the reflection in her eyes. Her mother, on the other hand, loved it. And perhaps she loved it because Maradyn hated it.

Fear, boredom, hate, love . . . it all remained relevant to her. All eyes remained trained upon her. She could tell much from a look, and she assumed her own look was that of satisfaction. The attention should be on her, was meant to be on her. She stood one day from her wedding, and only two or three days from that to the crowning of Jerryn Pratt. Allura Rowe, no . . . Allura Pratt, *Queen* Allura Pratt . . . it felt good to say.

Only a few more days before she became the most powerful woman in Amon.

"Beautiful, child," softly spoke her mother, and the seamstress gave a silent sigh of relief.

"It is beautiful, is it not?" she replied, a genuine smile upon her face.

All things considered, a wedding was still something to be excited for. The dress was a strapless, sleeveless gown, all white save for a thin blue outline around the waist. Blue was the color of her House and her father's favorite color. She wished that her friends back home could have made the trip, but she understood they could not wait. It would take almost two months at minimum to travel the length of Amon for them to attend, and that would be a nonstop ride. It took her seven weeks to make the same trip to witness the crowning of Yelium Aylmer II. That felt like a lifetime ago now.

No . . . her friends, her extended family . . . none of them would be present to witness her wedding. But thus was life. This was not exactly the most orthodox wedding as it were. So far as she could tell, there would be more soldiers than guests in attendance. As a matter of fact, outside of her mother and her uncle Lurey, there would be no one else in attendance for House Rowe. Jerryn's mother and father would be in attendance, along with First Pratt's family, and that was the entire invitee list, save for the political people that would need to be present.

It did not matter. All of this was for formality anyways. Should she choose, she could remarry Jerryn in front of the crowds in the center of Corovium. She would be the queen, why not? But for now, she just needed to get it over with. They could have just signed papers and been done with it but her mother wanted a wedding of some kind. Only her mother knew the reasoning for such. Perhaps it was meant to show her that she still loved her daughter, but somehow she doubted such. Her mother always had angles, always played things to work in her favor. Finding that angle was the challenge.

"I wish Gerald was here," Allura stated, stepping down carefully from the raised platform she stood upon.

"I am sure your brother would be happy for you," her mother stated. "But someone must run Argonus in my absence. Now enough talk. You are to be married in one day. You should enjoy your last night."

"Mother?" she inquired curiously.

"I know that your friends are not present in the capital, but I am sure that the last thing you want to be doing before you wedding is worrying about any of the details. The rest is done. Go enjoy yourself."

"If I may," Maradyn offered up, "Joanna Leir wanted me to extend to you an invitation for dinner tonight, just a few of the girls only. She will be family soon, I thought perhaps you wouldn't mind the arrangement to meet and get to know one another? I believe Lillianna is excited about meeting you as well. You of course could bring anyone you like with you."

"Of course."

I have such a long list of people I have befriended here in the capital. Perhaps I should invite that killer I met in the tavern? He seemed to have liked me. Can I invite my personal guard? I mean he will be there whether I want him to or not. At least he is pleasant on the eyes. Very pleasant on the eyes . . .

"Might I speak with my fiancé privately before I depart as well?" Jerryn questioned to the women in the room.

Christina nodded. "Let's leave them be, ladies."

Quickly the other women in the room scuttled away and the door closed firmly behind them, leaving her future husband pacing about, his eyes wandering.

"So I gather you will not be joining me on this dinner tonight with your family?"

"No," he answered. "Joanna's husband, Winston, and a few others from our guard have offered a night of cards and alcohol."

"So I go spend time with your family, and you get right and drunk, basically."

"You should probably get used to that."

"Ah yes, you are turning out to be everything a girl could ever dream of."

The back of his hand connected to the cheek with blinding quickness, and she felt the vicious sting for the long seconds after. His eyes burned of anger as he glanced at his own hand, as if it had a mind of its own, as if someone else wielded such a horrid weapon.

"Never forget," he hissed, "this is what you wanted."

It certainly was. All the way up until she got it. The reality did not quite live up to the dream.

"I will see you on the altar," the young Pratt made claim as he also departed, leaving her alone with likely a flushed red face to match her bruised pride.

Perhaps a queen was all that Amon truly needed at the end of the day. As long as an heir was on the way . . . why would the people need anything more?

--

Clouds loomed overhead this late afternoon and though they did not threaten to cause rain, they did well to block the afternoon sun, which Philip found a pleasant change of pace. He stared down a tavern he had yet to visit. This would be the twelfth he had visited this day, each prior not yielding any information he desired. But then again, he was not so certain he knew what he would find.

Caution would be a better play, but I need to know what I am up against. I need to know the truth.

If he was to believe that House Rowe stood as the possible kidnapper or murderer of Rayden Pratt, all to wed a different man they wanted to be king . . . it changed the game quite drastically. How would his brother react to such? A wedding took place tomorrow. The courts granted their approval of the union already. How could they go against such now? And if they did, they would be declaring war against Argonus. They could not wage war against Argonus and defend against Ursan at the same time.

And then came the other thought, the one he desperately tried to bury but it continually bobbed to the surface. If they truly were so quick to remove Rayden Pratt from the picture, precisely how long until they turned their attention to him and his family. How long until he woke up with a bag over his head, arms and legs tied together on a long boat ride out into the Vurid Sea?

Caution truly was the better play. But Philip had no capacity for caution.

Soldiers still stood silently around him, more ghosts than anything else. They never spoke and never questioned his movements. For another few days, Philip was still the ruler of Amon, for whatever that was worth. And thus he did what he had been doing all day; he walked into the tavern.

The place was rather empty, but the day was still young for getting drunk. Still, half a dozen patrons sat about and went against the norm, drinking themselves into a blissful stupor, or so it appeared. Behind the counter was a heavyset Argon, his thick beard humorously countered his balding head. The First made his way directly to him.

"Are you the owner of this place?"

He nodded. "Aye, First. I'd gather that would be me."

"So you know who I am? A good memory or just well informed?"

"We have never met, if that's what you mean," the barkeep answered. "But I just assume anyone walking the streets with armed escort must be someone important. And you are a tan fellow, so that would likely make you the First. Guess I was right."

"You've got a good eye. Might be that you remember who was working last week, the day we had the storm roll in, the day the Ursan left the capital."

"Again, gather that would be me."

"What can you tell me about that night? Anything odd?"

"Such as?" he pried.

Philip shrugged. "Odd guests."

"I wish my memory was what it once was. Seem to recall something, but damned if I can remember the details."

Philip did not bother to waste any time with haggling. He reached in his shirt and produced a coin purse, to which he tossed onto the counter.

"How is that memory now?"

The barkeep smiled, showcasing the multitude of missing teeth. "Much better. I would gather I had a few rougher than normal patrons in here, ones that I am not familiar with. And to be honest, I am familiar with them all. They played some card game that they fought constantly over. But outside of that, they were well behaved. Loud, but minded their business. Overheard them talking about taking a trip east soon, saying it was their last night in the capital. Not sure about much else than that, but they certainly weren't locals. All different races, too."

Cards . . . men going east . . .

"Anything else?"

"Yeah, we also had a brief visit with an Argon girl. Young, had to be a House lady by the looks of her. She didn't spend much time here. Looked like she was getting out of the rain. She minded her own business until the black fellow went up and spoke with her for a few minutes. Not sure about the contents of their talk, only that when they were done, she left, and the black guy and the rest of his men paid for their drinks and left. That is about all I can tell you. Strange night indeed."

"The black fellow . . . Fallneesian I presume?"

"Sure, sorry. *Fallneesian.* Isn't it easier to just say the black one, tan one, pink one, pale one?"

"Maybe so. Regardless, do you remember if he had eyebrows?"

The barkeep's face shifted some in thought. "Now that you mention it, no, no he didn't."

The First nodded toward the Argon. "You have been a great help. Thank you."

To which the barkeep smiled, shrugged his indifference, and went back to attending his counter.

Philip turned about and left the tavern, moving back into the streets.

"Shit," he cursed beneath his breath, staring back up to the capital. What he had learned did nothing for him. A young House lady entering a dicey bar and speaking with some unsavory men . . . *his* unsavory men. What exactly did that prove? He could no more pin Allura in that room than he could admit to the existence of the Moon Divide. And how did she know of their existence? And why would Deso agree to kidnap . . . or kill . . . Rayden Pratt?

He had no proof, only guesses at what took place here a week ago. And still, all signs pointed to House Rowe. But what was he to do? Confront Allura directly? No, that would not bode well.

But then again, he was still Philip Pratt, ruler of Amon.

--

She was the only Argon at the dinner table, minus her personal guard that floated some in the recesses of the room. In a way, Allura felt embarrassed. It was a feeling none to pleasing or familiar. All of the House names that traveled with her to attend the crowning of the new king had long since made the return trip home after the assassination, long since left her alone in Genethur with nothing save her mother and uncle. So she sat there, wine glass in hand, a fake smile toward Joanna Leir and Lillianna Pratt, daughters to the First, along with several other Donovinian girls attached to names they only thought mattered in this world. Daughters of court officials and the such. Nobodies. No one deserving of sitting across from the future queen of Amon.

"Do you think you will be able to fix the courts quickly, milady?" one of the lesser girls nervously questioned to her.

"Don't pester her with those kinds of questions," Joanna swiftly defended. "She is about to get married. I am sure that her thoughts on are other things, not on political things. Let the girl enjoy married life first before her and Jerryn start to fix our country."

"There is little luxury for patience," Allura noted.

That quieted the room some, at least for a few seconds.

She took a long sip from her glass.

The little one, Lillianna, then spoke up. "Do you think there will be a war with Ursan?"

"Do you want war, little one?"

"I am thirteen," she snapped, her face turning red the moment the words escaped. "I . . . it's just milady, I . . . it's only . . ."

"I believe," Joanna interrupted nervously, "that my sister is *very* sorry and thinks she is older than she really is."

"Let her speak for herself," Allura demanded. "When I was thirteen, I thought the older girls didn't spend enough time listening to my point of view, even though I thought it was quite valid. Go ahead, Lillianna Pratt. Tell me, do you want war in Ursan?"

Her eyes met hers. "If they have Rayden, then yes."

Allura turned back to Joanna. "Honesty of youth should be treasured, not suppressed."

"Words I will remember, milady," was the elder sister's response.

"So," Allura continued, turning back to the girl. "You miss Rayden? As do I."

"You didn't love him, though, did you?" Lillianna inquired, though not harshly, just inquisitively.

"No, but this remains a political marriage. I read books of dashing princes fighting for the honor of beautiful princesses when I was your age. I believed that life would end up that way. Never quite turns out the way you expect. But I believe you can learn to love someone. Not quite as romantic as all the books, but certainly love nonetheless."

"I know that you can't marry Rayden, even if you are able to rescue him, but . . . I want to be here when you and Jerryn declare war against Ursan."

"Lilli," cautioned the elder sister.

"What?" was Lillianna's defensive response. "I don't want to go. I want to stay here!"

"And I believe that is enough for you, Lilli," Joanna stated firmly. "Perhaps it is time you went to your chambers."

"I did not excuse her," Allura clarified. "Tell me, Lillianna, where exactly are you meant to be going."

She gave a look, one that told Allura that the girl was not supposed to say anything. But the question had been asked.

"Mother wants us gone after the wedding. We are heading back to Astrona."

Allura smiled at the comment. "How is your writing, child? Have you kept up with your studying?"

"Yes, milady. My writing is superb, or so my instructors have told me."

"It is true, milady," Joanna agreed. "Lilli is head of her class in all things, albeit brash and outspoken, two things that she could use less of, that is for certain."

"Horseback riding?" continued Allura.

Lillianna nodded. "Yes, milady. I have also trained in archery and some swordplay, and my dance instructions have gone quite well. My singing is not really anything to boast, I am afraid."

"Neither is mine," admitted the future queen. "Well I will have words with the First of Amon. Flame's embrace, I think I would like my lady-in-waiting to be at my side, not off in another country."

The little one's eyes widened and Joanna's narrowed. The other twats at the table gasped at the proclamation.

And so now the games truly begin.

--

"You may enter, First Pratt."

The guard moved aside and Philip walked in, Christina sitting alone at her balcony view of the city.

"You come very heavily accompanied, First Pratt, for a mere conversation with me."

He turned back to the soldiers behind him. "Wait outside for me."

One or two of them looked to argue, but thought better of it. Soon the room emptied and only he and the House lady remained.

"Is this the kind of conversation that might be better accompanied with wine?"

Philip allowed himself a smile. "I would gather it may be the perfect conversation to have such."

"Then on the counter to your left, bring it here."

He grabbed the dark red wine that sat alone atop a table along with two glasses, then made his way out to the balcony. Christina sat nonchalant, her eyes out to the vast city of Corovium before her. Philip poured two glasses, handing one to her.

"I miss my home, Philip. How did you survive here for so many years?"

The First took a sip from his glass, the wine going down smooth. "I do miss Astrona. It has been many years since I've seen it. How did I survive? I suppose by burying myself into work for many long years. I love Amon, more so than Donovini, it saddens me to say. At the end of the day, all I ever wanted was to make this a better world for all of us, not just my own people."

"I agree, First." Christina pointed outward to the city, waving her arm about some for emphasis. "We should start thinking of fortifying our walls. Corovium is not built to sustain a siege, but it can be. We need high walls around the perimeter. We need to begin working on it."

"So you believe war comes to us?"

Taking a slow sip, she placed the glass down, standing to face the First. "The throne is here, First Pratt. Those that want it will come *here*. They can denounce our claim all that they desire, they still must understand that the rest of Amon bows to that wooden chair. Ursan, Donovini, Argonus, Fallneese . . . we are about to be above them all. And we must begin to think as such and prepare."

"We? As in you and me?"

"Of course. You are the First of Amon. I will be beside the king and queen at all times. We must put our petty differences aside. We must seize control of Amon."

"And what of your daughter? Do you control her as well?"

"Allura?" she stammered. "Of course I do. The girl will obey me. She will not do anything without my consent."

Philip moved over to her, close enough to smell her perfume, close enough to garner a watchful however curious eye from the House lady.

"How long have you known of her affection for Jerryn Pratt?"

Christina smiled at the inquiry. "For some time now, I am afraid. Young love, it is such folly."

"And far would she have gone for this *love*?"

"How do you mean?"

The First took a sip, then placed the glass down. "I have a witness stating that she was in a particularly rough tavern on the night Dehyllo left the capital, speaking to men that I know to be of lesser standards than most, the same men that might have been seen sneaking away with Rayden."

Lady Rowe's face tightened at the comment. "And you can surface proof of this? Is your witness certain without doubt that it was my daughter?"

"Certain, yes. But he is a barkeep. It doesn't matter how reliable he is, he's still just a barkeep. I can't prove anything. But that doesn't make it any less true."

"And that is why you have come to me. To inquire the truth for yourself?"

"You may be a cold woman, Christina, but you are not a monster. I know that you couldn't have cared less at who your daughter married, so long as she married someone. I question whether your daughter saw things the same way. I will do my own investigation, as I can contact the men I believe she hired, if that in fact happened. It would do her well to simply confess and let us know if he still lives."

Lady Rowe turned from him, her face flushed. From either embarrassment or anger, he could not immediately say.

"Monster or not," she started, "what you ask of me is to interrogate my own daughter. It is . . . a difficult thing for you to ask. What happens if she is guilty, First Pratt?"

I will fucking kill her.

"I don't know, Christina. She would go to trial the same as the rest of us in the same situation. And it would be better for her if she confessed."

"Better for who, I wonder?" Reaching for her wine glass, she turned to the First, though her eyes remained intent on the floor. "Have you spoken to Nicolas of this?"

"No, nor will I until I have something to tell him. Which you could and should help me in."

"And what if Allura does not tell me what you wish to hear?"

"Then I hope it's the truth. And if I find out differently, I will hold no mercy for her."

Not that I have much to begin with.

--

Candles were already lit in her room as she entered late that night. Allura's guard moved into the room first, which was nothing new, examining the corners and the extra rooms, ensuring she was alone. Satisfied, he nodded to her.

"Well . . . go," she stated, pointing to the door.

The guard bowed his head some and walked out, closing the door. She could feel the heat from the bath in the next room, likely prepared moments before she arrived back in her chambers. As she kicked off her heels and slipped off her dress, there crept an eerie feeling at that fact. Her every move now was monitored. Her personal guard, which she barely remembered seeing much of weeks ago, now seemed to be at her every step. Food was prepared fresh and hot the moment she sat down, baths prepared at the perfect moment, clothes preselected before she woke. Ants that bounced about, tracking her breathing and walking and what times of the day she had to piss.

The fact that everyone watched her did not disturb her. Allura thrived in such. The fact that everyone seemed to know what she was going to do before she did it . . . now that was the more disturbing of facts.

Clothes off, she slipped into the warm water and sighed heavily, the water soothing her skin. An empty glass stood beside her tub along with a bottle of wine. She reached over, poured herself a glass, and leaned back with her arms over the sides. It was time to think of her next move. She had many to make. Being queen would be difficult, that she knew. Many enemies, very few friends. In fact, she had no friends here in Corovium to speak of. She could bring in her friends from her capital of Tessenul back home, but that did her little good. If she were to succeed as ruler, Allura would need new friends. Powerful friends. Influential ones.

"Relaxed?"

Allura half screamed, dropped her wine glass, and nearly slipped up and out of her tub before recognizing the voice as her mother's. Christina sat patiently, legs crossed in the corner of the room, barely visible through the faint light of the candles.

"Earth and Flame, Mother," she hissed. "You damn near scared me death. Why the hell didn't my guard tell me you were here? Remind me to replace him tomorrow."

"Alex does his job well, especially since I am the one who assigned him to you many weeks ago. He follows your every movement upon my command, since I can barely trust you anymore."

"Is he protecting me, or are you just using him to spy on me?"

"Your safety remains at the very top of his priorities. And at the time he was assigned to you, I was trying to find out when you planned to stop your frequent visits with Jerryn. Now it doesn't so much matter, but I needed to know at the time. I needed to know if love was going to cloud your decisions. I needed to know that you truly wanted to aid me in ruling Amon."

Allura was uncertain where this line of talk led toward. "I have no intentions of being just a puppet, Mother."

"No, I gather not. Especially based on recent actions." Christina stood and moved over to her, grabbing the fallen but intact glass and splashing some wine within. "So I gave you a chance to confess to me if you had something to do with Rayden's disappearance. I asked you if it could be traced back to this House. You told me no. That was a lie. So now I would gather you need to tell me the truth."

The water was still warm, but she felt a cold chill through her body. "What answer would you like me to give?"

"A truthful one this time," was her reply.

Allura bit down on her lip for a few seconds, ensuring to feel a bit of the pain before releasing. "Who knows what I did?"

"First *fucking* Pratt of all people," she said, the words coming out like the plague. "Now tell me this, child. Does Rayden still live?"

This will not be good.

"I don't know."

"You don't know," she calmly repeated. Then she exploded. "You don't *fucking* know? You have someone removed and you don't know if they live or die?"

"I wasn't really specific in those details."

"You weren't *specific*?" Now Christina laughed. Never a good sign when she laughed. "You are forever a disappointment. Must I clean up *all* of your messes, child?"

Emptying the contents of the glass, she dropped it again, this time shattering on the ground. She then moved out from the back room and continued to the main one, not looking back.

"Where do you go now?" Allura called after her. "Are you not going to ask me why? Are you not going to ask me how? Are you not going to ask me anything about it?"

"No," she responded, pausing as she turned to face her. "I will ask your guard if he remembers the way back to your tavern. Yes, child, he was with you even then, even when you did not see him. As for you, you have a wedding tomorrow. Get a new glass, get some wine, get some rest."

"And what of you?"

"I have to clean up after your foolishness. Which means I need to see if we can find this witness to your stupidity . . . and put them in the dirt."

--

Philip did not place one foot in the door to his chambers that evening before Jessica nearly attacked him.

"What are we going to do?" she howled, arms flailing about like a mad woman. "I will not have my child here one moment longer, not one *fucking* second longer than this wedding!"

"Calm down, Jessica. What are you talking about? What's going on?"

"It's our new queen. She has selected Lilli to be her lady-in-waiting! I will not allow it! I won't!"

Fallen gods . . . if you exist, you do so just to mock me. I hope you find humor in this all.

"I will speak with Jerryn *after* the wedding. I am sure that we can have him explain to Allura that Lilli is too young for the role, and has already been asked to return to Astrona."

"And what if she says no?" pressed Jessica.

To which he shrugged. "She is not the queen yet. She can make no demands of us."

"Don't be a fool, Phil. Not with me." Jessica ran her fingers through her hair, over and over, doing all that she could to not scream any further. "She can and will make demands. That girl is an arrogant shit, and you know it. And Jerryn will allow her to do what she pleases."

"I will talk to Nick," he assured. "He will make this right."

"Your brother was once a proud warrior. But he aligned himself with that woman." Jessica paced the room, her face flustered and in pain. "Nicolas has made a horrible decision for this family."

"At least someone else agrees with me," he muttered.

"I have always agreed with you," stated his wife, though there was no smile upon her face when saying the words. "You only have little trust in my confidence."

"It's not that. I just choose to not burden you with what I deal with daily. It is . . . it just is."

Her frown deepened. "Would you have me here when it is all said and done?"

"What?"

"Would you like me to stay?" She restated. "Or would you like me to go with our daughters? Assuming any of us can leave, of course."

"I don't want any of you to leave. But I understand why Lilli and Jo should." Philip shrugged. "I cannot imagine my brother's pain. To lose two of his children to the politics of this place . . ."

"I did not ask about our children. I asked of me. Should we gain permission from the Rowes, I would leave with Lilli and Jo to ensure they make it safely to Astrona. Do you want me to return?"

"Damn you woman, why would I want you to leave my side in the first place?"

"I don't know," was her reply. "I feel that at times, you would prefer it if I left."

"That is not the case."

"Would it be the case if Dylinn were still here?"

He waited a moment. What response was there to give? He could lie. Certainly he could do that. He had been doing such for more years than he could remember. He could be honest and simply own up to his affair to the former queen. What good that would do, he was not so certain. And then there was the easy option. He could say nothing at all.

He did not choose the easy option yet, though his hesitation made it so.

"I love you Philip. I know in your own way that you love me too. But you love this country and your work more than your family. You can argue with me all you like, it is truth. I have given you two beautiful daughters. I have given you my support. I have given you your space when you needed it. I even allowed this affair to go on unnoticed and played the ignorant wife. I understand how it is to be a House lady. Do you think I'm the only one that deals with such? Do you believe that Nicolas or Edmond don't have their own mistresses? Do you believe that I am the only one dealing with the fact that my husband has found solace elsewhere? I accepted it, and I accepted you. I moved to this capital of backstabbing and cutthroat dealings, I bore our youngest daughter away from our homeland, all for you. And what do I get in return? Very little, save your lack of attention.

"You are not that fucking special, Philip. Your brothers might have had their affairs, but at least they had the decency to pick whores to do such. There was no emotion in that. They didn't love their whores. But you . . . I have to have the one Pratt with feelings. I have to have the one that might actually have *loved* his mistress. And I bet she loved you. Didn't she? Well fuck her, Philip. And fuck you too."

Philip wanted to say a great many things, not all of them positive. Lashing out seemed like a great idea at the time, but the better part of him gave caution to such. Instead he kept his silence, kept his lips tightly shut.

"So nothing? Very well," she announced. "I will do as I have always done tomorrow. I will pretend. After the wedding, I will pack and leave for Astrona with our children far and away from the dangers of the capital. Ensure the soon-to-be queen does not stop us. And as for you and me, perhaps you will feel like talking more later."

Not likely.

--

The morning came. It was time for Allura's wedding . . . or a full on military assault based on how many members of the Imperial Army stationed about her chambers. All of her handmaidens were present: one for makeup, one for her hair, one tendering her dress, one for her nails. She literally felt as if she hung by drawstrings, being pulled in every direction. But their work, steady and amazing, was worth it. Allura gazed into the mirror and saw a radiant beauty. If there had been a mark where Jerryn struck her the day before, it was gone. If she had been stressed and found any pimples or blemishes on her face or exposed shoulders, they had disappeared. Circumstances apart, this was how she envisioned herself on this day. Everything was so close to perfection, so close to her dreams, and yet . . .

Her shadow kept himself tucked away in the corner, silent as always, the look of a killer upon his brow. And why not? He was a killer. She did not bother to speak to him, did not bother to question whether or not the task was done. If Christina set this man out to kill whatever witness she spoke of, then it would be done. Her mother was not known for leaving doors half open.

But there were things that even her mother could not protect against. First Pratt knew but did not have the proper evidence as it seemed. If he knew for certain, she would be in a locked cell right next to the Second. That, and the wedding would have been canceled.

So what now?

Allura whipped her head toward her personal guard. He turned his attention to her.

"I wish my lady-in-waiting present," she demanded.

"As you command, Lady Rowe."

"And have her belongings brought upstairs to our new suite. She lives within our chambers now."

It was time to make her move.

--

"I sent a bird carrier to the coast," explained the First.

Afeon nodded inside his cell. "If anything, be thankful she stumbled upon the Divide. The Guild would have just killed Rayden and been done with him. I doubt Deso and the rest of them would have killed your nephew, assuming they knew who their target truly was."

"You assume they cared one way or the next, even knowing who he was."

"Deso would have cared for certain, and that is fact." Afeon shrugged. "The other men of the Divide might have been every part of what they truly were. Not Deso. I'm not sure what he was before the Divide, but there is still a human being left within him. Regardless, until you get word back from him, there is little to be done of this wedding."

"Even if Deso makes a claim that collaborates with this barkeep, it will still not be enough. I need him in Corovium with Rayden alive. I need my nephew to stand before myself and the courts and explain Allura's treason against House Pratt. The only thing the letter from Deso will do is stall the courts from approving the crowning."

"You have given your word to pushing through the succession," noted the Second. "You cannot back down from your word on rumors and speculation alone."

Philip shook his head. He could not know for certain what to make of the situation. His knowing of Allura's treason made him furious, made him want to kill her himself. And yet doing so would only condemn his family. Admitting that she had Rayden removed also admitted Brocusk's innocence in that crime, which may have also had him rethinking the assassination of Yelium. If not Ursan, certainly Rowe. But he could not place his arms around that one either. Nothing made sense.

Not even his recent decision to descend into the dungeons to speak of current affairs with his prisoner, who was quite innocent of any crime.

"How are you holding up?"

Afeon flashed a devilish grin. "It is the vacation of my dreams, First Pratt. Ironic, as you were the one that placed me here, and yet now you are regretting your decision perhaps."

"I regret sending the Guild after my niece, but I would not retract that command. You are no stranger to these kinds of decisions. I did what I had to do."

"You are incorruptible, First Pratt. It is of your more . . . annoying qualities. You fail to realize that you are the most powerful man in Amon. What have you done with your power? Have you abused it? Have you seized the power for yourself and damned those below you? No. You should have named yourself the king. You should have named yourself a god. Instead you played within the rules."

"You say such as if it were a curse," recognized Philip.

"You had an opportunity, one that I would have taken in your place, First Pratt. You are likely a better man than me."

"Why Afeon, I didn't know you cared so much for . . ."

"But I will live longer than you."

His tone changed at his last statement. No longer the witty, sarcastic ass that he was, his voice darkened, challenged.

"You say that behind bars, Second."

"You presume that I cannot leave whenever I choose." He flashed a wicked grin.

"Then when do you choose?"

"It's all about timing," was his response. "Now you should go. You have a wedding to witness and a world to give away."

Philip stood from his stool and pressed it back against the stone wall. "You are a difficult man to like, Afeon."

The Second bellowed a healthy laugh at that. "Come now, First Pratt. What am I at the end of the day? Take away the politics and the clothes and my intelligence, and what am I still? An Ursan. Unlike those in the courts, I have never lost my edge, never lost what got me through my upbringing. We all endure hardships in my country, First Pratt. We are stronger because of it. Do you think these bars will break my will? They strengthen my resolve. Look at me, now look at yourself. Can you claim such confidence? Ha! I am safer inside this cell then you are outside. Eyes will be upon you, First Pratt. Allura knows that you have ousted her, with or without proof matters little. You *know*. How long into her rule before you start looking over your shoulder? How long until she decides that one less Pratt is probably for the best?"

"Good day to you, Second. I will hopefully remember to visit you before your sentencing. We have such uplifting talks."

He wasted no more words with him. Philip stormed off, the chuckling of the Second following him felt the same as fingernails being bent back . . . slowly.

--

Her uncle Lurey Hillan held his arm out and she placed hers through it. Lillianna Pratt took her place just behind Allura, donning a mighty grin upon her young face. The little one was excited, more so than Allura and she was the one minutes away from marriage. The doors to the large reception hall on the first floor opened and the music began.

Allura took her first step inside the room and the short list of those in attendance stood and turned to her. From her side, her mother stood in attendance along with Fourth Lijid Nulittan as well as several high court officials from both Fallneese and Argonus, including Gillar, the head of the courts. From the opposing side, Nicolas and Maradyn stood at the front, with First Pratt and his family behind, along with a few Donovinian representatives from the courts as well. Jerryn stood tall, a half smile upon his face, and Joanna's husband, Winston Leir, stood as his best man.

The rest of the room was filled with soldiers, headed by Second General Brocusk, which outnumbered the guests. Damned if this did not appear more like a hearing than a wedding. The distance between the entrance and the head of the room was not terribly long, but it felt like eternity to cross that distance. Allura focused straight ahead, determined not to move her eyes to the left, not to lock eyes with any of the Pratts. Jessica would want her dead for taking in Lillianna. Philip would want the same for knowing of her involvement with Rayden. Had he told Nicolas yet? If so, add that to another wishing her death.

Would they allow this wedding to take place? Could they stop it?

Don't look at them. Just look at Jerryn. Look into those brown eyes of his.

Did he know?

Fuck it, don't look at him either. Just look at the priest. He's probably the only one who doesn't know how much of a shit I am.

Lurey gave her a gentle kiss on the cheek and released her, taking his place next to her mother at the front of the ceremony. As she took a step up to the platform, Lillianna just a step behind her, she stood equal to Jerryn, their hands clasped.

And for a moment, she felt happiness.

--

And for a moment, Philip thought he might *actually* vomit.

Words, vows, and a kiss later, and it was done. Jerryn and Allura were now official. After the fake claps as if anyone truly felt the blessed union of these two, the wedding moved to the next room where they had their cake and wine and plenty of food. Wine had a way of making any tense room a bit more relaxed. Eventually conversations broke out, and eventually people began to enjoy themselves. All save for him, of course, and perhaps Christina across the room. She could not mask her worry any more than he could mask his. Whatever grasp she thought she had on her daughter slipped away the moment Allura went rogue.

After a few hours, it was done. The two newlyweds retired to their new chambers three stories up, the entire floor once owned by House Aylmer. Some lingered and drank more wine, while others moseyed off to whatever destination they needed to be other than here. He was counted within the lingering, along with the head of the courts, Gillar, who fast approached.

"A lovely ceremony, if I must say so myself," the bald, fat little Fallneesian stated.

"Earth moving," mumbled the First.

"By Shadow, I would think that was sarcasm if I didn't know any better. So tell me, First. When do you vote? This should be done as soon as possible."

"Why the rush, Gillar?" questioned Philip, only half interested in the response.

"We need the courts fixed. We need to start rebuilding broken relationships. Despite what you may think of me, I have done my work with the whole of Amon in consideration."

"Then we are two men of the same breath."

"Yes, but don't let anyone know, lest they think we actually could get along, despite the hatred between us."

"As far as your vote is concerned, you have just as much stake in the speed of things if not *more* than I do. Now if there is nothing else . . ."

"There might be something else," added the Fallneesian. "Pending on who I am speaking with. Am I speaking to the First, or am I speaking to Philip Pratt?"

"You are always speaking to the First," sternly responded Philip.

"Too bad then."

As he turned to walk away, Philip reached over and grabbed his shoulder lightly. "Speak, Gillar. You got this far with it."

He smiled. "I just wanted to let you know that your niece lives. Word has reached me that the Guild has lost her within Ursan. I thought that might give you some comfort."

Philip sighed heavily. That *was* good news. Though surviving in Ursan would prove difficult even with the Druid at her side. Still . . . at least she was still alive. "Have you heard anything else?"

"Nothing that would interest you, I wouldn't think. They believe that two Guild members are responsible for aiding her elude through Donovini unscathed, and they hunt their own more fiercely than they hunt Katlynn."

"Two of their own? Do you know their names?"

"Well, one was a Jade something. The other was Wode. I forget the first name, but the last name was certainly Wode."

Nathanial . . .

"It is good news," Philip stated, no hiding the relief in his words. "And damn well received. Thank you Gillar."

"Of course. I will let you share that with Maradyn. I am certain she wishes to hear it."

"That she will," he agreed. "It might brighten her mood."

"Funny," Gillar humored. "You would think this wedding would do the trick?"

There was little reason to retort. The Fallneesian already moved away, his smirk could be detected from the other side of his shiny bald head.

--

Allura struggled with her dress, Jerryn had little trouble with his shirt. His skinny chest stood bare and somehow he managed to keep his wine glass upright. His shitty grin seemed plastered on his face, looking about as dumb as she felt trying to get her damn dress off.

"Should I start without you?" slurred her husband, his free hand reaching into his pants as he started stroking himself. He was not doing much other than flopping around his limp dick, though.

"You are drunk," she whispered, turning about, untying some of the strings from the back, loosening it to the point that she was able to start slipping away and out from the top. Finally out of her dress, she worked on her undergarments, only to turn back and see Jerryn off in the next room, pouring himself another glass.

"Should have brought up the bottle from downstairs," he continued, speaking to absolutely no one save for himself. "Better than this. What year is this? Not a good year. I don't think anyways."

Her clothes now off, Allura reached down and began to touch herself, knowing full and damn well that Jerryn was too drunk to be able to pronounce the word foreplay much less perform. She watched him clank down an entire glass of wine, then pour himself another.

"Jerryn," she called out. "Come here."

Her husband put down another drink, poured another, then stumbled over, still grinning, still looking quite pleased with himself. And why not? He was days from becoming king. He was about to spend the rest of his life fucking her, which was quite an honor she presumed. He would get drunk and fat and piss away his life while she ran Amon. What easier life would there be for him? Why not be happy? Why not smile?

Back into the bedroom, Jerryn made it half way in before tripping on her dress, the upper half of his body landing on the bed, his lower half slumped over and hanging onto the ground. His wine flew across the bedroom and shattered against the wall, red wine pouring downward like a blood.

"Are you okay?" she stated, rolling over to rub his back.

He only moaned in response.

"Jerryn?"

Then came a loud, single snore.

"Oh fuck me, are you serious?"

Followed by a series of snores. She shook him a bit, but that did not deter his unconsciousness. Jerryn Pratt, future leader of Amon, was passed out and snoring by late afternoon, drooling from the side of his mouth. What a glorious wedding this had been.

Allura sat for a minute, thinking. So angry, so disappointed, she could not focus on one centralized thought. And so she stood and walked across the room, made her way to the door and opened it. There stood her shadow, her personal guard, who did all that he could to pretend not to stare at her nude body.

"Alex is it?" she questioned. He nodded in response. "Do you serve me, or my mother?"

"You, Lady Rowe," he responded, his eyes adverted.

"Lady *Pratt*," she corrected. "And good, then get in here."

He did as commanded and she shut the door behind him. There was confusion in her guard's face, but not of fear or trepidation. Only curiosity. He was a handsome Argon, but a killer, a tool, a sword.

"Did you kill someone last night?"

"Yes, Lady Pratt."

"But I did not ask you of this. Why did you do such?"

"Your mother asked this of me. She technically commands me until you ascend to the throne."

"What if I needed someone killed now? Would you do such for me?"

"Yes, Lady Pratt."

"Would you do whatever I ask of you?"

He bowed his head some. "Yes, Lady Pratt. I am bound to you. I must follow your every command."

"Good. Now take off your breeches," she commanded. "Someone is going to fuck me tonight. Might as well be you." He hesitated. "Do you defy me?"

"No, Lady Pratt."

Hesitant still, but his pants came down nevertheless, and his larger than life cock came into full view. *Finally, something positive about this day.*

"Don't you *dare* kiss me," she hissed toward him. "Touch me, whatever you need to do to get it up, but don't you *fucking* kiss me. Now let's get this done."

He reached out and played with her nipples, then reached between her legs and placed his fingers within her. It did not take long for him to harden, after which he grabbed her by the hips and lifted her up just enough to place himself within her standing upright.

Everything leading up to this exact moment was a disaster. But this part . . . this part made up for it.

Weddings did bring out the best in people.

--

If you can't figure out why they call them the Moon Divide, then you can't figure out why they call them the Moon Divide.
-- Tauven Ulfini, Major in the Imperial Army

XVII

First General John Shonnen stared heavily at the latest note before him within his tent. It felt heavier than the previous ones he received since the death of the elder Yelium Aylmer. This letter reeked of despair. This letter oozed of the impotence of the First of Amon. John did not hate him for such; he pitied him. He pitied his inability to use his power to help, pitied the loss of his nephew and niece, pitied the decision to forcefully comply with a union with House Rowe.

But what did he know? Shonnen was but a soldier, ignorant himself to the politics of the world. Or at least that was the lie he told himself regularly. It was a simple thing he required; necessities, primarily water and food. The ability to hunt for as many men that served underneath him was impossible nowadays. They of course did, but what amount of game could serve some thousands of people? The smarter animals had fled the shores of Argonus long ago. The foolish ones were long since dead. Thus they primarily lived off the fish in the ocean, but even that was a difficult task. Men grew tired of eating fish every day, thus they also grew hungry. Hungry men grew testy. Testy men fought and killed other testy men.

Many men that claimed Argonus as their home country had already departed the army . . . or rebellious force, or whatever it is they were calling themselves. As it stood, Shonnen and his officers were the only men still *officially* associated with the military. The remainder of soldiers that followed their command had been disbanded by the boy king. Thus while they stood stationed in Argonus, many of the Argons simply left, distraught. Others began to disperse as the Guild ceased delivering them supplies. Twenty thousand men turned into fifteen in a night, fifteen turned into ten in another few weeks. But still he had over eight at his command, eight thousand men that had nowhere to go.

He knew what First Philip asked of him. A wise man in his stead would do such. But the fallen gods would curse him where he stood should he make such a play.

The flaps of his large tent came open and the face of his major, Baldin Ascotte, came into view. A mere pup in his role just the same as John, Ascotte was in his early thirties, which was young to be a major in the Imperial Army. A Donovinian, same as he, but neither of them had seen home in many long years.

"Add Colonel Pullman to the missing," stated Ascotte.

"Tell me you jest," he responded.

But the major shook his head. "Couple of the boys saw him ride out last night, heading northwest. No sign of his return since."

Shonnen nodded unwillingly. "We knew it would happen eventually. He was an Argon."

"He was also an officer still, General. And still a member of this army. He abandoned his duties. That's a crime punishable by death."

"He was a man all the same," corrected Shonnen. "And we have been asked to head home."

"Sir?"

John Shonnen waved him inside and Ascotte complied, walking in and taking a seat across his desk.

"Since Pullman has officially deserted, you are promoted. Baldin Ascotte, you are now a colonel of the Imperial Army. Congratulations."

"That was quite lackluster, sir, but still much appreciated. I love being promoted due to recently vacated positions."

"Good, then perhaps your former captain will feel the same. Tell Captain Ulfini that he is now Major Ulfini in your stead. And since our former lieutenant also went the way of Pullman, that leaves us vacant in lower officers."

"Excellent, General Shonnen. I am feeling confident that the three of us can best eight thousand men the moment they turn on us."

Shonnen picked up the letter from First Pratt and tossed it before the new colonel. "The First of Amon regrettably cannot help us. This was our last real hope of getting out of this in one piece. To sum it up, Brocusk removed every Ursan from the courts and now the courts will not make any decisions yet until they fix their current situation. Until the marriage and then approved succession takes place with Jerryn Pratt and Allura Rowe, he can do nothing to aid us. The Guild is owed money that has yet to be approved by the crippled courts, and the Guild will not resupply us until the back funds are paid."

Ascotte picked up the letter and began to breeze over it. "Anything in here about *when* that crowning is planned to happen?"

"Soon. But not soon enough. Even after the crowning, Jerryn will not be able to wave his hand and force the Guild to supply us again. King or not, the Guild is a difficult thing to budge. So there is no time table for our men to be reinstated. And since that is the case, we are to follow through with our initial command from King Yelium Aylmer II. First Pratt has asked us to disband the rest of our men and return home."

The newly promoted colonel dropped the letter back on the table and gave a stern look to him. "When they say disband, I hope he understands that means abandon. These men have been out here for years. They are young, they have no homes to return to, and should we leave them, they will simply raid the nearest town and pillage. The moment we leave, they lose what is left of their sanity and dignity."

"They are losing that every second we sit about and talk about this," added the general. "It seems so long ago when First Pratt asked us to guard this coast. By the fallen gods, we haven't patrolled in months. What is the purpose of that? Let whatever horrors lie beyond the Terrandonan come. At the least, that gives our men purpose away from their hunger."

Ascotte clasped his hands together and placed them under his chin. "Do you worry about it ever? What we've seen?"

"We don't know what we've seen," answered General Shonnen. "Missing men to the sea could be a great many things. Do I think it could be what lies across the sea? Certainly I do. I remember my letter to Pratt all those months ago asking for additional support. He probably laughed at that letter, thinking I was a terrified fool. Difference between him and me, Major Ascotte, is that I'm a religious man. I believe that the gods protected us from whatever horror lies across the sea. And now the time draws close."

"I know you have kept us out here because of your sense of duty to the men, to the country, to your religion. I know you have done nothing wrong to this point, General, and I have backed your every move. But at what point do you feel this is a lost cause? Our men are literally dying. If something came across that sea now, they would wipe us out without a fight regardless."

"So you suggest we follow through with what First Pratt suggests?"

But Ascotte only shrugged. "I have no suggestion, General. There is no right answer here. At least none that I can figure. Abandoning our men seems heartless and folly. So what else then? Do we continue to fish until only the strongest of us are left alive? We can't live this way much longer, and you know this."

"I am more concerned about water than food at this point. Our supply runs dangerously low. If perhaps we . . ."

The tent came open again and Tauven Ulfini stepped through, the slightly older Fallneesian captain and soon-to-be promoted major.

"My apologizes sirs, but we have . . . well we have visitors, of a kind."

"Say again?" the general queried.

Ulfini straightened and fixed his uniform. "We have visitors. A few more men, maybe fifty or sixty. I didn't really count. He says he is here on the request of First Pratt but will not speak with anyone else about the matter save you."

Ascotte turned to him. "Your reinforcements?"

"A bit late," mumbled Shonnen. "And at the oddest of times."

"Are we to disband them too?" questioned Ascotte.

John Shonnen could only laugh. "Well, I suppose we should introduce ourselves first."

--

Rayden Pratt rubbed back against the stubble of his now bald head. Deso felt it best that he not be noticeable. True or not, Rayden was a slave to his will. It took only two days on their boat ride through the Sullein River to reach the heart of Donovini and the remainder of the trip to the east coast was made on foot, which took about a month. The summer was upon them in full effect, and the trip, to say the least, was anything but pleasant. Deso might have led the Moon Divide, but no one could have deciphered such by their actions. They were brutal, sadistic, foul mouthed little deviants. Criminals, by every definition of the word.

And now he was one of them, he supposed. Rayden was very much an outcast; finding the acceptance of cutthroats was both difficult and unrewarding. He still had trouble understanding how he ended up here in Argonus, against the vast coast of the Terrandonan.

The thought had crossed his mind to find a moment to confess his real identity to First General John Shonnen. He did not know the man personally, but by name alone. Certainly he would believe him and aid him in returning home. That thought dissipated the moment they arrived and he saw the eyes of the men of the Imperial Army. These were not soldiers, not to the likes of those within the capital. These men's loyalty looked to sway with the passing winds, and identifying himself as a Pratt was not likely going to win him any favors amongst them. No, it would likely end up killing him.

He had been a boy the first and only time he had seen the Terrandonan Sea. Much had remained the same in his memories, with the lush greens and low plains that scattered throughout Argonus. The green fields led all the way up to the white sands of the beach, only the sporadic tree sprouted from time to time. Argonus, while had its share of forests, was mostly flat and vast, a sea of open plains and fields. The ocean, while fiercer in his younger days, still had an intriguing green tint, almost turquoise by the looks of it. But whatever he remembered of the viciousness of the waves when younger, that had all but died to the subtle cascading of waves that barely seemed to bother washing ashore much less crashing downward.

And the army of men that sat about the coast looked to have lost a war, except they fought no war at all. They were hungry, broken down, and looked agitated. Thousands upon thousands of men scattered the beach, some out in boats fishing, others working the fires used to cook what they apparently could scavenge. These were desperate men. And somehow the Moon Divide did not sense fear, nor had the decency to care. The moment they marched near the army, they set up their tents and camped upward from the beach, a small blotch of higher elevation that rose just enough to be in sight of the rest of the soldiers below. Here several of them entered into the interior of the camp and produced empty boxes to which they simply took without asking and returned to their encampment to use them as tables and chairs.

After a higher ranking officer asked who they were and what they were doing, Deso sent him off to find the general. Then came the glasses and the bottles of wine, followed by their deck of cards. This was not going to sit well with the remainder of the soldiers, Rayden could tell. Outside of a decent meal, these men did not look to have had a stiff drink in some time. Eyes began to wander and the Divide did not give those eyes much notice.

They stood sixty-three in all, including himself. There were four large groups that swiveled together, each one more a representation of power it seemed. The larger group comprised of twenty men, Deso included in that bunch. The other groups trickled down from there, about fifteen in another, fourteen or so in the others. Only those in the main group played the particular game of cards that never seemed to end, and even then only six of them within the group played it. Those six were of the highest men in the camp, excluding only Deso, as he said he was removed from the game many years back.

There might not have been leadership within the Divide, but there was certainly respect. Deso might have garnered the most based on his stature and his apparent ties to Philip Pratt, but these other men were respected for various other reasons, ones that Rayden could honestly claim he had no desire to know.

"You going to join us, Breeches?" asked Flint, a short, Argon fellow.

"In the drink or the game?" was his response. "Because you know I will take the drink."

"Bah," Nails, a massive Ursan fellow wailed. "Skinny Donovinian bastard doesn't know a good hand from a rock in the face."

"That, and I cautioned him against your game," Deso stated. He sat with the group, but just a few steps away, his wine glass filled first amongst the criminals. "Boy is in debt well enough to me. And if he doesn't have the coin to throw in, he doesn't have any stake in it."

"He's already in debt to you," offered up Scythe, a tall, lanky Fallneesian. "Not so sure why you don't just give him some money to spend. Maybe he can pay you back sooner."

"Yah, what's the hurry?" Nails added. "Is he going somewhere? Thought he was one of us now anyways."

A badly scarred Donovinian named Mortar could only laugh. "Just because Deso says he is doesn't make him one of us. He ain't drawn blood that I've seen. Skinny shit doesn't even look like he could hold a blade upright."

"Bet he could hold some cards upright though," Flint made note.

"Just sit the fuck down, Breeches," Deso ordered, pointing to the box beside him. "Pour him a drink, and no, I'm not lending him money. Just play your damn game."

Chained it was called, and from as far as he could tell, not a single one of them knew how to play. They all talked a good game, and pretended such, but damned if they did not argue over the rules a majority of the time. There seemed less playing and more fighting going on. And Rayden, while no jack of all trades, considered himself a decent player of cards. He had no idea what the rules were, despite analyzing the game since day one of his kidnapping. All he knew was that there stood a lot of coin on the game, and no one seemed to win the pot. He had thought it dangerous to carry that much gold amongst a group of criminals, but there did seem to be honor amongst thieves, as no one even thought to look at the coin with ill intent. That and if they were to be believed, the amount carried with them was a mere portion of what was truly held inside the vaults of Corovium. But Rayden had trouble believing that.

Scythe's twin brother, Haze, grabbed the deck and chuckled some to himself. "Remember when Deso went all in like a dumb ass?"

Aaron, an Argon with a scar that went down across his blinded right eye, laughed loudly at the comment. "Ha, he thought he won! Thought we were on the third engagement, but we were on the fourth. Went all in on three nines. Can you believe that?"

"If it was the third it would have beaten you all and ended the fucking game," Deso huffed, only mildly annoyed.

"How does the game end?" Rayden inquired.

"When someone wins all the money," Haze stated, shuffling the deck.

"And how often has that happened?"

All six men looked at him from the table, each with a half-smile upon their face.

"It hasn't," Deso answered for them.

Rayden turned to the Fallneesian leader. "So . . . this has been the same game going on over and over again until someone wins. How long has it been going on?"

"I don't know," mumbled Scythe. "What do you guys think? Ten years? Something like that. Most of these other losers around you all bought in at some point in time too. Once you run out of money, you are out. Only way to lose."

"Ten years," he repeated in awe. "And so you are the last six men playing this game over that many years?" None answered as Haze began to deal the cards. "Exactly how much money are we talking about that's in that bag of coins there?"

The men on the table chuckled to that. "That there is just recently acquired gold," noted Mortar. "We are like everyone else in Amon and have to deposit money to the bank vault in Corovium every now and again."

"Well then . . . how much money does the winner of this game take?" he pressed further.

Scythe shrugged his shoulders. "Don't think anyone knows anymore. A lot. Think of a number. It's more than that."

Rayden turned to Deso. "And I guess you went all in once, lost everything, and were removed from the game completely."

"Stupid fucking game anyways," he mumbled. "I just wanted to end the damn thing."

Rayden could feel the crowds of men forming on the beach, mostly curious parties if nothing else, as the form of the higher officer appeared with two others following. Both a tad younger than he would have presumed for high ranking officers. Two Donovinians approached: one that he did not recognize, but the other he knew immediately to be John Shonnen. He might have been in his late thirties, if not early forties. Very young for his status but walked with a sense of pride that had others step aside and back away from him as he made his way toward the criminals of the Divide.

Well this should be interesting, to say the least.

As John walked his way up to the camp, none of the men stood or acknowledged him. Each of the six studied their cards, drank their wine, and gave no notice. The rest of the Divide continued to unpack and pitch tents, oblivious to the commanding officer within their presence. Even Deso did not look back when approached. He grabbed beneath him a sealed letter and held it upward.

"For you, General," he stated without looking.

John certainly did not look too pleased at the lack of respect. He took the letter but did not immediately open it. "Who are you all?" he demanded, his voice low and commanding.

"Just the men you asked for, General."

"I *asked* for reinforcements," John corrected. "There can't be more than . . . what, fifty of you?"

"Sixty-three," Deso corrected. "First Pratt said that is all that you needed. We are part of a . . . let us just say, special unit." He finally stood and faced the General. "Captain Deso. Good to meet you, First General John Shonnen. Situation seems a bit dire around here."

The general gave a questioning glare to the Fallneesian, and with good reason. He broke the seal and unrolled the letter, reading the contents out loud. "I am Captain Deso. Signed . . . Captain Deso." The letter dropped from his hand.

"Well, what more did you want? A letter from First Pratt? He said to take my men and march out here. That's what I did. But doesn't look like you need men, General. It looks like you need food."

"Captain Deso . . . I certainly don't recognize that name within the Imperial Army. What is your first name?"

"Deso."

"The general asked you a direct question, Captain," barked the other Donovinian man that stood beside the general. He lacked the understanding of what these men truly were to be properly frightened. He should have been though. "What is your full name?"

"Deso," he repeated. "We carry no last names in my unit. We are but mere ghosts."

"Ghosts? Well did First Pratt give you any instructions on exactly how you were to aid us?" stammered the general. "Especially since he is asking us to disband my men and return home."

"Fun tour of duty, *Captain,*" Flint stated, while throwing down the first card of the game.

"Sign me up for a second fucking tour," laughed Aaron.

Deso ignored his men. "We were sent here for support. You still lead your men. So, do you disband your men as commanded?"

The general turned away, his glare hesitant. "These are matters we should speak in private and with the rest of my commanding crew, Captain Deso."

"You can speak candidly in front of my crew," Deso responded. "They truly don't care about our conversation regardless. So tell me. If you are unsure, then food must be a priority. So I am here to support. Do you need food for your men?"

"Fucking double jacks!" hollered Scythe.

John turned to the men playing cards, then back to Deso. "Live game has up and gone in this area, and travel gets tougher as men grow weaker. We fish regularly, but that is not enough to feed men daily. The only other food source left would involve us to raid a town or city, which would bring House Rowe and their guard down upon us. We are but the eight thousand men left, Captain Deso. The guard for Argonus would outnumber us, and at our weakened state, would destroy us."

"Fair enough assessment, I suppose," Deso answered. "But why would you presume to attack and assault a city? The Guild has an outpost not too far from here."

The stare returned from the general was a blank one, emotionless, confused. "You understand that would call down the Guild upon us quickly, and that would spell our death."

"Then disband your men."

"And where would they go? How would they live?"

"Then keep them together and feed them, help them survive. You have no money, nothing to barter with. Seems like numbers is the only thing you have."

"There must be another option, Captain Deso. I will not send these men to war in this state."

"Well, assuming these men can be fed," continued the Fallneesian, "what would be your next move? Wait until you get another letter from First Pratt?"

"We cannot hold out that long, unfortunately."

Deso shrugged, then turned to him. "What do you think, Private Breeches?"

I think that I want to go home. I think I should have stayed in the capital that day and not gone out. I think I should have stopped and talked it out with Allura. I think too damn much as it is.

"I think that the end result is the same from every angle," started Rayden. "These men look stretched to their very end. They will need food. Should you disband and abandon your post as per suggestion, these men will either begin attacking themselves, or they will unify and attack a nearby village. Either way, it doesn't end well. You could try to negotiate with a nearby village . . ."

"Thank you, Private, but we tried that already," the general responded. "We are known to be trapped here and no one will aid us. These men are not part of the Imperial Army any longer and no one owes them anything. I've even asked House Rowe for enough supplies to get us back to the capital, only to be told that doing such would be considered a donation, since these men were no longer soldiers. And Gerald Rowe isn't fond of handing out donations apparently. Not even to be rid of us."

"Well tell you what," started Deso, his arms crossing at this chest. "That Guild outpost only holds about two hundred men or so. Let me take my men and see if we can negotiate something."

"We already tried that too," John offered.

"I haven't," Deso followed.

John Shonnen stood for a few seconds, possibly in quandary of his choices, of the suggestion brought before him by a captain he just met. It was a long silence.

"Fair enough, Captain Deso. If the First Pratt sent you, I presume you are worth your own weight. Go have words with the Guild. Do not be upset when they turn you down at the gate."

"Takes more than that to get me upset," the captain said. "And everyone should be grateful for that."

--

A drizzly, cloudy night ruined what would have been a pleasantly cooler one than recent days. The summer months, while not nearly as brutal here as in Donovini, still bore down heavily. The start of the cool night felt uplifting as the breeze cut across Rayden's shaven head, a feeling that he was slowly growing accustomed to. But the rain, warm and uncomfortable against his skin, did not feel quite the same.

The outpost was southwest by a good part of the day and by night they finally reached it. Not vast by any means, the structure was basically a small fort; the walls stood but forty, maybe fifty feet from the ground if Rayden were a guessing man. This outpost held its fair share of supplies, especially lasting supplies like dried meat and grain. Deso seemed to believe that the food stored inside could sustain these Guild men a year without a restock of fresh supplies. It would only hold the army three weeks, maybe four. But that would be enough to regain their strength. It would be enough to get them to march away from the coast and perhaps home.

That was, of course, assuming that the Guild agreed to share, which seemed doubtful. Deso, however, did not seem worried during their trek. Whatever plan he had, he did not share it with Rayden. All the same . . . he had not expected him to. He was, after all, just a prisoner. More free than the average prisoner. But despite that fact, still captive.

The shock had passed after the first two weeks of his captivity. Angry, regretful, curious . . . all of the emotions mixed together, not one dominating the other. Rayden still found despise toward Jerryn and Allura, still allowed their union to get under his skin. With him gone, did they get married? Was Jerryn now the king of Amon? They lied to him, deceived him even, and that was the more troublesome part. But he regretted leaving the way he did. A disappointment to his father, a failure to his sister . . . he could have talked things out with his brother. He could have found a way to forgive him and get through things. He *chose* to storm out, to make the scene. He *chose* to enter that bar and get right and drunk. Certainly he was curious at who wanted him dead. Both Allura and Jerryn seemed likely suspects, but who knew? Deso knew but refused to say. Rayden was dead, he repeatedly told him, and dead men no longer carried grudges. But Rayden, or Breeches, did carry grudges, dead or not. He wanted to know who hired the Divide to kill him. And when he found them . . . well he had not thought that far ahead. First he would have to figure out how to escape the clutches of the Divide, much easier said than done.

And after that? Back home to Astrona, hide behind my father's walls? Or back to Corovium and take what's mine?

Funny, the throne within his grasp and he pissed it away without a care. Now that it was far and away from his grasps . . . perhaps he would have liked another opportunity to sit upon the throne. Dreams long gone now.

"What do you see?" questioned Deso, who stood quietly beside him.

Rayden realized that he had been thinking and paying very little attention to the fort before him.

"Walls," he answered. "Fifty feet at their highest. Guards posted on all four points. At least it appears that way. Getting dark."

"Ever killed anyone in your former life?"

Rayden shook his head.

"Have you been in a fight?"

"I have dueled," he answered. "I was trained with the sword."

"I said a fight," repeated Deso with intensity. "I did not ask if you played fighting. I asked if you had been in a fight, a *real* fight."

Again, he shook his head.

Deso's expression remained stoic. He unbuckled the straps to his belt that holstered his sword and tossed it over to Rayden. Instinctively he caught the weapon.

"Your father and uncles were men of the sword. Born such by their father, the great Landon Pratt. Did you know your grandfather well?"

Rayden turned his gaze back to the fort before them. "Of course I did. He was . . . not the man that legend suggests. He was full of sorrow."

"A great burden to live to the expectations drawn by others," answered Deso. "But his skill with the blade is still legend. Hopefully some of his born ability passed to you. But until that proves to be true, I suggest you stay close to me when the fighting starts."

"The fighting?" mumbled Rayden in a voice that unintentionally made him sound more fearful than baffled.

"Yes, boy. We are going to need supplies if we are stationed with this army. And if the general has not figured out a way to get them supplies, then I suppose we shall. I won't have a few thousand men raiding my camp for the money and food that we have."

"I thought we were going to negotiate."

"We are," replied the Fallneesian. "But we do it our way."

"Meaning . . ."

"We kill them until they don't want to die anymore." He flashed a wicked smile to Rayden. "No better negotiation tactic than that, or so my dad used to tell me."

--

All that came to the Divide came from different backgrounds, for different reasons. When his uncle selected the members, it was done so strategically. At first thought, Rayden had always believed that the Moon Divide were nothing but criminals selected solely to fill numbers to perform less than admirable jobs. In other words, expendable men. As his unfortunate time passed amongst them, he began to understand differently. Each were gifted killers, each with unique skills of survival, and they all shared one common trait; they feared nothing.

He did not share that similarity with the Divide, one of the many reasons he had no business breathing the same air as them.

One of the men raised a blowgun and a dart flung through the night sky, landing into one of the Guild men atop the fort tower. Another did the same to the east, and both men simply dropped in a heap and out of sight, mostly silent in their slumber . . . or death he supposed. Rayden could not be certain what poison laced the darts and what effects it caused. In either case, they were no longer in vision and it took less than seconds for them to reach the wall, three grappling hooks spinning, spinning, then tossed high and over the parapet.

Deso tested the strength twice, then started up, turning back only to point to Rayden. Little need for words when his face spoke volumes. He wanted Pratt up next. All for the best, Rayden figured. The closer he remained to Deso, the more likely he had to live.

I mean, if he wanted me dead . . . pretty sure he would have just done it a long time ago and been rid of me. Dead men eat less food.

Deso ascended another few feet up the wall, Nails nudged Rayden against the back, and young Pratt took to the rope. Deso made the climb look far easier than it was. The rope was not thick and quite difficult to grasp, as he presumed it would have to be to reach great heights. One thing for certain, it was not built for comfort. Where he could see the men beside him climbing the other two lines with little effort, all arms and back strength, Rayden could not fake this part. Seeing himself fall behind Deso by many strides, he pressed his feet against the wall and began to walk up. Yet even that proved challenging.

By the time he reached the top, even only the fifty feet or so that it was, his hands were on fire. Nothing felt better in his mind at reaching the top . . . foolishly so, knowing full and well that death awaited just over it. Feet over the parapet, he landed and drew the sword given to him by Deso. The Fallneesian's hands shined dully in the moonlight, the appearance of perhaps brass knuckles or something similar. He pointed to the body before them with authority, a still breathing, sleeping body.

The Fallneesian did not have hesitation in his eyes, even though Rayden had it in his heart. Rayden's sword came down onto the neck; the Guild member did not even wake from shock. He simply gurgled the blood, his eyes still shut, then simply stopped breathing. It felt . . . easier than he would have thought. Maybe easier than he would have liked. But it made him feel ill all the same.

The courtyard below them was empty, save for the many supplies and horses within. Fear showed within the animal's eyes as they could smell death just as easily as if it were freshly brewed tea. Deso did not wait for the horses to give them away. As others began to pile over the wall, he moved with purpose toward the nearest door along the parapet, Rayden now directly behind. The door opened and a staircase led downward before them. Which was convenient, as that was the direction they needed to travel.

Quicker work of the stairs than the rope, Deso hit ground level first, Rayden second, and they stood amongst a sea of sleeping men. Maybe two hundred at minimum if he was guessing, which was far more than what entered the fort, and that was not a guess. The beds lined up individually in several rows, positioned from east to west along the wall. Snores and heavy breathing of both naked and half-naked men filled the room, masking the steps from the members of the Divide that fast approached.

So what now?

He of course knew but was not prepared.

Deso threw the first blow, his metallic knuckles landing down hard onto the first sleeping man in the room. Crunching could be heard, along with a soft grunt, and then a lot of blood. Nails pushed passed Rayden, his two-handed hammer now gripped firmly as he raised and dropped the heavy, metal creation down onto another defenseless man, nothing more than a loud thud, and then a lot of blood. Rayden simply moved aside and allowed the men of the Divide to pile in and start the slaughter, to which they got another twenty or thirty seconds of before the first scream could be heard from a waking Guild member.

Vastly outnumbered, the element of surprise gone, and yet the Divide did not falter. Deso pushed forward, his fists connecting with furious accuracy, connecting with one man's temple who in turn dropped as if his head turned into stone. Another Guild member's hands rose in defense, to which he punched downward into his groin, then drove an uppercut into the chin. Nails swung his hammer around as if it were effortless, a mere toothpick in his hands. At times, two men were caught in the swirling motion of his weapon, and what the hammer left behind was nothing less than horrifying.

Though the men in the front were caught in a whirlwind, those in the rear began to compose, arming themselves with whatever lay scattered about, their own weapons or not. One of them must have thought it a good idea to get out into the courtyard; better odds there than in a narrow sleeping chamber. Here, their numbers would only favor them if the Divide got tired of swinging. Their numbers did not aid them inside the room. Out there, they could overwhelm them, swarm them, kill them. It was a good thought, a wise thought, or at least it must have seemed that way.

Up until one of the Guild members lifted the bolt across the door and opened it. First through the door were the twin Fallneesian brothers, Scythe and Haze, both wielding similar looking halberds, both extending out with the pointed ends and stabbing anything that stood before them. Mortar was not far behind, taking the first opportunity to step around the brothers as his long scimitar began to whistle through the chambers, slicing through victims with ease.

The Guild members might have been skilled, and were likely all well worth the coin spent on them, but they were caught unprepared. Who would have dared attack them? After all, they were the Guild. And yet here they stood, advantage in numbers only, and that advantage dwindled quickly. Boxed in by thirty men on both sides, the Divide pressed relentlessly. Deso did not stop his assault, his fists breaking through swords, turning face into mush. His drive rallied those behind him and those looking to meet him in the middle of the battle. Rayden spotted both Flint and Aaron manage to work their way around Nails and Deso, finding their way into battle, laying down killing blows with fresh hands and eager swords.

Meanwhile Rayden watched, paralyzed, uncertain of what he was meant to do in the wake of all of this chaos.

Why am I here? What did I do to deserve this?

The thought of escape cleared from his conscious. The thought of ever being able to leave these men abandoned. They were masters of their art, and their art was killing. Worse yet, they seemed to enjoy it. This was who they were. This was the Moon Divide.

And now he was one of them, he supposed.

He no longer felt horrified as much as he felt unworthy.

--

"I counted twelve myself," Flint bolstered some as they began to load the wagons within the fort of any and all supplies.

"Bah, that's only because you can't fucking count," Nails responded upon approach, barrels being dragged behind him.

The men of the Divide were in full motion, getting the horses calmed and ready for travel, wagons fully stocked with everything and anything that they could load. The battle had been successful, for whatever that was worth, and almost injury free. The Divide suffered but three losses, bringing their total to an even sixty. Their deaths were not mourned, but praised. They were now free men, Deso had claimed. It is what they all hoped for themselves. Meanwhile the Guild members of this fort were completely decimated. This was not an act taken lightly, Rayden knew. The Divide, however, did not seem to care for such things.

"Well me and Scythe took at least twenty a piece," Haze mentioned, tossing a sack of unknown contents onto the wagon.

"Ladies, ladies, you're all pretty," laughed Aaron.

"Besides," grunted Mortar, pointing to Rayden, "we all had more fucking kills than Breeches."

The group of named men laughed some, all turning to him, shaking heads.

"How many did you get there, Breeches?" Aaron questioned, his lone eye staring him down. "One? One fucking kill? Impressive."

"I'm not like you," mumbled Rayden.

"What was that?" Deso stammered from behind him, coming up so quickly that Rayden nearly stumbled backwards onto his ass. He might have just done so if Deso had not grabbed him by his tunic and pulled him in close. "You *are* one of us now, boy. So I suggest you grow a fucking sack and act the damn part." He then turned to the others. "And lay off the lad. He killed a man tonight. Quite a few less than the rest of you, but that was one less man to deal with, one less possibility of a sword in your back. So be thankful. A kill is a kill. And we all still live and breathe, so there will be a next time."

"Earth and Flame, Deso," spat Mortar. "We're just harping on the kid. No need to get all fucking uptight about it, *Captain*."

"Lieutenant Captain Deso? Or Captain Lieutenant Deso?" laughed Flint.

"Just get the fucking wagons loaded," barked Deso. He turned to face Rayden again, and pushed him off just a bit. "You too. Get to work."

--

"Those men were no soldiers," Ascotte stated.

Shonnen sat in his tent, his hand rubbing against his chin. Of course he knew that. The dumbest in his squadrons would have known the same. That fact, however, changed very little.

"First Pratt sent me a notice in one of his letters of this man Deso," the general responded. "Soldiers or not, First Pratt sent them. Of course, he sent them when we were an army, not a large group of renegades."

"Then why did you send them out to that outpost? They will not get anything accomplished, save for getting themselves killed."

Shonnen only shook his head. "New faces, men well fed and with plenty of money . . . best to keep them away from our men. Best have some distance while I figure out what I'm going to do with them. That's before any of our own men get ideas circulating around in their heads. We have one advantage at the moment. We aren't living any better than our men on the beach. I am just as hungry and thirsty as the rest of these men. But this new group of men . . . they are something else. I would hate to send First Pratt a note that his trusted men were killed for their supplies and I was powerless to stop it."

"And what if they are killed from the Guild?" Ascotte questioned.

"At least we wouldn't be to blame," he answered.

"Plausible deniability is something at the very least," Baldin Ascotte made claim. "What are you going to do with them should they return?"

The short silence between the men as Shonnen thought over that very question allowed them to hear the bustling of commotion outside their tent. They stared at one another for not but a moment after when Major Tauven Ulfini poked his head through their tents.

"And . . . they're back," the Fallneesian noted. "You might want to come see this."

--

He would not have believed it had he not seen it with his own eyes. The new soldiers simply rolled in, horses in tow with wagons filled with food and supplies. As much as they transported, they might as well have attached chains to the fort and brought it along for good measure. It was an improbable task given to the captain, an impossible one by all means, one that Shonnen feared to question as to how he succeeded in acquiring goods from the Guild.

But he would ask regardless. Shonnen was, after all, the leader of . . . well whatever this army had become.

Captain Deso rode on horseback at the front of this parade, a smug smile on his face. His appearance all but displayed the kind of man that he was. Carefully shaven beard to his jaw line showed attention to detail, but the lack of eyebrows and hair meant he lacked patience. Muscular, but to the point of obsession on his conditioning told him that he strove to be better than those around him. And based on his company, having such an attitude might have kept him alive.

Deso was a killer. He did not need to know anything about the man personally to know what his gut feeling warned him. This man was dangerous. Friend or foe, he could not tell.

"The negotiations went a bit awry," the so-called captain called out. "But we managed to make it out with enough supplies to last us a while."

"You have food in store?" the general questioned.

"A shit ton," replied the captain. "And plenty of water too."

His men were noticing the scene quickly, and more and more soldiers began to move upward from the beach, hunger in their eyes. A horrible kind of hunger.

"Hold there!" the general called out, waving Ulfini toward him. "We need these men fed in an orderly fashion, and the supplies need to be rationed out. Get a squadron up here immediately to begin the distribution."

The major turned to the gathering soldiers. "Sergeant Major Hollins!" Ulfini called out. "Report, Hollins!"

The crowd of men cleared and the elder Ursan took his steps out to face his officers. Shonnen was beginning to like his choice in the new major. Hollins was an excellent selection to calm the masses. A man amongst men, well respected, and moreover, controlled those that remained of the first squadron.

"Captain Ulfini," he recognized.

"It's Major now, Sergeant Hollins."

"Apologies, Major."

"Get your men front and center. I need these supplies quickly sorted and stored. I need someone on distribution. We feed men by squadrons, tail end to front. Your men will be responsible for the rationing. Let's figure out how long this is going to last and take care of this accordingly. I want everyone fed, everyone happy, but I don't want a grain of fucking rice dropped or wasted. Every man gets the same meal, and they will fucking enjoy it. Understood, Sergeant Major?"

"Sir, yes sir," announced Hollins. He immediately turned to the onlookers and began barking out orders, to which men began to hustle about with clean and precise direction.

The general pointed to the captain. "My tent, *now*. You too, Colonel. Major, stay with the men, make sure things are orderly."

"Yes, General Shonnen," Ulfini stated.

Captain Deso dismounted and in no immediate hurry, dusted himself off some, shook out his legs, then casually moved toward the general. Shonnen gave him his back as he worked his way towards his tent. Inside, both he and Ascotte waited patiently for the nonchalant captain to arrive, which took a great . . . many . . . seconds.

And when he did push back the tent flap, he still sported that grin.

"You seem quite proud of yourself," Colonel Ascotte noted. "Or maybe just fond of your antics."

"Well . . . I did bring back goods. Which at last check . . . you were in pretty desperate need of."

"And exactly how did you get this food from the Guild?" Ascotte pressed further.

"How else do you get something from the hands of the unwilling?" When the two of them said nothing in response to his question, the captain shook his head. "Pry it . . . from their cold, dead hands. Isn't that an Ursan saying? Or maybe it was something my dad said. Get the two confused every now and again."

"You killed them?" the general questioned.

To which Deso nodded. "Mostly. I'm sure there are a few that are still bleeding to death while we stand here and talk. It was pretty sloppy work, to be fair and honest."

"But . . . there are but sixty of you," Shonnen stammered.

"Aye, and about two hundred of them. Bad odds by most." He shrugged. "Not to my men. Maybe that's why First Pratt sent us. We are the best at what we do."

"And what do you do, Captain?" Ascotte pestered further.

"Kill."

I believe it.

"It's not that these men won't appreciate the food. They will love you for it. But they do not understand the consequences." Shonnen turned back to his desk and took a seat upon it, facing his two officers. "The Guild will come for us now. Fed men or not, we are trapped here on this coast."

"It will take the Guild some time to realize their outpost is sacked," stated the colonel softly. "We may have time to figure out our next move, despite my dislike of the captain's bravado and lack of respect."

"Hate to disagree, but the Guild will find out quickly," rebutted Deso. "Guild communicates freely and often with one another, enough that a late to report would result in an investigation, which would involve them finding an empty fort and a lot of bodies. But that is the least of your concerns."

"*Least*?" baffled the colonel.

"Aye. You can just say a rogue element of your former army ran off and sacked the fort. You had no part of it. Easy enough. You would have to hide the evidence of course, but you would easily lie and play this incident off. What you need to figure out is what to do next. Your men are about to be fed, and we have enough food for a few weeks, maybe even a month if we ration correctly. What are you going to do?"

"You seem to have all the fucking answers," hissed Ascotte. "Why not tell us?"

"Fair enough," Deso replied. "I'd march the fed men up to Tessenul while they still have spirit."

To which the general choked some in his reply. "The capital? To what end?"

"Their end," was his reply.

"Are you mad?" stammered Ascotte.

"Aye. But it won't take Gerald Rowe long to come down upon you. You think the Guild will come for us? No, they will wait along the Donovinian border. Let us starve out here, kill each other. You do not fully understand how they operate, but I do. They are not an army, General Shonnen. They aren't even honorable fucking men. They are just men that like coin. They don't move without profit in mind. Revenge? No fucking coin in revenge. Besides . . . war is expensive. They also have no honor to bruise. Now I did just put a dent in their pocket, to which will upset them some. Not enough to strike. But . . . I can see them speaking to House Rowe. Make them do their work for them."

A crazy killer, but rational one. It made sense. The Guild would take the assault on their fort personally, but would not waste their own time or resources in coming for the army themselves. But they would, however, quickly tap their resources. Gerald Rowe only watched over the capital for Christina Rowe while she was away. He would likely be easily swayed to their direction. He could not appear weak while Lady Rowe looked to expand her power in Genethur. He could not lose his relations with the Guild, at least if he looked to one day become the House lord.

They were moving the pawn many steps ahead, but that was what leaders did. They planned in advance, predicted their enemy's movements. Deso was a leader of men, killers or otherwise.

"Take the capital," mumbled Shonnen.

"Aye," replied Deso.

"Insane," stated Ascotte. "We should . . ."

"Should what, Colonel?" Shonnen inquired. "We move north or west, we pour into Ursan. Brocusk would have his men on us in a heartbeat, probably consider us invading his lands. South and southwest lies Donovini, and that places us far too close to Prillian and likely in the grasp of the Guild. We stay here and we die. We have nowhere to run."

"Thanks to Captain Deso and his attack on the outpost . . ."

"That has our men lining up for food," Shonnen swiftly retorted. "Without food, we would have no ability to leave this coast. With food, we have options. Albeit limited options . . . options nevertheless. We can feed our men and make for the border and hope to somehow avoid resistance from the Guild, but our movements could not be hidden. We are too large of a force to nimbly move across an entire country. So perhaps attacking the Guild was foolish . . . but it was a better option than what we were currently doing. Which was plenty of nothing."

"But . . ." started the colonel.

"It's done," the general interrupted. "We were stuck here until Captain Deso assaulted that outpost. Now we have enough supplies to move away from the coast. Like the tactics or not, we had no better plan. In fact, our plan was far worse, being we didn't have a plan. For the time being, our men get to eat something other than fish and bones today, so that's something. Stammering over what ifs is pointless. We took the outpost. We took from the Guild. Now we must decide what to do. It's no different from when Captain Deso arrived. The same decision sits upon us. Only now . . . our men are less likely to turn on each other."

"But General Shonnen," pleaded Ascotte, "you need to think this through. Rowe's guard would outnumber us four to one, maybe more."

"Interesting, we faced similar odds," Deso stated with a smile.

"One victory, if you can call it that, and you are ready to storm the capital of Argonus?"

The captain chuckled. "Rowe will come for us. After we now supplied our men here on the coast . . . after that attack . . . we are now a threat. If the Guild doesn't send word to Lord Rowe, they will find out on their own regardless. So why make him wait? Best to be proactive than reactive, or so my dad always told me, I think."

"And who was your father, *Captain*?" queried the colonel with heavy sarcasm. "I'm sure he was a man of great honor."

To which Deso maintained his half grin. "No, he was a son of a bitch."

Colonel Ascotte huffed a bit. "I'm sure you are quite proud."

Deso only shrugged. "Through my experience, sons of bitches have a tendency to outlive honorable men. You know why? They don't let morals or ethics get in the way of survival. They don't do what's right so much as they do what's necessary. You stand here on the beach and rot if you want, wait for the fallen gods to give you some sort of sign. It would be the honorable thing to do. Or . . . you could take action. Personally, I like living. Call me what you will. Call me a son of a bitch like my father if it pleases you. But I *do* have his knack for staying alive."

"A good family trait," humored Shonnen.

"Aye. Especially if you enjoy breathing. And whores."

The general could only smile. "Dismissed Captain. Make sure your men are well rested. We will speak more of this in the morning."

Deso nodded, waved his hand in a fake salute, and ducked back out of the tent.

"Tell me you are not considering this," his colonel stated with heavy insistence. "We're talking about attacking a capital city. Despite our men being disbanded, *we* are part of the Imperial Army. What you speak of is high treason. And for what exactly?"

"The lives of our men," answered Shonnen.

"We march to that city . . . men are going to die on both sides. We would kill others just to save our own? We are meant to protect people, not assault the capital of the country that has housed us for years."

"And what happens when they march their army across the plains and box us in here at the beach? What if we had the chance to get ahead of that before it happens?"

"If that happens, we just hand over the captain," noted Ascotte. "We sent him to negotiate and he went rogue, took out the Guild. Because that's *exactly what happened!* We can get ourselves out of this alive."

"We might," noted John. "But do you think the Guild would pardon anyone here save for the officers? Do you think our men would be saved from this situation if the Guild requests us dead?"

"A situation we could have avoided if . . . but no what ifs, right?" Ascotte sighed heavily. "John . . . we are still officers of the Imperial Army. This is a crime against the crown. Even if we do this thing, we will be traitors to the throne. Even if we sack the capital somehow, our men would be fed and housed for a short time until the remainder of the Imperial Army showed up and killed us all. We would literally be doing this to survive a few more months. Is that worth it?"

I am considering a great many things. But I am an honorable man . . . that wants to stay alive. I want to keep my men alive too. Does that make me the same as Deso? No, but it does make me desperate.

As the Ursan say, if death comes, move quicker.

By his estimation, they had best move fast.

--

At the end of the day, I couldn't care less what people think of me or my father. I know that we are not the popular Pratts, if such a thing exists. We are not head of our House, we are not within the king's council. We are simply men that honor our family name.

At times, I feel like we are the only ones left in that category.

-- Luther Pratt, House Lord of Donovini

XVIII

"I appreciate your situation, First Pratt," began Gillar, coughing some as he repositioned himself within his chair. "However, we are a bit in a conundrum."

First Pratt stared about his office. The Third bore an intense look about him, likely worry brought on by his sister to press these proceedings. Lurey Hillan was many things, though his honesty might have been a fault more than a positive for him. But the Third shriveled like a grape in the summer heat when it came to Christina Rowe. Beside him sat Lijid Nulittan, who might as well been sleeping for all it mattered. He sat silent as a corpse, soaking in all that transpired within the room, but added nothing.

"We need a king to fix the courts," the court head continued after he finally seemed comfortable, and his expensive, imported chair groaned at the Fallneesian's weight. "But as you tell me, you do not have full approval."

Lurey chuckled. "You might understand that the Second is not exactly cooperating based on his current situation."

"But he did pledge his alliance to the union on the throne?" Gillar inquired.

To which Philip nodded. "That he did, as did Dehyllo during the chaos in the courts."

"And did you get his written word on such? Either Brocusk or Afeon?" When Philip shook his head, the short Fallneesian only shrugged. "My hands are tied, gentlemen. You need to have Afeon honor his word if you seek Jerryn Pratt to become king. I suggest you revisit him. I cannot call for the courts when we do not even know *how* to vote without the Ursan members present."

"But I don't believe that Brocusk's act in the courts vetoed his decision to approve Jerryn's succession," pleaded the First. "This was an independent act. He does not believe in our power to rule this country, nor does he believe that his people mattered within the courts. He said they gave their written consent . . ."

"To the union," Gillar interrupted. "That they did, First Pratt, but the union of the two Houses and two countries does not gain you a throne. A unanimous vote from the king's council grants your nephew the throne without the need for court approval. Dehyllo left Afeon here in Corovium likely to make that happen. And you locked him in a dungeon. That decision was yours, not ours. We cannot help you. If you want the throne, I suggest you revisit with him and make amends somehow."

Of course he knew this would be the case. Gillar would not step any further than required. He would not risk his position in the courts to show favoritism to any side, no matter how obvious the choice should be. For Gillar, this was about his own positioning with both his peers and the Guild, to which lined his pockets handily. No need to hastily throw support behind anyone just yet, not when sitting idly by could yet gain him profit.

And for Philip, it was the only time where Gillar's greed and lack of conviction played directly into his own hands.

His witness to Allura's whereabouts during Rayden's kidnapping mysteriously disappeared. Likely gutted and dropped into the Vurid Sea. *What else did I expect? Why did I trust Christina to be honest?* And perhaps she was, at least honest with herself. The throne was right there, right for the taking, and all that stood between her and her goal was her daughter's foolish and careless act. But Christina did her part. She questioned her daughter and Allura denied claim, so said Lady Rowe. But in all likelihood, she buried her daughter's mistake.

But with no way to know for certain, the First would have to proceed as planned. The wedding done, now it came down to the crowning. And the longer he stalled, the more he hoped to hear word from the coast, primarily from Deso. If the Divide took Rayden, was he still alive? Philip would start praying to the fallen gods if that were so. And if his nephew lived, how quickly could he get him to the capital? In time to stop this crowning and prove Allura's part in her treason against House Pratt? Her execution *would* void the contract between Rowe and Pratt, as severe as that would be. And then . . . and then what exactly?

Should I do as Afeon suggested? Should I just claim the throne?

It was never as simple as that. For Afeon, for an Ursan, conquering was the same as an election. Earn respect or take respect; either way, respect is given. But the First believed that the people needed to see someone gain the throne through the laws set in place, not force and brutality. The union of the four races, the four countries was to end the barbaric wars of their past, to become one as a people. They did not want to see them divert back to their old ways.

So while Gillar sat with a smug grin on his chubby face, thinking that he had the council dead to rights, the First played his part. He gave the appearance of someone pushed against a wall, looking left and right for a way around the bully. In reality, the wall was exactly where he wanted to be. Everything went as planned.

But the knock on his door changed everything. It opened slowly and a soldier appeared through the crack, in his hands a sealed parchment. He held it out, hesitation on his face.

"Sorry to interrupt, First Pratt, but this message came for you. I was told to give it to you post haste," the soldier stammered.

It must have been bad news. Good news never interrupted meetings to be delivered. Good news could always wait. Only bad news had this sense of urgency.

"Bring it forth, soldier," Pratt stated, waving him onward.

And so he did, nervously walking across and handing Philip the scroll. As he turned to catch the seal, Philip could clearly see the mark of Dehyllo Brocusk.

"Dismissed, soldier."

"Yes, First. Just so you know, your brother received an identical parchment, sealed all the same."

Philip nodded and the soldier shuffled off, closing the door behind him. Lurey leaned in some, Gillar's eyebrows rose, and even Lijid might have woken up long enough to peak some interest.

Grasping the letter opener upon his desk, he cut through the seal and unraveled the scroll. Carefully he read the contents. He of course wished that he had not.

"Fuck," he mumbled.

--

Nicolas Pratt waltzed into her mother's chambers holding a parchment in his hands. He clutched it as if it were the last torch remaining in the Shadow Realm. Allura could only smile. At least the warrior's scowl returned to his face, the one that gained him respect across borders. There was fierceness in his eyes . . . and desperation.

She normally did not care for his presence, especially unannounced, but even Allura sat up some at his grandiose entrance. In honesty, Christina, Jerryn, and she had not been discussing much of importance. Until Jerryn was crowned, there stood little *to* discuss, annoyingly so. If First Pratt did his job, she would already be queen. But his loyalty was in question. Speculation or not, Philip believed that she had something to do with Rayden's disappearance. Unfortunately for him, there no longer stood a witness alive to defend his claim.

The House lord gazed about the room, spotting the three of them, then turned to the guard that stood just off in the shadows.

"A moment alone," barked Nicolas.

"He stays," Allura commanded. She could detect a hint of a smile on Alex's face, but just a smidgeon, just enough to not enrage the elder Pratt. "You may say what you must in front of those present."

She was beginning to gain the confidence of a queen, and her mother allowed her to do such. Mistakes . . . she was certainly filled with them. This Rayden business would not go away, if even her mother never spoke of it again. She could tell much from a look, and her mother gave her one of eternal disappointment. That being said, Christina still needed Allura to be seen as a powerful, decisive woman. How else could she run the country behind the scenes? Of course, Allura would not be the puppet, despite what her mother had in mind.

"Very well," Nicolas stated. He moved over with the letter and handed it to her mother. "The time for politics is over, Lady Rowe."

Christina did not question his statement. She took the parchment and opened it, taking only a few seconds to read the contents. Satisfied, she handed it to Allura. Jerryn moved closer to her on the couch as she opened it for both of them to see.

The Pratt Brothers,

I have two young Pratts in my possession now. If you wish this to be easy, concede the throne to me and I shall deliver them back to you. There are no other negotiations. If you do not like my demands, then come and get them back yourselves.

-- *Dehyllo Brocusk*

"Katlynn . . . Rayden . . ." murmured Jerryn.

"Who else?" Nicolas angrily questioned.

Maybe Katlynn if she wandered too far north. But not Rayden. It can't be possible. Luther maybe? But he should be back in Astrona with his father. Who does he have, exactly?

"Nicolas," cautioned Christina. "I know what you are thinking, but we need to approach this calmly."

"To Shadow with your calm," blasted the elder Pratt, his nostrils flaring as he spoke. "I will have my children back to me. And we will not do so by seceding the throne."

"You speak of war," Allura interrupted, now standing to face Lord Pratt.

"I speak of retribution, child," he harshly responded.

Christina though took a step closer to Nicolas. "Retribution not so easily achieved, Nick," she claimed.

"We do not command the Imperial Army just yet," added Allura. "Gillar cannot fix the courts, Afeon will not cast a vote toward us . . . thus we wait."

"Waiting is no longer an option," barked Lord Pratt. "They use my children as bartering tools. How long do you suppose they will let them live? When they do not hear from us? When they presume we have denied their wishes?"

"He will have to parlay if we request it . . ." started Allura, but her mother swiftly interjected.

"You do not know Dehyllo, child. There will be no parlay. There will be no negotiations. We will adhere to his demands or we will wage war. Those are the only two options. And since we cannot give him the throne, then we must risk open war."

"With what army mother?" she hammered back. "This is a moot point until we gain the throne." She turned back to Lord Pratt. "You must convince your brother to name Jerryn Pratt the new king."

"He . . . he does not listen," admitted Nicolas.

"Because it is not his way," Christina replied. "You must understand. Philip loves Amon the way he has created it. To simply bypass some of the laws placed generations before our time . . . well that would go against all that he holds sacred."

"Fuck his feelings," Allura cursed with intensity. "Make him see things our way."

"How can I make my brother do . . ."

"*Make him*," she restated, staring down Nicolas.

"My daughter is right," said Christina. "Dehyllo will respect war. It's what he truly wants in his heart. A throne taken tastes better than one given. He wants us to march an army north into Ursan and face him. Doing so, he will keep your children alive. That will be the only thing keeping you moving, keeping your men driving north. Killing your children will not yield anything positive for him. He wants you to have a sense of urgency to face him, in which case he needs your children alive"

"If we wage war," Nicolas continued.

"Which is what you want," rebutted her mother. "Isn't it?"

Allura shook her head. "Which we cannot do until Jerryn sits upon the throne."

To which Jerryn, finally deciding to make his presence felt, cleared his throat. "I will get them back, Father. I promise you."

Well said, you fucking moron. Will you be leading the charge against Dehyllo? Something tells me no. Not many women in Dehyllo's forces to punch or slap around. The only thing you will be conquering is another bottle of wine.

Nicolas, however, only nodded to his youngest son. He hovered for but another minute, then turned for the door. No more useless words, no more encouraging advice. Nicolas had one objective, and that was to convince his brother to bend the laws he helped defend for almost as many years as she had lived. Not an easy task for anyone.

But life was filled with unpleasant tasks. Allura had a feeling that there were many more yet to come.

--

Philip was getting used to the downward steps, the long hallway, the dank, stale air that hung like death itself within the dungeon. He did not know what that said about him, but it did not bother him like it once did. He also began to get used to the cold stare of the Second, one that all but told his feeling of superiority. Afeon did not seem to fear death, at least up to this point. But now things had changed. Arrogance and confidence would be shaken, as nothing could save him from the inevitable. The Second was going to die and there was no changing that now.

Defiant until the end. But knowing the play of Lord Brocusk, knowing what that meant for him would break him. No man could face death with a smile.

"Hopefully," the Second began, "you did not share this news in thinking that I would run to your support."

But of course he would not break either. Why would he?

"You understand how damning this piece of evidence is for Dehyllo, don't you?" questioned the First.

Afeon nodded. "Utterly. This looks like he kidnapped Nicolas's children. Which we know cannot be entirely true. Likely he has Katlynn."

"We know she was last tracked crossing into Ursan. No surprise that she would stick out there. No surprise that Dehyllo might find her on his way back to Antuannee."

"But two Pratts? Who is the second?"

"If instincts serve me well, no one that you would bother to know."

"Valuable?"

Philip nodded. "Still a heavy bartering tool." *Assuming my brother still holds some love for his bastard.*

The Second nodded. "Either way, add this to the fact that he removed his people from the courts, and the public will begin to believe him responsible for a great many things, perhaps even the assassination of King Yelium. So tell me, First Pratt, you come to inform me of my lord's moves in order to hopefully force me to side with you. Why would you presume I would?"

"Firstly, to live."

"Do you truly believe I will make it through this alive, regardless of my decisions to vote or not?"

No.

"Yes."

Afeon smiled. "You are an impressive liar, First Pratt. If you see me dead in either scenario, why do you think I would simply change my stance and vote for Jerryn Pratt to take the throne?"

"Because you are a man of reason. Because you know that war will do us no good as a country. If you believe that something lies across the Terrandonan . . ."

"Do not preach to me my own beliefs."

"Then know that I have spent my life preventing war. Give me a chance to prevent it."

"And how do you surmise that you can do such?" mused the Second.

"Make Jerryn king. Let me speak with him and I will have him hold off at sending in the Imperial Army. I will go speak with Brocusk myself and convince him to . . ."

"Ha! Can you truly be serious with me, First Pratt? If you cross the border into Ursan expecting to negotiate, Dehyllo will return your head on the next bird back to the capital. If kidnapping Pratts will not gain him war, he will start killing Pratts. Trust me. You will not leave Ursan alive."

"What does he gain by this war?"

Afeon gave a knowing stare. "Amon. As he told you, the throne is a means to an end for him. We gain the throne, we gain an army. We gain an army, we stand a chance at what awaits us. This is about survival, whether you understand it or not. Divided, we are nothing. Only together can we hope to overcome."

"And war is your way of uniting us?"

The Second shrugged. "No, but it is a way of conquering us. Dehyllo tried it your way, First Pratt. You and your politics ensured that would not happen. Now you will try it his way."

The First gazed heavily, desperately at Afeon. "If you do not give me a chance to fix this, many will die."

"Yes, yes they will. Senselessly. And my vote, one way or the next, cannot save that. All I can hope is that whatever comes across the Terrandonan does so swiftly, and hopefully our petty differences can be swept aside long enough to unify. Besides, I thought you were waiting from your word back from the Divide. Me voting for Jerryn puts Allura in power all the same as him."

"This letter changes everything," claimed the First. "If I don't act now, my brother is going to start a war all on his own. He's going to get my family killed."

"Perhaps. But that is life."

He was wasting his time per usual with Afeon. "You will be remembered in the histories of Amon as a traitor."

"Where is the Historian, First Pratt?" inquired the Second. "He does not seem to be around. Don't you find that odd, to be gone at such a pivotal time in our capital?"

He had not thought of it, but Aldric disappeared almost immediately after . . .

Dylinn.

"What the Historian decides to write of me in his books is of his own choosing," continued the Second. "My people will remember my defiance and my honor intact. I was left behind for but one purpose. And my time is coming, First Pratt. Of that I can assure you."

"Hopefully while your head is still atop your shoulders, Second."

To which Afeon could only laugh. "We shall see, First Pratt, if your end is any different. At least mine will be glorious."

"Glorious or not, dead is dead, Second. Sorry to say, but I am trying to live."

"Good luck with that, First." Afeon returned his shitty grin. "Good luck with that."

--

The day pressed onward and Allura spent those hours doing very little but wait. There had been no word from Nicolas or Philip Pratt, no word from her mother, no word at all. The entire fourth floor was hers now, once occupied by the Aylmers. It was hollow. Capital guards stood by the stairwell, mostly just occupying space. Alex hovered about just outside in the hallway. Jerryn napped soundly in the adjacent room since his return from his own personal meetings. And Lillianna steadily combed Allura's long, blonde hair. Would it always be this lonely?

The lack of communication or knowledge of where they were did not aid in her feeling of alienation. By now she would have presumed, or at least would have *enjoyed* the thought of the deciding vote being beaten out of Afeon, but that kind of act seemed far below the standards of the First. On the surface, he seemed to be doing all that he could to push forward Jerryn's succession. But somehow she doubted such. Allura had nothing directly to point to that would claim otherwise, but she could tell much in a look. First Pratt wanted her dead and buried. Deep and forgotten. He did not have it in him, of course, but that did not stop him from finding new ways to infuriate her.

There was so much to do, so much she had planned that she forced in the recesses of her mind. There stood little point in getting further ahead than step one. First she had to grasp the throne. Once hers, the wheels would begin to turn. And once they did, there would be no stopping them.

"Are you nervous about becoming the queen?" Lillianna questioned softly from behind her, still placing the comb through her hair.

"No, child. I am eager, not anxious."

"I think I would be," the girl continued. "I think all I've ever wanted was to get married to someone powerful and handsome, and have lots of babies."

"That is dream of most House girls, and that is not a slight against your age." She turned to the young Pratt, her light brown eyes wide with an equal mixture of fear and respect. The girl was excited about being here, thrilled with being selected to serve the future queen. Her peers would be jealous beyond belief. But Lillianna showed the proper amount of angst, knowing perhaps how dangerous Allura truly was.

Lillianna was both intelligent and shunned. Her father too busy, her sister too annoying, her mother too self-loathing . . . the girl was desperate for someone to guide her.

"I'm a second born of a second born," she claimed. "What else is there for me?"

"Anything you desire," Allura answered. "I know it is easier for me to say, being a first born of a House lord. But when my father died, there was little known of what would happen to my name. My mother was not a rich noble nor of some prestigious name. Hillan does not echo amongst these halls with the same intensity as does Rowe. My mother knew that her reign as House lady would be short lived if she showed weakness. I learned much from her."

"I guess you never figured you would be queen . . ."

"Any more than you figured that you would be my lady-in-waiting," Allura assured the young Pratt.

Lillianna hesitated a moment before questioning, "Can I ask how your father died?"

"You may," Allura stated. "I was young, younger than you. I would love to tell you it was something heroic or fantastical, but it was nothing so grand. Edfeld Rowe was an accomplished hunter and had an agreement with Brocusk to hunt Draywolves during certain times of the year. While on an excursion with his closest friends and associates, he fell victim to another's inexperience. As the story was told, one of the men missed his mark with an arrow and mortally wounded my father. Edfeld did not make the trip back to Tessenul alive."

"I am sorry."

"Don't be, child. Look where I am now. I did not get here because I wallow."

"What of the man that killed your father? Accident or not, I presume your mother did not take such an event lightly?"

Allura exhaled loudly and intentionally. "To say the least, child. My mother's wrath is unflappable."

Lillianna did not appear surprised. "Did she have him killed?"

"She had *all* of them killed, publicly."

"All of them?" baffled the girl.

"Ignorance can normally be forgiven. Incompetence is a different thing altogether. But enough of me. So what of you? What do you *truly* desire?"

Lillianna shrugged some. "I don't know, milady. I suppose I haven't given it much thought."

"I think you have. You are just afraid to speak of it."

A solid knock on the door caught the girls' attention, and Alex opened the door enough to slide through.

"Jessica Pratt is requesting an audience . . . alone," he claimed.

Allura nodded. "Wait minute, then send her in."

Her personal guard bowed some, then closed the door. Allura caught a soft smile on the face of the young Pratt. "I wouldn't mind starting with him."

To which Allura chuckled some. "Lillianna Pratt," she stammered. "A bit young for such talk."

"What? He is *gorgeous*." The young one shrugged. "To die for, really."

You have no idea, my young Pratt. No idea at all.

"Off to your room for now," commanded Allura. "We will discuss this more later. Right now, I fear your mother wishes to discuss you with me."

"I don't want to go home."

"You are home." Winking once to Lillianna, she waved her off. "Now go."

She nodded and shuffled along, opening the door and departing without another word. It took another minute or so before the door opened again and now Jessica Pratt entered. Her face had the look of someone with a premeditated speech. A fire raged behind those dark brown eyes, and it was certainly not unexpected. Allura had avoided her since the wedding. She had only moved Jessica's youngest daughter onto her floor and barred her from leaving. What was there really to discuss?

But the elder Pratt closed the door firmly behind her, gave a glance around the room to spot the sleeping Jerryn, then locked her eyes onto Allura.

"I know you are busy," started Jessica, "but I have been requesting a meeting with you ever since the wedding."

"And I certainly have not been ignoring you, if you feel as such," Allura replied. "My mother and your brother-in-law have been hording my time, as well as the bliss of a new marriage." *Oh, sometimes I make myself laugh.* "I hope that you can understand that I had full intent to give you the proper time. And as it is, you have picked an excellent time, as I await word from my mother on . . . current affairs."

"Well my troubles are trivial based on what you are currently dealing with. And my request is quite simple. I am looking to take leave temporarily while I escort my children back to Astrona."

"Are you now?" Allura retorted with a half grin. "Do you not feel safe here in the capital?"

"It is not my safety I am concerned with. Katlynn is unjustly a fugitive and Rayden is missing. The Pratt children are being marked and I *refuse* to sit about and watch one of my girls disappear."

Allura moved across the room and poured herself a glass of wine. Motioning for a second glass, but Jessica only shook her head in response. She took a sip before continuing.

"You do understand that I have constant guard here, from both House Rowe as well as the capital guard."

Jessica frowned deeply. "And that saved the other Pratts? Or how about Yelium Aylmer II?"

"No, I gather not. And you feel the road is a safer place for you? Be an easy target, especially with as many people seeing you leave. And what does that say to the people of Corovium, to watch the First's wife and daughters flee the capital?"

"Fuck the people and this capital!" Jessica exclaimed, her face reddening. "My children come first and these people couldn't care less about them."

"That may be true, but that does not help you escape your responsibility as the wife of the First, and a lady of this House."

"*This House*?" baffled Jessica, almost laughing through it. "You say such as if you have been part of this House for a lifetime. It has been a few meager days, Allura. By some strange spell alone you now care for the wellbeing of *this House*?"

"I do care for the wellbeing of this House, and have since the second I said my vows in marriage to your nephew, and the moment I became *your* House lady." Allura took another sip, her smile impossible to mask. "I think that you forget that House Pratt as it once existed is no more. When Nicolas and Christina signed their names to that document, they understood the consequences of that action. They forfeited their rightful claim as the House name and agreed to the union of a new nation. That nation would be ruled by the new House lord, Jerryn Pratt, and his wife, Allura Pratt.

"Like it or not, I am *the* House lady. You are nothing but the wife of the First to me. Your daughters stay. And if it comforts you any, I will have Joanna and her husband moved onto this floor as well to ensure their safety."

"To Shadow with that, you will not order me," softly breathed Jessica. "I will take my girls in the night, when you least expect it if I must. I will not stay here any longer than need be."

"If you flee with your children, I will have you rounded up as easily as the last batch of traitors to leave the capital."

Careful. No need to boast to her of your accomplishments. No need for her to know at all.

Jessica did not seem to notice her slip of the tongue. Instead she paced the room, fishing perhaps for some other way out of her current situation. But there was none. Jessica Pratt, once powerful and respected, was losing her luster along with the rest of the Pratts.

"This conversation is now over," announced Allura. "Return to your husband. Drink, eat, fuck, whatever it is that makes you happy. Let this thought of taking your daughters from the capital whisk away from your mind, never to return."

"And if it does not, Allura Pratt?"

Allura laughed some. "It will, Jessica Pratt, or you will find that tolerance is not one of my better virtues."

A gift passed down from mother to daughter.

--

Aldric . . . Dylinn . . .

It had not struck the First as odd, but it damn well should have. The fact that it had not up until now made him feel foolish. The Historian was the keeper of history, but in a way, he was more than that. Philip knew that along with the territory of recording events, secrets would be kept. It was part of what made the Kwyantin diplomatically immune. They did not meddle in the affairs of Amon. Silent observers, nothing more.

But why would Aldric and his apprentice not stay and record of the most intriguing changing of powers Amon has ever seen? Why, unless something far more interesting was happening elsewhere.

Philip needed eyes in the north and he knew that all too well now. The problem being was who to trust? Gillar? His trust might have been on shaky grounds, but he would not betray his home country, at least not for the First. If Orpay had remained, it would be possible to tap the Guild. Without direct contact with him, it would be pointless. The council, namely the throne itself owed the Guild money for the fruitless ordeal with the Imperial Army on the coast. And until those funds were paid, asking for favors would be like pissing in the Flame Realm.

It would have to be someone in the Imperial Army. For a brief moment in time, he still possessed the power to command them . . . to an extent. He would not need the approval of the council to send a solitary soldier northward in order to surmise the condition of Itopis and House Aylmer post assassination. The real question still remained, who to trust with that task?

Philip knew who and yet fought against every instinct possible. He would need to draft a letter, something official to give the soldier a reason to head north. From there, it was a collection of information only. The First moved toward his office with intent, but his door stood wide open as he approached.

As he turned inside, his brother sat on his expensive chair, his feet kicked on top of his imported desk. And why not? He was his elder after all.

"We need to talk," mumbled Nicolas.

To which the First could only chuckle. He moved across the room and sat down across from him. "Feels weird being on this side of my desk," Phillip noted.

"Feels equally as weird not being in control of my House any longer."

"To which you alone decided, brother," retorted the younger Pratt.

"I recall you agreeing to it somewhat. You know why I did it. And I will not have it mean nothing. I will not have this union be all for not because of fucking politics."

"But the marriage *was* politics, brother," the First commented. "Politics are fickle and unstable, and you damn well know that."

"Let me tell you what I know," started the elder Pratt. "You are going to figure something out. And you are going to make this happen."

"Make what happen? A crowning? Earth and Flame, Nick, it's not that easy."

Nicolas waved his finger to him. "I suggest you find a way. I have Christina breathing down my throat, that bitch Allura thinking she can command me, and now my children are at the mercy of Dehyllo. The time for complicated is done. The time for easy is upon us."

"Damn it, Nick, what do you want me to do?" pleaded Philip. "I just came from speaking with Afeon . . . *again*. He will not budge. He will not vote. Since he will not vote, we need to reach out to Dehyllo and request a new member for the council."

"And what happens when Lord Brocusk tells you to go fuck yourself?"

"At that point he would forfeit his claim to our country and we would treat him as any hostile force. We would have a unified front from all countries, including even the Guild. From there we would . . ."

"Enough!" Nicolas screamed, standing and slamming the palms of his hands against the desk. "No more politics! He has my children!"

"You don't know that!" Philip hollered back, on his feet now as well. "You are taking the word of a man we *know* not to trust. How do you know he does not just bait you, wanting you to engage war with him?"

"If that is his goal, he has accomplished it." Nicolas stood upright and straightened his tunic. "There were once days when we fought against our problems, brother. Remember the bandits that were holed up in the Uvull mines? Ah, glorious end to them. We rode in with reckless abandon, charging them without any idea how many hostages they had, without even asking for their demands. We filled those fucking caves with their blood. What happened to those days, Phil? Where are those men that led that charge?"

"They grew old," admitted the First. "Those days are over for us now."

"For you, maybe." His brother shrugged his shoulders. "I feel one good battle left in these bones."

"Don't be a fool, Nick."

"It's done. I have been away from Astrona far too long as it is. Maradyn and I ride back to Donovini at morning's break. Once home, I will gather the Astrona guard, stable boys, criminals, anything that breaths and ride north. I will meet with Dehyllo and get my children back or die."

"Oh, you will die. That is what you have chosen."

"Most certainly, if you do not get my son on the throne post haste. I left Jerryn specific instructions on what to do once crowned, namely in sending the army north to join me in combat."

"You are putting your life in the hands of politics that are out of my control, Nick."

"No, Phil," the elder retorted. "I am putting my life in *your* hands. And not just mine, but likely Edmond, Luther, and damn near everyone you know back home. At the end of the day, you are a Pratt. You may not live like the rest of us, you may have even forgotten how to. But you are still a Pratt. You will remember that before it's too late."

Nicolas was a fool, but still his brother nevertheless.

His morals or his family. The simplest decisions were often anything but.

--

Night crept through the capital building and something about darkness made even the bravest of souls second guess themselves. A sound from the corner, a creek from a door, a strange shadow cast against the torchlight. Each foolish in their own right, and yet all of them made Allura nervous while she followed Alex through the hidden dungeons of her new home.

She loved the games, loved the politics. Her move now was not about her impatience or her lack of understanding on how things were done. This was about setting things in motion, about getting done what First Pratt refused to do himself. Power dangled before her and she aimed to take it. If the First would not do what was within his ability, then it fell to her to take charge.

Christina did not know, nor did Nicolas or Jerryn. They all slept, and while they did, Allura made her move. Alex knew of the location of the dungeons. How he knew, she did not bother to ask. The man was like nothing she had known. Dangerous, silent, calculated. She did not trust him and would likely have him killed once the opportunity presented itself. If he were dead, no one would ever find out about their little sexual encounter on her wedding night, no one would find out the reason he killed that barkeep. But whether she liked it or not, she *needed* him. Until Allura claimed the throne, and perhaps a bit after even, she needed someone that could do a job without question, without hesitation. The problem came in his loyalty. Did he serve her or her mother? Or did he serve the highest bidder? Did he have standards and respect? Who was he really?

For the moment, he was the man that led her to the Second. And for the moment, that would have to do.

Alex took the torch from his hand and placed it against the sconce on the wall. He moved over the last cell and clanked against it with his sword a few times, then moved back toward Allura, giving her a nod as he walked by, allowing her privacy. She cautiously moved over to the cell, unsure of what exactly she expected to find. What she found was not surprising. Afeon had seen better days. He was thinner, his beard heavier, his hair fuller. He smelled of musk, he looked trodden, and yet still he sported the same, sadistic smile that she always remembered from her limited interactions with the Second.

"Allura Rowe . . . or Pratt now I suppose," he began, rubbing sleep from his eyes. "You caught me doing what most people do in the middle of the night, Lady Pratt. Sleeping. Only my bedroom is also my dining room, and my bathroom. A bit different from what you are accustomed to I would suppose."

"Perhaps now is not the time for witty banter," Allura claimed, her arms crossing before her. "Tomorrow you are going to die."

"But we barely know each other, Lady Pratt," followed the Second. "Seems a bit early for the hatred to have jumped to that finale."

"When you wake, someone will be here to cut out your tongue. Tomorrow you will stand before members of the court, members of my House, members of the Guild outside the west courtyard, and I will burn your body in front of everyone. I will show the evidence that Dehyllo has kidnapped Pratts, and I will place you in allegiance with him. Since you have no tongue, you will have nothing to say for yourself. After your body is nothing but ash, we will name Ursan as traitors to the throne and call for a vote without you. And then I shall take the Imperial Army and stomp your country into the ground."

Afeon smiled out of the side of his mouth. "Sounds like you got everything figured out. Why even bother waking me up then?"

"It is not the way I want this to happen. I give you one chance. Not to live, but to die with some form of honor. I promise that if you cast your vote in front of all that I gather tomorrow, I will leave your body intact and send it back to Ursan so that you may be buried with your people. I know what that means to you."

There stood a moment, a waver in his eyes at her proposition. The Ursan were all the same, so far as she could tell. They loved their land as if it bore gold coins from treetops. It meant everything to them to die with honor, and part of that was where their bodies rested when it was said and done. Allura, living so close to Ursan, spent much of her studies on their culture. Even savages such as the Ursan had minimum levels of esthetics, and part of that included respect for the fallen.

The First might have tried to speak to the Second as a man, and that was his ultimate mistake. Afeon might have dressed the part of a politician, but he was a barbarian like all the rest of his people.

"Your word means very little to me, you know this," said the Ursan.

"And yet you know that I speak the truth. I would much rather take the throne with your vote than by force. It would appease many people, including that dimwit First Pratt. It would be easier for me and would be better for Amon. But I will take this by force if I must. And once you're dead, I would honestly care very little about your body. I would be just as content to ship you home, so long as you aren't here any longer. It is easier for everyone."

"Except for me, I gather."

"A clean death versus burning you alive and kicking your ashes into the sands of Genethur." She shrugged. "It's easier for you as well, Second."

Another long pause took place between the two of them. "You could have said a great many things to me tonight, Allura Pratt. The First has spent quite some time pleading to me in different ways, as equals. You told it to me as it is. I am surprised you loathe the Ursan the way you do."

"I never said that . . ."

"You didn't need to. I can see it in the way you speak to me, as if I am inferior. But at least you spoke the truth to me. I am a dead man. If I wasn't one beforehand, Dehyllo all but sealed my fate. But to go home . . . it would mean everything to me."

"I promise it to you," she assured, and meaning it as well. She had some surprises left, for certain, but she took no pleasure in killing a man. Allura could only hope that in similar circumstances, someone would give her the opportunity to be buried on her own soil as well.

"I will cast my vote tomorrow, Lady Pratt. If you lie to me, I hope the gods are furious in retribution."

"The gods have left us, Second. Have you not heard?"

"They have fallen," he replied. "That does not mean they abandoned us."

As long as I have my throne, you can have your gods risen, fallen, upside down for all I give a shit.

"Then I shall see you in the morning, Second of Amon," she stated. "This will be over soon enough. You will be able to rest."

He said nothing. No witty retort, no grin. The Second of Amon only nodded once, then turned away, laying back down onto his bed. Maybe he understood better than most of the reality of his situation. How long can a man face death before he welcomed it?

She felt better about her meeting with Afeon. She felt . . . righteous.

--

Schill, yellow. Turitea, red. How do I still remember these things?

It was deep into the night, and a clear one at that. The kind of night that had the Twin Moons in full view, their light casting downward against the Vurid Sea, his mind reflecting on the former reasons for his late night escapades. It was strange how comfortable he was against the darkness. Certainly he was not alone; his guards still shadowing him discreetly. But his memories of Dylinn, the thought of her body against his . . . it was only part of his comfort with the night. He embraced the darkness because he lived so much of his life within it. Meetings with the Divide, overseeing tasks needed by King Aylmer . . . the Twin Moons watched, always watched.

If the fallen gods Turitea and Schill truly were observing, and if the Twin Moons were indeed their eyes . . . they had witnessed all of his worst exploits.

I barely like who I even am. But I know that I am not a wicked man. I wonder what people will think of me when I am in the dirt. The man that did all he could to save Amon, or the last man in charge when it burns to the ground.

The side door opening, he turned and watched Isani slowly approach, his eyes a bit cautious. His head recently shaven clean, and his red beard hung low and braided together. Philip could not say who the man was before he joined the Imperial Army, but it remained unlikely that the multiple scars on his face were from practicing within his squadron.

"It's apparently the perfect night for secret meetings, First Pratt," the Second General announced. "My men informed me that Lady Allura Pratt took a casual and short visit to the dungeons on this same night."

"Not unexpected, General." *But regrettable. Time is shorter than I thought.* "Moves are being made."

"It is a bit of a puzzle, is it not? Give me a sword any day over this nonsense. I do not know how you bear all of the games, First."

"Early years, I hated it. Middle years, I adapted. Later years, I worked it. Now? I just expect it and do what I can to stay ahead of it."

"And is this one of those times, First Pratt? Do you look to stay ahead of things?" questioned the general.

"In a way, General Brocusk."

Isani gazed away from Philip, looking toward the vastness of the ocean. "I have heard a rumor of my cousin. He may have admitted to kidnapping members of your family. Are you permitted to confirm or deny those rumors?"

Philip shrugged to the inquiry. "You will find out regardless, General. Yes, Dehyllo has taken two Pratts. Before you ask, he did not say which two. It is believed that he has Rayden and Katlynn, or he could have none for all we know."

"Not Dehyllo," mentioned Isani. "My cousin is a bastard for sure, but not a liar. If he claims to have two Pratts, then he indeed has two Pratts."

"Truth or otherwise, he has placed himself and Ursan in a difficult spot. He asks for war or submission, and you know which he would rather have. Outside of that, he is placing some of us in . . . impossible situations."

"There is little need to speak around the subject, First Pratt. My cousin has committed a crime against the throne. You have done all that you can do to protect Ursan and my family name. Dehyllo has done the opposite. And as I have told you before, I am part of the Imperial Army. I took my oath quite seriously when I made that decision."

"So then I might . . ."

"Can I speak freely, First Pratt?"

Philip exhaled a chuckle. "It has never stopped you before, Second General."

"You are left with few options. It has been months now since we have had a king and I know that Dehyllo and Afeon gave you their word to support the union of Rowe and Pratt. You have done what most men could not do."

"That being?" queried the First.

"Shown patience," was his reply. "Do you know how many men in similar situations would have simply seized the throne for themselves? To be honest, First Pratt, when I handed you the executive powers after the assassination, I half expected you to do so. Instead, you have shown honor."

"I am pleased you think such," Philip commented. "Now are you going to ask me why I called you out here this late at night?"

Isani's hands opened up and extended, a grin on his face. "My assumption is that this has something to do with Allura's late night meeting."

"It may. But only a part of it. You must understand this letter that your cousin has sent is damning, and not just for his name, but for Ursan. If a war takes place, I fear that those in charge will not hold back on their prejudice."

"You mean my last name."

But Philip shook his head. "I mean against Ursan."

His eyebrows rose. "I am part of the army, First Pratt."

"And I fear that will not save you, General Brocusk."

"And yet, this meeting is only in part of that."

"I will not lie to you. Part of the reason is that I fear something from another front. We are so focused on one side of the country, so focused on Dehyllo that I am afraid that we are missing something even more important. And so I entrust you with a task, one that will get you away from the capital before it's too late."

Isani crossed his arms. "I do not need saving, First Pratt. If Allura Pratt looks to have me killed because I am an Ursan, or I am a Brocusk, I will accept that. I *am* an Ursan. I would die with my honor intact, which is all that truly matters in this world."

"I am not doing this to save you, General. I am doing this because you are the only person I entrust."

The Second General laughed out loud for a moment. "A sad day when a Pratt must trust a Brocusk. What task is so important that you would ask it of me personally?"

"I ask that you find the Historian of Amon."

Isani did not even bother to flinch on his statement.

"Find the Historian?" the general repeated. "The Historian is not known for needing to be found."

"No, but he is also not known for being missing."

There stood a short pause between the men.

"And you think he should be here," Isani noted.

"Why wouldn't he?"

"And . . . his disappearance might have something to do with what exactly?"

The First smiled. "That, Second General, is exactly the task I have set upon you. You are to uncover both where Aldric is and why he has left."

"Well . . . it's a big world. Any suggestions on where I might start looking?"

"North," Philip advised. "More specifically Fallneese."

"Fallneese is a big country too," Isani stated.

"That it is." Philip shrugged. "I would start in the capital, Itopis."

--

I know much of fear. I have hunted greater beasts than Draywolves in my time, and even so, I can clearly remember my stomach drop the first time I came face to face with one. Just a boy in my father's House at the time, I damn near needed a change of pants. But you grow from the experience. Soon, you accept it. At some point, you embrace it. Fear becomes a drug, something you need to get you through the mundane life of ruling.

But it never goes away. I don't care what anyone tells you. Fear never goes away. You just start liking it, that's all.

-- Edfeld Rowe, House Lord of Argonus

XIX

She stood within the room, even though she kept her presence hidden. Brief moments Aldric would catch a blur of movement or hear a soft step somewhere behind him. All of these things were done on purpose. All of them were her way of letting the Historian know that she remained in charge. She would speak with him when ready, she would answer him when she felt so inclined.

Now, however, was apparently not the time.

Dylinn promised the Historian nothing save for the fact that she would allow him to speak with this shadow. She could not, however, promise him that he girl would ever respond. For a week straight he stood alone in the House lady's hall late in the evenings, the girl in the room with him, and for a week straight he asked basic questions. He asked for her name, for her origins, of the Shadow Realm, of House Aylmer, of her age, of her family. Each question was answered with the identical response.

Silence. Only this night he decided to ask no questions.

Aldric stood, still and speechless, listening to her. Her exhales, her steps, all the signs of her impatience, her frustration with him. It did not help answer any of his questions, but at least he was garnering a reaction of some sort. There was a breaking point in all mortals, and even she was human . . . or a reasonable facsimile. And if she would not respond to questions, perhaps she would respond to the lack of them. The annoyance of being forced to visit with the Historian day in and day out without words might do far more than the pestering of inquires as before.

So no questions on this day. He grew tired of hearing himself speak as it were. Instead he stood for only a few minutes, a few uncomfortably long minutes, then turned about and left the hall. He knew she watched him leave with heavy interest. Perhaps she wondered if he was now done with his questions. Perhaps she wondered if he would come back at all.

No matter what, the shadow would be thinking of him. And that was more progress than Aldric had made before.

--

"I have a pretty good feeling about this one," Erian claimed, tossing the book across the length of the table.

The library stood as their permanent lodgings during their imprisonment, and while equally as uncomfortable now as ever, it became . . . less irritable. *Perhaps when you lay your head down long enough, anything begins to feel a bit like home. Either that, or maybe just easier for people like us who barely have a home to begin with.* He sat down where the book had slowed and stopped, opening the page. It had the same look as the rest: journals of experiments.

"What differs this from the rest?" he inquired.

"I think we found our girl," was his apprentice's reply.

"Our girl?" repeated the Historian. "As in our assassin?"

He nodded, then waved his hand to the book, imploring the elder Kwyantin to dive in. And so flipped a few pages in and began.

. . . heading for Qeel. The girl we are looking for is named Niavona. She is supposed to be young and immensely talented from what we have heard. We cannot pass on this, despite it breaking our rules. Lord Aylmer was clear that we

are to only experiment on adults and the willing. I have a feeling this will be neither. She will . . .

"So we know this is recent, inside of two centuries," noted Aldric. "Aylmer ruled for seven generations of kings. Well, eight if you count the boy."

Erian sighed. "Just flip some more pages and read."

. . . younger than I thought. She is fifteen and does not speak to us at all. Certainly a strange one, and I am beginning to wonder if this is such a good idea. Her father seems in favor of us having her, but the mother wants us out of Qeel. I can't blame her. We are about to take her child from her.

I don't feel comfortable with this, in more ways than one. But I don't think my opinion is going to matter much. If Lyston wants to take this girl, then we will take her, whether the mother, father, or the gods themselves have said otherwise.

I understand him, because I have said the same thing. We have been on the cuffs of success many times, only to fail due to the strength of our volunteers. But none of them were masters of their Realm. None were extraordinarily powerful.

But Niavona is something else. Niavona may be a prodigy with her gift.

Tomorrow I will see about . . .

Aldric flipped through some more pages.

. . . wasn't much else we could do. I still can't believe it, and I think I have made myself ill. We just took a girl from her home. In the middle of the night we just went in and took her. Why would she even help us now? How can I even look myself in the mirror after this?

Aldric gazed up to his apprentice. "Fill in the gaps for me. This Niavona girl . . . who was she?"

"Just a girl from Qeel. She seemed like a typical, misguided teen searching for herself, and doing what she could to ignore her gift. These men from Itopis . . . they just took her."

The Historian nodded. "So what happened to this girl?"

"They took her back here. This is where she slept. They forced her to use her gifts, to open the Realms. She refused often. And when she refused, they refused to feed her. It was torture, Aldric, plain and simple."

"And why do you think this girl is *our* girl?"

"Because," Erian stated with confidence, "they sealed this room from the ordeal. It sounds like this was the end of the line from their experimenting. She might have been the last one. And Dylinn did say they uncovered her."

The Historian raised an eyebrow. "What happened?"

"I think you should ask her, Aldric," concluded his apprentice.

--

The mornings all began in similar fashion. Erian was left behind in the library where he would spend his entire day reading. Aldric moved back up the stairs, escorted per usual, through several halls and into Dylinn's den where he would eat breakfast with the former queen of Amon and discuss current affairs. Strange, as he still enjoyed this part of his day. Not the imprisonment, not the company, but the information. Aldric felt crippled without the knowledge, without the freedom to travel where he needed to be. His duty to his people was to record the histories of mankind . . . and sadly that was all that he knew to do. Without the knowledge, Aldric was naked, useless.

Dylinn waited for him patiently, sitting on one side of the bar counter, a plate of eggs and biscuits awaiting him. As usual, she did not dive into her food until the Historian sat down across from her and acknowledged her.

"Lady Aylmer," he stated.

She smiled, picked up a fork and motioned for him to do the same.

"Good morning to you, Historian. Have you gotten any further in your talks with my shadow?"

"No," he admitted. "But I do believe my apprentice has found her identity. I am eager to my next talks with her."

Dylinn barely looked interested in his revelation. "Do you truly believe that knowing her name is going to help you break through?"

"You never told me what helped you break through. How did you get her to do the things she has done for you?"

"Eat, Historian," was her answer.

And so he did. He began to consume the meal before him steadily, patiently, quietly.

"Last word from the capital," she started up, "has not changed. Without the courts intact, they cannot crown Jerryn Pratt. First Pratt still makes his attempt to convince Afeon otherwise, but it has not gone well so far. Other than that, Historian, there is little else to report in the world. I am attempting to get word from the situation on the east coast, but I have not heard from my sources within the Guild, which worries me. They are normally timely in their reports. Donovinian scouts tell me the drought continues, and Edmond is looking to remove men from the mines in order to work the canals in attempts to irrigate more water from Argonus."

"And what of your situation?" Aldric pried.

Dylinn smiled. "The men from the Guild have started to arrive, adding to the abundance of men coming in from the countryside. Good news, we are training and becoming a sizable force. Bad news, I cannot hide this many soldiers for long. Soon I will be questioned for assembling a force of this size. Thankfully, with the courts and the council crippled, no one is paying much attention to us or the east coast. All eyes are intent and focused on the capital and on Ursan. I am half tempted to seize control now while they are still in disarray."

"What prevents you?"

"First Pratt," Lady Aylmer replied. "He still has control of the Imperial Army. If I march south, he will cease all talks of succession until after the battle and he will embrace his executive power. If he won that war, it would unify all votes towards him. The public would love him. Nothing to satisfy the masses like bloodshed. From there, there would be no more talks of who would be king. They would crown him. And of course if I beat the First in battle, I would be a tyrant, a woman that charged in and claimed the throne by force. The public would hate me, the courts and council would not support me, and I would be killed swiftly and decisively. No, I need a silent battle, one that can be won quickly and with the least amount of bodies. Thus I need the army oblivious to us, and focused elsewhere."

"Ursan," replied the Historian.

"Or the east coast for all I care. So long as they leave. I need their forces deployed, allowing me an avenue to strike."

"Ironic, is it not? You need them to crown a king just so you can dethrone him."

"The line between noble and wicked is often times blurred. As much as you have seen, you should know this better than most."

"How do you really expect this to end?" Aldric questioned. "Do you really believe you will take the throne and make all of the changes you desire?"

"Do you care, Aldric, one way or the next? How many lives do you have in that head of yours? How many people have you known that died, and known their children and they died, and so on and so forth? How many times until we are just a blur to you?"

"Your lives may be quick," he answered, "but powerful. I remember them all to the finest of details. Do I care? Of course I do. I live on this world just the same as you."

"No, no you don't." She placed her fork down onto her plate and gazed intently at him. "I am no longer hungry. Will you walk the yards with me?"

"I do not believe I have much say in the matter."

To which Lady Aylmer flashed a half grin. "You always have a say, Historian. It just doesn't always amount to much."

--

Outside Itopis was amazingly organized and flowed as would an ocean to the shore. The blacksmiths hammered, the tailors sowed, the officers commanded, the soldiers trained. Each man different from the next, some of which Aldric knew or had met before in his many trips to Fallneese, but each of these unique men shared the common goal to reclaim the throne of Amon for Dylinn Aylmer. They worshipped her as if she were the vessel of the fallen gods. Ignorant to demons that plagued her, to the evils she committed behind locked doors, her servants stopped whatever task that stood at hand and smiled genuinely, bowed heavily.

The people loved her.

"Do you think they would love you so if they knew your exploits?" whispered Aldric to her as she nodded in respect to everyone that did the same for her.

"We are well beyond the point of return," she stated back in a hushed tone. "Even if you revealed my truths, they would no longer believe you. We have come too far in our venture to turn around. These people were promised blood, and I shall give it to them."

"And what if they find out the greater truth?"

Dylinn turned in bewilderment. "And the greater truth being what exactly?"

"That you have no intentions of taking these men to war."

To which she laughed some. "Oh I have every intention of *taking* them to war. I just have little intention of *using* them for war. How long will these men morn for the lack of excitement in exchange for a plethora of life? What happens at the end is all that truly matters."

"You cannot think that this will be a storybook ending, with you once again on the throne." Aldric shrugged. "There have been many names to sit upon the throne, many Houses to make claim to the power. But never has there been a case where a family name lost royalty only to reclaim it. It has never been done."

"So you suggest I am folly in my decision? You think it impossible?"

"I think it's improbable," he replied. "Your very strategy now weighs entirely on the play of others. Will Jerryn gain the throne? Will he drive his Imperial Army to war with Ursan? Will Orpay keep his end of the bargain and ensure the voting is in your favor?"

"I always play the odds," Dylinn responded. "A dangerous game, certainly, but what do I have left in life to lose, Historian? No children, no husband, I stand alone without a legacy to follow in my footsteps. All I have left is my country. Yes, if my acts are uncovered here, if the Imperial Army is sent for me, I will die as a traitor, and you can write of me as such in the histories. But if I am victorious, Fallneese will prosper from it."

"If you lose they shall crumble. A risky game to play, Lady Aylmer."

"Fallneese will be fine with or without me," remarked Dylinn. "The courts or the council would place a new House name in charge, stricter rules would follow, but Fallneese would remain. At the end of the day, it's just land, just a piece of the ground. And that's the beautiful thing about ground, Historian. It's always underneath your feet."

Men stopped and waved, some approached and greeted the former queen. But there stood little mistake that she remained the focus of thousands of eyes. Her movement commanded respect, the tone of her voice demanded action. Dylinn understood leadership better than most that had taken the throne before her. No one loved Yelium Aylmer II or his father, for as much as that was worth. And when they died, no one spent much time mourning, no one spoke of lifting statues in their name. They simply died, and the populace only looked for the next. Dylinn grasped the concept of popularity. Certainly there stood more than just fame to rule a kingdom . . . but when starting a war, it could not hurt.

Each day they walked the plains outside the walls of Itopis, and each time the army grew in size. Men and women began surfacing regularly, some for the combat but others only to aid. It took an extensive amount of food to feed thousands of soldiers, and cooks and merchants were needed, along with plenty of livestock. Several farmers must have lifted their entire barns and brought them for the journey based on how many creatures grazed within makeshift corrals. And as more Fallneesians arrived, the deeper the formations grew, the longer it took to make the entire distance to meet all of the new arrivals.

The Guild set up their own camp in the rear, a bit obvious in their distance from the rest of Dylinn's people. Unlike those that they passed in order to get here, only one paid the approaching House lady and Kwyantin any mind, a lighter skinned Fallneesian. This Guild member was mixed with something other than Fallneese, which was rather taboo anywhere else outside of the Guild. He seemed experienced, maybe in his mid-thirties, and basically a giant stack of meat. Built like statue, muscles on top of other muscles, and a look of no-nonsense on his face, the Guild member approached nonchalantly.

"Lady Aylmer, I presume," he claimed. "My name is Draven. I'm in charge here amongst these men."

"Well met, Draven." Dylinn extended her hand and the Guild member accepted it. "My guest here is Aldric."

"The Historian. We've met before. An honor, as usual." His arm waved back to his men. "We have just under two thousand to add to your support, Lady Aylmer. I believe that was the arrangement you had with Orpay."

"Very true, Draven. I also requested a more . . . specialized unit as well."

"That you did." He took a step closer and brought his voice down some. "And not all of my men know of this, so it would be best if we continued to speak of such things between us. I am not only in charge of these men, but I am also the one to lead your infiltration unit."

Dylinn crossed her arms and returned a stoic glare. "We will need to discuss things in thorough detail to ensure our plans are aligned."

"Agreed, Lady Aylmer. But we have only just arrived and are still setting up camp. I will need to report to one of your officers so that we might get in on the mix of work around here, as well as some meals."

"Certainly. I can have . . ."

"No offense, milady, but I can handle things," calmly stated Draven. "We are going to be looked at as outcasts as is, the last thing I would want to be labeled as would be a favored outcast. Guild or not, we are men no different from those in that camp, and we may yet fight side by side. We will need to build a rapport."

Lady Aylmer did not seem offended by his boldness, rather surprised instead. In either case, she softly shrugged to him. "Have it your way. If you receive any backlash, I expect you to let me know. I need to be informed of my own people."

"That will not be a problem."

"And I will want you at dinner tomorrow night, to discuss our strategies. Bring only those you trust completely."

Draven harbored the beginnings of a grin. "You can't trust anyone completely, save yourself."

"Then come alone."

"Very well, milady. I shall leave you to your duties, and I shall continue mine here. It was a pleasure meeting you."

"Indeed." Dylinn let Draven turn and walk a few steps away before calling back out to him. "Were you born here, Draven? In Fallneese?"

The young Guild member turned to face her again. "No. My father was born here in Molovand, if he was to be believed. My mother from Obline in Donovini. I was born in great city of Prillian."

"So your father Fallneesian, your mother Donovinian."

"And as you can imagine, Prillian is of the few places in this world where I am not judged by my parent's decisions."

"You will find no prejudice from me or my House. But tell me, being part of two different people, where do your loyalties lie between that blood?"

"Exactly where it should," he responded. "With the Guild. And more specifically, with myself."

Draven bowed his head a tad, then turned about again and walked back to his camp.

--

At dinner they sat once again inside the den adjacent to the throne room, his mind on anything but the food before him. He ate because it was required, both to stay alive and to appease Lady Aylmer. But his thoughts remained focused on speaking again to the shadow. It had been the same for days, with forced conversations and three meals a day, meetings with this person and that. Aldric was no more or less the same as the naked slave girl that Dylinn kept at her side from time to time: ultimately just a trophy on display. But the Historian paid little mind to Lady Aylmer. He endured with his head held high, all to learn more about the mystery assassin.

"You seem distracted this evening," claimed Dylinn in between chewing.

The Historian gazed down to the young, naked girl. The chain around her neck remained loose and she could easily slip out of it if desired. It was there for show, to represent Dylinn's power over her. She was frightened, but not worried. Aldric could tell that she knew that she could die at any point, that should Dylinn no longer need her services or grew annoyed with her, she would be replaced. But so long as she did as commanded and obeyed, there remained a place for her. Chained, a slave, but alive and needed.

He was no more or less than her.

"What is her name?"

Dylinn smirked as she placed her fork down. "What is it with you and names lately?" She pulled on the chain a bit. "Go ahead, answer him."

The girl looked up at the Historian. "Talia."

"And how old are you, Talia?"

"Nineteen," was her response.

Lady Aylmer returned to her plate of food. "Hopefully you are satisfied now."

He of course was not. "Your life was a difficult one, I know. But I do not believe that this is who you are."

Dylinn rolled her eyes some at his statement. "Did you believe me capable of doing the things I have done to Yelium, either of them?"

"No," Aldric claimed. "So much so that I left Corovium at a time of disarray to uncover if my fears were justified. I pitied you when you told me the truth of Yelium's son. It added to a life that I know has taken its toll. But does that mean that you would lash out onto others? What crime has this girl committed to deserve such a treatment?"

Dylinn tugged on the chain. "Answer him."

Talia turned away from his eyes. "I killed a man."

"Tell him why."

"Vengeance," was the girl's answer. "My brother was framed and taken from me for crimes he did not commit."

"The Historian of Amon is not interested in your propaganda, slave," interrupted Dylinn. "Her brother was a criminal, one of our most notorious ones at that. She believed him framed when he was finally apprehended and sentenced, but she was a child at the time. Memory is a funny thing for us, Historian. For you, you remember everything as you see it. For the rest of us mortals, we remember things how we want to remember them. For her, she believed so passionately that her brother was innocent that she grew up with the premeditated decision to kill the one who she though responsible for her brother's death."

"I thought my brother was dead," Talia stated.

"Silence," snapped Dylinn. "You speak when given permission. And yes, she believed her brother dead for his crimes when she decided to commit her own. Needless to say, I had a soft spot for the girl and had her removed from execution myself. Upon my return she humbly agreed to be my slave. Work in my estate and sex with me is better than the execution block I would presume, yes?"

"Yes, milady," Talia responded.

"And her brother?" the Historian inquired.

"Alive, in a manner of speaking. He is . . . serving a different type of sentence. But they will never see each other again. She is my prisoner for life, and he is doing the same elsewhere. So you see, Historian? You assume that I have simply chained up some random girl and made her a sex slave. But in reality I rescued her. You have become vastly more judgmental in your old age."

"Well I suppose you truly are merciful. But does all of this rectify any of the damage done to you?"

Not your wisest choice of questions.

Again Dylinn placed down her utensils. "Earth and Flame, Historian. My decision to keep you alive waivers and you ask me questions to poke at my resolve?"

"Why *do* you keep me alive?"

"To help me!" screamed Lady Aylmer. She placed her hands through her hair and took a few deep breaths to calm herself. "We do not walk the yards in front of my walls for the exercise. My men see you and it makes them feel just. The Historian of Amon here at such a pivotal time in our history shows them that what we fight for is pure and right."

"Despite the fact that I am here as your prisoner?"

Dylinn flashed a grin to him. "All they need to know is that the men we face are wrong, evil, and deserving to be purged. They do not need to know the political side of the fighting. You know as well as anyone that there are no right sides to a conflict. There are only sides."

"If there were right sides, you would not be on it," Aldric bravely retorted.

"To Shadow with your opinions, then. I suppose you believe the Pratts are upstanding and moral people that *deserve* the throne. They are willing to do whatever it takes to sit upon that wooden piece of shit, just like me, just like Dehyllo, just like Orpay, just like the Rowes. It is no different, only perspective. And for you, your gift to me is moral to my men, and what do you get in return? The most important person in all of Amon. I give you a creature that might possibly have all of the answers that you so desire."

"I believe her name is Niavona," started the Historian.

"Who cares what her name is?" stammered Lady Aylmer. "Your infinite amount of knowledge and all you have so far is her fucking name? For years I thought that stories of people that could actually cross over were stories told to scare children. I didn't *actually* believe that they could exist. And as you have been able to tell, this House has spent generations trying to create someone that can. What if they succeeded? Imagine what this girl has seen, what she can tell us. She has been to the other side!"

"Which is forbidden," he added.

"And neither you nor I made this girl cross over. That sin fell upon others before us, and perhaps they have paid the price for that in the next life. But why not try to find gain from this situation?"

"What do you think I have been doing?"

"Not enough," Dylinn stated, pointing harshly toward him. "Find out what she is. Find out what she knows."

"And what is your interest in all of this, besides curiosity?"

To which she shrugged her shoulders. "Better to know the killer inside your house than to not, I suppose."

You look to create others. You can hide your intentions all you wish, but if you could have an army of assassins like this girl, what foe could stand before you? What foe would want to, for that matter?

What makes you think I would bother telling you the secrets this girl has even if she told me? No, Dylinn, I would take my knowledge and die before I hand over the world to you.

Unless that's not it at all. Unless I have your intentions completely wrong. Unless you are just as frightened of this girl as I am.

--

Back in the main attendance hall, Aldric waited patiently for the shadow to reveal herself. She might have been there watching, or perhaps she had yet to arrive. It was difficult to decipher. A shadow by every definition of the word, the girl moved about with ease and without detection. An enigma, at least through his eyes. But Aldric was a patient man. *When you get to be over eight hundred years old, you better be patient at the very least.*

Through the corner of his eyes he could sense movement, subtle but there nonetheless. She did as commanded, showing to these little meetings as Dylinn had asked of her. But that was the extent of her obedience. All the books, all the information available to him, and nothing remained as valuable as this girl. The trick had become on how to harvest that information.

"Does the name Niavona mean anything to you?"

He could feel her presence move up beside him in a rush, nothing more than to show her power, nothing more than to display how quickly she could kill.

"Why won't you give up already, tall one?" she finally questioned. "Day in, day out, you ask me questions that I don't answer. Why don't you just go away?"

"I am a prisoner here," he replied. "I cannot just go away. So I will be back here every day to speak with you until you answer my questions."

"Or until I kill you."

There stood no humor in her tone. Idle threats were beyond her, as it would seem. "I suppose that would be one solution to both of our problems. I'd prefer one slightly less final than death." He turned to his left but the girl moved before he could see her. Again, he felt her behind him. "Niavona. Is that your name?"

Silence.

Aldric began to pace the room. "My apprentice read of a girl with that name, born in Qeel. She had exceptional ability in opening the Shadow Realm, and volunteered to aid in the research of developing that skill here Itopis."

"I was no volunteer."

"So then that is your name? It is a beautiful name, Niavona."

He waited a few, long seconds for her to respond. "I have not heard that name since I was a child."

"What do you remember from your childhood?"

"Almost nothing," was her answer. "My memory is not like yours, tall one. Live a hundred years, forget a hundred things. There is no face to my parents, no names either. If I had a last name, I no longer know of it."

"How old are you?"

"I don't know that either."

There was sadness in her tone, but honesty. "What did they do here?"

"You know what they did, tall one. But if it appeases you, and forces you to end your tireless questioning, I will speak of it. They kidnapped people here, mostly children. Children were easier to get, both young and not developed enough in their skill to fight back. Some were given willingly, though, and I felt worse for them. To succumb to what they did to us on top of knowing that their parents gave them up . . . it was difficult for them to shoulder."

"How many were with you here when they took you?"

"Maybe seven or eight locked away in that dungeon, each with the ability to open the Shadow Realm. Prisoners, all the same as you."

"So why only the Shadow Realm? Why not . . ."

"Power," she interrupted. "I guess they used Druids and Pyromancers before, but they were having little success in their experiments. Most crossed and never returned. Those that actually returned were never quite the same. But Shadow . . . they were having better fortune with Shadowmancers. They could cross and return quicker. They could analyze information easier with them. And so . . . that's why the Shadow Realm. They made us open and cross over. Only seconds to start. But seconds to them was hours for us. Then after a time it became a minute. Then minutes. Then an hour, and so forth. Some never returned from the first time. Others were lost after the second or third time. Spending hours in Shadow is like . . . it's like nothing you can ever understand, tall one. Can you open any Realms?"

Aldric shook his head. "My people are not gifted with the ability."

Niavona let out a single chuckle to that comment. "If you say so, tall one."

He found that comment curious, but quickly moved back to the subject at hand. "Tell me, what is on the other side?"

"Darkness," answered the girl. "And within that darkness, madness. It felt as if a million roaches crawled upon the surface of my flesh, sadistic laughter in my ears, the sounds and the cold . . . it was unbearable. Seconds felt like lifetimes. And there was pain. So much pain. Like knives puncturing your eyes."

"But this torture from the Shadow Realm . . . it was all mental?"

"Oh it was real, tall one. This was no dream, no imagination. The pain and torment were endured. The mutilation and penetrations were endured. When you returned, so did your body in the condition it left, but that did not erase what was done to you on the other side. I do not know if evil exists, tall one. Such things are for religion. But the other side . . . it will make you disbelieve in the gods. No gods would create such a world."

"So if the pain felt was real, how did anyone endure it?"

"They did not. I did, only because I embraced madness. Those that were with me fought against it. Not me, tall one. They screamed, and cried, and fought. Some let the Realm swallow them completely, never to return. Others simply refused to return to Shadow and no manner of torture would ever force them to return. They thought death here in this Realm was far better than what they faced going back into Shadow. And I agree. And there were others still that went completely insane and were deemed useless and thus were killed."

"What kind of torture could they use to make you cross?"

Niavona shifted places again, moving to his right, still remaining out of sight. "They would not feed you, days at a time. Sometimes they would rape you, over and over again. Some days they would lose their creativity and just pull back toenails. That was always an effective way to make us go. We succumbed to torture and did what they asked to only receive a different kind of torture from the other side. I cried every night for some time. I cannot remember how long. Every day of torture blends into the next. But I began to learn how to survive in Shadow. I accepted the voices, I accepted the pain, and I no longer fought against whatever evil lie in wait on the other side. I let them do what they desired willingly. Eventually hours could turn into days, and I spend as much time on the other side as I did on this side. The researchers here thought I was special. I was the only one to survive because I was so much more powerful. It had nothing to do with the strength of my gift, but everything to do with the strength of my resolve."

Aldric crossed his arms, remained motionless for a moment. "And so they succeeded in creating someone that could cross Realms with ease."

"No," Niavona remarked to his surprise. "They succeeded in creating a girl that could live in Shadow. I was no more powerful than when we started. In fact, I was likely weaker for it."

"I'm not sure I understand."

"Neither did they." She came into view, or what he could see of her. Niavona stood before him, but she was more like mist than a body. It explained why he had difficulty focusing on her before within the shadows of the room. How could the eyes focus on something so translucent? "I went from success to failure quickly. I knew they were likely to dispose of me at some point, so I spent more time in the Shadow Realm, longer than I had ever before. I *wanted* to be this creature they wanted. To not only cross the Realm of Shadow, but to cross them all. If I could just find a way to do it, I would be the most powerful person in Amon. It was all that I had left to live for. How could I have endured everything that I had for nothing? How could I just be some girl with incredible willpower, but not the girl with incredible power? How fair would life be if that were true?"

Aldric sighed heavily. "You should know well enough that life is anything but fair."

Niavona remained quiet for a few breaths, moving about, perhaps gathering her words. "I had thought for many years that to open the way into the Realms was like opening a door. You crack that door and grab what you need, then quickly close the door behind you. Enough to feel the exhilaration of the power but not long enough to find the pain and madness. But I was wrong. The door does not open into another room. It opens into a hallway first."

"Again, I don't understand."

"The door, tall one. It opens and shuts, but there is a place in between. The smallest of gaps, nearly impossible to see, and the only reason I could was because I crossed over so often that I could feel the space in between our worlds. And then I realized something that not even these people that experimented on me knew. The key to traveling between Realms was never to cross over and return. That gained nothing. But there remained a space between the Realms, a place where you can exist within both . . . that is the beginnings of what they should have sought all along."

Aldric gazed at the fog like appearance of the girl and began to comprehend. "It is what you are doing right now. Like some kind of purgatory."

"Yes, in a way," she confirmed. "When someone reaches out to touch the Realms, *any* Realm, there is a space between this world and the next. It is a space that you can physically visit. And within that space, I learned of a new kind of ability. I gained all the powers from the Shadow Realm without the madness, all the physical interactions with this world without the body. Here I require no sustenance, no sleep. I cannot die. Here I am a true immortal. You cannot kill what does not exist within your world . . . and I do not exist."

The Historian moved up to her, and she allowed him to do such. His hand extended to the mist and passed through, only wavering about like ripples in water.

"Can you return to our world?" asked Aldric. "Can you return to your body?"

"Not any longer. My body is in a strange kind of stasis. No matter that I am not within this world of existence, time cannot be altered or deterred. It passes all the same as with you or any other living being. So should I step back into this world from this space I exist in now, all of the time that transpired while I was gone would come over my body in a flash. And it has been countless years, tall one. I would be nothing but dust within seconds of breathing air for the first time."

"You traded your body for immortality?"

"It was not my choice." She moved closer, uncomfortably so. She might have been mist but she still had presence, she could still harden her body enough to kill, quite obviously.

"What happened when your captors found out about your new ability?"

"They never had a chance to find out what I was," Niavona replied. "Once I found this space, once I discovered what I was capable of within this void, I started killing them quickly. Could have killed them all, but . . . I was overtaken by vengeance that I fell to his intelligence."

"His?"

"Lyston. He was the one that took me. He was in charge. At the end of his miserable existence, he left me with the ultimate pain." She moved away, back into the shadows of the room in a blink of an eye. "He died saving others. He was a martyr, a hero. He deserved nothing, but was immortalized within these walls."

"How did it happen?"

"He lured me," she continued, pointing downwards, "back inside that library. I was killing anything and everything once I discovered that I had become everything they wanted, and everything they should have feared I would become. I killed everyone. The people that experimented on me. The guards that watched us. The people that served us slop for food. I was without remorse. But I saved Lyston for last. And so he knew that I would chase him down there in the library. He knew that I would come for him. And I did, like the fool I was. I chased him, but it was a trap. Once I found my way in there, his living assistants had rushed in and trapped us both inside that room. From there, they caved it in to ensure I couldn't find a way to dig myself out. We were trapped."

"Could you not just . . . move through the door and rubble?"

"Fool," she mumbled. "You don't understand how this works. I am in between worlds, tall one, and being such I am still shackled by many of the same rules of physics. I am quicker and stronger based on the power from the Shadow Realm, and despite my appearance I *still* have existence in this world, meaning I cannot just pass through objects. If that were the case, what exactly is keeping my feet to the floor? I have to open doors just as you do."

"So they trapped both of you in that room. I presume you killed off this Lyston?"

"No."

After she did not immediately follow up her reply, the Historian pressed further. "No?"

"No. I let him starve and dehydrate, just as he had done to the children for who knows how many years. Lyston begged for death, begged me to end his life. And so I did not give it to him. He lasted several days. They were . . . most unpleasant days for him."

"And so you remained in between the Realms all of that time until Dylinn uncovered you?"

"What other choice did I have? It was that or death. And before you ask, yes, I did often times think of death. It was just as easy as returning to Amon, stepping back from this void between Realms and I would have vanished from this world completely. But I didn't. And do you know why? Because I'm not done killing yet."

"But in the end . . . you *did* become what the researchers had wanted, am I right in that?"

"No," she said again, surprising him. "They wanted someone that could cross multiple Realms, tall one. I cannot do that. I have found this hallway, a way for me to live in both Amon and Shadow at the same time, and neither all the same. But I have not seen a way through Earth or Flame. But if there is a path through to them, it starts here. Of that I know for fact."

"But how can you know for certain?" he inquired. But the girl did not respond to that inquiry. "Well then tell me this. Do then do you work for Dylinn as a means to kill?"

"For now. The world is wicked. The way it has existed thus far has failed. Lady Aylmer looks to change that, so I will help her, so long as there are people to kill along the way."

"And what if her little plan fails, what then? What if she loses against the new king and queen and is hung for treason?"

"Then I will start killing people, tall one. And before you ask how many and who, I am not so sure. Every leader of every country, every councilor and court official, every Guild head, I will kill and keep killing until the emptiness inside me fills. And when enough blood has spilled and I feel Amon has changed because of it, I will return to Amon and breathe one righteous breath before I return to dirt."

And who could stop you? You cannot die.

And suddenly he had no more questions to ask.

"I think you have answered all that I care to know for now."

"Perhaps I can offer you one more bit of information," Niavona claimed. "It is the last bit that I have. You ask how I can be certain that the gateway to the other Realms is within this void? I am not alone here in this convergence."

"Someone else has found the same thing as you?" he baffled in horror.

"Yes."

"He is a Shadowmancer like you?"

"No, a Druid. He is much older than I, or so he claims. And he claims a great deal, tall one. He even speaks about you."

Aldric felt both fear and an eagerness about the girl's words. "Who is he?"

"He has never told me his name. Maybe he no longer remembers it, who know? But he told me to tell you something, and this is the only time I shall play his delivery girl, so listen closely. The answers you seek wait for you inside the vessel."

"But . . ."

What sense does that make?

". . . what vessel? Who or what is the vessel?"

"Maybe it's a riddle, tall one."

"There must be more."

"There is no more!" she yelped, as would a child throwing a tantrum. "At least not for you. He did make the mistake of telling me about your people, your kind. He told me what you are responsible for."

"*What?*"

"The Realms, tall one. You unleashed the Realms."

And there it is again, for the second time in my life. Jaa claimed the same thing . . . but what does it mean? I have spent seven hundred years looking for that answer since his death, seven hundred years and now I am left with this? The vessel? How am I to know what that means?

"And make no mistake, before my time is done in this life, I will kill every Kwyantin for your mistakes."

"Convenient for you that there are so few of us," answered the Historian.

"Ha, you really are a fool." She moved away, fading from his sight. "Do not come again, Historian. I have nothing else to tell you, and I do not want to start my rage against your kind just yet. Besides . . . they may yet do me the favor of helping out my cause. So much to purge, so little time."

"I don't even know what you mean?"

"Good," she snapped in response. "If you come tomorrow or any day after, I will kill you. We are done here, Aldric, Historian of Amon. We are done."

And then she was gone.

--

You don't need war to see tragedy. It's all around you. Every moment of every day. All you can do is surround yourself with love and those that you truly trust and hope that at the end of the day, you can smile.

Nowadays, I am finding it harder and harder to smile.

-- Maradyn Pratt, House Lady of Donovini

XX

Allura was alone in her bed and uncertain as to why that would be. Slowly she stood and glanced about her room, realizing quickly that it did not feel very familiar. The walls, the tapestries . . . in fact, Allura had no idea where she was.

"Hello?"

"Good to see you're awake."

As she spun about to the voice, she knew before meeting the dark eyes of the stranger it would be him. With blinding speed, the hired killer placed his hands around her throat and squeezed.

"Did you believe I would let you become queen today? No, not today. Someone as wicked as you deserves to die."

Her hands reached his arms, but he was far too strong for her to do much of anything. There could be no screaming, no crying. She faced her death from the bald Fallneesian, powerless to stop him. And his grin went from ear to ear.

"Nothing is for free, Queen Pratt."

No, she had not been foolish enough to believe so. And she had to admit, she had spent very little time thinking of the best ways for this life to end. But even if she had, this certainly would not have been it.

"Are you okay?"

The voice did not belong to the Fallneesian.

"Allura?"

And now woke from her dream, Jerryn hovering over her with mild concern on his face. Her hand reached her own forehead and was rewarded by a thick layer of sweat.

"Just a dream," she mumbled to her husband.

Just a dream. Just a stupid, fucking dream.

"You were crying," was his response.

Her eyes locked onto his. "I'm fine. What time is it?"

He stretched his arms over his head, his skinny bare chest displaying his ribcage during such. "Early," he yawned while speaking. "I was about to dispatch your lackey guard for breakfast."

"Not today," she replied, rubbing the sleep from her eyes. Allura stood and moved over to her robes, placing them over her exposed body. "We need to make an open appearance today for breakfast, as we will be joined by several court officials that I invited."

His face crinkled some in disapproval. "And I presume there is a reason for such?"

"I spoke with Afeon late last night." She paused, checking for some reaction from the House lord. When none returned, she moved to her closet and began riffling through her dresses. "Today you will become king of Amon."

And then after a delayed reaction, the reality sunk in for her husband. "Say again?"

"Afeon has agreed to declare you as the next king of Amon in a rather public display today. The council will be present, along with several key members of the courts. So we need you dressed as a young king would dress, and appear as one should appear. We need prestigious and refined."

"I think I am about to be sick," muttered Jerryn.

Ah, the true sign of a leader. Vomit.

Despite her thoughts, she strode over and stroked his dark hair with one hand, the other rubbing one of his shoulders steadily. "Not every day that you find out that you are going to be the leader of the world. I know this is a lot to soak in, but we've had some time to prepare."

"Time can't prepare you for something like this."

"No," she admitted. "It cannot. But you have people surrounding you. We had this discussion before at the expectations. You can be as involved as you want to be. Your father, my mother . . . they want to take this power and run with it. Let them. All you have to do is declare war against Ursan, then sit back and let others do their job for you. Your uncle has been First for almost as many years as we have been alive. He knows what needs to be fixed the moment you have the power. He will come to you, not the other way around. Sure you will have some documents to sign, but who cares? You will be able to live whatever lifestyle you choose."

"So you are telling me to just sit down, take the power, and shut up?" he queried.

"Flame's embrace, Jerryn, I am telling you to fucking relax. Isn't this what you wanted? To be able to be king without much in the way of responsibilities? We are going to make that happen."

She moved back to her closet and began again to look for a dress to wear at breakfast while Jerryn still stood about naked in just about every meaning of the word.

"How did you get him to agree?" Jerryn asked.

"I promised to give him what he wanted," she replied. "A clean, honorable death."

Jerryn only blinked for a moment after her statement, taking some time to register. "You are going to kill the Second?"

"No, you are," corrected Allura. "You cannot declare Ursan enemies of Amon and expect to imprison or release the Second of Amon. No, you must show harsh punishment for such wicked behavior."

"I know, but . . . I'm not so sure about this."

"About what?" she stammered, stopping again to turn to her husband. "Did you not promise your father that you would get your brother and sister back?"

"I know what I said," Jerryn snapped toward her, pacing within the room. "I don't think I am ready for the finality of it all."

Now she understood. "You are not ready to kill a man, regardless of his crimes."

"Is that such a fault?"

"Yes," was her immediate response. She disrobed and grabbed out a long, free flowing red dress, nothing too fancy but would serve fine for breakfast attire. As Allura dressed, she could see the distraught in Jerryn's face.

Like a lost puppy . . .

"Jerryn, my husband, my king . . . you are going to kill *a lot* of people during your reign. It is the only way people will respect you. It's the only way to stop the war Brocusk has started from spilling into the streets of Corovium. It's the only way to ensure that no one will come in and do to you what they did to Yelium Aylmer II."

"So rule by fear, then?"

"Fear equals respect."

Jerryn shook his head. "And how does this make us any different from Ursan?"

"Earth and Flame, Jerryn," stammered Allura. "This is not good versus evil, the righteous vanquishing the unjust. This is not some storybook tale that we read as children. This is just us versus them. And in case you haven't been keeping track, they are winning. They have your family held hostage. We would be fools to not sink as low as our enemies, to use their tactics against them. At the end of a war, people don't care how you won. They only care that you won."

"But I don't want to kill anyone. I told you I never wanted this to begin with, and now you would have me kill someone on my first day!"

"You would only say the words," Allura stated cautiously, knowing full well her husband's temper. "If it would get you to put some clothes on, I can declare the war against Ursan myself."

He moved across the room swiftly, long before she had time to react. His hands reached over to the straps on her dress and took firm hold of it, pulling her to his face. "You would like that, wouldn't you," he hissed. "Emasculating me on my first moment as king."

"Do you want the power or not, Jerryn? Either be king or move aside and let others rule in your stead. But do not grow upset with me for striving to gain the throne for us, striving to get your family back to you."

"As if you care about my family," Jerryn stated through clenched teeth.

"I did care about you," she earnestly admitted. "But I need a king and moreover, I need a man. I'm pretty sure I picked the wrong brother."

Bad idea.

Jerryn's hand rose and crossed her face hard and fast, and she could almost instantly taste the blood filling inside her mouth. He held her up and struck her again, this one with more force, this one with the feel that he was ready to close his fist and strike her with full intent to injure. Her husband lifted his hand again and this time held it above his head, in obvious conflict on whether or not she deserved another one.

And before she uncovered the results of his decision, Alex barreled into Jerryn, to which lifted him clean off the ground and slammed him solid against the floor. The initial impact stole his breath, the connection with the floor must have sent such a pain through him that Jerryn could do nothing but wince, tears rolling from his closed eyelids.

"What have you done?" muttered Allura to her guard.

Alex did not turn to face her. His stare remained focused on Jerryn Pratt.

"You have hit Lady Pratt once too often," her personal guard warned. "You are not king yet, and I am sworn to protect her . . . from anyone that would inflict her harm." Alex then motioned for her. "Come, let us find Lillianna. You are going to need some makeup now."

"You . . . I . . ."

"Come, now," he commanded.

Her personal guard likely committed suicide in striking a man about to be king in less than a day. And an unstable man at that. Of course Allura should have celebrated his brash behavior, as if Jerryn decided to kill Alex, that was one way to be done with a man that had far too much sensitive information stored away in his mind. But how could she be pleased if he was removed from her presence?

After all, he was the only person that cared for her, duty or otherwise. He was the only person that made her feel safe.

--

Philip woke alone, which was most recently not new. He stood and took a moment to gather his senses, gazing toward his open bedroom door. Jessica had again not taken his invitation to join him. Instead his wife had opted to spend her night in the living room, where she currently tidied up.

So much else to worry about, so much else going on in the capital, in the world for that matter . . . and yet here he was, a man with many faults who committed irreversible damage in his marriage. For the life of him, he could not determine if the better man would place his broken marriage before Amon, or the other way around. Certainly there was merit behind either answer, and yet he found himself hovering in between.

He loved his wife. Philip knew when he first saw her on the streets of Astrona that she would be his. Very little kept the First from his goals in life. But now those achievements crumbled around him, from the country he helped build to the relationship he took for granted. Both spiraled out of control and Philip was at a loss for how to stop them from reaching the bottom.

Might be too late for that, old man.

Rubbing the sleep from his eyes, he walked out to the living room, Jessica barely giving him notice as she continued to move about and clean. They of course had servants to do these tasks for them. Jessica cleaned for the sake of cleaning, as there was little else to do at the moment. Words were short, conversations nonexistent.

She did manage to stop long enough to shoot him a glance of absolute indifference. "Nicolas dropped by to say goodbye."

"So . . . he left?" When she did not answer, he realized it was a foolish question. *No, he decided to say goodbye when he changed his mind to stay, you idiot.* "Why did someone not wake me?"

"I didn't wish to bother you, and neither did your brother," was her answer. "Good to see someone still has it in them to leave this capital."

"That fool is leaving to wage war against Ursan. And the circumstances are different. Jerryn will not deny his father and Allura has no need for him to stay here. Christina would probably prefer it with him gone because that gives her more power."

"You are the First of Amon!" she snapped, then quickly stood upright and took a deep breath. "You had this country within the palm of your hand, able to do with it as you pleased. All your work, all that you spoke of, all that has taken away my husband, this fucking country and the land and the courts . . . you had it all, and you pissed it away. You could have seized the power and done what you pleased. I could have been gone with Lilli and Joanna by now, heading back home to Astrona."

"Be fair, Jessica. You are talking about conquering the throne. How different would that be from . . ." He stopped himself, hearing again her words. *She says this as if my time to change things has ended.* "What's going on?"

Her hands went to her hips, her eyes elsewhere in the room. "Allura Pratt has called for a meeting with the courts and all the councilors, as well as the respective families of them. There is an informal crowning tonight of Jerryn Pratt."

"*Informal?*" Philip baffled. "When did . . ."

"Apparently Afeon agreed last night to cast his vote in favor of Jerryn," Jessica interrupted. "You are about to give up your executive powers tonight, my dear husband. And we are trapped here in the capital. Trapped."

What did she say to him to make him agree? How can this be happening?

"I must speak with him," the First claimed, quickly moving back into the bedroom to find some clothes.

"Of course," she murmured.

Philip stopped, pondering on the argument that was about to take place, wondering if any of it was worth it.

"This is bigger than us, Jessica," he calmly remarked.

She now turned to face him.

"What exactly *isn't* bigger than us in your mind?" she returned. "We have been here eighteen years, and I am fairly certain that every minor issue that has ever surfaced is vastly more important than our marriage."

"Earth and Flame, I have been running this country!"

"And this country is going to Shadow. Good fucking job!"

Silence. It was the frightening kind of silence, the kind that all but declared that neither of them had much to say to the other.

"Go," she demanded. "See Afeon. Or whatever. It doesn't matter to me. Just . . . just go."

Pants and a shirt on, he nodded toward his wife, then moved for the door. He paused for a moment, thinking to say something, *anything*. But there were no words to describe his dedication to this job, no words to justify his adultery, no words left to say that had not already been said.

And so he opened to door and just left.

--

There was no public breakfast for Allura, not anymore. She ate what the servants brought up for her, and she did so out of instincts only. Word was sent out to the court officials that were in route to cancel the morning breakfast, but that the crowning would still be on schedule at dusk. Nothing was going to stop her from becoming queen, not even a few bruises on her face.

Allura had no desire to look into a mirror, and by the expression on Lillianna's face, it must have been a sight. The little one's expression tightened as she worked on covering up as best as she could the marks left behind by her husband, but the girl was just a teenager, not a god. Nothing was going to hide this completely, though Lilli worked diligently to prove otherwise.

"Why did he do this?" the young girl whispered, anger in her voice.

"Do not concern yourself with this," Allura cautioned.

"My future queen has been hit by my cousin," she remarked. "It's going to be hard *not* to concern myself with this, milady."

"He is under a lot of stress." Even saying the words made Allura feel hapless. She attempted a smile, but winced from the pain. "I suppose all women say such foolish things after they are hit."

Lillianna paused from her work, staring intently at Allura. "Is this the first time he hit you?"

"My child, we just discussed about not concerning yourself with this."

"So . . . no then," she deduced. "I am sorry, milady, but this . . . angers me. And embarrasses me."

"There should be no reason for you to be embarrassed. This was not you."

"But a member of our family. Someone once told me, I think as a slight toward me, that the last born are the worst born. But isn't it the truth? Jerryn is nothing in comparison to Rayden. Certainly I am not living up to expectations as of yet. Luther is a total ass for the most part. Maybe there is some truth to that saying."

"You prove that statement wrong, my child," stated the newest Lady Pratt. "You are far more elegant than your sister. We've previously started the discussion of being a second born does not determine your fate. You can . . . Luther isn't an only child?"

The look returned on the face of Lillianna Pratt all but clarified that she might have stepped beyond her means. Her mouth agape without words to fill also made it quite obvious that she had no idea where to go from here. *Lie? Tell the truth? She is wise to be cautious. Loyalty is a bitch, and I am* the *bitch.*

"I am sorry, but I might have said something in error."

Allura placed her hand on the girl's shoulder. "Careful on your next words. Remember, I may be the future queen, but I am currently the House lady in our new alliance. How am I to run this House if secrets are kept from me *about* my House? Tell me, Luther is not first and only born to Edmond Pratt?"

Slowly she shook her head. "No. But the only born from my aunt Karen."

"A bastard," Allura grinned. "Interesting. What is his name?"

"Nathanial Wode."

"Wode," she repeated. *Where have I heard that name before? I know that last name.*

Lillianna took a step back and nodded her head some. "Well, milady, I believe I have done as well as I can. It is not . . . entirely noticeable. And please, do not let anyone know that I spoke about Nathan."

"I won't, child." *I have little need. Nathanial Wode, I remember. The Guild tracks him down for aiding in Katlynn's escape. At least now I know who Brocusk has.*

--

Philip pulled up the same chair as usual, moved it to the front of the Second's cell, and sat down yet again, facing the diminishing Ursan.

"Where would I be if I did not get my regular visits from the First of Amon?" he mused, a smile working its way across his smug bearded face.

Defiant . . . until the end as it would seem.

"You apparently don't have to worry about that much longer, from what I understand," answered the First. "Why don't you tell me exactly what deal you made with Allura?"

"Strange that she does not confer with you on decisions as important as this, would you not agree?" Afeon only shrugged a bit. "She made me an offer, First Pratt, something that I might add you never did. She promised that my body would be taken back to Ursan after the public execution for my traitorous ways."

Philip could barely comprehend the words. "Say that again. She is going to kill you publicly?"

"That, my friend, was inevitable and you know it. If I'm going to die . . . I would at least rather keep my honor intact."

"By admitting your traitorous ways and losing your head? What sense does that make, Afeon? Where was your defiant attitude from before? You said these bars would not break your will."

"They have not. I accepted a deal, nothing more. The deal was as good as I was going to get. By the rope, but at least I can take some comfort in knowing that I got something out of this bargain. Besides, I thought you wanted me to vote so that you could convince Jerryn to slow the war."

"My mind changes by the day," replied the First. "By the fucking minute as of late. My brother already heads home to Astrona to gather up any able man and march to Ursan. I cannot stop this war. Best I can do now is get him the Imperial Army so that Dehyllo will not slaughter him completely in open combat."

"And now you look to war, when you were once content at stalling this vote. Have you heard any word back from Deso?"

"Not a sound." Philip slumped back heavily into the chair. "Maybe I was wrong, but it's hard to say."

"You cannot stall forever, First Pratt. The people *need* a king. That throne has been vacant long enough. At least it's Jerryn who takes it. It might have been easier with Rayden, but life is not easy. It will be important for you to ensure that Jerryn takes command. If Christina takes over, you will not live very long. She knows you suspect her daughter of treason. And once crowned, treason will be the only thing that can get her off of that throne."

"I know," Philip affirmed. "I know. But there is little I can do now. If you cast your vote this evening . . ."

Philip could only shake his head. *What am I going to do? Send war to Ursan? I cannot stop it any longer. What am I meant to do?*

"Dehyllo calls for war," Afeon noted. "Know that no matter what happens, I look to you with honor. You have done all you could to ensure the right people sat upon the throne. We might have disagreed at who you thought was right or not, but I certainly never argued your tactics, save for the fact that they were *too* by the book. And I don't know if you even understand how much power you have. You hated Yelium Aylmer II, but there was no hesitation in you that he would be crowned. You also had no intentions of handing the throne to Lord Brocusk, so you throw your support, unwilling or not, to Rayden Pratt. So much so that you risk your life by speaking to Christina about the possibility of her daughter committing treason. That is dedication to your job! You have fought hard to ensure we have not seen war in your tenure, even in the roughest of times. But war is inevitable, I fear. And the people of Amon will know that this was not your war, but one you did everything possible to prevent."

Philip stood and straightened his tunic. "I wish I could believe your words. But fault is placed solely on those at the top. That's you and me and Orpay and dead kings and soon-to-be crowned kings. I'm to blame as much as any, and I can't figure out how I'm supposed to stop this."

"Maybe you aren't meant to stop this," added the Second.

The First sighed heavily. "Well I suppose there is nothing to really say, Afeon. You have made your decision."

"She was going to kill me tonight, one way or another. I caution you, First Pratt. Do not underestimate Allura. She was likely behind Rayden's disappearance, and now has managed to sway my vote. She is far more powerful than I might have judged previously. She ultimately might be more dangerous than even her mother."

"Apparently so," Philip admitted. "Strange. We have been so focused on Christina and what she might do with the power, and did not ever really think about her daughter as anything other than a puppet."

"Ha! It's always the unexpected, is it not?"

Philip crossed his arms about his chest and gave a single nod toward the Ursan. "It was an interesting run, you and me, Afeon. I certainly will not look forward to tonight. Nor am I sure how you are going to live up to your own statement. You know, how you are going to live longer than me."

"Stranger things have happened," announced the Second.

"Of that, I agree."

"Farewell, First Pratt. Despite it all, it has been an honor."

"And to you, Second, I wish you well in your journey . . . to whatever lies beyond."

The First held his gaze for a moment longer, then turned and began his departure from the dungeons.

--

The sun rose high and the heat beamed down onto the rear courtyard with ferocity. Not even the steady costal breeze could cut through the discomfort. Still, not a stray cloud moved across the sky. A clear day, a hot day, a perfect day for a crowning. Despite it all, Allura smiled. Only a few hours away until she would be queen of all of Amon.

Who would have thought that when I left Tessenul a few months ago, I would be standing here in Corovium, ready to rule all of Amon?

She had of course dreamt of such a day in her wildest of fantasies. But never once had she foreseen the possibility. And yet . . . here she stood.

"Things are coming along nicely, milady," Lillianna mentioned beside her.

That they were. The servants scuttled about, getting together chairs for the assembly, erecting a stage for Allura and her husband, placing down a wooden block to be used for the execution. They moved with fluidity and purpose, almost a bit of eagerness perhaps in their step. The buzz had made its way around the capital by now. They were about to witness a crowning, informal or otherwise. All that mattered was that someone was about to take the throne.

"They are ready for a leader," she claimed, her lady-in-waiting gazing intently to her while she spoke. "It has been a long time for them. Many months have come and gone since King Aylmer fell to his illness."

"Strange," noted Lilli. "No one seemed that upset when he died. Maybe they expected it. I don't know. But I just remember there was a bit of . . . I don't know what a good word is. Relief maybe? That might be too harsh."

"Or maybe not. Human nature is a difficult thing to suppress at times. I think we were all ready for a change."

"But someone died. Shouldn't *someone* be upset?"

"I would gather his wife was upset."

Lilli shook her head. "She didn't seem so. I mean, she wasn't even at the crowning of her son. Left pretty quickly too."

That is . . . odd. And why didn't I notice that before?

"You are a very perceptive girl, Lillianna Pratt."

To which she shrugged. "At least someone around here notices."

"It is my job to see the little things. How else am I expected to run this country if I cannot see such detail?"

"Well, it's my father's job too, but he never notices much of anything." Lilli turned away, a hardened look appearing on her flawless, thin face. "He completely missed my birthday this year."

Philip is not only an ass, but a shitty father as well.

"You are thirteen, are you not?" Lillianna nodded to the question asked. "How often does a girl become a teenager?"

"I believe only once, milady."

Allura leaned over and placed her hand upon the girl's shoulder. "When this is all said and done, we will look to celebrate your birthday properly. Of that I promise."

The young Pratt beamed a smile toward her just as Alex, who had been spending the last hour or so hidden away and out of view, revealed his position from behind them and moved up nonchalantly.

"Sorry to interrupt, my ladies," he began, "but your husband is making his way outside, Lady Pratt."

She frowned to his statement. "Maybe it would be best if you checked in with my mother."

Please don't leave me.

"If it's all the same, I feel fine right here," was his response.

"Do as you will." Inside, though, she could not have been happier to his stubbornness and his current loyalty.

"Well I for one am going to say something to him," snapped Lilli.

"And because of that, you can go check in on your sister and ensure she is getting prepared. Then I need you ready early so that you can help me dress."

Allura could tell much from a look, but she did not need her gift to read the young Pratt girl. She wore her emotions directly onto her face. Currently, disappointment and confusion.

"But why? I have plenty of time to . . ."

"I send you away," Allura interrupted, "because I am certain that you *will* say something to your cousin that you may regret. Remember, he will be king."

"I don't care about that."

"But I do. Think about the words and you will understand what I mean. Now go."

She hesitated, then forced a smile and nodded nevertheless as she made her way to one of the side doors, reentering the capital. Not but a few seconds after, Jerryn appeared from the opposite door, his step a bit more cautious toward her, more than likely based on her current company.

He did not look into her eyes as he approached. His gaze darted about from the ground to the ocean to the sky and back again. Fear, guilt, anger even . . . it was all there, written without words across his face.

"Allura," he began, his tone hushed. "Can we speak?"

"You *are* speaking."

"Privately?"

Allura turned to Alex, then back to Jerryn. "To Shadow with that."

His fist balled up at his side, his eyes now locked to the earth beneath him. "I am sorry, I lost control."

"Nothing has changed," she assured him. "You are about to be king in a few hours, so you should go upstairs and get changed soon." When Jerryn's eyes finally met hers, they reflected his confusion. "Too much is at stake in Amon for us to be at ends with one another. You want your brother and sister back. Very well. In order to do that, we need the army. The only way to gain control of the army is to be the king. So be the king. I made no jest before. If you do not feel comfortable with declaring war or executing Afeon, I will do this for you."

"I can do it," the words spoken claimed, but the tone said otherwise.

"Very well. Think of your family and the promise to your father. It will get you through these tough times."

"It's just . . . the pressure is all. I haven't been myself lately."

"Have you heard the old Ursan saying about that?" When he shook his head, she flashed a smile. "You are only your true self in moments of fear and panic."

"What does that mean?"

"It means what you want it to mean, Jerryn," she sighed while spoken, her tolerance and bravery only available with Alex by her side.

"I said that I was sorry."

"I heard you," she hissed under her breath. "What is done is done."

"Please don't say that," he whispered. "I . . . this isn't me, you know that. I just . . . I don't know, Allura. I truly am sorry. I just . . ."

"We have discussed this before, remember?" She leaned in closely to him, now her words only for him. "I will run this country. You can do what you do best . . . drinking and fucking. But you will no longer be fucking me if you ever strike me again. No more childish romance or otherwise, Jerryn. This is now a business venture for us both. I want this, to rule Amon. You can live carefree for the rest of your life. Make the occasional public appearance, and other than that, just do whatever and whoever you want. You have the life just around the corner that you always wanted. All I need from you is to keep it together for another couple of hours."

"I know, and I am okay with that," Jerryn replied.

"Good," she said, taking a step back. "Now I am about to head back upstairs and check on Joanna and Lillianna, then I will be needing to get ready. You need to do the same. At dusk, you will be king."

"Okay."

And I will be queen of Amon. And you may need to be dead soon, my love.

The list of people I need alive is narrowing.

--

Dusk drew upon them and the time had finally come.

Chairs lined to the left and right of the stage and they already filled quickly. Gillar and other members of the court sat on the right, while immediate family of the newly formed union of House Pratt and Rowe to the left. Both Lurey Hillan and Lijid Nulittan took the stage, as the councilors were set to sit alongside Jerryn and Allura when they arrived. In front of the stage lay the execution block, and Philip Pratt stood solemnly between the two. He would play mediator at the proceedings, being that for the moment he still held executive powers and he still was the only one that could call the vote for the succession to the throne.

A small part of him was relieved for this all to be done. He could go back to being the First and only the First, a job he had performed well for many years prior. No more politicking for position, no more fighting for every inch of every mile. Jerryn would be king. Done. He was a far better councilor than leader, to be honest. Much better behind the scenes than in front of the crowds.

The skies were clear and the heat was intense. The summer months were upon them and it started in brutal fashion. Philip wondered how badly it struck Donovini. The drought had continued, and now with the heat rising . . . he could only imagine the suffering. And instead of focusing on aiding them, they were heading to war. Nicolas would take a bunch of angry, thirsty, rebellious people into a war they wanted nothing to do with, and had nothing to gain in doing such. This was not a war for land or supplies or wealth. It was a personal war. *Most wars are personal one way or the next I would gather.*

Jerryn and Allura came through the side doors, both dressed elaborately, both appeared ready and calm. His nephew wore a light armor to the affair, with a cape drifting behind him. A bit much, but it seemed to fit him just well. Allura, on the other hand, went with an evening gown normally reserved for a ball of some kind, fluffed out at the shoulders and the neckline, below the hips the dressed flared out and extended beyond by some measure. Lillianna dressed in a more casual manner, with a standard long dress and her hair beautifully done, placed up with several flowers stemming from it. Christina Rowe emerged dressed similar to her daughter, but toned down just a bit to not draw attention away from the star of the evening. Members of the Imperial Army escorted them in full force, along with the capital soldiers and Allura's personal guard as well.

All in all, better than the grandiose entrance by Yelium Aylmer II during his crowning.

Hopefully this ends better.

As they made their way to the stage, the soldiers and guards all surrounded the bottom of the structure while Lilli barely gave Philip a glancing notice as she moved across to join her mother and sister. It hurt, like hot candle wax on his flesh, but he could not think upon it at the moment. There would be a time for repairing his relationship with his now teenage daughter. Philip understood that everything was a bit more dramatic at a young age. He would fix it, when time permitted.

Jerryn sat calmly down upon one of the makeshift thrones, Allura refrained from such. Instead, she stood and faced the members of the court that were in attendance. She was a wicked person, of that he had little doubts. She had something to do with Rayden's disappearance. She somehow convinced Afeon to forfeit his life. Wicked . . . and yet she looked the part of a leader.

"Gillar, I thank you for assembling the members of the court here today," she announced, her voice commanding as it hushed the masses.

"It is my honor, Lady Pratt," the short Fallneesian responded. "All of us wait patiently as to the reasoning behind this visit."

"Of course. As I am certain that you have heard, I spoke with Afeon last night. He has agreed to appear before us today and cast his vote of succession."

"I cannot help but notice the execution block before us," Gillar beckoned. "Am I to assume that is for the Second?"

Allura nodded. "I would just as well let him speak upon the matter." Turning her attention to one of the doors, she waved onward. "Bring in the Second."

And so they did.

--

Allura watched as Afeon was escorted to the wooden block, and after a whisper from one of the soldiers, the Second willingly took to his knees. His arms were bound behind his back, but that did not kick the smile across his face. She tried to ignore it. She still had the intent at honoring her end of the deal and did not need a reason to back out of her word. Annoyance was not a good enough reason.

But he did not speak to her, nor the crowds, nor the courts as his first words formed. He turned to Philip Pratt. "Might I address the courts freely, First Pratt?"

The First shrugged. "I don't see why not, Second."

"Gillar," Afeon called out, "it's a pleasure to see you here."

"The same, Second," the Fallneesian replied. "What brings you before the execution block, if I might ask?"

"Treason against the throne." The Second still managed to smile. "Lord Brocusk has kidnapped two Pratts and is ransoming them back. He demands the throne or is preparing himself for war. Such an act is treasonous, as it goes against every law that we hold sacred. Being that I represent House Brocusk and all of the Ursan people as a member of this council, I stand guilty of those crimes, and should be treated as the criminal that I am."

"Your crime of being an Ursan?" laughed Gillar. "Or your crime of being a representative of a power crazed lord?"

"Both," answered Afeon.

"First Pratt," the court head started, "this does not seem like a just reason to imprison a man. Is he charged solo with being guilty by association?"

The First stole a look over at her, as if to curse her existence with his eyes. "He is being held because Lord Brocusk has committed treason against Amon, and Afeon is too closely tied to not suspect his involvement in this act."

"It is I that called this meeting together," boomed Allura, her aggravation growing to their lack of attention toward her. "This is not a trial against Afeon. His imprisonment was decided by the First of Amon, who holds all executive power. It is not in your right to question his moves, Gillar."

"My mistake, milady," the Fallneesian made claim. "By all means, continue."

Her mother took a step forward, eager for the opportunity to take over these proceedings, but she would not give her that chance. A single open palm raised by Allura stopped her mother in her place. And so Allura continued.

"What Lord Brocusk has done is demand something that no one here has the authority to give. He demands us forfeit an empty throne, one that has yet to be claimed. Brocusk has only asked for war in all reality. It is because of Lord Brocusk's actions that I find myself in the need to take action myself. The time to delay this vote has ended. Should we all sit here and wait for Dehyllo to march his men to our very capital and burn it to the ground? We have waited long enough. So I spoke with the Second of Amon last night, to which he has agreed to come before you and cast his vote. Are you prepared to honor your word, Second?"

"I am a man of honor, Lady Pratt," was his response. "I believe everyone here knew this was bound to happen. So why delay further?"

First Pratt began to pace between the stage and the Ursan, his movement representing his trepidation over the vote. It had to be done, they all knew such. Someone had to take the throne eventually.

It might as well be me.

First Pratt spoke clearly, but softly. "With all four council members here representing all four countries in their current format, I call for the vote on the succession of our throne. I cast my vote for Jerryn Pratt, member of the newly formed union of House Rowe and Pratt."

"Jerryn Pratt," Lurey, the Third of Amon proclaimed.

"Jerryn Pratt," Lijid, Fourth of Amon stated through uninterested eyes.

She smiled toward the Ursan.

Say the fucking words.

But he only bellowed in return.

"The only true king, Lord Dehyllo Brocusk," Afeon stated through his own laughter.

She could not even believe the words, nor did the rest in attendance by the looks on their faces.

"The vote must be unanimous," mumbled Philip. "The vote would then turn to the courts."

Gillar stood and waved his arms. "We are unprepared to vote currently. We have not decided what to do with the departure of our Ursan members. We have yet to figure this situation out yet." His eyes met hers. "I am sorry, Lady Pratt, but you have wasted our time. If Afeon will not vote for Jerryn, we have no king."

"I will not vote for this union," hissed Afeon. "I come before you as the messenger of the true king, Dehyllo Brocusk. He left me behind to speak with you all, to let you know that you are all fools in your games. While you vote for this boy and all of his inexperience to rule this country based on a marriage of names, the warrior that is Dehyllo pities you all. Together we have the strength to fight what awaits us across the Terrandonan. If we fight against each other, all is lost. This boy will not lead you to prosperity. He will only lead you to death. Lord Brocusk still gives you this last chance. Vote him as king, and all will be placed as should be. We will prepare for war against the unknown and join as one entire nation under his leadership. No more countries, no more House names. One country, united. Do so, and you will avoid so many unnecessary deaths."

Allura felt her face flared and flustered, angry beyond all words and expression. "You fucking Ursan! You have *no* honor!"

"I keep my word for those that are worth doing so," he replied. "You are not worthy of my word, Lady Pratt. You are not even worthy of that last name."

"I regret that you force me to such . . . extreme measures. But I will not lay and wait for your lord to destroy us all." She waved again to soldiers against a side door. "Bring forth my prisoners!"

--

First Pratt spun about, not knowing what to expect, not certain what she had planned. But as the Ursan women and children came, all bound by chains, he realized how gravely he underestimated Allura Pratt.

About thirty in all, Philip watched as they marched to the front of the stage, guards from House Rowe pushing them forward. The women and children varied in age, upwards to probably forties or fifties, the children as young as perhaps six or seven. Philip knew these people. They were the wives and children of the court members from Ursan. They were the ones that fled the capital on the night Rayden Pratt went missing. Afeon and Gillar both gave equal looks of shock and worry.

"These are all that are left alive from our recapture of the Ursan deserters," Allura claimed. "As you all know, leaving your position within the courts is an act against the throne, and an act against the throne is punishable by death."

"They were under command by their lord!" Gillar yelled.

"But they are under oath to Amon, not their lord, Gillar," she snapped back toward the Fallneesian. "Amon always comes before the House or the country. You should be wise to remember that."

"These people are innocents," Afeon pleaded. "Leave them be. I am the one that you want dead."

"The condition of how they leave today is entirely up to you, Second of Amon," Allura said. "Twice you have pledged your vote to my House, and twice you have broken that word. If you truly care for these people, you will honor your word. Who do you vote for?"

There was hesitation and yet a sense of understanding in his stare toward Allura. "Lord Dehyllo Brocusk."

"The true king!" an Ursan boy blurted out, maybe thirteen at best.

Allura turned to the child. "Kill that one first."

"*No!*" Philip screamed, but it was far too late.

One of the members from her personal guard slammed the hilt of his blade into the back of the child and as the boy fell to his knees, the sword turned and buried into the back of his neck. He was dead in an instance. The remaining prisoners did not flinch, did not budge from their stances.

"Fuck you, Allura!" Philip exclaimed. "Stop this immediately! I command you to stop!"

"This is House affairs, First Pratt," she answered him. "These people are in allegiance with Lord Brocusk, who has in turn kidnapped members of my House. I am within my rights to execute those found treasonous against the throne. These people have all been given the opportunity to deny Dehyllo as their lord and succumb to imprisonment and labor for their crimes. They would not do such. So no, First of Amon, I do not believe I will allow you to stop the actions in my House affairs. You may have executive powers, but they are still limited. Only a *king* can stop my actions, to which we have none."

Allura again turned to the kneeling Afeon. "Who do you vote for?"

"Lord Brocusk," he said through gritted teeth.

"Kill two more," she demanded. Now the crowds became nervous and uncomfortable as two more, one woman and one child fell victim to the blade. Blood emptied into the grassy courtyard and some in the audience began to leave. Others called out for the actions to stop. But the Ursan people did not waver, still Afeon would not submit.

Christina now took a step forward, her voice calm and desperate. "Please stop, child. This is not the way. This is madness."

"Afeon has the power to stop this!" yelped Allura Pratt. "There is war upon us, and these are now times of war! Cast your vote to Jerryn and I will end this slaughter and instead end your miserable life. You can still maintain your honor!"

"I have retained my honor, as have all of these people you kill today," retorted the Second. "My vote goes to Dehyllo Brocusk."

Another fell dead and Philip could not even find the presence to move. She was right, of course. He had no power to stop this. If they admitted treason, much as Afeon had done, executions could be performed. If they were given a chance to denounce their lord and live a different life . . . well they should have taken that opportunity.

But this . . . this was sickening. He could not stop this, but the House lord could.

"Jerryn!" Philip begged. "Stop this! I know you! You cannot approve of this!"

He gave an empty stare back. Either he was equally as powerless to stop his wife or he simply did not care.

"Vote!" Allura demanded.

"Brocusk!" Afeon answered.

Another dead body.

"Lady Pratt!" Gillar yelled while moving toward the chaos. "We are prepared to vote!"

"What?" she mumbled.

"Jerryn Pratt," the court head stated. "Jerryn Pratt. We vote for Jerryn Pratt. Earth and Flame, Allura, just please stop. We vote for Jerryn Pratt."

And now we have a new tyrant.

Allura did stop, at least long enough to stare like a drunken idiot toward the court head. "So you have the power . . . so you just . . ."

"The vote passed to the courts, and as the court head, I am announcing that the succession to the throne falls to Jerryn Pratt, under House Rowe. Now stop this insanity."

Jerryn was on his feet, but said nothing. He only turned his sight down to First Pratt. *What else can I do here? What else I am supposed to do?*

"As the courts have made this official, I relieve my executive powers to you, Jerryn Pratt. You are now the king of Amon, ruler of all four countries and the lands that encompass them. Hail to you, my king."

No applause, no roar of approval from the crowd. Only a stunned silence followed, one only fitting and equal to the bodies that lay lifeless before the very stage where Jerryn Pratt stood.

"You have one chance to claim your allegiance to me," Jerryn announced to Afeon.

"Ursan no longer recognizes this throne," was his answer, "or any man or woman that sits upon it."

"Then you and all of Ursan are traitors," claimed the king. "And we must now go to war against those traitors. Ursan men and women must deny their allegiance to Lord Brocusk and kneel before me. All those that will not kneel before this throne's authority will die. And it starts with you, Afeon. Kill him."

A soldier from behind Afeon gave him a shove forward and the Ursan slowly complied, placing his neck onto the block. Calling for an axe, the solider waited while one was fetched.

It was an intensely hot day for early summer. The beads of sweet fell from his face, just drops at first, then in droves. It was easily hotter now, he realized, then it was when these proceedings started.

He barely noticed, but Afeon turned his head just enough to see him.

"Take a step back, First Pratt."

Impulsively he did.

A young soldier rushed across the courtyard and placed the axe in hand of the executioner, and he in turn moved into place with the weapon. Though it raised high above his head, it never made it back down, as the soldier dropped the weapon outright, holding his hands as if they touched fire.

Afeon stood, his hands unbound somehow. The heat radiated from him as would an oven. Quickly the heat circulated about him until his very flesh began to steam, his clothes slowly burning away.

Flames' embrace . . .

He then erupted into flames.

--

Pyromancer!

There was no time to react. Or if there had been, Allura simply lacked the capacity to do so. A swirling ball of fire that was once the Second of Amon charged her with such speed that she knew instantly that death awaited. The fractions of seconds were but a blur for her. In one moment, Afeon stood from his executioner's block. The next second, he turned into body of fire. And then he curled up and hurled toward them in a ball of fire that hovered before her face. Allura just watched it, paralyzed in a stunned fear . . . but then hands pressed against her shoulders and she allowed herself to be shoved intensely to the floor. The impact of the fire hit whoever helped her, and did so with deathly precision. Screams could be heard, burning flesh could be smelt almost instantaneously, and the charred remains of something once mortal fell atop the stage.

Soldiers and guards were on her almost immediately, Alex first before the rest. His hands grabbed her arm and snatched her up, running while surrounded by members of the Imperial Army. The yelling from fear echoed, panic ensued, and yet again, a crowning had turned into an assassination attempt.

Allura turned and watched as the ball of fire already moved beyond them all, heading to the beach in speeds that could not be matched by the fastest of horses. Turning a corner, the thing that might have been Afeon hovered and skimmed the coastline until it removed from sight completely.

"I want him dead!" she screamed. "Let me go and hunt him down!"

"We will," Alex replied. "But not before you both are safe."

They moved beyond the panic of rushing bodies that piled inside the capital, Allura sneaking a look behind to see that Jerryn had his own entourage escorting him as well, and the First somewhere behind all of that. Outside of those Ursan that Allura had killed, there looked to be only one fallen from the Pyromancer attack, the body abandoned on the stage completely engulfed in flames, motionless.

Afeon was a Pyromancer. A fucking Pyromancer this whole time!

"Ursan bastard," murmured the new queen. "How *dare* he attack me? I want his fucking head intact when we find him."

"Allura," started Alex.

"Dead, Alex! I want his fucking heart!"

"Allura," he repeated softly. "Your mother is dead."

She turned back to the stage, the fire from the body now spreading to the wooden structure that once held the new king and queen.

"How . . .?"

He shook his head. "She shoved you out of the way. Christina took the full force of the attack that was meant for you. It was so quick, but it was . . . I'm so sorry, my queen."

Guards surrounded her, people rushed and pushed their way through and around each other. It was Yelium Aylmer II all over again. Only this time the assassin had come only a half second away from killing her. But he failed nonetheless. Instead, however, he seemed to have killed her mother.

She felt her eyes water from rage.

Don't you fucking cry. Not for her.

She wasn't even on the list of people I needed alive.

--

Lost and Found

Killing is easy. In battle, the only thing on your mind is survival, and staying alive normally involves killing someone else. It doesn't always involve thinking about the morality of it all. It's just instincts.

Doing the right thing? Now therein lays a challenge.

Nicolas Pratt, House Lord of Donovini

XXI

Up a ways along the Terrandonan coast sat the capital of Argonus, Tessenul. An impressive structure in many ways, the capital sat just a mile or so from the beach on small patch of land that rose just high enough above sea level for John Shonnen to catch a breathtaking view of the ocean beyond. At midday, the waves could still been seen rolling in steady lines, like rows of soldiers in formation, each marching one after the next. *Where does it end? Does something truly lie beyond the horizon?* Questions without answers, he knew, and he had little time for philosophy.

Especially with war afoot.

Tessenul was a large structure completely encased by a forty-foot wall with archery stations all along the parapet on all four sides. The doors were pure steel with spikes protruded out to prevent battering rams from damaging the integrity.

"The Rowes certainly don't lack caution, do they?" Colonel Baldin Ascotte jested, though his face showed no such signs of humor.

Major Tauven Ulfini nodded solemnly beside him. "If everyone hated you, you would build some pretty sturdy walls yourself." The Fallneesian shrugged his indifference. "If anything, sir, this will be . . . difficult."

"Impossible would be the word I'd use," the colonel added.

"But necessary," Shonnen concluded, staring down both of his officers with a look that he hoped would end their banter.

"We still have a chance to pull back and away," Ascotte made claim.

"And go where, Colonel?" pried John. "We've been through this every which way we can. We cannot make it back to Genethur with the amount of supplies we currently possess. We also cannot avoid the Guild any longer, not after the attack against their outpost. So we must find a compromise."

"Maybe Lord Rowe will take up our offer of sanctuary," said Ulfini without any conviction behind his words.

"Maybe I'll be king of Amon too," the colonel added.

The three officers sat steadily upon their horses, the white flag heaved downward before them. A few rows of soldiers were no more than statues behind them while the remainder of the army kept a firm and clear distance down the elevated terrain. The white flag had been seen and the guards within Tessenul had sprinted off to fetch their House lord some time ago, or so they had hoped. That had been long enough to ponder on the fact if their summons would be answered at all, but there was little rush in the matter. If Gerald Rowe looked to gain advantage through wasting away their time, he found the wrong group of men to do such with. Patience was all they had, the only tool they used for many long months and years.

But ultimately the parlay was all but a formality. There would be no parlay, of that he had very few doubts. If anything, John would love it if Lord Rowe emerged through the gates and had the willingness to negotiate much as Ulfini had suggested. But he had plenty of dealings with Gerald in the past, even before this mess with their disbanding. Willing and able were not virtues he would label the House lord with.

Shonnen heard the gallop of the lone horse approaching before he turned and watched it ride upward to meet them, his new captain atop the steed looking no worse for wear.

"Good morning, sunshine," Baldin stated to Deso. "Glad you could join us this morning, being this whole thing was your idea."

"It doesn't look like I missed anything," the captain made claim, rubbing his thumb across where his eyebrow would be if he had them. "And I caught some extra sleep, so a win-win situation for me."

Shonnen reached his hand back and one of his soldiers moved upward toward them, placing a small scroll into his palm, to which he then extended to Deso.

"This came in addressed to a *Second Lieutenant Deso,*" the general announced as the muscular Fallneesian took hold of the scroll. "Addressed from the First of Amon."

"Must be an old note," he mumbled.

"Well . . . in a way, it is," Major Ulfini confirmed. "Bird went to the coast and we weren't there. Not the most dependable means of communication, nor the smartest of carriers. Should be glad you got the note in the first place."

Deso broke the seal and unraveled the scroll, taking a few seconds to read over whatever the contents were. After a moment, he turned to face them. "Do you have a squire?"

"I have soldiers, Deso." John nodded and motioned back to one of the young men behind him. He immediately approached with a quill and parchment. "Say what you must, he will transcribe it for you."

"Very well," the captain began, clearing his throat a bit. "Address this to Lord Philip Pratt, second within House Pratt, First of Amon, head of the Imperial Army, holder of the executive powers, and ruler of the four countries." He waited for the solider to write down his dictation. "When are caught up, write the word *yes*, then sign it *Captain* Deso of the special forces unit within the Imperial Army."

"That is all, milord?" the soldier baffled. "Just . . . yes?"

"Yes, now seal the fucking thing and send it back to him," snapped Deso.

The general would have thought to ask about the contents of that letter if he would have presumed that the alleged captain would have responded honestly. No point in wasting his breath, he figured. Whatever it was, First Pratt apparently felt that only Deso need know. And so the new letter was resealed and the soldier moved back toward the main army to send it away.

And then the doors to Tessenul came open.

Chains rattled and wheels grinded against each other as the two doors slowly began to part ways and the illustrious city lay just within. At the entrance on horseback, Shonnen could easily make out Gerald Rowe. A good looking lad, young and stupid, long blond hair, a strong build. The House lord did well to appear like he was all business, but in reality was nothing more than a boy in power. Beside him rode the former colonel of the Imperial Army, the deserter Frederick Pullman. No doubt now back in charge of the House guard, or at the very least a military advisor. The rest of the entourage that rode alongside Lord Rowe were unfamiliar to Shonnen, but all had the appearance of hardened men.

He brings his ugliest and toughest to stand behind him during our parlay. The sign of someone frightened. He gains courage from his company.

The group of Argon men waited for the doors to fully open before galloping along their horses to meet with Shonnen and his officers at the clearing before the city.

"First General John Shonnen," called out Gerald as he approached. *"What . . . the . . . fuck?"*

"Afternoon to you as well, Lord Rowe," Shonnen returned. "And good to see you in good health, Frederick."

"He speaks for himself," Baldin spoke as he spat on the ground. "Fucking deserter. Rot in Shadow."

Gerald clapped his hands in delight. "Well, well. This parlay is starting off marvelously. So we know each other and don't need to waste time with pleasantries. So please, save me the trouble of asking and just get to the part where you tell me why you are here and what exactly do you want."

"We ask for sanctuary," John commented. "For me and my soldiers."

"Earth's warm bosom," murmured Lord Rowe. "I barely liked dealing with you when your men were actually part of the Imperial Army. Those men down there are nothing but a rogue faction. Disbanded by the king."

"And that king died," continued Shonnen. "It was a foolish decision by a foolish boy. But now we look to you for aid. House my people for a few weeks, allow me to get word back to First Pratt as to our current state. I'm sure we can have this situation sorted out."

"Interesting, because by sorted out . . . it sure looks like you brought the bulk of your army, lined up in battle formations. Is that the kind of sorting you figured would take place here? This doesn't look all that friendly to me, General Shonnen."

"They marched here in formation, but we have no intent to fight you if we can avoid it. We only look for sanctuary."

"You marched them here under a false pretense," claimed Gerald. "What exactly makes you think I would allow them entrance into my city?"

"A heart, maybe," Shonnen continued. "Some of these men have spent up to two years on this coast, serving Amon as they were commanded. These are not thugs and cutthroats, but honorable men that served their country."

"And so that explains the attack on the Guild post?" Gerald inquired. "Oh yes, that has already reached me. I have already received a letter from Orpay. *Orpay*! The head of the Guild nearly has me dead to rights because of your *honorable* men. So what would you have me do? Orpay wants your men dead, General. He even has the audacity to threaten me in this matter. But I can understand. You've lost control of both this situation and your men. Orpay wants you taken care of, and I'd have the right mind to do it if I didn't figure you would just run yourself into the ground at some point."

Frederick Pullman sat up tall atop his steed. "We are prepared to offer you entrance, General. You are still a part of the Imperial Army, as are your officers. That much we are well aware of. You may march into Tessenul, the doors will close, and that will be that. No treason, no charges, no questions asked. We'll put this entire mess behind us. But you will need to send word to both First Pratt and to Orpay and confess to the attacking of the Guild outpost. Between the two of them, they will decide what is to become of you and your officers."

"And my men?" he pressed.

Pullman shrugged his shoulders. "These conditions are for you and your officers, no others. And that *very* generous offer is because of your service to your country and for no other reason whatsoever. It is also a onetime offer."

John did not dare turn to face his officers. They were just offered a way out . . . but none of them would take that offer. That did not make it any less tempting. A horrid image of him abandoning his men came at the general vividly, and he did all that he could to flush it out of his thoughts. No, he did not want his men to see him at his weakest.

Thankfully, Deso was a piece of granite.

"I think it will be more fun to take your precious city," the captain threatened.

Pullman turned his steed to face the captain. "You . . . I do not know. Who are you, soldier?"

"That is Captain Deso," Baldin Ascotte made claim. "He and his men come handpicked by First Pratt to aid our men."

Gerald laughed. "So, a well-connected man, I presume. Well-connected men do not scare me."

"Do I look well-connected to you?" Deso inquired, agitated. "I've got a monster of a hangover at the moment, so if you don't mind, can we wrap this up so we can start killing all of you and raping your women?"

"So these are the honorable men that you would ask to come into my city?" Gerald stated, appalled. "But that's the play, isn't it? If we do not allow you entrance, if we turn you away . . . you plan to simply storm the walls and try to take it from us."

"I'd much rather it not come to that," John noted.

"General, this is folly," Lord Rowe stammered. "We hold the position, we outnumber you at least three to one. Don't be a fool."

"Funny," Deso began, "the Guild thought the same thing, I gather. They outnumbered us about three or four to one. Had a big fucking wall there too. Ask them if that mattered. Oh, that's right, I killed all of them. Dead men don't answer many questions."

"Lord Rowe," Shonnen called out, trying to ignore Deso's bravado. "These are desperate men, but soldiers nevertheless. They are trained with the sword, with strategy, and obey. They did not come here for war. They came here for shelter. We have, at the moment, nowhere else to go. I will submit a parlay to the Guild once you allow us entrance and meet with Orpay myself. I am certain we can work something out. In the meantime, you have my word that my men will not cause issues, and if I am wrong, I would be held personally accountable for such."

"Here's the thing," Lord Rowe started, "I am House lord while my mother is away. My sister is now *the* House lady of this new union, which would . . . in all likelihood . . . make me the next in power here in Tessenul and all of the original borders of Argonus. What kind of leader would I look to my people if I just let some seven or eight thousand hungry, desperate men into my city and allowed them to ravage through my supplies? What would I have to gain by doing such? What would my people have to gain? Your men are not the military anymore. They are just men. We do not take refugees here anymore than we take any outsiders save for the Guild. And you are not the Guild either, General Shonnen. You are now at war with them, whether you realize that or not. And that puts us at a bit of a crossroads, doesn't it?"

"You're more worried about Orpay and the Guild than you are about the soldiers right here at your front door," Ascotte mumbled.

"I agree with the colonel," Deso stated. "Time to worry about the Guild later. The time to worry about us is now. So what if your people question your motives. Who fucking cares? Better to look questionable than dead, or so my dad used to say."

Pullman turned to both the colonel and the major. "The offer stands, now or never. Ascotte, Ulfini, if you would just step forward, you can enter our gates and be done with this madness."

Ascotte chuckled toward the former colonel. "And then I would be in the same position as you, Frederick. Both a coward and scared."

"You've got a bunch of guards," Ulfini noted. "We've got a bunch of soldiers. We will take the damn thing by force if we must, but we'd rather not. This is *your* last chance. Allow us a peaceful entrance and a parlay attempt with the Guild."

"Fuck you," Gerald cursed, a devilish smile flashed toward them. "I will see that your bodies are swept together and burned for all to see."

Pullman looked hesitant, though not scared for himself, but for his former friends. "You are making a mistake," he pleaded. "Just come with us. This does not have to end with blood."

"It's done, Frederick," Shonnen said. "Go back to your walls. We will be seeing each other soon enough."

"Lord Rowe," Deso called after the House lord. "Do you still share words with your sister?"

"Careful, cunt," Gerald hissed. "Parlay or not, I will have you killed here and now for disrespect of a House lady."

"It was not a slight, but a question," the captain defended.

The House lord seemed cautious. "Then yes would be my answer, of course."

"Would you deliver a message to Allura? Tell her that you met a dark skinned Fallneesian without eyebrows today. Tell her that I said it was a pleasure working with her, and if she is curious, the prize is still very much intact."

Gerald returned a puzzled look to Deso, and Shonnen could only assume that he must have done the same. "You have met her before?" inquired the House lord.

"Aye," Deso answered. "Tell her what I said. She will understand what it means."

At least that makes one of us.

--

The sword began to feel lighter in his hands, his swings were slowly becoming more fluid. It rose to Rayden's shoulder, sweat emerging from his palms as he repositioned his grip. He took a step left first, then moved right as his swing came hard and fast, true as the day was hot. It could not have been a better strike, there could have been no better swing.

And yet Scythe easily ducked the attack and punched Rayden in the face. The tall Fallneesian let off a bit at the end of the punch, so it was a passing pain, nothing lasting or damaging, but enough to have Rayden back off and his eyes water all the same.

"It was a good swing, kid," Mortar claimed, the Donovinian sitting upon the grass before them, only half paying attention to begin with.

"The kid is a natural," Haze, Scythe's twin, agreed, who seated himself next to Mortar. "Did you have any warriors in your line, before you were damned to the Divide?"

Rayden waited a moment, regaining his composure from the impact to his face. Scythe, who stood defenseless, only smiled patiently at him in return.

"My father was a . . . guard of sorts," he claimed. "His father before him too. Both knew the sword well."

"Well you got a killer swing, Breeches," Haze reiterated, nodding his head while he spoke. "Very impressive. You've got no fucking aim though."

Mortar laughed some to that. "Couldn't hit me passed out drunk."

Scythe walked up calmly and forced Rayden to lift his sword arm again. "What did you do before you were sentenced? Guard like your father?"

"I thought we didn't talk about our past lives?" Pratt inquired.

The Fallneesian grinned to that. "Very true. Only curious. You *are* a natural, boy, but don't let that shit get to your head. You absolutely suck, and if you swing that like in this war we are about to get ourselves into, you are going to die. Battle isn't pretty. Just look at Mortar over there."

"Fuck you," the badly scarred Donovinian responded.

"Style gets you nothing in close combat," Scythe continued. "Especially in a battle where you are pressed so closely against the person next to you, all you can do is look for one kill shot after the next. You watched us in that Guild outpost. What did you see?"

Rayden shrugged. "Their numbers didn't really amount to anything. You had the position and the element of surprise, and . . ."

"Wrong," he snapped, crossing his arms about his chest. "We did not worry ourselves with how or why. We simply went in and did our job. It wasn't pretty. As a matter of fact, it was damn sloppy. But Guild members? Always about whose cock is bigger, who has the newest armor, the sharpest blade. None of that matters. I am unarmed and you haven't even scratched me yet. What if I was like Deso, carried me a set of brass knuckles. Would have busted open your face already. You keep worrying about form and style, and you sure will look prettier than your opponent, and be a lot deader."

"So, suggestions?" Rayden inquired. "I am not a swordsman, but . . ."

"You've been coached," Mortar stated, now thumbing through cards.

"Aye," Haze added. "We don't care, kid. Not our business or our place. And like you said, none of us lived before the Divide. By the chain, you know. This is all the life we got. But you obviously came from some kind of money, and that money bought you some very expensive coaching lessons. All those lessons amount to about nothing out here in the real world."

"No one fights fair," concluded Mortar.

Scythe nodded in agreement. "They can't coach dirty. How can they? How do you coach the unexpected?"

Rayden gave a perplexed look in return, his sword arm dropping. "Well how do you coach the unexpected?"

His finger jabbed toward him. "Don't think." Scythe gave a solid jab to his shoulder, this one with force. Pain shot up and down his arm and then back up to his neck for a few seconds, but he shook it off the best he could. "Now lift your sword arm. Despite us being a bunch of assholes, we don't lose members willingly. Which means I've got a lot of work and not a lot more time to get you in some sort of condition to survive."

"Lot of work," Mortar mentioned.

"Glad it's you and not me," Haze stated to his brother.

Rayden was just glad it was someone.

--

"A lot of brave words out there, gentlemen," Colonel Ascotte mentioned, a frown across his face. "By all of us, I mean. Now exactly how are we going to get beyond those walls?"

Back inside his command tent, John Shonnen sat patiently, gazing at a map of the surroundings, staring with such intent as if the gods would point out weakened spots and vulnerable areas against the Tessenul wall. The fallen gods would not support this war. John knew they were all on their own.

"Bottom line," Deso stated, pointing on the map to the entrance to Tessenul. "We have to get those doors open. We won't be able to get ladders up to that wall easily, and not like we would be able to just get eight thousand men up and over."

"Agreed, Captain," Major Ulfini stated. "But that does us very little. It's not like they are going to just open the front doors and let us walk right on in."

The captain nodded his head. "Aye, no reason for them to just open the doors. So we will have to do that for them."

Shonnen raised an eyebrow to that statement. "Alright, Captain, you obviously have a plan. Spit it out."

"Small team is going to have to infiltrate," he explained. "I take my most trusted men with me, we find a way into the city walls, we figure out some way to get to the door mechanism and signal you, and you make a mad rush to the doors while we open them. What can possibly go wrong?"

Ulfini gave an interested look. "How do you intend to get anyone beyond the wall?"

"Always a way in," answered Deso. "Maybe not for an army, but four or five men, certainly."

"You do not lack confidence, Captain," Shonnen claimed. "While getting a few men beyond the wall might be possible, you'll need more than just a few to get anything done once you're on the inside. We need to think of a better plan."

"We can sit around and do nothing, I suppose," Deso sarcastically offered up. "But of course you already *have* been doing that, so how about we try something new for a change?"

Baldin Ascotte both laughed and shook his head. "Let us for the moment even presume you have a way to get beyond the walls. What exactly makes you think you would for one second pass as Argon and make it to the door mechanism? And even if you could do all that, I am certain it will be of the most heavily guarded location in the city, save for maybe the walls themselves. This plan is foolish."

"Oh I don't know," Deso pestered. "Taking the Guild outpost was far dumber than this idea, but that worked just fine. Besides . . . what's your suggestion?"

"Well, Captain, we just started discussing strategy, so I don't know," snapped the colonel.

"Enough," announced Shonnen, standing before map on his table. "The days have been hot on our march to reach Tessenul. We still have enough food to last for another few weeks, and so long as we lay siege here, we may yet gather more incoming supplies to last longer. The Guild will not show, and it is quite obvious that Rowe will not come out and meet us again. Time, gentlemen, is something we have in abundance."

"And when our supplies drain in three weeks or so?" Baldin inquired, his arms crossing before his chest.

John sighed audibly. "Let us hope we have a plan by then. Now leave me . . . except you, Captain Deso."

The other two officers eyed their newest member for a moment, then turned and left the tent. Time was not infinite, despite his statements, and decisions needed to be made about what happened after this move. What if the improbable *actually* occurred? What if they defeated Lord Rowe and claimed Tessenul, what then? They would be fully supplied and possess a city in hand. Eventually the Imperial Army, the *real* Imperial Army would come for them. Against that they stood little opportunity to survive.

But there would be no open combat with them. John had spent very little time contemplating the solution given by Deso after he sacked the Guild outpost. Taking Tessenul was practically insane, and the chance of success low at best. But this battle gave his men purpose again. No longer did they fight and kill each other, no longer did they hunger and thirst. Once fed and given an enemy and a purpose, the men looked strong again, eager to engage and fight for their general. And First General John Shonnen was proud of his men.

When this was all over, he fully intended to die for them. How else was this supposed to end? There had never been a way out of this situation, not from the moment that Yelium died. This war, if they managed to win, would call out the main army in the capital. Under parlay, John Shonnen would be given an opportunity to negotiate, to which he would surrender his life for the lives of his troops and his officers. A fair trade, and one that any opposing officer would be forced to take. Shonnen would be beheaded for his acts of treason . . . but his men would live.

There was no other way he could think of. But first he had to sack Tessenul.

"Chest in the corner over there," the general stated while pointing. "Good bottle of wine that I've been saving. I suddenly feel like a glass. Would you mind sharing one with me?"

"I'm not much for company," Deso replied, a smirk across his face. "But I could always use a drink."

The captain moved over and opened the chest, producing the bottle and two glasses. The wine placed onto the table, Deso produced a dagger and removed the cork, followed by the pouring of the dark merlot.

"Any family, Captain?" John questioned while he took a sip of the wine. Bitter at the first swish and swallow, but good nonetheless. "I've got two brothers, three sisters myself. I'm the middle child amongst them all. Been a long time since I've seen them, or even heard from them. What about you?"

"No." Deso took his glass and drained the contents immediately, his face unchanged. After a second, he shrugged. "A sister. But I haven't seen her in a long while. To be honest, I don't know for certain if she's alive or not. Been far too many years. A different life, General Shonnen. A dead life."

"You still seem to be breathing, Captain Deso."

He turned away and took an exasperating amount of time to respond. "No, no I'm not."

The general sat down, and motioned for Deso to do the same. "There is more than one way to get inside a city."

"Aye, truth there."

Shonnen took another sip from his wine. "Want to tell me your plan?"

--

Rayden felt more comfortable in his silent role as prisoner within the Moon Divide. They did not like him, that much was abundantly clear. He was handsome, prestigious in a way they could not relate, and somehow had an aura of superiority about him that they could not stand. But above all else, Rayden was a complete and total liability. *Who in their right mind would want me by their side in combat?*

But it became increasingly difficult to ignore his inability to just *fit in* with these people, for both himself and the Divide. They knew he did not belong, but thought better than to question it. Deso brought him along and that was enough for them. Not to say they were not curious, only that they knew better than to inquire too heavily on his past. It was one of numerous unwritten rules of the Divide. No last names. No questions.

As for him, the longer the days, the more he missed home. The more he missed home, the angrier he became. But it was a dangerous anger, one without direction. Who amongst him could he vent his anger? Deso? Certainly he could, as he was his original kidnapper, along with others from the Divide. But he also was the man who spared him as well. Would have been a lot easier to simply dump him off the side of the boat with a slit throat, but the Fallneesian chose otherwise. Likely he had his own agendas, but so long as he kept Rayden breathing, he had little intention of complaining. He could have thrown his anger toward others in the Divide, but they had less patience with him than even Deso. The fact that each of them could kill him without a weapon was also problematic.

So his anger had no release. The fact that he had not had sex since he left the capital certainly did not help matters any. Very little private time in a group of men to handle himself either, being someone was always watching his movements. What was left for him at this point? He could talk to the general, but he still found little merit in that. What exactly could Shonnen do for him at the moment? His hand was forced to start a siege in a war he never asked for. The sanity and stability of his men hung by the thinnest of fibers. Revealing himself to the general would add more shit than remove, and sadly shit was of the few things they had in abundance.

And thus there stood little for Rayden to do save for train with the sword. His arms ached, his body depleted, and he felt no better at the blade than when he started. Scythe spent more time telling him what a pathetic excuse of a fighter he truly was than show him how to improve on it. But at least he tried. And at least his brother and Mortar showed *some* interest in his survival. The others, well they cared little for anything other than themselves it seemed.

Well that and their stupid fucking card game.

Aaron sat upon one of the crates, rubbing the palm of his hand against the scar than ran down his blinded right eye. He threw down his cards against the makeshift table. "Double queens, should be enough."

The others at the table grunted, Nails more than the rest. "Lucky shit," he spat, throwing down his own cards. "Second engagement the only reason that shit rides."

"A winning hand is a winning hand," Flint claimed, his hands running through his unkempt blond hair. "Makes little difference when you get it, or what engagement. Only thing that . . ."

"Shut it," snapped Nails, veins protruding from his neck as he did. "Now deal the fucking cards."

Flint gathered the cards and began shuffling, a half grin on his face while he did. Rayden moved away from the card playing Divide members, heading over to where Scythe and Haze stood. Mugs in hand, they took in some ale from one of the casks they acquired from raiding the guild outpost.

Scythe extended his arm and handed Rayden a full mug of beer in his hand. "Take it," he mumbled.

"Thanks," responded the Pratt.

The tall brothers could only be distinguished apart by their hair. Scythe keeping his hair to mere stubbles, much the same as Rayden, while Haze grew his hair wildly and often braided it, not always evenly, not always logically.

Mortar walked by, grabbing a drink from Haze. "You can get another one," the scarred Donovinian claimed, then turned to Rayden. "Sparring with us does not make you one of us, you know."

"Cut him some slack," Scythe cautioned, finishing pouring another drink, to which he handed to his brother. "We were all new at some point to all this shit. Some of us handled things a whole lot worse than this one."

Mortar took a drink, and then shrugged. "It takes a while to sink in. You know, the life sentence and all. We serve the king, and the First, and the courts, and blah fucking blah, forever, until death do us part. It takes a bit of time to realize you won't see your family and loved ones anymore."

"You didn't have any loved ones," Haze pointed out.

"Didn't stop him from crying the first few nights," Scythe added.

"To Shadow with you both," hissed Mortar. "Not all of us are made of stone like Breeches here."

"Well you all better be," another voice claimed. As Rayden turned, Deso appeared from around the corner of the tent. His face a bit more serious than usual. "We got some work ahead of us, gentleman."

"Shit," Mortar cursed. "That doesn't sound good."

"No," admitted Deso. "It really doesn't."

--

The slow walk east allowed nightfall to finally draw before them, the Twin Moons providing plenty of light against the blackness of the sky. The named members of the Divide traveled with Deso at the lead, destination toward the coast. Their venture took them several miles outside of Tessenul to a small grate, barely tall enough to stand through, wide enough to only fit two at a time. The smell was horrid.

Nails spat onto the ground. "Got to be fucking kidding me."

Rayden concurred.

"The sewer," Flint painfully laughed in disbelief. "You want us to travel through the sewer?"

"To get into the city," replied Deso. "Only way we can get in undetected."

"Well, until they smell us when we reach the surface," Aaron stated.

"Aye, all is true, gentlemen," their Fallneesian leader agreed. "We are to enter into Tessenul, take to the door, and open it for the rest of Shonnen's men. And we have to get this done tonight."

"*Tonight?*" stammered Flint. "What happens if it is not tonight?"

Deso shrugged his shoulders. "Then they assume us dead and they come up with a new strategy. And if we can't get this done, we will likely be dead anyways, so good luck to them."

"Sound fine by me," Nails offered up. "Let's just signal the rest of the Divide and leave. Not our war."

"Enough of that," Deso harshly rebutted. "We work for First Pratt and the council. Like it or not, you chose this life." His eyes reached Rayden's. "All of you did, one way or the next. By the chain, you all did. We abandon this, you know what happens to us. We just become wanted criminals . . . another picture on the wall for the Guild to behead and collect some coins."

"They could try," Flint stated.

"And succeed eventually," Deso countered. "By the rope or by the chain. Every fucking one of you had your chance to take the rope. You chose the chain. Well . . . this is where it leads."

"If you'd have told me it led to the sewers back then, I might have taken the fucking rope," noted Aaron.

"Who put *you* in charge anyways?" Nails bellowed.

"First *fucking* Pratt," the captain answered. "But if you want to fight me for this prestigious job, be my guest."

The large Ursan chuckled in response. "No thank you. Don't really got the stomach to lead men into sewers. Get it? Because it smells fucking bad."

Aaron laughed a bit. "Hey, that was actually kind of funny. Who says the Ursan don't know a joke from a rock to their head?"

"Fuck you, Argon bastard," cursed Nails. "I'll put a rock to your fucking head."

"Earth and Flame," Deso exhaled. "Just get the damn grate open."

Being a leader was impossible, Rayden realized. He watched Nails bring his mighty hammer about and take a few solid clanks against the bolts. These men respected Deso, and yet gave him such a difficult time about his position. It was not that they did not want or need someone in charge, only that Deso had not wanted or desired the title to begin with. As much as he wanted to relate to his situation, Rayden knew better. When given Amon, he gave it right back. Allura had been willing to speak with him, willing to do the things required to be a leader. Love, emotion? Fleeting, and only now he understood. She loved Amon and that was more important to her.

But at that time, she was what he wanted. Rayden allowed his emotions to horde his actions. Did Deso hesitate when given his duty? Not likely more than seconds, knowing the man. He understood the charge and the responsibility of it and did his job. No, Rayden was not like him in any way, not even in the conviction of his loyalties. If he had a second chance, he would have married Allura, taken power, fixed things. If given a second chance . . .

Don't waste time with these thoughts. What good will they bring?

"So," Flint began, "are we going to discuss strategy at any point in time? Maybe a plan?"

Deso smiled. "I don't see anything wrong in doing what we normally do. Just figure shit out as we go."

"True," continued the wild haired Argon. "But to be fair, we've never exactly infiltrated a capital city with intent to sabotage the mechanism to the main doors to allow an army entrance. Maybe if we were ever going to change our standard operating procedures, this might be an opportune time."

Mortar crossed his arms about his thick chest and gave a glance upward to the Fallneesian twins. "What do you guys think?"

Haze shrugged. "No one asks for our input. That's pretty standard, so no need to start changing things now."

"Stick to what works," Scythe added.

"See," Deso noted, pointing to the brothers. "You don't need strategy when you have that kind of positive reinforcement."

Another solid hit and the bolts came loose, the grate denting inward enough for the large Ursan to simply push against it to force it the rest of the way.

For better or for worse, they now had entry into the main sewer pipe of Tessenul. But as the grate clanked inward, the men of the Divide stood about and gazed around to one another.

"Well," Scythe mumbled, "not everyone at once or anything."

--

In my line of work, loyalty is fleeting. Certainly I love my country, and I am not without pride. But my love for Fallneese does me nothing. My loyalty to House Aylmer does me nothing. Pride, sure. But it never clouds my profession, never prevents me from doing what must be done.

Ultimately, the Guild is unflappable, and I along with it.

-- Cylaa, a Member of the Guild

XXII

The rain had poured, moving in and out with such consistency over a three day period that kept the travelers drenched, muddy, and miserable. The trees offered some cover during the low points of the storm, but could not contain the downpours. Clothes tattered, stomach empty, body weak, Nathanial Wode felt a bit ashamed that while sitting down inside his wooden cell, he was actually relieved.

It was a long walk to Antuannee, after all. At least now as a prisoner within the Ursan capital, he could sit down.

His shirt long since removed, he had nothing save his ripped pants. And since the rain recently dissipated, the mosquitoes found a new home upon his flesh. And these were no regular mosquitoes. They were Ursan mosquitoes, which pretty much meant they were bigger and uglier than anything Nathan had ever seen. He felt the need to negotiate with these bugs on how much blood to leave him with after they were done. But they rarely seemed to listen to him.

His cell was located outdoors and in the middle of the forest city, in plain sight for all to witness. Antuannee was like no city, no village he had ever seen before. A mixture of both modern and tribal, they built the structures and homes *around* the existing forested area rather than tear down trees in order to create their civilization. There were no walls, no parapets, no gates, nothing to protect them against an invading force. Only trees, brush, moss, vines, and a whole lot of people.

The Ursan of the deep north lived up to every predetermined expectation that Nathanial had. Strength . . . the people were built like trees up here. Not tall by any means, but wide as a mountain range, thick as syrup. Warriors . . . every one of them looked more than capable of holding a weapon and using it, likely with extreme results. They did not pretend fight here or play in tournaments to prove who was the stronger. They fought, they killed. Respect was gained through the edge of a blade and the proficiency of the wielder. Dedication . . . as they all moved as one, each knowing purpose, each knowing what to do. There stood very little hesitation in Antuannee, very little chaos. It moved as would ants, with precision and attention to detail.

For the most part, the people left him alone within his tiny wooden cell. Just another Donovinian for all they cared. His few hecklers came from the guards that checked on him every now and again, feeding him whatever scraps they felt like, when they felt like. But Nathan paid very little mind to all that. He ate because it gave him strength, albeit minimal at best, and it would be needed if he were to make any attempt to escape. But first he needed to find out the fate of Katlynn and the rest of his companions, each who were taken from him at their arrival in the capital.

At the moment, however, surviving day to day felt like the real challenge.

The approaching footsteps caught him off guard, but he barely had energy or desire to move about to see who it was. He turned nevertheless and to his surprise, found a smiling Iero on the other side of the cage.

"Excellent to see you still alive, young Wode," the Druid claimed, in his hand a bowl of rice and meat. He placed his hands through a small hole in the cell for that exact purpose, and Nathan gladly accepted it, spending no time devouring the contents. "Slowly. You may get sick if you gorge yourself."

"Easy enough for you to say," responded Wode between bites. "How are you allowed to be here . . . unsupervised?"

"Threats go a long way in my loyalty, of that you can be assured." He shrugged some. "Dehyllo was very clear that if I open my Realm or try anything to either escape or aid in someone's escape, that he would kill all of you, even Katlynn. I'd prefer you all . . . alive."

"I'm surprised he's kept you alive."

"No more surprised than me, young Wode."

"And Katlynn?"

The Druid nodded. "Far better shape than you. She is not a prisoner, but a guest as Lord Brocusk would say.

But she is eating regularly, dressed appropriately, and thus far, taken care of."

"Jadenine?"

"Not so fortunate, I am sad to say. She is a prisoner as well, but kept in Dehyllo's throne room on display. An example is being made of her, as it would seem. But alive still, and that is a positive."

"And what of Feko?"

Iero's eyebrows raised some at the comment. "Feko departed immediately before the arrival of Dehyllo back in Vlate. He . . . warned us . . . in a manner of speaking."

"What do you mean?"

"He told us that we should leave and . . . take a walk. Well, specifically he wanted Katlynn to leave with him. When Tristan refused and sent him on his way, Feko ran off. Immediately following that we had the arrival of Dehyllo and his men."

Feko Hawbry . . . what more do you know about all this?

"Why didn't you listen?"

But the Druid only shook his head. "It was not my decision to make. Ultimately, it was Katlynn's. In the end, no one trusted him."

"Even you?"

The chubby Donovinian took a seat on the grass in front of his cage. "I trust that not everything that stands before you should be taken at face value."

"How else could anyone perceive Feko? He seemed crazy." The Druid did not immediately respond, but instead pulled out some sort of jerky that he had stashed away in one of his pockets and began to chew upon it. "What was he really, Iero? Did the fallen gods speak with him?"

"I would gather no," answered Iero. "But that is my guess."

"So then he was . . . *is* insane."

"Maybe. Maybe not as much as you believe."

"You said the gods didn't speak with him. That pretty much makes him as crazy as we thought."

The Druid shook his head some. "Just because it was not the fallen gods, you presume that *someone* wasn't talking to him. What if someone was in fact talking to him?"

Nathan felt more confused now than when they started this topic. "Such as?"

Iero turned away, staring at a few of the guards that cautiously watched the two Donovinians. "I felt the presence of a Realm around him."

"So . . . he *could* open the Realms. That explains the Draywolf encounter back in . . ."

"I didn't say he could open the Realms," corrected Iero, interrupting his statement. "I said I felt the presence around him, but not often."

"No more side talk," demanded Nathan, finishing his bowl and tossing it aside. "Feko wanted to protect Katlynn and was doing a pretty damn good job of it in all reality. He saved me in the Lis'rial. He led me right to her, which is what he wanted. It sounds like he might have been able to get her out of Vlate in time if you all had listened. I need to know . . . what was he?"

"You ask my opinion, young Wode? Very well, but trust me in that I am only guessing at things, and I have no facts to give you for certain. But I believe that he in fact *did* hear voices, or a voice, or something. There was a time when I in fact did feel a Realm about him, but it was not open. It was a strange feeling, one that I have felt before when the king was assassinated. As if someone was using the power of a Realm without actually opening the Realm. In either case, I do believe that perhaps someone, maybe on the other side, is talking to him."

"The other side?"

"Of the Realms," he concluded, a frown forming. "Faith is not required to believe in the Realms. You have seen them with your own eyes, or at least the power that comes from them. Who is to say what else lies there? Perhaps something yet discovered? In either case, yes, I believe that someone specifically is talking to him . . . but not as frequent as he speaks to himself. Perhaps it damaged a fragile mind, not knowing whether or not what he heard was real or otherwise. Let me see how you could deal with hearing voices, see how well you could contain the madness."

"Well what could possibly be talking to him, and for what purpose?"

"If I knew that, young Wode, I would not be wasting my time in trying to piece this all together. I don't rightfully know. I just know that there is more to Feko than any of us understand. Maybe something unexplained is plotting something and using him. Maybe he can open Realms and is hiding that from us. Or maybe he is just a raving lunatic. All possible. But again, you asked my opinion, and I gave it. But that is neither here nor there, I suppose. Feko is hopefully both safe and far away from here."

"Maybe," mumbled Nathan. "Guess he is safer than the rest of us right now."

"Very true."

Nathan hesitated, pondering on if he should even bother asking his next question. "What is going to happen to me?"

Iero stood and brushed off his pants. "Lord Brocusk is undecided . . . on if he needs two Pratts."

He nodded. It was, after all, not completely unexpected. When luck ran out, it certainly ran out.

"My thoughts and prayers are with you, young Wode. I must be getting back. I will bring you more food and water as soon as I am allowed."

As the Druid turned to walk away, Nathanial called out, "I know she is okay, but how is Katlynn holding up . . . to everything?"

Iero paused, not turning to face him. "I presume you mean to Tristan's death. I would say she is handling it better than we would. She's a tough one."

"Of course she is," he responded. "She's a Pratt."

To which the Druid spun about to face him. "So are you."

--

Katlynn moved with great caution around the throne room, as if any misstep would be her very end. This particular building was made of stone, but left several holes in the floor and ceiling for the trees to grow up and through, leaving four large trunks erected at random, an appearance like wooden pillars. The war table, or dining table more often than not, was nothing more than several dead trunks, sanded and evened out, placed together to form both seats and a top. If she were not a prisoner, there was a sense of admiration to this place. Everything, from the cups used to the swords crafted, were done with their surroundings in mind. They lived with the land rather than around it.

The young Pratt moved closer to Jadenine, who hung by chains from one of the trees. She had been left naked but unharmed in any way, on display for others to see and either pity or despise, pending on the heart of the beholder. From what she had seen, Jadenine had not spoken since her capture. For all intents and purposes, the Ursan woman looked broken.

Despite the naked Ursan beauty on exhibition, many eyes were upon Katlynn around the room, as they always were. Guards and sentries, all waiting for her to try something foolish, to open her Realm and attempt to flee or help others escape. But that was senseless at this point. She was a prisoner, all the same as Jadenine, though in much better condition. Katlynn was the jewel prize of Brocusk, his bartering tool against House Pratt. Far too valuable to mistreat and yet still his possession nonetheless.

Besides, she had little heart for retreat at the moment. Not to say she embraced despair either. Her emotions remained frozen, stagnant the moment since Tristan's death. There was no time to mourn. There was no time to even feel. And so she simply chose to shut down on the inside. It kept her feet moving in front of her, kept her eating and breathing and living.

That could not be said true of Jadenine. As she moved to Ursan woman, who hung lifelessly against the chains, she could see the desire to live removed from her brow, her purpose muddled and confused.

"As you hungry? Would you like me to find you some food?"

But Jadenine did not answer. Her only response was the closing of her eyes.

Katlynn took a step back and started her way to the table. The cooks had already prepared the evening feast and per usual, she was required to attend. There would be plenty of food leftover, enough that there stood little reason why not to share some with Jadenine.

But as she gathered a plate together, the doors opened and Dehyllo Brocusk entered, each of his three wives behind him solemnly. From eldest to youngest, Eili, Indulla, and Trayy, each a radiant beauty, each mothers to Dehyllo's many children. They were proud women, strong women, and despite sharing their husband, they felt honor in their duty to him. They bedded and birthed children with the strongest man in Ursan. To them, there was no wrong in him. Katlynn was certain that nothing in her words would ever change those women to think otherwise.

"Leave the food on the table," announced Brocusk, marching quickly ahead of his wives and toward Katlynn. "She will eat, but when she is ready."

"She starves to death on those chains," stated Katlynn.

Dehyllo laughed a bit, pointing to his servants. "Pour the wine. I am in the mood to have some drinks. So are my wives. So is Katlynn Pratt."

"I'm not thirsty for your wine."

"You will have some nevertheless," commanded the Ursan leader. He sat down as one of the servers approached and poured several cups of wine. "Sit, sit."

His wives sat on one side of the table next to Dehyllo, and Katlynn did as commanded, taking a seat across from him. A cup was handed to her and reluctantly she grasped it, taking the lightest of sips.

Dehyllo took a heavy swig from his cup, then pointed to Jadenine. "Zo. It is a name I have not heard in quite some time, a name we have not thought of in some time either. Did your friend here ever tell you the story of her people? Ever tell you of their dishonor?"

"Why don't you just tell me what you are going to do to us all?" she bravely inquired, ignoring his question and his obsessive need to hear his own voice.

Lord Brocusk allowed a grin to snake across his face. "I knew your grandfather, Landon Pratt. Did you know that? I had not unified Ursan completely at that time. It has been many long years, child, many of your lives put together to equal that amount of work that I have put in for this land. So although I was not the House lord of Ursan, I had many dealings with the Guild, and consequently, many dealings with Landon. Now there was a House lord if there ever was one. A warrior, someone that you would be proud of."

"I knew my grandfather," Katlynn quickly retorted.

"No, no you didn't," replied the House lord, taking another drink. "You were very young when he passed to the world beyond, taking his place next to the Schill and Turitea. And he had already handed down lordship of Donovini to Nicolas by then. Landon was old and sodden when you knew him, but I knew him when he was a champion, a sword arm that none could compare. They claimed him the greatest combatant seen in our generation, and I would wager I have not seen an equal since. His son's had that sword arm passed to them. It may not have been as clean and powerful as their father's, but most people pray for a third of what Landon possessed. And what did your father do with such a gift? He pissed it away."

She frowned to his statement, uncertain though of how wise it was to argue against her captor. "He fought in his time, and fought well."

"Yes, and for a brief moment in time was a proud representative of the Pratt name. And then one day he sent his brother to be a representative to the council. The once mighty Pratt brothers became the shitty Pratt politicians. They traded honesty with backstabbing, a fair fight with underplay."

"And what does that have to do with you kidnapping me? Why not just turn me into the Guild and be done with it? I don't understand any of this."

"Of course you don't," stated Dehyllo. "You have been on the run for some time now. You don't know that your father sold Donovini for the throne, giving part ownership to the Rowes. You don't know that Rayden has gone missing and apparently I am to blame for that. You don't know that Jerryn has married Allura Rowe as part of the union. You don't know that your uncle Edmond has thrown up the banner and called all in service to him, as he looks to foolishly march his army north into Ursan. Your people are about to go to war . . . for you."

Her stomach turned at hearing all of what was said. He gained nothing by lying to her at this point.

"Where is Rayden?"

"Dead, in a likelihood," he answered. "And no, I had nothing to do with it."

And now her heart plummeted as well. "Why do you think he is dead?"

Brocusk shrugged a bit. "Someone wanted him gone. Seems like the easiest way to make someone gone."

"But why would someone want him gone?"

"All politics, child. Can't you see? This is what those that play with politics go through. Scheming and plotting. Senseless, all of it."

"And yet you play it all the same."

He laughed softly at her comment. "No, child, I am done playing the game. All I wanted was to protect us all, unify this country. Who do you think pressed the issue at placing an army on the eastern coast? It was I. It took years to accomplish this, despite all of my attempts, despite all of the backings from the churches that supported my claims. Do you think I truly want to rule Amon? Child, that is not my place. I *need* an army. *We* need an army."

"You are a fool," she hissed. "You would create a war just so that you can gain an army. How many lives will end because of your idiocy? Lives that could be used to fight for you."

"Not when the throne belongs to your brother. We must kill or be killed. Unfortunate, but we are desperate men."

"And for what? You would do all of this so that you can prepare for the unknown? What happens when nothing comes across the Terrandonan?"

"I would be quite pleased at that," admitted Dehyllo. "As we like to say here, better to be prepared for nothing than unprepared for something. Certainly if nothing comes across the sea, I would look a bit foolish, but we would all be better for it. What happens on the opposite side of your statement? We do not prepare, and whatever comes for us kills us all? What then, Pratt?"

"But you would go to war and kill thousands upon thousands just to take Amon? What would that prove? You would lose that many people to war, just to try and gain others *for* war? It makes no sense."

"I tried it your uncle's way," stated the House lord. "Your government decided it was not to be. So now we do things my way. Yes, Edmond Pratt comes for me. I have already sent out my men to notify my country that our banner has been raised as well. All of Ursan will converge here to Antuannee and prepare for combat. But you . . . you are the prize. You are what they travel for. You may despise me now, child, but when this is all over, you will come to understand what I have done."

"I will fucking kill you at the first chance I get," she promised, the words leaving her mouth like fire.

But Brocusk only laughed. "You have such spirit! Careful, though, as the rest of your companions live based on my patience alone. Speaking of which, isn't it about time to tell me who the other Pratt is? I am beginning to think that I don't need two of you. Maybe you can convince me otherwise."

"The bastard son of Edmond Pratt," stated Jadenine, her voice cracking as she spoke.

Damn you, woman.

Lord Brocusk slammed his hand against the table in delight, standing immediately and moving toward his prisoner. "And so she speaks! And what a revelation you have revealed! Tell me, Zo, what makes you speak now? What has this bastard son done to you to make you feel so free to reveal him?"

Jadenine's eyes met Brocusk. "Because I hate you. I want you to know that you do not hold him as any bargaining chip as you do with Katlynn. The least you could do is kill us, give us a good end."

"An Ursan deserves a good end," Dehyllo agreed. "But your bastard is a Donovinian, and you are the daughter of a traitor. Neither of you are Ursan."

"Fuck you," Jadenine cursed, drool coming from her mouth while she spoke.

"No, you do not understand. I let you live. Do you hear my words? *I let you live*! I gathered all of Ursan, all of the named men and women of his great country and began to unify. But your father, he would not listen to reason. He demanded battle and bloodshed instead of loyalty. I offered him more land and more people under his watch than he already had. He said he wanted to be free and left alone. Your father was a fool, could not see the bigger picture, could not see what I was trying to accomplish. When I offered him the chance to be my second in command, in charge of the unified force with me, he turned me down again, called me a tyrant and not a leader of men. I *begged* him not to have me go to war with him, but he wanted it.

"I arrived in peace the day your brother died. I came there with my top named men and looked to negotiate. I thought bringing the best warriors this country had ever seen would help persuade him to reason. Seeing men of his equal, men he respected having come to terms with the reality, that unification was necessary, that maybe he would fall suit. But instead he took this as challenge, and decided instead of peace talks, he decided a championed duel to settle things. And beyond that, he sent your brother as his champion. Vilihame was a good man from what I knew of him, a powerful one. He had a Draywolf as a pet, if you remember. But your father was a fool to challenge me and even more of a fool to place his son in this battle."

"You burned my brother alive," she hissed.

"All within the laws of our people," Dehyllo defended. "Yes, I will not lie, sending the Pyromancer after your brother was a bit . . . brutal. But the stipulations were set without that clause. Your brother was a great swordsman, and any good warrior knows that one error in a swing could end your life. I had a chance to end this war before it began, a chance to finally unify all of Ursan. I was not about to risk that against your brother's arm. I looked to end it and have your father submit. Instead . . . he defied the laws of our land. He cursed your people and your name for eternity.

"I can remember seeing you, your village in fire and blood, and I saw you. I let you live because I knew that you would become strong, become someone worth of the name your father stained. Instead you use my gift as a means for hatred and revenge. You piss away all that I have given you."

"You took it all away!" she screamed.

"It was justice!" he hollered back. "And look how far our people have come because of it! We are on the verge of besting the Donovinians and having them bow before us. Once they do, Argonus and Fallneese will do the same. Your father halted our stance, brought our production to a standstill. Only I moved this country forward! Only I look to save Amon! No one else has done what I have or sacrificed all that I have sacrificed in order to save us!"

"You are fucking lost," Jadenine said, a chuckle inside of her breath. "You will lose this war once the Imperial Army joins in. And perhaps you forget, the Guild is still assigned to acquire Katlynn, and more importantly, reacquire both myself and that bastard son and kill us for treason."

Brocusk crossed his arms, turning back a second to Katlynn as if she was to lend him some sort of wisdom, then back to Jadenine. "The Guild fights for profit and the Imperial Army has some time before they would reach us."

"But if Pratt takes the throne," Jadenine continued, "how long will it be before the army shows? And the Guild has reason and profit to come as well. First, you have their prize in Katlynn, who is worth *a lot* of money. Second, removing you would give Orpay a great chance to take a larger stake into Ursan, being this is the largest exporting country in Amon."

"Let them come," he boldly stated. "Let them all come."

"Oh they will," Jadenine continued, laughing while she did. "You are so fucking stupid, thinking that your actions would not be judged by anyone."

"The fallen gods will know that I am right," was his reply. "All of you will know this at your end. And speaking of such, I believe that I am no longer in need of a second Pratt after all."

"No!" screamed Katlynn, but someone was already upon her from behind, her hands quickly tied behind her back.

"Bring her," he demanded. "She should see this bastard die before us all."

--

One of the guards laughed, opening his cell. "Your time has finally come, you brown skinned son of a bitch."

He watched as a crowd began to come together, Dehyllo at the front of this particular mob along with Nathan's cousin at his side, bound and screaming at him. Maybe she pleaded for his life. Maybe she cursed Brocusk's existence. There was no way of knowing. Iero had all but warned him this was coming though.

Why keep two Pratts when you can have one? And if you are going to keep a Pratt, you might as well keep the more important one.

He did not see Iero or Jadenine, though his eyes did search for them. A part of him still hoped perhaps for his luck to return. A part of him *expected* that luck to return. Once, he was a powerful member of the Guild, carving his destiny into stone in Prillian, and with one false step, it just crumbled away.

"Earth and Flame, prisoner! Out with you!"

The guard kicked him in the side and Nathan wheezed in pain. Regardless, he moved to his knees, and from his knees to his feet, his hands pressed onto the pain. The food Iero gave him helped some, gave him some strength to stand. He moved out of the cell for the first time in days and stood as tall as he could against the House lord.

Dehyllo clapped his hands from the distance while he approached. "Bastard son of Edmond Pratt!"

The guard gave Nathan a solid strike in the back. "Kneel before Lord Brocusk."

He saw little room to do otherwise. Nathanial dropped to his knees.

"You had me fooled," Lord Brocusk continued. "I thought for a moment that you were actually someone of true importance. Instead, you are a bastard. I would not think that your father would march an entire army into my land for a bastard."

Nathan shook his head. "I wouldn't either."

"Ha!" Again, he slapped his hands together. "I love the Pratts! It's a shame that your family is the enemy of mine, boy. I think that we truly have the same philosophy. Too bad we sit on opposite ends. Go ahead and kill him."

"No!" screamed Katlynn, guards quickly restraining her.

Nathanial's eyes gazed the crowd. No Jadenine, no Iero, no Feko, no anything. Nothing and no one came for him, save for a guard who approached with a sword in hand. But his eyes then caught Ollifo within the crowd, the tall nephew of Dehyllo, the man that killed Tristan Crane.

"I have done nothing against your people or this land," claimed Nathanial.

The House lord gave an interested look in return. "This is true, but you are here without request, and you are the blood relative of my enemy."

"Yes, but being as I am in your land and you condemn me to death for no crime against Ursan, you should give me the same rights as your people," he remarked loudly, ensuring to silence all of the onlookers. "I should be allowed to die by combat."

"You are indeed a Pratt," breathed Brocusk, smiling from one side of his mouth. "I like it. Yes. You can die with a sword in your hand. But who would be your killer. Let's see."

"I would fight Ollifo, if it pleases the masses."

"My nephew," stammered Brocusk, clearly not pleased with his selection. "He has fought one of your people already and proven himself. He has nothing to prove in fighting you."

"Well if he fears to face me, then perhaps you should select someone else for me."

The tall, lanky Ursan took a few steps forward and out of the crowd. But of course Nathan expected him to do such. If he knew anything of these people, their greatest weakness was their pride.

He had no plan, he had no agenda. Nathan knew that death awaited him no matter what he did here. At the very least, he would take the man that killed Tristan with him into the next life.

"I will fight him," Ollifo announced and the crowd roared in response.

Brocusk could only wave his arms. "Very well, nephew. Give him a swift death. And you," he started while pointing to one of the guards, "give him your sword."

Reluctantly the guard who had previously approached to kill him now dropped his weapon before Nathanial Wode. When his hands touched the hilt of this weapon, it made him miss his own blades. This was a fine weapon, that much for certain, but nothing like the feel of his own sword. It of course would have to do. Using the sword to aid him, he lifted from the ground and stood upright. Still tired, still weak, but the adrenaline already coursed through his veins. Unfortunately, his stomach moved as well, tumbling about, and his free hand covered his mouth. It did not help, as he keeled over and sprayed vomit onto the grass before him.

The assembled crowd laughed in unison and the lanky Ollifo raised his fist into the air, pumping it about, rallying the masses even further to his cause.

"He fears me!" the Ursan screamed and the people voiced their support. "And you should fear me! I will remove your head just as I did your friend."

He wiped his mouth clean and adjusted the sword in his right hand. Heavier than he would have liked, but the grip was clean, the weight balanced.

"I do not fear you," answered Nathan, the sword spinning once around his hand before reclaiming his grip. "I just don't like killing. But I am pretty damn good at it."

"We shall see," Ollifo barked back.

The Ursan came forward, quick but awkward in his movement. Nathanial stood patient, watching him come closer, watching his sword arm raise to shoulder level. He would likely try to swipe at him, going for the body. Not as lethal but twice as accurate. Somehow Wode would have to be quicker. Somehow . . .

Ollifo's arm snapped forward in a thrust.

Steady, calm.

Nathan did not bother to deflect the kill strike. He spun about, his sword already moving with him, and he ended up just beside the attack. Now his sword came down hard on Ollifo's right leg, burying deep into his calf. The Ursan let out a solid yelp in pain and dropped instantly to his knees and Nathanial swiftly brought his sword up and down again, this time against the back of his right shoulder. The blade penetrated deep into his flesh and bone, and Ollifo screamed.

Wode kicked him to the ground and came down hard against his neck, his head separating from the body.

The crowd reacted with stunned silence. Nathan did not bother to acknowledge them. He picked up Ollifo's sword, testing the weight. Lighter by several precious pounds. He dropped the first blade and kept the new one, spinning it twice around his hand. His adrenaline masked his fatigue completely.

Shrugging to a stunned Dehyllo, he said, "Another?"

Lord Brocusk's face flustered with anger and his eyes gazed around to his people. "Where is Tennoi? Is he here?"

A huge man took a step forward, quickly grabbing a sword from a companion. "I will take care of him, Lord Brocusk."

This new opponent had arms about the size of Nathan's chest, and his girth was practically comically. He came forth in a trot, his sword swinging left and right frantically, high to low. Wode's stomach churned but he swallowed hard, breathing steadily to calm himself. He waited, patiently, cautiously. When the swing came close enough from the huge Ursan, Nathanial drove his sword forward, forcing his opponent to deflect the blow and break his stride.

With a smile, Nathan pressed the issue now, his sword thrust then burst into a sweeping strike to his side, narrowly deflected by the Ursan, but it pushed his opponent back several steps as he gathered himself. This beast of a man must have won by brute strength alone up to this point, because he was clearly outclassed. Not that he lacked skill, only fear worked in his favor and strength masked his true lack of grace and ability. Problem with Nathan, of course, is that he had no fear, at least none that he had discovered quite yet.

No wasted motions for Wode as he moved up, his sword now flipped facing down as he slid to his knees and swung low, cutting into the thighs of the Ursan, while his sword came upward and blocked against a downward attack. The clang of steel echoed into his ear before the Ursan's howl of pain, and Nathan sprung to his feet, the hilt of his blade connecting to the jaw of his opponent.

It was over. Blood sprayed from the Ursan's mouth as Nathan spun his sword back upright, centering himself, then slashed across his neck. Flesh opened, blood poured, and he dropped to the earth, silent and still.

Nathanial picked up the second sword, which was a bit heavier than his. It moved to his right and the other to his left. His eyes again reached Brocusk. "Maybe it would be fair to just send two at a time?"

If Dehyllo's stare had started in hatred, it seemed to vanish with every swing of Nathan's sword. Perhaps respect, perhaps understanding, but his expression changed nonetheless.

Two more moved forward without command of anyone, their swords out, and unlike Brocusk, wore their hatred all about their faces. This situation was of course rather foolish of him, but Nathan had no time to think why in Shadow he had made the challenge. It was done, and now there was only time to react.

Both men separated, north and south, both walking in a slow confident stride, much as would a pack of wolves around their helpless prey. But Nathan was far from helpless. He watched as the men circled about and waited for them to reach the apex, then he charged south. It did not surprise his opponent, though, who squared up and readied himself. Nathan swung with the right and his opponent rose his blade up to meet it, then jumped back some to avoid the thrust of his left arm. By now the other man had rushed up to meet him as well, and Wode spun about to narrowly miss a top to bottom swing, and then sprung away from both men, keeping them within his sight.

These men were skilled, unlike the other two. They turned to one another for a second, nodded to each other, then moved together toward him in unison. Nathan did not wait for their charge, but instead came to them with ferocity. It was a move they did not anticipate, and each had the look of confusion in their eyes. Nathan swung at the man to his right. It was a wild swing, one he knew the man would duck or block, of which he did the former, and Nathan followed it up by spinning all the way about and with a back swing, drew the first blood to the unsuspecting man to his left, cutting his arm deep.

Nathanial did not let up. A swing to the right, back to the left, he had both men on the defensive. But the injured man winced at every deflected blow, and that did not slip by Wode at all. He threw a devastating kick to the stomach to the uninjured Ursan, which forced him to stumble backwards and onto his ass. But instead of finish him, he turned to the bleeding man and put forth a flurry of strikes. They were blocked to the best of his ability, but he could only do so much. Four or five were defended, then one cut his attacking arm, another his chest, another his leg, and then the Ursan stood a bloody mess. Guard dropped, Nathan drove his weapon into his chest, and left the weapon embedded there.

His other opponent was back on his feet but breathing heavy, his composure not regained. Nathan was relentless. He stormed in, his sword swinging to the body, defended, then countered to the shoulder, which landed in overwhelming fashion, sliding in deep. The Ursan dropped his weapon and screamed in pain, and Nathan responded by sliding his sword out quick and stabbing him through the neck. He left this sword in place as well and stepped away, watching the Ursan fall lifeless to the ground.

Defenseless now, breathing heavy, he turned again to Brocusk.

"You are worthy of the name," whispered Dehyllo, moving toward him without fear. "I have seen this swing before. I saw your grandfather in battle. I swore I would never see a man wield a sword as he did again. I find myself . . . mistaken."

Nathanial said nothing in return. His arms rested on his hips, his breath erratic, his body returning to the state he had before the adrenaline fueled him to victory. But Brocusk gazed intensely upon him, an excitement in his eyes.

"You have earned your place to stand amongst us. Fight for Ursan."

Nathan was not exactly certain he heard the House lord correctly. "Fight . . . for *you*? Against my own people?"

"More than likely against the Guild," admitted Brocusk. "Everyone comes for us now. The Guild, the Imperial Army, your family. They will not fight together. And the Guild comes for you. You will have to fight them eventually, so fight them with us."

"I just killed your nephew, and you want me to fight with you?"

"Do you know how many relatives I have?"

"Well then tell me why I would fight for you?"

"Why wouldn't you?" he responded. "Tell me, Pratt, why did you join the Guild?"

Again, he felt a loss of words. "To live," he managed to say.

"And did your father embrace you? Does he love you as much as he loves that shit of a brother of yours, Luther?"

His teeth clenched together. "No," Nathan admitted.

"And why would he? Donovinians are so much about honor in blood. Why would he open his arms to his bastard child? No, Pratt, you were discarded. You joined the Guild to prove yourself, if not to him, to yourself. Perhaps to the world."

"What of it?"

"What of it? What of it, you ask?" Dehyllo laughed again, his hands clapping together. "What exactly do you owe your father? Do you truly think he comes here for you?"

Of course he's not. If they ride north, it's for Katlynn. As it should be . . . but still . . .

"You are a good man, Pratt. You know your place. I can see it in your eyes. You are the bastard, and she is the House name. It is as it was meant to be. It can't feel good, though. It lessens your worth. But you have proven your loyalty, your honor. You risked your position and life with the Guild to instead of capture Katlynn Pratt, help her escape. There is great honor in that. And how is it repaid? The Guild wants you dead. Your father likely has no idea you are even here or what you are even doing. Even if you managed to have saved her, would you have received a hero's welcome? Not likely. You would still have to answer for your treason with the Guild no matter the outcome."

"That means nothing," he lied.

"It means everything!" emphatically answered Brocusk. "What do you fight for? Yourself? What good is that? Your people want nothing for you, nothing of you. Why fight for them? We fight for Amon. What do they fight for? Power. Coin. Yet we are shunned, we are looked on as if we are evil. Flame's embrace, Pratt, this is war. Right and wrong is just a difference of opinions. But you . . . you want to prove your worth. What better way than to fight against a common enemy?"

Nothing he said was untrue. Nathan could not, would not fight against his father and his people. But what if the Guild came to assist his father? They would be trying to kill Nathanial no matter the side he fought for. It was a true thing that Brocusk spoke, yet how could he stand on the opposing side of his family name. But then again, it was not his family name. Wode was his name. Pratt . . . that felt more like a curse than a name. Nothing he could do could earn him that last name. He was forever a Wode, and that was all that he would ever be.

But who needed the Pratt name? Legends were made in war, through blood, through death. Names were carved into the histories written by the Kwyantin through battles such as these, win or lose, live or die. His father would not give him a name, would not give him a home. Who needed that? Perhaps there was some truth behind the words of Brocusk. Perhaps he grew tired of being just a bastard.

"Your grandfather would be ashamed of what your House has become," concluded Dehyllo.

"I met my grandfather once," he admitted, his eyes wandering. "He . . . seemed strong, even near death."

"None stronger," Dehyllo agreed. "But we have yet to see your worth."

Nathanial Wode, the hunter, the killer. In Antuannee, far away from his home of Astrona, he was no longer a bastard within House Pratt. Here, he could be whatever he desired.

"There is a greater battle ahead," continued Lord Brocusk. "Not against the throne or the Guild . . . but a battle for our very existence. I know it's coming. We need men like you to fight. Not for me or your father or your country. But for Amon."

"Katlynn remains unharmed," he immediately stated.

Brocusk nodded. "Only if you fight for me. If not, who knows? Your father would be none the wiser to her life or death."

"Jadenine Zo is released to me."

Dehyllo frowned a bit to this. "I am not yet done with Zo."

"Yes you are," replied Nathan. "She belongs to me."

"Very well, it is done. What else?"

Nathan knew better than this. In fact, he knew exactly what he should do. *I should just tell him to kill me, that I will not fight for him or against an imaginary army across the sea.* Problem was, of course, he could no more convincingly say those words than he could admit that self-preservation was vastly more important than almost anything or anyone else.

That and in all likelihood, the fate of his companions, especially Jadenine, depended on his decision. What he was doing was clearly not thought out and clearly not wise. But what was wise, what was easy, and what was right rarely, if ever, aligned.

In fact, through his experience, they were not even in the same Realm for the most part.

His eyes did not deter from Dehyllo. "I will fight the Guild. But not for you. I will fight against the Guild because I must. And I will fight for Amon. I will not fight against my own people, though. But . . . we share a common enemy. I could fight beside your people against them if they come."

There was little other way to keep his companions alive then to say these words. He would say anything in order to appease the House lord. But there was some truth in them as well.

"Excellent, Pratt. We will begin the induction of you into our people by . . ."

"And one more thing," he interrupted the House lord. "Stop calling me Pratt. My name is Nathanial Wode."

--

Life. Death. It's all you really think about before the battle starts, all that really goes through your head until the first swing of your sword, or the first sword swung at you. After that, it's all just chaos and screaming and doing your damned best to not trip over the next guy and fall on your own blade.

It's never pretty. In fact, the pretty ones normally die first from my experience. That tough, ugly, ruthless son of a bitch . . . he never gets what is coming to him, not in battle anyways. Those kind of men, they get what is coming to them at other times. But when the battle begins, well that's the playground of the wicked.

And the wicked always win.

-- *Baldin Ascotte, Colonel of the Imperial Army*

XXIII

Shonnen gazed to the Twin Moons as the sun nearly dipped completely beyond the horizon. Dark settled in and only the red and yellow light from the moons illuminated the night. He stood alone for the moment near the top of the incline, in sight of the walls of Tessenul, watching carefully. If Deso could make it though, if he could somehow get the doors open, it would be complete anarchy behind the walls, which of course gave his men a chance to take the capital.

It was both the worst and best chance they had at ending this swiftly.

He had little idea who Deso truly was. Captain, second lieutenant, or swindler. At this point it hardly mattered. Results were all that truly mattered in battle. A lord could be toppled by a peasant with none the wiser. Status and prestige were terrible armor and worse shields. John was no fool. He knew Deso was far more than he claimed. But then again, John was no fool. He knew better than to ask.

For the moment he stood alone, standing along the front of the small incline, just inside the vision of the guards that carefully watched him in the distance. Below Shonnen was his army, preparing for the unknown. They had no idea whether or not they would see battle this night. Some eager, some anxious, and likely others indifferent. He was a strange mixture of them all. If there would be a battle, best to get it over with. But there would be much death, something he wished it possible to avoid. Then again, if postponing meant clearer heads, perhaps another solution would present itself.

None of those thoughts were more dominate than the next. And so he stood there, stoic, numb.

Sergeant Major Hollins slowly made his way up to the general, in no apparent rush to interrupt his thoughts.

"General," announced the elder Ursan. "If I might speak freely, it would make my job easier if I knew what to tell the men. They have no idea whether or not we are about to fight or if we are preparing for a siege."

"I'd imagine that would be good information to have," concurred Shonnen. "I'm looking for an opening, Sergeant Major. If I should find that opening, we will strike . . . immediately."

"So you need the men ready?" Hollins inquired.

"That would be correct."

His arms crossed about him. "Difficult to tell desperate men to hurry and wait, General."

"Then I am glad that it is your job and not mine, Sergeant."

After a brief moment, Hollins chuckled some, then nodded. "To be honest, General, I am just ready for this damn thing to be over and done with, one way or the next. I know that we have only been here for a half a day, but . . . well after a year and a half of duty for me, I suppose I'm just ready to finish this."

Shonnen eyed the soldier suspiciously. "You don't think we will live through this?"

"That is up to the gods."

"I didn't take you as the religious type, Hollins."

"Is that . . . humor, General? Have you known an Ursan that is *not* religious in some way or another?"

"The Imperial Army can change men, Sergeant."

To that, the soldier nodded. "It does not change men, only the perception of their country and the Houses that represent them. For instance, I look differently at House Brocusk and his sheep, General."

"Is it truly that way in your country?"

"Sadly yes," Hollis replied. "I took the oath to join the Imperial Army because of my love for Ursan. Our land is part of Amon and the army protects that land. I pledged my loyalty to the Imperial Army, but that did not change my love for my people, my country."

"Despite what Lord Brocusk feels?"

"He is but a man. He is not above the gods or the lands below them. Although clearly Dehyllo thinks otherwise. I have no regrets, General, if that is what you are getting at."

"Nor should you," stated Shonnen. "Do you pray?"

"I do. Do you?"

"I haven't in some time."

The soldier moved a few steps closer, leaning in. "I believe that if there were an appropriate time, General, you have found yourself upon it."

Hollins smiled, a sad, pitiful one, then turned and walked back to his men. Shonnen watched him leave, his words heavy onto his conscious.

Turitea . . . Schill . . . guidance in this time of need. Give blessings and grant wisdom to those that risk their lives for us all.

--

"Fuck! You stepped on my foot!"

"Well move them from underneath mine and that won't happen!"

"Horseshit, just don't step on them!"

Rayden could barely see his hand in front of his face and could no better tell who was even arguing, likely Flint and Aaron, but he could not be certain. All he knew was that they had traveled for well over an hour in the sewers, which smelled worse than his imagination could even fathom. Though he was able to keep his latest meal inside, he did have several moments of gagging where he thought otherwise.

But not even the darkness of the sewer could disguise the deep, penetrating voice of Deso.

"Shut up," he hissed toward them all. "We are underneath this city and I would prefer if we at the very least made it out from this literal shithole before we die. So keep your voices down and move ahead."

How are these men so damn good at what they do? They don't even like each other.

"And Breeches!" Deso continued. "Catch up to the rest. You're lagging behind."

He was curious how the Fallneesian could even tell that when he himself had no idea. Rayden shrugged it off and moved up quickly, nearly bumping into someone, catching himself in the process. As he fell into line, he found it bizarre that the thought of death had yet to really reach into his mind. Maybe being next to such prolific killers suppressed such thinking, or maybe the adrenaline that coursed through him, numbing his senses to the reality. More than likely, though, he just had little left to live for.

And that, he realized, was the secret to the Moon Divide.

Deso repeatedly told him the workings of dead men. Dead men held no grudges, dead men asked no questions. Dead men had no fear either, Rayden supposed. It was not their skill or bravado or their heroism that made the Divide so feared, so powerful, so successful. It was not their previous criminal backgrounds or their ties to the council and the king. It was not their extensive training or dedication to their craft.

At the end of the day, the Moon Divide just did not give much of a shit about anything, not even staying alive. That was what made them the best at what they did.

And Rayden was one of them, he supposed. He could honestly say that the reasons for him living were miniscule. The rest of the world already presumed him dead and moved along with their meager lives. Word had spread of the marriage of Jerryn and Allura, his brother now the House lord of Donovini in Rayden's untimely death. How long before he gave up that title to become King Jerryn Pratt, ruler of Amon? How long before Allura Rowe tired of her husband and stabbed him in the back? *Wretched bitch.*

He took a deep exhale. What good were such thoughts now? He would die a second time tonight, only this time as Breeches, a man of the Divide. All the same, he guessed. Very rarely does anyone get to choose how they die. But if he were choosing, spending an hour or so in the sewer before getting skewered in the streets of Tessenul . . . not exactly at the top of his list.

Ahead of them, Rayden spotted a light overhead before he heard the booming voice of Nails.

"There's our entrance," the Ursan stated.

"Impressive," Aaron added, who stood directly in front of Rayden. "You spotted the only thing we can all see. Earth's warm bosom, I saw it and I've only got one eye."

"I can make you have no eyes, you Argon fuck!" Nails blasted.

"Enough," Deso demanded, pushing through the men. "Find the stairs and let's get onto the streets."

Now his heart pounded heavier against his chest. He might not have feared death, but it did not exactly make him wish to dive toward it either. But that was exactly what they were about to do. It took a moment of stumbling about in the dark before Scythe called for them over to a ladder, and one by one they began their ascension.

For as much chatter as the named members of the Divide had between them leading up to this very moment, it baffled Rayden at how swiftly they could convert into a killing mode. Not only were there no more words, but they barely made a sound as they moved. First to the ladder and first to the summit, Scythe took a moment while he fiddled with the grate at the top of the sewer, prying open a side, then bending back and away enough to slide through. The light from the Twin Moons poured through the opening and Rayden watched as those above him made their way up and out. Nails, Flint, Haze, then Rayden climbed onto the cobble streets.

He barely had time to stand before Mortar made his way up and grabbed him by the back of his shirt, pointing him to the west. They stood in the middle of the street, at least for the second they emerged, and in the midst of a compact housing area. In the depths of the evening, only the torches from steel lamps lit the street and barely at that. The first three members of the Divide that surfaced waved him onward as they all stood in the darkness of a side alley. Mortar jumped ahead of Rayden in a hurry and Pratt sprinted right behind him now.

In the narrow street, Rayden pressed against the wall of a building and watched as Aaron and Deso made immediate work of the distance between them. Eight in all, the members of the Divide gazed at one another, each likely curious at how they managed to live the mere seconds they had so far. Strange, he realized, how empty the streets were. Certainly the hour was late, but not late enough to be devoid of all life. No lights emerged from the houses, no voices echoing in the streets.

Deso must have spotted the confusion and casually pointed northward. Rayden's eyes met the direction and he saw the tower in the distance, a colossal menace that dwarfed the rest of the capital. No doubt the estate for the Rowe's, and it was large enough to house much more than just House lords and ladies.

The women and children are there, the men are being armed and placed against the parapet and the surrounding wall. Of course the city is barren. They are readying for war. And you knew that, didn't you Deso? You knew they would not be organized enough to have patrols set up. You knew that they would evacuate houses and clear the streets. You knew that this would be the least organized that they would ever be and the best opportunity to pull a stunt such as this.

Exactly who were you before the Divide?

Even with the empty streets, the men remained silent. Deso now ducked low and moved with haste, the others trailing closely. Tessenul was vast, but difficult to grasp the scope while they bounced from street alley to the shadows of houses, only to move back between buildings. It might have been as large as his capital of Astrona, or perhaps larger. Difficult to say. Only once before had he visited the capital, negotiating aid with his father for the droughts that Donovini suffered. But he had no time to explore then any more than he did now. The houses varied in sizes, from one floor up to four stories tall. Moving south, they passed several market plazas and assorted shops that mixed in with the homes of the civilians. All remained the same. Silence, emptiness, the night was still.

They crossed away from whatever housing area they had emerged from and found their first glimpse of the southern wall. Still some distance away, but their destination was now in sight. The spacing between the buildings widened with a commercial area now before them. Deso took a single step out into the main road before pressing back into the side street, his fist into the air.

Rayden could hear voices but could not make out words from the noise. At least two approached, but unaware and lackadaisical in their speech to one another. The Divide pressed against the wall, with Deso closest to the street but Scythe moving up amongst the men, placing him next to the others. The captain pointed two fingers into the air as he peeked out from the shadows. But they waited . . . all of them . . . patiently.

As the voices came close, Scythe sprung out into the open. One arm wrapped around the first Argon guard's mouth, the other arm wielded a short dagger that planted into a second guard's neck. Before the first soldier could put up much of a fight, the tall Fallneesian took a quick, firm hold of his head and spun it about, snapping. It all happened within seconds, with the guards hitting the cobblestone as the only sound made. Haze moved out into the open and helped his brother drag the bodies into the darkness of the alley.

And just like that, they were back on the move.

They were slower now in their step, more cautious. The closer they came to the wall, the more small patrols they found. Some only two or three men, others much larger clusters. But most of them spoke freely and gave away their position before they posed much of a threat. Deso kept them hidden, allowing the patrols to pass before moving up and down the streets of Tessenul. The guards did not expect this move from the army. They did not take their duties seriously, as if they had, they would have spotted the Divide by now. A silent patrol would have caught a misstep. Instead, the Moon Divide were like the wind.

Rayden's heart felt like it would burst at every wide street they crossed. Every stride he anticipated a scream from one of the guards or a pedestrian of some kind, *something* to give them away to the masses. And then that would be the end. But it did not happen. Instead they were invisible, travelers of the dark, and Deso was their only source of light. He maneuvered the streets as if he knew them, as if they were his home. And who knew, Rayden supposed. Perhaps the Fallneesian truly did know these streets.

In either case, guards were avoided, and the wall fast approached. The closer they got, the more sounds appeared about them. Guards were no longer patrolling, but simply occupying. They crowded some streets that forced the small group to divert and head down other pathways. In other areas, namely in taverns and brothels, they poured out; still relaxed, still disbelieving that a battle would take place anytime soon. And in other places still, they slept; some inside inns and others inside homes of the commoners that once lived within them.

Though travel was slower, it moved nevertheless, Deso always finding the right place and the right time to move the named members of the Divide. Rayden did the only thing he could: follow.

And as the wall loomed before them, they pressed against a large house that sat still some ways from the large entrance doors, but their goal had at last come into view. But so ended whatever luck they had carried with them to this point. Voices and laughter carried upward down the wall and a large group approached. Only this time the alley was far too wide to conceal them. Deso spun about, his eyes moving about.

Fall back!

But Rayden did nothing. The voices and footsteps approached, and he waited his orders, as if he were an official member of the Imperial Army, as if he took his role within the Moon Divide seriously. He did not run, he did not panic. He waited . . . as patient as his nerves would allow.

The Fallneesian then pointed to Flint and subsequently to the door to the large house. In seconds the short Argon surfaced a thin dagger and went to work on the door. *Not quick enough.* The voices approached, the mumbling and incoherence of the noise became words and sentences. As he could hear them, so did the realization that they were directly around the corner. Instinctively Rayden pressed his hand against the hilt of his sword, only to have Scythe place his large hand against his shoulder, shaking his head calmly.

Then he heard a soft click as Flint opened the door and the Divide practically dove inside, silent in their rush. Rayden pressed in right beside Scythe, and Deso was the last to move in. Flint then shut the door quietly and firmly behind them, pressing his back against the wood as he slid down and exhaled deeply.

They all remained low as they listened to the guards moving around the corner just outside, laughing away, ignorant to their presence.

And then after some time, silence came again.

The house was dark and quite empty, which was yet another stroke of luck. Many of the houses had already been claimed as barracks, but there had apparently not been enough time to truly start provisioning all of them. Guards were likely without complete understanding yet of what their duties were, where and whom they were reporting to, and the such. This was war. And war was chaotic, or at least that was what his readings told him of war. What did any of them truly know of it?

Deso gathered himself for a moment, then pointed upstairs. After Flint turned and locked the door, the named men of the Divide moved to the stairs, Rayden right in line as they made it to the second floor. The captain quickly entered one of the bedrooms facing south and ducked low, inching toward the window. Rayden remained at the other side of the room, watching as Scythe and Nails worked their way toward Deso.

After a moment of studying the room, Nails decided to break the silence.

"Shit."

Scythe nodded his head. "Couldn't have said it better."

Rayden decided to move a bit closer, gazing out the window himself. What he saw was easily discouraging. The main doors to the capital were clustered with men, Argon guards standing about everywhere. Sporadic and without purpose, but there nonetheless. The wall was more sparsely guarded, with men intermittently placed about the parapet. But there were thousands upon thousands of men, either on the wall or by the door or roaming the streets.

And they were only eight.

"We are good," continued Scythe, "but not this damn good."

"What the fuck do we do now?" Flint added.

"You grab your sacks," snapped Deso. "I'd wager the mechanism is upstairs. And besides, we are all dead men, last I checked."

"True," Mortar stated, moving up to the window as well. "But I suppose we all thought we would have a fighting chance at life, not just throw our lives away. And for what?"

"First Pratt asked we support General Shonnen," Deso declared. "And so that is what we are doing. We serve the council, we serve the First, and that is that."

"By the fucking rope all of the sudden," muttered Nails, who moved back to the hallway to sulk.

"Fair enough," replied Aaron, who still stood by the doorway. "What's the plan?"

Deso took a moment, still gazing carefully through the window. "We wait."

"What exactly are we waiting for?" Haze questioned bluntly.

Their leader flattened his back against the wall, his head away from the window opening. "Hope that our general comes through with that distraction I ordered."

--

Timing was everything, and that was only assuming that the captain had made it anywhere near the main doors. But Shonnen had given him enough time. Either he succeeded or failed, lived or died, but either way, he had to take the chance.

Both Colonel Ascotte and Major Ulfini approached with the sergeant major, each looking as if they had just waked. Which of course was of no coincidence, since he had Sergeant Hollins do the waking.

"Have you slept at all?" mumbled his friend, Baldin Ascotte.

"No," John replied. "And hopefully you have all had enough. Major Ulfini, take the entire seventh squadron and storm the eastern wall."

Tauven Ulfini rubbed out some sleep from his eyes, then stared blankly in return. "Say again, General?"

"It's time, Major."

Hollins took a few steps forward. "Seventh is only about six hundred men, General."

"I can count, Sergeant Major."

The Ursan sergeant straightened himself some, remembering his place in the military. "Of course, General, but perhaps you might have me lead my men to the wall in the Major's stead?"

"Not a chance, Hollins," John swiftly replied. "I need you here in case all of this actually works."

"All of what?" Baldin questioned, then sighed heavily. "Of course. Our devoted captain and his band of honorable men. You went ahead with his plan, didn't you?"

"That was my call to make, *Colonel*."

"Sorry, *General*. And so now what? We are some sort of distraction so that he can try and get the door open?"

"We are exactly that," John confirmed.

"And if your captain is already dead?" pressed Baldin.

Shonnen crossed his arms, hating the words before they even left his mouth. "Then my error in judgment costs us only the seventh."

His officers turned to each other for a moment, then back to him.

"Sergeant Hollins," Ulfini began. "Gather me the seventh. We have a war to start."

--

Back downstairs, the eight members of the Divide sat patiently, listening carefully as patrols moved about and around them, waiting for some sign that General Shonnen had given the word to attack. But each passing Argon guard gave worry to Rayden; every moment that escaped was another that might cause their discovery. All it took was the unlocking of one door to undo them, end them, and this ridiculous plan would be for not.

If Deso was worried, then Rayden was a free man. The captain adjusted the shining knuckles on his hands carefully and with precision. But his confidence did not transfer to his men, who in turn moved positions, stood from one side of the room to the next, heading upstairs then back down, all of the things that would suggest nervous men. But these men were not capable of such. They were antsy, ready to get to whatever end they were meant for. Rayden Pratt could easily relate.

After the clear passing of another patrol, Scythe moved up toward Deso and sat beside him. "What's the plan after we get this door open?"

"How do you know that's not the whole plan?" Deso returned in hushed tone.

To which the tall Fallneesian shrugged. "Suppose I've known you long enough to know better than that."

"Aye," their leader responded. He gave a quick look about, noticing that his men were all carefully listening to the conversation. "Second the fighting starts, we make to the top of that wall and get to that mechanism. Nothing different than any other mission, so do not stop for the fallen. Priority one is to get to that mechanism. Priority two . . . we make for the tower."

Scythe raised an eyebrow to that statement. "We're going after Rowe?"

"About fucking time," Nails claimed. "Was wondering when this whole thing was going to make sense."

"Sense?" blurted Rayden instinctively, feeling a fool the moment he did.

Nails moved in closer, leaning over to him. "Aye, sense, boy. We aren't the military, despite what our fearless leader thinks. And this thing we're doing, not really our kind of job. Now infiltrating a tower and killing a House lord . . . a bit more our style."

"I would prefer not to kill him," Deso interjected. "He can end this damn battle before it gets too ugly, if we can get to him."

"It can end with his head on a fucking pole too," responded the large Ursan.

"You can't beat every problem to death with your damned hammer," Aaron noted.

"How would you like me to beat *you* to fucking death with my damned hammer?"

Flint chuckled at the two. "Both of you shut up."

"All of you shut up," hissed Mortar. "Can you hear it?"

The room drew silent . . . but the world outside this house was not. There was a roar far in the distance, followed by frantic yelling, then pandemonium. Rayden moved over close enough to peek outside the downstairs window to witness guards ramming into each other, searching for someone to command them, looking for somewhere to go. After a good minute of disorder, a few barking men were able to contain the guards and gather some sense of unity as they formed up and pushed east, away from the southern entrance.

The distraction as promised was working, but certainly not as complete as they would have liked and not nearly enough by his estimation. While guards began to move in droves to where there seemed to be the start of a battle, they had thousands upon thousands to begin with. There still stood a sizeable chunk leftover, guarding the doors, preventing their passage. Thousands of men . . . distracted men . . . but thousands nevertheless. The mechanism to open those doors, however, was located upon the parapet above them. Probably. More than likely anyways. Not like they could see it from their current perspective.

"Our distraction isn't going to last very long," Deso announced, standing now, as did the rest of the Divide. "I'd love to say it's been an honor or something like that, but I can't fucking stand any of you."

"Likewise," replied Nails.

"Aye," Mortar added.

"Hey Breeches," Flint called over. "Let's try to increase that kill count. This time there will be plenty left over for you."

"If I live through this," Rayden started, his sword now unsheathed, "you will have to deal me in to that stupid game of yours."

To which Flint laughed in response. "About time you saw the light, you skinny Donovinian shit."

Deso then moved up to the door and unlocked it. His hand reached the doorknob and held his ground for a moment . . . a long moment. Perhaps the longest moment of Rayden's life. He could not think, could not formulate his fears or his emotions. All that had led up to this point felt trivial and irrelevant. It changed absolutely nothing. Fair or unfair, just or unjust, none of that would keep him alive beyond a second outside that door. The only thing that would keep him alive was himself.

"Don't . . . think," whispered Scythe from behind him.

He took a deep inhale.

His sword felt somewhat lighter in his hands.

Deso threw open the door. The sounds of the outside world were void to Rayden. He could hear his breath, feel the sweat on his skin, see his legs push him forward out the door, but he no longer commanded any of it. Instincts controlled him, primal ones at that, and the young Pratt was on the streets before any part of his better conscious could persuade him otherwise.

Along the main street before the wall, there were still a few men running eastward, heading away from the doors, but they were sparse and without leadership. Deso led the way directly through a space between them, and Rayden did not hesitate to follow. The Argon guards were so frantic, so lost in the commotion that they barely noticed the eight men of varying races simply run through them as they sprinted along the wall. For a second it seemed as if they would simply walk right up and hit a switch, but life could not be so easy. Rayden of all people knew such. A single yelp from behind them had several others turn to face this new group, who of course ran the opposite direction of the rest. But the Divide did not stop. The stairs loomed just before them, the mechanism on the top of those stairs.

Deso did not make the stairs. About a dozen men stood in close proximity of them and he took them by storm. One, then two down by his fists as he cleared the way. Haze was the next up the stairs, followed by Aaron and Rayden directly behind. He did not look back to see if their leader needed help, if he stood any chance to live. There was no time for that.

On the parapet, Haze did not turn to the direction of the door, but instead met a direct charge of several guards that moved toward them all. Aaron did not stop either, turning toward the direction of the door, Rayden again moving just behind him. The mechanism was within sight now, along with about thirty men that stood between them. There was no room for second guessing. Aaron's two long blades went to work quickly, one guard gutted with his sword held high in the start of a swing, another went down to a quick jab while he held his stance.

Form, style . . . Rayden understood. All that he had learned as a boy and a teenager, all that had been taught to him, it was all shit here. He felt Scythe behind him and watched as his giant halberd went to work on the closest guard he could find. Rayden now had two members of the Divide in front of him along with just under thirty Argon guards, and behind those guards a single lever that would open one side of the doors that could let in the Imperial Army.

Rayden leapt up to the parapet and leapt along the top of the crenellated wall. Several guards watched in awe as he bounced from one notch to the next, bypassing a majority of the guards before hearing the roar of approval from the distant Imperial Army. There stood no fear of the guards to his right, no fear from the fall to his left. Driven by instincts, he moved forward with fury in his step. He could feel the earth shake as thousands began to storm the capital. It had begun and the doors had yet to be opened. His sword came down on an approaching guard, and then he dove back into the fold, back down onto the parapet. The hilt of his blade hit one guard on the chin, blood gushing outward, then a swift stab to another, then an arcing slice to a third. He was beyond the masses now, only one left to his side that he gave a kick to the groin. Now Rayden gave a dead sprint, nothing between him and the lever as he wrapped his left hand around it and pulled.

--

The door began to open and Shonnen heard his men bellow in anxious anticipation during their approach. Archers rained down onto his men, but there were not enough of them against the walls to do much damage. They had focused upon the attack to the eastern wall and had insufficient numbers here to repel them completely. But the focus of his men was the opened door, to make their way into the capital before the Argon guards found a way to shut them.

John's sword and shield were in hand, but he was further back from the masses. His men were far too eager for blood to allow their general anywhere near the front. An arrow landed beside him, taking down a soldier just to his right. Shonnen kept his shield high to deflect anything else inbound. He watched as the guards inside the capital were so unprepared, so unsure of what to do that they rushed out into the open to meet the charge of his soldiers. Steel clashed, blood spilled, and the battle had begun.

It did not take long for the first wave of the Argonus guard to be crushed under Shonnen's men, and the Imperial Army, or remnants of what once was, poured through one side of the open door. But with only one side open, they funneled through slowly and many simply pressed against each other, waiting their turn to enter Tessenul. This was where the archers above on the parapet began to do the most damage, as they simply pummeled arrows downward on the stationary men.

"Raise those shields!" screamed Shonnen and his orders were echoed throughout the masses. Even with them raised, men fell injured in staggering numbers, but they pressed onward. Had a majority of the Tessenul guards not been battling his seventh squadron along the eastern wall, the losses would have been catastrophic. John stole a glance upward, enough to see that the battle against the wall no longer seemed to take much precedence, that Captain Deso had accomplished his end and at the very least, it was not countered. Those along the wall did not seem to be fighting anyone other than the soldiers pouring into the capital, and if there was a battle along the wall, it was beyond his sight.

As he closed in to the wall, an arrow punctured straight through his shield, the tip of the arrow only inches away from his eye. It made the general hold his shield up higher, all the way until he was pushed and shoved and forced through the opening of the door. Immediately he spotted Sergeant Major Hollins, who stood atop several wooden boxes, exclaiming orders to his men. They had already taken the front doors, and now they seemed to be moving to the walls. Shonnen traveled with the flow of the men until he approached the sergeant, to which he then forced himself over.

His shield dropped as he climbed atop the boxes to make his way to Hollins. "Status, Sergeant!"

Hollins turned to him. "We have the courtyard secure, General! We need to take the wall, and then press to the eastern wall to aid the seventh!"

"We need to split these men, Sergeant! We need to get men to press north toward the tower! They still have thousands in between us and Rowe!"

Hollins gave a look that Shonnen would have given back to him in the same situation.

"They're all yours, General!"

John stared down as the men simply pushed forward, some upward, others eastward, others simply running to find something to kill. They were more like caged animals at the moment then trained soldiers. No words would stop them until their adrenaline calmed. If he was not in the middle of war, he would have laughed.

--

Rayden held his ground, with members of the Divide fighting from the back end of the wall toward him. He stood long enough to kill three more guards, long enough for the first wave of soldiers to enter Tessenul. After which, and rightfully so, the guards quickly lost interest in the small infiltration group. They scampered about, looking for their bows to attempt to suppress the army which was filtering through. Haze and Mortar were already moving back down the stairs, and Pratt took the opportunity given. With the guards panicked and otherwise occupied, and the number of corpses not easily counted, he simply leapt about and over bodies until he made the stairs unchallenged.

The guards slammed into the incoming Imperial Army, but it was like holding back an ocean wave. The Argon men had no leadership, no idea what to do or where to go, so they did what instincts alone suggested; they moved toward the storm. Rayden, however, spotted his companions already sprinting down the streets from whence they came, and he ran quickly to catch up. On the streets, he felt a swing before it reached him, and he did not bother to square up or fight back, but kept moving, allowing the guard to meet the air between them. Another Argon moved between him and the side streets and Rayden dove forward in stride, sword puncturing an arm. The blow was not lethal but it was not meant to be. It was meant to stall and hurt the man, which it of course did, and allowed him to continuing forward without pause. A kill strike would have involved him plunging his sword into the man, or cutting accurately into him, each requiring him to stop. But that was not the plan at this point. The plan was simple. Get to the tower.

Scythe waited for him in the alley and upon seeing him, waved him onward. He ran beside the tall Fallneesian as they moved from back street to alley.

"Everyone make it out?" he managed to ask Scythe while they ran.

"Not without new scars," he stated between breaths.

"To the tower?

"Aye," he responded. "Going to be fun."

For some reason, Rayden realized that Scythe's definition of fun was utterly different from his own.

--

After some time and some screaming as well, the men were back in line, at least for the most part. A portion had broke off and ran eastward to aid the seventh. Another chunk stormed northward, likely to hit the tower, or simply to find more to kill. But the courtyard now belonged to the Imperial Army, along with the southern wall. Organized, together, Shonnen reformed the front lines, Hollins set formations, and he and Baldin watched as they prepared to take the capital.

"We took some serious losses just getting in here," Colonel Ascotte made note, pausing for several precious seconds.

"But . . ."

Baldin shrugged. "Captain Deso came through. The losses versus the entry were . . . acceptable."

"Remember to tell him that when you see him."

"*If* he lives, I will." Baldin shook his head. "In either case, they still outnumber us. Likely a majority of them are gathering around the tower. But as long as we stick to formations, numbers should not matter as much. Streets have a way of negating numbers, and skill comes more into play."

"You speak as if we have done this before."

"No, I suppose we haven't. But the theory is right."

Shonnen nodded. "Let's test that theory."

Ascotte turned to the front lines. "Sergeant Major!"

It took only a few seconds for the elder Ursan to find his way to the officers. "Reporting, Colonel."

"Let's get this moving. Head to the tower, *slowly*. We are going to run into pockets of Argon throughout the capital. Keep it tight and together, Sergeant."

"As you command, Colonel."

Hollins moved back to his men and began screaming to them, calling for them to remain in formation at all times. Within seconds they were on the move, the thunderous sounds of thousands of feet hitting the stone echoing through Tessenul. What fear it must have caused for those inside, knowing that but a day before, all was well with the world. The perfection of the capital of Argonus, wealth and status . . . nothing could ruin such a day, such a life. And in the next moment, an invading force made it through the walls and began to destroy their fragile world.

It certainly did not please him. None of this would help him sleep at night. But it had to be done. It would be justified at the end of the day when he sacrificed himself for their freedom, all of them, even the Argons that they would take prisoner on this night.

"General," Ascotte beckoned. "Let's see this through."

--

The army finally made their approach, but they were still off by some distance. No mistaking the sounds of thousands of men marching, armor clanking and swords clashing. But they would be in for a battle they would not rightfully expect. Conquering the wall might have been one thing, but taking Tessenul was still far from their grasp. While Rayden and Scythe moved through the streets with relative ease, that was solely based on their lack of numbers. Even when spotted by a much larger force, they were not pursued. There stood little point, he gathered. Chase two men, or prepare for some six or seven thousand inbound? The choice was obvious.

But there were still many men left quite able to fight, and by quick glance, they were slowly coming together and organized. Blockades were being placed, archers looked to be setting up inside houses . . . it would be a battle . . . an ambush. While they might have been taken by surprise to start, someone now unified them and gave them purpose. General Shonnen would be in for a surprise if he thought this battle won. In fact, Rayden was uncertain still of their chances to take Tessenul at all.

Perhaps this was the reason Deso had them charge the tower. Taking Lord Rowe would end this, or so they all hoped. But what were the odds of their success? No better or worse than the general's, he presumed.

The rain started when they reached the tower. Drizzle at first, then lightning moved through the clouds above, and then it poured. The two members of the Divide simply pressed on, Rayden completely drenched within mere seconds from the storm. Still between houses and buildings, Scythe held up a closed fist and Rayden pressed against the wall. The tall Fallneesian gazed out, the tower now looming just before them, and the distinct sounds of battle could be heard over the rain and the thunder.

"They're already at it," stated Scythe, his halberd out as he charged the main street.

Rayden took his sword into his hand and did the same, quickly seeing the long, narrow bridge that connected the city to the tower littered with members of the Divide, bloody and engaged in battle. Clearly outnumbered by the guards that poured from inside the tower, and yet still Deso and his men moved forward, closer to the archway entrance.

Scythe charged down the bridge and nearly plowed into his own men in order to force his way to the front lines. Rayden eyed the side of the bridge, as it was not very steep and simply hovered some ten feet or so above a small channel that surrounded the tower. The water was not too deep, at least from his perspective. In fact, the bridge and moat were just for appearance as it appeared. *All for show, but I bet they wished the architect took his job more seriously.* He spotted a window that was accessible just within reach of the water. Sword sheathed, the young Pratt wasted no thought on the matter. He dove off the bridge and landed into the water, allowing himself to be carried downward as he swam toward the tower. The muffled sounds of the fight still audible, along with the drumming of rain against the surface of the moat. It only took maybe thirty, forty seconds for him to reach the tower, coming to the top for air upon doing such. The guards, if they noticed, did not pay him any mind quite yet. Sword unsheathed, he hammered the hilt of his blade against the glass window, shattering it. Carefully avoiding the glass, he lifted himself up and into the tower.

Not careful enough, though, as he saw the blood before he felt it, a deep cut on his left hand from the glass. Cursing to himself, he gazed about the common room here for but a moment, then moved across and opened the door. Two dozen guards covered the tower entrance to his left, each waiting their turn to find the space to move through and battle the invaders on the bridge. Behind them stood the spiral stairwell that led upward to the heights of the tower. He moved across with careful steps, watching as the guards kept their focus to the battle just in front of them, paying little mind to their rear. He found no issue slipping right by and making quick work of the stairs.

Of course it dawned on him that he had absolutely no idea where he was going.

"Earth and Flame," he mumbled to himself, continuing upward, stopping on each floor for a hesitant second. Once he saw no resemblance of life, he pushed onward. Four, five, six floors in with the same result. On the seventh floor, he found his first signs of life. Three children sat on the stairs themselves, staring downward at the battle and of course, now at him. The small Argon kids, two boys and one girl, a stunning glossiness returned in their eyes.

Rayden paused for a moment, certain that he looked of death to these kids. "Lord Rowe?" he managed to inquiry.

And one of them, the girl, pointed upward. "Next floor," her voice cracked in fear.

Not another wasted breath as he took to the stairs again, and the sounds of battle now reached the interior of the tower. If it had been any other men, any other seven soldiers, he would not have presumed them make it behind some thirty or so guards. But the Divide . . . they were far from ordinary men. And these guards were anything but elite.

The stairs conquered one more floor, he nearly found his head removed as an axe whistled from around a corner, and he ducked just in time to watch the weapon plow into the wall above him. The arms of the assailant yanked once without avail to remove his weapon, the axe embedded deep into the wall itself. Rayden made him pay, his sword coming upward and removing the guard's arms at the elbows. The Argon did not even bother to scream as his body must have gone through some kind of shock, he only glared at the open wound and fell to his knees, the blood ushering out by the buckets.

Rayden kicked him over and turned to face the direction from which he was attacked. Three men stood within the hall, staggered back in a defensive formation. They were afraid, having watched their companion lose his arms, and Rayden supposed they had that right. The young Pratt took a step toward the first guard, and in response the Argon dropped low with his sword held up to his ear. *Standard defensive stance. I bet he is thinking about his swing.*

And then Pratt snapped into motion, moved with experience he clearly did not have, as he came close enough to fake a swing. The Argon fell for the fake, moved his weapon to defend, and Rayden reeled back and kicked him between his legs. The guard fell to the earth, sword dropped and hands over his genitals, Rayden moved over him and rammed his weapon down through him. The second guard stormed him, a careless swing that Rayden merely muscled through in defense, then countered with a quick cut to the neck. The third Argon dropped his sword and threw his hands up.

"Let me go!" he pleaded.

Rayden motioned for him to move beyond him. The man ran with his arms in the sky, his pants clearly wet from fear. He let the Argon reach parallel to him before shoving the coward against the wall and driving his sword through his gut. He let him fall to the ground with his companions, then turned his attention to the door that they defended.

Reaching the handle, he turned the knob and flung open the door. Almost immediately a knife, poorly thrown, reached the door and simply thudded to the ground. Before he could fully chastise the sloppy, errant toss, the once wielder of the weapon charged toward him with another dagger in her hand. He spun about, dodging the attack, and punched the girl in the stomach. She dropped the weapon and he grabbed her by the neck, holding her firm and in place.

"I give up!" screamed an unseen man.

Rayden turned about, staring around the room, and found a solitary man, ducked low and behind a desk.

"Show yourself!" demanded Rayden.

And so he did, hands raised and shaking, the House lord of Argonus slowly stood from his hiding place. He met him once, many years ago. Of course Rayden had hair then, and looked more . . . prestigious he supposed. But if Rowe recognized him in return, he made no indication by his actions.

"You'd let a girl die in your defense, you spineless shit?" Rayden lashed out to Gerald.

"Just don't kill me," pleaded the boy.

And as Rayden stared at him, he realized just that; Gerald Rowe was nothing more than a boy, younger than he by several years. What did he know of war? What did he even know of running a country? The young Pratt fared no better when given his opportunity to rule Amon. At least this boy took the position given to him; he was just too arrogant and ignorant to realize that desperate men fight to the death because it is all that remains for them. Most guards were no more loyal than their paycheck.

But his attitude did not entirely relieve him of guilt. Gerald Rowe was notoriously bigger than his breeches . . . the irony of that thought not completely slipping Rayden's mind. This battle, this conflict could have found a different resolution had Lord Rowe been willing to negotiate, willing to listen to some sort of reason from the other side. But Rayden did not need to sit in to those conversations to know that the House lord would have things done one way: his way, or no way.

That mentality rarely, if ever, yielded positive results. More often than not, it yielded plenty of blood, plenty of second guessing.

"And please," begged Lord Rowe, "let my cousin go."

The girl remained calm, despite the blood from his hand now covering her dress. He then remembered that he cut his hand on the glass. And as he remembered, the pain began to surface through his adrenaline. And so he released the girl, though her eyes remained closed, her breath steady. Rayden wondered what she must be thinking.

"This ends now," demanded Rayden. "Can you get word to the front to throw down arms?"

The lord nodded quickly like an idiot.

"Well then, Lord Rowe, I suggest you do such."

After all, who liked a drawn-out battle? Certainly not Rayden Pratt, or on this day, Breeches of the Moon Divide.

--

People love to think that war involves two sides of massive numbers. So I would gather that many of those out there would say that I have never seen a war. But I guess my definition of war is different from most. A war needs two people, and only two people. Flame's embrace, if the readings of our histories are even true, most wars started with conflict between exactly two people. Because at the end of the day, that's all it takes. Two men . . . unable to see the same thing equally . . . unable to find common ground.

No, I've seen my share. Battles, wars, call them whatever you like. Let the histories speak of me as they wish. But in the end, I won them all. And do you know what I got for winning? Three ungrateful sons, a bad back, pains in places you never knew you could have pains, and nightmares that never, ever go away no matter how hard you pray to the fallen gods.

I'm beginning to think that my definition of winning is different from most too.

-- Landon Pratt, House Lord of Donovini

XXIV

There had been heavy rain overnight, and the mixture of grey and black clouds still hung overhead ominously in the morning over Corovium. Philip had barely slept as is, nor had he for several nights, and the thunderstorms certainly did not help any in that. He sat up in his bed, staring out his window toward the Vurid Sea, alone of course. Jessica had left their chambers entirely after the death of Christina, deciding instead to stay with Joanna and Winston. It was not in spite of him, though certainly that must have come into some play when the decision was made. Jessica was scared, for their children and for herself. And she had every right to be.

Two people assassinated, a kidnapped House lord, and fugitive House lady. The capital as of late was becoming more dangerous than the Ursan wilderness.

But Amon had a king and queen. Certainly not the ceremony that any of them wanted nor expected, but a ruler nevertheless. Jerryn wasted little time in his rule to announce his war against Ursan, to march the Imperial Army east to meet with Nicolas and his force to invade Ursan. About fifty thousand men left the capital, leaving less than ten thousand to defend it. That number would have normally felt . . . adequate at best. But nothing made the First feel safe as of late. Certainly not Allura. She wanted him dead, no doubts there. Doing so would cause a war within the capital, pit the Pratts and Donovini against the Rowes and Argonus. And being there already stood a war with Ursan, it would leave all of Amon in complete shambles, and place her rule in jeopardy.

No, Allura would need to find a safe way to kill him, one that could not point back to her. But without Christina there to pull in the reins, and with Jerryn seemingly under her control, there stood reason for him to believe that his days in the capital were limited. So what to do? Flee? Leaving his position would place him in the same fate as the Ursan court officials and their families. Apparently Allura took treason *very* seriously. He could not doom his family by simply running. But as to his next move, he had yet to figure it out.

And then there was Afeon . . . a Pyromancer . . . all the years he had known him, and never once had he suspected him anything more than the lackey of Dehyllo. The world was full of surprises. Philip hated surprises.

The knock against his door startled him. Of course it did.

"Enter," he called out loud enough for his guards outside to hear.

The door opened and a young courier entered with a small scroll in his hand. Must have been bad news, he figured. Far too early in the day for good news.

"This came for you, First Pratt, early this morning by bird carrier," the boy stated, his voice cracked and low.

Philip only waved him forth and the boy moved up and handed him the scroll. A quick bow and a step backwards, the courier turned and made his way back out of his chambers. The First cut the seal and read the contents.

First Pratt,

A few days into Fallneese and your damn instincts were right. Something is afoot here. Well I suppose I should rephrase that. Nothing is afoot here. I have moved through a few villages and they are all the same. Empty. Like the whole damn country has gone up and disappeared.

Plenty of tracks are heading north. Looks like they are assembling for something big. I am following the trail now, hopefully have something more for you in the coming week. All signs point to Itopis, but we shall see.

Nothing on the Historian yet, but maybe where I find all the people, maybe I will find a giant Kwyantin. Time will tell. I wish you would have told me what you knew before you sent me out here. I'd be lying if I said I wasn't a bit nervous.

I realize you have no way of sending me a message back, so hopefully you are still alive, lest I write to a ghost. If you are still alive, stay that way. Trust no one. And if you are dead, whoever is reading this, send word to whoever is in charge now in Corovium. Smells like war here. -- Second General Isani Brocusk

"Earth and Flame," mumbled Philip as he tossed the scroll aside.

Dylinn . . . what in Shadow are you doing?

--

The throne room looked clean, sharp, in a way it had not looked since as long as she had been alive, or at least remembered. All banners that had once represented Fallneese and House Aylmer had been removed and replaced with banners from both Pratt and Rowe. While the side room still suffered from damage from the battle with the Druid and the Shadowmancer, it was being worked on each day. Still, it would take some time to make it whole again. Paintings were placed along the wall from her favorite artists in Argonus, decorative weapons hung on display throughout, a wide fountain now sat in the middle of the room, and the members of the Imperial Army stood about in full armor, rotating out every hour on the hour, enough to keep the illusion of safety.

But it was an illusion, of that she knew. Her mother was a victim of that illusion.

The Ursan man that knelt before her was skinny and smelt of feces. Pale complexioned all the same as the rest of his race, he looked calm, at ease. He had spent the last several days in the dungeons along with any other Ursan from the capital. Any that claimed their loyalty to Amon and abolished their connections with Dehyllo were set free. Those that did not were killed.

She sat alone on the throne on this day. Jerryn did not have the stomach to sit through the prosecutions any longer.

"What is your name?" she questioned the Ursan.

"Heldon, my queen," was his answer.

"What do you do here in Genethur?"

"A tailor, my queen, and a representative of our goods from Ursan."

"Explain," she pressed.

Heldon gave a cautious glance toward her before eyeing the ground again. "My supplies only come from Ursan directly, and I fashion items that originate from my homeland. I do not work for the Guild, not directly anyways. I service a . . . particular clientele."

"The Ursan," she deduced.

"Yes, my queen. Not that I have any offense to others from outside my own people, but our style and culture is quite . . . unique I suppose."

"I would agree with that. And do you have any family in the capital?"

He nodded. "A wife, three children, my queen."

"Are they in the dungeons as well?"

"They are."

"Good, Heldon. Because your health and theirs is very reliant on the decisions you make today. Do you understand what I am saying?"

"I do."

"Good. So let us get to it then. Are you here, prepared to swear your loyalty to your queen, king, and Amon?"

"Of course, my lady. Since the moment I arrived in Corovium, I swore loyalty to any that held the throne. At the end of the day, I love Amon. I live upon Amon. And the king and queen of Genethur rule Amon. I bow to this throne, my queen, and the one that sits upon it."

"Thus you serve King Jerryn and Queen Allura Pratt?"

"I do," he answered.

"Excellent. You are almost a free man, Heldon, free to return to your honorable work here in the capital. You will be able to take your family with you as well. I will just need you to do one thing for me. I will need you to denounce your allegiance to your House lord, Dehyllo Brocusk."

Heldon turned his eyes to her and held them steady, saying nothing.

"Your House lord has committed treason against this throne, the same throne that you claimed loyalty to. They have kidnapped members of my family and assassinated my mother. They no longer acknowledge this throne as power, and that makes Ursan enemies to the throne, which also makes them enemies to Amon. Denouncing them allows you to join Genethur as a refugee. All you have to do is say the words. All you have to do is do the right thing. Denounce Dehyllo Brocusk as your House lord."

The Ursan shook his head. "That is something I cannot do, my queen. Dehyllo Brocusk is my House lord, and the true king of Amon."

She bit against her lip hard. "Then you have made your decision, Heldon." She pointed to one of the soldiers, who walked over, drew his sword, and buried it into the Ursan's back straight through. *Yet another mess on my floor to clean*. "Make sure his family dies as well, all of them."

Before his body even hit to floor, she turned to her right, Alex standing tall beside her. "How many so far have denounced Dehyllo since we started this?" she questioned.

"Including the Guild?" he retorted with an inquiry.

"No, excluding them. We know they only work for money. So except for the Guild, how many Ursan have denounced Dehyllo?"

"Then including Heldon?"

"Well of course," she smiled in response.

"Well then none, Queen Pratt."

"Outstanding."

Just another dead Ursan, I suppose. One less we have to kill in this war.

The throne room doors opened, and one of the guards bellowed, "Gillar, the court head, my queen!"

Allura turned to the now lifeless body spilling blood onto her floor. "Someone clean this up," she announced.

"Don't mind me," Gillar stated. "Continue your executions as planned, my queen."

Her mood went from pleasant to sour by his words alone. "What can I do for you, Gillar?"

"Well," the Fallneesian started, "far be it from me to let you know that there is a more to running a country than just killing people."

"Fuck you, Gillar. What do you want?"

"I have your recommendation, along with First Pratt's I might add, to start building fortifications here in Corovium."

"Do you question the move?"

Gillar shrugged. "It is curious. But being that we are now marching to war, I do not question your motives, Queen Pratt. We should be cautious. We *will* make enemies. So we should build this wall. There is just one major problem with this."

A soldier picked up the dead Ursan by his arms and dragged him across the throne room, another soldier behind him attempting to wipe up the blood. Gillar did not seemed bothered by the body, perhaps because it was becoming nothing new as of late.

"I suppose," she began, "that you are here for that very reason, Gillar. So just tell me."

"It costs money to build a giant wall surrounding our capital, Queen Pratt. A shit ton of money. And here is the thing. Your predecessors on the throne did not do well with our financial situation."

"And?" stammered Allura. "I have councilors and courts to deal with my finances."

"Well you used to," stated Gillar. "The one in charge of all financial situations in our council was a fucking Pyromancer that tried to kill you. And he is no longer here. And neither is one million, one hundred and seventy-three thousand gold coins that were owed to the Guild."

She returned a blank stare to the court head. "Say again."

"That was how much the throne owed the Guild, my queen. That is how much was signed off by our courts and removed from the treasury for transport to Orpay in Prillian. I've done some researching, though, and have found that the money never made it to Prillian."

"So, let me get this straight. The throne owed over a million gold to the Guild. For what exactly?"

"The war effort on the coast, my queen."

"And so that money was removed . . . well where is it?"

The short, chubby Fallneesian shrugged. "If I were a guessing man, somewhere where Afeon would be able to acquire it."

The ignorance of this council and these courts infuriated her to no ends.

"Do you aid me in running this country, Gillar?"

"That I do, as well as the council."

"Well you have done a shit job before I have arrived. I don't know how your relationship was with Aylmer, but we will be reforming a new relationship here amongst us."

"I'd be more than happy to, my queen," replied Gillar. "But that does little to help our current situation. We owe the Guild money, and until it is paid, they will not help us construct this wall. We also do not have the proper supplies in order to make this wall. With Donovini at war with Ursan, I decided to send word to Lady Aylmer in request of labor and supply support. I have heard nothing back from her as of yet."

"Then we do this on our own," answered Allura.

He nervously shifted position. "But that requires money, my queen."

"Then find it."

"It is . . . not that simple."

"I suggest you make it that simple," she hissed. Allura then waved her arms. "I am surrounded by incompetence. Send word to my council. I want a meeting with them, as with you Gillar. The four of you together, so that we can straighten a few things out."

"Ma'am, I don't believe there is anything that needs to be sorted. I suppose I could take a look at raising taxes in order to . . ."

"No, Gillar, the wall must be constructed *now*. I am not waiting for tax money to be collected so that we can negotiate supplies. We are about to be at war. We will have a dinner tonight to finalize the plan, and you *better* have something by then, or I will find a new court head."

His eyebrows raised some. "You understand I am voted on by the people."

"They can only vote for the living."

"Indeed." He wiped the sweat forming upon his forehead. "Then I will see what I can get done before our meeting tonight. By your leave, my queen."

Gillar bowed, fake smiled, then turned to leave the throne room. Allura watched him go, wondering silently if she would be adding him to her new list of people she needed dead.

--

Philip straightened himself, then knocked on the door to his daughter's chambers. In no immediate rush, Winston Leir opened the door, a startled look on his face.

"First," he stated, waving him in.

His son-in-law should be surprised, Philip gathered. His wife had left his side days ago, moved in with him, and this was his first visit. And it was anything but casual. As he strode in, Joanna smiled widely and stood from her couch, moving over to embrace him.

"Father," she whispered. "You should have come sooner."

He should have done a great many things. That changed little to where they all stood today.

"Matters have been . . . hectic, Jo," he answered. Jessica spotted him from the balcony, her face hardened and emotionless, but she managed to maneuver her way back into the main living room, back to where the rest of the family convened. Lillianna did not stand to greet him. Her face almost as cold as her mother's.

You deserve this. All of this.

"So," started his wife, "what is the bad news?"

Always too damn smart, woman. That is why I love you.

"It's time to leave the capital. Tonight." His family gazed about to one another as if they did not comprehend the words.

"Glad you finally see the big picture. Of course there is the problem with Allura and her banning my children to leave." Jessica pointed her finger distinctly toward him. "And if you even dare suggest that I leave without my children . . ."

"Don't be a fool, you are taking everyone," answered the First.

Joanna folded her arms. "What has changed your mind?"

Too much like your mother.

All eyes fixated upon him. "Nothing has changed my mind. I always felt it best for you all to leave once this all started. It just . . . it wasn't as easy as you make it. But you are right. Something has changed. I fear war is coming to Corovium, and walls alone that we try to build will not stop what is to come. To Shadow with Allura. I will stay and deal with any consequences that take place in having my family return home to help maintain Astrona while Nicolas marches our people to war." He turned to Jessica. "You need to be with Maradyn and Karen, helping the wives of my brothers run Donovini in their absence. You no longer need to be here, any of you, and wait for war to march upon us. It's time to leave, while leaving remains an option."

"And how do you suggest we do such?" Winston queried. "Allura Pratt has barred us from leaving the capital building, much less the capital itself."

"Who guards your rooms? The Imperial Army? I believe I still have plenty of sway over them."

Jessica did not seem pleased over his statements, if anything could please her these days. "And what of you? You staying . . . how do you think Allura will react? We have all been witness to her . . . shall we say, hammer."

"I doubt she could easily kill the First of Amon," stated Philip. "Not without the courts. She might be a tyrant in the works, but she does not have that kind of power, at least not yet. Thus the reason that now is the appropriate time, especially since I have a reason for you to head back home to begin with. I can tell Allura that you are needed home to help Maradyn, which is true, but mask the reality. It's not safe here."

"I'm not leaving you here alone, Father," Joanna claimed.

"There really is no option, my child," the First responded. "I need you out of here before we have a war flooding the streets. That, and maybe you can convince Nicolas and his men to think twice before marching into Ursan with the Imperial Army. I don't care how many numbers they have, Dehyllo will be able to match them. And any number that he is short, he gains advantage on understanding the terrain and having the foresight to plan ahead of this invasion. That and we now know that he has a Pyromancer on his side." He paused, gazing about at each of his family, realizing how deeply he loved them all. "I just need you away from what is likely to come here."

"I do not like the idea of leaving you behind," Winston said, though his voice had the distinct feeling of relief. "But I understand. Besides, I should be with Luther and the men on the battlefield."

"No you do not!" Joanna nearly shrieked. "You are not a warrior. My cousins are all warriors, but you . . . you are not."

"Neither are the boys that your uncle is likely recruiting for the war," responded his son-in-law.

"We can deal with that later," Philip interrupted. "Right now, you will leave the capital. We will take tonight to gather what you need for the road and sneak out while . . ."

"I'm not leaving," Lillianna firmly made claim, interrupting Philip.

When he turned to meet the eyes of his daughter, he recognized them immediately. Firm, demanding, unwavering. This was his daughter, through and through, and she was every bit just like him.

"I was born here," she continued, her voice steadfast. "This is all that I know. And all the things you say about Allura . . . but she has been one of the only people in the capital to ever show that she cared for me."

"How can you say that?" Jessica stammered.

"Because it's true!" she exclaimed, turning to Philip again. "You didn't even remember my birthday."

"I remembered," he softly stated. "It's just . . ."

"Your work," Lilli finished. "It's always your work. Allura is busy too, but she spends time with me."

"You have seen her cruelty first hand," the First continued, taking a few steps toward his youngest. "She *murdered* those Ursan women and children in front of everyone in attendance. And for what? To get what she wanted?"

"To get what she earned," Lillianna defended boldly. "And those Ursan . . . they deserved what they got."

Jessica now moved across the room, grabbing Lilli by her shoulders. "How *dare* you even think such a thing? What did they do besides keep their loyalty to their country? Would you denounce your people and your country just to stay alive?"

Lilli gave her an awkward stare in return. "Wouldn't you?"

"No!"

"Even if by doing so, you would kill your children?" Lilli pressed further.

"Well . . . I mean . . . more the reason why you should despise someone for forcing those to choose such a thing!"

But Lilli would not budge. "Or realize what fools they are for choosing their leader over their family. I realize how important family is. I know why you are doing this, Father. But I do not *feel* a part of this family. I won't tell Allura. I won't stop you. But I'm not coming with you."

"Well . . . you don't have an option," Jessica concluded.

Lillianna's face grew red, and tears began to form on her eyes. "Yes I do."

Don't say what I think you . . .

"Then I *will* tell Allura you are all leaving if you make me go."

The room became as still as death on her comment. There had been good reason for Allura to give her lady-in-waiting title to Lillianna Pratt. Young, influential, and of course, daughter of her adversary. She would give Lilli what Philip had failed to do for years. She would give her attention. And sadly, his daughter was young enough to fall for the bullshit.

"We are your family, Lilli," Joanna pleaded.

"So is she," answered the youngest. "She is a Pratt."

"She is a Rowe," hissed the First.

"She is the House lady," again retorted his youngest.

A standstill, by all means. There stood no resolution to this here, not until cooler heads prevailed.

"We do not have to decide anything this second," Philip claimed. "We can talk more about this later. We know that danger awaits if we stay here. Lilli, I need you to think about this, long and hard. I do not want you out of here because I want you away from Allura. I want you out of here because of the war that comes for us. When we build our walls, we will all but invite those to come and destroy it. And when they run through our streets, they will leave nothing but death behind them. There is no prejudice in war, my child. Only unadulterated hate. I want you away from this city because death comes for us all here. You are too young and too pure to be here for that day. I want you in our home country."

Lilli shook her head. "Genethur is my home country, Father."

She bolted beyond them, reaching the door and disappeared from sight.

And he did not know what else to do besides watch her leave. Allura had planted a seed, and it was growing in the worst of ways.

--

Alex moved through her chambers, examining the rooms one by one. Once satisfied, he returned to the entrance and nodded to her.

"Anything else, my queen?"

Allura shook her head and waved him off. He closed the door firmly behind him and she exhaled deeply. The world could not see her cry. But she wanted to, desperately. When her mother died, Jerryn did not even bother to embrace her, tell her that things would be okay. Something, anything would have been better than his apparent lack of concern, as if her death interrupted his otherwise perfect day. She no more wished for her friends to be in the capital than this very moment. Someone to just embrace her tightly, someone to let her cry into their shoulder.

She did not have that. In the capital, she had nothing. And so she breathed, pretended to everyone that her mother's death was just another day, when in reality it crushed her. Her father died when she was young, but before this death, Christina was a loving mother. Warm, smiling . . . she was everything that a mother should be. Allura never knew for certain if her mother loved her father, *truly* loved him, but his death changed her forever. Like day to night, she became a different person, but she had to. They would have taken the House title from her had she not been what she was. But despite it all, despite the bitterness and the arguing and the disappointment, Allura wanted her mother to love her, to be proud of her. What child would not?

And though Christina never gave her an inkling of a thought that she loved her, that she was proud of her, in her last actions . . . she saved her. Easily her mother could have done nothing as did the rest of them, including Allura. She had never seen a Pyromancer before, and likely neither had Christina. But motherly instincts being what they were she presumed, she shoved her aside, the ultimate notion of love.

And that was why she fought the tears. It was why she looked for a shoulder to cry upon. Not because her mother died, but because she died to save her.

Allura moved over to her bar and poured herself a glass of wine. The afternoon wound down and dinner would be soon. A meeting still loomed ahead with the council and Gillar to figure out the funding situation with building the wall, so her day was far from done. All morning she had taken care of Ursan families, all of which were killed upon the throne room floors. All save for the Guild members, of course. They denounced Dehyllo before they stepped before her. The rest from this morning, no different from yesterday or the day before, refused to denounce their House lord and died. They were more than half way through the prisoners at this point. She was hoping to have the executions wrapped up before week's end.

She sat upon her couch and took a sip. A moment to relax, of her only ones. Her mind wandered from her mother, to her day, then back to Alex. She had been thinking quite a bit of her only night with him lately. Jerryn stumbled into bed drunk last night and gave her quite an underwhelming experience, which he did not seem to be concerned with. He finished, and that was all that truly mattered for him. Alex, on the other hand, was the exhilarating feeling of fucking a complete stranger. Nervous, uncertain, and yet liberating all at once. Did not hurt that he was well endowed and knew how to use it either. She had thought more than once to invite him in at different times, to have another encounter with him, but thought against it. In reality, she was amazed he still lived. If Jerryn was not occupied with drinking himself stupid daily and nightly, he would have killed her guard and had him replaced the moment he became king. Situations reversed, Allura would have certainly done such. Not only that, she would have spent no time complaining about that either. Alex knew of her involvement with Rayden's disappearance, and of course fucked her on her wedding night, both of which could get her killed. With Christina now gone, his death would remove the last traces of evidence remaining. She *should* have pushed for his execution. After all, he roughed up the king a bit.

But for some reason, she was relieved he still lived. At least he was trying to protect her.

"My queen," whispered the soft voice of a girl behind her.

Allura nearly dropped her glass from her startle. When she turned, she could see the frail look on the face of Lillianna Pratt.

She immediately turned to the door. "Alex!" she screamed. To which the door immediately opened, and his eyes instantly spotted her lady-in-waiting. "You are the worst fucking bodyguard in the capital!"

Lilli spoke first and quickly. "I'm so sorry, my queen. I did not know you would be back by . . ."

"I am not upset with you, little one," quickly stated Allura. "You may come here any time you wish." Turning back to Alex. "You are worthless. I just wanted to show you that this teenage girl was able to slip your careful attention to detail."

"It will not happen again," was his response.

"It could have been an assassin," Allura continued. "Then there wouldn't have been a next time."

"Would you like me to escort Lady Lillianna Pratt to her chambers?"

"No, escort yourself back outside," she snapped.

Alex nodded again and closed the door. Lilli clearly had fear, or at the very least, worry written all about her.

"I am so sorry, my queen. I did not mean for Alex to be in trouble. This was the only place I knew to . . . well to be alone. I didn't expect you to be back already. When I heard Alex searching rooms, I didn't know whether or not to let him find me or just to keep hiding."

"It's fine, truly it is." There was clearly something Lilli kept from her. "Come, sit."

The girl did as asked, moving over to the couch across from her and sat down calmly. Her tanned skin beautifully dark, her eyes a golden brown, the girl was gorgeous. Allura realized for the first time that she would become a beautiful woman in her adulthood. One thing to say about the Pratts, she thought . . . easy on the eyes.

"Are you . . . sad, my queen?"

The girl was clever. She would read people well for being so young.

"I don't have time to be sad, little one," was her answer.

Lilli took a moment, her eyes down to the table between them. "When will you have time to be sad?"

If her body would have allowed her to cry, Allura would have taken the moment to do such now. But she could not, would not allow herself weakness. Not even in front of the girl.

"I mourn in my own way, I assure you. I loved my mother, and she loved me. But she also loved Amon with a passion that I can only hope to replicate. She taught me what was truly important in life. Should I sit back and cry . . . I would not do my mother justice. There will be a time and place for tears, Lilli, I promise you. But now is not the time." She placed the glass of wine down and smiled genuinely. "So, do you want to tell me why you were hiding in my chambers?"

"I was . . ." she hesitated. She was searching for a lie.

"Remember our conversation from before? How am I expected to run my House while secrets are kept from me?"

"I know, my queen. But I came here to ask something from you, but it is . . . difficult to ask."

Allura shook her head. "Do not fear to ask a question. So, what is it that you would like from your queen?"

Lilli's eyes gazed up to meet her own. "I want you to send my mother and my sister back home."

Curious . . . is this your words or your mothers?

"This is not the first I have heard of this request. Your mother came to me personally over a week back and informed me should would like to take all of you with her back to Astrona."

"She was frightened for us," admitted Lilli. "I know that she still is. But she honors your request to stay. But my uncles are preparing for war and my mother's place should be by my aunts, helping to run Donovini while Uncle Nicolas and Uncle Edmond are away to war."

"And your sister?"

"Winston should be at war . . . with the rest of his people."

"*His* people?" stammered Allura. "They are your people as well, little one."

"I was born in Genethur, my queen."

"Where you were born has nothing to do with who you are, Lilli. The earth beneath you does not change the fact that you are Donovinian."

"The Ursan would disagree," was her retort.

"And that's why we are fucking killing them," Allura replied hastily. "Genethur was given a name and a place as a sign of peace. Do you know why there are no walls? Because it was to show that there was no fear of war, no fear that our people would resort back to our primal ways of combat and death, to fight over pieces of the land. Foolish. No walls, no wars. But times have changed, little one. You are right to be concerned for your mother, your sister, for your brother-in-law. But never forget who you are. You are a Donovinian. It is something to be proud of, not disputed."

"Proud," she mumbled. "My cousin, your husband, is busy getting himself drunk nightly in local bars in the city. What is there to be proud of about that?"

"Do you know why he does such?" Allura waited a moment, but Lillianna gave no indication that she knew the answer. "I *asked* him to do such."

"But . . . why?"

"The people are frightened, little one. Do you know what frightened people do? They panic. They make brash decisions. Two assassinations . . . they worry for their own safety now, as does your family. The king does not need to be in hiding. He needs to be among them, with them, drinking with them and being a fucking idiot. They *need* that. It does two things. First, it keeps morale high, which drives fear away. Second, it keeps the focus away from the capital. If the public knew that all we have done thus far in our rule is execute traitors, I suppose you could imagine what could happen. The Ursan could gain the sympathy of the masses, and the last thing we need is to martyr these traitors."

"So you asked him to go and get drunk?"

"I did, with a thousand or so from the Imperial Army with him."

Lillianna gave a single nod. "So . . . do you disagree with sending my family away?"

"I think . . ."

The door came open, and Alex held a scroll. "A message for you, my queen."

"And you felt the need to interrupt me because of that piece of news?"

Her personal guard gave a bit of a frown. "It's from your brother, from a bird carrier. I thought it might be important."

"And what exactly would my brother have to tell me that is important enough for you to interrupt me? Just throw it on the table there and I will look at it when I have the time."

Alex shrugged his indifference and did as commanded, again shutting the door.

"Anyways," Allura continued, "I think that there is some validity to your concerns. But you mentioned nothing of yourself in your request."

"Because my place is by your side," was Lillianna's answer.

To which Allura smiled to the young Pratt. "Yes it is."

--

Philip sat down in his familiar chair in his even more familiar office. Still the First, for all that truly mattered, he supposed. The work still piled before him, as it normally had as of late.

Well . . . it certainly isn't going to clean itself, now is it?

He started to riffle through the top stack of his papers, organizing and situating, when he caught sight of a sealed scroll from the Imperial Army near the top of his stack. The seal clearly from First General John Shonnen.

One of his guards opened the door slowly. "First Pratt, your wife is approaching."

"Fine. Tell me, when did this scroll arrive?"

The guard poked his head into the room and gave a quick glance to his table. "The one from the coast? Today, First. But . . . it wasn't marked with anything indicating that it was urgent, so I left it on your table."

He found his letter opener and cut the seal, suddenly finding himself in a hurry.

After all, good news normally had patience. Good news could always wait.

As he opened the scroll, it had quite the extensive introduction for him, and another rather lengthy closing from *Captain* Deso. The word in between the introduction and closing was the most important word he had read in quite some time.

Yes.

Yes, to the question he had sent Deso quite some time ago. Was Rayden Pratt in his possession and was he still alive?

"Philip," stated the familiar voice of his wife, and the First met her gaze. Scroll dropped for the moment, he rose and moved across the room.

"What is it?"

"The queen has asked that I leave the capital, along with Jo and Winston. She has made it clear through her messenger that we have very little option in leaving."

"Lilli?" he asked, but Jessica only shook her head to his question, tears already forming in her eyes. "Do you think that she . . ."

"Of course she told her," Jessica snapped.

"I will find a way to get her out of the capital."

"Phil . . . you can't even get yourself out of the capital." Her hands reached out and touched his face, soft and perfect, as her touch always had been. "Promise me you will look after our baby. She is not as grown as she would think. Allura is dangerous and she just doesn't understand that now."

But the First shook his head. "Don't worry about Lilli. I need you to understand that this could be a blessing for us, though it clearly doesn't seem as such. I need you to take this opportunity and get to Nicolas. I need you to tell him that Rayden is alive."

But his wife returned a puzzled look. "Well of course he is, or else he would not be marching his army into Ursan."

"That's what I mean. He is alive, and he is *not* in Ursan. He lies on the eastern coast under the supervision, one way or the other, of a member of the Moon Divide."

"What?" she stammered.

"Allura hired a member of the Moon Divide to take care of Rayden, not knowing that they swear loyalty to the First of Amon. And Deso knew me well enough to know my family as well. Instead of killing him, he removed him. Maybe he thought it safer for Rayden away from the capital, maybe he has a different plan. All that truly matters is that I know for a fact that Nicolas's son is alive, and he is part of the Imperial Army on the east coast."

"Why would Allura want him dead?"

"She was involved with Jerryn, probably for some time now. Clearly before their recent visit to the capital. And she must have cared for him enough to have Rayden removed so that she could have Jerryn instead."

"Then . . . who does Dehyllo have?"

Philip shrugged. "Maybe Katlynn. Maybe no one. I need you to deliver this message to him for me. I cannot trust sending this information out on a bird carrier. I *need* you to do this for me."

"And do you really believe your brother will deter his plans for war?"

"I don't know," honestly answered the First. "But it's the best chance we have at some sort of peaceful resolution with Ursan."

She nodded to him, a sad one at that. "I will do as you ask. Will you do as I ask?"

"Do not worry about Lilli."

Jessica frowned. "How can I not? Every fiber of my body is telling me to send my guards up and just take her with us, knocking her unconscious if we must."

"The queen would have you hunted and killed."

"I don't care about me. I care about my children."

"Then get Jo out of here," pleaded Phil. "I will . . . I will think of something."

His wife turned her eyes from him. "I won't be returning." Her voice was firm, final in the statement. "War or not, peace or not, I will not be returning to the capital."

I know. Earth and Flame . . . are these the last words we will ever speak to one another?

"Jessica . . ."

"Don't."

"I love you."

She grabbed his shirt and brought him close, kissing him passionately, slowly, deeply. She then embraced him, held him tightly and he felt her warmth. Then, quite abruptly, she pushed him back far enough away to swing her open palm across his face, the sound echoing inside his chambers, the pain exploding against his cheek.

"You've got a fucked up way of showing it, Philip Pratt." She turned from him, pausing at the door, contemplating perhaps more to say, more to do. But she did not turn to him, did not dare face him one last time. Instead she opened it and took her first steps toward Donovini in all likelihood, her first steps out of his life forever.

The scene already replayed inside his head, and he wished he would have said something more.

But in the end, what more was there to say?

--

The night upon her and Allura stormed back into her chambers. The meeting had been, for the most part, a failure. First Pratt did not show to the meeting, as he claimed he wanted to spend time with his daughter before her immediate departure from the city. Gillar showed but had very little input as to how they could simply come up with the materials to build a wall without buying them. Her Uncle Lurey suggested that they start to tear down some of the lesser areas of the city in order to use those materials for the construction, to which Allura immediately threw out. Ousting people from their homes was not a smart way to start a reign as ruler of Amon. And Lijid, not surprisingly, added nothing.

About thirty minutes to eat, thirty minutes to stare at each other and throw out ideas, and they conceded to wait for First Pratt. All in all, a waste of one hour of her life.

I am the fucking queen. Why can I not just go to the vault of money and simply take what is mine? This is my country. Does the treasury not exist because I allow such?

Clearly she was upset, but things were beginning to compile. Her losses, her lack of a husband and lover, her lack of friends and family . . . and now she began to feel a crippling effect of leadership. Perhaps there stood a bit of validity to Dehyllo and his tyrant ways. Here, everything had to be done through proper channels. She might have been the ruler of Amon and she might have been able to execute traitors at will, but that was because the law was written out accordingly to allow her to do such. Perhaps killing, the easiest of her executive powers, was in place purposefully for stress relief. Consequently, however, she could not just waltz in and take money from the treasury, despite the fact that she made the decisions on how that money was spent, how it was collected. She should have the power to simply take. But the laws prevented that. It had to be loaned to her. And what bank would willingly loan the throne money when they just loaned over a million to the throne to repay the Guild, money that the Guild did not receive, money that no one currently knew the location to.

So in came a series of dire questions. How important was this wall? In the mind of Allura, not very important. In the mind of her mother, detrimental. Walls invited far more trouble than an open door. Challenges were often accepted by those that felt instigated. It was human nature. An open door was inviting, welcoming, humble. A wall shouted to others to keep out, making those on the other side curious what lied within. But many suspected that war was upon them, and not just the army that marched toward Ursan. So if a wall needed to be built, then so be it. Problem was money . . . the problem was *always* money. So she would visit with the First in the morning. Likely he would be upset for her sending away his wife and daughter . . . but that was something he would have to live with.

She poured herself a glass of wine, then remembered that she had not finished her first glass. Turning, she spotted the scroll from her brother that Alex had dropped off. She took it in hand, then grabbed a blade and cut the seal.

My sister,

I do not wish to alarm you with opening this letter to hear of foul news, so I want to assure you that things are under control. Having said that, Tessenul is currently under siege from John Shonnen. His men are hungry, skinny, and of no real threat. We outnumber them by quite a bit, but Shonnen certainly has enough men to form a siege against our supplies.

I defer to my commander, Frederick Pullman. He believes that we should not have a long, drawn out battle with General Shonnen. If they storm the walls, there have been some thoughts to just allowing him inside. Pullman is beginning to set up blockade after blockade, trap after trap. Our walls can defend us against their numbers, but eventually we will be forced to confront them. The choices are simple, and yet we must tread carefully. Pullman believes that if we simply sit back and wait, eventually our supplies will run thin while they raid nearby villages and steal from our supply lines. Also they will take every incoming supply until word gets back to the Guild that this siege takes place. At some point we will become just as hungry and weak as they are, if not more so.

But if we lightly defend the wall and keep the option to open the doors to them, it would be chaos at first. Should Shonnen gain entry, he will likely head to the tower. Here is where he will face his end, as Pullman is confident that his plan of ambush will annihilate the former army. Best to get this whole thing over with quickly, he thinks. We have the numbers, we have the position, we might as well use it to our advantage while we can.

If you are wondering why they face us, it's because they've grown desperate since they have been disbanded. They attacked a Guild outpost, and Orpay wants me to kill them for it. And so now they want sanctuary or war. I cannot give them sanctuary. Orpay has threatened to cut us off if we do anything but kill these men. So then it must be war.

There is so much to tell you, but this damned battle has got in the way. Please do not worry. These men that battle us are desperate, and are not worth a thought. Do not send the Imperial Army to me. I can handle this. I need to handle this.

How is mother? Please do not have her worry over this. I will send the First General back alive if I can so that he can answer for his war crimes. I do miss your ridiculous sense of audacity here back home. Your friends always ask how you are doing. I always lie and tell them you are doing great. But how would I know? You don't write. And when you do, it's barely worth noticing. Is Jerryn everything you had wanted? I hope you are doing well. I worry about you.

Speaking of which, I met an officer today on the side of the First General. He was at the parlay before we shut our doors completely and armed our wall. Though to be honest, he did not act like an officer. He was very clear in sending a message to you. His name was Captain Deso, apparently handpicked by First Pratt himself. Not so sure I believe that, but it would make sense that he knew you if it were true. He was a Fallneesian, very dark complexioned with no eyebrows. He wanted me to tell you that it was a pleasure working for you. And he said that prize was still intact, whatever that means. I . . .

The letter dropped from her hands without another word read.

"Earth and Flame," she murmured.

Rayden Pratt lived.

"Alex!" she screamed and the doors immediately opened, her personal guard entered with a start. "Close the door."

He firmly shut the door behind him and turned to her. "What is it, my queen?"

Allura walked over and used a match to light a large candle by her bar. She took the scroll and let it catch on fire, watching the edges blacken and turn to ash, the smell filling the room.

"Tell me, Alex, my mother once asked you to kill for her. You did so without question, did you not?"

"That is true, my queen," he answered solemnly. "She asked the bartender to disappear. So I interpreted that my own way."

"And if I asked you to do such now . . . would you?"

"You are the queen. I am at your disposal."

"Good. I have been haunted by my poor decision with this Rayden thing for too long. I need people . . . gone."

"How gone?" he inquired.

Allura smiled. "Someone once told me, no better gone than in the dirt."

"I'm inclined to agree with that. So . . . who exactly are we talking about?"

"Three men, three that know of my involvement with this. I need them all dead. One is a Fallneesian named Captain Deso of the former Imperial Army to the east."

"You want me to leave your side? Travel to the east coast?"

"This is important," she assured. "My reign on the throne could depend on the death of these men."

"It also means that I am not here to protect you any longer."

"I am aware." *I don't like it, but I am aware.* "The second is Rayden Pratt himself. He is with Captain Deso, in some capacity or the next. If he is not, ensure you torture the captain until you find out where he is hiding Rayden. When you do, kill him."

Alex's eyebrows crunched in, concern clearly on his brow. "It will be done . . . if it is your will."

"It is my will. You will do this . . . without question. As with my mother. Right?"

He nodded, but with some reluctance. "I am your protector, in all ways, in all things. I will kill these men. Who is the third?"

Allura smiled. "The First."

His eyes widened. "Say again."

"Kill Philip Pratt."

--

I was on the western coast, a prisoner in Fallneese, searching for an escape, desperately looking for the vessel. Little did I know that the vessel was desperately looking for me. All of Amon crumbled around me, with Dylinn marching south against the capital, the Pratts forming their men for the march north against Ursan.

It was easy to see why the conflict on the eastern coast seemed trivial at the time. How could we have known that the fall of Amon began with the Battle at Tessenul? How could we have foreseen what was to come?

Then again, how could we have not?
-- Aldric, Historian of Amon

XXV

It was a bloody mess. The books, the stories . . . they never really painted the full picture, or at least all of the finer details. War seemed glorious, righteous. But from where John Shonnen stood, it was bodies smashing into bodies, men grabbing anything they could, yanking, pulling, biting . . . especially biting. Very little room to swing a sword when pressed against each other. So men from both sides resorted to kill in any way they could. In fact, many were trampled underfoot. All it took was a misstep before one man, friend or foe, was forced into the spot, forced to step on the fallen, forced to press down and brace themselves against the opposing wave. Glorious and righteous . . . well this was neither. This was organized madness, and the smell of musk, blood, vomit, piss, and defecation could make even the strongest of stomachs nauseous.

War . . . if the Historian ever asks for my accounts of this, I will make sure to include the smell in my descriptions.

The General watched as they cleared through the intersection, but this was rough going. After the first surprise attack, they had been better prepared. But being prepared and finding success were two completely different things. Pullman's strategy against them had consisted of archers well hidden inside of houses and atop the roofs. His soldiers hid down alleyways and poured from inside of homes. Their numbers in these small packs were nothing in comparison to the Imperial Army, but since they were bottlenecked, the numbers did not stack up the way they should have. Besides, his former colonel clearly had no intentions of winning on all of these smaller skirmishes. He intended to start thinning their numbers. And of that, he was succeeding.

Once, the attack came head on. Another time, the archers sent down waves just ahead of them while they were flanked by another smaller group. Each time, even suspecting the attack, the Argons killed many of his men at the cost of their own lives. John's men were desperate enough to consider each wave they survived a victory, but he knew better. The Argons were winning this war, and winning it quickly. Already down to half of his force, they pushed forward with determination against this next wave but they were struggling. The strength of the men on the other side were men that had yet to fight; well fed men that were at the very least in shape. Not skilled, but healthy. His men were tired men, beaten down in more ways than one. Numbers alone were winning them these battles against much smaller forces, but that would not hold for long.

In the middle of his men, screaming and commanding, was Sergeant Major Hollins. He did the best he could, but his men were ravenous. Given an objective, they simply tore through anything in front of them or were cut down in their effort. Hollins himself looked wounded, but that did little to stop him. He had his own archers scale the tops of houses and rain down a barrage of arrows onto the pack of Argon soldiers. The tactic was effective in the simplicity of it, using the strategy against them. Problem was, of course, the archers on the other side of the open plaza. They focused less on the oncoming army and more on the archers, which of course forced those archers to start aiming at the other archers.

War . . . organized madness.

Baldin Ascotte still stood by his side, shield at the ready, but his weapon sheathed. No point in drawing a weapon in the crowd they were in. Though in the back half of the formation, the two officers were still surrounded, anxious men all about them that could do little but hold up their shields in defense of the rare archer attack that reached their ranks. Men that he had known for years fell about him in staggering numbers and it left him numb. A pointless battle. What was it for? Survival, he reminded himself. Irony of course in the amount of deaths just for the sake to survive.

Turitea . . . Schill . . . find a way to stop the death. Find a way to ease this suffering.

--

The blunt end of his knife pressed hard against the girl's neck with his right arm, his left arm wrapped around the front of her, just above her breasts. It was a tight squeeze and it did not seem necessary, but Rayden's nerves were getting the best of him. He had arrived this far on adrenaline alone, but now that the moment had ended and he had an opportunity to think, doubt crept into his mind. As Gerald Rowe moved ahead of them both, slowly making it down the stairs, he wondered exactly why he simply did not just take Gerald as a hostage. What was keeping him from just running the moment they made it down the stairs?

Because this girl is important enough to him to not run. If he was my hostage instead, who knows how he would react, how his guards would we react. Maybe they wouldn't care. Maybe they would just let me kill him, then kill me.

The girl might have been seventeen or eighteen or somewhere in that range. He blew away her shoulder length brunette hair from his own face.

"I'm not going anywhere," she stated, her voice steady and firm.

"No shit," he mumbled back in her ear as his dagger pressed a bit harder.

She squirmed for but a second to get more breathing room. "As in you can ease back a little and let me breathe. Might keep some of my hair out of your mouth too."

"You've got a strange attitude toward a man with a knife at your throat."

"And blood all over my dress."

Rayden gave a quick look at his hand, the cut no longer continually bleeding but it remained filled with the color red nevertheless. His mind too clouded, his tension too coiled to feel the pain. But it would come sooner than later.

"I've had worse," he lied.

"Well you should get that looked at."

"I appreciate the concern," he snapped.

"It's not concern. I would just rather you not bleed on me. And don't feel too special. I'm pretty much this way with everyone. Besides . . . you aren't going to kill me."

She whispered the last part, and Rayden frowned to that comment. "Did you not see the bodies of the men that you walked over to reach these stairs?"

The girl exhaled loudly in doubt. "I did not question your skill. I only question your character. Takes a cold man to kill a defenseless woman."

"You weren't so defenseless a few minutes ago," he commented. "So being that you tried to kill me, I might have to disagree with you."

"But you won't disagree, will you?" He could feel her smile as they continued down the stairs. "I can see that in your eyes. I know sadistic. If you have heard stories of the Rowe's cruelty, I must assure you, they are all accurate."

"From my understanding, it was mostly on the Hillan side."

"Ha, well I suppose it is a good thing that I am from the Rowe side of the family. Now about that grip . . ."

"Shut up."

"Fair enough."

Their decent concluded, the sounds of battle ongoing. The bridge remained the battleground, and men from inside the keep still waited their turn to die apparently. Gerald raised his hands and yelled out to his men.

"Drop you weapons!" he screamed, to which his men within the tower whipped about. "Surrender! We are surrendering!"

There stood a few awkward seconds as the men stared blankly at their House lord, bewildered perhaps in his cowardice or just perhaps in the situation entire. Certainly they had no desire to surrender, even though it had appeared from his vantage point that they were losing severely to the Divide. But it did not matter. Their House lord gave a command and they in turn dropped their weapons, one after the next, each less enthusiastic about the task than the previous.

"Move them into the next room and close and lock the door," commanded Rayden.

Gerald pointed to the other room. "You heard him," the House lord mumbled. "Who's got the key?"

One of the guards reached in and handed the House lord a key, then the men began to pile into one of the side rooms. Those from outside began to disengage cautiously with the Divide, backing themselves step by step into the keep and into the room with their companions. When they were all gone, Gerald locked them in, and the members of the Divide slowly moved inside the tower.

"Fucking Breeches," murmured Aaron, the first to enter through the doors. He was an absolute bloody wreck. "Gather you right about showed me up this time. Makes the whole Guild outpost thing go away real fucking quick."

Scythe and Haze moved through next, followed closely by Mortar and the remainder of the named men of the Divide. They were all in bad shape. How they were even alive was the better question.

Deso moved in, his arm cut deep at the shoulder, but otherwise looked better than most of the Divide. "Good work, Breeches," he commended, a rarity from his experience. "But we got this now. Let the bitch go."

"Can't say I blame you for holding her tight," noted Mortar, who looked to have gained a few more healthy scars about him.

"Aye, I'll drink to that," Flint chimed in with a grin upon his face.

"What won't you drink to?" questioned Nails, whose large frame piled into the entryway.

Rayden hesitated, but the glare from Deso felt absolute. He released the girl and she in no immediate rush moved away from him and over to Gerald. The House lord moved his eyes amongst the Divide. "Who are you?" he inquired.

"Captain Deso of the . . ."

"Who are you *really*?" he pressed.

Nails chuckled. "Dead men, something we will likely have in common here shortly."

"Shut up, Nails," snapped Deso before turning back to Gerald Rowe. "We need to get you to the battlefield, cease arms so that we can discuss the terms to your surrender."

"Terms?" queried the House lord.

"Yes, Lord Rowe," answered Deso. "You are still the House lord here, correct? Well General Shonnen has no intentions of taking power, I hope you realize. He met you for a parlay. You spit in his face. Be wise and meet him again, and you will yet retain your rule of Tessenul."

"How certain can you be of that?" continued Gerald.

To which Nails bellowed loudly. "Like you have some sort of fucking choice?"

"Well . . . fair enough. Shall we go then?" Gerald inquired.

"We won't need to go very far," Flint made note, pointing outside. "I think the battlefield is coming to us."

Rayden moved quickly into view of the door and caught sight of a larger force forming, a big man with elaborate armor at the front. Maybe thirty soldiers at first as they came from the main road and adjacent streets, but the number increased as the seconds passed. Forty, maybe fifty, and they did not seem to be in any immediate rush. Perhaps they had not known that the House lord was now captive . . . but there was something in the way they approached . . .

Deso must have sensed it as well.

"Get ready to close these doors," he commanded, pointing to the twins.

Scythe nodded, his arms pressed against a deep wound in his arm. "Aye," he responded.

The captain took a step out onto the bridge leading to the tower, pointing out toward the oncoming force, primarily the one in charge. "Cross that bridge alone, or find your House lord dead!"

The leader rose a closed fist upward to the soldiers that trailed him and they stopped several paces away from the bridge in response. But he did not cross the bridge at all, rather decided to speak up loudly from the distance between them. "Captain Deso, was it?"

"Aye. Frederick, right?"

"That is correct. Used to be a colonel in the Imperial Army, before I realized that following the general would get us all killed. So . . . interesting seeing you here."

"Like I said," continued Deso, his arms gesturing toward the air around them, "big fucking walls, false sense of security."

He huffed in response. "Mind if I see Lord Rowe?"

The captain nodded. "Breeches, bring the prisoner."

After taking a moment before realizing he had been called, Rayden moved over and waved the House lord over, to which Gerald complied. He placed his hand firmly on the shoulder of Gerald and guided him over to the door. Part of him realized who this was, brother of the woman that married his brother. He was family now. *Maybe I should give him a hug?* In reality, he had a strange desire to kill him.

Rayden allowed the lord to make his way directly to the entryway but not through, stopping him there.

"Are you okay, my lord?" called out Frederick.

"As well as I can be," answered back Gerald. "They have Jennifer as well in here."

Hard to tell faces from this distance, but Rayden got the impression that kidnapping did not sit well with the former colonel. "Let the girl go, Captain. Not very prestigious of you to hold a woman hostage."

"We will let the girl go once you lay down your arms," Deso stated. "Lord Rowe is calling for an immediate surrender."

"Surrender?" baffled the large Argon. "Why surrender when we are winning this battle?"

"And yet I have the upper hand in this situation."

"Depends on what side of this bridge you're standing on, I suppose," announced Frederick.

"I'm standing on the side where we fucking kill your lord and that bitch inside," snapped Deso.

"And then we kill you," answered the former colonel, shrugging his indifference. "Maybe a fair trade?"

"How *fucking* dare you!" screamed Lord Rowe and Rayden tightened his grip. "I am in command of this capital. *Me!* You are lucky I let you inside these walls, you fucking deserter! You *dare* take my hospitality and stab me in the back!"

"I do this for your honor, Lord Rowe," continued Frederick. "What would it look like, you surrendering the capital of Argonus while you babysat for your mother?"

"I surrender to end this bloodshed on our streets!"

"You surrender because they have a blade to your throat!"

Deso sighed heavily. "Fuck this. We do this our way now. Nails, give me a knife."

Nails grunted, grabbing a thin narrow dagger sheathed at his side and handed it to the captain. Deso did not even wait for a blink of the eye. Once the weapon was in his hands, he sprinted across the bridge, causing the men to stumble about in startle. Once he made it a quarter distance across the structure, the dagger released from his hands in a grunted heave, and Rayden watched in amazement as the dagger soared through the open space between Deso and Frederick. The former colonel had seconds to react and used those precious seconds reaching for his shield. It did him little good strapped to his back.

The dagger found a new home in Frederick's neck, and while he reached instinctively for the blade, blood poured effortlessly from the wound. The men around the former colonel simply froze in uncertainty, watching as he grabbed the weapon, attempted to pull it out, then simply dropped to his knees and eventually to the ground altogether.

Deso stood his ground almost half way across the bridge now, staring down the some forty or fifty men that now focused on him.

"Any of the rest of you defy your House lord?"

Silence.

"Good," said Deso. "Make your way back to the front and lead the way for us. Your House lord wishes to see his men and declare the surrender."

And to his amazement, the men across the bridge complied, turning about one by one, heading back toward the interior of the capital.

Deso spun back and met the eyes of Rayden Pratt and Rayden could not help but feel slightly inadequate in comparison. This man might have been a killer, but he also had a wonderful way with people.

--

The archers might have run out of arrows the general presumed because they had finally ceased firing upon his men. Still trapped in a wall of bodies, the plaza that opened up between two housing areas crowded with both battle and death. Men were having trouble finding each other, and both sides had to pause on occasion to move bodies aside in order to continue killing. It was appalling, and if Shonnen had given any chance to think upon the situation, he would have been sick. As it were, he had a feeling that sleeping would prove difficult in the coming days, presuming he lived at all.

Hollins still rose above others, sending men in varying directions, plugging holes in their defenses, charging different weakness in the opposition when needed. And all things considered, he performed admirably. By some standards they were actually winning this current skirmish. The problem being, of course, there were more. There was always more. Every alley, every home, every open space, Argon guards filled it. They were winning one street at a time, but there were many streets between them and the tower. Should they make it, there would be nothing left of them. Shonnen knew this. Baldin certainly knew this as well. Even Hollins likely understood. But what options stood for them now? Retreat back to the entrance? They would lose as many turning back as they would pressing forward. There was but one path remaining for the former Imperial Army, only one obvious conclusion. Death here, death of starvation on the beach, death to the Guild that would hunt them down eventually. It was all the same. There never really was another way for this to end.

From behind John came a surprising roar, and as he turned, he could see a small batch of soldiers coming in, making their way through the crowd. It took a few moments before he could recognize his major, Tauven Ulfini, make his way through the approving ranks.

Shonnen smiled as the major slowly approached. "I see you managed to make it through after all."

"Might be because someone got the gate open," replied his major, a smile returned on the Fallneesian, but it quickly removed. "Not much left of the seventh, as you can see."

"Not much left of any of us, but we can use whatever we can get, Major."

"Agreed. I will push them to the front. I see Hollins hasn't given up quite yet."

"Ha!" exclaimed Ascotte from beside him. "The man's not smart enough to quit."

"Fair enough," Ulfini replied. "Any word from the captain?"

Shonnen shook his head. "He did his job, Major. As do we all."

"He will be honored," the major noted.

"If we live, Major. Only if we live."

--

The doors to the tower closed and barred, Rayden smiled if only to himself. *A lot of good barring these doors will do. Wouldn't have exactly stopped my entrance.* Mortar and the twins, Scythe and Haze, dressed their wounds and said very little for a change. They were left behind, Deso deeming them too injured to continue. Rayden was left to guard the girl, Jennifer, in case they needed her. He would have argued but currently his hand crippled him enough for Deso to give pause. Though now properly wrapped and cleaned, pain was still an issue along with his grip. But despite the injury, this girl was important . . . somehow . . . or at least they guessed such. Rayden should have known who she was. Sadly, he had paid little attention to the world outside of his own. Anyone outside of his capital of Astrona had not mattered, save for Allura, for what good that had done.

He knew Gerald but never met him in his single trip to Tessenul before this insanity. Of course he also knew Christina and Lurey, but that was the extent of his knowledge of the Rowes and the Hillans. He had never met Edfeld while he lived or any other members of their extended family. Certainly there were many, and this girl was obviously one of them.

She was tall, maybe even equal to his height, if just a bit under. Very attractive, as were most of her family to some extent. Her hair a bit wavy but not wildly so, her face slightly littered with freckles around her nose. Pleasant on the eyes, but behind the exterior stood a Rowe: calculated, devious, power hungry. Jennifer strode across the room to come closer to Rayden.

"I am thirsty, my lord."

Rayden frowned to her comment. "I am no one's lord."

She shrugged. "Well what else am I to call you?"

"Breeches," he stated, then turned back to stare out the window, gazing into the night, finding nothing but a disturbing quiet returned.

"I am Jennifer Rowe. So . . . what's your real name?" she pushed.

"We don't have names," he answered. "Not anymore."

She took a few steps closer. "They don't have names," Jennifer whispered, motioning back to the three members of the Divide subtly. "You, though . . . you have a name."

"Ah, so you have known me for an hour, said but a handful of sentences, and now you know me to be what? Different from them?"

"Am I wrong?"

"And stupid. Now sit back down. You test my patience."

Though she did stop talking for the moment, she only crossed her arms and remained exactly where she was, like a child pouting. Rayden ignored her, again staring out into the dark of the night, listening to the sounds of battle. They were distant still. He wondered how exactly Deso could get Gerald close enough to combat to attempt to end it. Of course he did not question that it was possible. Deso was making a ridiculous habit of proving others wrong. Rayden did what he could to avoid being one of those people.

"Three fucking aces does not beat full queens and jacks on the fourth engagement," blurted Mortar.

Of course they are playing cards.

He heard Haze huff loudly. "It does on the seventh engagement."

"Aye, it does," Scythe complied.

"Of course, he's your brother," hissed the badly scarred Donovinian. "You've got to follow his lead."

"Don't you think," started Jennifer, "that this is an inappropriate time to play cards?"

Rayden turned, if for nothing else out of morbid curiosity. She really had no idea who she spoke to.

The three members of the Moon Divide gave nearly identical stares toward her, one that all but told their awe at her audacity, or moreover, her ignorance.

"You must be a House lady," Mortar claimed. "Probably an important one."

"Well as a . . ."

"I didn't ask you, now did I?" he snapped, interrupting her immediately. "I stated a fucking fact. Only a House lady is dumb enough to not know when to just stand there and keep quiet."

"I am not some sort of pet, told to stand in a corner and behave!" she unwisely screamed back.

"No," agreed Mortar. "You are insurance just in case Gerald Rowe dies. If the young shit dies, then I am going to presume you would take charge. I'm guessing that based on how everyone seems to think you matter. So if that is true and if Gerald dies, then we try this all over again with you as our hostage."

"True or not, you cannot harm insurance," she presumed.

The scarred Donovinian chuckled at her last comment. "How astute of you. You are right, though. But nothing says I can't gag you and tie you on the top of the fucking tower neither. Or maybe you don't need one of your fingers. I mean you have so many of them, what's missing one going to matter much. You'll live through it, I'm sure of it. So . . . nothing? No witty fucking retort? Nothing at all? Good." Mortar immediately turned back to the game, and the three members of the Divide began cursing and playing again.

The girl took a cautious step forward to Rayden again.

"See," she whispered. "You are not like them."

"You don't know me as well as you would think you do."

And then she winked toward him. "As a matter of fact, I know you far better than you would like me to. And I might add, shaving your head does not change your face . . . for future reference." Jennifer smiled, curtseyed, and then walked back closer to Mortar and the twins.

Shit.

--

In one moment, John was certain that they were on the verge of making it through the plaza, just significantly weaker than when they started. The seventh joined in on the front and surged through with furious aggression. And then it broke and the Imperial army pressed through the Argon guards like a broken dam. It was momentary success, he knew, as their numbers still dwindled even with the addition of the seventh. But at least they would be out of the cursed plaza and onto the next trap laid forth.

And in the next moment, the fighting just . . . ended.

"What the . . ." started Ascotte.

Men simply began to stop, some screaming could be heard but not deciphered at the other end of the plaza, and the guards of Argonus began to simply drop their weapons. *Surrender?* It felt asinine for them to give up the fight when they were clearly winning . . . and yet the soldiers yielded in overwhelming numbers. Hundreds, then thousands of weapons and shields hit the cobble streets of Tessenul, hands raised into the air, and many of Shonnen's men turned back to him in anticipation of their next command.

"So . . . what do we do now?" questioned Baldin.

Thousands of Argon men must have thought the same thing. *I don't rightfully know. I only half expected to win this battle.* The Argon men began to drop to their knees in full submission, and the reality began to sink in for John that they truly had won this battle, this war. He had no explanation for it, no reasoning behind such a . . .

"Unbelievable . . ." mumbled his Colonel, pointing outward into the distance.

The general eyed where his friend pointed. Down a side street at higher elevation clearly stood a crowded circle of soldiers around a young, blond haired man which might have been Gerald Rowe, but John could not tell from this distance. But the man next to him . . . no distance could mask his identity.

"Colonel," started Shonnen, "I believe you are going to owe the captain your thanks after all."

To which Baldin nodded. "That I do, General. That I do."

--

It took half a day to sort out the mess and Rayden could barely figure out where in Shadow he was supposed to be. Deso, Nails, Flint, and Aaron had made it through to the front lines successfully with Gerald Rowe, and the House lord did the rest. The fighting had ended and neither side seemed disappointed in the announcement. Some of the soldiers and guards seemed confused at the cause of the victory or defeat, pending on which side they stood on. But it mattered very little. History would tell of the victory by General Shonnen and likely never even speak of the true hero of the war, Captain Deso.

But a part of him smiled at his own work. Perhaps none of it would have been possible if not for him. And no one would likely know of his exploits. The Divide were not known to bolster outside their own ranks. What he did would never make the pages of history, and that did not necessarily bother him.

Breeches was very different from Rayden Pratt, he realized. It had been a long time since anyone called him by his real name, and he was beginning to simply live life by the very minute, which was normally advisable when traveling with the Moon Divide. But doubt and anger crept back into his thoughts the moment the Rowe girl all but ousted him. She could have been meeting with Shonnen and Gerald and telling them exactly who he was. And then . . . well he had no idea what would happen then. Would the Divide, or primarily Deso kill him on spot if his identity was discovered? Would Shonnen be able to shield him against his wrath? And moreover, would Rayden really want him to?

Rayden Pratt was weak. He allowed his younger brother and bride-to-be make a fool of him and ultimately remove him completely from the capital and his family. Breeches . . . well he was someone different. There was no thought when he moved across the wall to hit the door mechanism, there was no thought when he dove off the bridge to enter the tower alone. He reacted to the moment, something that he simply could not do before.

He would have time to be Rayden again, time to get his revenge against Allura and Jerryn and anyone else that crossed him. He did not know how, but he would. But for the time being . . . he *needed* to be Breeches, a man of the Moon Divide. And though he was a long way off from being on equal ground as the others . . . even they gave him a nod of respect as of late. The Divide might never tell the tale of Breeches the hero to anyone outside of their own, but they would know. And for some reason, earning their respect made him proud.

No, Rayden was not worried. There was something in the wink that the girl gave him. She could have at any point called him by his name and been done with it. But that was not her intent. Jennifer Rowe had a reason for approaching him the way she did. Perhaps she had a plan, perhaps she knew her next play but kept it a mystery from him. But something told him that he had far from seen the last of that girl.

Inside the large kitchen in the tower, the named members of the Divide sat and waited for word from Deso. They were all worse for wear, but nothing that time and stitches would not heal. He unraveled the bandages on his own hand to change the dressings, the blood stopped but the wound open and jagged. He spent no time examining it as he simply placed new bandages upon the injury.

"I heard we suffered a few more losses," noted Flint, breaking the obtusely long silence.

"Ha," coughed Aaron. "But I heard our men took down damn near five times what the other squads had, at a fraction of their numbers. Only about fifty of them in all, and killing hundreds upon hundreds."

"He said this, he said that," stated Nails as he spat onto the kitchen floor. "Can't trust shit people say. They probably say our illustrious general won the war."

"Well he didn't exactly lose the war either, Nails," Aaron defended. "Give the man some credit."

"I'll give you a fucking boulder in the face, you Argon shit," hissed the large Ursan.

"Flame's embrace, give it a rest," Mortar called out, laughing some in the process. "We lost some more men of the Divide. They are free men now."

"Died in combat," added Flint. "Damn sure hope we get that same chance when it's our time."

"Ain't my time," bravely declared Nails. "No time soon."

"It'll be our time," Breeches offered up, the men turning to him. "Today, tomorrow, ten years from now. Doesn't matter. It'll always be too soon. *Always*."

Deso opened the side door, his face the same stoic, stern expression that he had known from the beginning. He motioned them all to him.

"General wants to see us up in the command room," their leader claimed. "Let's get this over with."

--

John was tired and could not remember the last time he slept. The tea that was prepared did well to keep him at least falsely awake, but his body knew the truth. He needed sleep and plenty of it if he were to recover not only in body, but his mind. But the general did not know how much he trusted sleep in this place. Obviously the hours of negotiation between his officers and Gerald and Jennifer Rowe were to alleviate some of that stress. But talk did not change facts. Gerald surrendered his men in fear of his life. How quickly, if he felt he had the upper hand, would he turn on him in if given the opportunity? Fear alone would not hold Tessenul for as long as he needed it. They simply did not have the numbers for a lengthy occupation.

` He would have thought that talks of surrender would have been easier than they had been. But Gerald was intent at keeping power, control. He was willing to give all of the soldiers pardons for their crimes against Amon if he retained power. John would be his personal advisor, but he would ultimately have the final say. Of course that was simply ludicrous and Shonnen had no intentions of agreeing to those terms. His counter proposal was simple: the Imperial Army would occupy under *his* command, and Gerald would be kept under arrest. Of course this would allow him, in reality, to keep his men alive long enough until the *real* Imperial Army showed, and John was subsequently arrested. He did not share that last point, of course, but it stood as reality. They only needed maybe two months, he figured, until his tenure as First General would end. Having Gerald in charge dampened his plans quite a bit.

Thankfully it was Gerald, not him, that finally grew weary of the talks.

"Maybe we should just call it a day? We've been at this for hours." The House lord shrugged. "What do you think?"

Shonnen nodded. "You will have to remain my prisoner. Both of you," he motioned to Jennifer Rowe, "until we reconvene."

"I doubt that is necessary, General," assured Gerald. "You won this war. Clearly you . . ."

"Then we will continue talks until we come to some sort of conclusion, my lord."

Gerald turned to Jennifer, but she did not turn. Her gaze met his intensely. "Maybe a break would be good for all of us," she stated. "And yes, that only seems fair, General Shonnen. The cease of arms is only because of the capture of Gerald. Since we have yet to fully negotiate the terms of surrender, then we should remain your prisoners here."

Jennifer, unlike her cousin, gave thought to her reasons, and reason to her thoughts. It was . . . refreshing at the very least.

"Earth and Flame," muttered Gerald. "I will not be a prisoner in my own *fucking* house."

"Yes you are and it's done," she snapped back. "I am sure that we will be allowed within our rooms under supervision, correct First General? No need for the dungeons."

"Agreed," the general concurred. "Remaining here under constant guard is sufficient enough."

The doors opened slowly and Captain Deso strode through the hallway, his men halting some ways back as he came through the entryway alone.

"General," stated the Fallneesian, a grin suppressed upon his face.

"Captain Deso, it's good to see you intact and well," stated Shonnen. "There will be time later to honor your work with metals and glory."

"I require neither," he replied.

"It's not about what you require, Captain."

"Okay," he continued. "Then I *want* neither."

Baldin leaned forward in his chair. "No need for modesty, Captain. You have earned the praise. That was an amazing job you did at getting the doors to this city open, not to mention storming this very tower."

"Kissing my ass won't win you my favor, Colonel," noted Deso, who then promptly shrugged. "But it's a good place to start."

"Fair enough, Captain," John continued. "I called you up here for a reason. Sent out a small scouting unit consisting of about three of Gerald's men to patrol the area, ensure we did not have any other forces outside the walls that did not know of their House lord's surrender. They did not return. I then sent out some of my men. They also have not returned."

"General," interrupted Major Ulfini. "The captain and his men are badly wounded. Maybe we should find another."

"Damn near everyone is either wounded, tired, or hungry," Shonnen commented in earnest. "I sent two lesser squads and have heard back nothing. I would just like to know what has happened to the men that I have sent out. No one better for the task than your men."

"We are wounded," Deso stated, "but far from hapless. Aye, it will be done. Where did you send the last batch of men?"

"Closer to the coastline," replied John. "I don't expect trouble of any kind, Captain. Saying that, I . . ."

"Understood, General. We will head to the coast, see if we find any traces of your men. Anything else?"

John shook his head. "You've done enough, Captain. Report back to me once you find something."

Deso gave a half attempt at a bow, more in mockery, then turned and left. Every time he walked away, John presumed it to be the last time he would see him. And yet he continued to surprise.

He was not a solider . . . at least not like any soldier he had ever known. John had no idea whatsoever who Captain Deso *truly* was. Soldier, killer, captain, criminal. The general did not know. He only knew that he needed a thousand more of him.

--

Rayden Pratt was tired and he could not remember the last time he slept. Mortar and the twins were left behind, as Deso considered them too injured to be useful. So Deso marched ahead of the rest, outside the walls of Tessenul heading east, with Aaron, Flint, and Nails trailing. There was little to no conversation, not even the occasional complaint from Nails, which was truly a rarity. They were strong men, powerful men, but even they had their breaking point. Even immortals could sleep and eat, he presumed. A trek through a sewer, suicide mission to unlock the mechanism to open the doors to the city, a second suicide mission to capture the House lord . . . well even that could take its toll against the strongest of men. And he was convinced that he stood amongst the strongest in Amon.

There still stood a sparse forested area before they broke way to the ocean, but the smell hit his nostrils long before sight ever would. It was a different smell, though he would have never had noticed such or cared such until now. His journey had started at the western coast, along the Vurid Sea, traveling with his family to Genethur to witness the crowning of a new king. If he were to guess how things would have ended up then, this would have been his last possible scenario. But here he stood, tired and injured, hungry and beaten down, moving toward the Terrandonan Sea, and noticing the subtle differences in the smell and the taste of the salt water in the air from west to east.

But life was a surprise in itself. If he spent his day trying to piece together the reasoning behind it all, he would be wasting the day. Some would tell him everything happened through the eyes and consent of Turitea and Schill, the fallen gods. *Maybe.* But Rayden hated rationalizing reality with faith.

Despite the differences, the smell still reminded him of Genethur. While it was not fond memories, it did make him miss his family. Breeches . . . Rayden . . . it did not matter. He still loved his family. Admitting love did not admit weakness. While he was a stronger man around the Divide, and a man that he liked better than the previous one he had been, he was still a Pratt. He still wondered if his sister was alive and well. Did his mother and father think him to be dead? All for the better, he presumed. All the better, because a part of him died back in Genethur, a part that he did not want back.

It was not until he nearly toppled over Deso that he realized that their leader had come to a dead stop. Rayden narrowly sidestepped him and halted his movement as well. They had not quite yet reached the beach, just inside the last bit of forested area, but the white sands and the blue of the water could be seen through the gaps of the trees. And that was not the only thing in view.

Before the small group stood two men, massive in structure, some eight, maybe nine feet in height. Long but not narrow, these were beasts of men, arms bulky and chests wide. They seemed every bit as startled to see the Divide as they did to see them. Life was a surprise in itself, after all. These men, if he could call them such, were heavily armed, lightly armored, and completely stationary. One of these giant men had his hand upon a sword, the other had a spear in hand, sword sheathed on his hip. They stood silent, as did Deso and his men, studying one another, waiting for one of them to make the first move.

They were not friendly, that much was clear. But what exactly were they?

The spear holding giant spun his weapon about, changing his grip. Breeches reached for his sword.

The giant launched his spear through the air, and in a devastating spray of blood, impaled Aaron straight clean and through, launching him back some ten feet in the process.

Whoever these giants where, they had absolutely no idea who they just fucked with.

Deso somehow moved before even him, and Nails had his hammer out in a rush. Breeches unsheathed his sword and approached the first intruder that threw the spear, taking an intentional wild swing toward him just to gather some space. The giant took a step backward, then withdrew his own sword. He came down hard with the weapon, but Breeches managed to spin away just in time. Flint took a step forward and stabbed toward the giant and missed, and paid dearly as the large assailant took his free hand and punched him hard into the chest. Rayden, though, did not miss with his second attack, slicing deep into the giant's side, blood coming from the open wound.

He was not done, however. The giant kicked Breeches square in the gut, which not only knocked out every bit of air in his lungs, it also took him off his feet and sent him back a few yards. He landed hard onto his back, the sharp pain numbing for a moment, but his adrenaline kept him alive, kept him from allowing the pain to paralyze him, kept his mind focused. With a sword on its way downward, Breeches managed to roll away with inches to spare. Flint was back on his feet and charged the creature, and this time he did not miss. His sword buried into the giant man, and in response the creature screamed. Sword dropped, he snatched Flint as if he were a doll, squeezing the very life from him. Rayden gathered himself and found his breath again. He leapt to his feet and rushed the giant, burying his blade deep into his side, sword sliding into flesh all the way to the hilt. He kept it there for a moment, watching as the grip slowly released from Flint, as the eyes of this giant man slowly began to grow distant. As he removed his weapon, the giant first dropped Flint, then fell to his knees, plummeting dead onto the earth after.

He turned to the second giant, who was holding off well against Nails and Deso, but was backing off against the assault. Now with Flint and Rayden charging toward him, the beast must have known the reality. There stood no chance for him to best them, no chance for him to walk away from this situation alive. And so he did not fight. Instead the giant dropped his sword altogether and simply screamed at the four of them. It was not meant to give fright, from his standpoint anyways. This scream was a calling, a reckoning. Deafening in the volume, long in its length, the giant man ended with a laugh. It was not a sad laugh, not a nervous laugh at the end of life. It was pity. He knew something that they currently did not, and the giant found humor in such. And why not?

What is life if you can't enjoy the simple things?

Flint, Nails, and Breeches approached the giant and struck at once, mauling him quickly, ending whatever smile he had upon his face. When it was done, the four members of the Divide breathed heavily and stared toward each other.

Nails was the first to move, Flint close behind him, heading back toward the lifeless body of Aaron. The Ursan knelt down and went silent, his hands pressed against the earth before him. The two men hated each other from what Breeches could tell. But hate and respect were two entirely different emotions, he presumed. The Ursan said nothing, did nothing. He simply knelt before the body, silent, motionless, respectful.

Flint, however, was not so silent. He screamed, kicking sand as he took his sword and heaved it into the forest. Even men of the Divide could mourn death.

Before he could truly reflect on any of the madness, Deso was already on the move, pressing beyond the trees to the beach. Rayden joined him in a dead sprint.

What he found behind the trees was not what he expected . . . but maybe it should have been.

"Those were scouts," hissed Deso, his own voice only now showing signs of humanity, normality, surprise.

A lone boat sat against the shoreline, bodies of men lay before it. Likely the corpses of the previous patrols sent out by John Shonnen who stumbled upon these giants. But that was the least of their concerns. Deep against the horizon of the Terrandonan Sea sat a line of blackness. It was difficult to decipher at first, but as his eyes came into focus against the morning sun, he began to recognize what he saw.

Ships. Thousands of them. Far too many to count, littered against the horizon of the ocean, a dark shadow in front of the rising sun. Rayden turned to Deso, but his eyes did not remove from the Terrandonan Sea. Perhaps he knew exactly what Breeches thought, perhaps he did not. But his eyes reflected the same understanding as him.

There was truth to the warnings placed before them. But it was far from mystical, far from magical, far from religious. Turitea and Schill, the fallen gods, their rising high kept some kind of demon at bay, kept the ocean wild and impassable, kept Amon protected from whatever lay across the sea. In the end, it was all horseshit. There *was* something across the sea. Thousands upon thousands of approaching boats all but validated that fact, and upon those boats were likely hundreds of the very same giants that they just killed.

They were right to listen. They should have been scared. There was reason for the Imperial Army to guard the coast. There were reasons for the ministers to preach of the coming storm. But they had it all wrong. There were no monsters across the sea. There were no demons or anything of the such that came for Amon. History was at play here. A war several millenniums old, a race that once dwelled and dominated Amon, and somehow they disappeared. The sea raged and kept them at bay, and if that was the workings of the fallen gods, only faith could answer that question. But the sea no longer protected them. And the threat was very real. The approaching army was just not what he had expected, if he had expected anything at all.

Because this was not the first giant he had seen, nor apparently would it be his last.

"By the rope or the chain now, First Pratt," Deso mumbled to himself.

Against the eastern coast of Argonus, an army approached on the calmed Terrandonan Sea.

An army of Kwyantin.

**

17033556R10425

Printed in Poland
by Amazon Fulfillment
Poland Sp. z o.o., Wrocław